I0587463

John Webster, Jonas Moore

The Displaying of Supposed Witchcraft

John Webster, Jonas Moore

The Displaying of Supposed Witchcraft

ISBN/EAN: 9783337376116

Printed in Europe, USA, Canada, Australia, Japan

Cover: Foto ©Andreas Hilbeck / pixelio.de

More available books at **www.hansebooks.com**

THE
DISPLAYING

OF SUPPOSED

WITCHCRAFT.

Wherein is affirmed that there are many sorts of

𝕯𝖊𝖈𝖊𝖎𝖛𝖊𝖗𝖘 𝖆𝖓𝖉 𝕴𝖒𝖕𝖔𝖘𝖙𝖔𝖗𝖘,

AND

Divers perfons under a paffive *Delufion* of

MELANCHOLY and *FANCY.*

But that there is a *Corporeal League* made betwixt the
DEVIL and the WITCH,

Or that he fucks on the *Witches Body*, has *Carnal Copulation*, or
that *Witches* are turned into *Cats, Dogs,* raife Tempefts, or
the like, is utterly denied and difproved,

Wherein alfo is handled,

The Exiftence of Angels and Spirits, the truth of Apparitions, tne Nature of
Aftral and Sydereal Spirits, the force of Charms, and Philters;
with other abftrufe matters.

By *John Webfter*, Practitioner in Phyfick.

*Falfa etenim opiniones Hominum praeoccupantes, non folùm furdos, fed & caecos faciunt, ità ut
videre nequeant, quae aliis perfpicua apparent.* Galen. lib. 8. de Comp. Med.

LONDON,
Printed by *J. M.* and are to be fold by the Bookfellers in *London.* 1677.

To his Worſhipful and honoured Friends *Tho-mas Parker* of *Braiſholme*, *John Aſheton* of the *Lower-Hall*, *William Drake* of *Barnolaſ-wick-coat*, *William Johnſon* of the *Grange*, *Henry Marſden* of *Gisburne* Eſquires, and his Majeſties Juſtices of Peace and *Quorum* in the Weſt-riding of *Yorkſhire*.

Worſhipful Gentlemen and honoured Friends,

I Do not dedicate this piece of my Labours unto you, there-by to beg protection for it, as fearing either its weak-nefs, or the malevolent cenfures of the ignorant; for I very well know, and have experienced, that it is the ufual property of idle and pragmatical perfons to pleafe their own malignant humors, with the condemning and fcoffing at the painful lucubrations of others. And I have ever judged that nothing ought to be publiſhed, that like a Noun Subftan-tive cannot ſtand by it felf, without being fupported by any other adjoined help. Neither is this forth of a vain confidence or an overweening of mine own abilities, though I very well know that fome are as much in love with the brood of their own brains, as others are with the fruit of their loines : Be-caufe I have for many years been as wary and vigilant, as any could be, to watch over my felf, that I might both know, and keep a clear diftinction, betwixt flattering Phantafie, and true and found judgment. But I ſhall in brief ſhew you the true reafons of my prefenting of this poor piece to your reading and judgments.

1. The firft reafon is, becaufe you have all been Gentle-men, not only well known unto me for many years, as being my near Neighbours, but alfo with whom I have been freely admitted to a Noble and Generous converfe, and have been trufted, and honoured by you in your Domeftick concerns, wherein by my Medical Profeſſion, I might be ſerviceable to

you,

*you, or your Families, far beyond my poor Merit and Deſert.
And having been for many years a due obſerver of your de-
portments in your places of truſt as Magiſtrates, for being but
as a ſtander by, and looking on, may (perhaps) have noted
as much, as thoſe that are Gameſters, I was moved to preſent
this piece of my labours unto you, by reaſon of that knowledge
and acquaintance, rather than to others, whoſe abilities and
integrity I did not ſo well underſtand. And (I hope) I may
without ſuſpicion of flattery (of which I am ſure both your
ſelves, and others that know me, will acquit me, that if I
be any way guilty, it is rather in being too plain and open)
ſay, that you have been, and are true Patriots to your Countrey, and not only Juſtices of the Peace, but true conſervers of
it, and Peace-makers amongſt all your Neighbours; and really
this is one of the chief cauſes why I have dedicated this Treatiſe unto you.*

*2. Another reaſon is, you have all fully known me, and
the moſt of the particulars of my life, both my follies and
frailties, as alſo my other endowments and abilities, and therefore in reference to theſe, I thought none more fit than your
ſelves, to whom I might tender this laborious piece. For it
is not unknown unto you, that (excepting my Phyſical Practice, which age and infirmities will not ſuffer me very much
to attend) I have for many years laſt paſt lived a ſolitary,
and ſedentary life, mihi & Muſis, having had more converſe
with the dead than the living, that is, more with Books
than with Men. And therefore I preſent this unto you, as being better able than moſt others to whom I am unknown, to
judge what I am like or able to perform in ſuch a ſubject as
this is.*

*3. Alſo it is not unknown unto you, that I have had a
large portion of Trouble and Perſecution in this outward
world, wherein you did not like many others ſtand aloof off,
as though you had not known me, but like perſons of Juſtice,
and true Magnanimity, durſt both look upon and aſſiſt wrong-
ed innocency, though beſmeered over with the envious dirt
of malicious ſcandals, and even in that very conjuncture of
time, when the whole giddy Troop of barking Dogs, and ra-*

venous

venous Wolves, did labour to devour me. But then, even then did put to your helping hands, and were free to declare, what you knew of mine innocency: which was so Generous, Noble and Christian a kind of just commiseration, that I should for ever account my self a wretched person, if I should not have deeply impressed in my breast and memory, which no time, nor adversity can ever obliterate. But being in a condition that I may truly say with the Apostle S. Peter, Αργυριον και χρυσιον εχ υπαρχει μοι, *Silver and Gold have I none (which I know you expect not) and therefore the greatest power I have is my weak pen, thereby to testifie my thankfulness for your unparallel'd kindness. And therefore I offer this Treatise as a perpetual and monumental memorial to all Posterities, of my gratitude, and your goodness.*

And further, to whom can a subject of this nature be more suitably and fitly presented than to such Magistrates as your selves, who have often occasion to be cumbred and troubled with the ignorant, envious, and sometimes knavish accusations against people suspected of Witchcraft, Sorcery, Charming and Inchantment? Wherein to free the guilty, and condemn the innocent, is equally abominable to the Lord: And therefore much judgment, caution, care and diligent inspection ought to be used in the examining and determining of these matters, wherein I have used as much perspicuity and plainness as was possible to distinguish betwixt those that are Impostors, Cheaters, and active Deceivers, and those that are but under a mere passive delusion through ignorant and superstitious education, a melancholy temper and constitution, or led by the vain credulity of inefficacious Charms, Pictures, Ceremonies and the like, traditionally taught them. The one sort of which deserves to be punished for couzening of the people, and taking upon them, and pretending to bring to pass things that they have neither skill nor power to perform; but the other sort rather merit pity and information, or the Physicians help than any punishment at all. And I make bold to mind you of this one thing especially that in things of this nature great heed ought to be taken of the conditions, qualities, ends and intentions of the Complainants and Informers, who are often

more

more worthy of punifhment, than the perfons accufed. For many forth of a meer deluded fancy, envious mind, ignorance and fuperftition do attribute natural difeafes, diftempers, and accidents to Witches and Witchcraft, when in truth there is no fuch matter at all. And fometimes they counterfeit ftrange fits and difeafes, as vomiting of preternatural and ftrange things, which if narrowly lookt into and examined are but Juglings, and deceitful confederacies, and yet for malice, revenge or fome other bafe ends, do accufe others to be caufers of them.

And though you fhould find fome confidently confeffing that they have made a vifible and corporeal league with the Devil, and that he hath carnal copulation with them, and that he doth fuck upon fome parts of their Bodies, and that they are Tranfubftantiated into Dogs, Cats, and the like, or that they fly in the air, and raife Tempefts; yet (I hope) I have fufficiently proved by the word of God, the true grounds of Theologie and found reafon, that there never hath been any fuch Witch exiftent in rerum natura, and fo you may know what credit may be given to fuch Fables and impoffibilities.

So wifhing that you may long live in Health and Happinefs, to do his Majefty and your Countrey fervice, which is, and fhall be my faithful prayer for you, I take leave fubfcribing my felf

Your Worfhips

moft Faithful Friend,

and Devoted Servant.

John Webfter.

THE
PREFACE or INTRODUCTION.

Knowing certainly that all writings once publifhed, do equally undergo one fate, as to ftand or fall by the common cenfures, judgments and opinions of Men; therefore have I affixt'd no Epithete, as forefeeing this Treatife (like a Man once at Sea that is forced to hold out againft all weathers) muft abide the cenfures of all fort of perfons, how various foever their minds and principles be. And though mens fancies and opinions be commonly as different as their faces, yet I fhall enumerate fome few general forts, that may be fufficiently comprehenfive to comprife the moft of other fubordinate particulars, and that in this order.

1. Firft, that which a Man hath found true by experience in fuch like cafes, may very reafonably induce him to expect the like again; as after I had printed my book of the Hiftory of Metals I met with fome that were no more learned than Parrots, who could not write true Englifh, and whofe greateft skill was in the feveral ways of debauchery, and other poor Pedanticks that were hardly mafters of Grammar, and yet this crew, and the like were rafh and bold enough, to cenfure my painful endeavours, and to fcoff at it as a mere collection. And therefore in publifhing of this piece, which is a dark and myfterious fubject, I may very probably meet with fome troops of fuch rafh ignorants, to whom only I fhall return this fharp, but fuitable refponfion. It is an ordinary thing for many that never could fhape a fhoo, to reprove and find fault with the Shoomaker: but fuch wife men (fit only for *Gotham*) may learn thefe two Proverbs, *There is none fo bold as blind Bayard*, and *A Fools bolt is foon fhot*, and their heads may be fitter for Feathers, than the Laurel, and when any of them have made fuch a collection as my former Book, or publifht fuch a piece as this, then I fhall give them a better anfwer, and not before, *Lactucas non effe dandas hifce Afinis comedendas, cum illis fufficiant cardui.*

a   2. There

2. There are another generation that seem wise in their own eyes, whose brains are like blown Bladders filled with the wind of over-weening and self-conceitedness, and these usually do huff, snuff, and puff at every thing that agrees not with their Capricious Cockscombs, when their abilities for the most part lie in the scraps they have gathered from the Theaters, or from the discourses had in Taverns and Coffee-houses, and if they can but reach some pittiful pieces of Drollery and Raillery, they think themselves fit and able to censure any thing though never read nor seen, except the Title Page. To these I have little to say, as being but such airy and frothy Vaporoso's, as the least blast of sound reason maketh them vanish into smoak and nothing; but only wish them to take into serious consideration, the saying of the Wiseman : *Seest thou* Prov. 26. 12. *a man wise in his own conceit ? there is more hope of a Fool than of him.* And the counsel of a learned Father is proper for such vain confidents : *Expedit benè timere, quam malè fidere ; & utilius est, ut infirmum se homo cognoscat, ut fortis existat, quàm fortis videri velit, & infirmus emergat.*

3. There are another sort that are so critically envious, that they can allow of nothing that is not their own production, and beareth not the test of their approbation, and cannot but stigmatize the labours of others how good or beneficial soever they be, because they shadow their fame, and tend not to the advancement of their own reputation : even as divers sorts of insects do feed upon the excrements of other animals, so these feed their own humours, and please their own fancies by the calumniating, and blacking the labours of others. These being guilty of peevish morosity cannot look kindly at any thing of anothers, without frowning, distast, and censuring ; but we have little to say unto such as these, but shall leave them to the gall of their own breasts, and the spleen of their own minds, having neither intended our labours for any such, nor valuing their censures how sharp and bitter soever they be. For *nulla felicitas tam magna est, ut malignitatis dentes vitare possit.* And therefore it is discretion to bear that patiently for which humane prudence can find no remedy.

4. Others there are who are grown obstinate in their minds and

and wills, concerning Spirits, Apparitions, Witchcraft, Sorcery, Inchantment, and the like, and are grown pertinacious
and resolute to stick to and hold those opinions that they
have imbibed through ignorant education: not considering
that perseverance in a good cause, and well grounded opinion
is laudable and commendable, but pertinaciousness in a bad
and ill grounded tenent, is as bad and hurtful. And it is every wise mans duty to study the cultivation and improvement
of the goods of the mind, and never to be ashamed to learn that
of which they were ignorant before. For the minds of men
are not only darkned in the fall of *Adam*, but also much mis-
led, by the sucking in of errors in their younger and more
unwary years, from whence they ought to endeavour with
might and main to extricate and deliver themselves. But he
that is wilfully setled upon the lees and dregs of former opinions, though never so erroneous, hath shut forth all further
light from shining into his understanding, and so is become
wilfully blind. To such as these we shall only propose the example and practice of the Apostle, who saith: *When I was a* 1 Cor. 13. 11.
child, I spake as a child, I understood as a child, I thought as a
child: But when I became a man, I put away childish things. And I
advise them not to refuse the counsel of S. *Augustine*, who saith:
Ad discendum quod opus est, nulla ætas sera videri potest : quia etsi
senes magis decet dicere quàm discere ; magis tamen decet disce-
re, quam ignorare. And they need not be ashamed to imitate
Socrates, who did wax old every day learning something.

5. As we have not intended this Treatise, and Introduction
for such conditioned persons as we have enumerated before,
so there are others to whom we freely offer and present it,
and shall shew the grounds and causes that moved us to undertake such a mysterious, and dangerous subject. And those
are such as have an humble, lowly, and equal mind, that they
commonly read Books to be informed, and to learn those
truths of which they are ignorant, or to be confirmed in those
things they partly knew before. It is to such as these only
that we offer our labours, and therefore shall candidly declare
unto them the causes and reasons of our undertaking which
are these.

1. Though there be a numerous company of Authors that

have written of Magick, Witchcraft, Sorcery, Inchantment, Spirits, and Apparitions, in fundry ages, of divers Countrys, and in various languages : yet have they for the moſt but borrowed one from another, or have tranſcribed what others had written before them. So that thereby there hath been no right progreſs made truly to diſcover the theory or ground of theſe dark and abſtruſe matters, nor no preciſe care taken to inſtance in matters of fact, that have been warrantably and ſufficiently atteſted : But only rhapſodies, and confuſed heaps of ſtories and relations, ſhuffled together, when not one of an hundred of them bore the face either of verity, or truth-likelineſs, whereby the underſtandings of Readers have remained uninlightned, their memories confounded, and their brains ſtuffed with Whimſies and Chimera's. And though there be nothing more common than diſputes of Witches, and Witchcraft, both in words and writing, yet not one of great multitudes that hath plainly told us, in what notion, or under what acceptation, they take the words, nor what deſcription is agreed upon, of either of theſe, that their exiſtence, or not being, their power and operations might be known and determined : But all the diſputes as yet concerning them have been looſe, wild, and *in vagum*. And therefore to remedie this, as far as ſuch a ſubject would allow, and our abilities ſtretch, we were moved, and have attempted to clear thoſe difficulties. And if we do not (which is epidemical to mankind) flatter and deceive ourſelves, we have in ſome meaſure reaſonably attained, as having plainly laid down the notion and acceptation of the words, Witches and Witchcraft, in which we grant them an exiſtence, and in what ſenſe and reſpect we grant them none, which is more (as we conceive) than yet hath been performed by any. And though our inſtances of matters of fact be neither ſo punctual nor full as might be wiſhed, for things of this nature are deep and hid ; yet are they the beſt we could ſelect or chuſe ; and this is one chief reaſon why I undertook to treat of this ſubject

2. Though the groſs, abſurd, impious and Popiſh opinions of the too much magnified powers of Demons and Witches, in this Nation, were pretty well quaſhed and ſilenced

lenced by the writings of *Hierus*, *Tandler*, Mr. *Scot*, Mr. *Ady*, Mr. *Wagstaff* and others ; and by the grave proceedings of many learned Judges, and other judicious Magistrates : yet finding that of late two persons of great learning and note, who are both (as I am informed) beneficed Ministers in the Church, to wit Dr. *Casaubon*, and Mr. *Glanvil*, have afresh espoused so bad a cause, and taken the quarrel upon them ; And to that purpose have newly furbished up the old Weapons, and raked up the old arguments, forth of the Popish Sink and Dunghills, and put them into a new dress, that they might appear with the greater luster, and so do with Tooth and Nail labour to maintain the old rotten assertions, the one in his Book called, A Treatise proving Spirits and Witches *&c.* the other in a Treatise called, A blow at modern *Sadducism* &c. Finding these (I say) as two new Champions giving defiance to all that are of a contrary judgment, I was stirred up to answer their supposed strong arguments, and invincible instances, which I have done (I confess) without fear, or any great regard to their Titles, Places, or Worldly Dignities, but only considering the strength or weakness of their arguments, proofs, and reason. For in this particular that I have to deal, it is not with the men, but their opinions and the grounds they would lay their foundations upon. And if I be censured for dealing too sharply and harshly with them, they must excuse me, for I profess I have no evil will at all against their persons, no more than against a *non*-Entity, but was justly zealous for the truth, and bitter against such opinions as they have vented, which to me seem dangerous, and in some respect impious, as (I suppose) I have fully proved. And this was another reason of my writing about this subject.

3. Another reason that made me undertake this subject, was the horrid absurdities the tenent of the common Witchmongers brings along with it, as not only tending to advance superstition and Popery, but also to be much derogatory to the Wisdom, Justice, and Providence of the Almighty, and to cry up the power of the Kingdom of darkness, to question the verity of the principal Article of the Christian Faith, concerning

concerning the Refurrection of Chrift in his true numerical Body, and generally to tend to the obftruction of the practice of Godlinefs and Piety. Thefe after I had ferioufly weighed and confidered them, did move me to labour as far as the light of Gods word, the grounds of true Theology, and the clear ftrength of reafon would guide, and direct me, to undertake the confutation of them as far as I was able, and if I have failed I humbly defire thofe that are more able to handle the matter more fully if poffible.

If any be moved that I feem to maintain fome things that are Paradoxes, I hope I may crave leave, as well to difcede from the opinions of others, as others have done from thofe that went before them. And I defire them not fo much to confider, either the novelty or ftrangenefs of the opinions, as the weight and ftrength of the reafons that are laid down to fupport and ftatuminate them ; for if the arguments be found and valid, the Tenents built thereupon cannot be weak and tottering. And however I acknowledge my felf to have humane frailties and fo may err, yet I have no mind or will pertinacioufly to perfevere in an error, and thefe things that we have treated of lying fo far from the ken of our fenfes, and experiments of this nature, either fo rare, or uncertain, that we may rationally expect pardon, rather than reprehenfion.

But I fhall fay no more, but let the Book fpeak for it felf, only defiring the Readers, firft to perufe and ferioufly to confider, before they cenfure, that fo I may have caufe to bid them, Farewel.

Dated *February*
23. 1673.

THE

THE
CONTENTS.

CHAP. 1. *Of the false, irrational, and unchristian censures, that have been, and yet are cast upon learned Men for writing of abstruse subjects: As also for treating of Apparitions and Witchcraft, especially if they crossed the common stream of vulgar opinion.* Page 1.

Chap. 2. *Of the Notion, Conception, and Description of Witches and Witchcraft according to divers Authors, and in what sense they may be granted, and in what sense and respect they are denied.* p. 19.

Chap. 3. *The denying of such a Witch as is last described in the foregoing Chapter doth not infer the denying of Angels, or Spirits. Apparitions no warrantable ground for a christian to believe the existence of Angels, or Devils by, but the word of God.* p. 37.

Chap. 4. *That the Scriptures, and sound reason are the true and proper mediums to prove the actions attributed unto Witches by, and not other improper ways that many Authors have used. And of the requisites necessary truly to prove a matter of fact by.* p. 43.

Chap. 5. *That these things now in question, are but barely supposed, and were yet never rationally nor sufficiently proved: And that the Allegations brought to prove them by are weak, frivolous, and absolutely invalid: with a full confutation of all the four particulars.* p. 63.

Chap. 6. *That divers places in Scripture have been mis-translated thereby to uphold this horrid opinion of the Devils omnipotency, and the power of Witches, when there is not one word that signifieth a familiar Spirit, or a Witch in that sense that is vulgarly intended.* p. 106.

Chap. 7. *Of divers places in the Old Testament, that are commonly wrested, and falsly expounded, thereby to prove Apparitions, and the power of the Devil, and Witches.* p. 136.

Chap. 8. *Of the Woman of Endor that pretended to raise up Samuel, and of some other places in the Scriptures, not handled yet, and of some other objections.* p. 165.

Chap. 9. *Of Divine permission, providence and prescience.* p. 183.

Chap. 10. *Whether faln Angels be corporeal, or simply incorporeal, and the absurdity of the assuming of Bodies, and the like consequents.* p. 197.

Chap. 11. *Of the knowledge, and power of faln Angels.* p. 215.

Chap. 12. *If the Devils or Witches have power to perform strange things, whether they do not bring them to pass by mere natural*

means.

The Contents.

means, or otherwise? And of Helmonts opinion concerning the effects caused by Devils or Witches. p. 241.

Chap. 13. That the ignorance of the power of Art and Nature, and such like things, hath much advanced these foolish and impious opinions. p. 267.

Chap. 14. Of divers Impostures framed and invented to prove false and lying miracles by, and to accuse persons of Witchcraft, from late and undeniable authorities. p. 270.

Chap. 15. Of divers creatures that have a real existence in nature, and yet by reason of their wonderous properties, or seldom being seen, have been taken for Spirits and Devils. p. 279

Chap. 16. Of Apparitions in general; and of some unquestionable stories, that seem to prove some such things. Of those Apparitions pretended to be made in Beryls and Crystals, and of the Astral or Sydereal Spirit. p. 288.

Chap. 17. Of the force and efficacy of words or charms, whether they effect any thing at all, or not, and if they do, whether it be by natural or diabolical virtue and force. p. 321.

THE

THE
DISPLAYING
OF SUPPOSED
WITCHCRAFT.

CHAP. I.

Of the false, irrational, and unchristian Censures, that have been, and yet are, cast upon Learned men, for writing of abstruse Subjects : As also for treating of Apparitions and Witchcraft, especially if they crossed the common stream of vulgar Opinion.

BEING about to treat of the mysterious and abstruse Subject of Witches and Witchcraft, I cannot but think it necessary (especially to make the things we handle more plain and evidential) to imitate Architectors, who when they intend to raise some fair Fabrick or Edifice, do not only provide themselves of good and lasting Materials, but above all take care to lay a firm and sure foundation, which they cannot well accomplish, unless the earth and rubbish be removed, that a firm ground for a foundation may be found out. So before I lay the foundation of what I intend in this Discourse, I shall labour to remove some censures and calumnies, that are usually cast upon those learned persons that labour to unmanacle imprisoned truth, and to adventure to cross the stream of vulgar Opinion, backt with seeming Authority, Antiquity, or universality of Votes, especially if they have intermeddled in Subjects occult and mysterious.

And these Censures (how unjust soever) have often deterred the
B   most

most able and best learned from divulging their opinions, or publish their thoughts upon such difficult and intricate matters, which (I conceive) ought not to be done for these reasons.

Reaf. 1.   1. Because the best part of a man, as naturally considered, is his Courage, Resolution, and Magnanimity, which should make him resolute and couragious to declare and maintain, what he upon sound and rational grounds apprehends to be truth, and not at all to fear the censure or judgment of others, who may have had no better means to inform themselves, or perhaps have been less diligent, and however are subject to the same errours and mistakes of Mankind, who must all confess the verity of that unerring Oracle, *Humanum est errare.* And therefore he must needs be a person of a poor, base, and low spirit, that doth conceal his own sentiments of the truth, for fear of the censure or calumnies of others.

Reaf. 2.   2. He that is afraid to declare his thoughts, for fear of censure or scandal, must of necessity be very weak in his Morals, as having little affection for verity, which is the chief object of the intellect, and consequently ought above all things to sway and lead the affections. And to be frighted from owning or declaring of the truth, for fear of the vain, aery, groundless, and erroneous censures of others, must needs speak a man weak in the grounds of Morality, and to have small affection for vertue, whose guide is verity.

August. de Agone Christi.   The Learned Father said exceeding well to this purpose : *Qui veritatem occultat, & qui prodit mendacium, uterq; reus est. Ille quia prodesse non vult, ipse quia nocere desiderat.*

Reaf. 3.   3. He that conceals the truth that he knows, for fear of the censures of others, must needs have little of Christianity in him,

Prov. 23. 23.   for we are commanded to buy the truth, and not to sell it; but for a Christian to conceal the truth, and not to dare to declare and defend it, for fear of the vain and perishing censures of men, is to make absolute sale of the truth, and that for the worst of all prises that can be. For what a weightless and worthless prise are the judgments and opinions of vain man, whose breath is in his nostrils, and whose life is but a vapor, that a Christian should, for fear of such vain censures, be afraid to declare or defend the truth? Therefore let the subtil Politicians and *Machiavillians* of this Age, who have in a manner turned the truth of the Christian Religion, and the most certain Rules of Providence into Atheism, and becom'd vain Idolaters, to sacrifice to the falsely adored and deified fancies of their own craft and cunning, think or say what they

Gregor. Homil.   please, yet the rule of pious *Gregory* will ever hold true : *Ille veritatis defensor esse debet, qui quum rectè sentit, loqui non metuit,*

Chrysost. sup. Math.   *nec erubescit.* And that of *Chrysostom* ought never to be forgotten by a good Christian, and one that fears God, who saith : *Non solùm proditor est veritatis, qui mendacium pro veritate loquitur : sed qui non liberè pronuntiat veritatem, quam pronuntiare oportet, aut non liberè defendit veritatem, quam defendere oportet.* But as there have been some that have been affrighted with the feigned

                                          Bugbears

Bugbears of malevolent mens cenſures and ſcandals ; ſo there have been others, to whom Nature hath given greater Magnanimity, who were better principled in their Morals, and better rudimented in the Chriſtian Religion, that have ſcorned and undervalued thoſe cenſures as vanities and trifles, and theſe were thoſe

——————*Quos Jupiter æquus amavit,*
Et meliore lu.) finxit præcordia Titan.

Theſe were thoſe that for the advancement of Truth and Learning, and the benefit of Mankind durſt undertake

Ire per excubias, & ſe committere Parcis.

And feared not the tempeſtuous ſtorms of venemous tongues, or malicious minds, of which we ſhall here enumerate a competent Catalogue.

1. In the firſt place we need not travel far, either in regard of time or place, to find Precedents of ſuch as have undergone no ſmall cenſures and ſubſannations for vindicating Truth, and labouring the advancement of it, though againſt common and deep-rooted Opinion. So ill entertainment new Inventors and Inventions have always found amongſt the preſent Maſters of ſeveral Profeſſions, and thoſe that made the World believe, that they alone had gained the Monopoly of all Learning. Our learned Country-man Doctor *Hackwell* in his Preface to his Apology, hath ſufficiently proved this particular : whoſe profound Piece of proving no decay in Nature (a truth now ſufficiently known, and aſſented to) found no ſmall oppoſition, both from the Learned in Theology, and other perſons, and underwent many ſharp cenſures, until men had more conſiderately weighed the ſtrength and cogency of his Arguments, which carry ſufficient evidence to confute rational perſons. Our learned and moſt induſtrious Anatomiſt Dr. *Harvey*, who (notwithſtanding the late Cavils of ſome) firſt found forth and evidenced to the World that rare and profitable diſcovery of the Circulation of the Blood, did undergo the like Fate : who for eighteen or twenty years together did groan under the heavy cenſure of all the Galeniſts and expert Anatomiſts almoſt in *Europe*, and was railed upon, and bitterly written againſt, not only by ſuch as *Alexander Roſſe* and Dr. *Primroſe*, but by *Riolanus* and others, and not forborn by that famous Phyſician of *Roterodam*, *Zacharias Sylvius*, who ingenuouſly confeſſeth thus much : *Primum mihi inventum hoc non placuit, quod & voce & ſcripto publicè teſtatus ſum ; ſed dum poſtea ei reſultando & explodendo vehementiùs incumbo, refutor & ipſe & explodor : adeò ſunt rationes ejus non perſuadentes, ſed cogentes : diligenter omnes examinavi, & in vivis aliquot canibus eum in ſinem à me diſſectis, veriſſimum comperi.* Which was a moſt candid and free retractation and confeſſion of his own errours, and may be propoſed as an example to all raſh and unadviſed Cenſurers. Neither could this moſt clear and evidential Verity (which falls under ocular Demonſtration and manifeſt Experiments) find countenance in the World, until that *Wallæus*, *Plempius,*

Praf. in Harvai Exerc. Anat.

B 2   *pius,*

pius, and divers other judicious and accurate Anatomists, had found the truth of *Harvey's* opinion, by their own tryals and ocular inspection: so difficult it is to overthrow an old radicated opinion. For I have known some years ago, that a person for owning or maintaining the Circulation of the blood, should have been censured and derided, as much by other Physicians, as one should be now for denying the same: so hard it is to root out an opinion (though never so false and groundless) if once setled in the brains of many, and hath had a long current of continued reputation and belief. And it is much more to consider the ignorance, stupidity, and perversness of those, that in this Age of Knowledge dare take upon them to censure (nay to condemn) that Society of persons, and their endeavours, who have a just, pious, merciful, and learned King for their Founder, and the greatest number of Nobility and Gentry, renowned both for divine and humane Knowledge, that can be chosen forth of the three Nations for their Members, and whose undertakings and level are the most high, noble, and excellent that ever yet the World was partaker of. And yet (which may be wondred at) I have not only met with many, that do censure and misjudge their vast and laudable enterprise, but even have been bold to appear in Print to censure and scandalize their proceedings, as is manifest in that Piece styled *Plus ultra*, written by Mr. *Stubbs* of *Warwick*, wherein he hath effected as much as Dogs do by barking at the Moon. But it is plain, that highness of place, or greatness of parts exempts no man from evil tongues, or bad censures. And to this purpose I cannot but add Dr. *Casaubon*, who as he had a long sickness of body, so doubtless he wanted not some distemper of mind, when in his Treatise of Credulity and

Pag. 3.

Incredulity, he uttered this. "If I may speak my mind (he saith) "without offence, this prodigious propensity to innovation in all "kinds, but in matters of Learning particularly, which so many "upon no ground, that I can see, or appearance of reason, are "possessed with; I know not what we should more probably a-"scribe it unto, than to some sad Constellation or Influence. Alas! poor man, he was so blind, that he could see no ground or appearance of reason for the usefulness of Experimental Philosophy, nor for the Institution of the Royal Society, but must ascribe it to the Stars: it is a wonder why he ascribes it not to natural Melancholy, as he doth almost all strange Effects, in his Book of Enthusiasm, or why not unto Demons or Witches, as he doth the most things in the Treatise quoted.

2. That learned and painful person *Renatus des Cartes*, who brought in, revived, and refined the old Doctrine of Atoms, ascribed to *Democritus*, and other of the Ancients, found for a long time much opposition; insomuch that when he lived at *Utrecht* in *Holland*, the Aristotelian Professors of that University became so inflamed with envy at him, that their Scholars raised the Rabble of the City at the sound of a Bell, to drive him out of Town. And

yet

yet this mans Philofophy hath had the luck to triumph in that
Univerfity, where fo much contempt was poured upon him; for
Henricus Regius, the publick Profeffor of Phyfick there, hath publifhed a Book of Natural Philofophy, agreeable to the Principles
and defign of *Des Cartes :* and is in a manner generally received
and applauded; and by the honourable Mr. *Boyle* much made ufe
of, and by him ftyled the Corpufcularian Philofophy.   So was not
that muft learned and diligent Mathematician *Galalæus* imprifoned
for feeing more than others could by the help of his Optick Glaffes,
lofing (as one faith) his own liberty in Prifon, for giving the Earth
liberty to fetch a round about the Sun? And yet now to what
great height of improvement are Telefcopes arrived unto, and
what credit is given to the Obfervations made with them? though
in their birth their firft Author and Ufer fo much oppofed and punifhed; for all Inventions that are new (as well as Opinions) are
in their beginnings oppofed and cenfured, not confidering, that all
acquired Knowledge, and all Arts and Sciences were once new, and
had their beginnings.

3. When *Jofephus Quercotanus* and Sir *Theodore Mayern* did labour to introduce the practice of Chymical Phyfick into the City
of *Paris*, what cruel cenfures and fcandals did they undergo by all
the reft of the Phyficians of the Colledge, fo that they were accounted illiterate and ignorant Fellows and dangerous Empiricks,
not fit to practife in the King of *France* his Dominions, and fo were
fentenced by the Colledge, and prohibited to practife? So far did
ignorance, felf-intereft, and blind malice prevail againft thefe two
perfons, of fo much Worth and Learning, infomuch that the former
was made Phyfician to the King of *France*, and lived to fee defpifed
Chymiftry to flourifh, where it had been moft contemned, himfelf
to be honoured, and his Chymical Works to be publifhed, and to be
had in great and general efteem with all that were Lovers of Learning.   The latter likewife out-lived the malice of all his enemies,
and faw himfelf advanced to be Phyfician to two potent and renowned Kings of *England*, and to have the general practice of the
moft of the Nobility and Gentry of the Kingdom, and to live to
a fair old age, and to dye vaftly rich.   So that even the braveft
men, for their noble endeavors for the good of Mankind, have always found harfh ufage.

4. It hath fared no better with divers perfons that have written
of abftrufe and myfterious Subjects, fuch as were *Arnoldus de Villa
Nova* and *Raimundus Lullius*, who, becaufe they handled that fecret and fublime Art of the Tranfmutation of Metals, were by the
ignorance and malice of *Francis Pegna* and the *John Tredefchen* of   *Mund. fubter.*
Rome, *Athanafius Kircherus*, with fome others, branded with the   *lib.* 11. *fect.* 2:
name of Magicians., taken in the worft fenfe.   *Facile eft reprehen-*   *pag.* 277.
dere & maledicere, fo apt are men through over-weening pride and
felf-conceitednefs, as though they were ignorant of nothing, to
take upon them to cenfure all things, when Artifts only are fit to
                                            judge

jndge of thofe proper Arts, in which they are verft and bred in, and not others : For it is not fufficient for a man to be verft in many parts of Learning, but alfo in that very Science or Art, in which the Queftion is propounded : as for Example ; Suppofe a man to be well read in School Theology, Metaphyficks, Logick, Grammar, Rhetorick, Ethicks, and Phyficks, yet for all this how unable were he to refolve one of the difficulteft Propofitions in *Euclid?* no more can any perfon, though never fo generally learned, if he perfectly do not underftand the method, terms, ground, matter, and end of the Writers in myftical Chymiftry, be any competent Judge of their Art, nor of the nature of Tranfmutation. And this might juftly have bridled *Kircher*, and many other rafh and vain Cenfurers to hold back their judgment, until they perfectly underftand the matter, about which they are to give judgment, and to have

Prov. 25.12. confidered that Maxime of the wifeft of men : *Seeft thou a man wife in his own conceit ? there is more hope of a fool than of him.* But notwithftanding thefe groundlefs flanders againft *Arnoldus*, that he was guilty of Diabolical Magick, from which the Pen of learned *Nandæus* hath totally difcharged him, though he otherwife (accor-

Hift. Magic. c.14.p.177. ding to his petulant humor and prejudiced opinion againft the Art of Tranfmutation, of which he was no competent Judge, for the reafon foregoing) caft fome unworthy reflections both upon him, and *Lully*, yet he confeffeth (which is but the bare truth, as every learned Phyfician doth fufficiently know, that have heedfully read his Writings of the Art of Medicine) in thefe words, "That it is "certain, he was the learnedeft Phyfician of his time, equally ac-"quainted with the Latine, Greek, and Arabian Tongues, and one "whofe Writings fufficiently witnefs his abilities in the Mathema-"ticks, Medicine, and Philofophy, the practice whereof gained him "favour and imployment about Pope *Clement*, and Frederick King "of *Sicily*, who certainly would never have made ufe of him, if he "had thought him a Conjurer or Magician, fuch as may judged "he was. As for *Lully* (notwithftanding the malevolent froth of fome rafh, malicious, and ignorant Writers) he was guilty of no other Magick but what was natural, lawful, and laudable, as his profound and learned Works (if his blind Adverfaries had ever taken pains to have perufed them, who frequently cenfure and condemn thofe things they never faw, read, or underftood) do witnefs beyond all exception, and is all juftified by the teftimonies of fo many learned and judicious perfons, that more cannot be faid to his praife and vindication. The moft of his learned Works being kept in the Library at *Oxford*, written in an ancient hand : which would never have been done, if they had not been highly efteemed and pri-

D. Arte Lullian. Præf. fed. For as *Zetznerus* the great Stationer of *Stasburgh* faith : "*Tantæ* "*fuo fuiffe ævo authoritatis atq; æftimationis legitur, ut juftiffimi* "*Arragonum Reges eum in privilegiis eidem conceffis, magnum in* "*Philofophia magiftrum, & mirandarum artium & fcientiarum* "*authorem nominârint.* Laftly, one Father *Pacificus* in his Jour-

ney

ney from *Perſia* 1628. came into the Iſle of *Majorca*, where *Lully* was born, and to his great admiration found the Statue of *Lully* there in Wood curiouſly coloured, and he honoured as a Saint (whom he had before judged an Heretick) as alſo a Society of Profeſſors following the Doctrine of *Lully*, and called *Raymundines* or *Lulliſts*, and that they affirmed, that by Divine illumination he had the perfect knowledge of Nature, by which he found out the univerſal Medicine, by a certain *Aurum potabile*, by which he prolonged his life to the 145. year of his age, in which year he ſuffered Martyrdom. This I have produced to ſhew how inconſiderately and ignorantly the beſt learned of an Age may be, and often are wrongfully and falſely traduced and ſlandered, which may be a warning to all perſons to take heed how they paſs their cenſures, until they underſtand perfectly all that is neceſſary to be known about the Subject they are to give judgment of, before they utter or declare their ſentence.

5. *Roger Bacon* our Country-man, who was a *Franciſcan* Fryar, and Doctor of Divinity, the greateſt Chymiſt, Aſtrologer, and Mathematician of his time, yet could not eſcape the injurious and unchriſtian cenſure of being a Conjurer, and ſo hard put to it, that as *Pitts* ſaith, he was twice cited to *Rome* by *Clement* the Fourth, to purge himſelf of that accuſation, and was forced to ſend his Optical and Mathematical Inſtruments to *Rome*, to ſatisfie the Pope and the Conclave, which he amply performed, and came off with honor and applauſe. To vindicate whom I need ſay little, becauſe it is already performed by the Pens of thoſe learned perſons, *Pitts*, *Leland*, *Selden*, and *Nandæus*, only I ſhall add one Sentence forth of that moſt learned Treatiſe, *De mirabili poteſtate artis & naturæ, & de nullitate magiæ*. Where he ſaith thus: *Quicquid autem eſt præter operationem naturæ vel artis, aut non eſt humanum, aut eſt fictum & fraudibus occupatum.* Another of our Country-men Dr. *John Dee*, the greateſt and ableſt Philoſopher, Mathematician, and Chymiſt that his Age (or it may be ever ſince) produced, could not evade the cenſure of the Monſter-headed multitude, but even in his life time was accounted a Conjurer, of which he moſt ſadly (and not without cauſe) complaineth in his moſt learned Preface to *Euclid*, Engliſhed by Mr. *Billingſley*, and there ſtrongly apologizeth for himſelf, with that zeal and fervency, that may ſatisfie any rational Chriſtian, that he was no ſuch wicked perſon, as to have viſible and familiar converſe (if any ſuch thing can be now adays) with the Devil, the known Enemy of Mankind, of which take this ſhort paſſage, where he ſaith: "O my unkind Country-men, O unnatu-"ral Country-men, O unthankful Country-men, O brain-ſick, raſh, "ſpiteful, and diſdainful Country-men, why oppreſs you me thus "violently with your ſlandering of me contrary to verity, and "contrary to your own conſciences? Yet notwithſtanding this, and his known abilities in the moſt parts of abſtruſe Learning, the great reſpect that he had from divers Princes, Nobles, and the

                                                                                moſt

Vide Relat. Parvit. impr. f. Gallic, 1631.

Lib. 1. de Script. Anglic.

Cap. 1.

moſt Learned in all *Europe*, could not protect him from this harſh and unjuſt cenſure. For Dr. *Caſaubon* near fifty years after Dr. *Dees* death, hath in the year 1659. publiſhed a large Book in Folio of *Dees* converſing for many years with Spirits (wicked ones he meaneth.) But how Chriſtian-like this was done, to wound the mans reputation ſo many years after his death, and with that horrid and wicked ſlander of having familiarity with Devils for many years in his life time, which tends to the loſs both of body and ſoul, and to regiſter him amongſt the damned, how Chriſtian-like this is, I leave all Chriſtians to judge? Beſides, let all the World judge in this caſe, that Dr. *Caſaubon* being a ſworn Witchmonger, even to the credulity of the filthieſt and moſt impoſſible of their actions, cannot but allow of the Law that doth puniſh them for digging up the bones of the dead, to uſe them to Superſtition or Sorcery; what may he then think the World may judge him guilty of, for uncovering the Dormitories of the deceaſed, not to abuſe their bones, but to throw their Souls into the deepeſt pit of Hell? A wickedneſs certainly beyond the greateſt wickedneſs, that he can believe is committed by Witches. It is manifeſt, that he hath not publiſhed this meerly as a true relation of the matter of fact, and ſo to leave it to others to judge of; but that deſignedly he hath laboured to repreſent *Dee* as a moſt infamous and wicked perſon, as may be plainly ſeen in the whole drift of his tedious Preface. But his deſign to make *Dee* a Converſer with evil Spirits was not all, he had another that concerned himſelf more nearly. He had before run in a manner (by labouring to make all that which he called Enthuſiaſm, to be nothing elſe but impoſture or melancholy and depraved phantaſie, ariſing from natural cauſes) into the cenſure of being a Sadducee or Atheiſt. To waſh off which he thought nothing was ſo prevalent, as to leap into the other end of the balance (the mean is hard to be kept) to weigh the other down, by publiſhing ſome notorious Piece that might (as he thought) in an high degree manifeſt the exiſtence of Spirits good and bad, and this he thought would effect it ſufficiently, or at leaſt wipe off the former imputation that he had contracted.

But that I may not be too tedious, I ſhall ſum up briefly ſome others, by which it may be made clear, that thoſe dauntleſs Spirits that have adventured to croſs the current of common opinion, and thoſe that have handled abſtruſe Subjects, have never wanted oppoſition and ſcandal, how true or profitable ſoever the things were that they treated or writ of. *Trithemius* that Honour and Ornament of *Germany* for all ſorts of Literature, wanted not a *Bouillus* to calumniate and condemn him of unlawful Magick, from which all the Learned in *Europe* know he is abſolved, by the able and elegant Pen of him that ſtyles himſelf *Guſtavus Silenus*, and others. *Cornelius Agrippa* run the ſame Fate, by the ſcribling of that ignorant and envious Monk *Paulus Jovius*, from whoſe malicious ſlander he is totally acquitted by the irrefragable evidence of *Wierus*, *Melchior*

Melchior Adams, Nandæus, and others. Who almost have not read or heard of the horrid and abominable false scandals laid upon that *totius Germaniæ decus, Paracelsus*, by the malevolent Pen of *Erastus*, and after swallowed up with greediness by *Libanius, Conringius, Sennertus*, and many others? for not only labouring to bring in a new Theory and Practice into the Art of Medicine, but also for striving to purge and purifie the ancient, natural, laudable, and lawful Magick from the filth and dregs of Imposture, Deceit, Ceremonies, and Superstitions : yet hath not wanted most strong and invincible Champions to defend him, as *Dorne, Petrus Severinus, Smetius, Crollius, Bitiscius*, and many others. Our Countryman Dr. *Fudd*, a man acquainted with all kinds of Learning, and one of the most Christian Philosophers that ever writ, yet wanted not those snarling Animals, such as *Marsennus, Lanovius, Foster*, and *Gassendus*, as also our *Casaubon* (as mad as any) to accuse him vainly and falsely of Diabolical Magick, from which the strength of his own Pen and Arguments did discharge him without possibility of replies. We shall now come to those that have treated of Witchcraft, and strongly opposed and confuted the many wonderful and incredible actions and power ascribed unto Witches : and these crossing the vogue of the common opinion, have not wanted their loads of unworthy and unchristian scandals cast upon them, of which we shall only name these two, *Wierus* a learned person, a German, and in his time Physician to the Duke of *Cleve* ; the other our Country-man Mr. *Reginald Scot*, a person of competent Learning, pious, and of a good Family : what is said against them in particular, I shall recite, and give a brief responsion unto it.

1. There is a little Treatise in Latine titled *Dæmonologia*, fathered upon King *James* (how truly we shall not dispute, for some ascribe it to others) where in the Preface these two persons are intimated to be Witches, and that they writ against the common opinion, concerning the Power of Witches, the better to shelter and conceal their Diabolical skill. But indeed this groundless accusation needs no confutation, but rather scorn and derision, as having no rational ground of probability at all, that they should be such cursed Hypocrites, or dissembling Politicians, the one being a very learned and able Physician, as both his Writings do witness, and that upright and unpartial Author *Melchior Adams* in his life hath most amply declared : the other known (as not living so very many years ago) to be a godly, learned, and an upright man, as his Book which he calleth, *The Discovery of Witchcraft*, doth most largely make it appear, if his Adversaries had ever taken the pains to peruse it. So that all rational persons may plainly see, that it is but a lying invention, a malicious device, and a meer forged accusation.

2. These persons are accused to have absolutely denied the existence of Witches, which we shall demonstrate to be notoriously false, by these following reasons.

C

1. Could

1. Could ever any rational man have thought or believed, that Mr. *Glanvil*, a person who pretends to such high parts, would have expressed so much weakness and impudence, as to have charged Mr. *Scot* with the flat denial of the existence of Witches, as he doth in these words (speaking of him? and pretends this to be a Confutation of the being of Witches and Apparitions; and this he intimates in divers other places, but without any quotation, to shew where or in what words *Scot* doth simply deny the Being of Witches, which he doth no where maintain : so confident are many to charge others with that which they neither hold nor write.

Considerat. about Witchcraft, p. 76.

2. Mr. *Scot* and *Wierus* do not state the Question, *An sint*, Whether there be Witches or not, but *Quomodo sint*, in what manner they act.   So that their Question is only, What kind of power supposed Witches have, or do act by, and what the things are that they do or can perform : so that the state of the question is not simply of the Being of Witches, or *de existentia*, but only *de modo existendi :* wherein it is plain, that every Dispute *de modo existendi*, doth necessarily grant and suppose the certainty of the Existence, otherwise the Dispute of the manner of their Being, Properties, Power, or Acts would have no ground or foundation at all. As if I and another should dispute about the extent, buildings, and situation of the great City *Peking* in *China*, or about the length, breadth, and height of the great Wall dividing *China* from *Tartary*; we both do take for granted, that there is such a City, and such a Wall, otherwise our Dispute would be wild, vain, and groundless : like the two Wise-men of *Gotham*, who strove and argued about the driving of sheep over a bridge; the one affirming he would drive his sheep over the bridge, and the other protesting against it, and so begun, one as it were to drive, and the other to stay and stop them, when there were no sheep betwixt them.   And this might be a sufficient document to Mr. *Glanvil*, to have been more sober, than to have charged *Scot* so falsely.   And do not the ancient Fathers differ in their opinions *circa Angelorum modum existendi*, some of them holding them to be corporeal, and some incorporeal ? yet both these parties did firmly hold their existence : so that this is a false and improper charge, and hath no basis to stand upon at all.

3. What man of reason and judgment could have believed, that Mr. *Glanvil* or Dr. *Casaubon*, being persons that pretend to a great share of Learning, and to be exact in their ways of arguing, would have committed so pitiful and gross a fault, as is *fallacia consequentis ?* For if I deny that a Witch cannot flye in the air, nor be transformed or transubstantiated into a Cat, a Dog, or an Hare, or that the Witch maketh any visible Covenant with the Devil, or that he sucketh on their bodies, or that the Devil hath carnal Copulation with them; I do not thereby deny either the Being of Witches, nor other properties that they may have, for which they may be so called : no more than if I deny that a Dog hath rugibi-

lity

lity (which is only proper to a Lion) doth it follow that I deny
the being of a Dog, or that he hath latrability? this is meer incon-
fequential, and hath no connexion. So if I deny that a man cannot flye by his natural abilities in the air like a Bird, nor live continually in the Sea as a fiſh, nor in the earth as a Worm or Mole,
this doth not at all infer that I deny the exiſtence of man, nor his
other properties of riſibility, rationality, or the like. But this is
the learned Logick, and the clear ways of arguing that theſe men
uſe.

3. A third ſcandal Mr. *Glanvil* throws upon him is this, where
he ſaith thus: "For the Author doth little but tell odd tales and *Pag. 76.*
"ſilly Legends, which he confutes and laughs at, and pretends this
"to be a confutation of the Being of Witches and Apparitions. In
"all which, his reaſonings are trifling and childiſh; and when he
"ventures at Philoſophy, he is little better than abſurd. Dr. *Ca*-
"*ſaubon*, though he confeſſeth he had never read *Scots* Book, but Of Credul. and
"as he had found it by chance in friends houſes, or Book-ſellers Incredul. p.40.
"Shops, yet doth rank him amongſt the number of his illiterate
"Wretches, and tells us how Dr. *Reynolds* did cenſure him and
"ſome others. To theſe, though they be not much material, we
ſhall give poſitive and convincing anſwers.

1. There is no greater ſign of the weakneſs of a mans cauſe, nor
his inability to defend it, than when he ſlips over the ſubſtance of
the queſtion in hand, and begins to fall foul upon the adverſe
party, to throw dirt and filth upon him, and to abuſe and ſlander
him: this is a thing very uſual, but exceeding baſe, and plainly
demonſtrates the badneſs of their cauſe.

2. If Mr. *Scot* hath done little but told odd tales and ſilly Legends, Mr. *Glanvil* might very well have born with him; for I
am ſure his ſtory of the Drummer, and his other of Witchcraft are
as odd and ſilly, as any can be told or read, and are as futilous,
incredible, ludicrous, and ridiculous as any can be. And if the
tales that *Scot* tells be odd and ſilly, they are the moſt of them taken from thoſe pitiful lying Witchmongers, ſuch as *Delrio*, *Bodinus*, *Springerus*, *Remigius*, and the like, the Authors that are moſt
eſteemed with Dr. *Caſaubon*, and other Witchmongers, of whom
we ſhall ſay more hereafter.

3. For Mr. *Glanvil* to give general accuſations without particular proofs, as to ſay *Scots* reaſonings are trifling and childiſh, and
when he ventures at Philoſophy, he is little better than abſurd, do
plainly manifeſt the mans malice, and diſcover his weakneſs: For
dolus verſatur in univerſalibus, and no man ought to be condemned without particular and punctual proof, as to the time, place,
and all other circumſtances, which Mr. *Glanvil* could not do, and
therefore he only gives general calumniations without ground; and
if *Scot* were little better than abſurd, then he the better agrees
with Mr. *Glanvil*, whoſe Platonical Whimſeys are as abſurd as any,
as we ſhall ſufficiently prove hereafter.

4. Dr. *Caſaubon* muſt needs have been highly elevated with the deſire of cenſuring, when he would condemn a man without reading his Book, or ſerious weighing the force of his arguments, this concludes him of vaſt weakneſs, and of great perverſneſs of mind, as all rational men may judge ; for in effect it is this, *Scot* is an illiterate Wretch, and his Book full of errors, but I never read it, but as I have looked upon it at a friends houſe, or a Book-ſellers Shop : is not this a wretched ground whereupon to build ſo wretched a foundation, as thereby to judge him an illiterate Wretch ? And to cenſure him by the report of others, is as unjuſt, weak, and childiſh as the former ; and though Dr. *Reynolds* were a learned man, it doth not appear for what particular point or errour he cenſured *Scot*, and therefore is but a general and groundleſs charge, ſheltred under the colour of Dr. *Reynolds* reputation, an evidence, in Reaſon and Law, of no weight or validity.

5. For Dr. *Caſaubon* to rank him amongſt illiterate Wretches, is againſt the very Rule of the Law of Nature, that teaches all men, that they ſhould not do that to another, which they would not have another to do unto them. . And ſure Dr. *Caſaubon* would not have another to judge and condemn him for an illiterate Wretch, and therefore he ought not to have condemned Mr. *Scot* to be ſo. And as it is againſt the Law of Nature, ſo it is contrary to the rules of modeſty and morality to give a man ſuch ſtigmatizing titles : nay it is even againſt the rules of good manners and civil education, but that ſome men think that it is lawful for them to ſay any thing, and that nothing what they ſay doth miſbeſeem them. And laſtly, how far it is againſt the Rules of Chriſtianity and Piety, let all good Chriſtians judge.

6. The falſity of this foul ſcandal is manifeſt in both the particulars therein couched. 1. For Mr. *Scot* was a learned and diligent perſon, as the whole Treatiſe will bear witneſs ; he underſtood the Latine Tongue, and ſomething of the Greek, and for the Hebrew, if he knew nothing of it, yet he had procured very good helps, as appeareth in his expounding the ſeveral words that are uſed in the Scriptures for ſuppoſed Witches and Witchcraft : as alſo his quoting of divers of the Fathers, the reformed Miniſters, and many other Authors beſides, which ſufficiently prove that he was not illiterate. 2. And that he was no wretched perſon, is apparent, being a man of a good Family, a conſiderable Eſtate, a man of a very commendable government, and a very godly and zealous Proteſtant, as I have been informed by perſons of worth and credit, and is ſufficiently proved by his Writing.

I have not been thus tedious to accumulate theſe inſtances of men that have been cenſured, for oppoſing vulgar opinions, or writing of abſtruſe Subjects, as circumſtantial only, or for a flouriſh, but meerly as they are introductive, neceſſary, and pertinent to the purpoſe I intend in this Treatiſe, as I ſhall make manifeſt in theſe Rules or Obſervations following, and ſhall add ſufficient reaſons to confirm the ſame.

1. That

1. That the generality of an opinion, or the numerousness of *Rule* 1.
the persons that hold and maintain it, are not a safe and warrantable ground to receive it, or to adhere unto it : nor that it is safe or
rational to reject an opinion, because they are but few that do hold
it, or the number but small that maintain it. And this I shall labour to make good by these sure and firm arguments following.

1. Because the Scriptures tell us thus much : *Thou shalt not fol-* Exod. 13. 2.
low the multitude to do evil. And that there are many deceivers :
For many shall come in my Name, saying, I am Christ, and shall de- Mat. 24. 5.
ceive many. And woe unto you, when all men shall speak well of Luke 6. 26.
you : for so did their fathers to the false Prophets. From whence
it is plain, that first we are to consider and be assured, that the
matter be not evil ; for if it be, we are not at all to be swayed
with the multitudes that follow it, or that uphold it : so if the
opinion be evil, erroneous, or false, we ought not to receive
it, or adhere unto it, though never so many do hold or maintain it. So that in truth and substance, we are not at all to consider, whether there be few or many that hold it, but simply,
whether it be true or not. For as *Plato* tells us : *Neq; id conside-*
randum quid dixerit, sed utrum verè dicatur nec ne. For the multitude have been by all good Authors and Learned men always
esteemed the most erroneous, as *Seneca* saith : *Quærendum non quod* Lib. de vit.
vulgo placet, peßimo veritatis interpreti. And *Lactantius* teaches beat. Lactant.
us this : *Vulgus indoctum pompis inanibus gaudet, animisq; pueri-* Duimar. Instit.
bus spectat omnia, oblectatur frivolis, nec ponderare secum unam- l. 2. c. 3.
quamq; rem potest. And our Saviour gives us a proof and instance
of the errour of the multitude, and that in matter of fact. Did
not almost all the Jews under divers Kings Raigns applaud and
approve of the doctrine and opinions of the false Prophets, though
utterly erroneous ? insomuch that *Elijah* said, that he only was left
of the true Prophets, though the false ones were many and numerous. So that the Rule is proved to be true, both by the precept
and example of the Scriptures.

2. If we consider the generality of Mankind, either in respect of
their inclinations and dispositions, or their breeding and education,
we shall not find one of an hundred, either by nature inclined, or
by education fitted and qualified to search forth and understand
the truth. And then if there be an hundred to one drowned in
ignorance and errors, and so few fitted to understand the truth of
things either divine or natural, then it must needs follow, that it is
not safe to embrace or adhere to an opinion, because of the great
number of those that hold or maintain it, but rather to stick to
the smaller number ; though neither simply ought to be regarded,
but truth it self.

3. Again, if we consider those numbers, that either by nature
are inclined, or by education trained up in Learning, to enable
them to judge rightly betwixt truth and truth-likeliness, how few
of these that prove any thing excellent in those parts of Learning
                                                         wherein

wherein they are bred, we may eafily fee the verity of this Rule fufficiently proved, that it is not fafe to embrace or adhere to an opinion, becaufe the numbers are great that hold or maintain it.

4. If the multitude that hold the opinions, whether of fpiritual or natural things were to be followed, meerly becaufe of the great numbers that hold them : then if we look and confider the Writings of the beft Geographers, Travellers, and Navigators, we fhould either be of the opinions of the Pagans, who are the moft numerous part of Mankind, or the Mahumetans, which are many in refpect of the paucity of Chriftians.   And then what horrid, blafphemous, idolatrous, impious, and diabolical opinions muft we receive and hold, both concerning God, Angels, the Creation, and the moft of the operations that are produced by Nature ? So that the arguments of Dr. *Cafaubon* and Mr. *Glanvil*, drawn from the univerfality of the opinion, and the great multitudes of thofe that hold it, are vain and groundlefs.

5. If the comparifon I ufe be thought too large, and the rule be put only as to the greater part of the Learned that are in *Europe*, yet it will hold good, that the greateft part of the Learned are not to be adhered to, becaufe of their numeroufnefs ; nor that the reft are to be rejected, becaufe of their paucity.   For it is known fufficiently, that a Bifhop of *Mentz* was cenfured and excommunicated for holding that there were *Antipodes*, by fome hundreds of thofe that were accounted learned and wife : fo that it is plain, that the greater number may be in the errour, and thofe that are few be in the right.   And did not the greateft number of the Phyficians in *Europe* altogether adhere to the Doctrine of *Galen*, though now in *Germany, France, England,* and many other Nations the moft have exploded it ? And was not the *Ariftotelian* Philofophy embraced by the greateft part of all the Learned in *Europe* ? And have not the *Cartefians* and others fufficiently now manifefted the errours and imperfections of it, and efpecially the endeavors of the honourable and learned Members of the Royal Society here in *England*, and the like Societies beyond Seas by their continual labour and vigilancy about Experiments, made the errours and defects of it obvious to all inquifitive perfons? So that multitude, as multitude, ought not to lead or fway us, but truth it felf.

6. If to all this we add, that truth in it felf is but one ; for *unum* and *verum* are convertibles, and that errour or falfity is various and manifold, and that there may be a thoufand errours about one particular thing, and yet but one truth ; it will neceffarily follow, the greateft number holding an opinion, cannot be fafe to be followed, becaufe of their multitude, and the reafon is errour, is manifold, truth but one.

Rule 2.   2. It is not fafe nor rational to receive or adhere to an opinion becaufe of its Antiquity ; nor to reject one becaufe of its Novelty. And this we fhall make good from and by thefe following reafons.

1. Becaufe there is no opinion (efpecially about created things)

things) but it hath once been new; and if an opinion should be rejected meerly because of novelty, then it will follow, that either all opinions might have been rejected for that very reason, or that novelty is no safe ground only, why an opinion should be opposed or rejected.

2. Antiquity and Novelty are but relations *quoad nostrum intellectum, non quoad naturam*; for the truth, as it is fundamentally in things *extra intellectum*, cannot be accounted either old or new. And an opinion, when first found out and divulged, is as much a truth then, as when the current of hundreds or thousands of years have passed since its discovery. For it was no less a truth, when in the infancy of Philosophy it was holden, that there was generation and corruption in Nature, in respect of Individuals, than it is now: so little doth Time, Antiquity, or Novelty alter, change, confirm, or overthrow truth; for *veritas est temporis filia*, in regard of its discovery to us or by us, who must draw it forth *è puteo Democriti*. And the existence of the *West-Indies* was as well before the discovery made by *Columbus* as since, and our ignorance of it did not impeach the truth of its being, neither did the novelty of its discovery make it less verity, nor the years since make it more: so that we ought simply to examine, whether an opinion be possible or impossible, probable or improbable, true or false; and if it be false, we ought to reject it, though it seem never so venerable by the white hairs of Antiquity; nor ought we to refuse it, though it seem never so young, or near its birth. For as St. Cyprian said: *Error vetustatis est vetustas erroris.*

3. In regard of Natural Philosophy, and the knowledge of the properties of created things, and the knowledge of them, we preposterously reckon former Ages, and the men that lived in them, the Ancients; which in regard of production and generation of the Individuals of their own Species are so; but in respect of knowledge and experience, this Age is to be accounted the most ancient. For as the learned Lord *Bacon* saith: "Indeed to speak truly, *Antiquitas seculi, juventus mundi,* Antiquity of time is the youth of the World. Certainly our times are the ancient times, when the World is now ancient, and not those which we count ancient, *ordine retrogrado,* by a computation backward from our own times; and yet so much credit hath been given to old Authors, as to invest them with the power of Dictators, that their words should stand, rather than admit them as Consuls to give advice. *Advanc. of Learn. l.1. c.5.*

3. It is not safe nor rational to resolve to stick to our old imbibed opinions, nor wilfully to reject those that seem new, except we be fully satisfied, from indubitable grounds, that what we account old is certainly true, and what we reckon to be new is undoubtedly false. And this will appear to be a truth, partly from the weakness of their arguments, that seem utterly to condemn all recession from ancient opinions, as vain, foolish, and unnecessary; as also from other positive reasons. *Rule 3.*

1. Some

1. Some give the reason why they will not recede from an opinion that their Predecessors held ; for that their Forefathers were as wise, if not wiser than they. But this, if strictly considered, is very lame and defective; for their Predecessors were but men, and so were liable both to active and passive deception, and were not exempted from the common frailty of Mankind, who are all subject to errours. And therefore, unless they were assured that their Ancestors in former Ages, held the certain and undoubted grounds of truth, it is nothing of reason in them, but meer perversness of will, rather obstinately *errare cum patribus*, than to learn to follow the truth with those that are coetaneous with them, which is foolish and irrational. Further, there are more helps now, and means to attain the knowledge of Verity, than were in the days when their Ancestors lived, and it must be a kind of the greatest madness to shut their eyes, that the light of truth may not appear unto them.

2. This kind of reasoning hath no more of reason in it, than if one should say, that because his Grandfather and great Grandfather were blind or lame, therefore they will be so too: or that their Ancestors never learned the Greek or Latine Tongues, nor to write or read, neither will they learn any more than they did : or that their Predecessors were ill husbands and unthrifts, and that therefore they will continue the same courses: or that because their Forefathers followed drunkenness and luxury, therefore they will continue the same cariere of vices, as many of our debauched persons do now adays, having no better reasons to alledge for their exorbitant and vicious courses, but what the Prophet condemned, *The fathers have eaten sowr grapes, and the childrens teeth are set on edge.*

3. How far would they run back to state the beginning of their Ancestors? If as far as their first Originals, then they must all be Savages, Barbarians, and Heathens. And if they state it distant from their first Originals, then their Predecessors had the same reason to have continued, as those did that preceded them. But if their Ancestors varied from, and left the steps and opinions of those that went before them, then if they will do as their Ancestors did, they must leave their courses and opinions, as they had done of those that preceded them.

4. Some say they cannot recede from the opinions of their Predecessors, because it would be a shame and disgrace unto them. But that which we call shame and disgrace consists in the opinion of others, and we ought not to receive errour, or reject truth, by reason of the censures or opinions of others : *Si de veritate scandalum* *Augist. lib. de Liber. Arbitrio.* *sumitur, utilius permittitur nasci scandalum, quàm veritas relinquatur.* And to leave an errour to entertain truth, is so far from being a shame and a disgrace, that there cannot be a greater honour or glory : for *errare humanum est, sed in errore perseverare belluinum ac diabolicum est.*

Rule 4.   4. Those effects that seem strange and wonderful, either in respect of of Art or Nature, require much diligence truly to difcover and find out their caufes; and we ought not rafhly to attribute thofe effects to the Devil, whofe caufes are latent or unknown unto us: and that for thefe grounds.

1. It hath been common almoft in all Ages, not only for the vulgar, but alfo for the whole rabble of Demonographers and Witchmongers to afcribe thofe ftrange and wonderful effects, whether arifing from Art or Nature, unto the worft of Gods Creatures, if they did not themfelves underftand their caufes, and to cenfure the Authors that writ of them, as Conjurers and Magicians, as I have made manifeft in my former Inftances, and might be further made good and illuftrated by the effects of healing by the Weapon-falve, the Sympathetick Powder, the Curing of divers Difeafes by Appenfions, Amulets, or by Tranfplantation, and many other moft admirable effects both of Art and Nature, which by thefe felf-conceited Ignorants are all thrown upon the Devils back, and he made the Author and effector of them, as though he had a kind of omnipotent power: of which the learned Philofopher and Phyfician *Van Helmont* gives us this account: " *Credo equidem cum pietate* De Inject.mater. " *pugnare, fi Diabolo tribuatur poteftas naturam fuperans. Verum* pag. 597. " *naturæ ignari præfumunt fe naturæ fecretarios per librorum lectio-* " *nem: quicquid autem ipfos latet, vel adynaton, vel falfum, vel* " *præftigiofum, atq; diabolicum efto.* And a little after he adds this: " *Pigritiæ faltem enim immenfæ inventum fuit, omnia in* Ibid. pag. 598. " *Diabolum retuliffe quæ non capimus, nec velim Diabolum invoca-* " *tum, ut noftris fatisfaciat quæftionibus per temerariam poteftatum* " *attributionem.*

2. Whofoever fhall read *Pancirollus de rebus memoralibus noviter repertis*, may eafily be fatisfied, what ftrange and ftupendious things Art and the Inventions of men have produced in thefe latter Ages. And no man can rationally doubt, but that many more as ftrange or far more wonderful, may in Ages to come be found out and difcovered; for there is a kind of bottomlefs depth in Arts, whether Liberal or Mechanical, that yet hath not been founded, but lye hid and unknown unto men. And if thefe for their wonderfulnefs fhould (as former Ages have ignorantly done) be afcribed unto the power of Satan, and their Authors accufed of Conjuring and Diabolical Magick, no greater wrong could be done unto Art and Artifts, and it would be a kind of blafphemy to attribute thefe ftupendious effects (as the Vulgar and Witchmongers ufe to do) unto the Devil, the worft of Gods Greatures, and the Enemy of Mankind.

3. The third argument I fhall take from Mr. *Glanvil* (which is the greateft piece of truth in all his Treatife) and convert and retort it againft him: and is this (he faith) *We are ignorant of the* Pag. 103. *extent and bounds of Natures Sphere and Poffibilities.* Now if we be ignorant of the extent and bounds of Natures Sphere and Poffibilities, then it muft needs be folly, madnefs, and derogative

againft

againſt Gods power in Nature, to attribute thoſe effects to wicked, fallen, and degenerated Demons, that we do not know but are produced by the courſe of Nature. And to aſcribe the products of Nature to ſuch wicked Inſtruments is blaſphemous, in depriving Nature of the honour due unto her, and robbing God of the honour and glory belonging unto him, for the wonderful power wherewith he hath endowed his Creatures, who were all made to

Rom. 1, 20. ſhew forth his power and Godhead, *and the Heavens declare the glory of God, and the Firmament ſheweth his handy-work :* and as one ſaid very well, *Natura creatrix eſt quædam vis & potentia divinitùs inſita, alia ex aliis in ſuo genere producens.* So that the honour that is due unto the Creator, Conſerver, and Orderer of Nature ought not to be aſcribed unto the Devils ; for in doing this, the Witchmongers become guilty of Idolatry, and are themſelves ſuch Witches as are mentioned in the Old Teſtament, who by their lying Divinations led the people after them to follow Idols; therefore the effects that belong unto Nature, are to be attributed to Nature, and the effects that Devils produce, are to be aſcribed unto them, and not one confounded with another. And much to

De Civit. Dei lib. 10. this purpoſe the learned Father hath a very conſiderable paſſage : " *Quicquid igitur mirabile ſit in hoc mundo, profectò minus eſt quàm* " *totus hic mundus, i. e. cælum & terra, & omnia quæ in eis* " *ſunt, quæ certè Deus fecit: nam & omni miraculo quod ſit per ho-* " *minem, majus miraculum eſt homo. Quamvis igitur miracula vi-* " *ſibilium naturarum videndi aſſiduitate vileſcunt, tamen ea quum* " *ſapienter intuemur, inuſitatiſſimis rariſq; majora ſunt.*

4. Though theſe men ſhould believe the power of the Devil to be great by his Creation, and not leſſened by his Fall (which is doubtful or falſe) yet can he not exert, or put this power into execution, but when, where, as oft, and in what manner, as God doth ſend, order, direct, and command him : and could not enter into the herd of Swine, until that Chriſt had ordered and com-

Job 1. 11. & 2. 5. manded him; nor to touch *Job* or afflict him either in his goods or body, until that God had given him licence and order with expreſs limitation how far he ſhould proceed, and no further. In all which there appeareth nothing at all of his power, but his malice and evil will; and what was effected, was the hand of the Lord, and he but the bare Inſtrument to execute and perform the command. Therefore to aſcribe to the Devil the efficiency of thoſe operations we do not clearly underſtand, is to allow him a kind of Omnipotency, and both to rob God and Nature of that which belongeth unto them ; for the Almighty doth work whatſoever he pleaſes both in Heaven and Earth, and it is he that worketh all in all. And the Devil is but as Gods Executioner to fulfil his will

2 Pet. 2. 4. in tempting men, and puniſhing the wicked, and can act nothing but as God commands him, except the acts of his wicked and depraved will ; for he is with all his Angels delivered into chains of darkneſs to be reſerved unto Judgment. To this purpoſe there is

a very

a very true and Christian saying of St. *Augustine* in these words:
" *Diabolus plerumq; vult nocere, & non potest, quia potestas ista est* _{dig. q.}
" *sub potestate : nam si tantum posset nocere Diabolus quantum vult,*
" *aliquis justorum non remaneret.*

5. The last Rule I shall observe is, That men, if they mean to *Rule 5.*
profit by reading Controversies of this nature, they must prudently and deliberately consider the design that Authors have had in
writing. For though it be the general pretence of all, that they
write to confute errours, and to maintain truth, yet very few in
Disputes of this nature have sincerely performed this pretended
end. For some have written (as we shall hereafter make manifest
in due place) upon designed purpose, thereby to establish some
points in their corrupted and superstitious Religion. Some because
of their own lucre and profit arising by the upholding of these opinions of the great power and performances of Witches, as did all
the Inquisitors and their Adherents, having a share in the condemned Witches goods. Others have written in these Subjects meerly
for ostentation and vain-glory, to get a name that they were learned and able persons : of all which the judicious Readers ought to
beware of, and to consider. There is another main scandal that
Witchmongers usually (especially of late) cast upon those that oppose their gross, impious, and blasphemous opinions ; but I cannot seasonably give answer unto it, untill I have laid down the
state of the question, upon which the substance of this Treatise is
grounded, and therefore shall proceed to its Explication.

CHAP. II.

*Of the Notion, Conception, and Description of Witches and
Witchcraft, according to divers Authors, and in what
sense they may be granted, and in what sense and respect
they are denied.*

THose that are Masters in Ethicks teach us, that every Vertue
hath on either side one Vice in the extreme, and that Vertue
only consists in the mean, which how hard that mean is to be kept
in any thing, the Writings and Actions of the most Men do sufficiently inform us. This is manifest, that not many years ago the
truth of Philosophy lay inchained in the Prisons of the Schools, who
thought there was no proficiency to be made therein, but only in
their Logical and Systematical ways: so that (in a manner) all liberty was taken away both in writing and speaking, and nothing
was to be allowed of that had not the Seal of Academick Sanction.
And now when Philosophy hath gotten its freedom, to expatiate
through the whole Sphere of Nature, by all sorts of inquiries and

tryals,

tryals, to compleat a perfect History of Nature, some are on the other hand grown so rigid and peremptory, that they will condemn all things that have not past the test of Experiment, or conduce not directly to that very point, and so would totally demolish that part of Academick and Formal Learning that teacheth men Method and the way of Logical procedure in writing of Controversies, and handling of Disputes. Whereas what is more necessary and commendable for those that treat of any controverted point in Writing or in other Disputations, than a clear and perspicuous Method, a right and exact stating of the Question in doubt, defining or describing the terms that are or may be equivocal, and dividing the whole into its due and genuine parts, distinguishing of things one from another, limiting things that are too general, and explaining of every thing that is doubtful? Those that would totally take away this so profitable and excellent a part of Learning, are not of my judgment, nor can be excused for having run into that extreme that is extremely condemnable. Let Experimental Philosophy have its place and due honour; and let also the Logical, Methodical, and Formal ways of the Academies have its due praise and commendation, as being both exceedingly profitable, though in different respects; otherwise, in writing and arguing, nothing but disorder and confusion will bear sway.

    I have premised thus much, because the most of the Authors that have treated about this knotty and thorny Subject of Witches and Witchcraft, have been as confused and immethodical as any. For whereas the learned Orator *Cicero* tells us, that *omnis discursus à definitione debet proficisci*; and that it is also true, that what is not aptly and fitly defined or described, as far as the Subject will admit of, is never perfectly understood: yet have the most of these Authors (which are numerous) laid down no perfect description of a Witch or Witchcraft, nor explained fully what they meant by that name, notion, or conception. And therefore, lest I become guilty of the same fault, I shall lay down what the most considerable Authors that have treated of this Subject, do mean or intend by this word *Witch*, and *Witchcraft*, and shall fully explain in what notion or sense I either allow or deny them, and their actions, and that in this order, and in these Particulars following.

Lib.14. Method. c. 9.

    1. Though an argument taken *à denotatione nominis* be of little weight or validity, and that the industrious and sharp-witted person *Galen* doth seem to make little account of words, that is, in this respect, when we would only understand the nature of things,

Id. c. 1.

yet in another respect he concludeth thus : " *Verùm qui alterum* " *docere volet quæ ipse tenet, huic prorsus nominibus propter res uti* " *est opus.* Now the handling of Controversies is chiefly and principally to inform others, and teach them the truth, and to discover errours; therefore in this respect the explication and denotation of words is exceeding profitable and necessary : and so *Plato in Cratylo* tells us: " *Nomen itaq; rerum, substantiam docendi discernen-*
                                                                         " *diq;*

" *diq; inſtrumentum eſt.* And it being a manifeſt truth, that words are but the making forth of thoſe notions that we have of things, and ought to be ſubjected to things, and not things to words : if our notions do not agree with the things themſelves, then we have received falſe *Idola* or images of them ; but if we have conceived them aright, and do not expreſs them fitly and congruouſly, then we ſhall hardly make others underſtand us aright, nor can clearly open unto them the doctrine that we would teach them.

2. But to come to the ſignification and acceptation of the words that thoſe Authors, who have magnified and defended the power of Witches, have uſed to expreſs their notions by, we ſhall find them to be ſo far fetcht, ſo metaphorical, and improperly applied, that no rational or underſtanding man can tell us what to make of them. And if we take the notion, as they do, of a killing and mur-thering Witch, with the reſt of the adjuncts, which they couple with it, we ſhall not be able to find a proper and ſignificative word, either in the Hebrew, Greek, Latine, French, Spaniſh, Italian, or High-Dutch, but a multitude or a *Ferrago* of words, whereof not one doth properly ſignifie any ſuch thing, as they would make us believe, by the notion that they maintain of a Witch : of which we ſhall principally note theſe.

1. For the Hebrew words uſed in the Old Teſtament we ſhall not mention them here, but afterward, where we ſpeak of the miſ-tranſlation of them, and therefore ſhall purſue them in the Latine and other Languages. And firſt they ſometimes uſe the word *La-mia* in the Latine, Λάμια in Greek, which *Geſner* and others tell us doth ſignifie a terreſtrial Creature, or a voracious fiſh, as alſo a Spe-ctrum or Phantaſm. And this was ſuppoſed to be a Creature with a face like a Woman, and feet like a Horſe or an Aſs, ſuch as (in-deed) neither is, nor ever was *in rerum natura,* but was only a fig-ment deviſed to affright children withal. But if we will believe Poetical Fables, the Romances of *Philoſtratus* concerning *Apollo-nius,* or the lying Diary of his Man *Damis,* we muſt take it to be a Spirit or Apparition, ſuch as the Greeks called *Empuſa,* that went upon one leg, and had eyes that they could take forth, and ſet in, when they pleaſed. And ſuch a monſtrous Fable and Lye was a ſufficient ground for doting Witchmongers to build their incredi-ble ſtories of the power and actions of Witches upon, having no proper word for ſuch a Witch as they falſely believe and ſuppoſe. Though there be a Text in the Lamentations of *Jeremiah,* that Lament. 4. 3. hath given occaſion or colour to this vain opinion, eſpecially as the vulgar Latine renders it, which is thus : *Sed & Lamiæ nudaverunt mammam, lactaverunt catulos ſuos. Filia populi mei crudelis, quaſi ſtruthio in deſerto.* The French render it, *The Dragons have made bare their breaſts :* and ſo have alſo the Italians in their Tranſla-tion retained the words Dragon and Oſtrich ; and alſo the Septua-gint render the words δράχοντες and ςρυθόν. And *Luther* in his Tran-ſlation hath kept the ſame words, though the Germans call *Lamia*

𝔈in

Ein Rachtsgeist. But our own Translation hath come more near the truth : *Even the Sea-monsters draw out the breast, they give suck to their young ones : the Daughter of my people are become cruel like the Ostriches in the wilderness.* And *Arias Montanus* gives it thus : *Etiam draco*—— תנין *Tannin* (which signifieth a Dragon, Serpent, Whale, or other Sea-creatures) *solverunt mammam, lactaverunt catulos suos : Filia populi mei in crudelem, veluti ululæ in deserto.* But none hath come up close to the mark but *Junius* and *Tremellius*, who render the place thus : *Etiam Phocæ præbent mammam, lactant catulos suos, quomodo filia populi mei, propter crudelem inimicum, est similis ululis in deserto.* And the Notes upon the place do make it plain : " *Vox quidem Hebræa latè patet, significans serpentes &* " *reptilia magna, sive terrestria sive aquatilia ; sed cùm non omnium* " *reptilium sint mammæ, neq; aquaticorum sint ii quos Propheta vo-* " *cat catulos ; necesse fuit hunc locum ad Phocas, id est marinos vi-* " *tulos accommodari, qui à natura sint quasi Amphibii. Nam Dra-* " *conibus accommodari non potest, cùm volucrium solus vespertilio* " *mammas habeat : serpentium terrestrium nulla species mammata est,* " *ac proinde hæc ad marinum istud genus referri debent.*

2. Another far fetcht and improperly applied name to Witches, is *Strix*, and so some Authors call them *Striges* ; when as the word *Strix* doth properly signifie a nocturnal bird, *à stridendo sic dicta*, that do use to suck the dugs of Goats, and also of young children, which we shall shew hereafter to be a Truth, and no Fable, as *Ovid* saith,

Nocte volant, puerósq; petunt nutricis egentes,
   Et vitiant cunis corpora rapta suis.
Carpere dicuntur lactentia viscera rostris,
   Et plenum poto sanguine guttur habent.
Est illis strigilis nomen ; sed nominis hujus
   Causa, quòd horrendâ stridere nocte solent.

This is that sort of bird that *Gesner* calleth *Caprimulgus*, and the Greeks Αιγοθήλας, the Germans Rachtvogel or Rachtraven, the Hebrews לילית *Lillith*, as is said in *Isaiah* : *Quin & ibi subitò quievit strix (seu lamia) & invenit sibi requiem.* It is taken to be a kind of Owl, litter bigger than an Ousel, and less than a Cuckow, they are blind upon the day, and flye abroad upon the nights, making an horrible noise, and were to be found about *Rome, Helvetia,* and *Crete* or *Candy,* and do certainly suck the dugs of Goats, that thereby they waste away and become blind. And that they are also sometimes found in *Denmark,* that learned Physician and laborious Anatomist *Bartholinus* doth make manifest, and that they do suck the breasts or navils of young children. Now what affinity hath this to a Witch or Witchcraft ? but that Witchmongers would bring in any allusion or Metaphor, though never so impertinent or incongruous ? For if it were transferred to the actions of Witches, yet as *Calepine* tells us : *Ab hujus avis nocumento striges appellamus*
mulieres

muliéres puellulos fascinantes suo contactu, & lactis mammarúmq̃ oblatione. So that if the affimulation were proper in any proportion or particular, thofe Women they do account Witches, do but hurt the little children with the virulent fteams of their breath, and the effluviums that iffue from their filthy and polluted bodies, and fo wrought by contact and contrectation, by which the contagious poyfon is conveyed, but not by Witchcraft.

3. There is another word that they apply to Witches, as infignificant and improper as the other, and that is *Sortilegus*, Κληρομαντις, a Teller of Fortunes by Lots or Cuts: and *Lambertus Danæus*, who in other things was a judicious and learned perfon, yet doted extremely about this opinion, calling a Witch *Sortiarius*, deriving it from *Sortilegus*, which the French call *Sorcier*. Now what affinity or congruity hath cafting or ufing of Lots with that which thefe men call *Witchcraft*? furely none at all. For though Lots may, like the beft things, be abufed and wrefted to a vain or evil end, yet are they not altogether evil, but that a civil and lawful ufe may be made of them, as is manifeft this day at the famous City of *Venice*, where their chief Officers are chofen by them. And alfo there hath been a godly and divine ufe made of them even by the Apoftles themfelves, in the deciding of the Election of *Barfabas* and *Matthias*, upon the latter of which the Lot fell, and fo he was numbred with the eleven Apoftles. And *Solomon* tells us, *The lot is caft into the lap, but the whole difpofing thereof is of the Lord.* And fure thefe men were at a lofs to find a fuitable word to fix upon thefe Creatures, to whom they afcribe fuch impoffible and incredible actions, when they were fain to bring this appellation of *Sortilegus*, that hath no kinfhip at all with fuch Witches, as they mean and intend. Act. 1. 26. Prov. 16. 33.

4. Sometimes they call them by the name *Saga*, which fignifieth no more than a Wife and fubtil Woman, being derived *à fagiendo* to perceive quickly, or to fmell a thing quickly forth, which the Germans call 𝔘𝔫𝔥𝔬𝔩𝔡, which is no more than *malevolus*, or evil-willed.

5. They ufe the word *Veneficus, venefica*, and *veneficium*, and this in its proper fignification and derivation from the Latine, doth import no more than a Poyfoner, or to make poyfon, *venenum facere*, and fo might perhaps be given unto them, becaufe by Tradition they had learned feveral ways to poyfon fecretly and ftrangely, as doubtlefs there may be divers hidden and not ordinarily known ways (as we fhall fhew hereafter) by which either by fmelling, tafting, touching (and it may be by fight) they could kill and deftroy, though the means they ufed, and the effects produced, were meerly natural ; yet becaufe the manner was very occult and unperceivable, it was through ignorance and want of due infpection into the matters accounted Diabolical ; when there was no more of a Devil in the bufinefs, than is in a Thief or Murtherer, but only in the Ufe and Application, which is to fteal, kill, or deftroy.

ſtroy. And this, though now improperly and abuſively called
Witchcraft, doth but ſignifie poyſoning, and ſo the French call it
Empoiſonnement , and the Italians *Veneficio* or *Avenenatione*, and
the Germans **Bergifftung**, which all amount to one purpoſe. And
this *Veneficium* or poyſoning the Greeks call Φαρμάκιυσις and Φαρμακεία,
from Φάρμακον *Medicamentum v.l Venenum* ; for ſometimes it was
taken in the better ſenſe for a curing and healing Medicine ; and
ſometimes in the worſe for poyſon that did kill or deſtroy. Neither can it be found in any Greek Author to ſignifie any more, than
ſuch men or women that uſed Charms and Incantations , and were
believed by the Vulgar to effect ſtrange things by them, when in
truth and indeed they effected nothing at all but by natural means
and ſecret poyſons, and from thence had theſe names. And the
Poets ſpoke of them to adorn and imbelliſh their Poems withal,
according to common opinion; not that either they themſelves believed the things to be ſo done, as the Vulgar believed, nor to give
credit to ſuch falſe Fables and impoſſibilities ; but to make their
Poems more delectable and welcome to the common people , who
are uſually taken with ſuch fond Romantick ſtories and lyes. But
after the year 1300. when the Spaniſh Inquiſitors, the Popiſh Doctors and Writers had found the ſweetneſs and benefit of the con-
fiſcated Goods of thoſe that they had cauſed to be accuſed and condemned for Witches, in their ſenſe then theſe words either in the
Greek or Latine were wreſted to ſignifie a Witch that made a viſible
and corporeal League with the Devil, when in the true ſenſe of them
they did but ſignifie a ſecret Poyſoner. So that all things were
hurried , though never ſo improper and diſſonant, to be made ſerviceable to their filthy lucre and avaritious ſelf-endedneſs. *Templum
venale Deüſq;.*

6. Laſtly, For Withcraft they uſed the Latine *Faſcinum* and
Faſcinatio, and ſo they called a Witch *Faſcinator* and *Faſcina-
trix*, and this the Greeks called Βασκανίος, Βασκανία, *Faſcinum, Faſcinatio*, alſo *invidia, odium, ſeu invidentia,* Ἀπὸ τῦ Βασκανίν *à faſcinan-
do, ſeu oculis occidendo :* the Germans call it **Zauberp**, and **Ber-
zauberung**, and ſometimes **herwerk** ; the French *Enſorcellement*
and *Sorcelerie* ; the Italians *Leſtrigare & amaliare, amaliamento* ;
the Belgicks **Betoobenge** : the Saxons called them and it *Yicce* and
Yicce-cpeepc, from whence we have the name Witch and Withcraft,
that ſignified *Saga, Venefica, Lamia*, and *Faſcinum, Magia, Incan-
tatio, Faſcinatio, Præſtigium :* of which (becauſe we ſhall have
occaſion to ſpeak more of it hereafter) we ſhall here only note
theſe few things.

1. It is taken ſometimes for Envy and Malice, becauſe thoſe that
were ſuppoſed to uſe Faſcination, did direct it to one Creature
more than another through their envious minds, as may be perceived by ſome few Authors : And ſo was accounted a kind of eye-
biting, whereby (as the Vulgar believed) children did wax lean,
and pined away, the original whereof they referred to the crooked

*Vid. Alexand.
Aphrod. lib. 2.
Probl. 53.*

and

and wry looks of malicious perfons, never examining the truth of
the matter of fact, whether thofe children that pined away, had
any natural difeafe or not, that caufed that macilency or pining
away ; nor confidered, whether or no there was any efficiency in
the envy or wry looks of thofe malicious perfons, but vainly afcribed effects to thofe things that had in them no caufality at all to
produce fuch effects.

2. Sometimes this kind of Fafcination was afcribed to the fore
or infected eyes of thofe that were accounted caufers of hurt there-
by in others, and in this fenfe *Virgil* faith : *Nefcio quis teneros ócu-*   *Eclog. 3.*
lus mihi fafcinat agnos. And by this no more could be under-
ftood, but that thofe that had infected and fore eyes might infect
others, and this was nothing but contagion, or corrupt fteams iffuing from one body to another, which may happen in many difeafes,
as is manifeft by the Writings of divers learned Phyficians, as in bodies infected with the Plague, French Pox, Leprofie, Ophthalmies,
and fuch like.

3. Sometimes Fafcination is taken for fome kind of Incantation,
that by virtue of Words or Charms doth perform fome ftrange
things ; but concerning this there is fuch incerrainty of the opinions of the Learned, fome flatly denying that Words or Charms have
in them any natural efficacy at all ; others as ftrongly affirming it,
that of this point it is very difficult to make a clear determination :
and therefore we fhall fay but this of it here, that the Angelical
Doctor did conclude well in this particular, in thefe words : " *Ad*   *Sup. epiſt. D.*
" *fciendum autem quid fit fafcinatio, fciendum eſt quòd fecundùm*   *Paul. ad Galat.*
" *gloſſam fafcinatio propriè dicitur ludificatio fenfus, quæ per artes*   *c. 3.*
" *magicas fieri confuevit, puta, cum hominem facit aſpectibus alio-*
" *rum apparere leonem, vel cornutum, & hujuſmodi.*

Having been thus large in confidering the names and denomina-
tion given to thofe perfons that are efteemed Witches, and finding
them to be fo improper, impertinent, various, and uncertain, let
us now proceed to the notion and acceptation of Witchcraft and
Witches, to try if in that we can find any more certainty or confo-
nancy, and herein we fhall produce fome of the chief defcriptions
that are given of them by feveral Authors ; for to quote all would
be tedious and fuperfluous. Thofe that are or may be accounted
Witches we rank in thefe two orders.

1. Thofe that were and are active deceivers, and are both by
practice and purpofe notorious Impoftors, though they fhadow
their delufive and cheating knaveries under divers and various pretences ; fome pretending to do their Feats by Aftrology (which
is a general Cheat as it is commonly ufed) fome by a pretended gift
from God, when they are notorioufly drunken, debauched, and
blafphemous perfons, fuch as of very late years was the Cobler that
lived upon *Ellill* Moor, named *Richmond*, and divers others that I
could name, but that in modefty I would fpare their reputations :
fome by pretending skill in Natural Magick, when indeed they can

E   hardly

hardly read Englifh truly ; fome by pretending a familiar Spirit, as one *Thomas Bolton* near *Knaresborough* in *York-fhire*, when indeed and in truth they have no other Familiar but their own Spirit of lying and deceiving : fome by pretending to reveal things in Cryftalglaffes or Beryls, as was well known to be pretended by Doctor *Lamb*, and divers others that I have known. And fome by pretending to conjure and call up Devils, or the Spirits of men departed ; and fome by many other ways and means that are not neceffary to be named here ; for errour and deceit have a numerous train of Followers and Difciples.   And the exiftence of fuch kind of Witches as thefe (if you will needs call them by that name, and not by their proper titles, which are, that they truly are Deceivers, Cheaters, Coufeners, and Impoftors) I willingly acknowledge, as having been, and are to be found in all ages, and thefe forts are alfo acknowledged by *Wierus*, Mr. *Scot*, *Johannes Lazarus Guticrius*, *Tobias Tandlerus*, *Hieronymus Nymannus*, *Martinius Biermannus*, and all the reft, that notwithftanding did with might and main oppofe the grofs Tenent of the common Witchmongers.

And of this fort were all thofe feveral differences of Diviners, Witches, or Deceivers named in the Scriptures, as Mr. *Ady* hath

A Candle in the dark, p. 12,13.

fufficiently declared in this paffage, which we fhall tranfcribe.   " A
" Witch is a man or woman that practifeth Devillifh crafts of fedu-
" cing the people for gain, from the knowledge and worfhip of
" God, and from the truth, to vain credulity (or believing of lyes)
" or to the worfhipping of Idols.   And again he faith : " Witch-
" craft is a Devillifh craft of feducing the people for gain, from the
" knowledge and worfhip of God, and from his truth, to vain cre-
" dulity (or believing of lyes) or to the worfhipping of Idols.
" That it is a Craft truly fo called, and likewife that it is for gain,
" is proved *Act.* 16. 16, 19.   The Maid that followed *Paul* crying,
" brought in her Mafter much gain ; and that it is a Craft of per-
" verting the people, or feducing them from God and his Truth,
" is proved *Act.* 6. 7, 8. *Elimas the Sorcerer laboured to pervert*
" *Deputy from the Faith.*   So likewife *Act.* 8. 9, 10, 11. it doth
" more plainly prove all thefe words : *And there was a man before*
" *in the City called Simon, which ufed Witchcraft, and bewitched*
" *the people of Samaria, faying, That he himfelf was fome great*
" *man, to whom they gave heed from the leaft to the greateft, faying,*
" *This man is the great power of God, and gave heed unto him, be-*
" *caufe that of long time he had bewitched them with Sorceries.*
" How bewitched them with Sorceries ? That is, feduced them
" with Devillifh Crafts : (as the Greek and alfo *Tremelius* Latine
" Tranflation do more plainly illuftrate.) In this fenfe fpeaketh *Paul*
" to the *Galatians* 3. 1. *O foolifh Galathians, who hath bewitched*
" *you, that you fhould not obey the truth?* And that a Witch or
" Witchcraft is taken in no other fenfe in all the Scripture, it ap-
" peareth by the whole current of the Scriptures, as you may fee
" in this Book.   But againft this Mr. *Glanvil* and the reft of his
                                                        opinion

opinion will object and say, that it is hard and severe that **Cheaters** Object. p. 78. and Impostors should be ranked with Inchanters, and such as converse with Devils and with Idolaters, and that of this it is hard to give a reason. To this we shall give this full responsion.

1. We are to consider in what precise respect actions are in Sacred Writ called sinful and wicked, and wherefore they have such severe punishments annexed unto them, and we shall find that this Levit. 20. 10. is not *ratione medii vel actus, sed finis*. As for instance and illustra- Deut. 22. 22, tion : we shall find that the Law was peremptory in point of adul- 23, 24. tery, which saith : *If a man be found lying with a woman married to an husband, then they shall both of them dye.* Now the act of copulation, as it is an act, is all one with a lawful wife, and with the wife of another man (that is, one generically considered) and yet the one is lawful, as agreeing with Gods Law and Ordinance, and the other is unlawful, sinful, wicked, and therefore to be punished with death, because it is an aberration from the Divine Ordinance, and contrary to the Command of God, who saith, *Thou shalt not commit adultery.* So though the things committed by these persons, were or might be performed by natural or artificial means, that simply in themselves were not sinful, or so severely punishable, yet were they evil in regard of the end, which was to deceive and seduce the people to Idolatry.

2. Therefore the true and punctual reason why these persons (termed Witches or Diviners) are by the Law of God so severely to be punished, is, because they drew the people to Idolatry, the thing that God most hateth, and against which he hath pronounced the most severe and terriblest judgments of all. Nay these people were the very false Prophets, especially of one sort, and the 2 Chron. 33. very Priests to the Idols, as is manifest in the wicked and filthy 1, 2, 3, 4, 5, 6, Idolatry of all sorts set up and practised by *Manasses*, even all the 7, 8. sorts (or the most of them) mentioned in the Scriptures. And God declareth himself to be a jealous God, and that he will not give his glory to another, but is the only Lord God, and him only we ought to serve ; and therefore will most severely punish those that attribute that unto Idols, that is only proper unto himself : and for this cause, and upon this ground are all those terrible Comminations used in the Scriptures, and especially against this sort of people, who were the chief Instruments of promoting Idolworship, ascribing the power of a Deity unto them, when the Prophet tells us, *Their Idols are silver and gold, the work of mens* Psal. 115. 4, 5, *hands ; they have mouths, but they speak not ; eyes have they, but* 6, 7. ibid. Psal. *they see not ; they have ears, but they hear not ; noses have they,* 135. 17. *but they smell not ; they have hands but they handle not ; feet have they, but they walk not, neither speak they through their throat ; neither is there any breath in their mouths.*

3. That many great and abstruse things may be lawfully done by Natural Magick, is well known to the best Naturalists, and how great Feats may be performed by the Mathematicks and Me-

chanical

chanical Arts, are well known to the Learned; and that there is and
may be a lawful use of Astrology, and many things may be foretold by it, few that are judicious are ignorant; that the Progno-
sticks in the Art of Medicine are necessary, and of much use and
certainty, all learned Physicians know very well; that observing of
times, and many other such like things may for divers respects be
lawfully practised.   But if all or any of these be used to draw people to Idolatry, and their strange effects ascribed unto dumb and
dead Idols, then what horrible sin and abomination were this, and
no punishment could be too heavy for it.   And so it is in the case
of these sort of people called Witches or Diviners, they perswaded
the multitude, that their false Gods (or rather Devils) in their

2 King. 1. 4.   Idols, could foretel life or death, and so led the people a whoring
after them, as *Ahaziah* sent to inquire of the god of *Ekron*, whether he should recover or not, and therefore he had that sharp
judgment, *That he should not come down from that bed whither he
was gone up, but should surely dye.*   And did not the Priests of *Baal*
(which were the same rabble named *Deut.* 18. 10, 11, 12, 13, &c.)

1 King. 18.   obstinately labour to make *Ahab* and all the people believe, that the
Gods (or Devils) that they worshipped in their Idols, could and
would answer by fire, and pertinaciously persisted in their obstina-
cy, *cutting themselves with knives and lancets from morning until
the time of the offering of the evening sacrifice,* and yet nothing was
effected ? so that they were justly guilty of that punishment which
they received, which was death, for ascribing that to a dead Idol,
that none could perform, but the only true God of *Israel*, and yet
in the mean time could neither by their own skill, nor the skill of
their Idols foresee that sudden death that fell upon them : which
punishment fell deservedly upon them, for labouring to deceive the
people, and confirm them in Idolatry, in ascribing that unto a dead
stock, which was only in the power of the Almighty to perform.
So if all those fine Knacks and neat Tricks that *Athanasius Kircher*
performed at *Rome* by the help and means of the Loadstone, and
mentioned in his Book *de Arte Magnetica*, had been by him ascribed unto some Saint, thereby to have drawn the people to the adoration of that Saint, and so to Idolatry, it had been active imposture, deceit, and knavery in him, and he might justly have been
inrolled in the Catalogue of these Witches or Diviners, and had
really been an active Impostor, as they were, and so had deserved
the same punishment: when on the contrary for ascribing effects unto
their true and proper causes, and clearly shewing the manner and
means of producing those effects, he hath justly deserved the title
of a learned and honest man.   And though a common *Hocus Pocus*
man, or one that playeth Tricks of Leger-de-main or slight of
hand, to get a livelihood by, do labour to make the ignorant multitude believe that he doth his Feats by virtue of his barbarous terms
or non-significant words, or by the help of some familiar Spirit;
must therefore a prudent or learned person believe the same, and
                                                            not

not labour to underſtand that thoſe pretences are but uſed the better to deceive the ſenſes of the beholders, and ſo that pretence but a cheat and impoſture?

4. We affirm that all theſe mentioned in the Scriptures (nay, and that the Prieſts attending all the ſo famouſed Oracles) were but meer Cheaters and Impoſtors, and that for theſe reaſons. 1. They could not be, nor were ignorant that all their numerous Idols were but the works of mens hands, and that they could not of themſelves move, ſee, hear, ſmell, or breathe, much leſs eat and drink; and therefore were notorious Cheaters and Impoſtors in labouring to make the people believe the contrary. 2. They could not be ignorant but what anſwers were given, and what acts were done, were performed by themſelves, and not by the Idols, and yet they laboured to make the people believe the contrary, as the *Bramines* and Prieſts do to this day all over the Eaſtern parts of *Aſia*, and in many other places, and ſo muſt needs be notorious Knaves and Cheaters; becauſe, as *Iſaiah* ſaith, *With part of the wood whereof* Iſa. 44. 15, 16. *he hath made himſelf an Idol, he maketh a fire and warmeth himſelf.* 3. They could not be ignorant that their Idols could not, nor did declare any thing truly that was to come, but what Anſwers were given, or Divinations were uttered, were of their own deviſing and invention, and no other Devil in the caſe, but Diabolical inſpirations in their minds. And this is manifeſt by their pitiful ſhuffling equivocations (eſpecially of all the Oracles) their reſponſions being always ambiguous, and bearing a double ſenſe, which cauſed *Cardan* to ſay: "*Oracula, ſi non eſſent ambigua, non* "*eſſent oracula.* And commonly (if not always) they were given in the favour of thoſe that gave the largeſt gifts, which made *Demoſthenes* ſay, that the Oracle at *Delphos* did φιλιππιζειν, becauſe it always ſpoke in favour of *Philip* and his proceedings. And it was with the Oracles, as with the Temple of *Neptune*, All the Offerings of thoſe that eſcaped ſhipwrack were preſerved, and to be ſeen; but of thoſe that had ſuffered ſhipwrack, there was no memorial nor knowledge of their number: ſo, many have noted ſome few Hits of the Oracles, but few have noted their Miſſes, which doubtleſs were far the greater number. For ſo it is here in this North Country with our Figure-flingers and pretended Conjurers, Piſs-Prophets, and Water-Witches, that if they hit once, it is cryed up and told every where; but if they erre an hundred times, it is ſoon buried in ſilence and oblivion, and one fool will not take warning at anothers being cheated and deceived. And that their Idols did not, nor could declare truly what was to come, is manifeſt by the Prophet who ſaith: *Let them bring them forth* (that is, their Idols) Iſa. 41. 22, 23. *and ſhew us what ſhall happen: let them ſhew the former things what they be, that we may conſider them, and know the latter end of them; or declare us things for to come. Shew the things that are to come hereafter, that we may know that ye are gods: yea do good or do evil, that we may be diſmayed, and behold it together.* Yet theſe

miſera-

miserable, cheating, diſſembling Wretches that would have had the
multitude to have believed, that their Idols could have foretold
truly almoſt any thing; yet neither their Idols, nor the Gods (or Devils) they pretended to be in them, nor themſelves could foretel or
foreſee their own deſtruction, as is manifeſt in the Prophets of *Baal*
in the time of *Elijah*, who went up to Mount *Carmel* to advance
the worſhip and power of their Idols, but did not foreſee it ſhould
be all their deſtructions and deaths. Doubtleſs thoſe that in the
Book of *Daniel* are called Wiſe-men, Magicians, Aſtrologers, Sorcerers, and Chaldeans were endowed with much rare knowledge,
both in reſpect of Nature and Art: for if their knowledge had
been Diabolical, without queſtion *Daniel* would hardly have in-
terceded for them, yet could they not reveal what the Kings dream
was that was gone from him, nor foreſee that they run the hazard
of their lives; but did conclude that none other could ſhew it,
except the *gods whoſe dwelling is not with fleſh*. 4. In matters
of fact it appeareth, that they were active deceivers and deluders,
as is manifeſt when *Pharaoh* had dreamed two dreams, that he called and ſent for all the Magicians and Wiſe-men of *Egypt*; but they
could not interpret them unto him. *Junius* and *Tremelius* render
it: *Omnes Magos Ægypti, & omnes Sapientes ejus*. The vulgar
Latine (or that which is improperly called St. *Hieromes* Tranſla-
tion) gives it: *Miſit ad omnes Conjectores Ægypti, cunctóſq; Sapientes*. And theſe doubtleſs *Pharaoh* would not have ſent for, but
that either upon his own knowledge he knew that they profeſſed
the ability of the interpretation of dreams, and (perhaps) as the
ſequel ſhewed, greater matters; or elſe upon common repute, or relation of others, and that muſt needs ariſe from their own profeſſion of the knowledge of ſuch abſtruſe matters: and ſo of neceſſity
muſt have pretended greater matters, than when they came to tryal
they were able to perform, and ſo muſt needs be Impoſtors. And
the Woman at *Endor* (falſely called a Witch, or a Woman that
had a familiar Spirit, when in the Hebrew ſhe is only called the
Miſtreſs of the Bottle, as we ſhall manifeſt hereafter) muſt needs be
a Deceiver and Impoſtor, becauſe ſhe pretended to bring up whom-
ſoever *Saul* deſired, which was a thing abſolutely not in her power, as I ſhall undeniably prove afterwards. And notwithſtanding the ſtories of *Euſebius*, and the ſtrong endeavours of Doctor
Hamond to make it good, that *Simon Magus* was a perſon that
had peculiar and corporeal converſe with the Devil, and by that
league and converſe could perform ſtrange and wonderful things;
yet was he but a notorious Impoſtor, as appeareth by two reaſons.
1. The Text ſaith, *That he gave out that himſelf was ſome great
one*, that is, that he had great skill, and was able to perform wonderful things. This ſheweth his preſumption and pretence, the certain badge of a Deceiver and Cheater. 2. But could do little, except ſome petty jugling Tricks of Leger-de-main, confederacy, and
the like; *becauſe he wondred, or was amazed, beholding the Mira-*
cles

Dan. 22. 11.

Gen. 41. 8.

1 Sam. 28. 11.

Act. 8. 9.

cles and *signs which were done*, *and those were*, *that unclean Spirits*, *crying with loud voice*, *came out of many that were possessed
with them* : *And many taken with palsies*, *and that were lame*, *were
healed.* Now if he had been any great Magician, or could have
performed any great things, he could not have so much wondred
at those things that *Philip* wrought: or if he could have flown in
the air, as *Eusebius* (or those that have foisted such incredible lyes
into his Writings) pretendeth, then he need not have been so amazed at the miracles and signs that the Apostles wrought, nor to have
offered to have bought the gift of bestowing the Holy Ghost, but
only because he was a notorious Dissembler and Impostor. And if
he had been in league with the Devil, surely he might have cast forth
Devils by the power of *Belzebub* the Prince of Devils: all which
do plainly conclude him to be an absolute Cheater and Impostor.
And the story of *Bel* and the *Dragon* (though but an Apocryphal
piece, yet very ancient, and of sufficient credit as to matter of fact)
doth evidently demonstrate, that these sort of people were abominable Cheaters and Impostors, and were not endowed with any supernatural power, nor had assistance of any visible Demon, but only
the Devil of deceit and cousenage in their own breasts, and so
were, as *Cardan* saith, *Carnales Dæmones ipsis Dæmonibus calli-
diores.*

5. And though by the Laws of our own Nation these kind of
people were to be severely punished, as appeareth by the Statute
1 *Jac. cap.* 12. yet had they respect in that Act, not only to the punishment in respect of what these persons could or did do, but also
in regard of their being Impostors and Deceivers of the people; ⟨*Instit. p.3. p.4 5.*⟩
for so the Lord Chief Justice Sir *Edward Cook*, the best Expositor of
Law that hath written in our Language, doth expound it in these
words. The mischiefs before this part of this Act were : "*That di-
*"*vers Impostors, men and women*, *would take upon them to tell or
*"*do these fine things here specified*, *in great deceit of the people*, *and
*"*cheating and cousening them of their money or other goods* : *there-
*"*fore was this part of the Act made*, *wherein these words* [*take up-
*"*on him or them*] *are very remarkable. For if they take upon them*,
"*&c. though in truth they do it not*, *yet are they in danger of this
*"*first branch.*

6. And whereas in the objection Mr. *Glanvil* mentioneth converse with Devils, if he mean mental, internal, and spiritual converse, such as Murtherers, Adulterers, Thieves, Robbers, and all
wicked persons have with Satan, we grant it; for so had the Jews
and the High Priests in conspiring and acting to put our blessed
Saviour to death: *it was their hour*, *and the power of darkness.*
But if he mean a visible and corporeal converse, then we plainly
affirm that there is not, nor can be any such, whereby any such
strange things (as Witchmongers fondly and falsely believe) can
be performed or effected. Therefore by way of conclusion in this
particular, we grant that there are many sorts of such kind of
Witches,

Witches, as for gain and vain-glory do take upon them to declare hidden and occult things, to divine of things that are to come, and to do many wonderful matters, but that they are but Cheaters, Deceivers, and Couseners.

2. And as there are a numerous crew of active Witches, whose existence we freely acknowledge ; so there are another sort, that are under a passive delusion, and know not, or at least do not observe or understand, that they are deluded or imposed upon. These are those that confidently believe that they see, do, and suffer many strange, odd, and wonderful things, which have indeed no existence at all in them, but only in their depraved fancies, and are meerly *melancholiæ figmenta.* And yet the confessions of these, though absurd, idle, foolish, false, and impossible, are without all ground and reason by the common Witchmongers taken to be truths, and falsely ascribed unto Demons, and that they are sufficient grounds to proceed upon to condemn the Confessors to death, when all is but passive delusion, intrinsecally wrought in the depraved imaginative faculty by these three ways or means.

1. One of the Causes that produceth this depraved and passive delusion, is evil education ; they being bred up in ignorance, either of God, the Scriptures, or the true grounds of Christian Religion, nay not being taught the common Rules of Morality, or of other humane Literature ; but only imbibing and sucking in with their mothers and nurses milk, the common gross and erroneous opinions that the blockish vulgar people do hold, who are all generally inchanted and bewitched with the belief of the strange things related of Devils, Apparitions, Fayries, Hobgoblins, Ghosts, Spirits, and the like : so that thereby a most deep impression of the verity of the most gross and impossible things is instamped in their fancies, hardly ever after in their whole life time to be obliterated or washt out: so prevalent a thing is Custom and Institution from young years, though the things thus received, and pertinaciously believed, and adhered unto, are most abominable falsities and impossibilities, having no other existence but in the brains and phantasies of old, ignorant, and doting persons, and are meerly *muliercularum & nutricum terriculamenta & figmenta*, and therefore did *Seneca* say : *Gravissimum est consuetudinis imperium.* And that this is one main cause of this delusion, is manifest from all the best Historians, that where the light of the Gospel hath least appeared, and where there is the greatest brutish ignorance and heathenish Barbarism, there the greatest store of these deluded Witches or Melancholists are to be found, as in the North of *Scotland*, *Norway, Lapland,* and the like, as may be seen at large in *Saxo Grammaticus, Olaus Magnus, Hector Boetius*, and the like.

2. But when an atrabilarious Temperament, or a melancholick Complexion and Constitution doth happen to those people bred in such ignorance, and that have suckt in all the fond opinions that Custom and Tradition could teach them, then what thing can be
imagined

imagined that is ſtrange, wonderful, or incredible, but theſe people do pertinaciouſly believe it, and as confidently relate it to others? nay even things that are abſolutely impoſſible, as that they are really changed into Wolves, Hares, Dogs, Cats, Squirrels, and the like; and that they flye in the Air, are preſent at great Feaſts and Meetings, and do ſtrange and incredible things, when all theſe are but the meer effects of the imaginative function depraved by the fumes of the melancholick humor, as we might ſhew from the Writings of the moſt grave and learned Phyſicians; but we ſhall content our ſelves with ſome few ſelect ones. 1. That diſtemper which Phyſicians call *Lycanthropia*, is according to the judgment of *Aetius* and *Paulus*, but a certain ſpecies of Melancholy, and yet they really think and believe themſelves to be Wolves, and imitate their actions: of which *Johannes Fincelius* in his ſecond Book *de Mirac.* giveth us a relation to this purpoſe. "That at *Padua* in the year " 1541. a certain Huſband-man did ſeem to himſelf a Wolf, and " did leap upon many in the fields, and did kill them. And that " at laſt he was taken not without much difficulty, and did confi- "dently affirm that he was a true Wolf, only that the difference " was in the skin turned in with the hairs. And therefore that cer- "tain, having put off all humanity, and being truly truculent and " voracious, did ſmite and cut off his legs and arms, thereby to try " the truth of the matter; but the innocency of the man being "known, they commit him to the Chirurgions to be cured, but " that he dyed not many days after. Which inſtance is ſufficient to overthrow the vain opinion of thoſe men that believe that a man or woman may be really transformed or tranſubſtantiated into a Wolf, Dog, Cat, Squirrel, or the like, without the operation of an omnipotent power, as in *Lots* Wife becoming a Pillar of Salt; though St. *Auguſtine* was ſo weak as to ſeem to believe the reality of theſe transformations: of which we ſhall have occaſion to ſpeak more largely hereafter.

2. Another ſtory we ſhall give from the Authority of that learned Phyſician *Nicolaus Tulpius* of *Amſterdam* to this effect. A certain famous Painter was for a long time infected with black Choler, and did falſely imagine that all the bones of his body were as ſoft and flexible, that they might be drawn and bended like ſoft wax. Which opinion being deeply imprinted in his mind, he kept himſelf in bed the whole Winter, fearing that if he ſhould riſe, they would not bear his weight, but would ſhrink together by reaſon of their ſoftneſs. That *Tulpius* did not contradict him in that fancy, but ſaid that it was a diſtemper that Phyſicians were not ignorant of, but had been long before noted by *Fernelius*, that the bones like wax might be ſoftned and indurated, and that it might be eaſily cured, if he would be obedient: and that within three days he would make the bones firm and ſtable, and that within ſix days he would reſtore him to the power of walking. By which promiſes it was hard to declare, how much hope of recovering health it had

Schenck. obſerv. medic. lib. 1. pag. 129.

Obſervat. medic. lib. 1. cap. 18. pag. 38.

F   raiſed

raised up in him, and how obedient it made him. So that with Medicines proper to purge the atrabilarious humour within the time appointed, he was at the three days end suffered to stand upon his feet, and upon the sixth day had leave given to walk abroad : and so found himself perfectly sound afterwards ; but did not perceive the deceit in his phantasie, that had made him lye a whole Winter in bed, though he was no stupid, but an ingenious person in his Art, and scarce second to any.

3. *Thomas Bartholinus* the famous Anatomist, and Physician to *Frederick* the Third King of *Denmark*, tells us these things : "That "it is the property of melancholy persons to fear things not to be "feared, and to feign things *quæ nec picta usquam sunt, nec scripta.* "A *Plebeian* (he saith) with them abounding with melancholy "blood did imagine that his Nose was grown to that greatness, "that he durst not go abroad, for fear it should be hurt or justled "upon by those he met. And that a famous Poet at *Amsterdam* "did believe that his Buttocks were of glass, and feared their "breaking, if he should sit down. Another Old man of prime "Dignity did suspect that he had swallowed a nail, which being "lost, he could no where find, and thought himself much tortured "by its being fixed in him. But was restored to his health, by "having a Vomit given, and the Physician conveying a nail into "the matter that he cast up. And that a certain man in *England* "would not make water, for fear that all the blood in his body "should have passed forth by that passage, and therefore straitly "tyed the yard with a thred for some days, which swelling he was "not far from death, but that his Brother by force untyed it. The Books of Physicians are very full with such relations, and we in our Practice have met with divers as strange as these, and cured them. Also he tells us this : "A certain Student of a melancho-"lick Constitution, distracted with grief for the death of a Sister, "and wearied with lucubrations, did complain to (*Bartholinus*) "of the Devil haunting of him : and did affirm that he felt the evil "Spirit enter by his fundament with wind, and so did creep up his "body until it possessed the head, lest he might attend his Prayers "and Meditations with his accustomed devotion, and that it did "descend and go forth the same way, when he bent himself to "Prayers, and reading of Sacred Books. Before these things he "used to be filled with unheard of joy from his assiduous Prayers "and watching, that also he had heard a celestial kind of Musick, "and therefore despising all mortal things, he had distributed all "things to the poor; but that now piety waxing cold by too much "appetite after meat, and his brain troubled with that wind, that "he had heard a voice of one in his brain upbraiding him with "Blasphemy, and that he felt hands beating, and a stink passing "before his nose. By all which *Bartholinus* guessed, that it was "Hypochondriacal Melancholy, and by good Counsel, proper Phy-"sick, merry Company, and rightly ordering of him, he was per-"fectly cured.

4. To

4. To thefe we will only add this that is related by *Marcellus Donatus*, Phyfician to the Duke of *Mantua* and *Montferrat*, to this purpofe. "That he knew a Noble Countefs of their City, "that did moft earneftly affirm, that fhe was made fick by the "Witchery and Incantation of a certain ill-minded Woman; which "was apprehended by a learned Phyfician to be, notwithftanding "her fancy, nothing elfe but Hypochondriacal Melancholy, which "he cured by giving her proper Medicaments to purge that hu-"mour, and ordering her Waiting-maid to put into the matter fhe "voided Nails, Feathers, and Needles; which when with a glad "countenance fhe had fhewed to her Miftrefs, fhe prefently cryed "out that fhe had not been deceived, when fhe had referred the "caufe of her difeafe to Witchcraft, and afterwards did daily re-"cover more and more.

Hiftor. medic. mirab. l. 2, c.1. p. 33.

3. And as ignorance and irreligion meeting with a melancholick Conftitution, doth frame many perfons to ftrange fancies both of fear and credulity: fo when to thefe is added the teachings of thofe that are themfelves under a moft ftrong paffive delufion, then of all others thefe become moft ftrongly confident that they can perform admirable things. As when a perfon hath by education fuckt in all the groffeft fables and lyes of the power of Witches and familiar Devils, and therein becometh extremely confident, heightned with the fumes of black Choler, and fo thinks, medi-tates, and dreameth of Devils, Spirits, and all the ftrange ftories that have been related of them, and becometh malicioufly ftirred up againft fome Neighbour or other: And fo in that malicious and revengeful mind feeketh unto, and inquireth for fome famed and notorious Witch, of whom they believe they may learn fuch craft and cunning, that thereby they may be able to kill or deftroy the perfons or goods of thofe that they fuppofe have done them injuries. Then meeting with fome that are ftrongly deluded, and confidently perfwaded, that they have the company and affiftance of a familiar Spirit, by whofe help they believe they can do (al-moft) any thing, efpecially in deftroying men or cattel, they are prefently inftructed what vain and abominable Ceremonies, Obfer-vances, Unguents, Charms, making of Pictures, and a thoufand fuch fond, odd fopperies they are to ufe, by which they believe they can do ftrange Feats. And from this do proceed their bold and con-fident confeffions of lyes and impoffibilities, that notwithftanding have abufed fo many to take them for certain truths: fo that ac-cording to the Proverb, *Popery and Witchcraft go by Tradition:* and we fhall find none of thefe deluded Witches (if they muft be fo called) but they have been taught by others, that thought them-felves to be fuch alfo. And this is a truth, if we may truft the confeffion of *Alizon Denice* at the Bar at *Lancafter*, who faith thus: "That about two years agone her Grandmother called *Elizabeth* "*Sotheres*, alias *Dembdike*, did (fundry times in going or walking "together, as they went begging) perfwade and advife this Exa-

Relat. of Lan-cafh. Witches.

"minate

" minate to let a Devil or a Familiar appear to her, and that she
" this Examinate would let him suck at some part of her, and she
" might have and do what she would.

But besides these two sorts of Witches, whose Existence we deny
not, there is an acceptation of the word *Witch* in another sense, the
Existence of which I absolutely deny, and that is this according to
Mr. *Perkins*. " A Witch is a Magician, who either by open or se-
" cret League wittingly and willingly consenteth to use the aid
" and assistance of the Devil in the working of Wonders.

But the full Description and Notion that the common Witchmongers give a Witch is this. " That a Witch is such a person to
" whom the Devil doth appear in some visible shape, with whom
" the Witch maketh a League or Covenant, sometimes by Bond
" signed with the Witches blood, and that thereby he doth after
" suck upon some part of their bodies, and that they have carnal
" Copulation together, and that by virtue of that League the
" Witch can be changed into a Hare, Dog, Cat, Wolf, or such like
" Creatures ; that they can flye in the air, raise storms and tempests,
" kill men or cattel, and such like wonders. This notion of a Witch
may be gathered from the Writings of these persons, *Delrio* the Jesuit, *Bodinus*, *Jacobus Springerus*, *Johannes Niderus*, *Bartholomeus
Spineus*, *Paulus Grillandus*, *Lambertus Danæus*, *Hemmingius*, *Erastus*, *Sennertus*, and many others. As also from the Writings of
our own Country-men, Mr. *Perkins*, Mr. *Bernard* of *Balcombe*, the
Author of the Book called Demonology, Mr. *Gaule*, Mr. *Giffard*,
and divers others, who have from one to another lickt up the Vomit of the first Broacher of this vain and false opinion, and without due consideration have laboured to obtrude it upon others.
Yet was it in a manner rejected by the most of the Learned, who
had duly weighed the matter, and read the strong and convincing
arguments of *Wierus*, *Tandlerus*, *Nymannus*, *Biermannus*, *Gutierrius*, Mr. *Scot*, and the like, until of late years Dr. *Casaubon* and
Mr. *Glanvil* have taken up Weapons to defend these false, absurd,
impossible, impious, and bloody opinions withal, against whose arguments we now principally direct our Pen, and after the answering of their groundless and unjust scandals, we shall labour to overthrow their chief Bulwarks and Fortifications.

CHAP.

CHAP. III.

The denying of such a Witch as is last described in the fore-
going Chapter, doth not in'er the denying of Angels or Spi-
rits. Apparitions no warrantable ground for a Christian to
believe the Existence of Angels or Devils by, but the Word
of God.

HAving declared in what sense and acceptation we allow of
Witches, and in what notion we deny them, left we be mis-
understood we shall add thus much : That we do not (as the
Schools speak) deny the existence of Witches *absolutè & simplici-*
ter , sed secundùm quid, and that they do not exist *tali modo,* that
is, they do not make a visible Contract with the Devil, he doth not
suck upon their bodies, they have not carnal Copulation with him,
and the like recited before, and in these respects, and not otherwise,
did *Wierus, Gutierrius* and Mr. *Scot* deny Witches, that is, that neither they nor their supposed Familiars could perform such things
as are ascribed unto them.   And that Dr. *Casaubon* and Mr. *Glan-*
vil should charge those that hold this opinion with Atheism or
Sadducism, is to me very strange, having no ground, connexion, or
rational consequence so to do : yet doth Dr. *Casaubon* affirm it in Of Credulity
these words : " Now one prime foundation (faith he) of Atheism, and Increduli-
" as by many ancient and late is observed , being the not believing ty, pag. 7.
" the existence of spiritual Essences , whether good or bad, sepa-
" rate, or united, subordinate to God, as to the supreme and original
" Cause of all ; and by consequent the denying of supernatural
" operations: I have, I confess , applied my self, by my examples,
" which in this case do more than any reasoning, and (the Autho-
" rity of the holy Scriptures laid aside) are almost the only con-
" vincing proof.   And Mr. *Glanvil* is so confident (I might justly
say impudent) that he styled his Book , *A Blow at modern Sad-* Preface.
ducism , which, I confess , is so weak a blow, and so blindly le-
vell'd , and so improperly directed , that I am sure it will kill or
hurt no body : and tells us this boldly and roundly.   " And those
" that dare not bluntly say, *There is no God* , content themselves,
" (for a fair step and introduction) to deny there are Spirits or
" Witches.   Which sort of Infidels , though they are not ordinary
" among the meer Vulgar, yet are they numerous in a little higher
" rank of understandings.   And those that know any thing of the
" World, know that most of the looser Gentry , and the small Pre-
" tenders to Philosophy and Wit, are generally deriders of the be-
" lief of Witches and Apparitions.   And the whole design of his
Book is to prove those men to be guilty of Sadducism, that deny
the existence of Witches understood in his sense , and this we oppose,

pose, and the state of the question we lye down thus.

That the denying the existence of Angels or Spirits; or the Resurrection, doth not infer the denying of the Being of God; nor the denying of the existence of Witches (in the sense before laid down) infer the denying of Angels or Spirits; and that they do unjustly charge the Authors of this opinion with Sadducism, we shall prove with irrefragable Arguments.

Argum. I.   1. There can be no right deduction made, nor no right consequence drawn, where there is no dependency in causality, nor no connexion of dependency. For as in the Relative and Correlative, the denying of the one necessarily destroys the other, yet *fundamentum Relationis non destruitur*; so a father without a child, as a father, doth neither exist nor is known, and yet the foundation of those two terms, of Paternity and Childship, which is Man, doth remain. So he that denieth Creation, doth destroy the Relative, which is Creator; yet the foundation, which is God, doth remain: and the denying of the Creation, doth not infer the necessary conclusion of denying the Being of a God, because there might be a God, though there were no Creation, because God is supposed to be, both in respect of causality and duration, before Creation. So what relation can Mr. *Glanvil* feign betwixt the Being of God and the Being of Angels or Spirits? For they both belong to the Predicament of Substance, and not that of Relation; and there is less relation betwixt the Being of a Witch and the Being of Spirits: so that the denying of the one doth not infer the denying of the other. And though there were relation (which Mr. *Glanvil* cannot shew) the foundation of that Relation (which is so necessary, that Relatives cannot subsist without it) might remain, though the Relatives were taken away: and therefore the denying of the existence of Angels or Spirts, doth not infer the denying of the Being of God; and therefore the Authors of this opinion are wrongfully and falsely charged with Atheism: and the denying of the existence of a Witch (in the sense specified) doth not infer the denying of the Being of Spirits; and therefore *Scot, Osburne*, and the like, are falsely and wrongfully charged with Sadducism.

Argum. 2.   2. Though it be a true Maxime, that *de posse ad esse non valet argumentum*; yet on the contrary, the possibility of that can never be rationally denied, that hath once been in *esse*. But it is apparent, that the Sadducees denied the Resurrection, and that there were either Angels or Spirits, that is, they denied that Angels or Spirits, whether good or bad, did separately exist, and that they were nothing but the good or bad motions in mens minds: yet these men were no Atheists; for though they denied the Resurrection, and held that there were no Angels or Spirits, yet they held and believed there was a God, and did allow of, and believed the five Books of *Moses*, else would not our Saviour have used an argument, whose only strength was drawn from a sentence in the third Chapter of *Exodus*, the sixth verse. So that even the denying of
the

Mat. 22. 23.
Act. 23. 8.

the Existence of Angels and Spirits, doth not infer the denying of a God; much less doth the denying the Existence of a Witch, infer the denial of the Being of Angels and Spirits; and therefore the charge of Atheism and Sadducism is false, injurious, and scandalous.

3. Those things that in their Beings have no dependence one *Argum. 3.* upon another, the denying of the one doth not take away or deny the being of the other; but where the being doth meerly exist in dependency upon another superior Cause, there take away or deny the being of the first Cause; and thereby you take away and deny the being of all the rest that depends upon it. So he that denies the Being of a God, doth necessarily deny the Being of Angels or Spirits; but not on the contrary. For he that denieth the Existence of Angels and Spirits, doth not therefore necessarily take away or deny the Being of a God, because the Being of a God is independent of either Angel or Spirit, and doth exist solely by it self. And therefore if *Wierus* or *Scot* had denied the Existence of Angels and Spirits (which they did not) yet it would not have inferred that they were Atheists; and therefore are falsely accused by Dr. *Casaubon* and Mr. *Glanvil.* And though they should have denied the Existence of Witches (which they did not *simpliciter, sed tali modo*) yet it would not have inferred, that they were guilty of Sadducism, because Spirits or Demons have their Existence without any dependence of the being of Witches; and therefore it is but a poor *fallacia consequentiæ* to say, he that denies a Witch, denies a Demon or Spirit.

4. The denying of the Existence of Spirits, doth not infer the *Argum. 4.* denying of the Being of a God, because in the priority of duration God was when Spirits were not, for they are not immortal *à parte anté.* So likewise the denying of the Existence of Witches, doth not infer the denial of the Being of Spirits, for in the priority of duration Spirits were existent before Witches; for *Adam* and *Eve* could not be ignorant that there were Spirits, both good and bad, and yet then there were no Witches. So that a Spirit having, in respect of duration, a Being before that a Witch can have any; the denying the Existence of the latter, doth not infer the denying of the Being of the former, but is meerly inconsequent, agreeable to no Rules of Logick, except that of Logger-head Colledge.

5. Many properties or proper adjuncts may be ascribed unto a *Argum. 5.* substance, the denying of which adjuncts, doth not infer the denying of the being of the substance. So that to deny that a Horse hath fins like a fish, or wings like a bird, doth not infer the denying of the being of a Horse. Therefore it is injurious and scandalous in Dr. *Casaubon* and Mr. *Glanvil*, to charge Dr. *Wierus* and Mr. *Scot* with Atheism and Sadducism, when indeed (as we shall prove hereafter) their own Tenents tend to blasphemy, impiety, vanity, and uncharitableness.

Another thing that we oppose is, that Apparitions are no warrantable

rantable ground for a Christian to believe the Existence of Angels and Spirits by, but the Word of God, which these cogent reasons do sufficiently prove.

Argum. 1.   1. For to say that the Apparitions of Spirits, good or bad, do prove their Existence, is but *petitio principii*, a begging of the question, that first is in doubt, and ought to be proved. For how come we to be assured, that the Apparitions that are made, and really by unquestionable Witnesses attested for truth (not to speak of melancholy Fancies, and Fables, Knacks of Knavery and Imposture, and other ignorant and gross mistakes, which are often believed to be Apparitions, when they are no such matter) that they are made by good or bad Spirits? for that is the thing in doubt, and so is but a circular way of arguing by way of begging the question, or proving *ignotum per ignotius*; for Apparitions do not prove the Being of Spirits, except it be first proved, that those Apparitions be made or caused by Spirits.

Argum. 2.   2. There are many Apparitions that are produced by natural and artificial Causes, and need not be referred to supernatural ones, as are all those *Idola*, Images, or Species that we see in Glasses, which cannot be denied to be Apparitions, and yet arise from natural Causes. So the Apparition of Comets, new Stars, and many other sort of strange Meteors, as sometimes three Suns, the Rain-bow, *Halones*, and the like, that have natural Causes to produce them, and are no proof of the Being of Spirits. Nay as the best and most credible Historians have left upon Record, and hath been known to be a certain verity in divers parts of these three Kingdoms, within the space of these forty years, strange and various Sights have been seen in the Air, both of Men, and Horses, and Armies fighting one with another; and yet were these no proof of the Existence of Spirits, because they may (and doubtlesly do) proceed from other causes, and not from the operation or efficiency of Angels or Spirits, either good or bad.

Argum. 3.   3. It is not certainly known what diversity of Creatures there may be that are *mediæ naturæ* betwixt Angels and Men, that may sometimes appear, and then vanish: so that if it be granted, that there be Apparitions really and truly, yet it will not necessarily follow, that these are caused by good or bad Angels, because they may be effected by Creatures of another and middle Nature; and so Apparitions no certain ground for the believing of the Existence of Angels or Spirits. For the most learned *Drusius* gives us this ac-

Jo. Drusii Præterit. l. 7. p. 289. count from one of the Commentators upon the Book *Aboth.* "De- "*bet homo intelligere ac scire à terra usq; ad firmamentum, quod* "*Rakia, id est, Expansum appellant, omnia plena esse turmis & præ-* "*fectis, & infrà plurimas esse creaturas lædentes & accusantes, om-* "*nésq; stare ac volare in aëre, neq; à terra usq; ad firmamentum* "*locum esse vacuum: sed omnia plena esse præpositis, quorum alii ad* "*pacem, alii ad bellum, alii ad bonum, alii ad malum; ad vitam &* "*ad mortem incitant. Ob id compositum fuit canticum occursuum,* "*quod*

" *quod incipit, Sedet in occulto Supremus*.   And if this be a truth,
here are orders and numbers enough of feveral forts to make Apparitions, and yet be neither the good or bad Angels.   And if
there may any credit be given to the relation that *Cardan* gives of *De Subtil. l. 19.*
his Father *Facius Cardanus*, which he had from his own mouth, and *p. 1202, 1203.*
alfo had left it in writing; then " there are mortal Demons, that
" are born and do die as men do, that can appear and difappear,
" and are of fuch moft tenuious bodies, that they can afford us
" neither help nor hurt, excepting terrors, and fpectres, and know-
" ledge.   And if there may be credit given to *Plutarch* (fo highly
magnified by Dr. *Cafaubon*) the God *Pan* of the Heathens muft have
been one of thefe mortal Demons, becaufe he tells us upon the credit of *Epotherfes* (a Tale of hear-fay) " That *Thamus* was by a *De Nymph. lib.*
" voice thrice calling upon him, commanded that when he came to *pag. 389.*
" *Palodes*, he fhould tell them, that the great God *Pan* was dead.
And that there are fuch mortal Demons, is ftrongly afferted by
Paracelfus, and by him called *Nymphæ, Sylphi, Pygmæi*, and *Sala-
mandræ*, and that they are not of *Adams* Generation, and that they
have wonderful power and skill.   And to this opinion do the
Schools both of the ancient and later Academicks wholly incline,
and feems to be favoured both by Dr. *Moor* and Mr. *Glanvil* himfelf; and if there be any fuch matters, doubtlefs from thence did
arife all the ftrange ftories and gefts that former Generations have
told and believed concerning the Apparition of thefe kind of
Creatures, which the common people call *Fayries* : of which the
Reverend and Learned perfon Bifhop *Hall* giveth us this touch : The invifible
" The times are not paft the ken of our memory, fince the fre- World, fect. 6.
" quent (and in fome part true) reports of thofe familiar Devils, pag. 303.
" Fayries, and Goblins, wherewith many places were commonly
" haunted; the rarity whereof in thefe latter times, is fufficient to
" defcry the difference betwixt the ftate of ignorant Superftition,
" and the clear light of the Gofpel.   And whofoever fhall ferioufly
read and confider that little Piece that was printed fome few years
fince, though written long ago, and by fome (that pretend to no
fmall fhare of Learning) cryed up exceedingly for a moft convincing Relation, to prove the Exiftence of Spirits, called, *The Devil of
Mafcon*, may eafily gather, that if the thing were truly related, as
to the matter of fact, that it muft needs be fome Creature of a
middle Nature, and no evil Spirit, both becaufe it was fuch a fport-
ful and mannerly Creature, that it would leave them, and not di-
fturb them at their devotions; as alfo (as far as I remember, for I
have not the Book by me) becaufe it denied that it was a Devil,
and profeffed that it hoped to be faved by Chrift.

4. That the Scriptures contain in them all things neceffary to *Argum. 4.*
Salvation, is fo clear a truth, that none but thofe that are wilfully
blind can deny it; for Chrift taught his Difciples *all things that* Joh. 15. 15.
he had learned of the Father, and the Father fending him to be the
Saviour of the World, and to preach the Gofpel of eternal Salva-

tion, was not defective in declaring all things that were necessary to accomplish the work and end, for which he was sent forth of the Father. And the glorious Apostle St. *Paul* tells the Disciples and Brethren, *That he had not shunned to declare unto them all the counsel of God*, which must of necessity be abundantly sufficient for their Salvations. And he telleth *Timothy, That he had known the Scriptures from a child, which were able to make him wise unto salvation. All Scripture is given by inspiration of God, and is profitable for doctrine, for reproof, for correction, for instruction in righteousness : That the man of God may be perfect, throughly furnished unto all good works.* Nay the Woman of *Samaria* had so much knowledge and faith, that she believed *that when the Messias was come, he would tell them all things.* Now to the obtaining of Salvation, there is nothing more necessary than to know what enemies men have to fight against in their Christian Warfare, which the Apostle tells in these words : *For we wrestle not against flesh and blood, but against principalities, against powers, against the rulers of the darkness of this world, against spiritual wickedness in high places : Wherefore they are to take unto them the whole armor of God,* πανοπλίαν τῶ Θεῶ, *that they may be able to stand against the wiles of the Devil,* μεθοδείας τῶ διαβόλν : and that made the Apostle say in another place, *We are not ignorant of his devices or crafts,* νοήματα. Now the Scriptures being able to make us wise to Salvation, it hath sufficiently declared the natures, powers, knowledge, and offices of both the good and bad Angels, and is a sure word of Prophecy, unto which it is good to take heed, and not unto old wives fables of Apparitions and Goblins, such as Mr. *Glanvil* would perswade us that they are tydings of another World, when we are taught by unerring testimony of Truth, *That those that have Moses and the Prophets, and do not hear them, neither will they be perswaded, though one rose from the dead.* And therefore we must be bold to tell Mr. *Glanvil*, that the Sacred Scriptures do with infallible certitude teach us, that both good and bad Spirits have most certainly an Existence, and therefore we need none of his feigned nor forged stories of Apparitions ; which if they were certainly known to be true and real, by undeceivable matters of fact, yet he that doth not believe what is written of the Being of Spirits by *Moses* and the Prophets, will not believe Apparitions, no not of a man, if he came from the dead. And therefore I will conclude with that precious and pithy Sentence of St. *Austin*, who saith : *Major est hujus Scripturæ authoritas, quàm omnis humani ingenii perspicacitas.* And believe not them that say, If you would know the power of Devils and Witches, go to the Writings of Dr. *Casaubon*, Mr. *Glanvil*, and to the rest of the Demonographers and Witchmongers, that amass and heap together all the lying, vain, improbable, and impossible stories that can be scraped forth of any Author, ancient, middle, or modern, when we are commanded to go *to the Law and to the Testimony, if they speak not according to this word,*

Act. 20. 27.

2 Tim. 3. 15, 16, 17.

Eph. 6. 11, 12, 13.

2 Cor. 2. 11.

2 Pet. 1. 19.

Luk. 16. 29, 30, 31.

Sup. Gen. ad lit. l. 2.

Isa. 8. 19, 20.

word, *it is because there is no truth in them.* And so I shall shut up this Chapter, wherein (I suppose) I have sufficiently proved, that the denying of such a Witch as I have described, doth not infer the denial of the Being of Angels or Spirits, and that Apparitions are no sufficient grounds for Christians to believe the Existence of Angels and Spirits by, but the Word of God; which was the thing undertaken to be proved.

CHAP. IV.

That the Scriptures and sound Reason are the true and proper Mediums to prove the Actions attributed unto Witches by, and not other improper ways that many Authors have used. And of the Requisites necessary truly to prove a matter of Fact by.

AS we have in the former Chapter proved, that Apparitions (though true) are no sufficient warrant to ground our belief upon, for the Existence of Angels or Spirits, but the Word of God: so here we shall endeavour clearly to manifest, that the Sacred Scriptures are the only Medium, joyned with sound Reason, of deciding this point of the power and operation of Demons and Witches, and not other improper Mediums brought in by divers Authors, and first we shall answer the Objection of Mr. *Glanvil,* that runs thus.

"That though the New Testament had mentioned nothing of *Object.* 1.
" this matter, yet its silence in such cases is not argumentative. He *Pag. 95, 97.*
" said nothing of those large unknown Tracts of *America,* nor gave
" he any intimations of as much as the existence of that numerous
" people; much less did he leave instructions about their Conver-
" sion. He gives no account of the affairs and state of the other
" World, but only that general one of the happiness of some, and
" the misery of others. He made no discovery of the *Magnalia* of
" Art or Nature, no not of those whereby the propagation of the
" Gospel might have been much advanced, *viz.* the Mystery of
" Printing and the Magnet, and yet no one useth his silence in these
" instances as an argument against the being of things, which are
" evident objects of sense. To which we answer.

1. He falleth into a common mistake in making the Proposition *Respons.*
universal, and *dolus versatur in universalibus,* when it ought but
to be particular: so for him to say, that no silence of Scripture is
argumentative, is too universal; for its silence in point of Geo-
graphy, as in describing *America,* and the people thereof, nor in
discovering the *Magnalia Naturæ & Artis* is not argumentative;
and we do not say, that all silence of Scripture is argumentative,

but

but yet we affirm that some silence of Scripture is argumentative. So we cannot universally say, that nothing hath a being but what is mentioned in Scripture; but we may very well affirm, that some things have no being, or truth of existence, because not declared in Scripture.

2. The Scriptures were not written to teach Naural Philosophy, Arts or Sciences, humane Policy, or the like; but were given, *that the man of God might be perfect, furnished for every good work :* and it is by them that we have the doctrine of eternal Salvation revealed unto us, and we positively affirm the sufficiency of the Scriptures unto Salvation, which thing no Orthodox Divine (we suppose) will deny, and *Bellarmine* himself did confess in these words: *Prophetici & Apostolici libri sunt verum verbum Dei, ac stabilis regula fidei.* And if it be a certain Rule of Faith, and the true Word of God, then whatsoever it is silent of, we ought not to believe, and so its silence is argumentative in that point. The Scriptures are utterly silent concerning Purgatory, and therefore it is a good argument to affirm there is no such place as Purgatory, because the Word of God is silent as concerning it; but if it had been necessary to have been believed, then there would have been mention made of it.

Lib. 1. *c.* 1.

3. And as the Scriptures are sufficient in matters of Faith, and *circa credenda*, and what they are silent in, are not to be received as Articles of our Faith, but to be rejected, as having no truth of Existence: So likewise what Worship God requireth of his people, is fully revealed in his Word, and therefore I am to reject the worshipping of *Mahomet* with the Turks, or Images, and praying to Saints with the Papists, because I have neither precept nor president in the Word, but it is silent in such matters; nay tells us, *That he is the Lord our God, and him only we ought to serve.*

4. Though Mr. *Glanvil* say, that God hath given no account of the state of the other World, but only that general one of the happiness of some, and the misery of others; yet Am I to believe as Mr. *Glanvil* somewhere in his Book affirmeth, that *Samuels* Soul was raised up by the Woman at *Endor,* and that those that he feigneth to make Leagues and Contracts with Witches, are the Souls of such as had been Witches when they lived, and asketh, Who saith that happy Souls were never imployed in any ministeries here below? Or am I to believe that both the Souls of the godly and wicked, do rove up and down here upon earth, and make Apparitions, because the Popish Teachers do hold it to be so? I hope not, and therefore I shall in part give an answer here to some of these, and handle that of the Woman of *Endor* in another place. 1. The Word of God doth particularly teach us the state and condition of the Souls after death, that they shall be like the Angels in Heaven; and all other things necessary to move and draw us to believe the immortal Existence of Souls, as that most able and learned Divine Dr. *Stillingfleet* hath asserted in these words: " The Scriptures give
the

Pag. 87, 88.
23.

" the moft faithful reprefentation of the ftate and co~ ~ion of the
" Soul of Man.   The World (he faith) was almoft loft in Difputes   *Origin.Serm..3.*
" concerning the Nature, Condition, and Immortality of the Soul,   *c.6.p.608.*
" before divine Revelation was made known to Mankind by the Go-
" fpel of Chrift; *but life and immortality was brought to light by the*
" *Goffel,* and the future ftate of the foul of man not difcovered in
" an uncertain Platonical way, but with the greateft light and evi-
" dence from that God who hath the fupreme difpofal of fouls, and
" therefore beft knows and underftands them.   A Sentence truly
pious and orthodoxal.   2. Hath not God in the holy Scriptures
amply and plainly taught us the ftate of the other World, in de-
fcribing unto us fuch a numerous company of Seraphims and Cherubims, Angels and Archangels, with their feveral Orders, Offices,
Minifteries, and Imployments ? and this is more than a general account, as may be feen at full in that learned and godly Piece of Bifhop *Halls,* called *The invifible World.*   And hath he not given us
a particular account of the very Kingdom of Darknefs, telling us
of the Devil and his Angels, and precifely in this enumeration ? *For*
we wreftle not with flefh and blood, but againft principalities, againft
powers, againft the rulers of the darknefs of this world, againft fpi-
ritual wickednefs in high places.   And this is more than a general
account, and we muft needs fay, that what he holds is very derogatory to the wifdom and goodnefs of God, and the fufficiency
and truth of the Scriptures.   3. Muft I believe him that the
fouls of the Saints do rove and wander here below ? when as Bifhop *Hall* faith, where he is fpeaking againft the opinion of thofe
that hold, that Souls do fleep until the Day of Judgment: " In-   *Invifib. World;*
" deed who can but wonder that any Chriftian can poffibly give   *p.112.*
" entertainment to fo abfurd a thought, whilft he hears his Saviour
" fay, *Father I will that they alfo whom thou haft given me, be with*   *Joh.17.24*
" *me where I am, and that* (not in a fafe fleep) *they may behold my*
" *glory, which thou haft given me.*   Sure if the Souls departed be
with Chrift where he is, and do behold his glory, then it is a Popifh Fable of Mr. *Glanvil,* to feign their coming upon Meffages
hither.   The faying of St. *Bernard* is remarkable in this cafe: *Ad-*   *Serm. c. 7.*
vertiftis tres effe fanctarum ftatus animarum, primum videlicet in
corpore corruptibili, fecundum fine corpore, tertium in corpore jam
glorificato.   Primum in militia, fecundum in requie, tertium in
beatitudine confummata.   And if the fecond ftate of holy Souls
be without a body, and be at peace and reft, then it muft neceffarily be a truth, that they do not wander here, nor run upon Errands; *For the fouls of the righteous are in the hands of the Lord,*   *Wifd. 3. 1.*
and there fhall no torment touch them.   And our Saviour told the
Thief upon the Crofs, *This day thou fhalt be with me in Paradife,*   *Luk. 23. 43.*
that is, as Dr. *Hammond* giveth the Paraphrafe: " Immediately after
" thy death thou fhalt go to a place of blifs, and there abide with
" me, a Member of that my Kingdom which thou askeft for.   Now
if the fouls of the godly, after their death, be immediately in a place
of

of bliſs, and abide with Chriſt as Members of his Kingdom, then they do not wander up and down here, as Mr. *Glanvil* and the Papiſts vainly fancy and believe; for as *Chryſoſtome* ſaith upon that place of *Lazarus* his being carried by Angels into *Abrahams* boſome. "What is it then that the Devils ſay, I am the Soul of ſuch "a Monk? Truly I therefore believe it not, becauſe the Devils ſay ": it, for they deceive their Auditors. 4. Or muſt I believe that the ſouls of the wicked do wander, and make Apparitions here, becauſe Mr. *Glanvil* and the Popiſh Writers tell me ſo? I hope not; for the Text telleth us plainly, that the rich man preſently after his death was in Hell in torments, and could not come hither unto earth again to warn his brethren, otherwiſe he would not have prayed *Abraham* to have ſent *Lazarus*. And whether it be taken for a real Hiſtory of things done, or but a Parable, yet the ſpiritual meaning of our Saviour muſt be infallibly true, that immediately after death the ſouls of the godly are by Angels carried into *Abrahams* boſome, and the wicked go down into Hell, from whence there is no redemption; and therefore do not wander up and down here, nor make any Apparitions: for I imagine that the authority of holy King *David*, a Prophet and a man after Gods own heart, is to be preferred before the authority of a thouſand Popiſh Writers, and he tells us, when the child was dead: *But now he is dead, wherefore ſhould I faſt? can I bring him back again? I ſhall go to him, but he ſhall not return to me.* And *Job* tells us: *As the cloud is conſumed, and vaniſheth away: ſo he that goeth down to the grave, ſhall come up no more, he ſhall return to more to his houſe, neither ſhall his place know him any more.* And therefore it was a vain argument of *Bellarmine* when he ſaid: "*Apparitiones anima-* "*rum ex Purgatorio venientium idem teſtantur.* To which the Proteſtants anſwer: "But who ſhall bear witneſs of theſe Appari- "tions, that they were not either ſeigned fables, or Satanical illu- "ſions? They were men, and might be deceived, even the beſt of "them, with whom doth reſt the faith of theſe Narrations. 5. And whereas he audaciouſly asketh, "Who ſaith that happy Souls were "never imployed in any Miniſteries here below? I ſhall tell him who they are that ſay, that happy Souls departed are never imployed here in any Miniſteries; and they are all the learned Divines of the Reformed Churches, and all thoſe that were true Sons of the Doctrine of the Church of *England*, ſuch as were Biſhop *Jewel*, Biſhop *Hall*, Dr. *Willet*, Dr. *Whitaker*, Mr. *Perkins*, and many more ſuch, the authority and reputation of the leaſt of which is far above the ſimple queſtion of Mr. *Glanvil*. And therefore ſaith the latter Confeſſion of *Helvetia*: "Now that which is recorded "of the Spirits or Souls of the dead ſometimes appearing to them "that are alive, &c. we count thoſe Apparitions among the delu- "ſions and deceits of the Devil.

  5. And as the Scriptures are ſufficient both in reſpect of matters of Faith, and concerning divine Worſhip, that their ſilence in thoſe

two

Concio ſecunda de Lazaro.

Luk. 16.22,23.

2 Sam. 12.23.
Job 7.9, 10.
Idem 10.20,21.

Bellarm. Enervat. tom. 2. *l.*5. *p.* 204.

Homil. ſect. 16.
pag. 484.

two particulars are fully argumentative, to deny whatever is not contained in them, as unfit to be received to either purpose. So in respect of a Christians warfare, all things for the obtaining of a perfect and compleat victory, and for standing and perseverance, are in them fully declared, and what they mention not is to be rejected, as wanting the seal of Divine Authority, whether it be in regard of eschewing what is prohibited, or in following what is commanded. And therefore we affirm, that what the Scriptures have not revealed of the power of the Kingdom of Satan, is to be rejected, and not to be believed, and what weapons we are to use against the wiles of the Devil, we are to be furnished withal, but have need of no others but what the Holy Ghost in the Scriptures hath made known unto us, the rest are to be cast off, as fables and lyes, or humane inventions, because the Scriptures are silent of any such matter, and that for these weighty grounds and considerations.

1. We shall take the Concession of *Bellarmine* himself, who saith: *Nullum est vitium ad quod sanandum non invenitur in Scriptura aliquod remedium.* And again: *Illa quæ sunt simpliciter omnibus necessaria, Apostoli consueverunt omnibus prædicare: & aliorum quæ sunt omnibus utilia.* And to the same purpose is the saying of St. *Austin: Titubat fides, si divinarum Scripturarum vacillet authoritas: porrò fide titubante, etiam ipsa charitas languescit.* *De Doctrin. Christian.* Therefore if there be no fault for which the Scripture doth not yield some remedy, then surely to make a visible League with the Devil, or to have carnal Copulation with him, either must have no verity at all in it, or that the Scripture hath provided no remedy for it, for of such things there is no mention. And if Faith must stumble, where the authority of the Scriptures is wanting, then surely the belief of all rational men must needs be staggering, to believe what these common Witchmongers affirm of the Witches visible League and carnal Copulation with the Devil, when there is no authority of Scripture at all to strengthen or countenance any such matter.

2. The Scriptures do fully and abundantly inform us of the Devils spiritual and invisible power, and against the same declares unto us the whole Armor of God, with which we ought to be furnished, as the Apostle saith: *Put on the whole armor of God, that* *Eph. 6. 11,12, 13.* *ye may be able to stand against the wiles of the devil. For we wrestle not against flesh and blood, but against principalities, against powers; against the rulers of the darkness of this world, against spiritual wickedness in high places. Wherefore take unto you the whole armor of God, that ye may be able to withstand in the evil day, and having done all, to stand.* And the Apostle St. *Peter* telleth us: *Be sober, be vigilant, because your adversary the devil,* *1 Pet. 5. 8, 9.* *like a roaring lion, walketh about seeking whom he may devour; whom resist stedfast in the faith.* And in another place: *For the* *2 Cor. 10. 4, 5.* *weapons of our warfare are not carnal, but mighty through God to*
the

the pulling down of strong holds, casting down imaginations, and every high thing that exalteth it self against the knowledge of God. From which Scriptures we may take these remarkable observations.

1. We are to consider the nature of this Warfare, that it is spiritual and against spiritual wickedness in high places, and not against flesh and blood; and the Holy Ghost could not be wanting nor defective, but superabundantly full in describing the nature of this warfare, that it is spiritual, not carnal; and therefore we are to prepare our selves against all spiritual assaults: but as for any visible, carnal, or bodily, there is not, nor can be any such, because the Apostle that declared by his Preaching and Writings the whole counsel of God, hath revealed no such thing as the visible appearing of Satan, much less of his making of a visible League with the Witches, or the sucking of their bodies, or the having carnal Copulation with them, which must of necessity be lyes and figments, because the Holy Ghost hath not warned us of any such, which we ought certainly to believe he would have done, if there had been

2 Cor. 2. 11. any such matter. And the holy Apostle, who was not ignorant of the devices νοήματα, notions or intentions of Satan, would not have omitted to have warned the godly, if there had been any such matter as a visible League, sucking of their bodies, or carnal Copulation, the thing being of so great weight and concern. For 1 Tim. 3. 7.
2 Tim. 2. 26. as one said well: *Grave est de vita & bonis periclitari, sed multò gravius insidiantem habere Satanam.* And he that so often hath given us warning of the wiles, devices, and snares of the Devil, if there had been any such dangerous snare as this, would without doubt have given us notice of it.

2. We are to consider the end of this Warfare, that it is for no less than a Crown, and that not a terrestrial, but a celestial one, not a fading one, but an everlasting one, a Crown of eternal life, of immortal glory, even for an house given of God, eternal in the Heavens. Therefore this being a thing of the greatest concern that belongs to a Christian, the Apostle would not doubtlessly omit any thing that had been necessary to the obtaining of such an inestimable prize, and such an important Victory; and therefore cannot in reason have concealed or omitted such a weighty matter as a visible League, and the like, if there had been any such thing.

3. We are to consider that this Armor prescribed for the Souldiers of Jesus Christ, is *the whole armor of God,* πανοπλίαν, the compleat armor of God (as Dr. *Hammond* renders it) perfect both for defence and offence. And therefore the Apostle describes it fully by a Metaphor, taken from such Arms as the *Roman* or other Na- Eph. 6. 14, 15, 16, 17, 18. tions in his time did use, saying: *Stand therefore, having your loyns girt about with truth, and having on the breast-plate of righteousness: And your feet shod with the preparation of the Gospel of peace. Above all taking the shield of faith, wherewith ye shall be able to quench all the fiery darts of the wicked. And take the helmet*

of

of falvation, and the fword of the fpirit, which is the word of God. Praying always with all prayer and fupplication in the fpirit, and watching thereunto with all perfeverance and fupplication for all Saints. And as it is a compleat and perfect Armor, both in refpect of defence and offence; fo it is a fpiritual, not a carnal, corporeal, or bodily armor, becaufe the warfare *is not againft flefh and blood, but againft fpiritual wickednefs in high places,* againft fpiritual enemies, not againft corporeal and carnal ones; for as the enemies are and the warfare, fo are the armor and weapons. From whence we truly urge, that the Apoftle led by the Holy Ghoft, and the Wifdom of the Father, and knowing the whole counfel of God (efpecially in this point) hath omitted nothing that is fitting armor for a Chriftian either of defence or offence, whereby he may be inabled to get the victory againft Satan, and all his fpiritual Army. And therefore that either Satan hath not power, or doth not affault Chriftians after a vifible, carnal, and bodily manner, or elfe that the Holy Ghoft hath been defective in prefcribing armor againft fuch affaults, and confequently that the armor of a Souldier of Jefus Chrift is not compleat, or elfe there is no fuch bodily affaults of Satan at all, as to tempt vifibly, to make a corporeal League, to fuck upon the Witches bodies, nor to have carnal Copulation with them. But we affirm, and that (as we conceive) with found reafon, that the Scriptures in this particular of a Chriftians armor, and the compleatnefs of it, is abundantly fufficient againft all fpiritual affaults whatfoever, and confequently that there is no other kind of affaults but meerly fpiritual, and therefore the Word of God, the moft proper *Medium* with found reafon, to judge of the power of Spirits and Devils by.

3. That the Scriptures and found reafon are the only true and proper *Medium* to decide thefe Controverfies by, is moft undeniably apparent, becaufe God is a Spirit, and the invifible God, and therefore beft knows the nature and power of the fpiritual and invifible World, and being the God of truth, can and doth inform us of their power and operations, better than the vain lyes and figments of the Heathen Poets, or the dreams of the Platonick School, either elder or later, nay better than all the notional and groundlefs fpeculations of the School-men, of whom it may truly be faid that, *Rivulo divinæ Scripturæ relicto, in abyffos vanarum opinionum incidêrunt.* Nay thefe can better inform us in this point, than the Writings of all Mortals befides, and therefore whatfoever may be faid to the contrary, may receive its anfwer from the Father: *Quod de Scripturis facris authoritatem non habet, eâdem facilitate contemnitur, quâ probatur.* Therefore he being *the King eternal, immortal, invifible, and the only wife God,* of none can we fo truly and certainly learn thefe things, as of him who hath plentifully taught us in his Word all things neceffary to Salvation, *that the man of God may be perfect, throughly furnifhed to every good work.* Nay *he is the Father of Spirits*, and therefore truly

Gregor. fup. Ezikiel. Homil. 6.
1 Tim. 1. 17.

Heb. 12. 5.

know-

knoweth, and can and doth teach us their Natures, Offices, and Operations.

4. The Scriptures (especially the Writings of *Moses*) considered only as Historical, are of more antiquity, verity, and certainty both as to Doctrine, Precepts, matters of Fact, and Chronology, than all other Histories whatsoever, whether of the Phenicians, Egyptians, Chaldeans, or Grecians, as the learned person Dr. *Stillingfleet* hath sufficiently proved. Now if there had been such an one as a Witch, that made a visible League with the Devil, and upon whose body he suckt, and with whom he had carnal Copulation, something of that nature would doubtless have been recorded in the Scriptures, of which notwithstanding there is not the least tittle or mention. And *Moses* who was so perfect a Law-giver, as in a manner to omit no kind or sort of sin or evil that men possibly could commit, but to forbid it, and make a Law against it, could never have left out such an horrid, unnatural, and hellish wickedness as carnal Copulation with the fallen Angels, if there had been any such matter. For he saith, after he had forbidden all sorts of Fornications, Adulteries, and Incests: *Thou shalt not lye with mankind, as with womankind: it is abomination. Neither shalt thou lye with any beast to defile thy self therewith: neither shall any woman stand before a beast to lye down thereto: it is confusion. Defile not your selves in any of these things: for in all these the nations are defiled, which I cast out before you.* Now it cannot be rationally imagined, that *Moses* having named and prohibited the less sins of bestial Copulation and Sodomy, would have left out that which is the most horrid and execrable of all others, to wit, carnal Copulation with Devils, if there had been any such thing either in possibility or act. And therefore we may conclude according to the rules of sound reason, that there is no such matter, and that the Scriptures are the most fit *Medium* to decide these Controversies.

5. The Scriptures and sound reason are the most fit Mediums to determine these things by, because there is nothing that any hath written upon this Subject (though the Authors be superfluously numerous) but if it agree not with the principles of right reason, and the rules of the Scriptures, they ought to be rejected. For what is not consonant to right reason, ought not to be received by any that truly are rational Creatures; and what agrees not with the Word of God, ought not to be entertained by any that are or would be accounted good or true Christians. And if all the gross fables, lyes, impossibilities, and nonsensical stories that Demonographers and Witchmongers have related and accumulated together, were brought to the test of the Scriptures and sound reason, they would soon be hissed off the Stage, and find few believers or embracers of them. But alas! all (nay few men) have the right use and exercise of their rational faculty, but men to see to are in themselves as beasts; and therefore we may all pray with the Apostle to be delivered from unreasonable men, or men without reason, or absurd men,

Vid. Orig. facr. l. 1. c. 1. p. 15.

Levit. 18. 22, 23, 24.

2 Thess. 3. 2.

men, that make no right ufe of reafon, ἄτοπων ἀνθρώπων.

6. The Scriptures and right reafon have declared all things concerning Spirits either good or bad, as alfo all forts of Diviuers (or Witches, if you will have them called fo) and the nature, power, operations, and actions of them, more than any other Book that was written before the time of our Saviours Birth (the dreams and whimfies of the Platonifts only excepted) or for the fpace of three hundred years after, and therefore are the moft fit Medium and Authority to determine thefe things by.   1. For firft it is manifelt, that all things are ordered by the wifdom of the Almighty, who hath done whatfoever he would both in Heaven, *and he doth* Dan. 4. 3⁵. *according to his will in the army of heaven, and among the inhabitants of the earth : and none can ftay his hand, or fay unto him, What doft thou ?* And thefe things God doth not by a naked prefcience, but by his divine will, providence, and ordination, as a learned Divine hath taught us in thefe words: *Eft hoc inprimis neceffarium & falutare Chriftiano nôffe, quòd Deus nihil præfcit contingenter, fed quòd omnia incommutabili & æternâ, infallibiltq; voluntate & providet, & præponit, & facit.* So it was only his will, decree, and determination, that Chrift fhould not be born, or affume humane nature vifibly, but at that precife time that he had appointed, according to the evidence of the Apoftle. *But when the* Gal. 4. 4. *fulnefs of time was come, God fent forth his Son made of a woman, made under the law.* And when that fulnefs of time was come that he fent him, then did the divine Wifdom and Providence ordain all means, objects and occafions, whereby the fulnefs of the Godhead that dwelt in him bodily, might be made manifeft, by working of miracles, both by himfelf and his Apoftles, therefore were there fo many feveral forts of Demoniacks, blind, lame, dumb, deaf, and difeafed, not by chance, but by the providence of the Father, and only and chiefly that the work of God might be manifeft in them, for the Evangelift tells us: *And as Jefus paffed by, he faw a man which* Joh. 9. 1, 2, 3. *was blind from his birth. And his Difciples asked him, faying, Mafter, who did fin, this man or his parents, that he was born blind ? Jefus anfwered, Neither hath this man finned, nor his parents, but that the works of God fhould be made manifeft in him.* Upon which place Dr. Hammond doth give this clear Paraphrafe : "And " fome of his followers asked him, faying, Sir, was it any fin of his " own, when his foul was in another body, or was it fome fin of his " parents at the time of his conception, which caufed this blind- " nefs in him? Neither his own, nor his parents fins were the caufe " of this blindnefs of his, but Gods fecret wifdom, who meant by " this means to fhew forth in me his miraculous power among you. And though the Doctor would bring in the opinion of *Pythagoras* of the Tranfmigration of Souls (of which vain traditional fancies he is almoft every where guilty) as received and imbibed in by fome of the Jews that then followed him : yet it appeareth plainly, that it was not interrogated by the Jews, but by his Difci-

ples, οἱ Μαθηταὶ, and therefore it is a wonder the Doctor ſhould be ſo
groſly miſtaken; and *Theophylact* tells us thus much plainly : *Neq;
enim Apoſtoli Gentiles nugas receperunt , quo anima ante corpus in
alio mundo verſans peccet , ac deinde pænam quandam recipiat in
corpus deſcendens. Piſcatores cùm eſſent, neq; audiverant tale quiddam , quia hæc Philoſophorum dogmata erant.* And ſo declareth,
that the Diſciples having ſeen Chriſt heal the man that had thirty

Joh. 5. 14.

eight years been impotent and lame, and had ſaid unto him , *Behold thou art made whole , ſin no more leſt a worſe thing come unto
thee*, did conceive, that this man being born blind, it had been a
puniſhment upon him, either for his own ſins, or the ſins of his pa-

Vid. Thom. A-
quin. caten. aur.
in loc.

rents, and ſo doubting asked the queſtion. And ſo alſo do St. *Au-
ſtin* and *Chryſoſtome* expound the place, which is both ſound and
rational. And of our Saviours reſponſion, *That neither had this
man ſinned, nor his parents*, the learned Father giveth a ſatisfactory
anſwer, ſaying : *Nunquid vel ipſe ſine originali peccato natus erat,*

Ut ſupr.

*vel vivendo nihil addiderat ? Habebant ergo peccatum , & ipſe &
parentes ejus , ſed non ipſo peccato factum eſt ut cæcus naſceretur.
Ipſe autem cauſam dicit quare cæcus ſit natus , cùm ſubdit : ſed ut
manifeſtentur opera Dei in illo.* And to the ſame purpoſe *Gregory*
hath this notable paſſage : *Alia itaq; eſt percuſſio , quà peccator
percutitur, ut ſine retractatione puniatur : Alia quà peccator percutitur, ut corrigatur : Alia quà quiſq; percutitur , non ut præterita
corrigat, ſed ne ventura committat : Alia per quam nec præterita
culpa corrigitur , nec futura prohibetur. Sed dum inopinata ſalus
percuſſionem ſequitur , ſalvantis virtus cognita ardentiùs amatur.*
From whence it is manifeſt, that as the Father in the fulneſs of time,
by his Decree and Providence ſent out the Son, *in whom dwelt
the fulneſs of the Godhead bodily*, with a purpoſe to manifeſt the
ſame by his great and wonderful Miracles : ſo in his divine Wiſdom he had ordered fit ſubjects and objects upon whom that power
might be made manifeſt. And therefore were there ſuch ſtrange
diſeaſes offered, eſpecially in Demoniacks, that can hardly be parallel'd in any one Country of that ſmall compaſs , and in ſo ſhort
a time , and all that the works of God might be manifeſt by that
ever-bleſſed Saviour of Mankind, Jeſus Chriſt. And though there
were ſo many perſons, ſo many ſeveral ways perplexed and afflicted both in their minds and bodies, as ſome made deaf and dumb,
ſome torn and contorted in their members , ſome thrown on the
ground, ſome into the fire, ſome driven to live amongſt the graves
and monuments, and yet all theſe cured by our bleſſed Saviour : Yet
is there no mention made of any that had made a viſible League
with the Devil, nor upon whoſe bodies he ſuckt , nor with whom
he had carnal Copulation, nor whom he had tranſubſtantiated into
Wolves, Dogs, Hares, Cats , or Squirrels; to have cured which
would have been as great a miracle as any of the reſt, but there
were no ſuch matters; and therefore we may ſafely conclude, there
never were, are , or can be any ſuch matters, whatſoever may be
ſaid to the contrary.
                 2. In

2. In the New Testament there is mention made of several sorts of deceiving Impostors, Diviners, or Witches, who were all discovered and conquered by that power that Christ had given unto the Apostles; as for instance: *Simon, which before-time in the same city used sorcery, and bewitched* μαγεύων & ἐξιστῶν *the people of Samaria, giving out that himself was some great one. To whom they* Aɛt.8.9,10,11. *gave heed from the least to the greatest, saying, This man is the great power of God. And to him they had regard, because that of long time he had bewitched them with sorceries;* ταῖς μαγείαις ἐξεστακέναι αὐτὸς, *seducebat populum suis magicis præstigiis,* saith *Tremellius;* and *Beza, Exercuerat artem magicam, & gentem Samariæ obstupefecerat;* who when he would have bought the gift of the Holy Ghost Aɛt. 13. 8. with money, was rejected by *Peter* as an Impostor and Counterfeit, and declared, *that he was in the gall of bitterness.* Such another was *Elymas* the Sorcerer (for so is his name by interpretation) ὁ μάγ@, who was stricken blind by St. *Paul.* Such an one was the Ibid. 16.16,18. Damsel that was possessed with a Spirit of Divination, which St. *Paul* cast forth. And such were the Jewish Exorcists, that took upon them to call over them which had evil Spirits, the Name of the Lord Jesus, saying, *We adjure you by Jesus whom Paul preacheth.* Aɛt. 19. 13,16. *But the man in whom the evil spirit was, leapt on them, and overcame them, and prevailed against them, so that they fled out of that house naked and wounded.* But amongst these several sorts of Diviners, Impostors, or Witches, there were none that had made a visible League with the Devil, nor upon whose bodies he suckt, nor that had carnal Copulation with him, nor were changed into Cats, Dogs, or Wolves: but if the Devil had had any such power, or had there been any such sort of Witches, the divine Wisdom and Providence would have ordained some of them then to have been made apparent, that his power by Christ and the Apostles, might have been shewed as well in the greater as in the less: and that for the more full manifestation of the Works of God, as for a more triumphant declaration of the power of Christ in conquering him and his Kingdom, and for a more ample warning and instruction to the Children of God to avoid the snares and wiles of the Devil; d Thess. 2. 9. but there being no such, then we must rationally conclude, that there now is not, nor ever was, or can be any such matter, but the vain believing of such figments and forgeries, is only the cunning and delusion of Satan, who works by lying and deceiving wonders τέρασι ψεύδους, of which St. *Chrysostome* saith thus: *Hoc est, omnem* Chrysost. in loc. *ostentabit potentiam, sed nihil veri, verùm omnia ad seductionem. Et prodigiis, inquit, mendacii. Aut ementitis ac ludificantibus, aut ad mendacium inducentibus.*

Having now sufficiently proved, that the Scriptures and sound Reason are the proper Mediums to decide these difficulties by, we shall in the next place shew the invalidity of some ways used by the most Authors, to prove and defend these Tenents, and *ab uno disce omnes*, take Mr. *Glanvil* for all, in his own words: " That Pag. 5.
" this

" this being matter of fact, is only capable of the evidence of authority and sense : and by both these, the being of Witches and
" Diabolical Contracts, is most abundantly confirmed. To which
we shall give this smart Reply. Not to make the Proposition universal, generally to deny the evidence of authory and sense; no, far
be it from me to run into that wild and senseless absurdity, which
were in a manner to destroy the credibility of all humane testimony:
But we shall here speak of the evidence of authority and sense with
this restriction and limitation, to these Particulars. 1. Those Authors that write of Apparitions and Spirits. 2. Those that treat
of Diabolical Leagues and Contracts. 3. Those that mention the
Devil sucking of the Witches body, carnal Copulation with them,
their being changed into Hares, Dogs, Cats, and Wolves, and the
like. These Authors we say are to be read with caution, and their
relations not to be credited, except better proof be given to evidence the matters of fact, than hitherto hath been brought by any,
and that for these especial reasons and necessary cautions.

   1. The Authors that have recorded stories of this nature, are to
be seriously considered, whether they have related the matter of
fact by their own proper knowledge, as eye and ear-witnesses of it,
or have taken it up by hear-say, common fame, or the relation of
others: and if what they relate, were not of their own certain
knowledge or αὐτοψία, then is it of little or no credit at all; for the
other that relates it, might be guilty either of active or passive deception and delusion, or might have heard it from another, or by
common report: of all, which there is no certainty, but leaveth
sufficient grounds for dubitation, and is sufficient to caution a prudent person altogether to suspend his assent, until better proof can
be brought. There is a story related by *Plinius Cæcilius* to his
Friend *Sura*, of a House in *Athens* that was haunted by a Spirit in
so terrible and frightful a manner, that it was left utterly forsaken,
and none would inhabit in it, until that *Athenodorus* the Philosopher adventured upon it, and abode the coming of the Apparition
or Phantasm, and upon its signs followed it to a place below, and
then it vanished: he marked the place, and went to the Magistrate,
and caused the place to be digged up; and found the bones of a
person inchained or fettered, and caused the bones to be buried,
and so the House remained free afterwards. It is a wonder to think
how many Authors have swallowed this relation (nay even *Philip
Camerarius* himself, who though a very Learned man, yet in things
of this nature too extremely credulous) and urged it for proof, as
a matter of great credit and authority, when we cannot discern
that it affords any credible ground to a rational man to believe it,
not only because the very matter it self, and the circumstances of
it, do yield sufficient grounds of the suspicion of its verity; but
chiefly because *Pliny* doth but relate it by hear-say, *exponam ut
accepi*, and of it and the rest he desires the opinion of his Friend
Sura, from whom we do not find any answer. The story taken
      from

*Epist. lib. 7.
pag. 252.*

from *Plutarch* (a grave Author, if he be confidered as an Heathen De *defect.oracul.*
and a Moralift) yet of no authority to decide fuch points as thefe p. *mihi* 700.
are) of the voice that called upon *Thamus*, and commanded him to
declare when he came at *Palodes*, that the great God *Pan* was dead,
which he performed, and that thereupon followed a great lamen-
tation of many : the ftory at large is related by many , and urged
as a matter of great weight and credibility , when indeed there is
no ground fufficient to perfwade any that it was true.   For if it
had been related by *Plutarch* as an ear-witnefs of it , yet was he
but an Heathen, that we know believed many fond, lying, and impoffible things , efpecially of their Gods ; and therefore in this
cafe to a confiderate Chriftian could be of no great authority.
And if his authority had been great, or of weight in fuch matters
as thefe, yet was he but *fingularis teftis*, which is not fufficient in
thefe things to be relied upon.   And laftly (to our prefent purpofe here) he doth not record it as a thing of his own certain
knowledge, but of hear-fay from *Epitherfes*, who was but a fingle
Relator , and a man of no certain veracity ; and therefore we can
have no rational ground to believe the truth of the ftory , but it
may be rejected with more reafon, than it can be affirmed by.   Of
no greater credit can his ftory be of *Brutus* his *malus Genius* ap- *Plutarch.in vit.*
pearing unto him, becaufe he received this by meer Tradition and *Marc. Brut.*
hear-fay, neither could it have any other rife , but from the rela- *pag.* 361.
tion of *Brutus* himfelf, whofe guilty confcience, and troubled
brain, fancied fuch vain things ; for thofe that were near *Brutus*
neither faw nor heard any fuch matter , and therefore muft have
been a deception of Phanfie, and no real Apparition *ad extra.*

2. And as evidence of the matter of fact recorded from the relation of others, is of no validity to a judicious perfon : fo if the
matter of fact be witneffed but by one fingle teftimony (though
an eye or an ear-witnefs) it is not fufficient, becaufe one fingle perfon
may be imperfect in fome fenfes, or under fome diftemper, and fo
be no proper Judge of what it fees or hears ; and the Word of Truth
tells us, *That in the mouth of two or three witneffes every word
fhall be eftablifhed* ; and therefore we are not (efpecially in fuch
abftrufe matters as thefe) to truft the evidence of one fingle teftimony.   To make clear this Particular, we fhall relate a ftory or
two from the credit of the Reverend and Learned Bifhop *Hall*, The invifible
joyned with his judgment of fuch weak and feigned Tales, one of World, p.245,
which runs thus: "*Johannes à Jefu Maria*, a modern Carmelite, 246, 247.
" writing the Life of *Therefia* (Sainted lately by *Gregory* XV.) tells
" us, that as fhe was a vigilant Overfeer of her Votaries in her life,
" fo in and after death fhe would not be drawn away from her care
" and attendance: For (faith he) if any of her Sifters did but talk in
" the fet hours of their filence, fhe was wont by three knocks at the
" door of the Cell, to put them in mind of their enjoyned tacitur-
" nity.   And on a time appearing (as fhe did often) in a light-
" fome brightnefs to a certain Carmelite, is faid thus to befpeak
" him ;

Jo. à Jeſu Mar.
lib. 5. de Vit.
Thereſ. cap. 3.

"him; *Nos cœleſtes, ac vos exules amore ac puritate fœderati eſſe*
"*debemus, &c.* We Citizens of Heaven, and ye exiled Pilgrims on
"earth, ought to be linked in a League of love and purity, &c.
"Methinks the Reporter (ſaith the Biſhop) ſhould fear this to be
"too much good fellowſhip for a Saint; I am ſure neither Divine
"nor Ancient ſtory had wont to afford ſuch familiarity: and many
"have miſdoubted the agency of worſe, where have appeared leſs
"cauſes of ſuſpicion.   That this was (if any thing) an ill Spirit
"under that face, I am juſtly confident; neither can any man
"doubt, that looking further into the relation, finds him to come
"with a lye in his mouth.   For thus he goes on; [We Celeſtial
"ones behold the Deity, ye baniſhed ones worſhip the Euchariſt,
"which ye ought to worſhip with the ſame affection wherewith
"we adore the Deity] ſuch perfume doth this holy Devil leave
"behind him.   The like might be inſtanced in a thouſand Appa-
"ritions of this kind, all worthy of the ſame entertainment.   This
is a ſtory from one ſingle perſon, a lying Carmelite, one that for
intereſt, and upholding of Superſtition and Idolatry, had feigned
and forged it; for in it ſelf it appeareth to be a meer falſity and
figment, as any rational man may eaſily diſcern, and ſo are a thouſand ſtories of this kind worthy of the like entertainment, that is,
The inviſible
World, p.305. to be condemned for moſt horrid lyes.   Another he tells us: "A-
"mongſt ſuch faſtidious choice of whole dry-fats of voluminous
"relations, I cannot forbear to ſingle out that one famous of *Mag-*
"*dalen de la Croix*, in the year of our Lord Chriſt 1545, &c. The
Ibid. p. 284. third from the mouth of another lying Fryar named *Jacobus de*
Pozali, in his Sermon, "That St. *Macarius* once went about to
"make peace betwixt God and Satan, &c.   Now whatſoever credit this Learned man (who in things of this kind appeareth to be
as vainly credulous as any) doth ſeem to give unto theſe, or what
uſe ſoever he would make of them, it is undeniably manifeſt to all
impartial judgments, that they were but abſolute forgeries and
knacks of Impoſture and Knavery, and (according to his own opinion) may juſtly be ranked amongſt thoſe thouſand Apparitions of
this kind, all worthy of the ſame entertainment, that is, to be rejected for abominable lyes or forgeries, and that for theſe reaſons.
1. Becauſe they are not atteſted by any ſincere and uncorrupt ear
and eye-witneſſes, but by reports and relations, and that of thoſe
that were corrupt and partial, or Accomplices to bring to paſs the
fraud and impoſture.   2. If they be run up to their firſt Author or
Venter of the Tale, he will but be found a ſingle Witneſs, which is
utterly inſufficient in evidencing truly a matter of fact.   3. The
Relaters of them did publiſh them for intereſt ſake, and upon deſign to advance falſe Doctrine, Worſhip, Superſtition, and Idolatry,
and therefore are not of validity and credit.   4. In themſelves (if
ſtrictly conſidered) they will appear to be lying, ridiculous, contradictory in themſelves, and contrary to the authority of Divine
Writ, and diſſonant to ſound and right reaſon, and therefore ought
to

to have no other entertainment, but as abominable lyes and forgeries.

3. But if matters of fact be witnessed and attested by many or divers persons that were ear and eye-witnesses, yet may their testimony bear no weight in the balance of Justice or right Reason, because they may be corrupt in point of interest, and so have their judgments mis-guided and biassed by the corruption of their desires and affections, or relate things out of spleen, envy, and malice; and so may not in these mysterious matters be fit authority to rely upon, nor competent evidence in these particulars, as Dr. *Casaubon* is forced to confess in these words: "In the relation of strange "things, whether natural or supernatural, to know the temper of "the Relator, if it can be known: and what interest he had, or "might probably be supposed to have had, in the relation, to have "it believed. And again, whether he profess to have seen it him-"self, or taken it upon the credit of others. And whether a man "by his profession in a capacity probable to judge of the truth of "those things, to which he doth bear witness. Every one of these particulars would require a particular consideration. For if there be interest in point of Religion, then all authorities, all colour of reason is drawn in to make good this interest, and verity is commonly stifled in this contest for selfness and interest, and the adverse parties stigmatized with all the filthy lyes and enormous crimes that can be invented, as is most manifest in these instances. The Popish party finding themselves hindred and opposed in point of the highest interest, have forged a thousand false stories and tales to make good the interest of their Party, and have left no dirt and dung unscraped up to throw in the faces of their Opponents; and so have each Party done against other, where religious interest was the quarrel, as Bishop *Hall* hath truly observed in this passage, where he is shewing the abominable corruptions of the Church of *Rome* : " A Religion that cares not by what wilful false-"hoods it maintains a part ; as *Wickliffs* blasphemy , *Luthers* ad-"vice from the Devil, *Tindals* Community , *Calvins* feigned Mira-"cle, and blasphemous death, *Bucers* neck broken , *Beza's* Revolt, "the blasting of Huguenots , *Englands* want of Churches, and "Christendom , Queen *Elizabeths* unwomanliness , her Episcopal "Jurisdiction , her secret fruitfulness , English Catholicks cast in "Bears skins to Dogs, *Plesses* shameful overthrow , *Garnats* straw, "the *Lutherans* obscene Night-Revels , *Scories* drunken Ordina-"tion in a Tavern, the Edict of our gracious King *James* (*An.* 87.) "for the establishment of Popery, our casting the crusts of our Sa-"crament to Dogs, and ten thousand of this nature , maliciously "raised against knowledge and conscience, for the disgrace of those "whom they would have hated, e're known.

Of Credul. and
Incredul. pag.
159.

A serious Dissuasive from Popery, pag. 38, 39.

The rise of this opinion that we are disputing against, that the Devil makes a visible and corporeal League with the Witches, that he sucks upon their bodies, hath carnal Copulation with them,

and

and that they are changed into Hares, Dogs, Cats, or Wolves, and the like, was soon after the thirteenth hundred year of Christ, when as *Frederick* the Second had made a Law temporal, for the burning of Hereticks. And not long after that, was the Inquisition set up in *Rome* and *Spain*, and then did the Inquisitors and their Adherents, draw in from the Heathen Poets, and all other Authors, whatsoever might carry any colour of authority or reason, the better to countenance their bloody and unjust proceedings, where they drew thousands of people into the snare of the Inquisition for pretended Witchcraft, which they made to be Heresie. And whatsoever these have written concerning these things, such as *Delrio, Bodinus, Remigius, Springerus, Niderus, Spineus, Grillandus*, and a whole rabble besides not necessary to be named, are nothing but lyes and forgeries, and deserve no credit at all for these reasons. 1. Because as many of them as either were Inquisitors themselves, or those that had any dependence upon them, or received benefit by their proceedings, are all unjust and corrupt Authors and Witnesses, as writing and bearing witness for their own ends, interest, and profit, having a share in the Goods and Estates of all that were convicted and condemned: and the Wolf and Raven will be sure to give judgment on the Serpents side, that he may devour the man, though never so innocent, because they hope to have a share of his flesh, or at least to pick the bones. 2. These Authors that were the first Broachers of these monstrous stories of Apparitions and Witches, and are so frequently quoted by others, (that ought to have been more wary, and might have seen reason enough to have rejected all their feigned lyes and delusions) were not only sharers in the spoil of the Goods of the condemned (who were judged *per fas & nefas*) but also had another base end and interest, to wit, to advance the opinion of Purgatory, praying for the dead, setting up the vain Superstitions of the virtue of the sign of the Cross, holy Water, and the like. And therefore they did forge so many stories of Apparitions, and Souls coming forth of Purgatory, and recorded so many false, lying, and impossible things from the forced, extorted, and pretended confessions of the Witches themselves, which were nothing else but an Hotch-potch of horrid and abominable lyes, not to be credited, because the Authors only invented them, to promote their own base ends and wretched interests.

Again, where Authors are engaged for interest sake, they fall into heat, passion, malice, and envy, and what they cannot make out by strength of arguments, they labour to make good by lyes and scandals, as is most apparent in this one Example we shall here give. *Henricus Cornelius Agrippa*, a person in his time well known to most of the Learned in *Europe*, and admired for his general and universal skill in all kind of Learning, having published a Piece which he styled, *A Declaration of the incertitude and vanity of Sciences and Arts, and the excellency of the Word of God:* wherein amongst other

other things he had sharply taxed the Monks and Fryars, and other Orders, of their ignorance, idleness, and many other crimes and misdemeanors, whereby certain Theologasters of *Lovain* (netled with their own guilt) did in bitter malice draw up certain Articles against him, therein accusing him of Errour, Impiety, and Heresie, and had so far incensed *Charles* the Fifth then Emperour against him, that he had commanded *Agrippa* unheard to make a Recantation. But he writing a strong, polite, and pithy Apology, gave them such a responsion, that afterwards they did never reply; by which, and the mediation of divers learned Friends, who gave *Cæsar* a right information of the end and drift of that Book, and of the things therein contained, He was pacified, and brought to a better understanding of the matter. Yet this could not protect *Agrippa* from the virulent malice of the Popish Witchmongers, but that they forged most abominable lyes and scandals against him, especially that wretched and ignorant Monk *Paulus Jovius*, that was not ashamed to record in his Book intituled, *De Elogiis docto-* *Lib.2.depræstig.* *rum Virorum*, that *Agrippa* carried a Cacodemon about with him, *Dæmon. cap. 5.* in the likeness of a black Dog, and that he died at *Lyons*, when it is certain he died at *Gratianople*. From all which horrid aspersions and lying scandals he is sufficiently acquitted by the famous Physician *Johannes Wierus*, one that was educated under him, and lived familiarly with him; and therefore was best able to testifie the whole truth of these particulars. But any that are so perversly and wilfully blinded as to have a sinister opinion of this person, (who *ab incunte ætate in literis educatus esset, quâ fuit ingenii fœ-* *Vit. Germ. me-* *licitate, in omni artium ac disciplinarum genere ita versatus est, ut* *dic. pag. 16.* *excelluerit*) may have most ample satisfaction from the modest and impartial Pen of *Melchior Adams*, who hath written his Life: as also from something that our Country-man, who called himself *Eugenius Philalethes*, hath clearly delivered: so that none can be *Anim. mag.* ignorant of this particular, but such as wilfully refuse to be infor- *præf.* med of the truth.

Nay where interest hath a share, truth can hardly be expected, though it be but in more trivial things, as even but for aery fame and vain-glory, as may be manifest in *Hierome Cardan*, who was a Inquir.into vul- man of prodigious pride and vain-glory, which led him (as the gar Errours, learned Dr. *Brown* hath noted) into no small errours, being a great pag. 34. Amasser of strange and incredible stories, led to relate them by his meer ambition of hunting after fame and the reputation of an universal Scholar. And of no less pride and vain-glorious ambition was his Antagonist *Julius Cæsar Scaliger* guilty, of whom it may truly be said, that he was of the nature of those of the *Ottoman* Family, that do not think they can ever raign safely, unless they strangle all their Brethren; so he did not think that he could aspire to the Throne of being the Monarch of general Learning, without stifling the fame and reputation of *Cardan* and others, against whom he hath been most fell, and impetuously bitter. But when

I 2   men

men fall out about profeſſional intereſt, then the ſtories that through
malice they invent and forge one againſt another, are incredible,
as is manifeſt in many Examples; but we ſhall but give one for
all, which is this.   When *Paracelſus*, returning from his Peregrina-
Vid. vit. Gom-
medic. pag. 29.
tion of ten years and above, was called to be Phyſical Lecturer
at *Baſil*, where he continued three years, and more, having by his
ſtrange and wonderful Cures drawn the moſt part of *Germany*, and
the adjacent Countries into admiration; ſo that he was, and might
(notwithſtanding the envy and ignorance of all his enemies) juſtly
be ſtyled, *Totius Germaniæ decus & gloria:* yet this was not ſufficient to quiet the violent and virulent mind of *Thomas Eraſtus*,
who coming to be ſetled at *Baſil*, and finding that he could not
outgo nor equal *Paracelſus* in point of Medicinal Practice, and
being ſtrongly grounded in the Ariſtotelian Philoſophy, and the
Galenical Phyſick, did with all poyſon and bitterneſs labour to
confute the Principles of Chymical Phyſick that *Paracelſus* had introduced; and leſt his arguments might be too weak, he backt
them with moſt horrible lyes and ſcandals, thinking that many
and ſtrong accuſations (though never ſo falſe) would not be eaſily anſwered, nor totally waſht off: which after were greedily ſwal-
lowed down by *Libanius, Conringius, Sennertus*, and many others:
ſo apt are men to invent, and ſuck in ſcandals againſt others, never
conſidering how falſe and groundleſs they are, or may be: for that
he wrongfully and falſely accuſed him in many things, will be manifeſt to any unbiaſſed perſon, that will but take pains to read his
Life, written by that equitable Judge *Melchior Adams*, and that
large Preface the learned Phyſician *Fredericus Bitiſkius* hath pre-
fixed to his Works printed at *Geneva* 1648.

    4. But if the Authors that report matters of fact in reference to
theſe four particulars that we have named, were ear and eye witneſſes, and not ſingle, but a greater number, and were not ſwayed
by any corrupt or ſelf-intereſt whatſoever; yet all this is not ſufficient to give evidence in theſe matters, except they be rightly
qualified in other things, that are neceſſarily requiſite to capaci-
tate a perſon rightly to judge of theſe nice and difficult matters,
ſome of the chief of which we ſhall here enumerate.   1. The perſons that are fit to give a perfect judgment of theſe matters, ought
to be perfect in the organs of their ſenſes, otherwiſe they may eaſily be deceived, and think the things otherwiſe than indeed they
are; ſo ſome defects or diſtempers in the ears, eyes, or the reſt of
the ſenſories, may hinder the true perception of things acted or
done.   2. They ought to be of a ſound judgment, and not of a
vitiated or diſtempered Phantaſie, nor of a melancholick Temper
or Conſtitution; for ſuch will be full of fears, and ſtrange imaginations, taking things as acted and wrought without, when they
are but only repreſented within.   Theſe will take a buſh to be a
Boggard, and a black ſheep to be a Demon; the noiſe of the
wild Swans flying high upon the nights, to be Spirits, or (as
                                                         they

they call them here in the North) *Gabriel-Ratchets*, the calling of
a Daker-hen in the Meadow to be the Whiftlers, the howling of
the female Fox in a Gill, or a Clough for the male, when they are
for copulation, to be the cry of young Children, or fuch Creatures, as the common people call Fayries, and many fuch like fancies and miftakes. 3. They ought to be clear and free from thofe
imbibed notions of Spirits, Hobgoblins, and Witches, which have
been inftamped upon their Phantafies from their very young years,
through ignorant and fuperftitious education, wherewith generally all mankind is infected, and but very few that get themfelves
extricated from thofe delufive Labyrinths, that parents and ignorance have inftilled into them. From hence it is, that not only
the ftolid and ftupid Vulgar, but even perfons otherwife rational
enough, do commonly attribute thofe fleights and tricks that our
common Jugglers play, unto the Devil, when they are only performed by Leger-de-main, or fleight of hand, Boxes, and Inftruments
aptly fitted ; and will not ftick to believe, and ftrongly to affirm to
others, that they have feen the Jugglers Familiar or Devil, when
it was but a poor Squirrels skin ftuffed with hair or mofs, and nimbly agitated by the hands of the Juggler : which makes me call
to mind a very lepid and pertinent Accident that once in my younger years happened in *Burrow-bridge* upon a great Fayr holden Hiftory 1.
there upon St. *Barnabas* day : I being in Company with divers
Gentlemen, whereof two were Mafters of Arts, and walking in the
Horfe-Fayr, we efpyed a great crowd and ring of people, and
drawing near, there was a perfon commonly known through moft
of the Northern parts of *York-fhire* by the name of *John Gypfie*,
being as black as any of that Tribe, with a Feather in his Hat, a
filk flafht Doublet, upon a fair Holland Half-fhirt, counterfeiting
himfelf half drunk, and reeling to and fro, with a fine Tape or
Incle-ftring tyed faft together at the two ends, and throwing it,
(as it were) carelefly two or three times about a fmooth Rod, that
another man held by both ends, and then putting the bout of the
Tape upon the one end of the Rod, and then crying, It is now faft
for five fhillings ; but no fooner reeling and looking afide, the man
that held the Rod did put off the bout of the Tape again, and ftill
John Gypfie, would cry and bet that it was faft, then would there
come two or three, and bet with him, and win, and go away (as
it were) laughing him to fcorn, yet ftill he would continue, and
pray the Fellow that held the ftick not to deceive him, and plainly
fhew the people, that it would be faft when the bout was put on,
then would the Fellow that held the ftick, ftill put off the bout when
John Gypfie looked away, whereby the people believed that he was
in drink, and fo deceived by him that held the Rod, and fo many
would come and bet with him, and lofe : fo that he ufed to win
much money, though the bout was put off every time, and none
could difcern any alteration in the ftring. This ftrange Feat (which
I confefs, as he handled and acted it, was one of the neateft that
                                                              ever

ever I saw in all my life) did so surprize all my Companions, and in part himself, that some of them were of opinion, that he had some stone in the Ring upon his finger, by virtue of which he performed the Trick. But the most part concluded, that it could not be done but by the power and help of the Devil, and resolved to come no more near *John Gypsie*, as a man that was a Witch, and had familiarity with the Devil. But I that then was much guilty of curiosity, and loth to be imposed upon in a thing of that nature, then also knowing the way and manner how all the common Jugglers about *Cambridge* and *London* (who make a Trade of it) did perform their Tricks, I slipt away from my Company, and went to the place again where I found him still playing; and thrusting in, I desired to hold the stick, which he refused not; and so in a short time I perceived how it was done, and so returned to my Company, and shewed them the sleight and mystery of it, which made them very much ashamed of their folly and ignorance. They may deride this story that list, and yet it may serve for instruction to the wisest, and there are hundreds yet living that knew this person, and where he was born, which was at *Bolton-bridge* near *Skipton* in *Craven*, and have seen him play this trick of fast and loose, as I have related it: so that if a man meet with a crafty cunning Fellow, he commonly by way of Proverb calls him *John Gypsie*. 4. They ought to be free in their judgments as *in æquilibrio*, and not to be radicated nor habituated in the belief of those things; for then they will hardly be diswaded from their opinions, but pertinaciously adhere unto them, though never so absurd, and will be apt to ascribe all effects, that they understand not, unto Devils

Vid. Resp. Rob. Flud. ad Foster.

and Witches, as is manifest in the Jesuit *Roberti Foster, Sennertus*, and many others, who attributed the effects of the Hoplocrism or Weapon-salve, and the Sympathetick Powder unto the operation of the Devil and Witchcraft, when they are but meerly natural.

Hiftory 2.

Which makes me call to mind a pretty story that happened when I was but a young Boy. For where I once learned at the School, there was one who was Rector of the Church, who was a very godly man, a good and constant Preacher, accounted very learned, and Bachelor of Divinity: this person being informed, that I and some other Boys could play some odd Feats of sleight of hand, especially to put a Ring upon our Cheek, and to throw it unto a staff holden fast by both the ends; this he by no means did believe could be done but by Diabolical means, and did advise and threaten us to desist from such practices, as devillish and damnable. So ready even the otherwise Learned may be, when once setled in these fond and absurd opinions of the too great power of Demons and Witches, to ascribe that unto them, which is performed by Nature and lawful Art.

CHAP.

CHAP. V.

That these things now in question are but barely supposed, and were yet never rationally nor sufficiently proved : And that the Allegations brought to prove them by are weak, frivolous, and absolutely invalid. With a full Confutation of all the four Particulars.

HAving in the preceding Chapter proved that the Scriptures and sound Reason, are the proper Mediums to decide these difficulties by, and also laid down the necessary qualifications requisite in an Author or Witness that would evidence these things as matters of fact : We shall here once again repeat the four Particulars, which we are about to confute, which are these. 1. That the Devil doth not make a visible or corporeal League and Covenant with the supposed Witches. 2. That he doth not suck upon their bodies. 3. That he hath not carnal Copulation with them. 4. That they are not really changed into Cats, Dogs, Wolves, or the like. And these four Particulars we affirm were never matters of fact, nor ever had a being, except only in the fancy as meer Chimera's, nor that they ever were or can be proved to have been brought to pass or acted ; and *de non apparentibus, & non existentibus eadem est ratio,* saith the great Maxime of our Law. But in the first place let us hear what the Patrons of this wretched and execrable opinion have to say to prove that they are matters of fact, or were ever acted or performed. And first we have Mr. *Glanvil* arguing at this rate : "All Histories are full of the exploits *Pag. 5, 6.* " of those instruments of darkness ; and the testimony of all ages, " not only of the rude and barbarous, but of the most civilized and " polisht World, brings tidings of their strange performances. We " have the attestation of thousands of eye and ear-witnesses, and " those not of the easily deceivable vulgar only, but of grave and " and wise discerners ; and that when no interest could oblige them " to agree together in a common lye : I say we have the light of " all these circumstances to confirm us in the belief of things done " by persons of despicable power and knowledge, beyond the reach " of Art and ordinary Nature. Standing publick Records have " been kept of these well-attested Relations, and Epocha's made of " those unwonted events. Laws in many Nations have been ena- " cted against those vile practices ; those among the Jews and our " own are notorious ; such Cases have been often determined near " us, by wise and reverend Judges, upon clear convictive Evi- " dence, and thousands in our own Nation have suffered death for " their vile compacts with Apostate Spirits. And a little after he saith : "And I think those that can believe all Histories are Ro-
" mances ;

"mances; that all the wiser World have agreed together to jug-
"gle Mankind into a common belief of ungrounded Fables; that
"the sound senses of multitudes together may deceive them, and
"Laws are built upon Chimera's; that the gravest and wisest Jud-
"ges have been Murderers, and the sagest persons Fools or design-
"ing Impostors. Bishop *Hall* maketh the like Objection, saying:
"Neither can I make question of the authentick Records of the
"Examinations and Confessions of Witches and Sorcerers in several
"Regions of the World, agreeing in the truth of their horrible
"pacts with Satan, of their set Meetings with evil Spirits, their
"beastly Homages and Conversations. I should hate to be guilty
"of so much incredulity, as to charge so many grave Judges and
"credible Historians with lyes.

These Objections at the first view seem very plausible, and to
carry with them a great splendour and weight of truth and reason;
but if they be looked into, and narrowly weighed in the balance
of sound reason, and unbiassed judgment, they will be found too
light, and will soon vanish into Rhetorical fumes and frothy vapours: which that it may be more clearly performed, we shall
rank them into the number of three, in which all their seeming
strength lyes, and these are they.

1. They pretend that these things are sufficiently proved by Historians of unquestionable credit and reputation.

2. That the Confessions of Witches themselves, in divers Regions, at several times and places, who have all acknowledged these
particulars, are sufficient evidence of the truth of these performances.

3. That so many wise and grave Judges and honest Juries could
not have been deceived, to put to death such great numbers of
these kind of people, called or accounted Witches, without sufficient proof of the matters of fact. To all which we shall give a
full response, in respect of the four particulars, mentioned in the
beginning of this Chapter, and shall commix and adjoyn such positive Arguments as will be cogent to all rational persons, whose corrupt wills have not perverted their judgments.

1. It is much to be admired, that Mr. *Glanvil* (but especially
Bishop *Hall*, a very Reverend and Learned person) should lye any
great stress upon such a weak foundation: For there is none of
these three Objections that will amount to a necessary Proposition, but only to a contingent one, which will infer no certain and
necessary Conclusion, nor bring forth any certitude or science, but
only bare opinion and probability. *Propositio contingens est, quæ*
sic vera est, ut falsa esse possit: and at the best the strength of all
these are but *testimonia humana*, which are but weak, and no sufficient ground for a rational man to believe them to be true, because *humanum est errare.* And the weight of these matters is not
a contention *de lana caprina, vel de umbra asini, sed de pelle hu-*
mana, for the lives and estates of many poor Creatures, and they
professed

profeſſed Chriſtians too, and therefore doth require ſtronger Arguments than contingent Propoſitions, to eſtabliſh a firm ground for the belief of this opinion.

2. It is one thing barely to affirm, and another thing to prove ſufficiently and fully : For though they boldly alledge, that theſe things are ſufficiently proved by Authors of unqueſtionable credit and verity, we muſt return a flat negative, and that for theſe reaſons. 1. Let them ſhew us any one Author of credible veracity, that ever was ear or eye-witneſs of the Devils making of a viſible and corporeal League or Bargain with the Witches, or that he ever ſuckt upon their bodies, or that he had carnal Copulation with them, or that by the experience of his ſenſes ever certainly knew a man really tranſubſtantiated and transformed into a Wolf, or a Wolf into a man, and we will yield the whole Cauſe. But we muſt aſſert and truly affirm, that this pretence of theirs, that theſe things are ſufficiently proved by Hiſtorians of good credit, is a meer falſity, and a lying flouriſh of vain words. There are (we confeſs) a multitude of vain and lying ſtories, amaſſed up together in the Writings of Demonographers and Witchmongers of ſtrange and odd Apparitions, Feats, Confeſſions, and ſuch like ; but never any one poſitive proof of any of theſe four particulars by any Authors of credit and reputation : and this we dare boldly aver to the world. 2. Let them produce any two Witneſſes that were of honeſty and integrity, ſound underſtandings and ability, that ever were preſent, and ear and eye-witneſſes of a viſible, vocal, and corporeal League made betwixt the Devil and the Witch ; or let them tell us who was by, and watched, and really and truly ſaw the Devil ſuck upon ſome part of the Witches body ; or who were the Chamberlains, Pimps or Panders, when the Devil and the Witch committed carnal Copulation ; or who were ever preſent when a Witch was changed into a Cat, a Dog, an Hare, or a Wolf. If they can but bring forth any two credible Witneſſes to prove theſe things by, then we ſhall believe them ; but we muſt aſſert that never any ſuch two could be produced yet : and therefore cannot but wonder at the ſhameleſs impudence of ſuch perſons, that dare affirm theſe things that never were, nor can be proved, and yet have not bluſhed to vent and trumpet forth ſuch execrable and abominable lyes to the World. Mr. *Glanvil* confidently affirms theſe things to be matters of fact, and *affirmanti incumbit probatio*, let him produce his Witneſſes, and if they be perſons of judgment, veracity, and impartiality, then we ſhall accept their proof ; but it is not figments, ſuppoſals, weak preſumptions, or apparent falſities that will perform it ; for that which never was acted, can never truly be proved, and things that appear not, are as though they were not ; therefore he muſt produce his teſtimonies, or loſe both his cauſe and credit, and muſt be taken for an Aſſertor of never-proved Fables. *Lying lips are abomination unto the Lord : but they* Prov. 12. 22. *that deal truly are his delight.*

K   Now

Now we know they use to do in this case, as Souldiers use, who when they are beaten forth of some Out-work or Trench, they then retreat into another that they think more strong and safe. And being driven from their weak Hold of a bare affirmation without proof, that these things are verified to have been matters of fact, and really performed, both by authority and the evidence of sense, which are both utterly false, then they flye to this assertion: That the Confessions of so many Witches in all Ages, in several Countries, at divers times and places, all agreeing in these particulars, are sufficient evidence of the truth of these matters. To which we shall rejoyn, that the Confessions of Witches, however considered, are not of credit and validity to prove these things; but are in themselves null and void, as false, impossible, and forged lyes, which we shall make good by these following Reasons.

Reas. 1.　　1. The Witch must be taken to be either a person *insanæ, vel sanæ mentis*; and if they be *insanæ mentis*, their Confessions are no sufficient evidence, nor worthy of any credit; because there is neither Reason, Law, nor Equity that allows the testimony or confession of an Idiot, Lunatick, mad or doting person, because they are not of a right and sound understanding, and are not to be accounted as *compotes mentis*, nor governed by rationality. For as by the Civil Law mad Folks, Idiots, and Old men childish, Bond-slaves, and Villains are not capable of making a Will to dispose of Goods, Lands, or Chattels: so much more are all these sorts of persons excepted for giving evidence by confessions, or otherwise in matters concerning life and death, which are of far greater weight and concernment. And that these persons are of unsound understandings, is manifest in all the points that they confess, and therefore are no proof, nor ought to be credited: and that for these reasons. 1. Because the things they confess are not attested by any other persons of integrity and sound judgment, and they must of necessity be lyars, because the Bond-slaves of the Devil, whose works they will do, and he was a lyar from the beginning. 2. Because they confess things that are impossible (as we shall prove anon) and *confiteri impossibilia insanientis est.* 3. There is no good end wherefore they make these Confessions, neither do they receive any benefit by them, either spiritual or temporal, internal nor external. And this doth sufficiently shew, that they are deluded, melancholy, and mad persons, and so their Confessions of no credit, truth, or validity.

Reas. 2.　　2. Their Confessions will be found null and false, if we consider the impulsive cause that moves them to make them, and the end wherefore they declare such false and lying matters, and that in these particulars. 1. The moving cause is not, nor can be the Spirit of God, which is a Spirit of truth and righteousness, nor any motion of true remorse for their sins, or any thing flowing from repentant hearts, because they are persons forsaken of God and his Grace, and given over to reprobate minds and senses, and therefore
the

the truth of the Word of God is fulfilled in them : *Because they* 2 Thess. 2. 10, *received not the love of the truth, that they might be saved, there-* 11, 12. *fore God shall send them strong delusion, that they might believe a lye. That they all might be damned, who believed not the truth, but had pleasure in unrighteousness.* 2. Neither is the end for the glory of God, or their own Salvation, because they are the Vassals and Bond-slaves of Satan, being kept Captive at his will, and are Rebels and Traitors against God and Christ, his Church and Truth, having renounced the Faith, and become Apostata's to the truth. 2 Tim. 2. 26. 3. The impulsive cause and chief end wherefore they make these and such like confessions, is sometimes, and in some persons meerly to eschew torture and bodily pains, and sometimes the quite contrary solely to escape the present miseries of a poor, wretched, and troublesom life; and therefore these confessions not at all to be credited, as being vain and feigned. 4. Sometimes they are by force, waking, craft, and cunning, in hope of pardon and life, to make such confessions as the base ends and corrupt intentions of the Inquisitors themselves, or their Agents, have infused into them, for the advancement of false Doctrine, Superstition, and Idolatry : such were the most (if not all) recorded by *Delrio Bodinus*, and the rest of the Witchmongers, to which no credit can be given at all. 5. But the chief end that Satan hath (who is the Forger, Contriver, and Deviser of these Confessions, if voluntarily and freely made, the principal Agent in all these matters) is to set forth the power and glory of his own Kingdom, thereby to lead men into, and continue them in lyes and errors; *for when he speaketh a lye, he speaketh of his own, for he is a lyar, and the father of it,* Joh. 8. 44. and the Witches are his Children, and the works of their Father the Devil they will do, and he was, and is a Murtherer and Lyar from the beginning. And thus far we acknowledge a spiritual and mental League betwixt the Witch and the Devil, by virtue of which they confess these horrible and abominable lyes, of the glory of him and his Kingdom; but other League or Covenant there is none, neither is there any the least spark of truth in all that they say or confess, because their sole end in making of these confessions, is to advance the credit and power of Satan. 6. The impulsive cause that often makes them to utter such confessions of strange and impossible things, is the strong passive delusion, that they lye under, contracted by ignorant, unchristian, and superstitious education, which they have suckt in with their milk, heightned with an atrabilarious temper and constitution, and confirmed by the wicked lyes, and teaching of others, which makes them confess these execrable things, which they in their depraved and vitiated imaginations, do think and believe they have done and suffered, when there was never truly acted any such matter *ad extrà*, but only in their mad and deluded Phantasies : and so no more credit to be given to them, than to the maddest Melancholist that ever was read or heard of.

K 2

3. That

3. That there is not any jot of truth in thefe Confeffions, is manifeft, if we confider the fubjective matter of them, as is plain by
thefe enfuing grounds. 1. For the moft of them are not credible, by reafon of their obfcenity and filthinefs; for chaft ears would
tingle to hear fuch bawdy and immodeft lyes; and what pure and
fober minds would not naufeate and ftartle to underftand fuch unclean ftories, as of the carnal Copulation of the Devil with a Witch,
or of his fucking the Teat or Wart of an old ftinking and rotten
Carkafs? furely even the impurity of it may be fufficient to overthrow the credibility of it, efpecially amongft Chriftians. 2. There
are many things that have no verity in them at all, that notwithftanding have verifimilitude; but thefe are not only void of truth,
but alfo of truth-likelinefs: for it is neither truth, nor hath any likelihood of it, to believe it for a truth, that the Devil fhould carry
an old Witch in the Air into foraign Regions, that can hardly
crawl with a ftaff, to dancing and banqueting, and yet to return
with an empty belly, and the next day to be forced, like old *Dembdike* or *Elizabeth Sothernes*, and *Alizon Denice*, to go a begging
with the fowr-milk Can : is this either probable or likely? would
it not much more have advantaged the Devils intereft and his Kingdom, to have furnifhed them with good and true meat and drink,
and not with fuch imaginary Cates, which would neither fill the ftomach, nor fatisfie the appetite? Had it not been more for the Devils benefit to have furnifhed them with plenty of gold and filver,
than to let them go ragged and tattered, begging their bread from
door to door? 3. As thefe confeffions have no truth-likelinefs
in them, fo they are things that are fimply impoffible to be performed by any created power, and therefore muft needs be falfe
and fictitious relations; for no Creature can perform any thing but
that for which by Creation it was ordered and defigued to; but
the Devils by Creation have no generative power given them, nor
members or organs to perform the act of copulation withal; and
therefore their having carnal copulation with the Witches, is a
moft monftrous fiction, and an abfolute impoffibility, and can have
nothing in it more than the ftirring up of the imaginative faculty,
and thereby to move titillation in the members fitted for the act
of generation, which is a thing that happens to many both men and
women, that are of hot conftitutions, and abound with feed, which
we call *nocturnæ prolutiones*, of which the Divines and Cafuifts
make that great queftion. *An nocturnæ prolutiones fint peccatum?*
And it is as fimply impoffible for either the Devil or Witches to
change or alter the courfe that God hath fet in Nature, as to tran-
fubftantiate a man or woman into a Cat, a Dog, or a Wolf; and
therefore are thefe confeffions meer impoffibilities and monftrous
lyes. 4. There can in found and right reafon no credit at all be
given to thefe confeffions, becaufe divers of them have been proved
to be utterly falfe, as is plain in the man that did confidently affirm, that he was a true Wolf, and that he had hair under his skin,
the

the woful tryal of which was his death, though a pregnant and undeniable proof, that the delusion was in the Phantasie, and that
there was no real change of the mans body into a Wolf; and
therefore doth flatly overthrow the credibility of these vain and
lying confessions. To the same purpose is the story related by *Ca-*   Lib. 1. of Pro-
merarius from *Johannes Baptista Porta*, a great Naturalist, and a   gnost.
person of competent veracity, which is this. "Once (saith he)   Hist. meditat.
" I met an old Witch, one of those that are said to enter houses in   lib. 4. cap. 13.
" the night time, and there to suck the blood of little children ly-   History 1.
" ing in their Cradles. Having asked her a question of something,
" she promised forthwith, that within a while she would give me
" answer. She puts forth of her Chamber all those that went in
" with me to be witnesses of that which should pass. Having shut
" us out, she strips her self stark naked, and rubs over all her body
" with a certain Oyntment, which we saw through the chinks of
" the door. The operation of the soporiferous juyces, whereof
" this Oyntment was compounded, made her fall to the ground,
" and brought her into a deep sleep. Upon this we open the door,
" and some of us begin to strike and knock her well-favour'dly;
" but she was so soundly asleep, that to strike her body and a stone,
" it was all one. Forth we go again, in the mean time the Oynt-
" ment had ended his working, and the old Trot being awaked,
" and having put on her cloaths, begins to tell tales of *Robin Hood*,
" saying, That she had passed over Seas and Mountains, and then
" gives us false answers. We tell her, that her body had never
" stir'd out of the Chamber; she maintains the contrary: we shew
" her the blows we had given her, she persisteth the more stifly in
" her opinion. By the testimony of this Author, who was an ear
and eye-witness of this passage, and other persons with him, which
manifests it to be good and sufficient evidence, it appeareth, that
the Witches are under a melancholy and passive delusion, promoted
by the help of soporiferous Oyntments, whereby they fancy and
think they are carried into far remote places, where they hear and
see strange things, and do and suffer that which is not at all performed, but only as in a dream, their bodies in the mean time lying immoveable, and so do but relate falsities and lyes, which is an
unanswerable proof of the absolute falsity of their confessions, the
thing that here we undertook to make good. And some late
Learned men (with Mr. *Glanvil* himself) giving too much credit to
the things related by the Witches in their confessions, to be true
stories of things really performed at a great distance, have been
forced to revive that old Platonical Whimsie, of the Souls real egression forth of the body into far distant places, and its return again,
with the certain knowledge of things there done or said, according
to the relation that *Pliny* gives us in these words: *Reperimus* (*in-*   Hist. nat. l. 7.
quit) *in templa, Hermotimi Clazomenii animam relicto corpore*   c. 52. pag.103.
errare solitam, vagámq; è longinquo multa annuntiare, quæ nisi à
præsenti nosci non possent, corpore interim semianimi: donec

*mato eo inimici (qui Cantharidæ vocabantur) remeanti animæ ve-
lut vaginam ademerint.* To which notwithstanding he doth not
seem to give credence. But these Relations of the Witches are
meer lyes and forgeries, and are but taught them by the spiritual
craft of the Devil, thereby to pretend to imitate the true Visions
that the Prophets had from God. And though there may be some
peculiar persons that have the way to fall into ecstasies, (as *Helmont* witnesseth of himself) and may thereby understand many
mystical matters, yet in it there is no real egression of the Soul
forth of the body, but a freeing or withdrawing of it from the
Phantasie and Senses, and then (as the Cabbalists and mystical Authors say) it is joyned to the intelligible World, and beholds
things as present; and though there may be something of truth in
it, yet few Authors of credit and veracity, have attested it upon
their own experience, and there may be much fallacy and danger
in it, and therefore we leave it to further search and inquiry. Another apparent ground of the nullity of the truth or credit of these
confessions, is that which a learned Divine in his Letter to Dr.

*Doctor. Epist.
pag. 641.
History 2.*

Wierus gives us, the substance of which we shall give in English,
which is this : "I have known (he saith) the year foregoing (he
" writ his Epistle *Anno* 1565.) many foolish things from the pri-
" vate confession of a certain old Woman, an Inchanter, who when
" she had heard in my Sermon the place in the 19. Chapter of the
" *Acts* explained, *That many of the Ephesians, being of those who
" had exercised curious Arts, had brought their Books, and burned
" them openly, &c.* She forthwith (he saith) came unto me with
" a mind plainly troubled ; and with tears pouring forth into my
" bosom the secrets of her breast, did receive Christian instruction ;
" and when she had understood, by the blessing of God, the vanity
" of Diabolical Impostures, and perceived them with opened eyes,
" she was easily converted to the light of truth, the smoak of lyes
" being laid aside. She, truth being once received, hath most con-
" stantly confessed, that it did appear to her more clear than the light
" at noon day, that Satan did only deceive and blind the eyes of his
" Vassals, and that there was nothing done in verity, and this she de-
" clared with a detestation of her Diabolical Art. And so concludes
it in these words : *Uno verbo dicam, me satis experientiâ didicisse,
bonam partem incantationum mera esse insomnia.* And whosoever
shall read, and seriously consider the Epistle of that excellent and
learned Divine, will find the most of those vain illusions laid open
and confuted : so that in all (or the most) of the things attributed unto Witches, we shall find no more of Diabolical operation in
them, than an internal, mental, and spiritual delusion, in making
the Witches to believe, and to draw on others to the same opinion,
that the Devil hath a kind of omnipotent Power and Soveraignty.

*Histor. Animal.
lib.8. cap. 24.*

Therefore did *Aristotle* well conclude : *Incantamenta esse muliercularum figmenta.*

Reas. 4.

4. A fourth Reason of the meer falsity and incredibility of these
Confessi-

Confeſſions is this : Is it poſſibly credible to a rational and unbiaſſed judgment, that the Witches (though never ſo many, at
ſeveral times and places) having made themſelves the Slaves and
Vaſſals of the Devil, both in ſoul and body, and being led by his
lying and deceitful Spirit (though making large and voluntary
confeſſions) can be conceived to have any touch of truth in them
at all ? Surely no more truth in theſe confeſſions, than there is in
the Devil, who was a Lyar from the beginning ; and therefore we
argue thus. Such kind of will, affections and inclinations as are in
the Devil himſelf, ſuch kind are in his Children. But the will and
affections of the Devil are againſt God, his Truth, and againſt all
Gods people, and his inclinations tend to continual lying. Therefore the will, affections, and inclinations of his Children (ſuch as
the Witches are, and are granted to be) are againſt God, his Truth,
and againſt all Gods people , and their inclinations tend to continual lying. The proof of the major and minor Propoſition is the
plain words of our Saviour, *Ye are of your father the devil, and the*
luſts of your father the devil ye will do, ϑιλετε ποιειν, *and he was a*   Joh. 8. 44.
murtherer from the beginning , and abode not in the truth, becauſe
there is no truth in him. When he ſpeaketh a lye, he ſpeaketh of his
own : for he is a lyar, and the father of it. And again St. *John* tells
us : *He that committeth ſin, is of the devil ; for the devil ſinneth*   1 Joh. 3. 8.
from the beginning. So that it may truly be ſaid of them, *They de-*   Pſal. 62. 4.
light in lyes, and their confeſſions are nothing but lyes. And if
they object and ſay, that here we confeſs a League with the Devil and the Witch, otherwiſe the Witches could not be his Children, Vaſſals, and Bond-ſlaves , which elſewhere we deny ; we
anſwer, it is a groſs miſtake , in not obſerving the diſtinction we
make betwixt a mental and ſpiritual League, ſuch as the Devil
and *Judas* made, and ſuch as all wicked men make with him, and
under this League we acknowledge all Witches to be ; but a viſible and corporeal League we poſitively deny, and ſo the objection is of no validity. And thus we ſuppoſe we have ſufficiently
proved, that there ought no credit at all to be given to the Confeſſions of Witches, no more than to Devils, who are all lyars.

Now let us proceed to their third main Objection : That ſo
many wiſe and grave Judges and honeſt Juries could not have been
deceived, to put to death ſuch great numbers of thoſe kind of people, without ſufficient proof of the matters of fact. Againſt which
we oppoſe theſe following Reaſons.

1. It is but an Argument at the beſt to drive the other Party in-   *Reaſ.* 1 :
to an abſurdity, which is not of any ſuch dangerous conſequence,
as may be ſuppoſed ; for it would but conclude, that many grave
and wiſe Judges and Juries have been impoſed upon, and deceived, which is but *argumentum ad homines,* and doubtleſs many
might, and have been. And do not we Chriſtians hold, that the
graveſt and wiſeſt Judges amongſt the *Turks* and *Perſians* have
been, and are deceived, and have done unjuſtly in perſecuting and
putting

putting Christians to death, because they would not submit to the
Religion of *Mahomet*, and yet we account it no absurdity or injustice to pass that censure upon them? And do not the Idolaters
in all those large Empires and Kingdoms of *Tartary*, *China*, the
Moguls Country, and the rest of those Countries in the East of *Asia*
persecute and put many to death, for not worshipping their Idols,
or embracing their Religion; and do we think it absurd to censure and condemn them of injustice, though in their own Countries
they be accounted grave and wise Judges? Surely we do not, and
there is the parity of reason in both the Arguments, for all are but
men, and so may erre.

Reas. 2.   2. But as for the grave, learned, and wise Judges, and understanding and honest Juries within His Majesties Dominions, we
affirm they are clear and innocent from these imputations, and that
for divers and sundry sound reasons. 1. Our Judges and Juries have
no such sinister and corrupt ends, to wrest the Laws, or wring forth
and extort feigned and false Confessions, because they have no such
ends as to uphold and maintain idolatrous and superstitious Tenents, as praying to Saints, magnifying of Holy-water, or setting up
of Purgatory, as had the Popish Inquisitors, and the Demonographers, and Witchmongers that writ for those ends. And therefore it is no absurdity to say or think, that they dealt unjustly in
their proceedings, which our learned and pious Judges are not, nor
can be guilty of. 2. The Inquisitors and their Agents had benefit
by the death of Witches, having a share in their Goods, and therefore no absurdity to conclude, that their proceedings were unjust,
partial, and corrupt, of which our Judges and Juries are clear, as
having no profit at all by the death of these wretched and deluded
people. 3. Our Judges are but sworn to the due execution of
the Laws made, and the Juries sworn to bring in their Verdicts according to their best evidence: now if the Witnesses forth of malice, envy, ignorance, or mistake swear to matters of fact, for which
death or other punishments are allotted by the Law, both the
Judges and the Jury are absolutely excusable; and if there be any
guilt in the Witnesses, or falsity in their Evidences, it lyes at their
own doors, and upon their own consciences, and the Judges and Jurors are clear, and not to be blamed, for no humane prudence can
altogether prevent, that Witnesses may not erre or swear falsely.

Reas. 3.   3. Have there not been many thousands of true and faithful
Martyrs, that have suffered and been condemned in many Ages, in
many and several Countries, at many different and distinct times?
And some of these have been condemned by such as were called
and accounted General Councils, Parliaments, High-Courts of Justice, and other places of great Judicature, before Judges that were
accounted wise, grave, and learned, and by Juries of honesty and
understanding: were there therefore no true Martyrs, and were
they all justly condemned and put to death? or is it absurd to be
guilty of such incredulity, as to think and hold, that so many grave
and

and wi.e Judges, and knowing Juries were deceived, and did unjuftly ? Let Mr. *Glanvil* or any other folve this Argument ; and carry the caufe ; or elfe we muft neceffarily conclude, that *opinio quæ à fe non propellit abfurda, per abfurda non premit adverfarium.*

Now having given a full and fatisfactory Anfwer to their main and ftrongeft Objections, and defeated the whole force of their firft and moft furious Charge, we fhall proceed to overthrow their main Battel, in proving the four Particulars mentioned in the beginning of the Chapter, to be falfe and impoffible. And in doing of this, we fhall handle the three firft promifcuoufly and all together, and the fourth about Tranfubftantiations or Change of Witches into Cats, Hares, Dogs, Wolves, or the like, we fhall handle by it felf.

1. And firft we acknowledge an internal, mental, and fpiritual League or Covenant betwixt the Devil and all wicked perfons, fuch as are Thieves, Robbers, Murtherers, Impoftors, and the like, whereby the temptations, fuggeftions, and allurements of Satan, fpirituallv darted, and caft into the mind, the perfons fo wrought upon, and prevailed withal, do affent and confent unto the motions and counfels of the evil Spirit, and fo do make a League and Covenant with the faid evil Spirit, as faith the Text : *According to* the *Prince of the power of the air, that now worketh in the children of difobedience.* He doth not only rule over them, but alfo worketh in them ; for men are either the Temples of God, or the Temples of Satan and Antichrift, *who fitteth in the Temple of God, and oppofeth and exalteth himfelf above all that is called God or worfhipped.* Such a fpiritual League or Covenant as this did *Judas* make with the Devil, whereby he agreed to betray his Mafter Chrift. *Then entred Satan into Judas :* not that effentially or perfonally he entred into *Judas,* but that he put it into his heart, βιβλnκότ⊕, to betray him : which wrought fo effectively in him in a fpiritual manner, that he took up that Diabolical refolution to betray his innocent Mafter : and this was entring into a fpiritual League with the Devil. For as *Theophylact* faith upon the place. *Hoc enim fignificat, fpofpondit, hoc eft, perfectam promiffionem & pactum fecit.* And another faith : *In Judam Satanas intravit, non impellens, fed patulum inveniens oftium : nam oblitus omnium quæ viderat, ad folam avaritiam dirigebat intuitum.* And again : *Miffio ifta fpiritualis fuggeftio eft, & non fit per aurem, fed per cogitationem : diabolicæ enim fuggeftiones immittuntur, & humanis cogitationibus immifcentur.*

2. We acknowledge that this fpiritual League in fome refpects and in fome perfons may be, and is an explicit League, that is, the perfons that enter into it, are or may be confcious of it, and know it to be fo ; for when a perfon refolves to murther, he cannot but know that he then maketh a League with the Devil, who was a Murtherer from the beginning. And it is manifeft, that in this

Eph. 2. 2.

2 Theff. 2. 4.

Luk. 22. 2.

Chryf. in Luc. 22. 3. Joh. 13. 2.

League, and in no other, were all the Priests that belonged to the
Oracles, who knew well enough that the Idols or false Gods they
worshipped, did give no answers at all, but the responsions given
were only of their own devising and framing, to uphold their credit; and more colourably to cozen and deceive the people, they
did pretend that they had answers from their Gods or Idols, and
thus far the Devil was in all their impostures and jugglings. And
so all the several sorts of the Diviners or Witches mentioned in the
Old Testament, were under a spiritual League with the Devil, and
did very well know, that what they did, was not by the finger of
God, but either by the help of Art, Nature, Leger-de-main, Confederacy, or such like impostures and cheats: and yet they pretended, as did *Simon Magus*, and gave out that they were some great
men, thereby to deceive others, when explicitly they plainly knew
that themselves were but dissemblers and lyars, and that for gain,
credit, and vain-glory they pretended to do those things, which
they could never truly perform. And under this spiritual League,
explicitly considered, are all our Figure-flingers contained, who
take upon them (far beyond the Rules of the true Art) to declare
where stollen Goods are, and to cause them to be brought back
again, and many other such vain and lying matters, which they
well know they have no power to perform, but that they willingly
and knowingly take upon them to pretend to do these things for
vain-glory and filthy lucre sake. And of this sort are all our pretending Conjurers, Diviners, Wizards, and those that take upon
them to reveal things by looking in Crystals, Beryls, and the like,
(of which we may perhaps speak more largely hereafter) that indeed know well enough they do but deceive and cheat others: of
all which we could recite very lepid and apposite stories, certainly
known unto us, or discovered by us; but Mr. *Glanvil* would account them but silly Legends and old Wives Fables, and therefore
we shall supersede here, and leave them to a fitter place.

3. There are others that are under this spiritual League, though
implicitly, as are all those that we have granted to be passively deluded Witches, those that by ignorant and irreligious education,
joyned with a melancholy temper and disposition, to which they
have added Charms, Pictures, and other superstitious Ceremonies,
which they learned by Tradition. By all which they become so
deluded and besotted in their Phantasies, that they believe the Devil doth visibly appear unto them, suck upon them, have carnal
copulation with them, that they are carried in the Air to feastings,
dancings, and such like Night-revellings; and that they can raise
tempests, kill men or beasts, and an hundred such like fopperies
and impossibilities, when they do nor suffer any thing at all, but in
their depraved and deceived imaginations. And so do blindly and
implicitly believe that the Devil doth perform all these things for
them, when indeed and truth he doth nothing but dart and cast in
these filthy and fond cogitations into their minds agreeable to
their

their wicked wills and corrupted desires, and so are fast bound in this spiritual and implicit League. And under this spiritual implicit League are also comprehended all those that are Witchmongers, and believe the verity and performance of these things, and think that the Devil can both hurt and also help, and that there is a bad and a good Witch, or with Mr. *Perkins*, a black and a white one, by which wicked opinion, the seeking unto Witches, Wizards, Mutterers, Murmurers, Charmers, South-sayers, Conjurers, Cunning-men and women (as we speak here in the North) and such like, is still upholden by the Authors and Favourers of this opinion, contrary to the direct counsel of the Holy Ghost, who saith : *And when they shall say unto you, Seek unto them that have familiar Spirits, and unto Wizards that peep and that mutter; should not a people seek unto their God? for the living to the dead. To the law and to the testimony: if they speak not according to this word, it is because there is no light in them.* And therefore saith one: *Admonet etiam, nos adversus impios cultus & superstitiones tutos fore, si in lege Domini acquiescamus.* The League or Covenant betwixt the Devil and the Witch, is that which is visible and corporeal, where he is supposed to appear in some bodily shape unto the Witch, and to have oral and audible conference with him or her, and so to make a League or Covenant; and this is the thing that we deny, and the consequents thereof, that he doth not suck upon their bodies, nor hath carnal copulation with them, nor carries them in the Air, nor for them, nor by them doth destroy or kill man or beast, raise tempests, or change them into Cats, Hares, Wolves, Dogs, or the like; and this we oppose with these following Reasons. *[Isa. 8. 19, 20.]* *[Calvin in loc.]*

1. Whatsoever the Devil worketh, it is to bring advantage to his own Kingdom, or otherwise he should act in vain. But whatsoever he worketh by a visible Covenant, is not for the advantage of his own Kingdom : and therefore it is in vain. The major is plain from the Text : *Be sober, be vigilant, because your adversary the devil, as a roaring lion, walketh about, seeking whom he may devour, whom resist stedfast in the faith.* The minor is manifest in these two particulars. 1. *Satan is that old Serpent, that was, and is more subtile than any beast of the field, which the Lord God hath created :* which notwithstanding the vain Cavils, and seeming Arguments of *Pererius*, must be understood of Satan the Adversary of Mankind, and not of the natural Serpent, which is not the most subtile beast that God hath created, there being many others more subtile than the Serpent; and the Scripture tells us of his cunning and wiliness: for the Apostle saith, *We are not ignorant of his wiles or devices* νοήματα. And the Apostle in another place calls them μεθοδείας, *his wiles*, which are so great, *that if it were possible, they might deceive the very elect.* So that he wants no cunning nor subtilty to know how to bring a sinner into his snare, and to hold him fast, and when he is fast, he knows he need do no more, *[Reas. 1.]* *[2 Pet. 5. 8, 9.]* *[Rev. 12. 9.]* *[2 Cor. 2. 11.]* *[Eph. 6. 11.]* *[Mat. 24. 24.]*

and therefore acts not in vain.   2. Before he need attempt a visible apparition to the Witch (if any such thing could be) he knows that the Witch is sure and fast in his snare by a spiritual Covenant already entred into, and therefore knows he need do no more, and he is too cunning to act to no purpose, and therefore doth St. *Paul* warn *Timothy*, *That a Bishop must have a good report, lest he fall into the snare of the devil*, all sins being the snares of the Devil, and when men are fast taken in them, they are in Satans fetters, and he labours no more but to keep them there.   And so the same Apostle speaketh of those that oppose the Gospel, *that they must be instructed in meekness, that they may recover themselves out of the snare of the devil, who are taken captive by him at his will.*   So that sins keep men in the spiritual snare of the Devil, and so are all those that are accounted Witches, in that spiritual snare, holden fast enough by their own consents and corrupt wills, and need no bodily apparition to make them surer: and so this visible League falls to the ground, as having no ground nor end why it should be made.   And for the Devil to appear like a Dog or a Cat, and speak, would sure not only fright and startle an old Witch, but even the boldest and most stout-hearted person.

2 Tim. 2. 25, 26.

Reas. 2.   2. The Witches by visible apparitions of the Devil (if any such thing could be) in any shape, could have no more assurance of Satans performances, than they have already, by mental perswasion, and the dominion of him in their hearts, *who is the Prince of the air, and worketh in the children of disobedience*, because by that visible appearance there is not brought any Hostages or Witnesses, which are absolutely necessary to confirm such a League or Covenant.   And these representations being made in their imaginations and fancies, wherein they think they see, do, and suffer these delusive Visions, they are most firmly and pertinaciously confirmed in the belief of them, that any Apparition externally must needs be vain and superfluous.

Reas. 3.   3. If the Witches be not superlatively mad (and if so, then so to be judged of, and all that in this point is believed of them either in doing, suffering, or otherwise, must be judged extreme folly and madness) they will not make a League with the Devil, knowing him to be the Devil, because they cannot but know that he was and is a Lyar and a Murtherer from the beginning, and hath deceived many before them, that were of the same way and profession.   And a visible appearance can afford them no certain security, but that he may and will deceive them still, and that he continueth a lyar and a deceiver.   But while the delusion is internal, and the imagination depraved, and led by the suggestions and motions of Satan, they then are so blinded, that they see not, nor understand the danger they run into, nor the certainty of the deceit they lye under, which a visible Apparition would sooner shake and overthrow, than any way confirm, and therefore is false and needless.

Reas. 4.   4. But how come the Witches certainly to know that the Devil

can

can perform such things as they would have done ? Surely by no means, but either by traditional hear-say or inward delusion ; the one they know not, but that it is a lye, and the other concludeth their passive delusion, to neither of which a visible Apparition like a Cat or a Dog, and speaking unto them, can bring any confirmation, except the Devil should bring them good store of gold or silver, or work some strange feat before their eyes, as to kill some men or beasts, or the like ; but none of these things are ever proved to be performed. And therefore it is not rational to believe that Witches do make a visible and corporeal League with the Devil, because by it they can have no certain knowledge, that he either can or will accomplish such things for them, as they desire.

5. The Devil cannot by his own power or will, either appear *Reas. 5.* visibly in what shape he please, neither can he when he will, nor as he will, perform these strange tricks, because he is under restraint, and can act nothing but as the will of God orders and determines : so God sent an evil Spirit upon *Saul*, otherwise he could not have *1 Sam. 16. 14.* troubled him ; and the Devils could not enter into the herd of *Mat. 8. 31, 32.* Swine, until leave was given them by our Saviour ; neither could he afflict *Job*, until that Gods hand was laid upon him, and God *Job 1. 10, 11.* ordered him to be an instrument in that affliction. And though the Devil be said *to walk about like a roaring lion, seeking whom* *1 Pet. 5. 8.* *he may devour*, yet must that walking about be only understood (and is so taken by all sound Expositors) of the evil and wicked intention of his will, according to which he is always ready seeking whom he may devour, if he be so ordered or permitted of God (ordering and permission in this point, being but all one act of the divine Will and Providence) and not in regard of his power or liberty to act or execute what he please, and when and as he list ; for the same Apostle and also St. *Jude* telleth us, *that he is kept in* *2 Pet. 2. 4.* *chains of darkness to be reserved unto judgment,* and by those chains *Jude 6.* he is kept, that he cannot hurt or destroy, when and where he list, but as he is sent and appointed of God, either to tempt or afflict the godly, or to punish the wicked ; and therefore the sentence of St. *Austin* is much to be weighed and considered, who saith : *Dia-* *Aug. super Psal.* *bolus plerumq; vult nocere, & non potest, quia potestas ista est sub* *potestate : nam si tantum posset nocere Diabolus quantum vult, ali-* *quis justorum non remaneret.* And therefore I cannot but transcribe here the opinion of that pious and learned person Bishop *Hall* up- *Of evil Aug.* on this very particular, which is this : " Could *Samson* have been *sect. 3. pag. 279,* " firmly bound hand and foot by the Philistine cords, so as he could *280.* " not have stirred those mighty limbs of his, what Boy or Girl of " *Gath* or *Ascalon* would have feared to draw near and spurn that " awed Champion? No other is the condition of our dreadful ene- " mies, they are fast bound up with the adamantine chains of Gods " most merciful and inviolable Decree, and forcibly restrained " from their desired mischief. Who can be afraid of a muzled and " tyed up Mastive ? what woman or child cannot make faces at a

" fierce

" fierce Lyon, or a bloody *Bajazet* lockt up fast in an Iron Grate?
" Were it not for this strong and strait curb of divine Providence,
" what good man could breathe one minute upon earth? The De-
" moniack in the Gospel could break his iron fetters in pieces,
" through the help of his Legion ; those Devils that possessed him
" could not break theirs; they are fain to sue for leave to enter
" into Swine, neither had obtained it (in all likelihood) but for a
" just punishment to those *Gaderene* owners: How sure may we
" then be, that this just hand of Omnipotence will not suffer these
" evil ones to tyrannize over his chosen Vessels for their hurt ?
" How safe are we, since their power is limited, our protection in-
" finite ? So that if the Devil be thus chained and restrained by the
omnipotent Decree and Providence, that he cannot execute any
evil, but as he is ordered of God, and that God doth not let him
loose but for just causes and reasons; then can it not be that the
Devil doth visibly appear and make Leagues with Witches, nor
work such strange things for them, because there is no just or reasonable end that can be assigned, why God should order him to do
these things; and therefore a visible League with Witches is meerly
false and fraudulent.

Reas. 6.   6. This pretended League must needs be a lye and a figment,
because of the effects that are feigned to follow, as to have carnal
copulation with the Devil, to raise storms and tempests, to flye in
the air, and to kill men and beasts. For if these things be done,
they are either performed by the Witches own natural power, or
by the Devils.   If by the Witches natural power, or the force of
her resuscitated imagination and strength of will to work *ad nutum* (as *Van Helmont* seems to hold) then the Devil operateth
nothing, but in playing the Impostor, and deceiving the Witch,
and that he may easily do by internal and mental delusion, and
needs no visible League to bring it to pass.   And if the Witch kill
men or beasts, or perform any of the fore-cited Feats by natural
means or Agents, then where is the Devils power, or wherein is
the Witchcraft or Fascination, or where is the effect of the League?
And if the Witch kill by natural means, then the natural Agent is
not simply evil, but in the use and application.   As a Sword is a
natural and lawful instrument for an honest man to use, to defend
his life withal, in using of it with his natural power and skill; but
if a Thief or a Robber, with his natural power and skill, use a
Sword to kill and murther an honest man withal, it is wickedness
in the use and end, but not in the agency of the Thief, nor in the
effect of the Sword. So if the Witch by any natural means (though
never so secret) do kill a man or child, it is murther; but wherein
lyes the Witchcraft ? Is it any thing else but *Veneficium* (as both
the Greek and Latine words do import) to kill by some secret
way of poysoning? Shew what Witchcraft there is in it besides.
If the Devil by his own power kill a man, or perform the Witches
carrying in the air, and the like, let us know how, or by what

means

means he performeth the fame? If what the Devil performeth in natural and corporeal matter, be (as the Fathers, School-men, and Divines moſt generally hold) by applying natural Agents, to fit paſſives, then the effect is natural, and ſo in killing any perſon, it is only wicked and diabolical, in regard of the end, which is murther, but what Witchcraft is there in the means and operation? And therefore *Guiterrius* ſtrongly concludeth thus. " If there be no " natural Faſcination, there can be no diabolical ; but there is no " natural Faſcination (as he thinketh he hath ſufficiently proved) " therefore he concludeth there is no diabolical Faſcination at all. There is no way to ſolve this Argument, but either in denying that the Devil worketh theſe things by natural means, and then it croſſeth the opinion of all the Learned in general, ancient, middle, and modern, or by proving that there is natural Faſcination, and then diabolical is but in vain and needleſs.

7. How can the Witches (if not maniacal in the higheſt degree) *Reaſ. 7.* believe, that the Devil who is a Lyar, and the Father of lyes, and whom they cannot but know hath in the like caſes deceived many, that have (in their opinion) made contracts with him, will prove true in the performance of his promiſe? Or that he who is the enemy of all truth and goodneſs, and laboureth to deceive all Mankind, will be faithful to perform his promiſe, or to do them any good, either real or apparent? Or (if the Witches be not incredibly mad) can they believe that he will perform without Hoſtages, Bonds-men, or Sureties? when we find that the weakeſt and maddeſt of Mortals, if he make a Covenant with another of known looſneſs and deceit, though for a thing of a far leſs value, than either ſoul or body, will he not require ſufficient Bonds-men and Security? Now what Bonds-men or Security can the Witches have?

8. And if the Witches be not beyond meaſure deluded and mad, *Reaſ. 8.* muſt they not rationally know, that if the Devil deceive them (as he is ſure to do) there is no recompence to be had, nor any that can compel him to perform bargains? Before what Judicature, before what Judges, by what Law muſt they call him to an account, or have him puniſhed? So that in all reaſon and ſound judgment we muſt conclude the Witches to be abſolutely mad, and then all theſe things alſo madneſs, lyes and folly, or that there is not, nor ever was any ſuch League or Covenant.

9. But if all this were granted, yet who are the Witneſſes to this *Reaſ. 9.* viſible League or Covenant, can the Witches name or find any? The things that cannot be proved by ſufficient Witneſſes, are never to be believed, and we have proved the nullity, impoſſibility, and falſity of the pretended Confeſſions of Witches themſelves, and therefore that no credit at all ought to be given unto them, and however no Law nor Equity ought to allow the Evidence of a Party, as in theſe caſes all Witches are. And though ſome few of them have been ſo exceedingly mad to make ſuch falſe and abſurd

Confeſ-

Confessions, yet if the Records of all Ages and Courts were fought, it will be found that many hundreds of them have suffered that never confessed the least tittle of any such matter ; and the supposed Witches of *Salmesbury* in the County of *Lancaster*, the tenth year See the Arraignment of Witches in *Lancast. Ann. 10. Jacobi.* of the Raign of King *James*, were so far from this confession, that they were cleared , and the accusation found to be false , and all acted by the imposture of one *Thompson*, or *Christopher Southworth*. And I my self have known two supposed Witches to have been put to death at *Lancaster* within these eighteen years, that did utterly deny any such League, or ever to have seen any visible Devil at all : and may not the confession of these (who both dyed penitently) be as well credited, as the confessions of those that were brought to such confessions by force, fraud, or cunning perswasion, and allurements ? But if there be any such League or Covenant betwixt the Witches and the Devil , how cometh the truth of this matter of fact (if ever there were or could be any such thing) to be certainly known and revealed ? Have any of the Pen-men of the holy Scriptures recorded, that there ever was, is, or can be any such League or Contract ? Or was it ever attested by any honest rational men, that were ear or eye-witnesses of such a bargain and contract ? Therefore we must once again conclude : *De non apparentibus & non existentibus eadem est ratio.*

Reas. 10.   10. As for the Witches either Males or Females, having carnal Copulation with Devils, either as an *Incubus* or *Succubus*, and their stealing of seed from a man, and conveying it into the vessels of the woman, it is in it self so horrid, monstrous, and incredible, that I cannot well believe him to be a rational person, or *sanæ mentis*, that believes it as a truth, and therefore cannot but think the rehearsal of it a sufficient confutation. Also herein I do appeal to all learned Physicians, who do know the way that Nature breeds humane seed, the causes that make it prolifical, and the members fit for its generation and reception, who (I doubt not) will deride this Tenent, and condemn it, as false and abominable. Moreover, the horrid absurdity of it hath been sufficiently demonstrated by *Wierus*, Dr. *Tandlerus*, Mr. *Scot*, Mr. *Wagstaff*, and others : and therefore all we shall say is this : " That Devils, whether concei-" ved to be corporeal or incorporeal, and to assume bodies (for the " one it must of necessity be) were not created of God to gene-" rate, neither have they, nor can have any seed, or members fit " for generation ; and therefore to copulate or generate is dero-" gatory from the glory of Nature, and blasphemous against God " and his Power. As for the Devils sucking the Teats, Warts, or such like excrescences of the Witches bodies, we should have passed it over as easily as the former, but only that Mr. *Glanvil* hath taken up the Cudgels to defend it : to confute which, we shall give these satisfactory Reasons.

Reas. 1.   1. There can be no rational end assigned , why the Devil should perform this action, for we must tell Mr. *Glanvil* that supposals are n.) proofs, and *ex suppositis supposita consequuntur*, and in a thing of this nature, arguments to prove it probable are insufficient. And *Pag. 18.* if (as he confesseth) for their being suckt by the Familiar, I say, (he saith) " We know so little of the Nature of Demons and Spi-" rits, that 'tis no wonder we cannot certainly divine the reason of " so strange an action: Now if he knew so little of their Nature, it must needs be vanity and arrogance to take upon him to declare so much : and if he could not certainly divine the reason of so strange an act, it was extreme folly and pride in him to bring in idle and vain conjectures and probability, where verity and certainty are expected. One while he supposeth them corporeal, which if granted, will not prove that they are recreated by the reeks and vapours of humane blood, because their bodies are of a more pure Nature, than to be nourished with gross, and sometimes (especially in melancholick old men and women) corrupted blood ; for if every thing be nourished by its like, then they cannot be fed with humane blood, for they have no flesh nor bones such as ours, that have need to be nourished with blood. And for his next, *perhaps, and may be, that it is a diabolical Sacrament*, we shall believe it when he proves it, and not before. But he hath a third supposal, which to him seemeth most probable, *viz.* ". That the " Familiar doth not only suck the Witch, but in the action infuseth " some poysonous ferment into her. If this had been most probable, why did he bring in the other two, that are less probable? surely he might have known that, *frustra fit per plura, quod fieri potest per pauciora*. And is his sucking now come to infusion and injection ? surely these will not accord : but enough of supposals.

2. But we must know of Mr. *Glanvil*, how he comes to know *Reas. 2.* that the Devils sucking of the Witches bodies is a truth, or ever was proved to be matter of fact, who were by and present that were ear or eye-witnesses of it ? A thing that never was proved ought never to be believed ; and if he recur to the Witches confessions, that is fully overthrown before, and we are sure that in these late years that are past, when so many pretended Witch-finders were set abroad in *Scotland* and *Northumberland*, they never manifested, nor could verifie any such thing, but were found and discovered to be notorious Impostors and Knaves, pretending to discover Witches by putting sharp Needles or Pins into the Warts *History.* and hollow Excrescences of divers persons, when the persons so dealt withal, did not see nor know ; and if the persons did not feel nor complain of pain, then (forsooth) they must be taken for Witches, and be burnt. So of many persons they got money and bribes, that they might not be searcht or stript naked, and of others for finding Excrescences upon them that were hollow and fistulous, and therefore when the Pin was thrust into the fistulous cavity, that was skinned within, and so indolent, they were then accounted guilty, and were either forced to compound with these notorious pretended Witch-finders, or to be prosecuted for their

lives.

lives. By which wicked means and unchristian practices divers innocent persons, both men and women lost their lives ; and these wicked Rogues wanted not greater persons (even of the Ministry too) that did authorize and incourage them in these Diabolical courses, as though this had been some way prescribed by God or his Word to discover Witches by, when it was an Hellish device of the Devil to delude Witchmongers, and bring poor innocent people to danger and death. Yet it had prevailed further, if some more wise Heads and Christian Hearts had not interposed, by whom the Villany was detected, and the Impostors severely punished ; and that this is a most certain truth, hundreds yet living can witness and testifie. And the like in my time and remembrance happened here in *Lancashire*, where divers both men and women were accused for supposed Witchcraft, and were so unchristianly, unwomenly, and inhumanely handled, as to be stript stark naked, and to be laid upon Tables and Beds to be searched (nay even in their most privy parts) for these their supposed Witch-marks: so barbarous and cruel acts doth diabolical instigation, working upon ignorance and superstition, produce.

Hi·tory.

Reas. 3.   3. But as this was never really proved *de facto*, that the Devil did suck upon the body of a supposed Witch, so the possibility of it likewise can never be demonstrated. For whether a Spirit be taken to be corporeal, or to assume a body, yet it neither hath nor can have such a body as our Saviour did appear in after his Resurrection, which was the same real and numerical body that he suffered in, and was by the sense of seeing and feeling distinguished from any bodies that Spirits can have and appear in, especially in solidity and tangibility ; for a Spirit hath not flesh and bones, as he was felt and seen to have. And where there is no flesh and bones, there cannot be any animal sucking, and we speak not here of artificial sucking or attraction, of which there is a great question, whether any such thing be at all or not ; but however the Spirits have no power to suck, because they have not flesh and bones.

Reas. 4.   4. That there are divers Nodes, Knots, Protuberances, Warts, and Excrescences that grow upon the bodies of men and women, is sufficiently known to learned Physicians and experienced Chirurgions. Some have them from their mothers wombs, some grow afterwards, some proceed from internal causes, some from external hurts, some are soft, some hard, some pendulous, some not, some fistulous, and issue matter, some hollow and indolent, and many other ways. And these are more frequent in some persons, by reason of their Complexion and Constitution, in others by reason of their Age, Sex, and other accidents and circumstances, especially in Women that are old, and their accustomed purgations staid, or by reason of Child-birth, and the like. Now if all these were Witch-marks, then few would go free, especially those that are of the poorer sort, that have the worst diet, and are but nastily kept. And for their being indolent, it doth argue nothing but ignorance ;

for

for many forts of Tumors and Excrefcences are without pain, as
well as fiftulous and hollow Warts.   And it is a woful errour, to
make that a fign and mark of a diabolical Contract, that hath natural caufes for its production.   And it is a ftrange kind of Logick
to argue or conclude, that men or women are Witches, and have
made a Contract with the Devil, becaufe they have fuch Warts or
Excrefcences that are indolent when pricked into: where is the
coherence, connexion, or juft confequence ? Let all wife men
judge.

As for that vain opinion, that Witches are, or can be really and
effentially transformed into Dogs, Cats, Hares, and the like, or men
tranfubftantiated into Wolves, it is largely by numerous pofitive arguments, confuted by *Cafmannus*, and by the Authors of that learned Treatife of Spirits and Devils, written in the Raign of Queen
Elizabeth, as alfo by *Wierus*, Mr. *Scot*, and others; fo that we fhall
not bring all that others have written about this point, but note
fuch things as are moft material, and have been lefs handled or regarded by others, and that in thefe Particulars.

Pfycholog. par. 2.
pag. 53. &c.
Dialog. Dif-
courf. pag. 149,
&c.
Difcovery of
Witchcraft, l. 5.
c. 1, &c.

1. It is taken to be a great matter with fome, becaufe St. *Augu-*
ftin feemeth to favour this opinion of transformation, and tells us
this: *Si enim dixerimus ea non effe credenda, non defunt etiam nunc,*
qui ejufmodi quædam, vel certiffima audiffe, vel etiam expertos fe effe
affeverent. And then faith: "And we, when we were in *Italy*, did
"hear fuch things of a certain Region of thofe parts, where certain
"Women that kept Inns, being skilled in thefe Arts (they did fay)
"were wont to give in Cheefe to Travellers that they could get to
"take it, from whence forthwith they were turned into Juments,
"and carried neceffary burdens, and when they had done, did again
"into themfelves, but that while they had not a beftial,
rational and humane underftanding. And yet concludeth:
vel falfa funt, vel tam inufitata, ut meritò non credantur. To
which we fhall return thefe fhort anfwers. 1. Though St. *Auftin*
were in many things a very Learned man, yet being but a man,
might and did erre, not only in this point, but in many others.
2. His Reafons to prove it by are weak and groundlefs. 3. He
fpeaketh nothing of his certain and peculiar knowledge, but by
common fame and hearfay; and therefore the matters alledged to
be done, are not credible. 4. He confeffeth that they are either
falfe, or fo unufual, that they are not worthy to be believed.
5. And when he hath faid all he can, he concludeth thefe Tranf-
formations (if any fuch were) to be but phantaftical, that is, to
feem fo, but not really to be fo, and what he meaneth by a phantaftical appearance, is not eafie to judge, whether it were a delufion
of the phantafie within, or of the fenfes without. 6. But in another place he telleth us this: *Non eft credendum, humanum corpus*
Dæmonum arte vel poteftate in beftialia lineamenta converti poffe;
fo that here is St. *Auftin* contradicting himfelf, or elfe he concludeth
nothing. 7. But his learned Commentator *Ludovicus Vives* doth

De Civit. Dei,
lib. 18. cap. 18.
pag. 583.

De Spirit. anima
cap. 26.

not give credit to those vain and lying Fables, but confuteth them
by the Authority of *Pliny* (who might have given St. *Austin* satisfaction, if he had read him) who tells us roundly : *Homines in lu-
pos verti, rursumq; restitui sibi, falsum esse confidenter existimare
debemus , aut credere omnia quæ fabulosa tot seculis comperimus.*
And further saith : *Mirum est, quò procedat Græcia credulitas. Nullum tam impudens mendacium est, ut teste careat.*

2. For essential Transformations we have examples in the Sacred Scriptures , but these not wrought but by a divine Hand and
an omnipotent Power. And such was that of *Lots* Wife, who
looking back contrary to command , was turned into a Pillar of
Salt, *& fuit in statuam salis,* as *Arias Montanus* renders it, which
accordeth with the Hebrew exactly, the vulgar Latine and others
say, *versa est in statuam salis :* and this by the divine finger was a
real transubstantiation, especially in respect of her body, the substance of which was really changed into an absolute Pillar of Salt,
without regression or returning back to what it was before , but
remained so still, and was standing in the days of *Josephus,* if credit may be given to what he writeth. Another example we have
in *Moses* his Rod, which God commanded him to cast upon the
ground, *and he cast it upon the ground, and it became a Serpent,
and Moses fled from before it. And the Lord said unto Moses,* Put
*forth thine hand, and take it by the tail. And he put forth his hand,
and caught it, and it became a rod in his hand.* This Rod afterwards *Aaron* threw down before *Pharaoh, and it became a Serpent,
and swallowed up the rods of the Wise-men and Sorcerers, and it afterwards became a rod again,* and *Aaron* used it in working some
of the rest of the Miracles. So that this was so true a transformation, that *Moses* himself was afraid when he saw the Rod a Serpent, that he fled from before it ; and that it was a real change,
appeared in that it swallowed up the Rods of the Magicians , and
still afterwards became a Rod again. So likewise all the Waters
in *Egypt* were really changed into blood : And our Saviour did
really change the Water into Wine at the Marriage in *Cana of Ga-
lilee.* And all these were true and real transubstantiations, which
neither Devils nor Witches can perform, as appeareth by these unanswerable Arguments.

1. All real Transubstantiations are wrought and performed by
a divine and omnipotent Power : but Devils and Witches have no
divine nor omnipotent Power. Therefore Devils or Witches cannot work or perform any real Transubstantiations.

2. All Beings that work real Transubstantiations, must work
contrary and different from that order and course that God hath
established in Nature : but Devils and Witches cannot work contrary and different from that order and course that God hath established in Nature. Therefore Devils and Witches cannot work any
real transubstantiations at all. Let all the Witchmongers in the
World answer these Arguments, if they be able.

3. We

---

*Hist. nat. l. 8.
c. 22. p. 114.*

Gen. 19. 26.

*Antiq. Judaic.
l. 1. c. 12. p. 17.*

Exod. 4. 3, 4.

*Exod. 7. 9, 10,
20.*

Exod. 7. 20, 21.

Joh. 2. 9.

3. We find also external Transfiguration, as of Christ in the Mountain; for the Text saith, in St. *Matthews* Gospel: *And he was transfigured before them, and his face did shine as the Sun, and his raiment was white as the light.* And *Mark* saith: *And he was transfigured before them, and his raiment became shining exceeding white as snow: so as no fuller on earth can white them.* And St. *Luke* saith: *And as he prayed, the fashion of his countenance was altered, and his raiment was white and glittering.* The word used in those places for the transfiguring or altering of his face by St. *Matthew* and St. *Mark* is μετεμορφώθη, from μετὰ *trans*, and μορφὴ *forma, figura*, the outward form, shape, figure, or lineaments; and this word is also used for the change or transforming of the mind, will, desires, and affections: For so the Apostle saith: *And be not conformed to this world: but be ye transformed by the renewing of your mind.* And again he saith: *We behold as in a glass the glory of the Lord with open face: and are transformed into the same image from glory to glory.* But St. *Luke* instead of this word expresseth it thus: τὸ εἶδΘ τᾶ προσώπα αὐτᾶ ἕτερον. *Tremellius* renders it: *Transformatus est aspectus vultus ejus.* And *Beza: Species vultus ejus alia,* which is nearest the Greek. So *Moses* face, when he had been with the Lord upon the Mount, the skin of it did shine, so that he put a veil upon it, when he spoke to the people, and put it off when he went in to speak unto the Lord. So that these were external alterations of both Christs and *Moses* face, by appearing glorious, resplendent, and shining like the Sun, and this was wrought by a divine hand and power. From whence we may note,

1. That though Christ was thus gloriously transformed (for so the word doth bear) yet we are not to imagine, that Christ was essentially changed into some other substance or nature; no, but that he was rather made there most resplendent in glory.

2. And where the Apostle wisheth the *Romans* to be transformed: Is it to be essentially transformed into any other substance or natural thing? Nay not so, but effectively into some other more sacred qualities, by the renovation of their inward mind. And again where he saith: *And are transformed into the same image from glory to glory.* His meaning is not, that we are essentially transformed into the very image of God; for so should he very shrewdly confirm that foolish opinion of some, who hold that men are deified in God, and that God also is hominified in men: But his purpose is, that we (by the operation of the holy Spirit) should proceed and grow (by degrees) from glory to glory, until we be truly conformed unto the similitude of that same glorious Image of God wherein we were first created; and so intendeth no essential transformation at all.

?. We are here to note the difference betwixt this Transfiguration, and that which may proceed from natural causes, as passions, affections, or diseases; and also from artificial or counterfeited Transfigurations. For it is wonderful to behold, how anger and

rage

rage doth alter the faces and countenances of some, and so give, sorrow, despair, and the like, in others, causeth horrible changes all over the external parts both of the face and body. Neither is any passion more prevalent than deep-rooted fear mixed with despair, as hath been manifested in some; that in a short time, nay even in the space of one night have had their hair, that formerly was black, turned into gray or white, as is testified by Authors of unquestionable veracity. And for diseases, it is almost incredible to think, what strange alterations Madness, Frenzy, the bitings of a mad Dog, Melancholies (especially that kind which Physicians call *Lycanthropia*, which is so wonderful, that it hath made many dotingly believe, they were really transformed) will produce and bring forth. Examples of which at large may be seen in *Schenckius*; of which we shall speak more fully anon, as also of artificial and counterfeited Transfigurations: and that Devils nor Witches can perform no such Transfigurations as this of Christ and *Moses*, is manifest by the Arguments laid down before, because these were brought to pass by a divine Hand and an omnipotent Power, which Devils and Witches have not, and therefore cannot operate any such things.

Observ. medic. pag. 80, &c. M. pag. 129.

4. Moreover in the Scripture there is mention of counterfeit, simulated, and hypocritical transformation, such the Apostle mentioneth in these words, speaking of the false Apostles: *For such are false Apostles, deceitful workers, transforming themselves into the Apostles of Christ.* And no marvel, for Satan himself is transformed into an Angel of light. Therefore it is no great thing, if his Ministers also be transformed as the Ministers of Righteousness, whose end shall be according to their works. The word there thrice used is from μετασχηματίζω, which cometh from ἔχω *habeo, possideo, teneo*, and from thence σχῆμα *habitus :* so that the compound Verb properly signifieth *effingo, assimulo*, and so of necessity must signifie in these three places. So the Apostle saith in another place : *The form of this world, σχῆμα, passeth away*, that is, the fashion, condition, custom, or usage of the world passeth away. This place of Scripture concerning Satans transforming of himself into an Angel of light (though plain in it self) hath been and still is most usually alledged by Witchmongers, to prove the Apparitions of Devils by : For thus they commonly argue; "If Satan can transform himself into an Angel of Light; much more (arguing *à majore ad minus*) into any other shape, and so may easily appear in "the form of a Cat, Dog, or in any other shape whatsoever, and this they think to be an invincible Argument. This way of argument were of force, if the Apostle in this place had meant or intended any real or essential transformation ; but that this is not the meaning of the Text, we shall prove by these following Reasons.

2 Cor. 11. 13, 14, 15.

1 Cor. 7. 31.

Reas. 1. 1. The very signification of the word here, doth not bear nor intend any essential transformation, but only feigning, pretending, and

and affimulating, as when *Judas* pretended charity and love to the poor, when he faid : *Why was not this oyntment fold for three hun-* Joh. 12. 5, 6. *dred pence, and given to the poor ? This he faid, not that he cared for the poor : but becaufe he was a thief, and had the bag, and bare what was put therein.* Though *Judas Ifcariot* hypocritically feigned and pretended this charity to, and care for the poor, yet was he not really a charitable man, or a lover of the poor, but a thief, and a moft covetous wretch. So thefe falfe Apoftles did pretend much zeal and piety to preach and promote the Gofpel, but therefore were they not really transformed and changed into true Apoftles, but were Deceivers, Diffemblers, and Hypocrites. So Satan often pretendeth heavenly, angelical, and divine things, and to do as the holy Angels do ; but it is in deceit, cozenage, falfity, and hypocrifie, and fo he is by counterfeiting and diffembling faid to be transformed into an Angel of Light, and not otherwife by any effential transformation at all.

2. The Text it felf doth plainly manifeft, that they were not Reaf. 2. transformed into true Apoftles, for then St. *Paul* had had no caufe to have written fo bitterly againft them ; but that notwithftanding that fhew, form, or pretence that they held forth, and though outwardly they feemed to perfonate the true Apoftles of Chrift, yet that was but an external and hypocritical fimulation; for really and truly they were falfe Apoftles, ψιυδαπόςολοι, and deceitful workers, ἐργάτει δόλιοι. And fo Satan may make what fhews or pretences he will of goodnefs, piety, and of heavenly things, and fo may counterfeit, diffemble and lye, yet ftill he remaineth a very accurfed Devil, and is never really changed from his damned and diabolical Nature.

3. Satan is fo transformed into an Angel of Light, as his Mini- Reaf. 3. fters are transformed into the Apoftles of Chrift. But Satans Minifters are not effentially transformed into the Apoftles of Chrift. Therefore neither is Satan effentially transformed into an Angel of Dialog. Difc. Light. For though Satans Minifters may pretend never fo much of Spirits and piety and zeal, and labour to perfonate and imitate the true Mini- Devils, p. 234. fters of Chrift, yet notwithftanding that pretended transformation, they ftill really and effentially remain as they were, that is, Deceivers and Hypocrites. And Satan for all his feeming and apparent perfonating and imitating the Angels of Light, he ftill remaineth in his effence and nature an Angel of Darknefs, and a lying and accurfed Wretch.

4. The Devil is never nor can be really and effentially tranfub- Reaf. 4. ftantiated into an Angel of Light, for then he could (indeed and in truth) be no longer a Devil, but his diabolical Nature would of neceffity ceafe. But all his transformation is, when he intendeth moft deeply to circumvent and deceive the fons of men, then he pretendeth the moft religious and the holieft fhews of all. Pretending in all outward appearance the holy affections, fincerity, and *Auguft. de Civ.* zeal of the holieft Angels of Light. For as St. *Auftin* faith : "Un- *Dei, l. 2. c. 26.* " lefs

" lefs the malignity of Satan be fleightly and cunningly covered,
" his deceivable purpofe is feldom or never effected.

Reaf. 5.　　5. The beft and moft found Expofitors, both ancient, middle,
and modern do expound the place as we have urged it, of which
Chryfoft. in loc.　we fhall name only two or three.　St. *Chryfoftom* tells us this : *Ope-*
rarii dolofi : nam operantur quidem, fed revellunt ea quæ funt plan-
tata : nam quoniam fciunt fe aliter non poffe effe acceptos, perfonâ
veritatis fumptâ, erroris actum fimulantes peragunt. And a little after
he faith thus : *Et multos Diabolus fic decipit, perfonâ in fe acceptâ,*
& non factus Angelus lucis : fic illi perfonam Apoftolorum circum-
ferunt, non ipfam potentiam, neq; fortes funt. Dr. *Hammond* gives
the Paraphrafe of this place thus : " For the truth is (he faith)
" thefe men that come to infufe falfe Doctrines into you, behave
" themfelves as cunningly as they can, and do labour to imitate,
" and feem to do thofe very things, that we true Apoftles do.　And
" 'tis no unufual matter for Deceivers and Seducers to do fo ; for
" Satan himfelf pretends to do thofe things that the good Angels
" do, makes as if he meant you all kindnefs, when he comes to de-
" ftroy you.　And therefore 'tis not any thing ftrange, if feducing
" Hereticks, imployed by him, do imitate the actions of the Apo-
" ftles of Chrift ; but according to the hypocrifie of their actions,
" fo fhall their ends be. See *Theophylact* and *Calvin* upon the place.
So that we pofitively conclude, that from this place of Scripture no
real or effential transformations of Devils can be proved at all.

6. There are natural Transformations by progreffion to perfection, as is manifeft in Infects, which at the firft to our view do
appear to be Worms, Maggots, Creepers, or Caterpillers, and yet
afterwards do become feveral forts of winged Creatures, as Buster-
flies of many and various kinds, Flies, and the ! ... as that Creature, which here in the North Fifhers do call a *May-Fly*, is firft but
a little Creeper inclofed in an Hull, as of pieces of ftraws, or the
like : and fo that which they call a Cod-bait, is like a yellow Mag-
got with a black head inclofed in a fandy cruftaceous Husk, and
yet towards the middle of *Auguft*, or the beginning of *September*,
becometh a fine yellowifh Fly, which the Fifhers ufe to bait withal,
and thefe are but gradual progreffions towards the perfection of the
Animalcle, as the learned Author *Johannes Swammerdanus* hath
Philofophical　declared in thefe words, as we find it laid down in the Philofophi-
Tranfactions,　cal Tranfactions : " Firft it lays down the ground of all natural
numb. 64.　" changes in Infects ; declaring, that by the word Change, is no-
" thing elfe to be underftood but a gradual and natural evolution
" and growth of the parts, not any Metamorphofis or Transforma-
" tion of them, and a great deal more of notable obfervations con-
" cerning the moft forts of Infects, as may be feen in the piece quo-
Vid. Barthol.　" ted in the Margent.　So likewife there are very many ftrange
Cent. 2. Hift.　transformations wrought by petrifactions both of Vegetables and
100. pag. 319.　Animals, or their parts, as may be feen by the Writings of many
Microgr. obfrv.　learned Authors, efpecially thofe noted in the Margent, to whom
17. pag. 107.　　　　　　　　　　　　　　　　　　　　　　　　　　　　　　　　　　we

we refer the curious Inquirer. These being natural Transfigurations (for so they may be properly called) we cannot rationally suppose that any man of judgment will imagine, that any such can be produced by Devils or Witches, because they are brought forth by natural Principles and Agents, which Devils or Witches cannot over-rule, alter, nor hinder, else the whole and certain course that the Creator hath set in the order of the production and generation of natural things, might be suspended, which is not possible to be performed without an omnipotent Power, which the Devils and Witches have not. Besides the most of these require a suitable time for their production and perfection, which must only be performed by the internal operation of Nature, or by Art accelerating the works of Nature, which Devils and Witches cannot bring to pass.

7. There are divers other Transformations (at least so accounted and called) which because they are not absolutely pertinent to our purpose, we shall only mention slightly. 1. External changes of the body in respect of diseases, and some by an extraordinary power, as that of *Moses*, to whom the Lord said: *Put now thine* Exod. 4. 6, 7. *hand into thy bosom. And he put his hand into his bosom: And when he took it out: behold, his hand was leprous as snow. And he said, Put thine hand into thy bosom again: And he put his hand into his bosom again, and plucked it out of his bosom, and behold, it was turned again as his other flesh.* Here we see that the same hand was made leprous white as snow, and was again restored as his other flesh. And this was done by a divine Power, such as neither Devils nor Witches can perform. So *Gehazi* of whom it is said: *The leprosie therefore of Naaman shall cleave unto thee, and* 2 King. 5. 27. *unto thy seed for ever. And he went out from his presence a leper as white as snow.* And here the judgment was permanent, and no restauration, and was a great Miracle, which Devils and Witches cannot perform. 2. There is feigned, and artificial transfigurations. So of *David*, of whom it is said: *And he changed his behaviour* 1 Sam. 21. 13. *before them, and feigned himself mad in their hands, and scrambled on the doors of the gate, and let his spittle fall down upon his beard.* And all this he prudently feigned, that he might escape from *Achish* the King of *Gath*, of whom he was sore afraid: So many Persons of Worth have disguised themselves strangely, that they might escape the hands of their enemies, or not fall into their power, and yet these were not done by the Devils Art, nor by Witchcraft. So a Stage-player transfigureth himself, sometimes to personate one person, and sometimes another; and though his outward habit, speech, and action be changed, yet he remaineth the same in Nature and Person that he was before those changes, and so maketh nothing for Witchcraft at all. 3. There are knavish Transfigurations and Counterfeiting for deceitful and wicked ends, as in those we call Gypsies, that discolour their faces and skins, to be more fit to cheat Di Monst. l. 2. and cozen. So likewise do many other vile and wicked persons c. 18. p. 565.

N counter-

counterfeit Sores, Ulcers, Leprosie, Dropsie, and such like diseases, as may be seen at large in *Ambrose Paræus* Book of Monsters, and we have seen and detected divers; and all this done only to deceive and abuse mens goodness and charity: But no more of Devil in any of these, but the wickedness of the mind, and the evil of the end and intention. Of a more wicked grain and temper are those, that for wicked and devilish ends counterfeit themselves to be possessed, and labour to make the World believe, that the Devil doth move in divers parts of their bodies, and doth speak in them, when it is nothing but only their own devilish cunning in lying and counterfeiting, as we shall have occasion to shew more fully hereafter. 4. There are also divers kinds of sportive and delusive Transformations, performed by those that use the Art of Leger-de-main or Juggling, wherein they pretend and seem to transubstantiate one thing into another, when by the agility of their hands, and the gesture of their face and body, they do but draw your eyes and attention another way, while they do but nimbly convey another thing in its place. And he that taketh these for Conjurers or Witches, and their Tricks for diabolical or Witchcraft, are surely under a devilish delusion, and are most strangely bewitched. And as for the changes wrought by *Pharaohs* Magicians, we shall particularly handle it in another place.

8. There are other Transformations mentioned in the Scripture, of which we shall now speak. 1. That transformation that the Grace and Spirit of God doth work inwardly in the minds and hearts of the Godly, which is not by changing their Nature or Persons, but by transforming their minds, and altering their wills and affections from sinful and earthly things, to those that are holy and heavenly: so the Apostle willeth the *Romans*, *that they be*
Rom. 12. 2. *transformed by the renewing of their minds*, and so they come to be changed from glory to glory, and this were blasphemy to say, that either Devil or Witch could perform it. 2. There is a transformation wrought in the minds of the wicked by the just judgment of God; for the Text saith, speaking of Antichrist: *Reveal-*
2 Thess. 2. 9, *ing even him, whose coming is after the working of Satan, with all*
10, 11, 12. *power and signs and lying wonders. And with all deceivableness of unrighteousness in them that perish; because they received not the love of the truth, that they might be saved. And for this cause God shall send them strong delusions, that they should believe a lye. That they all might be damned, who believed not the truth, but had pleasure in unrighteousness.* So in the case of *Saul* the Text saith:
1 Sam. 18. 10. *And it came to pass on the morrow, that the evil Spirit from God came upon Saul.* These therefore are inward judgments for wickedness, sent by God by the ministry of Satan, of which we shall speak more hereafter. 3. We lastly come to the main point, that is, concerning the transformation of *Nebuchadnezzar*, which the Witchmongers hold to be a real and an essential transubstantiation, therefore let us hear the words as they run in our English Translation,

tion, which are this : *And they shall drive thee from men, and thy* Dan. 4. 32,33:
dwelling shall be with the beasts of the field, they shall make thee 34, 36.
eat grass as oxen. The same hour was the thing fulfilled upon *Ne-*
buchadnezzar, and he was driven from men, and did eat grass as
oxen, and his body was wet with the dew of heaven, till his hairs
were grown like Eagles feathers, and his nails like birds claws. And
at the end of the days I Nebuchadnezzar lift up mine eyes unto
heaven, and mine understanding returned unto me. At the same
time my reason returned unto me. And a little before : *Let his heart* Lib. vers. 16.
be changed from mans, and let a beasts heart be given unto him.
From this place they commonly frame an argument to this purpose.
That *Nebuchadnezzar* being really and essentially changed from a
man to a beast or an ox, much more may Satan essentially transform
himself into the shape of any Creature, and consequently that he
may really change the Witches into Hares, Dogs, Cats, and the
like.   But we shall unanswerably prove that the assumption is
false, that *Nebuchadnezzar* was not transubstantiated, or essentially
transformed at all : And if he had been really so, yet that the consequence is invalid, and of no force, and that by these Arguments.

1. Because that being driven into the field, and eating grass as *Argum.* 1,
oxen, and having his body (it was his body, not the body of an
oxe, and therefore no corporeal nor real change) wet with the
dew of Heaven, do not at all conclude or infer, that his body was
really and essentially changed, nor in the external figure of it altered from what it was before ; for he might go upon all four, and
eat grass, and yet that doth argue no real change of his bodily
shape at all ; for so have divers persons done, that being young,
have been lost in Woods and Desarts, and have been brought up
with Bears or Wolves.   To which purpose take one story for all
from *Philip Camerarius*, that learned Counsellor of *Norimberg*, a Hist. medic. l.4.
man of great credit and reputation, in these words.   " In the year c. 5. p. 239.
" 1543. there was in the parts of *Hesse* a Lad taken, who (as he
" reported afterwards, and so it was found true) when he was but
" three years old, was taken away, and afterwards nourished and
" brought up by Wolves. These Wolves, when they got any prey,
" would always bring the best of it to a Tree, and give it to the
" Child, which did eat it : in Winter and time of cold, they would
" dig a pit, and strew it with grass and leaves of trees, and there-
" upon lay the Child, and lying round about it, preserve him from
" the injury of the weather : after they would make him go upon
" all four, and run with him, till by use and length of time, he
" could skip and run like a Wolf ; being taken, he was compelled
" by little and little to go only upon his feet.   He would often
" say, that if it had been in his power, he could have taken more
" delight to have conversed among Wolves, than among men : he
" was carried to the Court of *Henry Lantgrave* of *Hesse* to be seen.
And in the same Chapter he relateth another story to the same
purpose of one that he himself had known and seen, that was of

admira-

admirable agility, and more to the same end. Now must we conclude, that because this Boy did live and lye in the open air, was fed with raw flesh, and went upon all four, that therefore he was really and essentially changed into a Wolf? no, that would be inconsequent and ridiculous; and so would it be, if because *Nebuchadnezzar* lay in the open field, was wet with the rain and dew, and did eat grass as an ox, to conclude, that therefore he was really changed into a beast; the absurdities are both alike. This is as mad a kind of inference, as if we should say, Conies and Geese do eat grass like an Ox, therefore they are Oxen or Asses, when notwithstanding they still retain their essential beings and shapes, without any essential transformations at all.

Argum. 2.   2. Because the hairs of his head (as the Text saith) were grown like to an Eagles feathers, and for that also the very nails of his hands and feet were like the claws of a bird: yet it doth not prove that he was really changed into a beast, and that for these Reasons. 1. Because it would be more consonant to conclude, that he was rather transformed into some bird, having feathers and claws, than into a beast that hath horns and hoofs, though there was in him no corporeal transformation at all, but only a changed mind. 2. The Text is not according to the Hebrew Phrase used when there is real transubstantiaton, as in *Lots* Wife; *Et fuit statua salis*; but as *Tremellius* renders it: *Usquedum pili ejus ut Aquilarum plumæ crevissent, & ungues ejus ut avium.* And *Arias Montanus* thus: *Donec capillus ejus sicut Aquilarum crevit, & ungues ejus sicut avium:* which is exactly agreeable to the Hebrew. So that the assertion is not, that his hairs were changed into Eagles feathers, nor his nails into birds claws, but that they were *sicut* as the feathers of Eagles, and as the claws of birds; the hairs by being grown ruffled, squalid, and rugged, and the nails by being grown long, hard, and crooked for want of cutting, dressing, combing, and ordering; and more change than this the words or sense do not bear. 3. There was no other change, but what was by natural growth; for the Hebrew word רְבוּ doth properly signifie *multus fuit, succrevit in multitudinem:* so that the hairs were increased naturally in multitude and length, and the nails in magnitude and length, and so there was no essential change at all, but only an excessive augmentation of them both, he having lost the use of reason, whereby he could not use means to cut, cleanse, and order them. So that they did but grow squalid and ill-favour'd for want of using means to order and make them comely, even as many that have been lost, or left in Desarts, and desolate places, have after some length of time been found to be overgrown with hairs and ugly nails, that they have scarce been taken for men, but have appeared as savage and feral Monsters.

Argum. 3.   3. His restauration doth plainly testifie what kind of change it was; for that which was restored unto him, did bring him into the same condition that he was in, before this transformation; and

that

that was his knowledge or underftanding. Now therefore if his knowledge or underftanding did reduce him to the right ufe of reafon, and brought thofe conditions and qualities that he had before: Then it is moſt plain, that it was only his knowledge or underftanding that was taken away or changed ; and fo there was no other transformation, but what was internal in the mind, judgment, or imagination, by altering his will, defires, cogitations, condition, and qualities, and fo no eſſential transformation at all, nor no change of his external ſhape, but what grew naturally in regard of his hair and nails or skin, for want of due ordering and decent dreſſing. And that this is an unanſwerable truth, the words in the Text do ſufficiently teſtifie, which are in our Engliſh: *And mine* Dan. 4. 34, 36. *underſtanding returned unto me, and at the ſame time my reaſon returned unto me*; therefore it was only his underftanding and reafon, that had for a time been turned from him, and at his reftauration they returned, or came again. *Tremellius* renders the former Verfe: *Et mente meâ ad me reverſâ Excelſo benedixi.* And in the latter: *Mente meâ reverſâ in me.* In both Verſes *Arias Montanus* renders it: *Cognitio mea ſuper me reverſa eſt*; for the Hebrew word there uſed ירע, *ſcivit, reſtituit, cognovit, agnovit, propriè eſt mentis & intellectûs,* as *Avenarius* ſaith. And the Septuagint in Avenar. Diſti- both the Verſes do agree with the Hebrew, αἱ φρένες μυ ἐπ' ἐμὲ ἐπιςρέ- on. pag. 313. φησαν. And to this purpoſe doth the French, Italian, and *Luthers* Tranflation render it, only the vulgar Latine gives it by the word *ſenſus, & figura mea reverſa eſt,*which is altogether vicious. So that from hence we may ſafely conclude, that this transformation was only internal and mental, and no eſſential change at all : of which a moſt learned Divine tells us thus much : *Sunt nonnulli, inter quos* Palan. in loc. *eſt Johannes Bodinus, qui putant humanam figuram reverà fuiſſe ei ademptam. Ac ſanè Deus pro ſua omnipotentia miraculum hoc in rege iſto impio facere, & humanam ejus naturam in bruti animalis eſſentiam mutare potuit : ſed veriſimilius eſt regem alienatum mente, vel etiam maniacum factum, ademptâ ei divinitùs mente,ut patet ex ſequente verſ. 34. & in furorem verſum, ſive per iram, ſive per dolorem, ob acceptam ignominiam, quòd regiâ dignitate eſſet orbatus. Sic Ericus Rex Sueciæ in furorem eſt actus per iram & dolorem, quòd regno eſſet dejectus, Anno 1568.*

4. That this was only a mental and internal transformation, as Argum. 4. are many forts of Melancholy, eſpecially that which Phyſicians call *Lycanthropia,* or *Melancholia lupina, Rabies canina,* and the like, is moſt manifeſt by comparing it with ſome of theſe that we have named ; of which (though we have related ſome before) we ſhall give ſome few, from Authors of credit and veracity. 1. And firſt concerning the effects of that Madneſs cauſed by the biting of a mad Dog, we have a moſt ſad and deplorable ſtory recited by *Phi-* Obſer. medic. *lip Salmuth,* that experienced Phyſician of *Anhalt,* which we ſhall p. 57, 58. here give in Engliſh: "Many (he ſaith) do verily think that the "force of this poyſon will break out, and appear within a few
                                                                    "months

" months or years. But experience doth altogether testifie the
" contrary. As certain learned Authors do commemorate , that
" it hath laid hid in some the space of seven years, but in others it

History 1.   " hath broke forth in the twelfth. *Guainerius* also mentioneth a
" certain person, to whom the *Hydrophobia* did happen the 18.
" year after he was bitten by the mad Dog. Moreover (he conti-
" nueth) a most Noble person of *Hagen* hath told me, that a certain
" Noble man was bitten in the face by a little pretty Dog, which
" he much delighted in, and that the seeds of that poyson, as it
" were nourished in his bosom for a long time, at the last did sud-
" denly break forth. For after that for some years feeling no mo-
" lestation nor trouble from that bite , he addressing himself to a
" Virgin did marry. And the nuptial Supper being ended, and the
" Bride brought to the Marriage-bed, her Kinsfolks a little after do
" hear her complaining and lamenting. At which they laughed and
" jested, thinking it but to be the Venereal sport. But that howling
" continuing late, they by force do break the barred doors of the
" Chamber, and enter , and find that the Bridegroom had bitten
" with his teeth, plainly after the manner of a Dog, the face of the
" Bride, and also the shoulders and arms, and the fleshy places, and
" still did not give over the same sort of biting. Being much asto-
" nished with this sad spectacle and cruel wickedness, they with an
" ireful and provoked mind do forthwith slay him : and the new
" Bride also died the same day. Though this he had but by relation, yet it was from a person of great quality ; and if he had not
been reasonably assured of the truth of it , he would never have
writ it down amongst his Medical Observations. But this is also at-

History 2.   tested by other Authors of sufficient credit, of divers of this sort of
persons , that have both barked and bitten like Dogs, and this is

De Hydrop. l. 1.   testified by *Scribonius Largus* and *Rhases* , as *Baptista Codronchus*
c. 12. p. 99.   hath cited them ; and learned *Sennertus* tells us this : " That some
" (if bitten with Dogs) do bark like Dogs, and flye at whomsoe-
" ver they meet , and that against or besides their will. For (he

Sennert. de Hy-   " saith) *Gentilis* relateth in his Comment upon *Avicen* , that a cer-
drop. pag. 417.   " tain young man troubled with this rabiousness, did exhort his
" Mother, that she should not come near him, for he could not con-
" tain himself but bite those that came near him.   2. As concerning Wolf-melancholy , we shall only give a short relation or two,

De medind.   the first from *Donatus ab alto mari* , who confesseth that he had
morb. c. 9. p. 57.   seen two : of the one of which he saith : " This person (he saith)
" having formerly known me, did one day meet me when he was
" holden with this distemper ; but I truly fearing went aside, and he

History 3.   " looking at me a little went away. There was with him a multi-
" tude of men, and he did bear upon his shoulders a whole thigh
" and a leg of a dead man : At last being cured he was well, who
" afterwards when he met me again, did ask me, if I had not been
" afraid, when he found me in such a place when he was mad : by
" which it is manifest, that in him the memory was not vitiated.
                                   Another

Another take from that able Phyfician of *Delfe Petrus Foreſtus* in *Obſr. medic.*
Englifh thus : " A certain Country-man was in the Spring-time *l. 10. p. 440.*
" feen at *Alcmaria* with an horrid look, and mad, to ſtay about
" the Church-yard, and after to enter the Church, and did leap
" upon a Seat or Plank (as we have feen him) only climbing up- *Hiſtory 4.*
" wards, and another while downwards with great fury, and never
" reſting in one place.   He carried a long ſtaff in his hand, but did
" ſtrike no body, but did with it beat off the Dogs ; for he had
" his thighs and legs black and ulcered with black cruſts or ſcurff
" by the biting of Dogs.   His whole body did appear fqualid, very
" black, and melancholick, but pale in the face, and his eyes ex-
" ceeding hollow.   From the forefaid ſigns (he faith) I did judge
" the man affected with the *Lycanthropia* or wolfiſh Melancholy. He
" never uſed any Phyfician that I know of. And this both this Author, *Schenckius* and *Sennertus* do fufficiently confirm from *Paulus*,
Aetius, *Avicen*, and the like.   From all which it is clear and manifeſt, that *Nebuchadnezzars* diſtemper was but as ſome kind of
Melancholy, whereby the imagination was corrupted, and the uſe
of reaſon and right underſtanding for the time taken quite away,
as faith the Text : *Let his heart be changed from mans, and let a*
beaſts heart be given unto him.   That is, let his thoughts, defires,
and affections be made brutiſh ; for by the heart in Scriptures the
cogitations, will, and affections are underſtood, as, *my ſon give me*
thy heart, that is, the love and affections of thy foul and heart. So
that when it is faid, *Let a beaſts heart be given him*, that is, let his
mind, thoughts, and affections be made beſtial ; and ſo there was
a change of the conditions and qualities of his mind and heart, but
no real or eſſential change of his natural heart at all.   And in this
fenfe *Tremellius* doth take it, ſaying : *Obbruteſcat, nihil humanum* *Vid. Polan.*
fapiat, and ſo doth *Polanus, Rollock*, and others underſtand it ; for *Rolloc. & alios*
Polanus faith : *Debuiſſe animum ejus prorſus obbruteſcere, & men-* *in Dan. c. 4.*
tem judiciúmq; animi humani amittere : non enim intelligendum *v. 16.*
hoc de metamorphoſi aliqua in corpore facta, ſed de animo tantùm
obbruteſcente.   So that from theſe examples it appeareth, that many perſons, by reaſon of Melancholy in its feveral kinds, have been
menrally and internally (as they thought, being depraved in their
imaginations) changed into Wolves and other kind of Creatures,
and have acted their parts, as though they had been really ſo, when
the change was only in the qualities and conditions of the mind,
and not otherwife.   And ſo only was the change of *Nebuchadnez-*
zar, which notwithſtanding *Bodinus*, the Popiſh Writers, and
Witchmongers have falfely and ignorantly taken it to be a real
tranſubſtantiation, when it was only mental : ſo apt are men to miſtake and urge things amifs, when it lyes for their own gain or intereſt.   But if theſe perſons that thought themſelves really changed
into Wolves, had been covered with a Wolfes ſkin fitted to their
bodies, and gone upon all four, and ſo have acted the parts of
Wolves, then it might in all likehihood have more ſtrongly induced

ced them to have believed a real tranſmutation indeed, though that way neither had there been any change of ſubſtance, but only a counterfeit and cunning diſguiſement: of which we ſhall here inſert (for diverſion ſake) a pleaſant ſtory from the Pen of *Vincent le Blanc* of *Marſeilles*, and leave it to be judged of according to the credit of the Author, which runs thus: "As concern-

The World ſurveyed, part. 2. c. 19. p. 270. Hiſtory.

"ing the *Anthropolychi*, I have not heard (he ſaith) of any thing "ſo ſtrange, as that the Governor of *Bagaris*, related once to me. "He told me, that going with ſome of his Company from *Lionac* "to *Montpelier*, they overtook an old man with a Sack on his ſhoul- "ders, going a great pace towards the ſame Town, a Gentleman "of the Company out of charity told him, if he would, one of his "Servants, to eaſe him, ſhould carry his burden for him: at firſt "he ſeemed unwilling to be troubleſom; but at length accepted "the offer, and a Servant of the Commanders Chamber call'ed *Ni-* "*cholas* took the burden, and being late, every one doubl'ed his "pace, that they might get in in good time, telling the good old "man, they would go before, and he ſhould find them at the *White* "*Horſe*. The Servant of the Chamber coming in with the firſt, had "a curioſity to ſee what was in the Sack, where he found a Wolfes "skin, ſo properly accommodated for the purpoſe, that he had a "ſtrong fancy to diſguiſe himſelf in it: whereupon he got it upon "his back, and put his head within the Head-piece of the Skin, as "'twere to ſhew his Maſters a Maſquerade; but immediately a fury "ſeized him, that in the Hall where they ſupped, he made ſtraight "to the Company at Table, and falling on them with teeth and "nails, made a dangerous rude havock, and hurt two or three of "them, ſo as the Servants and others fled to their Swords, and "ſo plyed the Wolf with wounds, that they laid him on the ground, "and hurt in ſeveral places. But as they looked upon him, they "were amazed when they ſaw under the Skin a poor Youth wal- "lowing in blood. They were fain to lay him preſently on a Bed, "taking order for his wounds and hurts, whereof he was recovered; "and was long before he could be cured: But this cured him of "the like curioſity againſt another time. The Company by this "means had but a bad ſeaſoned Supper, and many of them were "ſick either of hurt or apprehenſion. For the old man Wolf, 'twas "not known what became of him; but 'tis probable, that hearing "of this tidy accident, he was cautious to appear. Now if this relation be true, as there is nothing in it that ſeems either impoſſi- ble or improbable, but that it might, then from it we may obſerve theſe two things. 1. To conſider for what end the skin of the Wolf was ſo fitted and prepared, which might be to act ſome part of a Tragedy or Comedy in, or in ſport to fright ſome perſons with- al; but then it is not likely, but that the old man would have ap- peared and ſought for it again, which he might have done without fear or danger. But I rather conjecture it was for ſome more per- nicious purpoſe, as in that diſguiſe to fright Travellers and Paſſen-

gers,

gers, that thereby they might (for without doubt the old man had
other Companions) more securely rob them, and so escape, and
not be discovered or apprehended, which might make him afraid
to be seen, or to seek it again. 2. We may note the curiosity of
the young man, and the strength of his fancy, being moved to see
himself, so fitly to appearance, to be so like a Wolf, and not to the
steams flowing from the Wolfes skin to work upon his imagination,
which we leave to the inquisition of Naturalists, that live in
Countries where Wolves are, to make tryal of.

So having sufficiently disproved their supposition or assumption,
that *Nebuchadnezzar* was essentially transformed into a beast, we
shall also shew the consequence that (if it had been true) they
would draw from it, to wit, that if *Nebuchadnezzar* were really
transformed into a beast, much more may the Devil transform himself into the shape of any Creature, and may change Witches into
Cats, Dogs, Hares, and the like, which can by no true Rules of
Argument be good, because it stands upon divers, or rather contrary efficients, namely God and the Devil. The one having of
himself an absolute and indeterminate power, and therefore of himself able to work what he will, where, when, and howsoever best
pleaseth himself. And so by consequence he might (if it had so
seemed good in his wisdom) have essentially transformed *Nebuchadnezzar* into an ox. The other (the Devil I mean) he hath
only a finite and limited power, and therefore utterly unable of
himself to accomplish any one work beyond the bounds of that
power: and so by consequence he cannot possibly transform himself essentially into any Creature whatsoever, without a special
power from God. Lastly we shall conclude all with this binding
Argument: what transubstantiations soever are wrought, the thing
transformed ceases to be what it was before, both in nature and
properties, as *Lots* Wife being transubstantiated into a Pillar of
Salt, did cease to be flesh, blood, and bones, as she was before, and
lost all the properties of humane Nature. So if Devils or Witches
be transubstantiated into other Creatures, they cease to be what
they were before both in Nature and Properties. And then by
consequence the Devil should cease to be a Devil in Nature and
Properties, and the Witches should cease to have humane Nature
and Properties in them.

Having laid down these positive Arguments, we shall in the next
place shew the horrid absurdities of these Tenents, to wit, of holding a visible Contract, that the Devil sucks upon the Witches bodies, that they have carnal Copulation together, or that they are
essentially changed into Cats, Dogs, or Hares, or that they can flye
in the air, or raise storms or tempests, and kill men or Cattel, and
the like, and that in this order.

1. These Tenents do derogate from the Wisdom and Power of *Absurd.* 1.
God in his Government of the World by divine Providence, because by these it is supposed that the Devils and Witches do ope-

O   rate

rate what, when, and howſoever it pleaſeth them , and ſo the life and eſtate of all Creatures ſhould be in their power to afflict, torment, or to deſtroy when they pleaſe , which is both falſe and blaſphemous.   For the Devils and wicked men are enemies and rebels againſt God, but yet conquered, and impriſoned, and chained cloſe up by his Almighty Power, that they are not able to act any thing at all (except the evil of their own wills) nor put that into execution , but as far as God doth licenſe and order them , which we ſhall make plain in theſe two particulars.   1. *The Devils are*

2 Pet. 2. 4.
Jude 6.

kept in chains of darkneſs unto the judgment of the great day, that is, though their wills be corrupt, wicked, and evil , and that they have a continual deſire, *like a roaring lion, to ſeek whom they may devour;* yet are they reſtrained from acting this evil, by the mighty Power of God , and can execute nothing at all , but only as far as God doth order and command them : ſo the Devils could not by

Mat. 8. 31,32.
Mar. 5. 9. to
14.

their own power enter into the herd of Swine, until Chriſt gave them leave : neither could Satan hurt *Job* either in his goods or body (though he ſtrongly and earneſtly deſired it) until he had leave

Job 1. 11, 12.
2. 5, 6.

and commiſſion given him from God.   No more can Devils or Witches perform theſe things that are pretended ; for it can never be proved that ever God did, or will give them order or leave to perform any ſuch filthy or wicked thing, for which there can be no reaſon or end aſſigned why God ſhould order ſuch things to be done; ſo far different and oppoſite to the rules of his Juſtice, Wiſdom, and Providence. 2, Nor can wicked perſons act what they pleaſe ; but God doth bridle and reſtrain them as he pleaſeth ; for though *Pilate* proudly thought and boaſted that he had power to condemn Chriſt, or to let him looſe, yet our Saviour tells him :

Joh. 19. 11.

Thou couldſt have no power at all againſt me, except it were given thee from above. Upon which place learned Dr. *Hammond* ſaith thus : " So that thou haſt neither right nor power to inflict any " puniſhment one me , were it not that God, who is my Father, " hath in his great Wiſdom and divine Counſels, for moſt glorious " ends, for the good of the World , determined to deliver me up

Rolloc. in loc.

" into thy power to ſuffer death under thee.   Of which another ſaith thus : *Verba hæc duobus modis accipi poſſunt : partim quia omnis poteſtas eſt à Deo , & divinâ ordinatione ; partim quia qui cum poteſtate eſt, nihil planè poteſt, niſi ex Dei efficaci diſpenſatione ac providentia.* So this is manifeſt in the exceſſive pride and boaſt-

Iſa. 38. 29.

ing of *Sennacherib* of his own power , and taking no notice of Gods inevitable Decree in his Providence, that it was he, even the Lord of Hoſts that had done it , and of ancient times had formed it, without which *Sennacherib* could have done nothing ; but becauſe he deſpiſed Gods Power and Providence, therefore ſaith the Lord: *Therefore will I put my hook in thy noſe , and my bridle in thy lips, and I will turn thee back by the way by which thou cameſt,* which was performed by the ſlaughter of his Army, and the ſending him back into his own Country : ſo little do mens purpoſes

and

and counfels prevail, when the Lords will and purpofe are againft them.

2. Thefe Tenents do divert and obftruct the power and practice *Abfurd.* 2. of Godlinefs : For while the Saints of God are taught, *that they are to fight the good fight of Faith* ; and if they intend to be crowned, they muft fight ftoutly, and gain the victory, knowing, *that they fight not againft flefh and blood, but againft fpiritual wickednefs in high places, and that therefore they are to take unto them the whole Armour of God :* Therefore they knowing that this warfare is fpiritual, and againft fpiritual enemies, and that the weapons.both offenfive and defenfive are alfo fpiritual ; therefore they ought always fpiritually to watch and ftand upon their guard, leſt their fubtile and cruel enemy the Devil take them unawares, or by his Stratagems furprize them. For he is that old crafty Serpent, that hath innumerable wiles, and while he intendeth one thing, he pretendeth another; and like a cunning Enemy, gives a falfe Alarm at the one fide of the Camp, while he affaulteth another, or making falfe fires or fhews he feemeth to march away, when in the dark of the night he intendeth to fall on. So leſt the Chriftian fhould be watchful and prevail, he laboureth by falfe Teachers, which are the Magicians and Sorcerers in the Myftery, to draw them from their vigilancy, by poffeffing their minds with thefe lying Tenents, that the Devil comes in the fhape of a Cat or a Dog to a Witch, and bargains with her, and the reft, that whilſt they are fet at gaze to look for him in a bodily fhape, they are made negligent in their fpiritual watch, and fo are diverted from the fpiritual combate, and thereby the power and practice of Godlinefs is diverted and obftructed. Therefore we are to give heed unto the counfel of the Holy Ghoft; to refift the Devil in his fpiritual affaults with the fpiritual weapons that God beftows upon us, and not to give heed to old Wives Fables, or the falfe Doctrine of Witchmongers, that make us watch for the Devil where he is not, and in the mean time not to refift him where he is, and that is within effectively in a fpiritual manner, for he worketh in the children of difobedience, and therefore a Devil within us is more to be feared, than a Devil without us.

3. Thefe Tenents do uphold that horrid, lying, and blafphemous *Abfurd.* 3. opinion, that our bleffed Saviour did caft out Devils by *Beelzebub* the Prince of Devils : For when they could not deny, nor difprove the plain and open matters of fact, that our Saviour did really caft out Devils, then they devilifhly invented and vented, that though he did fo, yet it was but by the help of the Prince of Devils, with whom he had a compact, and fo wrought by the greater power to over-power the lefs. Concerning which Mr. *Glanvil* is pleafed to Confiderat. about Witchcraft, pag. 95, 96. tell us this : "In his return to which he denies not the fuppofition "or poffibility of the thing in general, but clears himfelf by an ap-"peal to the actions of their own children, whom they would not "tax fo feverely. But by Mr. *Glanvils* leave we muft affirm, that

though

though it be a bold affertion, yet it is not true ; for our Saviour
doth abfolutely confute the fuppofition both in the general, and
alfo in reference to himfelf, by fhewing the abfurdities of it, and
that by thefe Arguments.

    1. They fuppofed that the Devils had a Prince or a Ruler that
was able to caft out Devils that were his Subjects, and inferior unto him, to which his anfwer is : *Every Kingdom divided againft it*
felf is brought to defolation, and every City or houfe divided againft
it felf cannot ftand. And if Satan caft out Satan, he is divided
againft himfelf, how fhall then his Kingdom ftand ? Upon which a

Vid. Dr. Ham-
mond in Math.
12. 25, &c.

moft learned Author doth thus paraphrafe : "If any King mean to
"uphold his Kingdom, he will not quarrel and fall out with his
"own Subjects, and caft them out, which are doing him fervice ;
"fuch divifions and civil diffentions as thefe will foon deftroy his
"Kingdom, and therefore cannot probably be affirmed of any pru-
"dent Ruler or Prince. And Satans cafting out Devils which are
"about his bufinefs (poffeffing thofe he would' have poffeft)
"would be fuch a civil diffention as this, and a breach. From
whence he neceffarily concludeth, that either Satan doth not caft
out Satan, or elfe that his Kingdom is divided, and cannot ftand,
but come to defolation. But Satans Kingdom is not deftroyed
nor brought to defolation ; therefore it is not divided againft it
felf, and confequently Satan doth not caft out Satan. Of this

Vid. loc. citat.

paffage *Theophylact* faith : *Quomodo enim Dæmones feipfos ejici-*
unt, quum magis inter fe conveniant ? Satan autem dicitur ad-
verfarius. And to the fame purpofe is that of S. *Chryfoftom : Si*
divifus eft, imbecillior factus eft, & perit : fi autem perit, qualiter
poteft alium projicere ?

    2. Our Saviour faith further : *And if I by Beelzebub caft out*
devils, by whom do your children caft them out ? For as the fore-
cited Author faith : " Why may not I caft out Devils by the Pow-
"er and in the Name of God, as well as your Difciples and Coun-
"try-men, the Jews among you (who being evil are therefore
"more obnoxious to fufpicion of holding correfpondence with Sa-
"tans Kingdom) do, at leaft pretend to do. When they in the
"Name of God go about to caft them out, you affirm it to be the
"Power of God, and fo do I. Why fhould you not believe that
"of me, which you affirm of your own ? *Si expulfio* (faith S. *Hie-*

Vid. Hieron. in
loc.

rom) *Dæmonum in filiis veftris Deo, non Dæmonibus deputatur,*
quare in me idem opus non eandem habeat & caufam ?

    3. Chrift further urgeth : *But if I caft out Devils by the Spirit of*
God, then the Kingdom of God is come upon you or *unto you.* "But
"if it be indeed by the Power of God, that I do all this, then it is
"clear, that although you were not aware of it, yet this is the time
"of the Meffias, whofe Miffion God hath teftified with thefe Mira-
"cles, and would not have done fo, if it had been a falfe Chrift. So
that he feemeth to conclude thus : " You Scribes and Pharifees feem
"to acknowledge, that there are real poffeffions by Devils, and
                                              "that

"that they may be thrown out, either by the Power of God or the
"power of Satan.   But I have shewed the absurdity, that Satan
"doth not cast out the Devils his obedient Subjects that are doing
"his service; and therefore that what I do must be by the fin-
"ger of God, and that must certainly denote unto you, that his
"Kingdom is come, and that I am the Messias.

4. He proceedeth: *Or else how can one enter into a strong mans
house, and spoil his goods? except he first bind the strong man, and
then he will spoil his house.*   "My dispossessing Satan of his goods,
"and turning him out of those whom he possesses, is an argument
"that I have mastered him, and so that I do not use his power, but
"that mine is greater than his, and imployed most against his will,
"and to his damage.   *Quòd enim* (as saith a learned Father) *non*   Chrysost. in loc.
*potest Satanas Satanam ejicere, manifestum ex dictis est : sed quo-
niam neq; alius potest eum ejicere, nisi priùs eum superaverit, omnibus est manifestum : Constituitur ergo quod & anteà, cum mani-
festiori abundantia.   Dicit enim : Tantum absisto ab hoc quòd utar
Diabolo Coadjutore, quòd prælior cum eo, & ligo eum : Et hujus
conjectura est, quòd vasa ejus diripio.   Et sic contrarium ejus quod
illi tentabant dicere, demonstrat.   Illi enim volebant ostendere,
quòd non propriâ virtute ejecit Dæmones.   Ipse autem ostendit, quòd
non solùm Dæmones, sed & eorum Principem ligavit : quod manifestum est ab his quæ facta sunt.   Qualiter enim Principe non victo,
hi qui subjacent Dæmones direpti sunt ?*

5. Lastly he concludeth: *He that is not with me, is against me :
And he that gathereth not with me, scattereth abroad.*   "And it's
"proverbially known (saith Dr. *Hammond*) that he that is not on
"ones side, that brings Forces into the field, and is not for a mans
"assistance, he is certainly for his Enemy, engages against him, doth
"him hurt; and consequently my casting out Devils, shews that I
"am Satans declared Enemy.   By all which arguments he flatly
overthrows the false supposition of the Pharisees.

4. These Tenents do overthrow the chief Articles of the Chri-   *Absurd.* 4.
stian Faith, to wit, the rational and infallible evidence of the Resurrection of Christ in the same individual and numerical body in
which he suffered : and this we shall elucidate in these particular
Considerations.

1. The whole strength of the Christian Religion consists in the
certainty of Christs Resurrection in his true and individual body.
For as the Apostle argueth: *And if Christ be not risen, then is our*   1 Cor. 15. 14,
preaching vain, and your faith is also vain : yea and we are found   15, 16, 17, 18.
*false witnesses of God, because we have testified of God, that he rai-
sed up Christ : whom he raised not up, if so be that the dead rise not.
For if the dead rise not, then is not Christ risen.   And if Christ be
not risen, your faith is vain, ye are yet in your sins.   Then also they
which are fallen asleep in Christ, are perished.   If in this life only
we have hope in Christ, we are of all men most miserable.*   So that
all these sad consequences must needs follow, and the whole Christian

ftian Religion be found a lye, if Chrift be not truly rifen from the
dead.

2. And though the Apoftle do enumerate fufficient Witneffes
of his Refurrection and appearance after death, *and that he was
feen of Cephas, then of the Twelve, after that he was feen of above
five hundred Brethren at once, then of James, then of all the Apoftles, and laftly of himfelf:* Yet all this Cloud of Witneffes will
prove little, but diffolve into vapour, if there were or are either
Angels or Spirits, that in their own or affumed bodies, may appear
in his form, fhape, and likenefs, and to fight and tangibility be in
all properties as his body was, to have flefh and bones, the print
of the nails in the hands and feet, and to eat and drink.

3. That the Apoftles held the opinion, that there was Apparitions and Spirits that did fhew themfelves in any form or likenefs,
is moft plain and evident; for when they faw Chrift walking upon the Sea, they fuppofed it had been a Spirit or Apparition, for
the Greek is φάντασμα, and cryed out.   That is, either being cruelly
affrighted and amazed, their Phantafies did reprefent ftrange
thoughts in their minds : or elfe (which doubtlefs was the truth)
feeing Chrift walking upon the Sea, which they thought was not
poffible for a man to do without finking or drowning, they in
great fear cryed out, and forgetting his former Miracles, did vainly
fuppofe it fome Spirit that had made an apparition in his likenefs.
But it is moft ftrange, that the Difciples that had feen and been eye-
witneffes of fo many Miracles wrought by him during his life, and
thofe that accompanied him at his death, as the renting of the veil
of the Temple from the top to the bottom, and the Earth-quake,
and the renting of the Rocks, and the Darknefs that was over the
Land from the fixth hour unto the ninth; and that after his Refurrection the Graves were opened, and many bodies of Saints that
flept arofe, and came out of the Graves, and went into the holy
City, and appeared unto many, of which they could not be ignorant;
It is (I fay) moft wondrous ftrange, that after all thefe they could
doubt of the verity of his Refurrection, and imagine that it was a
Spirit in his form and likenefs.   And moft efpecially, confidering
that his Sepulchre was made fure, the ftone fealed, and a Watch fet
to attend it, of which they could not be ignorant; and likewife
the certain affirmation and evidence of the two *Maries*, from the
mouth of the Angel, and their own fight who worfhipped him,
and held him by the feet, and *Peters* finding the Sepulchre empty,
and his appearing to the two Difciples that went to *Emmaus*, and
yet for all this at his next appearance, not to be fatisfied, but to be
terrified and affrighted, and to fuppofe they had feen a Spirit, is
beyond all wonder, but that doubtlefs the heavenly Father had fo
ordained it in his infcrutable Wifdom, that the infallible certainty
of his Refurrection might be more evidently and punctually proved.   For at his next appearing, when they were all together, Jefus himfelf ftood in the midft of them, and faid unto them, *Peace*

Mar. 6. 49.

Mat. 27. 51.
Mar. 15. 38.

Mat. 28. 6, 9.
Mar. 16. 1.
Joh. 20. 1.

Luk. 24. 37.

be

be unto you. But they were terrified and affrighted, and suppofed they had feen a Spirit, there the word is πνεῦμα. Now the caufe of this fuppofing that they had feen a Spirit, doubtlefs was becaufe as St. *John* tells us, *That Jefus twice had ftood in the midft of* Joh. 20.19,26. *them, the doors being fhut, becaufe of the Jews,* and therefore they could not poffibly imagine, that he could have a body that could make penetration of dimenfions, not confidering that he had an omnipotent Power, and therefore nothing could be impoffible unto him. Though it may well be conceived to be done without *Vid. Rollor. in* penetration of dimenfions, becaufe by his Almighty Power he might *Joh. 20.* inperceptibly both open and fhut the doors, and fo enter, and fuddenly ftand in the midft of them, and no humane fenfe be able to difcern it. But however it was, the Difciples did not then believe that it was Chrift with his individual body in which he fuffered, but either (as fome of the Fathers believed) that it was his very Spirit that he yielded up upon the Crofs, that appeared in his figure or fhape, that was fo pure, fine, and penetrable, that it could pafs through any Medium, though never fo denfe or folid: or fome other Spirit that affumed his form and fhape, which is far more probable and found. But howfoever it was, they did believe that it was fome Spirit in his likenefs, and not he himfelf, in that very numerical body in which he fuffered, as may be apparently gathered from the words of *Thomas* called *Didymus,* who ftrongly affirmed, faying: *Except I fhall fee in his hands the print of the nails, and put my fingers into the print of the nails, and thruft my hand into his fide, I will not believe.*

4. To the grounds of all thefe doubts our Saviour gives a demonftrative and infallible folution, which we fhall explain in thefe particulars. 1. He doth not at all deny the exiftence or beings of Spirits; neither that Spirits do not, or cannot make vifible apparitions: but doth grant both. 2. But he reftrains thefe apparitions to thofe infeparable properties that belong to Bodies and Spirits, that is, a body (that is to fay an humane body) hath flefh and bones, but a Spirit hath neither, as Chrifts or humane bodies have; and therefore faith a learned Perfon upon the place: *Docet fe non effe* *Rolloc. ubi fupr.* *Spiritum hoc modo: Spiritus, inquit, non habet carnem & offa. Ego verò, ut confpicitis, habeo carnem & offa: Ergo ego non fum Spiritus. Vide igitur ex fenfu & fenfibilibus: fenfu nimirum vifus; fenfu tactus: ex vifibilibus & tractabilibus fe corpus effe non autem Spiritum edocet. Per fenfum enim fides & gignitur & confirmatur.* So that whether Spirits be taken to be corporeal (and fo appear in their own bodies) or to be incorporeal (and fo to appear in affumed bodies) yet are they both to fight, and efpecially to feeling, not as humane bodies are that have flefh and bones. So that however they do, may or can appear (for it muft be confidered in that latitude, elfe our Saviours argument would not be irrefragable and convincing) they to the refiftibility of touching cannot be as flefh and bones are, for they to the fenfe of touching do refift, and

are

are folid, but fo the bodies of Spirits in what appearance foever have not, nor can have, otherwife our Saviours argument falls to the ground, and proves nothing. 3. He confirmeth this by the Difciples own proof of feeling and touching the prints or fcars of the nails in his hands, and the print of the wound in his fide, and thereby manifefteth that it was he himfelf, and the very fame individual body in which he fuffered, by which *Thomas* his great unbelief and doubting was unanfwerably fatisfied, by putting his fingers into or upon the very prints of the nails, and by putting his hand into or upon the wound or fcar upon his fide. And therefore though the fame power that raifed him from the dead, and rouled the fealed ftone from the Sepulchre, could have perfected his body to be without prints or fcars of the wounds; yet did the divine Wifdom referve them, thereby to cure the infidelity of his Difciples, and undeniably to confirm the truth of his Refurrection; to which *Vid. Caten. Auth.* purpofe one faid well: *Ibi ad dubitantium corda fananda, vulne-*
Tho. Aquin. in   *rum funt fervata veftigia.* And the further to eftablifh and fettle
locum. their Faith, he took a piece of a broiled fifh, and of an honeycomb, and eat before them; all which concluded him to have a true body, and that he was not a Spirit: from whence we draw thefe conclufions.

1. That howfoever Spirits do or may appear, they have not, or can have fuch a body, that in refpect of tangibility, is as flefh and bones. For flefh and bones are denfe, folid, and make fenfible refiftance to the touch; but the bodies of Spirits in their apparitions are not, nor can be fo. For as we deny not but there are and may be apparitions in any figure or fhape, yet they can but be as the figures and fhapes in the Clouds, which are often feen, and caufe much wonder, though (we fuppofe) many of them may be rather attributed to the affimilation made in mens fancies, than to their real exiftence in thofe forms or fhapes. So they may be as fhadows, or the fpecies of bodies that we fee near or afar off, or as the images that we behold of our felves and other things in Mirrours or Looking-glaffes: which though without doubt they be not non-entities, for *nullius entis nulla eft operatio*, but thefe affect the fenfes, which is an operation or action; yet do they all eafily yield to the touch, and have no firmnefs nor folidity, as flefh and bones have; and this is all that can be juftly deduced from our Saviours argumentation.

2. Either we muft believe that our Saviours argument is of no force and validity, which is blafphemous and horrid to affirm or imagine, he being the way, the truth, and the life, and in whofe mouth there was found no guile, and thereby overthrow the whole foundation of the Chriftian Religion: or elfe we muft for certain believe that Spirits whenfoever they appear have no fuch folidity or refiftibility as to touch, as flefh and bones have. And confequently that what ftrange things foever we may by fight and touch take to be the apparitions of Spirits, that to touch have the folidity of flefh and
bones,

bones, we muſt conclude that they are not Spirits, but muſt be
ſome other kind of Creatures, of whoſe nature and properties we
are to inquire ; for doubtleſs (as we ſhall manifeſt hereafter)
there are many ſtrange Creatures, that for their rarity or ſtrange
qualities, have been and are miſtaken for the apparition of Spirits.
For the Diſciples doubts muſt ſtill have remained unſatisfied, if
Spirits could appear to have bodies to touch, of that ſolidity that
fleſh and bones are of, and then the truth of our Saviours Reſurre-
ction falls to the ground, and the Chriſtian Faith is vain.

3. Therefore that Demons do appear in the ſhape of Dogs, Cats,
and the like, and do carry the heavy bodies of Witches in the air,
do ſuck upon their bodies, and have carnal copulation with them,
muſt ſuppoſe them to have bodies as ſolid and tangible as fleſh and
bones : and ſo overthrow the main proof of our Saviours Reſurre-
ction, and conſequently the very foundation of the Chriſtian Religion ; *For if Chriſt be not riſen our faith is vain, we are yet in our
ſins, and are of all men moſt miſerable,* as having only hope in this
life, and no further.   And this is ſufficient to ſhew the horrid and
execrable abſurdity of theſe opinions ; which objection Mr. *Glanvil* calls ſpiteful and miſchievous, but durſt not undertake the ſo-
lution, but with a plain ſhuffle leaves and over-runs it, as indeed
being too hard a morſel for his tender teeth.

And if any do object (as we have heard ſome do) that three An-
gels did appear unto *Abraham* in the Plains of *Mamre*, as he ſate ^{Gen. 18. 1, 4. 8.}
in the Tent-door, and did eat and drink, and waſhed their feet,
and therefore that they had fleſh and bones ; to that we return
this reſponſion.

1. It is a very froward and perverſe way of arguing, to make
one place of Scripture to claſh with another, when they ought all
to be expounded according to the Analogy of Faith, and it is a
perfect Harmony which we ought to labour to find out and re-
joyce in.

2. It is no perfect way of arguing from the Diſpenſations in the
time of the Patriarchs and Prophets, to thoſe that God uſeth now
in the time of the Goſpel ; for ſo they might argue that God ſhould
anſwer by *Urim* and *Thummim*, becauſe he did ſo in the time of the
Levitical Prieſthood, but that is now ceaſed, and the Apoſtle tells
us : *God at ſundry times, and in divers manners ſpake in times paſt* Heb. 1. 1, 2.
*unto the Fathers by the Prophets : But in theſe laſt days he hath
ſpoken by his Son unto us.*   So though God did then vouchſafe to
make himſelf manifeſt unto the Patriarchs by the viſible appearance of Angels : yet it is no rational conſequence that he doth ſo
now in theſe days.

3. It is manifeſt, that though they were in number three, yet it *Ibid. v. 17.*
is true that it was Jehovah that appeared unto *Abraham*, and Jehovah ſaid, *ſhall I hide from Abraham that thing which I do.*   Now
we do not find that the word Jehovah is communicable to any
Creature, but only to God himſelf ; and therefore the beſt Expo-
P ſitors

sitors do understand (notwithstanding what *Pererius* doth say to the contrary) that one of them was Christ the second Person in the Trinity, who after was to take humane nature upon him, and therefore did so appear.

4. However these Angels had with them the assistance of a divine and omnipotent Power, which cannot rationally be affirmed of the common and ordinary apparitions of Demons to Witches, and therefore doth conclude nothing against what we have laid down before.

CHAP. VI.

That divers places in Scripture have been mis-translated thereby to uphold this horrid Opinion of the Devils Omnipotency, and the Power of Witches, .when there is not one word that signifieth a familiar Spirit or a Witch in that sense that is vulgarly intended.

COncerning the words in the Hebrew and Greek, that are commonly alledged to prove these things, they have been wrested and drawn to uphold these Tenents by those Translators that had imbibed these Opinions, and so instead of following the true and genuine signification of the words, they haled them to make good a pre-conceived Opinion, and did not simply and plainly render them as they ought to have been. Which hath been observed by divers, especially by *Wierus*, who got the learned *Masius* (a great Hebrician) to interpret them, of which he hath given a full account, which was followed by Mr. *Scot*. As also Mr. *Ady*, who hath perfectly rendred them according to the Translation of *Junius* and *Tremellius*, and likewise Mr. *Wagstaff* hath prettily opened the most of them. So that our attempt here might seem to be superfluous and unnecessary, and may be condemned of arrogance and vain confidence. To which we reply, That it is far from us to compare our selves with those Learned men that were Masters of the Hebrew and Greek Tongues, being in comparison but a Smatterer in those Languagues, yet have in our younger years both studied and taught them to others, and as far as we undertake, we hope we need not fear the censure of the most rigid Critick; intending to note some things that others have omitted, and to handle them to the full, which others have but done briefly. And this we shall prosecute in this order.

1. We shall take the words in the same order as they are recited in *Deuteronomy*, and the first mentioned is in these words: *There shall not be found among you that maketh his son or his daughter to pass*

Wier. l.2. p.89.
A Candle in the dark, p. 10.
The Question of Witchcraft debated, p. 1. &c.
Deut. 18. 10.

pass through the fire. Now here we shall not enter upon that great Dispute, whether they really burned and sacrificed by burning their children unto *Moloch*, or that they only dedicated them to that Idol, by making them pass through the fire; but examine the reasons, why those that practised this kind of Idolatry are ranked amongst the Diviners or Witches, and were to have the same punishment, seeing it is no where mentioned, that these used any kind of Divination at all, and these we conceive to be the chief.

1. The Lord had promised his People to raise them up a Pro- *Reas.* 1. phet from amongst their Brethren like unto *Moses*, and that therefore they should hear him, and not go after other Gods or Idols. And therefore he sent them many and divers Prophets, of whom they were to inquire: so likewise they gave the Priest order to in- Vers. 14, 15. quire by *Urim* and *Thummim*, by which he gave answers, and therefore they were to hearken to his Ordinances, and not to follow after other strange Gods: For the Nations that he cast out had hearkened unto Observers of times and Diviners, but they were not to do so. And though these that caused their children to pass through the fire unto *Moloch*, used not Divinations, yet it was a wicked and abominable Ceremony, and the use and end of it to lead the people to Idolatry, and therefore is reckoned amongst the rest.

2. They are solely condemned, because the end of all their Di- *Reas.* 2. vinations and their other Feats, were only to draw and lead the people to Idolatry, and to serve other Gods. For it is manifest, that all ways and sorts of Divination were not in themselves evil and unlawful, for else Astronomy it self, that foretels the Entrance of the Sun and Moon into such Signs, and when Eclipses will happen, and the like, should be forbidden too, but they were not: so that the chief reason why they were condemned, was *sub ratione finis, non medii*, in regard of the end, and not of the means used, because all their Divinations, and other Arts, Crafts, or Feats, whether performed by natural or artificial means, or otherwise, had still for their chief and principal end the leading of the people unto Idolatry, and the serving of other Gods, which was above all things abominable and hateful unto God, who is a jealous God, and will not give his glory to graven Images. And therefore all Idol-Priests, or those that lead the people to Idolatry, are in the Scripture-sense Witches, Diviners, and the like. And that all Divinations were not forbidden, is most clear from that of *Solomon*, Prov. 16. 10. as *Arias Montanus* translates it: *Divinatio super labiis regis:* and that of *Isaiah*, where the Lord threatneth to take away the staff Isa. 3. 2. and stay of *Jerusalem*, that is, the mighty man, and the man of war, the Judge, the Prophet, and the prudent, *Divinum, sive Sagacem.* For it is the same word, and from the same root בזק *Divinavit:* For as *Avenarius, Schindler*, and others say, *Est verbum medium, nam modò in bonam, modò in malam partem accipitur,* of which *Tremellius* saith this: *Sagacitas, id est, consultissima prudentia in rebus dijudicandis, præcavendis, & veluti addivinandis: nam vox*

Hebræa media est five anceps, quæ non tantùm in malam partem ac-
cipitur, fed etiam in bonam. Therefoe was the Law fo ftrict, that
if any facrificed unto any other God, fave unto the Lord only, he
was utterly to be deftroyed, much more thofe that lead and inci-
ted the people to ferve and facrifice unto other ftrange Gods, were
to be rooted out.

Exod. 22. 20.

2. Is the word we have named before, to wit, קֹסֵם קְסָמִים, *Ko-*
fem Kefamim, Divinans divinationes : which, as we have fhewed
before, was taken *in bonam & malam partem*, and is by the Septuagint fitly rendred μαντευόμεν@ μαντείας, *vaticinans vaticinium*, and
is almoft with all Tranflators rendred in that fenfe and propriety :
fo that we need not complain, that it is one of them that is mif-
tranflated ; but concerning it, we may note thefe things.

1. That there were and are almoft innumerable ways, whereby
men have undertaken to Divine and foretel things to come, fome of
which were by lawful means and ways, as all prudent, fagacious,
and experienced men have done, and may do. Some by vain, trivial, foolifh, and groundlefs ways, as by the flying of birds, their
noife and motion, and fo of beafts, by cafting lots, dice, and the
like, which have no caufality or efficiency in them at all to declare
things to come, but were meerly vain and fuperftitious, with which
the Heathen World doth ftill abound, and they are not yet totally
eradicated from amongft Chriftians. The moft foolifh of which
was this, That when the Philiftins had kept the Ark of the Lord
feven months, they called the Priefts and the Diviners, to know
what to do with it, and they advifed them not to fend it away
empty, but to fend five golden Emerods and five golden Mice, and
to take a new Cart and two Milch-kine, upon which there had
com'd no yoke, and to tye them to the Cart, and to bring their
Calves home from them, and to lay the Ark in the Cart, and the
Jewels of Gold to be put in a Coffer by, thinking that if they
went up towards *Beth-fhemefh* that was the Ifraelites Coaft, that
if they did fo, then it was he that fmote them, otherwife that
it was but a chance that happened unto them. And this in refpect
of the Priefts and Diviners was only a cafual conjecture at Ran-
dom, though God in his Providence did order it according to his
Divine Wifdom for the beft. Like unto this was that mentioned
by the Prophet, a *Confulter with his ftaff*, as alfo that of *Ezekiel :*
For the King of Babylon ftood at the parting of the way, at the head
of the two ways, to ufe divination : he made his arrows bright, he
confulted with images, (Teraphim) he looked in the liver. And
befides thefe there were others that pretended Vifions and Revelations from their Gods or Idols ; but how far either Idols, or Devils, or their Priefts could truly foretel things to come, is very
doubtful and hard to determine, of which we fhall have occafion
to fpeak hereafter.

1 Sam. 6. 1, 2.
3, 7, 8, 9.

Hof. 4. 12.
Ezek. 21. 21.

2. We are to note, that though there were never fo many ways
of Divination ufed, and whether the means ufed to predict by,

were

were natural or supernatural, lawful or unlawful, frivolous and superstitious, or taken upon sound and rational grounds, yet were they all wicked and abominable, because they were used to withdraw the people from those Ordinances that God had appointed to give answers by, and to lead the people to inquire of vain and lying Idols, and their Priests, and thereby to commit Idolatry; and so whatsoever the means were, the end was wicked and damnable.

3. Moreover, what answers soever the Priests forged and gave (for it is manifest, that the Idols gave none at all; *for they had* Psal. 115.4,&c. *mouths and spake not, ears and heard not, eyes and saw not, feet and walked not, neither was there breath in their nostrils*) were nothing but lyes and conjectures of their own devising, and there an Idol in the Hebrew is sometimes styled אליל *nihiluu*, and therefore saith the Prophet: *The Prophets prophesie lyes in my Name, I sent* Jer. 14. 14. *them not, neither have I commanded them. They prophesie unto you a false vision and divination, and a thing of nought, and the deceit of their heart.* Unto which the Apostle alludeth, when he saith: *We know that an Idol is nothing in the world, and that there is* 1 Cor. 8. 4. *none other God but* r. That is, that an Idol taken abstractively, without regard to the matter of which it was made, as gold, silver, stone, wood, or the like, which were natural substances, or respect to the figure or shape which was artificial, and the work of the *Vid. Dr. Ham-* Work-man, it was plainly nothing, and had no real existence as a *mond. in loc.* God or Idol, but only in the Phantasies and minds of the blinded Worshippers; for it neither could truly foretel, nor act any thing of it self, but all that was done, was the lyes and inventions of the Priests that served them, and got their living by that villanous and lying trade. For God by the mouth of his Prophet doth set down the true difference of the true God, that could infallibly foretel and declare things that were to come, from the false Gods and Idols, and doth challenge them in this manner: *Shew the things that are* Isa. 41. 23. *to come hereafter, that we may know that ye are Gods: yea do good or do evil, that we may be dismayed, and behold it together.* From whence it is plain, that the only κριτήριον to distinguish betwixt the Divinations that are given forth by the Spirit of God in his Prophets or Apostles is, that they are plain, certain, and infallible, and the event never faileth to answer the Prediction, but those that are given forth by Satan and his juggling and lying Ministers, are always ambiguous, doubtful, and perplex, and evermore deceive such as trust in them, as was manifest in *Ahab*, when all the false Prophets bade him go up to *Ramoth Gilead*, and prosper, yet there was he slain. And as they never truly foretel things to come, so neither can the Idols do good or evil: all that is, or ever was done, was performed only by the cunning, confederacy, and juggling of the knavish and deceitful Priests; and therefore the Prophet admonisheth Gods people not to be afraid of them; *For they cannot* Jer. 10. 5. *do evil, neither also is it in them to do good.*

4. We

4. We are to note, that if a Sign or Wonder foretold do come to pass, we have no Warrant to ascribe the bringing of it to pass either to Devil or Witch, for the Lord telleth us this: *If there* Deut.13.1,2,3. *arise among you a Prophet or a Dreamer of dreams, and giveth thee a sign or a wonder. And the sign or the wonder come to pass, whereof he spoke unto thee, saying; Let us go after other Gods (which thou hast not known) and let us serve them: Thou shalt not hearken to the words of that Prophet or that Dreamer of dreams: For the Lord your God proveth you, to know whether you love the Lord your God with all your heart, and with all your soul.* So that what Divinations or Predictions soever be foretold by any, or what signs or wonders soever be brought to pass, if the persons that work or foretel them, perswade us to serve other Gods, or go to seduce us to Idolatry, we are not to follow them, but are to know that by them the Lord doth prove us, to try if we love him with all our heart, or not. And if there were no other means to distinguish a true Miracle from a false, yet were this infallibly sufficient to instruct and direct us.

5. We may note, that of all the several sorts of Divinations pretended, and of all the acceptations of this Hebrew word in all the Bible, there is nothing that doth imply any such kind of killing Witch, as is commonly imagined, nor none such as make a visible League with the Devil, nor upon whose bodies he sucketh, or hath carnal copulation with them, nor no such as are really changed into Cats, Hares, Wolves, or Dogs; which was the thing we undertook to prove.

3. The next word we are to consider, is עָנָן, which *Avenarius, Schindlerus, Buxtorfius,* and Mr. *Goodwin* do derive from עָנָן *obnubilavit, nubem obduxit, item præstigiis usus est.* From whence we may note these things.

1. That the most of all the Translators do some render it by one word, and some by another, that no certainty can be gathered from them at all, as though it did signifie divers and many sorts of these kinds of Augury, Divinations, or juggling Feats, when in reason we cannot but suppose that it only comprehended some one sort, and not so many as the Translators do ascribe to it. The Septuagint render it for the most part κληδονιζόμενος, sometimes ἀποφθεγγόμενος, Vid. Polyglot. in loc. and sometimes ὀρνιθοσκοπήσεσθε, which are all of different derivations and significations; some others render it other ways, as, *neq; auspicabimini, neq; observabitis horas, ne vaticinemini, ne ominemini, nec observet somnia & auguria, nec qui exercet Astrologiam, &c.* Now from such a diversity no man is able to draw a positive certainty.

2. They do not keep to one word appropriate to the Hebrew, which if they had not forgotten themselves, they would have done, and not left it uncertain. For *Arias Montanus* in the 19. of *Leviticus, vers.*26. renders it, *neq; præstigiabamini,* and in the 2. of *Isaiah, vers.* 6. translates it, *augures sicut Philistim.* In *Isa.* 57. 3. be

he calleth them *Filii Auguratricis*. And in the 27. of *Jeremiah, v.* 9.
Et ad Augures veſtros. Alſo *Micah* 5. 11. he renders it *Præſtigia-*
tores. Now what great difference there is betwixt any ſort of
Augury, and Juggling, or Leger-de-main; is known to any of in-
different reading. And the reſt of the Tranſlators are far more
wild, and more wide. And *Junius* and *Tremellius*, who of all o-
thers, one might have thought would have been more circumſpect,
yet fall into the ſame incertitude; for in *Deut.* 18. 10. he renders
it *Planetarius*, but in the place before-cited in *Leviticus*, they render it, *neq; utemini præſtigiis*, though in the Margent they mend
it, with this note, *neq; ex nubibus conjicite, vel ne temporis obſer-*
vationi plus æquo tribuite. And *Iſa.* 2. 6. *Et præſtigiatores ſunt*
ut Poliſchtæi.

3. But if there be any certainty in adhering to the primitive
ſignification of the Hebrew root, that plainly intendeth *obnubi-*
lavit, that it is without queſtion moſt ſafe and genuine to tranſlate
it *Planetarius*, to which the moſt learned *Andreas Maſius* (as he is
quoted by *Wierus*) doth incline in theſe words: *Veteres Hebræo-*   *Vid. Jo. Wie-*
rum dicunt id verbum ad eos propriè pertinere, qui temporum mo-   *de mag. Juſ.*
menta ſuperſtitioſè obſervant, atq; alia fauſta rebus gerendis, alia   *c. 1. p. 91.*
infauſta præſcribunt. To which agreeth Mr. *Thomas Goodwin*,   *Of Divin. lib. 4.*
ſaying: "But of all I approve thoſe who derive it from יבנ, a   *cap. 10. p. 183.*
" Cloud, as if the Original ſignified properly a Planetary, or Star-
" gazer.

4. But however thus far there is no word found, that ſignifieth
a Witch in the ſenſe we have laid down, nor any ſuch perſon that
hath a real familiar Spirit, either in them, or attending upon
them, ready viſibly to appear at their beck, this is not yet to be
found out.

4. The next is וּמְנַשֵׁ from the root נָחֵשׁ *nicheſch, auguratus eſt,*
obſervavit, augurium fecit, which our Engliſh Tranſlators have
erroneouſly rendred an Inchanter, which it no way ſignifieth, nor
hath any relation unto, having in the next verſe named a Charmer, as though Inchanter and Charmer were not all one, when the
word plainly (as Mr. *Goodwin* and the learned *Maſius* do confeſs)
importeth an Augur or Sooth-ſayer: That is, ſuch an one, who out
of his own experience draweth obſervations of good or evil to
come: of which we may note theſe things.

1. The moſt of all the Tranſlations given us in the *Plolyglot*, do
render the Hebrew word by *auguratus eſt*, and ſo underſtand it to
be an Augur or Sooth-ſayer, a Conjecturer, or an Obſerver, from
whatſoever it be that he taketh his obſervations, as from the flying
noiſe or motion of birds or beaſts, looking into their entrails, and
the like, and from thence taking upon them to foretel good or
evil to come, or what was hidden and ſecret.

2. The Hebrew word נָחֵשׁ, is by the Septuagint rendred οἰωνισ-
μα, *Augurium, Auſpicium*, that is, an Augur, an Obſerver, or a Conjecturer, which *Luther* tranſlateth: epn be bp Woegell geſchꜩep achte.
And

And in the Low Dutch Bible it is rendred agreeable thereto ; and the French render it *aux Oiseaux*, from the word *Oiseau*, *Avis*, *Volucris* ; and the Italians render it *Auguropista*, which are all to one purpose, and no difference at all , and so the gross mistake of our English Translators is most apparent, that make it to be an Inchanter or Charmer, to which it hath no relation at all.

3. This Hebrew word is taken *in bonam partem* , heedfully to consider, mark, or observe , as *Laban* said , when he laboured to stay *Jacob* from going from him : *I have learned by experience that the Lord hath blessed me for thy sake.* So that though *Labans* heart was not upright toward *Jacob*, nor he a sincere Worshipper of the God of the Jews ; yet so far had the Lord convinced him , by the faithful and industrious service of *Jacob* that he had experienced, and by tryal found that the Lord had blessed him for *Jacob's* sake. And the same word is used , when *Joseph* said : *Is not this the cup wherein my Lord drinketh, and whereby indeed he divineth, or maketh tryal ?* And again: *Know ye not, that such a man as I can certainly divine, or make tryal ?* And though *Pererius* hath made a large Dispute about this matter, and reciteth the Opinions of many Authors concerning it ; yet it is manifest, that *Joseph* knew his Brethren before, and had caused the Cup to be put into *Benjamins* Sack, and that all this was but done in a just and prudent way, the better to prepare his Brethren for his revealing of himself unto them , and so had reference to no unlawful conjecturing at all, though it was plain , that he had the special gift from God of interpreting of Dreams , and foretelling of things that were to come.

Gen. 30. 27.

Gen. 44. 5, 15.

4. It is too hard a task to enumerate all the several ways that the Heathens used, by observation to foretel things to come , and more difficult to declare all the subjects from whence they gathered the signs of their Predictions. The chiefest that the old *Romans* used, were *Augurium quasi Avigerium dictum, vel Avigarium, ab avium scilicet garritu quem auspicantes observabant :* And so *Auspicium, quasi Avispecium, ab avibus spectandis.* And these observations were taken, either from the teeding, flying, or noise of the birds. So they had their *Haruspices, Harioli,* and *Haruspicina,* which was derived *ab haruga, hostia, ab hara in qua concluditur & servatur.*

5. But all these sorts of Observations , Guessings , and Conjectures may be considered these three ways. 1. Some of them are natural, rational, and legal ; as is the Prognostick part of the Art of Medicine, Political Predictions of the change, fall, and ruine of Kingdoms, States, and Empires. Some Civil taken from the course and carriage of men, as when one seeth a rich young Heir that followeth nothing but vice, luxury, and all sorts of debauchery, it is easie to foretel that his end will be beggery and misery. Some from the due observation of beasts and fowls , which live *sub dio*, may easily conjecture the alteration of the weather. And so by observing

serving the change, or colour of the Stars and Planets, the Clouds and Elements, may easily foretel the change of weather. And we find that these predictions from the Signs gathered from natural causes, are not condemned by our Blessed Saviour, who saith: *When it is* *evening, ye say it will be fair weather, for the skie is red. And in* *the morning, it will be foul weather to day, for the skie is red, and* *lowring.* And again: *When ye see a cloud rise out of the West, straight-* *way ye say, there cometh a showre, and so it is. And when ye see* *the South wind blow, ye say, there will be heat, and it cometh to* *pass.* 2. There are some conjectures that are false, groundless, and superstitious, as were, and are all the predictions taken from the feeding, flying or noise of Fowls, or the signs appearing in the intrails of Beasts; for in all such like, there is no connexion betwixt the cause and effect, and they therefore are false and vain, and this was one of the reasons why they were forbidden amongst the Jews. 3. There were some that in regard of their use and end were wicked and Idolatrous, and in this respect all divinations and predictions are wicked and unlawful, if they be used (as was and is yet among the Heathen) to lead the people unto, or confirm them in, the worship of Idols, and false Gods. And from all this it appeareth, that yet we can find no proper or fit word for such a kind of Witch whose existence we have denied and are disproving.

5. The next word in this place of *Deuteronomy* is וּמְכַשֵּׁף *Ume-* *chasscheth*, which our Translators render a Witch, but in what sense or propriety, I think few can conjecture, for it comes from the Hebrew root, כָּשַׁף *Coscheth*, which *Avenarius* rendreth, *Fascinavit*, *effascinavit*, but *Schindlerus* translates it, *Præstigias, maleficia aut* *magiam exercuit, mutavit aliquid naturale ad aspectum oculi, ut a-* *liud appareat quàm est.* And by *Buxtorfius* it is rendred, *Præstigiæ*, and the derivations from it through the whole Old Testament, which is the most certain propriety of the word, as these following considerations will make manifest.

1. That the most of the Translators in rendering this word whether in this place, or in others, have been very inconstant, and one place not agreeing with another, as *Arias Montanus* in this place gives it *maleficus*, but in *Exodus* he makes it, *Præstigiatores*, and in the 22 and 16 of the same Book he makes it *Præstigiatricem*; and in another place where the very same word is used in the Hebrew, he saith of *Manasseh, & Præstigiis vacabat.* And yet in another place, he rendereth the very same word *veneficia.* So uncertain was this learned Man, and so inconsiderate in his versions, wherein he ought to have had a more special care. Now *Tremellius* in all the places named before, doth use the words *Præstigiato-* *rem*, and the words from the same derivation in the Latine, which sheweth certainty and constancy.

2. The most of all the translations in the Polyglott, do render this word doubtful and various: As *maleficus, magus, præstigias faci-* *ens, Incantator*, and the like, which are all dubious, and various,

and

Matth. 16. 2, 3.

Luke 12. 54.

Chap. 7. 11, 22.

Chron. 2. 33. 6.

2 Kings 9. 22.

Q

and no certainty can be produced from them. Only those we call the *Septuagint* do keep close to words of the same signification, deducted all from φάρμακον, which properly doth signifie no more than *venenum*, poison, though the circumstances do manifest that they were but Jugling and Imposture. And the High-Dutch, Low-Dutch, French and Italian translations do all render it with the same uncertainty, so that nothing sure can be drawn from them.

3. But to leave these uncertainties, it is manifest that this word doth signifie as *Burtorsius* and *Schindlerus* do render it, for they are best to be trusted, because they are not guilty of contradiction as the most of the others are; That is, a Jugler, or one that by himself, or the help of his Confederates, doth by sleight of hand, and such like conveyances perform strange things to the astonishment of the beholders. "And therefore doth Mr. *Goodwyn* tell us this: A Witch, "properly a Jugler. The original (he saith) signifieth such a kind of Sor- "cerer, who bewitcheth the senses and minds of men, by changing the "forms of things, making them appear otherwise than indeed they "are. And these Dr. *Willet* saith (speaking of *Pharaohs* Magici- "ans) were *Præstigiatores*, whom we call Juglers, which deceived "mens senses. And though learned *Masius* (speaking of those that "*Nebuchadnezzar* called to interpret his dream) doth make this ob- "jection, that if this word be translated *Præstigiatores*, he doth not "see, *quid illi ad explicandum somnium adferre suâ arte potuissent,* "*quæ tota fallax & delusoria est* : Yet is this of little or no force at all, for the rest that were called, were as well Impostors as these if not more, and the King and those with him knew not certainly (as the event shewed) that they could perform any such matter, but was ignorant of the manner of their delusions and cheats, and was only led by common rumour and belief, grounded upon the vain and lying boasts that such sort of people are apt to give out of them-selves, and the wonders they pretend to perform. So that from his and his Courtiers opinions of either the matter, or manner, of what they pretended to do, will no consequence be drawn, from what they truly could do, because belief and action are two different, things as might be manifested by the vain credulity of the vulgar, that those kind of deceivers can do strange things, but in trial and experiment they are found to be Cheaters and Impo-stors.

4. But that this word doth bear this signification is manifest from the things they performed, for in *Exodus* they are called בְּלָטֵיהֶם, *and they in like manner east down every man his rod and they became serpents* : not that their rods were really transubstantia-ted into true serpents as *Aarons* was, for that could not be done but by an Omnipotent and Divine power, which they had not; It was only done as Juglers, do seemingly, by sleight and cunning, and so had an appearance of true serpents, but were not so indeed ; or else in making a shew to throw down their rods, they secretly conveyed them away and threw down serpents in their stead, as
might

Moses and Aa-ron l. 4. c. 10. p. 191.

Com. upon Exod. c. 7. p. 72.

Chap. 7. 11.

might eafily be done by fleight of hand, as we fhall fhew more fully hereafter.

5. That this is the genuine meaning of this word is manifeft from the circumftances of fome other places duly weighed, and compared together: for one text faith as our Englifh Tranflators have rendered it, *And it came to paff when Joram faw Jehu that he faid, Is it peace Jehu? And he anfwered, What peace, fo long as the whoredoms of thy mother Jezebel, and her witchcrafts are fo many?* Now why they fhould tranflate it witchcrafts, cannot well be imagined, except it were to draw the Scriptures to fpeak according to their preconceived opinions, for the word ufed there is the fame we fpeak of, to wit, וּכְשָׁפֶיהָ, which though *Arias Montanus* rendereth, *& veneficia ejus,* that according to the Latine fignification is but poyfonings, or poyfon making, which doth not intimate Witchcraft in that fenfe that is vulgarly underftood, which *Tremellius* properly renders, *& præftigæ ejus*: and *Luther* renders it by the words **Toeverpe,** and fo doth the Low-Dutch: Though the proper High-Dutch word for *præftigiator,* a Jugler, be **Baeckler,** which is as *Calepin* tells us, that *Præftigiæ funt incantationes, delufiones, cujufmodi funt, quæ manuum quadam dexteritate alia apparent quam reverâ funt.* Now what whoredoms or fornications had *Jezebel* committed? Spiritual whoredomes, and not Carnal ones; for fhe had her felf gone a whoring after Idols, and ftrange gods, and as much as in her lay drew the people of *Ifrael* into the fame whoredoms, and for this it was that fo fearful a judgment fell upon her. And what Witchcrafts (if they muft be fo called) had fhe practifed or followed? Was it any other than in fetting up, maintaining, and defending the Priefts of *Baal* and of the groves, who practifed feveral forts of divination, jugling, impoftures, and delufions, whereby they were feduced and blinded to follow and worfhip the falfe god and Idols? And from this it is plain that all her Witchcrafts were only impoftures and delufions whereby the people were led unto idolatry: and fo the true fignification of this word is a deceiver and an impoftor, and intendeth no other kind of Witchcraft at all. And in the fame fenfe muft the word given by thofe we call the Septuagint which is τὰ φάρμακα αὐτῆς, *Pharmaca vel venena fua,* her poyfons, that is her deceits and delufions that fhe fet up by the lying Divinations, Juglings, and Impoftures of the Priefts, by which the people were feduced, and blinded and poyfoned with the filthy Doctrine and practice of Idol worfhip. And in the fame fenfe muft the words be taken in the Revelation where the words φαρμακεία, φαρμακεύς, φάρμακος are ufed. For the Text faith: *And a mighty Angel took up a ftone like a great milftone, and caft it into the fea, faying; Thus with violence fhall that great City Babylon be thrown down, and fhall be found no more at all.* And after: *For thy merchants were the great men of the earth: For by thy forceries were all nations deceived.* Thefe words are fpoken myftically of fpiritual *Babylon,* in which Antichrift ruleth, who (as the Apoftle

2 Kings 9. 22.

Chap. 21. 8.
22. 51. 9. 21.
18. 23.

Q 2   poftle poſtle ſaith) *ſitteth in the temple of God, and exalteth himſelf againſt all that is called god; and this is he whoſe coming is after the working of Satan, with all power, and ſigns, and lying wonders.* So that it is plain that his working being by lying wonders, his Merchants muſt needs be lyers and decceivers, and it is theſe Sorceries, impoſtures and deluſions by which all Nations are deceived, and cauſed to err: and ſo is no other Witchcraft but meer lying, deluſion and impoſture. And to this purpoſe doth Dr. *Hammond* Paraphraſe it in theſe words; ſpeaking of the deſtruction of *Babylon :* "And "three eminent cauſes (he ſaith) there are of this; Firſt, Luxury "which inriched ſo many Merchants, and made them ſo great. Se- "condly, ſeducing other people to their Idolatries and abominable "courſes by all arts of inſinuation. And thirdly, the perſecuting "and ſlaying of the Apoſtles and other Chriſtians. And in the ſame

Chap. 5. 20.

ſenſe muſt this word alſo be taken in the *Galathians,* which though tranſlated Witchcraft, muſt needs mean impoſture, deceit and deluſion by which people are led from the true Doctrine and Worſhip of Chriſt, to vain and lying Superſtition and Idolatry, and not bodily poyſoning.

6. Thus far we can find no ſuch Hebrew word as ſignifieth any ſuch kind of a Witch as Dr. *Caſaubon,* or Mr. *Glanvill* intend, or labour to prove, and therefore we may proceed to the next. Only we cannot but take notice of one other text, that our Engliſh Tranſlators have erroneouſly rendered, and that is this : where *Samuel* is rebuking *Saul* for ſparing *Agag and the beſt of the ſpoil,* he ſaith, *For rebellion is as the ſin of witchcraft, and ſtubbornneſs is as*

1 Sam. 15. 23.

iniquity and idolatry : Which *Tremellius* renders thus : *Quin ſicut peccatum divinationis eſt rebellio : & ſicut ſuperſtitio & Idola eſt repugnantia.* And *Arias Montanus* gives it thus : *Quia peccatum divinationis eſt rebellio, & mendacium vel Idolum, & Teraphim transgredi,* which both are agreeable to the Hebrew word קסם which ſignifieth properly Divination. So that this place noteth, not rebellion againſt an earthly or temporal King, but againſt the King of Heaven; and to diſobey his command, and to follow our own wills and judgments, and to perſevere therein, is as odious and deteſtable, as to ſet up lying Divinations thereby to follow Idols and falſe gods : for the following the fancies of our own brains, is to follow the divinations of our own counſel, and to make an Idol, and a Teraphim of our own frail, weak and blind judgments, and to forſake the pure and perfect Law of the Lord, which ought to be a lantern to our feet, and a light unto our paths, and is ſpiritual rebellion, even as the divinations of Idol-prieſts and Idol-worſhip were.

6. The next word in this place of *Deuteronomy* is וחבר חבר *utens incantatione, vel incantans incantatione, aut jungens junctiones,* from the root חבר *ſociatus eſt, junctus fuit alteri, copulatus eſt,* for ſo *Avenarius* renders it. And *Schindlerus* ſaith, *Incantator, vel qui conſortium habet cum Dæmonibus, conjurator, qui incantationibus*

*tationibus multa animalia in unum locum consociat vel congregat,
vel ne lædant associat.* From whence we may note thus much:

1. That it primarily signifieth to joyn together, as in that of *Genesis* speaking of the Kings that went to War, *All these were joyned
together in the vale of Siddim, which is the salt sea.* And in ano- Chap. 14. 3.
ther place, *And he coupled the five curtains together;* and in the Exod. 36. 10.
same sense in diverse other places: by all which it appeareth, that
when it is used for incantation or charming, it is because of some
conjunction or coupling together,

2. It is very remarkable that in all the translations in the Polyglot, there is no variance, neither do *Arias Montanus, Burtorfius,*
or *Tremellius* differ at all, and the Greek Translators do agree with
them, who render it, ἐπαίδων ἐπαιδῶ, and the Germane, Low-dutch,
French, and Italian Translators do accord herewithal, and it is
likewise so rendered in *Isa.* 47. 9, 12. and in other places. So that
it is plain it signifieth such as took upon them by strange words and
charms to prevent venemous beasts to hurt, bite or sting, and many other wonderful things; but what they brought to pass, or effected, besides deluding and deceiving of the people and leading
of them to Idolatry, is hard to determine, of which we shall speak in
another place.

3. There are divers opinions concerning this incantation or charming, why it should be accounted conjunction, or association; and
some, as *Schindlerus* and *Bithner,* do judge it is because they associ-
ate or bring together many Serpents or noysom Creatures into one
place, and then destroy them. But this is but a conjecture, for it
is by the best learned strongly disputed on both sides, whether
charms and inchantments can really and truly perform any such effects, and divers instances and examples brought both ways, some
for the affirmative, some for the negative, so that the matter of fact
is not certainly known or granted. Others by association do understand, the league or compact made betwixt the Charmer and the
Devil, by virtue of which such strange things are brought to pass
by them, and of this opinion was Mr. *Perkins* (if that Book of
Witchcraft, that goeth under his name, be truly his) who strengthen-
ing his conceit with that verse in the 58 *Psalm* thought that he had
found out an invincible argument to prove the Compact betwixt
Witches and Devils, and therefore it is necessary and expedient to
examine that text to the bottom to sift out the true translation, and
sense of that place, which we shall do at large as followeth in these
particulars.

1. Our English Translators render it thus, speaking of the deaf
Adder or Asp; *Which will not hearken to the voice of the charmers, charming never so wisely;* and in the margent, or *be the
mer never so cunning,* where they take no notice of the cr
of conjunctions, and consequently none of such a [1]
pact.

2. *Tremellius* gives it thus: *Quæ non auscult*

utentis incantationibus peritissimi, which piece of Latine were very difficult to put into perfect Grammatical construction, because
mussitantium is the plural number, but *utentis* and *peritissimi* are of
the singular, which we shall leave to the censure of Criticks, and
give the marginal note that is there added. *Surdæ*] *id est, calidè
agentis adversus incantamenta, ut sequentia exponuut, nam aurem
utramq; ab ea obturari*, &c. Of the deaf Adder] "That is to say, that
"acteth craftily against the incantations, as the following words do
"expound: For she stoppeth both her ears, By fixing one to the
"earth, and covering, and stopping the other with her tail; and
that *Hierome, Augustine, Cassiodorus*, and others do so expound
the place. Whether this be true of the Asp or not is much to be
doubted, for I find no Author of credit that doth averr it of his
own knowledge, and the thing is very difficult to bring to experiment, and the Psalmist might speak according to vulgar opinion,
of which there was no necessity that it should be literally and certainly true. Further he goes on and saith, *mussitantium*] "That is to
"say, pronouncing their incantations to charm her, whispering and
"very low; which study of charming, lest any should think that
"*David* doth approve of them in this place, he learnedly useth the
"very words of the prohibition, which God laid down *Deut.* 18.
"11. For (he saith) these fascinators in the Hebrew appellati-
"on are said to consociate society, because they apply the society
"of the Devil to their arts.

3. Those we call the Septuagint do render it thus: Ἥτις ἐκ ἀκούσε-
ται φωνῆς ἐπᾳδόντων, φαρμάκι τε φαρμακευομένη παρὰ σοφοῦ. And that which
is ascribed to *Hierome* in the eight Tome of his works printed at *Ba-
sil* 1525, gives two Latine versions to this, the one answering to the
Septuagint which is this: *Quæ non exaudiet vocem incantantium
& venefici incantantis sapienter.* The other according to the Hebrew thus, *Ut non audiat vocem murmurantium, nec incantatoris
incantationes callidas.* So that this maketh the meaning to be,
that the deaf Asp is so cunning in stopping of her ear, that she doth not
hear the voice of those that murmur, and mutter charms, though
it be a Charmer that uttereth the most cunning and powerful
charms: So that here is no regard had to conjoyning or associating
either of Serpents together, or of the society of the Charmer and
the Devil.

4 *Luthers* Translation of this place is remarkable, which is this,
Daß sie nicht höre die stimme des Gauberers, des Beschwerers
der wol beschweren kan. Which in English runs thus, That doth
not hear the voice of the Magicians or Charmers, the Conjurors
Exorcists, that well conjure can. And agreeable to this is the
sion of the Low-Dutch. So that the sense is, that the deaf Asp
her ear against the voice of the Charmers, those that have
it may be that common error and opinion had pre-
learned *Luther*, as doth appear by his exposition
ter to the *Galathians*, that he believed that
the

the Witch, and the Devil were in compact, and ſworn together)and that were moſt cunning in that art. But this doth but in a manner beg the queſtion, not prove it, for all will but amount to this, that the Aſp cannot be charmed, no not by thoſe that have the greateſt skill in the matter of incantation.

5. The French Tranſlators render it thus: *Lequel n'écoute point la voix des enchanteurs, ni du charmeur ſort expert en charmes,* Which will in no point hear the voice of the inchanter, nor of the Charmer that is expert in charms. And this proveth nothing at all of joyning ſocieties, nor of compacts. The Italian verſion giveth it thus, *Accioche non oda la voce de glivoce incantatori, del veneſico incantante incantationi di dotto.* In Engliſh thus, Which doth not hear the voice of the inchanter, of the Witch (if that be the ſignification of the word *veneſico,* a poyſoner) inchanting with the incantation of the learned : And this is moſt near the Hebrew of all the reſt, and beareth thus much, That the Aſp doth not hearken to the voice of the inchanter, of the Charmer which uſeth the charms that were framed and conjoyned by a learned Clerk : ſo that if aſſociating be compriſed, it muſt be underſtood of the framing and joyning of the charms, which doubtleſs was the compoſure of thoſe that were very learned, eſpecially if they work by a natural operation, of which we ſhall diſcourſe hereafter.

6. But now we come to the Hebrew it ſelf, which *Arias Montanus* renders thus, *Quæ non audiet ad vocem muſſitantium : jungentis conjunctiones docti.* And in the margent thus, *Quæ non obtemperabit voce incantantium, incantantis incantationes ſapienter.* Which we may thus Engliſh, Which hearkeneth not to the voice of the mutterers, of the learned joyner of conjunctions. And the other thus ; Which obeyeth not the voice of the Charmers, of the perſon charming charms wiſely. So that it may mean, that the Aſp hearkeneth not to the voice of thoſe that mutter or muſſitate the charms of the Charmer that doth wiſely uſe them, or of him that is a wiſe Charmer. But it is needleſs and improper to make an half period at *muſſitantium,* for then there will be no coherence in Grammatical conſtruction betwixt the former and latter part of the verſe : and therefore according to the order of Grammar, it ſhould be rendered thus : *Quæ non audiet ad vocem muſſitantium incantationes, docti incantantis.* And ſo the meaning is plainly this, that the Aſp doth not hearken to the voice of thoſe that mutter the charms of a learned Charmer. And ſo there is no intimation of aſſociation or compact either one way or another, but it doth meerly imply that the Aſp doth reſiſt and fruſtrate the charms of the mutterers that uſe them, though they be wiſe in the uſing of them, which doubtleſs is the moſt genuine rendring, and the true meaning of the place : or elſe it may be thus aptly tranſlated : *Quæ non audiet ad vocem muſſitantium conjunctiones jungentis docti* ; That is thus, Which hearkeneth not to the voice of thoſe that mutter the Conjunctions of a learned Joyner. So this way the ſenſe will be, that

ſhe

she resisteth the Charms, or Conjunctions of the learned Joyner or
Framer of them, and consequently that it hath not respect, either
to the associating or gathering of the Asps into one place, or an
association or compact betwixt the Charmer and the Devil, which
are both beg'd, and too far fetcht, and cannot be intended properly in this Metaphor. But it (if thus Translated according to *Arias
Montanus*) referreth punctually and properly to the cunning and
wise composure of the letters and words used in the Charm, that
if they had been never so cunningly contrived, or joyned together by
those that had the greatest skill of all others in framing and com-
posing of charms ; yet were they utterly inefficacious against this
kind of Serpent. And so we conclude this, having as yet found no
such Hebrew word as signifieth a Witch in the vulgar sense and
common acceptation.

7. Another word that followeth in this place of *Deuternomy* is
אוֹב שֹׁאֵל *requirens Pythonem*, which what it meaneth is more ob-
scured, and erroneously translated, than any of the rest. And
this our English Translators have ignorantly or wilfully, but
however erroneously rendered in all the places where it is used, to
be one that hath a familiar spirit. From whence note these things.

1. This word, as *Buxtorfius*, *Schindlerus*, and *Avenarius* observe,
hath two significations, the one is, *uter vel lagena*, the other *Python*, and so saith learned *Masius*, *significat vero vox Ob utrem vel
lagenam*; "From whence the Jewish Nation did call those Devils
"which did give answers forth of the parts of Men and Womens
"Bodies, *Ob*, and in the plural number *Oboth*; As it is only once for
Job 32.19. "bottles used in that of *Job, Behold, my belly is as wine that hath
"no vent, it is ready to burst like new bottles.* And to the same purpose speaketh *Schindlerus* in these words : "From thence it seem-
"eth to be called אוֹב *Pytho*, because those that had it, or were
"possessed with it, being puft up with wind, did swell like blown
"bladders, and the unclean spirit being interrogated did forth of their
"bellies give answers of things past, present, and to come, from whence
"also they were called ἐγγαστρίμυθοι, *ventriloqui*, speakers in the belly,
or out of the belly. So that in the sense of these men, it was a Devil or Spirit that spoke in them, as though they had been essentially and substantially possest with a Demon ; so prone were they to
ascribe all things (almost) unto the Devils power, not considering
that they had no other Devil, but that of Imposture and Delusion,
as we shall shew anon with unanswerable arguments.

2. The most or all the translations in the Polyglott do render it
Pythonem, *vel spiritum Pythonis* in this place of *Deuteronomy*, and
other places : But what is to be understood by *Python*, or the Spirit of *Python* is as difficult to find out, as the meaning of the Hebrew word *Ob*, because it must be digged forth of the rubbish of
Grecian lies: For some will have it to be derived from the word
ἀπὸ τῆ πυνθάνεσθαι, *à consulendi & interrogandi usu*. But that they
were called so rather from the Epithete given to *Apollo*, who (as
the

the Poets fabled) did soon after *Deucalions* flood slay the Dragon
Python, πύθων, so called a πύθως *quod est putrescere,* because he was
said to be bred of the putrefaction of the Earth; and so he was
called *Apollo Pythius,* and those that kept the Oracle at *Delphos,*
and gave answers, were called *Pythii vates,* and the Oracles *Oracula Pythia*: as may be seen in *Plutarch, Thucydides,* and *Lucian*:
and *Suidas* and *Hesychius* say, Πύθων *dicebatur etiam Dæmonium cujus afflatu futura prædicebant, & οἱ πύθωνες, è ventre hariolantes:*
From whence *Pythius Apollo* came because of slaying the Dragon,
nam πύθεσθαι *putrescere significat, ut est in his carminibus.*

> ——'Ο δ᾽ ἐπηύξαο φοῖβΘ· Ἀπόλλων,
> Ἐνͅαυθοῖ νῦν πύθευ ἐπὶ χθονὶ ϐωͺτιανοίͅῃ.

> ——*Sic inde precatus* Apollo *est:*
> *Putrescas tellure jacens campoqᵉ feraci.*

And from hence were the Pythian Games instituted:

* Ovid. *Metam. lib. 1.*

> *Neve operis famam posset delere vetustas,*
> *Instituit sacros celebri certamine ludos*
> *Pythia perdomitæ serpentis nomine dictos.*

Though, if we will believe *Natalis Comes* and some others, it was
not a Serpent or Dragon that *Apollo* slew, but a man whose name
was *Python,* and his sirname *Draco,* and from that Victory *Apollo*
was called *Pythius,* and those that kept his Oracle at *Delphos* were
called *Pythios vates,* Pythian Priests, or Diviners of *Python.* So
that all that can be gathered from hence is, that to have the Spirit
of *Python,* was to undertake such Divinations, as the Priests used
at the Pythian Oracle at *Delphos,* and that was no more in truth and
effect, but Cheaters and Impostors.

Mytholog. l. 4. c. 10. p. 36. 362.

3. Those that we call the Septuagint expressing the manner of
the performance of this kind of Imposture do (as *Masius* confesseth,
and is true) constantly call them by the name of ἐγγαστριμύθους, because
they did speak forth of their Breasts or Bellies, that was by turning their voices backwards down their Throats, which some of the
Latines imitating the Greek word have not unfitly called them *ven-
triloquos,* that is, speaking in their Bellies. And that there were
such in ancient times is witnessed by *Plutarch,* who saith, speaking
of the ceasing of Oracles, thus: "That it is alike foolish and
"childish to judge that God himself, as the *Engastrimuthoi,* (that
"is to say, the *Genii* hariolating forth of the Belly) which in
"times past they did call *Eurycleas,* now *Pythonas,* hiding himself
"in the Bodies of the Prophets, and using their mouth and voice
"as instruments, should speak. From whence we may note these
things. 1. That in *Plutarch* time who lived in the Reign of *Tra-
jan,* there were of these persons that could speak (as it were)
forth of their Bellies. 2. That though *Plutarch* was a very learned, sagacious person, yet he either knew not, or else concealed the
manner how these *ventriloquists* performed this speaking in their
Breasts or Bellies, it being nothing but a cheat and artificial imposture, as we shall shew anon, of whom his learned Translator *Adrianus*

*De defect. Ora-
cul. mibi p.
691.*

*In Præfat. de
defect. Oracul.*

R

anus Turnebus, and of these vanities speaketh thus.   "Therefore
" (he saith) we condemn all sorts of Divinations which are not re-
" ceived from the sacred writings, and do judge them to have been
" found out, either by the craftiness of men or the wickedness of
" Devils; but we rejoice to our selves that being Divinely taught,
" we here see far more than the most learned *Plutarch* did, who be-
"held but little light in this his disputation of the defect of Oracles.
3. We may note that these words (that is to say, the *Genii* hariolating forth of the Belly) which we have inclosed in a *Parenthesis*,
are not found in the Greek written by *Plutarch*, but are only added
as the conjecture of *Turnebus*.   4. *Plutarch* doth hold it childish
to believe that God doth hide himself and speak in the belly of
these couzening Diviners, and therein though an Heathen was wiser
than many that profess Christianity now, who believe it to be some
Spirit, when it is nothing but the cunning Imposture of those persons, that by use have learned that artifice of turning their voices
back into their Throats and Breasts.   5. As to matter of fact it is
manifest that in the time of *Plutarch* there were those that practised
this cunning trick thereby to get credit or money by the pretence
of Predictions and Divinations, and such an one doubtless was the
Woman at *Endor*, and the Maid mentioned in the *Acts* of the Apostles, of which we shall speak presently.

Also *Tertullian* a grave Author, affirmeth that he had seen such
Women that were Ventriloquists, from whose secret parts a small

Antiq. lect. 8.
10.

voice was heard as they sate, and did give answers to things asked.
And so *Cælius Rhodiginus* doth write that he often saw a Woman
Ventriloquist at *Rhodes*, and in a City of *Italy* his own Country,
from whose secrets he had often heard a very slender voice of an
unclean Spirit, but very intelligible, tell strangely of things past or
present, but of things to come for the most part uncertain, and
also often vain and lying; which doth plainly demonstrate that it
was but an humane artifice, and a designed Imposture.

Hist. I.
De Mag. In-
fam. c. 14. p.
141.

   " But most notable is that story related by *Wierus* from the mouth
" of his Sons who had it from the mouth of *Adrianus Turnebus*,
" who did openly profess that before-time he had seen at *Paris* a
" crafty fellow very like *Euricles* mentioned by *Aristophanes*, who
" was called *Petrus Brabantius*, who as oft as he would, could
" speak from the lower part of his Body, his Mouth being open, but
' his Lips not moved, and that he did deceive many all over by
" this cunning, which whether it be to be called an art, or exerci-
" tation, or the imposture of the Devil is to be doubted.   And
" further relateth that at *Paris* he deceived a Widow Woman,
" and got her to give him her Daughter in Marriage, who had a
" great Portion; by counterfeiting that his so speaking in his Breast,
" or Belly, was the voice of her deceased Husband, who was in
" Purgatory, and could not be loosed thence, except she gave her
"Daughter in Marriage unto him: By which deceitful knavery
" he got her, and about six Months after, when he had spent all
                                                                    "her

" her Portion, the Wife and Mother-in-law being left, he fled to
" *Lions*: And there hearing that a very rich Merchant was dead, who
" was accounted living a very wicked man, who had gotten his riches
" by right and wrong ; this *Brabantius* goeth to his Son called *Cor-*
" *nutus*, who was walking in a Grove or Orchard behind the
" Church-yard, and intimateth that he was sent to teach him what
" was fit for him to do. But while that he telleth him that he
" ought rather to think of the Soul of his Father, than of his
" Fame, or Death ; upon the suddain while they speak together a
" voice is heard imitating his Father's : Which voice although *Bra-*
" *bantius* did give out of his Belly, yet he did in a wonderful man-
" ner counterfeit to tremble : But *Cornutus* was admonished by this
" voice, into what state his Father was faln by his injustice, and
" with what great torments he was tortured in Purgatory, both for
" his own, and his Sons cause, for that he had left him the Heir of
" so much ill gotten goods, and that he could be freed by no
" means, unless by a just expiation made by the Son, and some con-
" siderable part of his goods distributed to charitable uses unto
" those that stood most need, such as were Christians made Cap-
" tives with the Turks. Whereupon he gave credit to *Brabantius*,
" with whom he discoursed, as a Man that was to be sent by God-
" ly persons to *Constantinople* to redeem the prisoners, and that he was
" sent unto him by Divine Power for the same purpose But *Cor-*
" *nutus*, though a Man no way evil ; and although having heard
" these things, he understood not the deceit : yet notwithstanding
" because of the word, that he should part with so much money,
" made answer that he would consider of it, and willeth *Braban-*
" *tius* to repair the day following to the same place. In the mean
" time being staggered in his thoughts he did much doubt, in re-
" spect of the place, where he had heard the voice, because it was
" shadowy, and dark, and subject to the crafty treacheries of Men,
" and to the Eccho. Therefore the next day he leadeth *Brabanti-*
" *us* into another open plain place, neither troubled with shadows
" nor bushes. Where notwithstanding the same tale was repeated,
" during their discourse, that he had heard before : This also being
" added, that forthwith six thousand Franks should be given to
" *Brabantius*, that three Masses might be said every day, to redeem
" his Father forth of Purgatory ; otherwayes that there could be
" no redemption for him. And thereupon the Son obliged both by
" conscience and religion, although unwillingly, delivers so many
" to the trust of *Brabantius* ; all lawful evidence of the agreement
" and performance being utterly neglected. The Father freed from
" the fire and torments afterwards hath rested quiet, and by speak-
" ing did not trouble the Son any more. But the wretched *Cor-*
" *nutus*, after *Brabantius* was gone, being one time more pleasant
" than wonted, which made his Table-companions much to won-
" der ; and forthwith opening the cause to them inquiring it, he
" was forthwith so derided of all, because that in his judgment he

R 2   " had

" had been fo beguiled, and cheated of his money befides, that
" within few days after he died for plain grief, and fo followed his
" Father to know the truth of that thing of him.

But to make this more plain and certain, we fhall add a Story of
a notable Impoftor, or Ventriloquift, from the teftimony of Mr. *Ady*;
which we have had confirmed from the mouth of fome Courtiers

Hift. 2.   that both faw and knew him, and is this: " It hath been (faith he)
" credibly reported, that there was a Man in the Court, in King
" *James* his days, that could act this impofture fo lively, that he
" could call the King by name, and caufe the King to look round
" about him wondering who it was that called him, whereas he that
" called him ftood before him in his prefence, with his face towards
" him: but after this Impofture was known, the King in his merriment
" would fometimes take occafion by this Impoftor to make fport up-
" on fome of his Courtiers, as for inftance; There was a Knight
" belonging to the Court, whom the King caufed to come before
" him in his private room (where no Man was but the King, and this
" Knight, and the Impoftor) and feigned fome occafion of ferious
" difcourfe with the Knight; but when the King began to fpeak,
" and the Knight bending his attention to the King, fuddenly there
" came a voice as out of another room, calling the Knight by name,
" Sir *John*, Sir *John*, come away Sir *John*; at which the King began
" to frown that any Man fhould be fo unmannerly as to moleft the
" King and him : And ftill liftning to the Kings difcourfe, the voice
" came again, Sir *John*, Sir *John*, come away, and drink off your
" Sack; at that Sir *John* began to fwell with anger, and looked
" into the next rooms to fee who it was that dared to call him fo
" importunately, and could not find out who it was, and having
" chid with whomfoever he found he returned again to the King.
" The King had no fooner begun to fpeak as formerly, but the
" voice came again, Sir *John*, come away, your Sack ftayeth for you.
" At that Sir *John* began to ftamp with madnefs, and looked out,
" and returned feveral times to the King, but could not be quiet
" in his difcourfe with the King, becaufe of the voice that fo often
" troubled him, till the King had fported enough.

Hift. 3.   I my felf alfo have feen a young man about 16 or 17 years of age,
who having learned at School, and having no great mind to his
Book, fell into an Ague; in the declination of which he feemed to
be taken with convulfion-fits, and afterwards to fall into Trances,
and at the laft to fpeak (as with another fmall voice) in his Breaft
or Throat, and pretended to declare unto thofe that were by, what
finful and knavifh tricks they had formerly acted, or what others
were doing in remote places and rooms. So that prefently his
Father and the Family with the neighbourhood were perfwaded
that he was poffeft, and that it was a fpirit that fpoke in him,
which was foon heightned by Popifh reports all over the Countrey.
But there being a Gentleman of great note and underftanding his Kinf-
man caufed him to be fent over unto me, to have mine opinion whe-

ther

ther it were a natural diftemper or not.   The Father and the Boy with an old cunning Woman (the made creature to cry up the certainty of his poffeffion, and the verity of a fpirit (fpeaking in him) came unto me, who all appeared to my judgment and beft reafon fit perfons to act any defigned Impofture. The Father having been one that had lived profufely, and fpent the molt of his means, being fufficiently prophane and irreligious: The Boy by his face appearing to be of a melancholy complexion, and of a fubtile and crafty difpofition; the Woman cunning, who would have forced me to believe whatfoever fhe related, thinking to impofe upon me as fhe had done upon others.   I prefently judged it to be neither natural difeafe, nor fupernatural diftemper, but only knavery and Impofture, and fo made the Woman filent, and told her fhe was a cheater, and deferved due punifhment, and that what fhe told, were the moft of them lies of her own inventing; and told the Father and the Son that I could foon caft forth all the Devils that he was poffeffed with; but then I muft have him in mine own cuftody, and none of them to come near him nor to fpeak with him.   A long time I expected to have feen him in one of his fits, but his Devil was too timerous of my ftern countenance and rough carriage.   Well after they three had confulted together, the Lad by no means could be gotten to ftay with me, no not for that night, nor be prevailed with again to be brought into my prefence; but away they went the Lad riding behind his Father, and when about a quarter of a mile from the Town the Father turned the Horfe to come back again unto me, the Lad leapt from off the Horfe, and run away crying from the Townwards as faft as he could.   They went that night to a Popifh Houfe where were concourfe of people fufficient, and many tales told of the Divinations of the fpirit in the Boy, but not one word either of me or againft me.   Soon after the Gentleman that was of kin to the Boy came over, and I gave him fatisfaction that it was a contrived cheat, and after he returned, he would have prevailed with them to have fent the Boy to me, but by no means could effect it; and fo he never after gave any regard unto them, and foon after it vanifhed to nothing.

I my felf alfo knew a perfon, in the Weft-riding of *Torkfhire, Hift. 4.* who about fome forty years or above, to have made fport, would have put a Coverlet upon him, and then would have made any believe (that knew not the truth) that he had a child with him, he would fo lively have difcourfed with two voices, and have imitated crying and the like.   And alfo the faid perfon under a Coverlet, and coming upon all four would fo exceeding aptly, even to the life, have acted a skirmifh betwixt two Maftiffs, both by grinning, fnarling and all other motions and noife, that divers underftanding perfons have been deceived and verily believed that there were two Maftiffs under the Coverlet, until their eyes have convinced them of their error: So delufive may art or cunning be, being feconded by ufe and agility.

I

Hiſt. 5.

I alſo have ſometimes ſeen a perſon that lived in *Southwark* near *London*, who holding his lips together, and making no ſound or noiſe at all, would notwithſtanding have, by the motion of the muſcles of his face, and the agitation of his head and hands and other geſticulations of his Body, made any of the beholders underſtand, what tune he had modulated in his fancy, which was very ſtrange and pleaſant to behold, and that which I could not have believed if I had not ſeen it.

Stow p. 864.
Hiſt. 6.

We might hereunto add the Story of the pretended ſleeping preacher, who had drawn many into admiration and belief that he did it either by Divine inſpiration or viſion, and yet was but a voluntary cheat and a deluſive Impoſture, as may be ſeen at large in *Stowes* Chronicle. We have been thus tedious in giving theſe examples, that it may appear how improperly Men fly to ſupernatural cauſes to ſolve effects by, that are and may be performed by natural means; and that Men need neither fetch a Devil from Hell nor a Soul from Heaven to ſolve theſe effects that mens cunning, art and craft are able to perform.

4. Next the more fully to explain this we may conſider the place in the *Acts* which is rendred thus, Παιδίσκω τινὰ ἔχυσα πνεῦμα ΠύθωνⒼ of which the learned and judicious *Iſaac Caſaubon* ſaith thus: " An "ancient interpreter readeth πύθωνα, and the *Syrian* verſion re- " dereth *ſpiritum divinationis*. It may be quere'd, ſeeing *Apollo* " underſtood, why S. *Luke* doth uſe the Epithete of him rather t[...] "the proper name: And the reaſon is becauſe the ancients did [...] "the Ventriloquiſts πύθωνας Pythoniſts. And it is plain [...] it "was Divination, that was telling of ſecret things, wheth[...] paſt, "preſent or to come, that the Maid pretended and under[...] : for "the text ſaith, *Which brought her maſters much gain by ſoothſay-* "*ing*; μαντευομένη, that is, by Vaticination. *Beza* in his La[...] tranſla-

Acts 16. 16.

p

Not. in Act. A-
oſt. in loc.

Vid. Beza
not. in loc.

tion ſaith in his Marginal Notes, " That that Spirit of Oracling, " was only an expreſſion alluding to the Idol *Apollo*, which was " called *Python*, and gave anſwers unto them that asked namely, " by the Prieſts that belonged unto it, of which Idol the Poets " feigned many things; ſo that they that had the Impoſture of Divi-

&

A Candle in
the dark, p.
67, 68.

" nation were ſaid by the Heathen to be inſpired by the ſpirit of " *Apollo*. And in this place of the *Acts*, S. *Luke* ſpeaketh after the " common Phraſe of the Heathen, becauſe he delivereth the error " of the common people, but not by what inſtinct the Maid gave " Divinations; for it is certain that under the Mask of that Idol, " the Devil plaid his deluding pranks, and this ſpirit of *Apollo* was " nothing, but as much as to ſay, an Impoſture, or deluding trick " of the Devil practiſed by the Prieſts of *Apollo*. So much ſaith *Be-* " *za*, who plainly expoundeth, " That that Spirit of Divination or " Oracling, was only a Devilish deluding Impoſture, and not a fa- " miliar Devil as many do fondly imagine: And whereas it is " ſaid in the verſe following, that S. *Paul* did caſt that Spirit out of " the Maid, it was, that he by the power of the Goſpel of *Jeſus* re-
"buked

"buked her wickednefs: fo that her Confcience being terrified, fhe
"was either converted, or elfe at the leaft dared not to follow that Luke 7. 47. 8.
2.
"deluding craft of Divination any longer : as when Chrift did caft
"out feven Devils out of *Mary Magdalen*, it is to be underftood
"that he did convert her from many devilifh finful courfes in which
"fhe had walked.   Thus far learned *Beza* and Mr. *Ady*, who both
feem to underftand no other Demon in the cafe than only a crafty
and devilifh Impofture and Cheat, and moft certainly it could be
nothing elfe.

5. But to come to the ftrefs of the bufinefs, thefe things are to
be confidered. 1. Some thought that they were really, and effentially poffeffed with an evil fpirit that did fpeak in them and gave
forth anfwers, and this is the moft common, though moft falfe opinion: which if it were true, it maketh nothing for thofe familiars
that are afcribed to our Witches, for by that they mean a vifible
Devil without them in the fhape of a Dog, a Cat or the like, and
both thefe are equally abfurd and falfe, as we fhall fhew anon.
2. Some thought that an evil fpirit *ab extra* did but work upon
their minds, and fo infpired them with thefe Divinations, and this
feems to have been the opinion of *Plutarch* and fome others of
the Heathen. 3. But others (which is that which we affirm) did
hold that they were but counterfeiting deluding Impoftors, and
what they did was only by Ventriloquy, Jugling and confederacy,
and that all their pretended Divinations and predictions, were nothing but lying conjectures and ambiguous equivocations. But to
open it fully we muft conceive that they did pretend and take upon them to foretel and declare things to come, which notwithftanding were but falfe forgeries and lies: for if they had really
had any certain foreknowledge of things to come, then when *Jehu*
was made King, and in fubtilty pretended to facrifice to *Baal*, and 2 Kings 10.
18, to 26.
fo got together all the Priefts to facrifice, if thefe bafe, lying, cheating Impoftors had really had any fkill in Divination, then they
might have known, that their calling together was not truly to
advance their Idolatry, but to take away their lives; and it may
fafely be concluded that thofe that could not forefee the danger
threatning their own lives, could not truly foretel contingent effects to others; and though the Scripture give us many fuch examples as thefe, yet to efchew prolixity this may fuffice to evince that
all their pretended predictions were nothing but conjectures, or lying forgeries.

And as they did take upon them to foretel things to come, fo
this Woman of *Endor*, and in likelihood the reft, did pretend to do it
by raifing up, or caufing to afcend thofe that were dead to give anfwers of the things demanded.

Now therefore the ftate of the queftion will be, whether this
Woman had really a familiar or fupernatural fpirit that gave her
anfwers, or that fhe raifed fuch an one, or that only fhe was a deceiver and Impoftor that could caft her felf into a Trance, and fo
                                                              fpeak

speak in her Breast, or that she had a place contrived for the purpose (as they had at the Oracle at *Delphos*) by which means she could speak, as in a Bottle or hollow cavity, and had other Confederates sutably fitted to accomplish her design. Here we shall only speak as to the significancy of the words relating to this matter, and shall handle the History of the matter of fact elsewhere : And in the first place we allow and grant that she had the cooperating power of the Devil, in her mind and will, leading her to take upon her to foretel things to come, of which she was utterly ignorant : so that we grant her under a spiritual league with the Devil, as all wicked persons are, but we deny that she had any other familiar spirit, but only the spirit of delusion and Imposture, as we shall make good by these arguments.

1. Because the word sometimes signifieth the persons pretending to be skilful in this sort of Divinations; for so the Woman saith unto *Saul: Behold thou knowest what Saul hath done, how he hath cut off* הָאֹבוֹת *Pythones*, that is, the persons that pretended, and practised that kind of Divination. And so again in that of *Isaiah : And thy voice shall be* כְּאוֹב *sicut Pythonis* as the voice of one that useth this kind of Divination. So that it is clear that the act is ascribed unto, and was performed by the persons practising this couzening craft, and not unto a familiar or Devil.

2. Sometimes it is taken for the means that they pretended they performed it by, as in *Sauls* deluded and despairing sense; for he saith, *Divina quæso mihi* בָּאוֹב *in Pythone, vel per Pythonem, and cause to ascend whom I shall name unto thee.* So that he vainly thought that she could call up, and make to ascend whomsoever he should name, so blind and deluded was he when the spirit of the Lord was departed from him, and was justly delivered up to believe lies, because he had not received the love of the truth.

3. It doth not appear that she had any familiar spirit, or called up any; for the name that is there given her is בַּעֲלַת אוֹב *Dominam Pythonis vel utris*; the Mistriss of the Bottle, or of the Oracle, for *Saul* saith, seek me a Woman that is Mistriss of the Bottle, or of the Oracle, for so it must signifie, if it be genuinely and fitly translated; and his servants tell him, that at *Endor* there is a Woman that was Mistriss of *Ob*, the Bottle or Oracle. For though some translate it *mulier habens Pythonem*, or as *Tremellius, mulier prædita Pythone*, it will but reach thus much, that she was possessed of or had in her power, this *Ob*, Bottle, or Oracle, that could be nothing but the fit contrived place to give answers, as they did at the Oracle. For if they meant that she had a familiar spirit in her Belly, then it was possest of her, more than she could be said to be possest of it. But there is another Text that doth fully agree with this, and will help to explicate it, and is this, speaking of the destruction of *Nineveh* or the Jewish Nation, and the causes of it : *Because of the multitude of the whoredoms of the welfavoured harlot, the Mistriss of Witchcrafts,* בַּעֲלַת כְּשָׁפִים, *Domina vel patrona*, the Mistriss, or Patroness

1 Sam. 28. 9.

Isai. 29. 4.

Nahum 3. 4.

Patroness of Juglings and delusions. So that in propriety of language she of *Endor* is called the Mistriss of *Python* or Oracle, because she could play the couzening feats that belonged unto it.

4. Amongst all the several ways of Idolatry that *Manasseh* set up, or caused to be set up, this is one אוב עשה, *& fecit Pythonem*, or *fecissetq; Pythonem*, he made *Ob*, or *Pytho*; and though Translators have been much perplexed, and hard put to it, to give a signification agreable to their preconceived opinion, yet have they, were it right or wrong, brought it to their minds, though it be utterly false and erroneous; for *Tremellius* renders it, *instituitq; Pythonem*, which though pretty near, yet is altogether short of the propriety, and the most of the rest have run quite Counter; but our English Translators the worst of all others, who give it, *and dealt with a familiar spirit*. When it is plain that this word must be taken in this place, as it is in the third verse of this Chapter, *he made groves, fecitq; lucos*, because the words are both from the same root which is עשה *fecit, confecit, perfecit*, and so it is, and must be taken in other places; and is especially manifest in these. *God said to Noah, make thee an Ark of Gopher wood*, and after, *a window shalt thou make to the Ark*. The Psalmist saith: *But our God is in heaven, he hath done whatsoever he pleased*, and again, *To him who alone doth great wonders*. We might add forty places more, where the word is used that cometh from this root and hath the same punctual signification; so that from hence we may conclude, 1. That *Manasseh* could not make a Devil nor a Spirit, and therefore that the word *Ob* doth not intend nor bear forth any such matter in true and genuine signification. 2. That he could not make a Man or Woman, and therefore the word properly doth signifie neither. 3. That he only could make, and cause to be contrived the Groves, in such as order, at the Idol-Priests might direct, as most fit for them to play their couzening and Jugling feats and delusions in. So he might make or cause to be contrived the μαντήον or place for the Oracle, and prepare those knacks and implements, wherewith and in which place the Diviner might either by him, or her self, or with the help of confederates bring to pass strange things, which they made the blind and ignorant people believe were performed by the God worshipped in and by those Idols, or by Demons and Spirits, or the calling up of the dead. When in truth there was nothing at all performed, but either in raptures, feigned and forced Furies, Trances; and thereby lying predictions and ambiguous equivocations were uttered, whereby the people were deluded and drawn unto Idolatry: or by giving dark and obscure responsions by Ventriloquy, speaking in Bottles, or through hollow Pipes and cavities, whereby they did peep and mutter; or lastly by having knavish confederates hidden in secret, and cunningly contrived places, and suitably habited to personate those that were desired to be raised up, as is most probable in this Woman of *Endor* and the forged and pretended *Samuel*: So

Margin notes:
2 Chron. 33.6.

Gen. 6. 14.16.

Psal. 115. 3.

Id. 136. 4.

that

that there was no Devil nor familiar but a couzening Knave or a
Quean, more crafty than the Demons themselves.

5. That they had no familiar Spirit is manifest, if we consider the
manner how they carried themselves in these cheating actions and
performances, for the Prophet tells us thus: *And when they shall*
say unto you, seek unto האבות *ad Pythones,* unto Oraclers, and
unto Wizards that peep, and mutter ; If they had a familiar Spirit or Demon, what need they chirp, peep, or mutter ? could it not
speak loud and plain enough? Yea doubtless it could if they had
any such, but it is to conceal their own deceit and knavery, lest
it should be found forth and discovered: And without such chirp-
ing and muttering they could neither perform their Jugling delusions, nor keep them from being known, and derided. *Tremellius*
his note upon this place is very remarkable: "The Prophet (saith
"he) aggravateth the heinous crime of those Witches from the va-
"nity of those Divinations, which the very manner of them be-
"trayeth: those seducers have not so much wit, that they dare speak
"to the people the thing they pretend to speak in plain and open
"terms, with an audible clear voice, as they that are Gods Pro-
"phets, who speak the word of God as loud as may be, and as
"plain as they can to the people ; but they chirp in their Bellies,
"and very low in their Throats, like Chickens half out of the
"shells in their hatching.   And this doth plainly declare their
knavery and cheating Juglings. The same Prophet in another place
speaking of the destruction, and bringing low of *Jerusalem* he saith:
And thou shalt be brought down, and shalt speak out of the ground,
and thy speech shall be low out of the dust. And thy voice shall be as
of a Pythonist, *Ob,* or as of an Oracler, *out of the ground, and thy*
speech shall whisper, peep or chirp *out of the dust.* The word there,
and in the former place used is from the root, עפעף *garrivit more*
avium, he hath peeped or chirped like a Bird. Now this doth plainly allude to these kind of Pythonists, or Oraclers, who in giving
their Oracles, or Divinations, did speak out of the ground, that
was from hollow Vaults and Caves contrived on purpose for them to
perform their tricks in, and such a place as this, called in the Hebrew *Ob,* did *Manasseh* make and prepare, *And thy speech shall be*
low out of the dust, like these deceivers who fall into Trances, and
lie upon their faces the better to conceal and hide their Impostures,
and so do change their voice, and mutter as it were out of the
dust, thereby to make the people believe that it is the Demon's or
Spirits voice that speaketh in them, when it is nothing but their
own counterfeiting. And thy voice shall be like one of these Oraclers, out of a low and hollow place, to whisper and chirp like a
Chicken coming forth of the shell, the more to make them believe
that it is the voice of a Spirit, and not their own, by craft and
cunning altered and changed. Upon which place learned and judicious *Calvin* saith thus much: " For the voice of them, who be-
" fore were so lofty and cruel, he compareth to the speech of *Py-*
"*thonists,*

Isai. 8. 19.

Id. 29. 4.

Calvin in loc.

" *thonists,* who when they did utter the Oracles, did give forth I
" know not what kind of murmur, from some low and dark place
" under the earth.

8. The next word that followeth in this place of *Deuteronomy* is
וְיִדְּעֹבִי from the root יָדַע *novit, ſivit, proprie eſt (ut* Avenarius *inquit)
mentis & intellectus.* Which word our Tranſlators (contrary to
their uſual cuſtom) have kept a conſtancy in, and alwaies have rendered a Wizard, a name (as we conjecture) not improper, for we,
in the North of *England,* call ſuch as take upon them to foretel
where things are that have been ſtoln, or to take upon them to help
Men or Goods, that the vain credulity of the common people have
thought to be bewitched, we (I ſay) call them Wiſe Men, or Wiſe
Women, without regard had to the way or means by which they
undertook to perform theſe things. Divers others do render it *ſcio-
lus,* which is proper and conſonant to the former.   The other
Tranſlations that we have either ſeen, or were able to underſtand,
are ſo uncertain, various, wide and wilde, that it were loſt labour
to examine or recite them; and the word Wizard (though a general one) is the moſt proper that we can find.   But we muſt conclude, that hitherto we find no ſuch word as ſignifieth a Witch in
that ſenſe we have allowed, and endeavoured to confute.

9. The laſt word mentioned in this Text of *Deuteronomy,* is a
Necromancer, or one that conſulteth with the dead. Now whether this were ſome ſpecial kind of Divination, or but a compre-
henſion of all the kinds, being but in all their ſeveral ſorts, a leading of the people to inquire of dumb and dead Idols, may be a great
and material queſtion.   And though no Interpreter or Commentator that we have ſeen, read, or do remember, do hint at any ſuch
matter, but ſtill ſtrike upon the common ſtring, that it ſhould
be ſome kind of Magick, whereby they could make the dead appear, and conſult with them: yet notwithſtanding all this we cannot
but propoſe our doubts in theſe reaſons following.

1. *Moſes* in this Text doubtleſly did not ſet down all the particular ſorts of Divinations and Impoſtures uſed amongſt the Heathen, for that had hardly been poſſible, but the chiefeſt kinds of
them.   And this is not rationally probable that he would do it by
a Tautology, or repetition of the ſame thing twice. For inquiring of the dead, or conſulting with them, was intended in the word
Ob, and the Woman of *Endor* ſaid; *Whom ſhall I raiſe up,* or cauſe
to aſcend unto thee? Whereby it appeareth that ſhe pretended
(and alſo *Saul* vainly believed, who ſaid; Divine unto me in or
by *Ob)* that ſhe could cauſe the dead to aſcend, and to have anſwers from them of things to come, as is manifeſt in the Story of the
pretended apparition and prediction of *Samuel.* And ſo this thing
ſhould be twice repeated in this place, which is not probable that
Moſes would have done.

2. He doth not forbid theſe ſeveral ſorts of Divination only becauſe they were evil and unlawful in themſelves (for ſome of them

S 2   might

might be lawful, and performed by natural or artificial means) but becauſe of the thing they all centred in, and the end they all tended to, which was to lead and draw the people to inquire of and to ſerve deaf, dumb and dead Idols. For though the Idols were Silver and Gold, the work of Mens hands, and had eyes and ſaw not, *ears and heard not, feet and walked not, mouths and ſpoke not,* neither was there breath in their Noſtrils : And though the common people could not but know this, for as *Iſaiah* ſaith they were

Iſai. 44. 19.

ſo blinded that, *None conſidereth in his heart, neither is there knowledge or underſtanding to ſay, I have burnt part of it in the fire ; yea alſo I have baked bread with the coals thereof, I have roaſted fleſh and eaten it, and ſhall I make the reſidue thereof an abomination? ſhall I fall down to the ſtock of a tree?* Yet notwithſtanding were they ſo deluded by the crafty Impoſtures, and ſubtile Divinations of all the ſeveral ſorts of theſe Jugling Prieſts, that they ran to ask counſel at theſe dead Idols, who (as they falſly perſwaded the people) did inſpire them, and gave them anſwers, when the Idols were all dead things, and gave no anſwers at all. And this is that conſulting with the dead, that all theſe couzening Prieſts did draw the people unto, and therefore in general is here forbidden.

Iſai. 8. 19.

3. The words of the Prophet, where he ſaith [*And when they ſhall ſay unto you, ſeek unto them that are Ob or Oraclers, and unto wizards that peep, and that mutter: ſhould not a people ſeek unto their God? for the living to the dead?*] do fully prove as much ; for the ſenſe muſt be this : That the people of God ought to ſeek unto their own God, who was and is a true and a living God, and to his Law & Teſtimonies, and not to thoſe peepers and mutterers that ſeek counſel of the dead Idols only ; and doubtleſs this is the true meaning of conſulting the dead.

4. This expoſition includeth no abſurdity, nor bringeth any inconvenience, and is genuine, and not wreſted ; whereas the other doth hurry in a whole heap of moſt abſurd doubts, queſtions and opinions. But if in this expoſition we be Heterodoxal, we crave pardon, and referr it to the judgment of thoſe that are learned, of what perſwaſion ſoever they be.

10. Another word that is uſed in divers places of Scripture is חַרְטֻמִּים, which though *Avenarius* doth derive from חָרַט *ſtilus* & אָשַׁם *clauſit*, yet the learned perſon *Maſius* ſaith, *Eſt autem ali-*

In Dan. c. 1. v. 20. p. 87.

arum nationum vocabulum, ab Hebræa lingua alienum & peregrinum, uſurpatum tamen ab Hebræis. And alſo the judicious *Polanus* is of the ſame opinion, that it is a word ſtrange and foreign from the Hebrew language. The Tranſlators are all ſo various about the proper derivation and ſignification of it, that it were but loſt time and labour to recite them : But it is manifeſt that it was a general word for one that was skilful in all, or divers ſorts of theſe Divinations, and might beſt be conſtantly rendred *magos,* and that for theſe reaſons.

1. It

1. It is the opinion of *Masius* and Mr. *Ady* that it is a general A Candle in the dark, p. 11. word, and signifieth one that hath skill in many of these kind of arts, (if they may be so called) the latter of which saith thus: "It "is taken in the general sense for *magus* a Magician; that hath one, " or all these crafts or Impostures. And the former quoting the sentence of *Rabbi Isaac Natar*, saith: *Hoc nomine vocatos esse ab Hebræis quosvis, qui inter gentes singularem profitebantur sapientiam; præsertim cùm ea ad superstitionem pertineret.*

2. Because that in *Exodus* 7. 13. those that there are called *Hachamim* and *Mechassephim*, that is *sapientes & præstigiatores*, as *Tremellius* renders it, which is most proper and genuine, are there called *Hartummim Mezeraim*, that is *Magos Ægypti*, the Magicians of *Ægypt*; by which it appeareth plainly that it is a general name, and may most properly be rendered a Magician.

3. It may most properly be taken for a Magician, because those that acted before *Pharaoh* are called by that name, and excepting their opposing of *Moses*, and their superstition, it doth not appear that they dealt with unlawful Magick, as we shall prove undeniably hereafter.

11. There is also another word which is used in divers places, which is למשׁ *mussitavit*, he hath muttered, or murmured, and is taken generally for any kind of murmuring for any cause whatsoever, as in this place, *But when David saw that his servants whispered.* And again, *All that hate me, whisper together against me.* 2 Sam. 12. 19 Psal. 41. 7. Isai. 26. 16. And in another place: *Fuderunt submissam orationem*, a low whispering prayer. In which places it is taken for any kind of low speaking, whispering or muttering. Of this we may observe these things.

1. Sometimes by a Metonymie it is taken for a low and modest speech, the art of Oratory, or Eloquence, as *Isaiah* 3. 3. *& intelligentem vel peritum eloquentiæ*, and sometime for an ear-ring *inauris*, as in the 20. verse of the same Chapter.

2. It is also ascribed unto Charmers or Inchanters as in the Psalm, *That doth not hearken unto the voice of the charmers:* Where it is Psal. 58. 6. plain that all Charmers were whisperers and mutterers, but not on the contrary, that all whisperers or mutterers are Charmers.

3. And whereas our English translation readeth it, *Surely the* Ecclef. 10. 11. *serpent will bite without inchantment, and a babler is no better;* It may as well be read, as *Arias Montanus* translates it, *Si mordeat serpens in non susurro, vel absq; susurro*, If the Serpent bite without hissing, or sibilation. And *Schindlerus* to the same purpose: *Si mordebit serpens absq; incantatione, vel murmure, id est sibilo.* And so *Avenarius: Si mordeat serpens absq; susurratione, id est absq; sibilo.* And though *Tremellius*, and the whole troop of Translators do render it, as our English Translators do, yet that will not make sense: for it would inferr that as a Serpent will bite except it be charmed, so will a babler do also. But who ever heard of a bablers being charmed? So that truly considered that cannot be the sense of the place.

But

But if it be taken exactly according to the Hebrew, then the sense runs thus, If the Serpent bite without, or in not hissing, and excellency is not to him that hath a tongue ; that is, The Serpent doth hurt with his biting, without making a noise with his tongue ; but a babler doth make a noise, but effecteth nothing, or speaketh to no purpose.

4. There is another Text in *Jeremy* which is commonly rendered thus: *For behold I will send serpents, cockatrices among you, which will not be charmed, and they shall bite you, saith the Lord.* But it may be as fitly read, To whom there is no hissing, and they shall bite you. And whether way soever it be read, the sense is good ; that is, their enemies shall be so fierce and cruel, that no words can stay or appease their fury ; or that they shall be so sly and cunning, that they shall destroy you, before they speak, or give you warning : And whether way soever it be, there is a pronoun in the Hebrew which is superfluous, a thing that is usual in that language.

Jerem. 8. 17.

5. But if in both places it be taken for charming, yet will it not prove the being and existence of such a kind of Witch, as we have denied and confuted ; nor doth it shew any fit appellation for such a one.

12. Moreover there is another word as much mistaken, and as falsly translated as any of the rest, and that is לַהַט, *Inflammatus est, flamme scebat,* and is understood a shining brightness, as in the Psalm: *Who maketh his Angels spirits: his ministers flaming fire.* And in another place, *& inflammabit eos dies veniens ;* The day cometh that shall burn as an oven. From whence we may note these things.

Psal. 104. 4.

Malach. 4. 1.

1. From this root doth come לַהַט *Flamma,* Metaphorically (as *Schindlerus* saith) a polished and shining piece of Metal, as a Sword or the like. But *Avenarius* tells us, it is, *Flamma rutilans, lamina fulgens & vibrans ;* as, *And he placed at the East of the garden of Eden, Cherubims, and a flaming or bright shining sword which turned every way, to keep the way of the tree of life.* And in another place, *The horseman lifteth up the bright sword, and the glittering spear.* Both places plainly shewing that it signifieth Metal so polished, that when it is shaken in the light, or shining of the Sun, and moved quickly, it doth then glitter like a red and shining flame.

Gen. 3. 24.

Nahum 3. 3.

2. There is also the word ראט *Involvit, velavit, arcanum,* and the like which the vulgar Latin do attribute to *Pharaohs* Magicians, when our translation saith, *And they did in like manner with their inchantments:* It is *& fecerunt similiter per sua arcana,* thinking the word there had been derived from ראט *arcanum,* when it is from לַהַט, *Flamma, lamina ;* a polisht and bright piece of Metal.

3. In all the places of *Exodus* where mention is made of the Magicians, *that they did in like manner with their inchantments,* the word is בְּלַהֲטֵיהֶם which if truly rendered, is this: And they did in like

manner

manner with their bright, glittering lamens, or plates of Metal. And how the Tranſlators could hale it by head and ſhoulder to ſignifie Inchantment, cannot be conjectured ; but becauſe the Magicians are there called, *ſapientes & præſtigiatores,* Wiſe Men and Juglers, they vainly thought that they wrought by a ſecret compact with the Devil, and ſo all muſt be done by their imaginary Witchcraft and inchantment, when it is plain that what they did was by natural Magick, and ſleight of hand, and not by Diabolical Magick at all. But let them ſhew us any one place in all the Old Teſtament, where any of the derivatives from this root, are tranſlated Inchantments, but only in theſe places of *Exodus,* and we will yield the whole cauſe.

13. There is alſo another Text which we have omitted of purpoſe until now, which our Engliſh Tranſlators do, according to their uſual manner, thus render : *And they ſhall ſeek to the Idols, and to the Charmers, and to them that have familiar ſpirits, and to the Wizards :* In which there is a word not uſed in that ſenſe in all the Old Teſtament beſides ; of which place we may note theſe things. Iſai. 19. 3.

1. The word there in doubt is אט, *Lenis, lenitas,* and it oft becometh an Adverb, *leniter, pedetentim.* The root אטל, *leniter inceſſit, Avenarius* ſaith it is not uſed in the plural number, and ſignifieth Inchanters or Diviners, and is האטים which he rendereth *Incantatores ;* becauſe as ſome think they do eaſily and gentilely pronounce their charms.

2. But *Tremellius* doth tranſlate it thus : *Conſulent ſua Idola, & præſtigiatores Pythoneſq; & ariolos :* And giveth this note, Their Idols, that is to ſay Devils, that give them anſwers, eſpecially the Idol of *Latona* in the Town called *Butun* over againſt the Sebenitick mouth of *Nilus,* of which *Herodotus* ſpeaketh : where he expoundeth alſo divers conſultations of theſe Idols. But how or in what ſenſe he holdeth that the Devils gave anſwers, except by the lying Impoſtures of the Prieſts, he doth not ſhew, nor *Herodotus* his Author neither.

3. But this place according to *Arias Montanus* is rendered thus: And they ſhall ſeek unto their vain things or Idols, and to their Diviners (that is this word *Haattim*) and to the Pythoniſts, or Oraclers, and to Wizards. But thoſe we call the Septuagint do render this place very odly, as they ſeldom do elſewhere, which is this : Καὶ ἐπερωτήσωσι τὸς Θεὸς αὐτῶν, ᾗ τὰ ἀγάλματα αὐτῶν, ᾗ τὸς ἐκ τῆς γῆς φωνοῦνται, ᾗ τὸς ἐγγαςειμύθοις that is, *And they ſhall ask their gods, and their images, or painted ſtatues, and thoſe that give their voice forth of the earth, and thoſe that ſpeak in their breaſts or bellies.*

14. There is alſo another word which is אטף, and ſignifieth (as *Avenarius* ſaith) *Sophus, ſapiens in Aſtrologia & in auſpiciis, augur, aruſpex. Rabbi Abraham* thinketh it ſignifieth a Phyſician, who knoweth the alteration of the body, by the pulſe of the arm, or by the urine. And *Schindlerus* tranſlateth it, a Philoſopher, an Aſtronomer and a Phyſician, and ſaith that ſuch were

Aſtronomers

Astronomers and Physicians amongst the *Chaldeans*, of whom *Strabo* saith : "There was a certain habitation appointed in *Babylon* for "their home-bred Philosophers, who were much conversant about "Philosophy, and were called *Chaldeans.* And further, "that "they were Physicians that could judge of the passions of the Body, "which dreams did imitate, by the Pulse and urine. And *Polanus* tells us that it is a *Chaldee* word because it is found no where else but in *Daniel.*

15. Lastly there is one word we shall touch more, and that is חָכְמָה, *sapientia*, the wisdom of Divine and Humane things, Magick or skil in naturall things; and cometh from the root חָכַם, *sapuit mente, sapiens fuit, sapientia præditus est.* And this is that 1 Kings 4. 30. wisdom that is ascribed to *Solomon*, of whom it is said : *And Solomons wisdom excelled the wisdom of all the children of the East countrey, and all the wisdom of Ægypt.*

So have we run over all the words in the Old Testament, that can any way concern this subject, and yet amongst them all there is not one that properly and genuinely, without stretching, wresting or mistranslating, doth, or can signifie any such Witch or Diviner, that can kill or destroy Men or Beasts, or that maketh a visible compact with a Devil, or on whose Body he sucketh, or that they have Carnal Copulation together; or such a Witch as is or can be really changed into a Cat, Dog, or such like, which was the task we undertook in this Chapter. And for the words that are in the New Testament, we shall handle them when we answer the objections made from thence. And therefore we would admonish Mr. *Glanvil*, and all other candid, and sober persons to beware of false or mistranslations, and not to labour to establish dangerous and erroneous tenents upon such slippery and sandy foundations : For one falsity once supposed or taken for good, doth bring a numerous train of absurdities at the heels of it.

CHAP. VII.

Of divers places in the Old Testament that are commonly wrested, and falsly expounded, thereby to prove apparitions, and the power of the Devil and Witches.

THUS far we conceive that we have sufficiently proved, that there is no word in the Old Testament, that in the original Hebrew, can genuinely and truly be translated, that doth signifie such a kind of Witch, whose existence we have denied. And now we shall proceed to answer those places in the Old Testament, that commonly are produced, to prove the Devils or the Witches
power

power in those particulars that we have oppugned. And because the whole stress lyeth upon the true interpretation of those places pretended to prove such matters by, we think it convenient and much conducible to the business in hand, to lay down those rules of interpretation, that the most learned Divines have declared and assigned; and that in these particulars.

1. That truly to understand the Scriptures according to the mind of the Holy Ghost that gave them forth, and by whose inspiration they were indited, it is most necessary that we implore the help of that blessed Spirit, that did reveal them to those that penned them; because, as S. *James* saith: *If any of you lack wisdom, let him ask of God, that giveth to all men liberally, and upbraideth not, and it shall be given him. For every good gift, and every perfect gift is from above, and cometh down from the father of lights, with whom is no variableness, neither shadow of turning.* And it is said of the Disciples of Christ: *Then opened he their understandings, that they might understand the Scriptures.* So that all Men whether wise or unwise, learned or unlearned, have need of the teaching and spirit of Christ to open their understandings to understand the Scriptures; and therefore have all men need of faithful and fervent Prayers, that God may enlighten their minds in the understanding of them; otherwayes, they are but as blind Men, that go without a guide, and so must needs fall into the Ditch of ignorance and error. *James 1. 5,17.* *Luke 24.45.*

2. That a most due and diligent collation and comparison be made of the several versions, with the Fountains and Originals themselves, that so the truth of the translations may be ascertained. For if an error in this point be committed, all the expositions and deductions drawn from thence, must needs be erroneous and vitious.

3. That there be a due comparing of the Antecedents and Consequents in the context, that the purpose, scope, theme, arguments, disposition and method, may be perfectly and maturely considered: otherwise the sleighting or omitting any one of these particular points, the whole place may be mistaken, and an error easily faln into.

4. There must a due and serious consideration be had of the Phrases and manner of speaking; especially in regard of that language it was first written in: For every several language hath its peculiar Phrases and forms of speaking, which may not be proper in another tongue, the not regarding of which may sooner lead into a great deviation from the genuine sense of the place.

5. That there be a most diligent comparing of the place of the Scripture to be explicated, with others of the same similitude or dissimilitude, For oftentimes one Scripture doth unfold and open another, and one Text doth enucleate and make plain another: Which for want of a due comparison one with another, may occasion the mistaking of the true sense of the place that is to be expounded.

T   6. And

6. And chiefly in explicating any place, regard muft be had to the Analogy of Faith : Becaufe the Scriptures do not contradict one another, efpecially in the Articles of Faith, and the chief points neceffary to be believed.

7. There ought a due comparifon be made with the judgments and fentiments of other Interpreters, according as the Apoftle faith : *That no Prophecie of Scripture is of any private interpretation :* Which ought to be rendered as learned *Beza* and Dr. *Hammond* give it : " No Prophecie of Scripture is *propriæ incitationis*, of a Mans own " or proper incitation, motion, or loofing forth ; for fo the Greek is, ¿δίας επιλύσεως ἡ γίνεται. Of which *Beza* gives this learned note. " The " Prophets truly are to be read, but fo that the gift of interpreta- " tion be begged of God, that the fame God may be the Au- " thor and Interpreter of the Prophetical writings. For though a Man have by nature never fo great endowments, of underftanding, judgment and reafon, or have never fo large and ample acquire- ments, or prefume never fo highly to be affifted with the Spirit ; yet his own fingle judgment ought not to be relyed upon in the expofition of the Scriptures ; but he ought to call in to his aid, and to confider the fentiment and opinion of others. For it is obvi- ous into what dangerous errors the *Arrians, Pelagians* and *Anti- trinitarians* of old, and the *Socinians* and *Arminians* of later years have faln, by making their innate notions and the ftrength of natural reafon to be the chief and principal rules for interpreting of the Scriptures by. And there is hardly any one thing that the Scriptures are more againft, or do more condemn, than the too much extolling and idolizing of Humane and Carnal reafon. *Be- caufe the carnal mind* τὸ φρόνημα τῆς σαρκὸς, *is enmity againft God, and is not fubjeĉt to the law of God, neither indeed can be* ; of which *Be- za* faith : *Probatio cur intelligentia carnis fit mors, quia, inquit, Dei eft hoftis.* And again, the Text faith : *For it is written, I will de- ftroy the wifdom of the wife,* τὴν σοφίαν τῶν σοφῶν, *and will bring to no- thing the underftanding of the prudent;* τὴν σύνεσιν τῶν συνετῶν. And again, *Hath not God made foolifh the wifdom of this world?* σοφίαν τῦ κόσμου τούτου. And the words of the Hebrew in that place of *Ifaiah* do fignifie all that height of wifdom or underftanding, that Men either have by Nature, or acquire by Art and Induftry. Neither is it fafe for a Man to rely upon his own fingle acquired parts, be they never fo vaft or great ; becaufe in the moft ages, the moft peftilent Errors and damnable Herefies have been vented and main- tained by Men that were of the greateft acquired endowments. And that it is often as vain to prefume upon having the guidance of the Spirit, as are the other two, is manifeft in the late times of Rebellion and Confufion ; where every Man pretending the Spirit, made fuch wild and extravagant expofitions of the Scriptures, as few ages have known before ; and is ftill kept up by the giddy troop of Fanatical Quakers, and the like.

There is another rule which the learned do ufe, in expounding of
the

2 Pet. I. 20.

Rom. 8. 7.

Ifai. 29. 14.

1 Cor. I. 19, 20.

the Scriptures, which is often either too far extended, or not rightly limited and applied, which is this; That Men in interpreting of the Scriptures should keep close to the literal sense, if it include not an absolute absurdity. Whereby Allegorical, Metaphorical, Mystical and Parabolical Expositions are not only cried down, but by some even abhorred and detested, which thing ought not absolutely and simply to be approved of; and therefore we shall make it plain in some few particulars.

1. In Historical relations of matters of fact, we ought to keep close to the literal meaning, and not to deviate a jot from it, otherwise we should overthrow the best part of the Christian Faith, and destroy the chief foundation of Scripture truths. But notwithstanding this, though we ought to hold to the literal sense in respect of the matter of fact, yet we are not always to be bound to the bare letter in the mood, means or manner of the performance. As may be plain in these examples. 1. It is apparent that our Saviour Christ cured the Man that was born blind, and the means and manner is described: *He spat on the ground and made clay of* John 9. 6, 7. *the spittle, and he anointed the eyes of the blind man with the clay. And said unto him, Go wash in the pool of Siloam (which is by interpretation, Sent.) He went his way therefore and washed, and came seeing.* Now as to the matter of fact, that the Man born blind was cured and had his sight restored, is a truth according to the sense of the letter; and that the manner, which was by spittle and earth made into Clay, and his eyes covered or anointed with it, and washing in the pool of *Siloam*, was also literally true, is manifest. But it were absurd so far to stick to the letter, as to believe that clay, and spittle, and washing in the poole *Siloam*, were true and real natural means to produce that effect; no, that were absurd, and therein the literal sense is not to be followed.

2. Again concerning *Ahab*, thus much is literally true in matter of fact that he was perswaded to go up to *Ramoth-Gilead* 1 Kings 22.19, by his false Prophets in whose mouths there was a lying Spirit. 20, 21, 22, 23. But the manner there declared of sending the lying Spirit into their Mouths, cannot rationally be presumed to be true in a literal sense, but in a Metaphorical; for that the Lord was set on his Throne, and all the Host of Heaven standing by him, on the right-hand and on the left, must needs be a Metaphor taken from an Emperour or a King that sits on his Throne, and all his Counsellors, Princes, Estates and Officers about him, to deliberate and consult what is to be done. And this is the highest and most apt Metaphor that the supream Majesty of Heaven and Earth can be represented by; not that in the literal sense it must be believed to be acted just in that mood and manner, but as the most apposite Metaphor that can be found to express the proceedings of the Heavenly Majesty by, and that for these reasons. 1. God is Infinite and is every where by his Power, Essence and Presence, and therefore cannot literally be said to be comprehended in any

locality, but after a Metaphorical sense and expression. For the Prophet saith: *Do not I fill Heaven and Earth, saith the Lord ?* And as *Solomon* confesseth: *But will God indeed dwell upon the earth ? Behold, the heaven, and heaven of heavens cannot contain thee: how much less this house that I have builded?* 2. God who is only wise, and before whose eyes *all things lie open, and naked,* cannot litterally be said to consult or deliberate, or to ask his creatures how a thing shall be done or brought to pass, because his wisdom is, like himself, Infinite, and need ask counsel of none, and therefore must the manner of the performance of the deceiving of *Ahabs* Prophets needs be Metaphorically understood, and not literally, which is the thing that we would demonstrate.

3. Further concerning Satans afflicting of *Job* in his Goods, Cattels, Children, Servants, and in his own Body, is a real truth literally so taken as to the matter of fact; but the manner of Satans appearing before God, with the Sons of God, cannot without manifest absurdity be understood in a literal sense but in a Metaphorical, that God who is Omnipotent, did command, order, send and limit him, what and how far he was to act. For otherwise *God is light in whom there is no darkness at all, dwelling in the light which no Man can approach unto;* but Satan is bound *in chains of everlasting darkness,* and therefore cannot be said literally to appear in person before God, but by way of a Metaphor. So when the Angel telleth the Virgin *Mary,* that she should conceive in her womb, and she not understanding how that should come to pass, because she had not known Man, the Angel answered, *the Holy Ghost shall come upon thee, and the power of the highest shall overshadow thee.* Though the matter of fact be an undoubted truth, and an Article of Faith, literally so taken; yet the manner of the Holy Ghosts coming upon her, and the power of the highest overshadowing her, cannot be understood in a literal sense, as though it were by that natural and humane way that Men and Women do beget and conceive Children by, for that were horrid and absurd, (as some late prophane, wretched and debauched Atheists have spattered forth) but after a Metaporical sense, and a most mystical meaning. So that it is plain that where a matter of fact may be literally and Historically true, yet the manner how that matter of fact is brought to pass may be, nay must be Metaphorical, or else an absurdity will follow, which was the thing undertaken to be proved.

4. There is nothing more common and usual in Scripture than Metaphors, as when Christ saith, *I am a vine, I am the door of the sheep, I am the living bread that came down from heaven:* Though they be Metaphors, yet the things signified and intended by them are as really and certainly true, as are the Metaphors themselves, and sometimes more true; because sometime the Metaphor is not used for the verity of its existence, but according to the common use and opinion, as *O foolish Galatians who hath bewitched you?* doth
intend

Jerem. 23. 24.
1 Kings 8. 27.

Rom. 15. 27.

1 John 1. 5.
1 Tim. 6. 16.

intend no more but an allusion to vulgar opinion, that held that men might be bewitched and inchanted. And so Christ in the true myftical and spiritual meaning is as really a spiritual vine, door and bread, as there are any of such things in nature, or being. But as that which is Literally and Hiftorically true in matter of fact, or meaning, is not to be deceeded from; so that which is a Metaphor ought not to be turned into a literal thing, nor on the contrary, the literal senfe ought not to be made Metaphorical.

5. Parables are Similitudes taken from things that may have been done, or that are supposed to have been done, and so the thing to which the comparifon is made, or from whence the Similitude is taken, need not always be a thing that hath been performed in all the circumftances and manner thereof; it is sufficient that the thing was poffible, or rationally probable to have been acted, or at leaft supposed so to have been. As for inftance in that Parable, where our Saviour faith: *That thofe that hear his words and do them are* Matth. 7. 24, *like a wife man that built his houfe upon a rock; and he that heareth* 25, 26, 27. *them, and doth them not, is like a foolifh man, that built his houfe upon the fand:* now it is not neceffary that there should be two fuch men, that in matter of fact did after that manner (though there might have been many men before the time of our Saviour that might have done fo) but it was sufficient that the thing from which the comparifon was made, was poffible, rational and probable. But the thing intended by the Parable or Similitude, is alwayes a spiritual truth and certainty. Concerning which learned *Beza* upon the Parable of the Rich Man and *Lazarus* doth give us this remarkable Marginal note: "Although Chrift doth relate an Hiftory, not-"withftanding he writeth spiritual things under Figures, which he "knew were fuitable to our fenfe. For neither are Souls endowed "with Fingers and Eyes, neither do they fuffer thirft, neither have "they mutual conference one with another. Therefore the fum is, "that faithful Souls after they be departed from their Bodies, do "lead a pleafant and bleffed life without the World: And that moft "horrible torments are prepared for the reprobates, which can no "more be conceived by our minds, than the immenfe Glory of "Heaven.

6. As for an Allegory, which is a continuation of a Metaphor, and properly fignifies a figure expreffing one thing by another, from ἀλλ⊙, and ἀγορέω, *enuntio*, and this is very frequently ufed in the Scriptures, as when the Apoftle fpeaking of the two Sons of *Abraham, the one from Hagar a bond woman, the other from Sarah a free woman,* faith: *Thefe things are an Allegorie,* ἅτινα ἀλληγορέμψα, which things do exprefs one thing by another; From whence we may note, 1. That Allegories that tend to edification, keeping the Analogie of Faith, and not perverting or overthrowing the literal fenfe, ought not to be fo much cried down nor condemned, as fome have done both against *Origen* and others. "For the Apoftle here, as *Beza* hath no-"ted, made it manifeft, that he had followed the footfteps of the
Prophet

"Prophet *Isaiah*, who did foretel that the Church was to be con-
"stituted of the Children of *Sarah* that was barren, that is to say
"of those who meerly and spiritually were by Faith to be made
"the Sons of *Abraham*, rather than of *Hagar* that was fruitful,
"even then foretelling the rejection of the Jews, and the vocati-
"on of the Gentiles. 2. Allegories may be used, and the literal sense
nevertheless preserved also for the History is literally true that *Sarah*
and *Hagar* were two living Women, the one *Abrahams* Wife a free
Woman, the other his Servant, and a bond-woman, and yet this
did not hinder but that thereby an Allegory might be used, and
they might, and did signifie and express another thing than what
was meerly contained in the letter.   3. We cannot here but add

De Civitat. Dei lib. 13. *c.* 21. *p.* 404.

the grave and learned opinion of S. *Augustin* upon this very point,
who rejecting the tenent of some that made Paradise and the things
therein contained, meerly corporal, and of some that made it only
spiritual and intelligible, doth run a middle course betwixt these
two extreams, saying thus : "As though Paradise could not be cor-
"poral, because also it might be understood to be spiritual: As
"though therefore there were not two Women *Agar* and *Sarah*,
"and of them two Sons of *Abraham*, one of the bond-woman, the
"other of the free-woman, because the Apostle saith that the two
"Testaments were prefigured in them; or therefore that water had
"flowed from no rock *Moses* smiting, because there by a figurative

Ut supra l. 15. *c.* 27. *p.* 475.

"signification Christ also may be understood, the Apostle saying,
"*and the rock was Christ*.   And after concludeth thus: "These
"and some others may be spoken of understanding Paradise spiritu-
"ally, and may be spoken without contradiction, while notwith-
"standing the most faithful verity of that History may be believed
"in the commendable narration of the things done or performed.
This same opinion this learned Father doth maintain in another
place, where he is speaking of the Ark of *Noah*.

Having premised these rules for the right expounding of the
Scriptures, we shall now come to the main things that we purpose
to handle in this Chapter.   And those that would uphold a kind of
omnipotency in Devils, and maintain their great power in Elementary and Sublunary things, the better to defend the great power
of Witches, do alledge divers places of Scripture, and expound
them in favour of their gross tenents, which now we shall examine
and confute in order as they lie.

1. The first colourable argument that they produce, is from the
Devils or the Serpents tempting and seducing of *Eve*, where labouring to prove the Devils power, and his visible apparition to Witches, and making a compact with them, they pretend that in the seducing of *Eve* he did visibly appear unto her and vocally discourse
with her, and to that purpose that he essentially entred into the
Body of the Serpent, and spoke through its Organs, or that he
assumed the visible and corporeal shape of a Serpent, and so discoursed, and had collocution with her.   To answer which (that
we

we may proceed methodically,) we shall lay down and labour to prove these two positions. 1. That if it were granted that he did it either way, it would be no advantage, thereby to prove the ordinary power of Devils or Witches.

2. That that place of Scripture, if rightly weighed and considered, will no way make it rationally appear, that the Devil performed that temptation any other way but only mentally; and that the History there in the manner and circumstances of it, is only to be Allegorically and Metaphorically expounded. And as to the first, if it were granted it proves nothing to the purpose, for the power of Devils or Witches, as these two Arguments will sufficiently evince.

1. From no single instance or particular proposition, can ever a *Argum.* 1. general conclusion be rightly drawn by any known and certain rules of Reason or Logick; for *Syllogizari non est ex particulari*, is known to any Tyronist in that Art. But if Satan for that once should have entred into the natural Serpent, or assumed his shape, it is a deceivable and vitious way of arguing, that therefore he hath such a power over all Bodies at all times when he pleaseth, or that he can assume what shape he please, and therefore it certainly and rationally concludeth nothing of validity.

2. In the temptation of *Eve*, there was something more extraor- *Argum.* 2. dinary than can be assigned in any other temptation whatsoever, except that of Christ. And therefore was there a more peculiar and extraordinary dispensation from God in that case than can be shewed in any others but that of Christ. For now it pleaseth God in his merciful providence, so to order and overrule the malice of his hellish will, and to restrain and bridle his envious nature, that though his will be never so wicked, yet is he kept in his chains of darkness, *and God will not suffer his people to be tempted, above* 1 Cor. 10. 13. *what they are able, but will with the temptation also make way to escape that they may be able to bear it.* Now *Adam* and *Eve* were in an extraordinary condition in respect of the Saints of God in this life, or of any other persons, and there was a more high and greater end in the providence of God in ordering and permitting of that temptation than there is or can be in any others, but that of Christ: And therefore from what the Lord permitted, and ordered to do in that temptation, or the liberty that he might grant him to exert his own power then, will no argument rationally follow that he can commonly and at his pleasure perform as much, and so maketh no firm conclusion.

And as concerning that place of Scripture in the third of *Genesis* the great and learned Jesuit *Pererius* doth undertake with tooth and nail to prove that it is to be literally interpreted, and that Satan did really enter into the Body of the natural Serpent, and spoke in him, or through his Organs; and laboureth (though in vain) to enervate and overthrow the strong arguments of his Brother in Religion, the most learned Cardinal *Cajetan*, Where he rejecteth the *Vid. Pererii* opinion of those that hold that the Devil did assume a Body in *Comment. in locum.* the

the shape of a Serpent; because (he saith) that Satan presently after the temptation ended must have deposited and put off the assumed body, but that the Serpent was after in Paradise, and therefore that he did not act it in an assumed Body. Therefore we shall also pass by that opinion of assuming of Bodies, as being a meer groundless figment invented by the dreaming Schoolmen, as we shall demonstrate hereafter. But to proceed in order, We shall first shew that the place must of necessity admit of an Allegory or Metaphor. And secondly, we shall lay down positive Arguments to shew the absurdity and impossibility of the Devils speaking in the Serpent, or by his Organs. And thirdly, we shall answer all objections that are material, and that in these particulars.

1. The thing that in that History is to be taken literally, is that *Eve* was tempted and seduced; but the instrument by which it was done, the manner and circumstances, must of necessity have an Allegorical or Metaphorical interpretation, otherwise no sense rationally can be made of the place at all.

Vid. Diaig. Discourses of Spirits and Devils. Dialog. 4. p. 110.

2. " There can no blame of the action be imputed to Satan himself, if neither absolutely, nor properly, nor Historically, nor " Allegorically, nor Metaphorically, nor no ways else he be named " in that very History of *Evahs* tentation, wherein the action it self " with the several circumstances is fully and plainly expressed. For " the action especially being so weighty a matter, was necessary to " be known in every point : And therefore it is not to be doubted, " but that the History concerning the same is so exactly set forth, " with every circumstance, as that any Man may be able to judge of " the principal Actors therein at the least. So then, although the " Devil in that History, be neither absolutely, nor Historically, " nor properly expressed by name; yet must we acknowledge him " to be therein Allegorically and Metaphorically set forth at the " least, or otherways impose no blame upon him at all concerning " the action. And therefore must *Pererius* needs confess a Metaphor in the place, or else the Devil cannot be made an actor in the business.

3. It was no natural Serpent but the Devil himself Metaphorically set forth by the name of a Serpent, who gave the onset upon *Evah* in that tentation. For by Allegories and Metaphors there is evermore some other thing meant than that which is literally expressed. And that this is so, is thus proved. If in that action the Devil himself be not Historically and properly, but Allegorically and Metaphorically, called a Serpent, because he is most crafty and subtile; then undoubtedly the objection of a natural Serpent to be used in that action is very inconvenient : But the antecedent is true, and therefore also the consequent.

4. The antecedent to that Hypothetical Argument foregoing is easily thus proved: It is an accustomed thing in the Sacred Scriptures to use the names of other creatures in setting forth to our sense the Intellectual Creatures themselves. Hereupon it is that in

the

the *Apocalypse* the Devil (by a perpetual Allegory) is called a Dra- Apoc. 12. 3,4, gon or Serpent: And therefore in this History of *Evahs* tentation, 5. by the like perpetual Allegory he is also called a Serpent. For no Id. 20. 2. Man can be so absurd and foolish to think that the Devil lite- rally and properly (in that of the Revelation) can be called a Dra- gon or Serpent; but only in a Metaphorical and Mystical sense, and therefore must in right reason be taken so in that place of *Genesis*; for one part of Scripture is alwaies best interpreted by another.

5. Again how can *Judah* literally *be a lions whelp*, or *Christ* Gen. 49. 9. *called the lion of the tribe of Judah*? must it needs be understood Revel. 5. 5. that Christ either assumed the shape of a natural Lion, or that he entred into the Body of a natural Lion? Surely not, that were most absurd to think or believe. Even so must it be accounted most absurd and abominable for *Pererius* or any other to fancy that the Devil may not properly enough in an Allegory, or My- stical sense be called a Serpent in that action of tempting of *Evah*, without either assuming the shape of a Serpent, or entring into the Body of a natural one. I appeal to all rational Men to judge if the absurdities of both be not alike, if barely and literally taken. But this being one of *Cajetans* Arguments, was too hard a morsel for the teeth of *Pererius*; and therefore he past it over without an answer. Further when our Saviour called the Pharisees, and Sad- ducees *a generation of vipers*, must any Man be so extreamly mad Matth. 3. 7. as to believe that naturally and literally they were generated by vipers? Must it not be understood that they were called so from their poysonous and wicked minds, by way of Metaphor? Yes surely: and so is the Devil called a Serpent by a Metaphor, or else literally so taken, both appellations are equally absurd. And let *Pe- rerius* or any other unloose this knot.

6. How can the Devil be a very *murtherer from the beginning*, John 8. 44. (which he is Mystically so considered) if he had no hand in the de- stroying of *Evah* and *Adam* both in Souls and Bodies? But if by the Serpent the Devil was not understood, then he stands acquit- ted, and was not guilty of the murdering *Adam* and *Evah* both in Souls and Bodies. But we must affirm that all learned and ratio- nal Divines, whether antient, middle or modern, that have expound- ed or commented upon that place, do by the words of our Saviour *calling Satan a murderer from the beginning*, understand the mur- dering of *Adam* and *Evah* both in Souls and Bodies; And we dare referr all those that have taken, or will take pains to examine them upon that piece of Scripture, that they shall be found as we have averred.

7. *Moses* (in that action) doth purposely intitle the Devil by the name of a Serpent, because (by his effectual creeping into the interiour senses, as also by infecting Mens minds with venomous perswasions) he doth very lively represent the nature, disposition and qualities of the venemous Serpent. And in this same sense was the Apostle jealous over the *Corinthians*, lest as *that Serpent* ὁ ὄφις 2 Cor. 11. 3.

(which

(which muft neceffarily be underftood of Satan by a Metaphor of that Serpent) *beguiled Evah through his fubtilty,* fo they might by the cunning of Satan in his falfe Apoftles *have their minds corrupted from the fimplicity that is in Chrift.*

8. The Serpent that tempted *Evah* in Paradife, is there faid to be *more fubtile than every beaft of the field,* the which (if the writing of fuch as have obferved and defcribed the nature of all forts of animals be true) cannot be avouched truly of the natural Serpent. For there are many other creatures more fubtil than the Serpent. And therefore it muft needs be underftood of the fpiritual Serpent, that is, Satan who is (indeed) the old Serpent.

9. *Mofes* doth therefore purpofely attribute fpeech to the Serpent which tempted *Evah,* to the end we (knowing by experience that fpeech cannot properly accord with a natural Serpent) might the rather be induced to believe that the fame muft metaphorically be underftood of the fpiritual Serpent. For we may with like abfurdity imagine that *the olive, the fig, the Vine-trees and the Bramble* did vocally and articulately fpeak one to another; as to fuppofe that either the Serpent, or the Devil in the Serpent did ufe an articulate voice and difcourfe unto *Evah;* they are both alike credible, and both alike abfurd.

Judg. 9. 7, 8, 9, 10, &c.

10. The punifhment inflicted by God, hath no conveniency at all with the natural, but with the fpiritual and myftical Serpent, which is the Devil. For neither can the going upon her belly, nor the eating of duft be any punifhment at all to the natural Serpent, becaufe (before the tentation) both thofe properties were peculiarly allotted unto her, fhe taking her name from her creeping condition, for *Serpens* is derived *à ferpendo,* and in the Hebrew fhe is called וֶמֶשׂ *reptile à* רֶמֶשׂ, *reptavit, ferpfit.* Neither yet may we imagine that the faid Serpent being of fome better form before the tentation, was then (by the juft judgment of God) transformed into a viler proportion, property or fhape, fhe being in the Hiftory of the Creation accompted amongft the creeping Creatures.

11. *Mofes* maketh no mention at all of the Serpents coming to *Evah* about that bufinefs, nor of her departure after the action, nor of any one fpecial property whereby fhe might be effentially difcerned to be (indeed) a true natural Serpent, nor of any manner of amaze, or fuddain fear in *Evah* at her fuddain approach and extraordinary fpeech: whereas yet *Mofes* himfelf was afterwards horribly afraid at the only fight of a Serpent. And where it is faid,

Exod. 4. 3.

Thou art curfed above all the beafts in the field; there the very bruit beafts (to the horrible confufion of Satan) are preferred before him; not in abfolute power, but in an efpecial regard of that happy continuance and timely confervation of their original nature. For, the beafts of the field, they do not forgo any heavenly happinefs, which they never yet had: But they continue forth their courfe in that felf fame primary eftate they took at the firft. But Satan is accurfed becaufe he kept not his firft eftate, but

but fell from it, and therefore is worse than the beasts of the field. Neither is this way of expounding the Scriptures metaphorically, where the literal sense includeth an apparent absurdity, either singular or novel, for both Antients and Moderns have allowed the same course, for S. *Augustine* saith : "When any thing is found in "the Scriptures which cannot (without an absurdity) be possibly "interpreted literally, That thing without doubt is spoken fi- "guratively, and must receive some other signification, than the "bare letter doth seem to import.   And *Gregory* saith : When the "order of the History becometh defective of it self in the literal "sense, then some mystical sense as it were with wide open doors "doth offer it self : yea and that mystical sense must be received in- "stead of the literal sense it self.   And therefore (saith *Peter Mar-* "*tyr*) that malediction or curse which the Lord did cast on the Ser- "pent, must be Allegorically understood of the Devil, and those "things which seem properly to accord to the Serpent indeed, must "metaphorically be transferred to Satan understood in the Serpent. So then, by all the premises it is very apparent, that it was the De- vil himself, and no natural Serpent, who set upon *Evah* in that ten- tation, he being only metaphorically set forth by the name of a Serpent : And therefore had no need in that action essentially to assume to himself the Body of a natural Serpent, for the better ac- complishment of the intended business.

Aug. ad Gen. lib. 11. cap. 1.

Greg. in Moral.

Pet. Martyr in Gen. 3. 1.

The next is to lay down positive Arguments to prove that the Devil did not essentially enter into the body of the Serpent and if he did, that yet neither he by himself, nor the Serpent, and he joyned, could thereby make any articulate sound or discourse. Which if the Devil in the Serpent be supposed (as it is) to perform any such matter, it must be either by considering him as an incorporeal or as a corporeal creature, but we affirm he could perform neither way, and that for these reasons.

1. If the Devil be considered as an incorporeal creature simply *Reas.* 1. and absolutely, then it will follow, that he cannot act upon any corporeal matter, because an incorporael substance can make no con- tact upon a body, unless it were it self corporael ; for, *quicquid agit, agit per contactum, vel mediatum, vel immediatum.* But both those are caused by the touch of one body upon another, as when ones hand by touching a straw doth immediately move it forth of its place, or else by blowing doth remove it, which is by the media- tion of the air ; but that which is meerly incorporeal can perform neither : Because that which is meerly incorporeal hath no super- ficies, whereby to touch the body to be removed ; and therefore can make no motion of it at all ; and where there is no motion, there can be no alteration, and consequently no speech nor articu- lation at all.   And therefore the Devil (if incorporeal) could not move the Organs of the Serpent at all, and so could not speak in the Serpent nor move his organs, if they had been fit for articulate prolation, which they were not.   Which was the thing required to be proved.   V 2   2. The

2. The Serpent by the ordinance of God in the Creation was specificated to an inarticulate sound, not to an articulate: but the Devil neither hath, nor ever had any power to change and overturn the course of Gods ordination in nature, and therefore hath not power, nor never had to make the Serpent speak articulately; for that were to overthrow the inviolable order of God set in the Creation, which no man of sound judgment did ever aver that the Devil could do,

3. I take it to be one of the most firm maximes that ever the Schools had, that, _immateriale non agit in materiale, nisi eminenter ut Deus:_ Therefore that the Devil being incorporeal and immaterial cannot act upon that which is material, as was the body of the Serpent, unless he had had a super-eminent and omnipotent power, which were blasphemous to attribute unto him, therefore could he not articulately speak in the Serpent unto _Evah_, because immaterial, and had no omnipotent power.

4. And if he be conceived to be corporeal, then he could either of himself speak articulately and audibly, or else not. And if he could do so of himself, then to enter into the Serpent was needless and superfluous. And if he could not, then the entring into the Serpent would not have contributed that faculty unto him, and so neither way he could have performed it; For a Frog creeping into the body of a Man, will not cause the Frog to speak, though it may make some noise or croaking.

5. Though the Devil being corporeal should have entred into the body of the Serpent, yet by no motion that could be made with or upon her organs, could they have been framed to have uttered an articulate sound, because they were not fitted for that purpose, but only to have made a sibilation or hissing. For in Instruments that are artificial, the several sounds and tunes made by them, are but agreeable to the diversity of their parts and their several compactions; so an Harp cannot (when made) be ordered to give forth a sound like a Trumpet, nor the noise of a pair of Organs; nor on the contrary: and if any of their parts be wanting, defective or broken, then the orderly sound and Musick is spoyled. And though a Parret or Paraquet may by vocal and external teaching be brought to learn and speak some words; yet it is not by the teachers entring into her belly, but by his outward, vocal teaching, whereby her senses and phantasie are audibly wrought upon, and not otherwise. But in this action ascribed unto Satan, he is not supposed to be able to speak articulately, nor to have taught the Serpent vocally and audibly, which if he could have done, yet were not her organs capable of any such matter; and therefore it had been more subtilty in the Devil rather to have chosen a Parret than a serpent.

The only objection worth taking notice of that _Pererius_ bringeth against the sound and reasonable opinion of learned _Cajetan_, is this: That _Adam_ and _Evah_ being in the state of innocency could not be

wrought

wrought upon by an interiour tentation, becaufe that neither the
fenfitive appetite nor the phantafie were corrupted ; and therefore
Satan could not internally work upon them, and therefore that
the whole tentation muft be extrinfecal. To which we return this
fufficient reply.

1. It is but a bare affertion without any proof at all, and he doth *Reaf. 1.*
but only fhelter it under the authority of S. *Auftin* and *Gregory*,
whofe authority in many other matters he doth often reject when
they agree not with his humour, end and intereft. But however
they are but *teftimonia humana* ; and we are not to regard what
the Men are that do fpeak, fo much as to confider the weight and
reafon of what they do fpeak.

2. He proceeds upon falfe fuppofition, that the fenfitive appetite *Reaf. 2.*
and confequently the Phantafie could not be wrought upon nor
drawn, but by a fenfible and exteriour object, when it is manifeft that the fight of the Serpent alone could not have ftirred the
fenfitive appetite ; for it is rationally to be fuppofed as a certainty
that *Evah* had feen the Serpent before that time. Neither could it
be the difcourfe with the Serpent, barely confidered as difcourfe,
that could have moved it ; for it is certain fhe had heard, and had
had audible, vocal and articulate difcourfe with her Husband before this time of the temptation. Neither could it be the beholding
of the tree of knowledge of good and evil, for by the difcourfe
it appeareth that fhe had before feen it, and it is probable that the tentation was in the view of it, and its fpecies that appeared to her eye
of the faid tree was the fame that it was before. So that it will be
moft manifeft that the tentation took effect from the ftrong lie that
Satan told her, *that their eyes fhould be opened and they fhould be as
Gods knowing good and evil*, and fo her deception was firft made
in her mind and underftanding, and thereby the will was drawn,
and the fenfitive appetite moved, whereupon *fhe took of the fruit
of the tree, and did eat*. And this may far more reafonably be
thought to be brought to pafs by a mental difcourfe and internal motions, than by external collocution, which muft firft work upon
the mind, before that the Phantafie or fenfitive appetite could at
all be moved or drawn.

3. If the tentation had been this way that *Pererius* fuppofeth it, *Reaf. 3.*
our firft parents could not have been feduced ; for Satans argument
lay not to perfwade *Evah*, that it was pleafant for the tafte or good
for the Stomach thereby to have drawn the fenfitive appetite and
the Phantafie, but that it was good and profitable to make them
wife, *and to be like Gods*, whereby he infnared her underftanding
with a fallacious and lying argument, thus framed, as learned
Pifcator lays it down: "That thing which will bring you Divine *vid. is. Pifcat.*
"Wifdom and Felicity, that thing ye ought to make ufe of. But *in locum.*
"the eating of this fruit can bring you Divine Wifdom and Felicity:
"Therefore the eating of the fruit of this tree, ye ought to make
"ufe of. And fo the feduction was not at all by the fenfitive appetite

petite (that could receive no more benefit by it than by the other fruits in the Garden) but by her underſtanding being blinded with a ſpecious ſhew of an apparent (not a real) benefit, and thereby her will drawn and led to put forth her hand, and to eat. And therefore conſequently there was no need at all of an extrinſecal tentation, which might and was brought to paſs by an intrinſick diſcourſe, working upon her underſtanding.

Reaſ. 4.   4. Surely if *Pererius* had been aware of the many inconveniences that this opinion of his doth hurry along with it, he would never have plunged himſelf into a Labyrinth of ſuch perplexities; ſome of which we ſhall here enumerate and ſo conclude.   1. If this opinion were true, that *Evah* by reaſon of her perfection in the ſtate of innocency could not be tempted nor ſeduced, but only by an external way and means : Then how could it come to paſs that the Angels in their Primitive Eſtate, which was as perfect (if not more) than that of *Evahs*, were without a tempter or any external means drawn unto that defection, who left their eſtate and ſtation, and abode not in the truth ?   2. How could the defection have been ſo general (for multitudes of them fell) if they had not had ſome way or means to have communicated their cogitations and intentions one to another?   For though we are not able to apprehend the manner how they diſcourſe or commune one with another, yet it muſt be taken for a truth that they have a way and means to manifeſt their cogitations one to another, which is ſome way Analogous to that which we call ſpeech or diſcourſe.   Therefore con-
Tom. 3. l. 3. c. cerning this point doth learned and judicious *Zanchy* thus conclude.
19. p. 156. "Therefore (he ſaith) that which we do by a ſenſible voice, the "ſame thing the Angels and bleſſed Souls in Heaven, yea the De-"vils in the infernal pit, and in the air, do perform, but without "voice, in a ſpiritual manner.   3. If this opinion were true, then the bleſſed Souls, being diveſted from their Bodies, ſhould not have a communion one with another, nor ſhould jointly praiſe and glorifie God together, which were falſe and abſurd; and therefore
Hieronym. in the learned Father ſaid well : "It is to be holden ſtedfaſtly that
Job. c. 24. "the offices of the Heavenly Hoaſt are by no means performed in ſi-"lence; ſeeing, we may read that the Angelical powers before the
Tom. 7. p. 187. "Throne of the Lord, do ſound forth his praiſe with unwearied
2 Cor. 2. 11. "voices.   4. The ſleights and ſubtil machinations (for he hath his Νοήματα or devices) of Satans Kingdom could not be carried on, if he had not a way and means to communicate them to the reſt of the Crew of his inferiour Fiends, and therefore doth plainly prove that there is a way of hidden, Myſtical and Spiritual diſcourſe, which the Devil might, and did repreſent to the mind and underſtanding of *Evah*, whereby ſhe was ſeduced, and that there was no need of a vocal and audible interlocution; and ſo much in anſwer to his objection.

The next place of Scripture that is commonly brought and urged thereby to prove the great power of Devils and Witches, is that
of

of *Pharaohs* Magicians, from whence they argue thus: If the Magicians of *Pharaoh* were able by the power and affiftance of the Devil to change their Rods into Serpents, the Water into Blood, and to produce Frogs; Why may not Witches, by the power and affiftance of the Devil, change themfelves and other things into ftrange and feveral fhapes, and do the reft of the feats that are afcribed unto them?

But though this be but *petitio prineipii*, a begging of the queftion, that by the affiftance of the Devil they did thefe things, which is neither fuppofed nor granted, but ought firft to have been proved; And though in the cafe of hardening *Pharaohs* heart, there might be (and was) a peculiar difpenfation from God at that time: yet it will not follow that God doth always difpenfe with, and give the Devil leave to operate the like things; and fo nothing firmly can be concluded from hence. Yet (I fay) though thefe be fo, we fhall pretermit them, and come to the full opening and difcuffion of the matter; and that in thefe two particulars. 1. How far the Devils power and affiftance did concurr with the actions and performances. 2. And wherein he did not concurr nor act at all.

1. We fhall grant that *Pharaoh* and the Magicians being Idolaters, and worfhippers of falfe gods, their ends were principally to magnifie the power of their Idols, and to manifeft that their fuppofed gods could work, and bring to pafs as ftrange miracles or wonders as *Mofes* and *Aaron* could perform by the affiftance of the God of the Hebrews; and in refpect of this end they had all the affiftance that Satan and his dark kingdom of Angels could afford them in a fpiritual and hellifh way; *for he is the Prince of the power of the air that worketh in the children of difobedience*, for fuch were both *Pharaoh* and his Magicians. And to this purpofe doth the Apoftle tell us, fpeaking of falfe and feducing teachers: *That they were like Jannes and Jambres that withftood Mofes, in their refifting of the truth:* fo that the Magicians of *Pharaoh* were condemned for refifting the truth of that meffage that *Mofes* and *Aaron* brought, and of thofe real miracles that they performed; and fo in refpect of the wicked end they aimed at, they were affifted with the power and concurrence of the Devil, and in that refpect only were his fervants and inftruments.

But as for the fecond particular, namely, the efficient caufes and means of the producing of thofe thing that the Magicians did, we affirm they were performed by the power of nature and art, and that the Devil was no efficient caufe of their production, and that by thefe irrefragable arguments.

1. Thofe that affirm that the Devil did or can produce fuch ftrange effects, do alfo acknowledge, that what he performeth in natural and elementary Bodies, is done by applying natural agents to natural and fit patients, which do truly bring to pafs fuch ftrange effects, and that he doth no more, but only make the local application of them.

Ephef. 2. 2.

2 *Tim.* 3. 8.

Argum. 1.

them. From whence it muſt neceſſarily follow that the effects flow
from natural agents, and ſo no cauſality at all can be aſcribed unto
him, except that fictitious one of being *cauſa ſine qua non*, which is
as much as no cauſe. And beſides that, there is no proof that he
maketh this local application; for if he be incorporeal, then it is
ſimply impoſſible that he ſhould perform any ſuch matter; and however, a man by natural power and means, if he know the fit and apt
actives and paſſives, may perform them himſelf, and ſo his aſſiſtance
is needleſs; and we have never yet met with any argument that bore
any convincing force that might induce us to believe that he is ſo
great a Naturaliſt.

Argum. 2.   2. There are many perſons that think themſelves no mean ſharers
in the moſt ſorts of learning, and others that are very ſtrait laced in
their pretended zeal for godlineſs, and in deteſting the works of Satan,
that even ſtartle and ſhew an abhorrency at the word Magick, if it
be but once named, as though there were no Magick but what is
diabolical, or that which they call diabolical were any other way
evil but only in the end and uſe: for there are many plants and minerals, that though poyſonous, are yet notwithſtanding good in reſpect of their Creation, and the good uſes that may be made of them,
as to kill noxious animals that are hurtful unto man. But if any
forth of malice and wickedneſs ſhould uſe them to poyſon and deſtroy Men and Women, it were wicked, and diabolical in the end
and uſe, yet were the means lawful and natural. So whatſoever the
Devil may do by wicked Men, his inſtruments, in leading and drawing them to make uſe of the great *magnalia naturæ*, to work ſtrange
wonders by, thereby to confirm Idolatry and Superſtition, or to reſiſt the truth and ſuch deviliſh ends, though the end and uſe may be
wicked and diabolical, yet the efficient cauſe is natural and lawful. And therefore we can find no other ground or reaſon of dividing Magick into natural and Diabolical, but only that they differ
in the end and uſe: for otherwiſe they both work by a natural a-
gency and means, ſeeing the Devil can do nothing above or contrary
to that courſe that God hath ſet in nature. Therefore may men do
without the aid of Devils whatſoever they can do, ſeeing they have
no advantage over us, but operate only by applying active things
to paſſive, like as Men do: And therefore ſaid that moſt learned
Philoſopher, Chymiſt and Mathematician, our Countreyman *Roger*
Bacon, excellent well in theſe words: *non igitur oportet nos uti*
magicis illuſionibus cum poteſtas Philoſophiæ doceat operari quod ſuffi-
cit. Therefore are thoſe men that came from the Eaſt to worſhip
Chriſt called Magicians, not becauſe that great knowledge they
had in the ſecrets of Nature was Diabolical or unlawful; for the
name of a Magician was honourable and laudable, until Knaves and
Impoſtors made uſe of it to cheat and couzen withal, and for wicked and ungodly ends; but becauſe they had made uſe of it for the
glory of God, and the good of mankind, therefore were they Magicians in the genuine, and beſt ſenſe, as working by lawful and natural

De ſecret. oper.
Art. & natur.
c. 5.

tural means, and to a good end: when the Magicians of *Pharaoh*
may be called Cacomagicians, becauſe they uſed the good and excellent cauſes and agents of nature to a wicked and Diabolical end,
namely to reſiſt the truth: and ſo the only difference of Magick is
from the end and uſes, and not from the cauſes or agents, that are
both natural. So what theſe Magicians of *Pharaoh* did, though it
were ſtrange and wonderful, yet was it meerly by natural means
and cauſes; and yet being for a wicked end was therefore Diaboli-
cal. So *Jacob* when he *ſet the pilled rods with white ſtreakes in*   Gen. 30. 37,
them, before the flocks in the gutters in the watering troughs, that   38, 39. &c.
when the Rams and the Sheep came up to drink, and coupled toge-
ther, they might conceive and bring forth ring-ſtreaked, ſpeckled
and ſpotted young ones; It came ſo to paſs, and is confeſſed by Pere-
rius himſelf, and the moſt of learned Expoſitors upon that place,
to be from natural cauſes, and was a ſtrange feat of natural Magick; but not evil becauſe not directed to a wicked end: but that
of *Pharaohs* though wrought likewiſe by a natural cauſes (for ſo it
was whether aſcribed to the Devil, that can but work by natural
means, or not) was wicked and Diabolical; becauſe they did it to
reſiſt *Moſes* and *Aaron* the meſſengers of the Lord Jehovah.

3. The moſt or all the learned Expoſitors that have Commented   *Argum.* 3.
upon this place of *Exodus* (as may be ſeen in Dr. *Willets Hexapla*
and divers other learned Authors) though they attribute theſe
things done by the Magicians to the power and aſſiſtance of Satan,
yet in the manner they do acknowledge them not to be done really
and in truth, but only in ſhew and appearance. But what they
mean by ſhew and appearance is not ſo eaſie to find out and determine; for if by it they mean, that they did it as Juglers and thoſe
that uſe the Art of Legierdemane do, that is, by ſhewing one thing,
and then by nimble ſleight and agility convey it away, and ſud-
dainly and unperceiveably ſubſtitute another thing in its place,
which they perform by leading the Eyes and attentions of the ſpe-
ctators another way with ſtaring and uſing of ſtrange and inſigni-
ficant words, then we ſhould be ſoon accorded, for ſo they might
probably and eaſily have been performed as we ſhall prove anon,
but this is not the thing they mean or intend. But ſome do mean
that the Devil did only deceive the Phantaſie and imagination of
the beholders, in cauſing them to imagine and believe that the rods
were changed into Serpents, when they were not changed at all,
but only their imaginations deceived in thinking them to be Serpents when they were but only rods, as melancholy perſons, Men
in Feavers, Phrenſies and Maniacal diſtempers do often think and
affirm that they ſee ſtrange things when they ſee no ſuch things externally, but the Phantaſie is only deceived with the ſpecies and
images of thoſe things within. This might be granted if *Pharaoh*
and all the Spectators could be proved to be Men under thoſe fore-
named diſtempers and the like, though yet that might (and doth
often) come to paſs from meer natural cauſes, where the Devil hath

X   nothing

nothing to do at all. But the beholders of these actions of the Magicians are neither proved, nor can rationally be supposed to be Men under any such distempers; but must be understood to be Men of several constitutions, tempers, and of sound health, and therefore not any way capable of any such illusions, neither could the Devil in a moment have so vitiated their imaginations, which we affirm he can no ways do, except the humours, fumes and spirits in the Body be first altered by natural causes, which cannot be done instantaneously, and if it could, then it would follow that no Man could certainly tell, when he were deceived in his imagination, when not: neither could it be, (as some imagine,) by casting a mist before their Eyes; for though Christ did hold the two Disciples Eyes going from *Emaus*, that they did not know him, it were blasphemous to think that Satan could do so also. And a mist casting before their Eyes might make them to see more dimly and confusedly, and cause things to appear greater than they were, but not to make one thing seem a quite contrary. But it never was yet proved that Satan could do such a thing, and what was never proved, may safely and rationally be denied. Some do suppose that the Devil did cloath or cover the Magicians rods with some such vestment of an airy substance, as might make the rods appear to the eye like Serpents; but this is as groundless a whimsey as any of the rest, and as it hath no proof, so it needs no confutation.

Argum. 4.   4. But to come more close to the matter, it is most plain and perspicuous that what they did was meerly by Art, or by Art and Nature joined with it; for if we may trust any thing to propriety of the words (as we have proved sufficiently before) they are called *mechassephim*, *præstigiatores*, that is Juglers, such as by sleight of hand, and nimble conveyance, could perform strange and wonderful things, and after they are called *Hartummin*, that is, Magicians, such as had skill in natural things, and by knowing their causes, and making due and timely application of them to passives that were suitable, could produce wonderful effects. And if we seriously consider the few things that they performed, they might easily be brought to pass by Legerdemain alone. For, as for holding a rod in their hands, and seeming to throw it down upon the ground, how soon might they throw down an artificial Serpent in its stead, and immediately and unperceivedly make conveyance of the rod? And if it be thought difficult or impossible, I shall unriddle the mystery, as I have sometimes seen it performed, and is but

Hist. 1.   thus. The Jugler that is to perform this feat is usually provided before-hand with a wiar so twined and wrested, that it may be pressed together with the little finger in the ball of the hand, and when let loose it will extend it self, like a spring, and make a pretty motion upon a Table, this is fitted with a suitable head, and a piece of neatly painted linnen, perfectly resembling a Serpent, with Eyes and all. This thus fitted he holdeth in his right hand betwixt his little finger, and the ball of his hand, then with his left hand

hand he taketh up a little white rod that he hath upon the Table, with which he maketh people believe he performeth all his feats: And then telling them a Story to amuse them, that he will like *Moses* and *Aaron*, transform that rod into a Serpent, then he presently beginneth to stare about him, and to utter some strange and nonsensical words, as though he were invoking some Spirit or Goblin, and so immediately conveyeth the rod either into his lap (if sitting) or into his sleeve (if standing) and then lets loose the Serpent forth of his right hand with pushing it forward, that what with the wiar, and the nimble motion of his hand, he maketh it to move a pretty space upon the Table, which he continueth, while offering with the one hand to catch it by the neck, he nimbly with the other puts it forward, and turneth it by touching the tail, and the mean while hisseth so cunningly, that the by-standers think it is the Serpent it self, and presently whips it up and conveys it into his pocket. And such a trick as this well acted might make *Pharaoh* and the beholders believe there was as much done, as *Moses* and *Aaron* did, but only that *Aarons* rod swallowed up their Serpents, or his Serpent theirs, which they might easily excuse. As for the changing water into blood, and the producing of Frogs, they were so easy to be done after the same manner, that they need not any particular explication, for by this the manner of their performance may most easily be understood. Though I once saw a Gentleman that was much delighted with these kind of tricks, and did himself play them admirable well, who performed it with a living Snake, that he had got for one of his Children to keep in a box; for in this North-Countrey they are plentiful, and are also innoxious; and it might have deceived a very wary person. So that it is very foolish and absurd to bring in a Demon from Hell, or an Angel from Heaven, or a Soul from above, to solve a thing that seems strange and uncouth, by, when the craft and cunning of Men (if duely considered and examined) are sufficient to perform the same, and much more.

5. And in this place of *Exodus* where our Translators, say: *and the Magicians did so* or in like manner *with their inchantments*, the word being *Belahatehem* ought to have been rendered, *suis laminis* (as we have proved before) that is, with their bright plates of metal, for the word doth not signifie Inchantments in any one place in all the Old Testament. And if truth and reason may bear any sway at all, it must be understood that they were deeply skilled in natural and lawful Magick (as generally the *Ægyptians* and the Eastern Nations were) though they did use and apply it to an evil end, namely the resisting the power of Gods miracles wrought by *Moses* and *Aaron*: and so by this word *suis laminis*, with their plates of Metal must be understood, Metalline bright plates framed under certain fit constellations, and insculped with certain figures, by which naturally (without any Diabolical assistance) they did perform strange things, and made the shapes of some things appear to the eye.

Argum. 5.

eye. And though we may be derided and laughed to scorn by the
ignorant, or hardly taxed and censured by the greatest part of Cy-
nical Criticks, yet we cannot so far stifle the knowledge of our
own brains, nor be so cowardly in maintaining the truth, but we
must assert, That anciently there hath been a certain lawful art,
whereby some sorts of metals might be mixed together under a due
constellation, and after ingraven in like fit Planetary times with
sundry figures, that would naturally work strange things; And this
piece of learning though it may justly be numbred amongst the
Desiderata, and might very well have been placed in the Catalogue of the *Deperdita* of *Pancirollus*; yet was it well known unto the ancient Magicians, and by them often with happy success
put into practise; And amongst those many noble attempts of that
most learned and experienced (though much condemned) person
Paracelsus, this part of learning was not the least, that he laboured
to restore. The truth of which we thus prove.

Argum. 1. 1. That there have been formerly in the World many such like planetary Sigills or Talismans, (as the *Persians* called them) is manifest
from the authority of divers Authors of good credit and account.
For the learned and most acute *Julius Scaliger* relateth this saying:

Exerc. 196. 6. "The novelty of this History also may sharpen the wits of the studi-
p. 637. "ous. In the Books of the *Arabick Ægyptians* (he saith) it is thus

Hist. 1. "written. That *Hameth Ben Thaulon* the Governour of *Ægypt* for
"the *Arabians* did command that a certain leaden Image or Picture
"of a Crocodile, which was found in the ground-work of a certain
"Temple, should be melted in the fire. From which time the inha-
"bitants did complain, that those Countreys were more infested
"with Crocodiles than before, against whose mischief that Image
"had been framed, and buried there by the more ancient Wisemen

Cap. 2. "or Magicians. *Junctin*, upon the Sphear of *Sacrobosco*, affirms
"that his Master who was a *Carmelite*, named *Julianus Ristorius à*

Hist. 2. "*Prato*, one that was not any whit superstitious, was intreated by
"a Friend of his to make one of these Images for the cure of the
"Cramp, which he was very much subject to. This learned Man
"resenting his Friends sufferings, taught him the manner how to

Vid. Gaffarel "make one: so that he, not content to make only one, made di-
Unheard of "vers of them when the Moon was in the Sign *Cancer*; and that
curiosities, p. "with so good success, and with such certainty, as that he im-
165. &c. "mediately found the benefit of it. *Confecit* (saith he) *plures ima-*
"*gines, pro se, & amicis suis : quibus effectis, unam pro se accepit,*
"*& liberatus est.* The same he reports of a certain Florentine, a
"very Pious Man, who made one of these Talismans, for to
"drive away the *Gnats*, which he did with good success. *Nico-*
"*laus Florentinus,* (saith he) *Vir religiosus fecit in una constella-*
"*tione annulum ad expellendum culices, quas vulgo* Zanzaras *di-*
"*cimus, sub certis & determinatis imaginibus; & usus fuit con-*
"*stellatione Saturni infortunati, & expulit culices.* Another Sto-
Epist. ad Vatit. ry take from an Arabick Cosmographer, cited by *Joseph Scaliger* thus:
"This

"This Talifman (he faith) is to be feen in the Countrey of *Hamptz,* *Hiſt.* 3.
"in a City bearing the fame name ; and it is only the Figure of a
"Scorpion graved upon one of the Stones in a certain Tower;
"which is of fo great virtue, as that it fuffers not any, either Ser-
"pent or Scorpion to come within the City. And if any one, for
"experiment fake, bring one of thefe out of the field into the City,
"it is no fooner at the Gate, but that it dies fuddenly. This Fi-
"gure hath this virtue befides; that when any one is ftung with a
"Scorpion, or bitten by any other Serpent, they need but take
"the Image of the Stone with a little clay, and apply it to the
"wound, and it is inftantly healed. Unto which Mr. *Gaffarel* addeth this : "If any one doubt (faith he) of the credit of this Cof-
"mographer, he may yet adventure to believe Mr. *de Breves,* as *Hiſt.* 4.
"having been an eye-witnefs of the like experiment : who fays in
"his Travels, that at *Tripoli* a City of *Syria,* within a Wall that
"reacheth from the Sea-fide to the Gate of the City, there is a cer-
"tain inchanted ftone; on which is figured, in Relief, or by way
"of Imbofsment, the Figure of a Scorpion, which was there pla- *Ut ſupra* p.
"ced by a Magician, for to drive away Venomous Beafts, which in- 164.
"fefted this Province, as the Serpent of Brafs in the Hippodromus
"at *Conſtantinople* did. And a little above the City, there is a cer-
"tain Cave, which is full of the Carkaffes and Bones of Serpents,
"which died at that time. And further *Gaffarel* faith: Now where-
"as he calls this an inchanted Stone, and fays that it was placed
"there by a Magician, you muft note, that he there fpeaks according
"to the fenfe of the inhabitants, who knew not how to give any o-
"ther account of the thing, as not underftanding any thing at all of
"the natural reafon of it.

2. And that the election of fit times according to the Configura- *Argum.* 2.
tion of the Stars and Planets, is of great efficacy and virtue, is fufficiently known to Husbandmen and Sailers, and of no fmall power
both in refpect of natural and artificial things, as we fhall fhew in
this inftance. *Lazarus Riverius* who was Counfellor and Phyfician
to the French King, a perfon of extraordinary learning and experience in the Medical profeffion, both in the Galenical and Chymical way, doth give us this relation faying: "I have not feldom *Obſervat. com-*
"experienced, and I have many witneffes of this thing, that Peony *municat.* 7.
"gathered under its proper Conftellation, to wit, the Moon incli- *p.* 329.
"ning (*inclinante*) being in *Aries,* doth loofe the *Epilepſie,* by ap- *Hiſt.* 5.
"plication alone : for the middle and chief root divided by the
"greater Longitude, I have (he faith) compaffed about the neck
"and the armes of a certain Virgin in the Hofpital, of eighteen
"years of age, who had been afflicted with this Difeafe from her
"childhood, and had the *Paroxyſmes* every day; but from that day
"feemed altogether to be cured. From whence it is manifeft how
"greatly the obfervation of the Stars is to be efteemed of in the
"Art of Medicine. Agreeable unto which is the judgment of that
Induftrious perfon *Galen,* who affirmeth that Peony by appenfion
doth

doth cure the *Epilepsie*, though he declare not the fit time for its collection.   From whence it is most clear that the careful and precise obfervation of the Heavenly influences is most neceſſary to a Phyſician, and to all others that would produce ſtrange and defired effects.   Therefore doth learned *Schroderus* tell us this concerning
the power and efficacy of thofe influences, faying: "The influen-
"ces of the Stars are *effluvia*, or Steams endowed with peculiar fa-
"culties, by which they make ſtrong (if they be in their ſtrength
"and vigour) things that are familiar to them, and do profper and
"promote their virtues; but on the contrary they debilitate, hin-
"der and make worfe things that are not agreeable to them.   And
this is that which *Mofes* fully mentioneth in thefe words, as they
are fitly rendred by *Arias Montanus*. *Et ad* Jofeph *dixit, Benedi-*
cta Domini terra ejus, de delicia Cœlorum, de rore, & de voragine
cubante deorfum : & de delicia proventuum Solis, & de delicia
ejectionis lunarum. Which our Tranſlation gives thus : *And of Jo-*
feph he faid, Bleſſed of the Lord be his land, for the precious things
of heaven, for the dew, and for the deep that coucheth beneath ; And
for the precious fruits brought forth by the Sun, and for the precious
things put forth by the Moon. The full evidence of the truth of
thefe influences of the Stars, and neceſſity and utility for due and proper feafons for the collection of Flowers, Fruits, Roots and Plants,
may be feen in that learned piece that *Bartholomæus Carichterus*
Chief Phyſician to *Maximilian* the Second, writ and dedicated
to his Maſter in the German Tongue.   As alfo, what is written in
the fame Language by thofe learned Germans, *Johannes Pharamun-*
dus Rhumelius, and *Ifrael Hebueras* that learned Mathematician,
in a Treatife which he calleth, *Myſterium Sigillorum herbarum &*
lapidum, which do compleatly verifie the certain efficacy and virtue of Planetary Seals, Images or Figures.

   3. Thefe things are confirmed by the effects of appenſions of many
natural things which produce ſtrange and wonderful effects, fome of
which we ſhall give in the words of that honourable perfon Mr. *Boyl*,
who faith : "That great cures may be done by bare outward ap-
"plications, you will fcarce deny if you disbelieve not the rela-
"tions which are made us by learned men concerning the efficacy
"of the *Lapis Nephriticus*, only bound upon the Pulfes of the wriſts
"(chiefly that of the left hand) againſt that ſtubborn and Anoma-
"lous difeafe the Stone.   And that which gives the more credit to
"thefe relations is ; That not only the judicious *Anfelmus Boetius*
"*de Boot* feems to prize it, but the famous *Monardes* profeſſeth
"himfelf, not to write by hearfay of the great virtues of this *In-*
"dian Stone, but to have made tryal of it himfelf upon perfons of
"very high quality : And that which is related by *Monardes* is
"much lefs ſtrange than thofe almoſt incredible things which are
"with many circumſtances delivered of that Stone, by the learned
"Chymiſt *Vutzerus*. And although it muſt be acknowledged that
"fome Stones that go under that name have been ineffectually ap-
                                                              "plied

"plied in Nephritick Diftempers. Yet the accurate *Johannes de*
"*Laet* himfelf furnifheth us with an anfwer to that objection, in-
"forming us that many of thofe Nephritick Stones (which differ
"much in colour, though the beft are wont to be greenifh) al-
"though not at all counterfeited or fophifticated are of little or no
"virtue. But that yet there are fome others of them which can
"fcarce be diftinguifhed from the former, but by tryal upon Nephri- *De Gemm. &*
"ticks, which are of wonderful efficacy, as he himfelf hath more *Lapid. i. 1.*
"than once tryed in his own Wife. *Garcias ab orta* mentions a *c. 23.*
"Stone found in *Balagat*, called *Alaqueca*; of which he tells us,
"that though it be cheap: *Hujus tamen virtus* (to ufe his own
"words) *reliquarum Gemmarum facultates exuperat, quippe qui*
"*fanguinem undequaq; fluentem illico fiftat.* *Monardes* (*cap.* 35.)
"relates the great virtues of a Stone againft Hyfterical futfocations,
"and concludes; *Cum uteri fuffocationem imminentem praefentiunt,*
"*adhibito lapide fubitò levantur, & fi eum perpetuò geftant (Hyfte-*
"*rici) nunquam fimili morbo corripiuntur: exempla hujufmodi fa-*
"*ciunt ut his rebus fidem adhibeam.* The fame Author in the next
"Chapter, treating of the *Lapis Sanguinaris* or Blood-ftone, found in
"*New-Spain* (having told us, that the *Indians* do moft confident-
"ly believe, that if the flefh of any bleeding part be touched with
"this Stone, the bleeding will thereby be ftanched) adds this me-
"morable obfervation of his own: *Vidimus nonnullos haemorrhoi-*
"*dum fluxu afflictos remedium fenfiffe, annulos ex hoc lapide con-*
"*fectos in digito continue geftando; nec non & menftruum fluxum*
"*fifti.* And to thefe for brevity fake, we fhall only mention the vir-
"tues of the Jafper, which is blood-red throughout the whole
"body of the Stone, which *Boetius de Boot* of his own experience *De Lapid. &*
"doth avouch in feveral trials to have ftopped Fluxes of Blood, on- *Gemm. l. 2.*
"ly by bare appenfion: As alfo the child of a famous Chymical *p. 102.*
"writer, who had his child (fuppofed to be bewitched) cured by
"hanging a piece of that Noble Mineral by *Paracelfus* called *ele-*
"*ctrum minerale immaturum*, of which *Helmont* tells us this : *Im-*
"*primis electrum minerale immaturum* Paracelfi, *collo appenfum, li-*
"*berat, quos fpiritus immundus perfequitur, quod ipfe vidi. Illius* *Mod. Intrand.*
"*potum verò plures à veneficiis folviffe, memini. Nemo autem, qui ap-* *p. 604.*
"*penfo illo fimplici, non praecaverit, ne injecta intromittantur : vel*
"*ab importunis ligationibus confeftim non folvatur.* All which do
manifeft the great and wonderful virtues, that God hath endowed
Stones, Minerals, Plants and Roots withal, that the Devil need
not be brought in to be an adjutant or operator in their effects.

4. And it is alfo manifeft that Metals may be fo artificially in fit *Argum.* 4.
Conftellations commixed together, that their effects will be rare
and ftupendious, as the aforefaid honourable perfon doth tranf- *Ut fupra. 209.*
cribe and relate to us in thefe words: "What *Monardes*, (he
"faith) mentions of the virtue of the *Lapis Sanguinaris* to cure
"Hemorrhoidal Fluxes, puts me in mind of a yet much ftranger *Helm. de*
"thing, which *Helmont* affirms, namely, That he could make a me- *Febr. c. 2.*
"tal,

" tal, of which if a Ring were worn, the pain of the Hæmorrhoids
" would be taken away, in the little time requisite to recite the
" Lords Prayer; and within twenty four hours the Hæmorrhoids
" themselves, as well internal as external, how protuberant soever,
" would vanish, and the restagnant blood would (as he speaks)
" be received again into favour, and be restored to a good conditi-
" on. The same Ring he also commends in the suffocation and ir-
" regular motion of the Womb, and divers other Diseases: But if
" *Paracelsus* be in any case to be credited in an unlikely matter, we
" may think by his very solemn protestations that he speaks upon
" his own experience, that he had a Ring made of a metalline sub-
" stance, by him called *electrum*, (which by his description seems to
" be a mixture of all the metals joined together under certain con-
" stellations) which was of far greater virtue than this of *Helmont*,

Paracelf. *in*
Archidox. mag.
l. 6. p. 714.

" For, *hoc loco* (says he) *non possum non indicare admirandas quas-*
" *dam vires virtutesq; electri nostri, quas fieri his nostris oculis vi-*
" *dimus, adeoq; cum bona veritatis conscientiâ præferre attestariq;*
" *possumus. Vidimus enim hujus generis annulos, quos qui induit,*
" *hunc nec spasmus convulsit, nec Paralysis corripuit, nec dolor ullus*
" *torsit, similiter nec Apoplexia, nec Epilepsia invasit. Et si annulus*
" *hujusmodi Epileptici digito annulari, etiam in Paroxysmo sævissi-*
" *mo, insertus fuit, remittente illicò Paroxysmo, æger à lapsu illico*
" *resurrexit,* &c. And though Mr. *Boyle* a person of a perspicuous
judgment, and of a great understanding, doth seem to question his
authority with a kind of dubitation, being in probability staggered
by the groundless censures of his greatest adversaries; yet we must
affirm that it is very hard that his veracity and experience (which
was as great as any Mans) should be undervalued, by reason of the
ignorance and idleness of those that judge him: who were never
able in regard of their ignorance to understand the meaning of his
mystical and dark way of writing, nor because of their supine negligence had ever made trial of those things he treateth of, with that
curious diligence and care that is requisite to accomplish such occult effects withal; not considering that, *Dii sua bona laboribus*
vendunt. But notwithstanding this, and the monstrous lies and
horrid calumnies of that pitiful Rapsodist *Athanasius Kircherus*,
we shall add one testimony more from the same Author, which in
English runs thus: " Also (he saith) I cannot here pass over one
" great wonder, which I saw performed in *spain* of a great Negro-
" mancer, who had a Bell not exceeding the weight of two pounds
" which as oft as he did Ring, he could allure and stir up many and
" various Apparitions and Visions of Spirits. For when he lift he
" did describe certain words and characters in the inward superficies
" of the Bell: After if he did beat and ring it, forthwith the Spirits
" (or shapes) did come forth or appear of what form or shape soe-
" ver he desired. He could also by the sound of the same Bell, ei-
" ther draw unto him or drive from him many other Visions and
" Spirits, as also Men and Beasts, as I have seen many of these per-
" formed

"formed by him with mine own eyes. But whenfoever he did begin
"any new thing, fo oft he did renew the words and Characters alfo.
"But notwithftanding he would not reveal (he faith) unto me,
"thofe fecrets of the words and characters, until I my felf more
"deeply weighing and confidering the matter, at laft by chance
"found them forth. Which notwithftanding, and the examples of
"which I here ftudioufly do conceal. But it is not obfcurely to be
"noted here, that there was more of moment in the Bell, than in
"the words: For this Bell was certainly and altogether com-
"pounded or made of this our *Electrum.*

5. And that there are great and hidden virtues both in Plants and *Argum. 5.*
Minerals, efpecially in Metals and Precious Stones as they are by Nature produced by Myftical Chymiftry prepared and exalted, or commixed and infculped in their due and fit conftellations, may not only
be proved by the inftances foregoing, but alfo by the reafons and authorities of perfons of great judgment and experience in the fecrets of
nature, of which we fhall here recite fome few. And firft that learned
and obfervant perfon *Baptifta van Helmont* tells us thus much : "But *In Verb. Herb.*
"this one thing (he faith) I willingly admit: To wit, that metals do by *& lapid. mag.*
"many degrees furpafs Plants and Minerals in the art of healing. And *vis til. p. 579.*
"therefore that metals are certain fhining glaffes, not by reafon of
"the brightnefs; but rather that as often as they are opened, and their
"virtues fet at liberty, they act by a dotal light, and a vital contact.
"Therefore metals do operate, by a manner attributed to the Stars,
"to wit by afpect, and the attaction of an alterative blafs or mo-
"tion. For the metals themfelves are glaffes, I fay the beft off-
"fpring of the inferiour Globe, upon which the whole central
"force, by fome former ages, hath prodigally poured out its trea-
"fure, that it might efpoufe moft richly, this liquor, this fweat,
"and this off-fpring of Divine Providence, unto thofe ends which
"the weaknefs of nature did require. But (he faith) I call them
"fhining glaffes, which have the power of penetrating and illumi-
"nating the *Archeus,* from its errors, furies and defects. Nei- *Vid. lib. de*
ther are thofe arguments of that learned perfon *Galeottus Martius, Doctr. promifc.*
for defending the natural and lawful effects of Planetary Sigills, *c. 24. p. 187.*
when prepared forth of agreeable matter, and made in their due conftellations, of fuch fmall weight as fome infipid ignorants have pretended, but are convincing to any confiderate and rational perfon,
as this one may manifeft, where he is fpeaking of the Figure of a
Lion ingraven in a Golden Plate in thefe words: "The Figure of a
"Lion (he faith) infculped in the fit hours, in a right conftellation,
"doth not act, but doth bring the beginning of the action, as S. *Tho-*
"*mas* and *Albertus magnus* do teftifie: not as a Figure and Image im-
"preffed Mathematically, but that it may effect this or that prepara-
"tion in the thing figured : which may in divers moods receive the
"Celeftial action without difficulty : Becaufe if the Image of a Dog,
"or an Horfe, or fome other Animal were infculped in a Golden
"Plate, there would not be that difpofition of the matter, which
                              Y   "doth

"doth accompany the Image of a Lion &c. From whence (he ſaith)
"we conclude, that this aptitude to draw in the Celeſtial virtue in
"the Figure, is not as Figure, but as the Gold is formed more denſe
"or thin, by the condition of the Image. For even in looking-
"glaſſes, the variety of the Figure, doth bring a moſt vaſt diffe-
"rence. For how much a Concave doth differ from a gibbous
"Looking-glaſs, is even known unto old Wives. Of theſe things

De ſecret. oper. artis & natur. c. 2.

also our learned Countrey-man *Roger Bacon*, who was ſecond to
none in the ſecrets of Art and Nature, doth teach us thus much:
"But they who know in fit conſtellations, to do their works ac-
"cording to the configurations of the Heavens; they may not only
"diſpoſe Characters, but all their operations, both of Art and Nature,
"agreeable to the Celeſtial virtues. But becauſe it is difficult in
"theſe things to know the certitude of Celeſtials; therefore in
"theſe there is much error with many; and there are few that know

Paracelſ. Ar-chidox. magic. lib. 1.

"to order any thing profitably and truly. But we ſhall ſhut up this
particular with that memorable and irrefragable reſponſion of *Pa-racelſus* to the common objection, which in Engliſh runs thus:
"But (he ſaith) they will thus urge; how comes it to paſs, I pray
"thee, that Metals, with their aſſigned Characters, Letters and
"Names, ſhould perform ſuch things, unleſs they be prepared and
"made by Magical and Diabolical power intervening? But (he
"ſaith) to theſe I return this anſwer. Therefore thou believeſt (as I
"hear) that if ſuch things be made by the help of the Devil, then
"they may have their force and operations. But ſhould not thou
"rather believe this? that alſo the Creator of Nature, God who
"dwelleth in the Heavens, is ſo powerful, that he in like manner
"can give and confer theſe virtues and operations to Metals,
"Roots, Herbs, Stones and ſuch like things? As though forſooth
"the Devil were more ſtrong, more wiſe, more omnipotent, and more
"powerful than the only Eternal, Omnipotent and Merciful God, who
"hath created and exalted their degrees, even of all theſe aforeſaid
"Metals, Stones, Herbs, Roots and all other ſuch like things that
"are above, or within the Earth, and do live and vegetate in the
"Water or Air, for the health and commodity of Man?

This argument we deſire that any of the Witchmongers or De-monographers ſhould anſwer, ere they conclude ſo ſtrongly for the power of Devils and Witches.

So we conceive we have ſufficiently proved that what *Pharaohs* Magicians did perform, might rationally, and probably be brought to paſs by Natural Magick or confederacy, and ſleight of hand, without any other Diabolical aſſiſtance than what was mental and ſpiritual in regard of the end, which was the reſiſting of *Moſes*. And by all they did, as in changing their Rods, bringing in of Frogs and changing Water into Blood, it doth not rationally appear, that they had any ſupernatural aſſiſtance, for then they could not have been ſo amazed at the miracle of turning the Duſt into Lice; for what skill did the Devil want that he could not perform this?

If

If by his power the former things were brought to pass, could there be more difficulty in doing of this, than in the bringing of Frogs? Neither could their Legierdemain have failed them but that they were surprized, and taken unawares, being not provided to play all kind of tricks, but only some few for which they had made provision. And so to excuse their own inability, they cryed out, *this is the finger of God* ; a pitiful shift to excuse their own knavery, and couzenage, for there could be no more of the finger of God in this than the former, but only a shift to put off their own shame. Exod. 8. 19.

Another place from whence they would draw arguments to maintain the power of the Devil and Witches, is the Story of *Balaam* in the Book of *Numbers*, from whence in the first place they would conclude that he used wicked and Diabolical Divinations, and that by words he could either bless or curse. In answer to which we shall give these pressive reasons.

1. Though it might be granted that he used Divinations that were not lawful, yet what is that to a killing and murthering Witch? Surely nothing at all. And though *Balak* believed that *whosoever he blessed were blessed, and whosoever he cursed, were cursed*, and therefore fetched him so far, yet there is nothing apparent to prove that *Balaam* could do any such matter, and from *Balaks* belief to *Balaams* performances proceedeth no argument, for his belief that he could either bless or curse, did not confer any power to *Balaam* to produce such effects withall. And *Balaams* blessings, or cursings might be intentional, and declarative, but could not be effective, for he confesseth a great piece of truth: *How should he curse, whom God had not cursed, or how should he defie, whom the Lord had not defied?* He might have done it verbally, but it would have been frustrate,, and to no effect, and therefore he concluded: *Surely there was no inchantment against Jacob, nor no Divination against Israel.* Reas. 1. Numb. 22. 6. Numb 23. 8, 23.

2. And though it be said, that he went not as at other times, to meet Auguries (for as we have before shewed, the word doth properly signifie that) It must be understood, and is manifest that at the former times he went to attend solitarily what the Lord would say unto him, and those two times that he went before was only to meet the Lord, to hear and receive what he would say unto him. But here he did not, nor had need to go, for the Spirit of the Lord came upon him, and he took up his Parable, and prophesied. Where though his going to meet the Lord, be called to meet Divinations, yet it cannot be taken in the worse sense, for unlawful Divinations, but for such as were sent him and taught him by God, by Visions, Angels, Trances, or other such like wayes as God in those times used to reveal his Will to his Prophets by: For from first to last, it appeareth that he neither professed, nor did (in this case) utter any thing but what the Lord commanded him, and so was no false Prophet. Reas. 2. Chap. 24. 1.

3. He was no false Prophet, that is, he had, nor used any Divi- Reas. 3.

nations,

nations, but what he had from God, is moſt clear from theſe par-
Numb. 22.18. ticulars. 1. When *Balak* firſt ſent meſſengers unto him, his reſponſion was: *If Balak would give me his houſe full of Silver and Gold
I cannot go beyond the word of the Lord my God, to do leſs or
more.* "Whereby it is apparent that he feared the Lord Jehovah,
"and calls him his God, thereby ſhewing the confidence that he had
"in him, and that he acknowledged him for his only God. 2. In the
"whole tranſaction of the buſineſs betwixt him and *Balak*, he never
"took upon him to declare any thing, but what the Lord would
"ſay unto him, neither did he at all vary from the ſame in the leaſt
Ibid 2. 24. 4,
15. "tittle. 3. He confeſſeth all along, *that he had his eyes opened, and
that he heard the words of God, and had ſeen the viſion of the Almighty, falling into a trance, but having his eyes open.* And theſe
were things that were not peculiar to any, but ſuch as were the true
Prophets of the Lord Jehovah. 4. The truth of his Prophecie,
which was of the Kingdom of Chriſt, and the Glory and Dominion
of it, with the proſperity of his people, doth plainly evince that
he was a true Prophet of the Lord, and that his Divinations came
Vid. Caton. Ant.
Tho. Aquin.
p. 10. from the Almighty. And this cauſed S. *Hierome*, and ſome other
of the Fathers believe, that by this Prophecie of *Balaam*, the *Magi* or Wiſe men were directed, to come to *Hieruſalem* to ſeek and
worſhip Chriſt the Saviour of the World.

Reaſ. 4. 4. Though this Prophet fell into hainous crimes, and enormous
ſins, as tempting of God, who when the firſt Meſſengers came
from *Balak* unto him, was poſitively commanded not to go with
them, and yet as though God would change his mind entertained
them again, whereby Gods anger was kindled againſt him. And
2 Pet. 2. 15,
16.
Jude 11. though he was drawn *to love the wages of unrighteouſneſs*, and ſo
was rebuked by the dumb Aſs, and though *he taught Balak to lay a
ſtumbling-block before the children of Iſrael*, and therefore had that
Revel. 2. 14. judgment to be ſlain among the Midianites: Yet none of theſe do
conclude at all, that therefore he uſed Diabolical Divinations, or
had not what he declared from Divine Revelation, no more than
Jonah 1. 3. &
4. 1. the flying of *Jonah* to *Tarſhiſh*, when he was commanded to go to
preach againſt *Nineveh*, or his repining at Gods mercy ſhewed to that
1 Kings 13. great City, manifeſted him to be a lying Prophet, or to uſe deviliſh
Divination. Neither the Prophets being ſeduced, *that cried againſt
the altar at Bethel*, before *Jeroboam*, by the old Prophet, *and his
being ſlain in the way by a lion, & his carkaſe left there*, did at all argue
that his Prophecie was falſe, or that he had not his meſſage from God,
but they only ſhew, that even thoſe that have been truly inſpired
by God and been truly taught by him, have notwithſtanding often
diſobeyed him, and have had therefore fearful temporal judgments
faln upon them, and yet no argument that they uſed unlawful Divinations.

From hence alſo the Witchmongers uſe to urge a frivolous, and
groundleſs argument which is this; that the Angel did ſpeak in
Balaams Aſs, and therefore the Devil may ſpeak in a Dog, or a
Cat

Cat to a Witch, but this is confuted by thefe reafons.

1. What the Angel did there was by command and commiffion *Reaf.* 1. from God, but we never read, nor can it be proved that the Devil is fent upon fuch idle, and ordinary errands, to work a miracle, to fpeak in a Dog, or a Cat, to a Witch; for God doth not work wonders for any fuch wicked and abominable ends. And if he be not fent of God, he cannot of himfelf perform any fuch matter, who could not enter into the Swine, without Chrifts leave and order; but is kept in chains of everlafting darknefs, from whence he is not loofed, but when God fends him as an inftrument to accom- plifh his will, which is always for good and juft ends, and not for fuch execrable and wicked purpofes.

2. They take up a falfe fuppofition, for the Angel was not in the Afs either effentially, or effectively, for at the very inftant that the Afs fpoke, *the Angel was ftanding in a narrow place, where was* Numb. 22. 26, *no way to turn either to the right hand or to the left,* and then *feeing* 27. *the Angel of the Lord fhe fell down under Balaam, and fpoke,* and the Angel could not both ftand in the narrow way and likewife be in the Afs, in the fame moment of time, except we fhould grant that abfurdity that a creature may be in two diftinct places at one and the felf-fame time, which was never yet allowed to any created being. But they openly belie, and falfifie the words of the Text, Verfe 28. for it doth not fay that the Angel fpoke in the Afs, but that the Lord, (the word is *Jehovah*) opened the mouth of the Afs. So that (we fuppofe) here is enough demonftrated that from none of the places of Scriptures hitherto enumerated, any colourable grounds can be drawn to uphold thofe particulars that we have laboured to confute, and therefore we fhall pafs to another Chapter.

C H A P. VIII.

Of the Woman of Endor that pretended to raife up Samuel, and of fome other places in the Scriptures, not handled yet, and of fome other objections.

COncerning the Woman of *Endor,* that our Englifh and many other Tranflators have falfly rendered a Witch, or a Woman that had a familiar Spirit, we have fpoken fufficiently, where we treated of the fignification of the word *Ob.* And there have fhewed plainly, that fhe is only called the Miftrifs of the bottle, or of the Oracle, and that what fhe there did, or pretended to do, was only by Ventriloquy, or cafting her felf into a feigned Trance lay groveling upon the earth with her face downwards, and fo changing her voice did mutter and murmur, and peep and chirp like a bird coming forth of the shell, or that she spake in some hollow Cave or Vault, through some Pipe, or in a Bottle, and so amused and deceived poor time-rous and despairing *Saul*, or had a confederate apparelled like *Samuel* to play his part, and that it was neither *Samuels* Body, Soul, nor no Ghost or Devil, but only the cunning and Imposture of the Woman alone, or assisted with a confederate. And though this might be amply satisfactory to all sound and serious judgments, especially if hereunto be added what Mr. *Scot*, Mr. *Ady*, Mr. *Wagstaff*, and the learned Authors of the Dialogue of Spirits and Devils have written upon this subject: yet because we have promised before to speak something of the History and matter of fact, and that Mr. *Glanvil* a Minister of our English Church hath of late espoused the quarrel, we shall confute his arguments and clear the case as fully as in reason can be required, and that in these particulars following.

1 Sam. 3. 19.
Id. c. 7. v. 13.

...I. The certain and infallible prophecies of *Samuel* so punctually coming to pass according as he foretold them, for it is said : *And Samuel grew, and the Lord was with him, and did let none of his words fall to the ground;* were manifestly known to all *Israel*, as in the case of the destruction of *Eli*, and his house, and by the overthrow of the *Philistines* at *Eben-ezer*, and in the anointing of *Saul* to be King, and in the case of sending Thunder and Lightning in Harvest time, and such like. And as these were publickly known unto all *Israel*, and they had seen, and tryed what infallible certainty followed upon them, so it was as generally known, that *Samuel* had told *Saul* that God had rejected him from being King over *Israel*, and that he had anointed *David* to be King in his stead; and therefore any rational Man, that knew these things, and also saw that *David* prospered in all things that he did, and that it was quite otherwise with *Saul*, might certainly know that the Kingdome would be transferred from him unto *David*, and so there needed neither spirit nor Devil be fetched up to predict this, being sufficiently known unto all, of which also the Woman at *Endor* could not be ignorant as a thing of concern to her, especially in the point of her practise which was meer couzenage and Imposture.

Confid. about
Witchcraft,
p. 8.

And therefore Mr. *Glanvils* argument concludes nothing, where he saith: "And this *Samuel* truly foretold his approaching fate, *viz.* " That *Israel* should be delivered with him into the hands of the " *Philistines*, and that on the morrow he, and his Sons should be " in the state of the dead, which doubtless is meant by the expressi-" on that [*they should be with him:*] which contingent particulars, " how could the couzener, and her confederate foretel, if there " were nothing in it extraordinary and preternatural ? To answer which we say, that there was no contingent particular that was foretold, but Mr. *Glanvil* might have foretold it, if he had been there, and known but that which was publickly divulged in *Israel*, without incurring the danger of being reputed a Witch or a Diviner.

1. Because

1. Becaufe *Samuels* prophecies were certainly known to come to pafs, and he had openly declared, that the Kingdom fhould be rent from *Saul*, and given to *David*.   2. She or her confederate might have gueffed as much, becaufe of the extream fear and confternation that *Saul* was in, for heartlefs and fearful Generals feldom or never win Battels.   3. Becaufe that he confeffed that God had forfaken him, and when he faw the hoaft of the *Philiftines*, he was afraid and his heart greatly trembled, and thofe that God doth forfake cannot profper.   4. The word *to morrow* in the Hebrew doth not precifely denote the day following, but the time to come, fo that how true foever Mr. *Glanvil* may think it, there was but a piece of ambiguous Equivocation in it, for it cannot be made out that it was fought the very next day, neither were all *Sauls* Sons flain with him, at that very time.   5. And if nothing muft be fupplied but meerly what is *totidem verbis* in the Text (as he urgeth againft Mr. *Scot*) then how will it be proved, that the Phrafe (*to morrow thou and thy Sons fhall be with me*) is to be underftood of the ftate of the dead, feeing the words (if literally to be taken) do imply a locality, not a ftate or condition?   6. But if it be fuppofed to be the Devil, how comes he to know contingencies fo certainly? It is a thing that is eafily affirmed, but was never yet fufficiently proved.   For if it be faid he gathered it from the Prophecie of *Samuel*, fo might the Witch have done without any affiftance of a Devil.   7. And if he take it to be *Samuels* Soul (as he feems to hold) how come departed Souls to know, and forefee what contingent effects are to fall out here below? Where reads he or finds any fuch Divinity except in Popifh Authors? But he may confult the Text: *Doubtlefs thou art our Father, though Abraham be igno-* Ifa. 63. 16. *rant of us, and Ifrael acknowledge us not.*

2. That this Woman was a meer diffembling and lying cheater, and ufed nothing but Impofture, is manifeft from thefe reafons. 1. Becaufe that fhe was but of the fame Crew and Stamp that *Manaffeh*, and *Ahab* fet up, is moft plain, but they were meer Impoftors and deceivers pretending to divine for other perfons, and in other matters, but could not forefee their own deftruction, and therefore in probability fhe was of the fame practice.   2. Becaufe fhe falfly faigned that fhe knew not *Saul*, of whom fhe could not be ignorant, he being fo publickly known, and feen, and was taller by 1 Sam. 9. 2.
& 10. 23. the head and fhoulders than any man in *Ifrael*.   3. If fhe had not known that it had been *Saul*, when he came to her at the firft, fhe would never have relyed upon his oath when he fwore by *Jehovah*, for there was none but the King that could protect her from deftruction.   4. She muft needs be a moft notorious diffembling cheater, becaufe fhe pretended to call up any, for fhe faid: *whom fhall I bring up unto thee?* which is moft certainly falfe, fhe had no fuch univerfal power, no nor all the Devils in Hell, if they had all affifted her.   5. She did plainly diffemble, for the Text faith, *and when the woman faw Samuel fhe cried out with a loud voice*; now if
fhe

she saw *Samuel* (whom she could not but know) why did she answer to *Saul*, when he asked, *what sawest thou?* She answered, *I saw gods ascending out of the earth.* Let Mr. *Glanvil*, and all men judge if this be not gross and palpable lying, Gods is plural, but *Samuel* was but one.

3. As it is manifest that this Woman was an active deceiver, and one that intended to cheat and couzen, so it is as plain that *Saul* was in a condition fit to be deluded, and imposed upon, even by those that had been less cunning and skilful than she was in the craft of cheating, which is apparent from these reasons. 1. The Spirit of the Lord was departed from him, and consequently, Wisdom, Prudence and Discretion, and so that which should have guided his Will, Affections and Actions in the right way, had totally left him. And when these are gone, what is man, but a fit instrument to undergo and suffer even the worst and lowest of delusions and abuses? 2. The Spirit of the Lord had not only left him,
1 Sam. 16. 14. but an evil Spirit from the Lord was come upon him that vexed and terrified him. And to what madness, folly and wickedness is not he subject to, who is led by the Spirit of lies and darkness? 3. The Lord had openly declared, that because he had rejected the word of the Lord, therefore the Lord had rejected him from being King over *Israel*, and that the Kingdom should be rent from him, and gi-
1 Sam. 15. 23, ven to one more worthy than him. Now what despondency of
27. mind, what torture and vexation of Spirit must needs be in him, that having been a King, is thus threatned to have his Kingdom rent from him and given to another, is easy to be imagined. 4. He must needs be under a most fearful consternation of mind not only because of these things named, but especially having before in his dangers and straights received counsel and advice from the Lord,
1 Sam. 28. 6. though he now *inquired of the Lord, yet the Lord answered him neither by dreams, nor by Urim, nor by Prophets.* The Lord answered him not by dreams; for the union and converse that had been betwixt him and the Lord before, was now broken by reason of his Sins and Rebellion. Neither did the Lord answer him by Urim, for the Urim was not in the possession then of *Saul*, but of *David*, Chap. 23. 6, 9. Neither did the Lord answer him by Prophets, for *Samuel* had left him, after his last denouncing judgment against him, and came no more at him until his death. 5. He must needs be in a most fearful case, and a fit subject for the most weak and simple Imposture of the World, because the *Philistines* were upon him with a potent and numerous Army, and he able to gather but few and weak forces, the best and most of the people being revolted from him, and were in their affections, or persons with and for *David*. And from hence may easily be collected, how facile a thing it was to delude, and deceive *Saul*, even by those that had far less craft than this Woman, who doubtless was devilish cunning in her couzening tricks.

4. There is much question who was the Penman of this first Book
of

of *Samuel*, but whofoever it was (for we cannot determine it) it cannot be rationally fuppofed that he had the Story of this tranf-action betwixt *Saul* and the Woman from Divine Revelation, for then doubtlefs it would not have been left fo ambiguous and doubtful, but the whole truth, both of the matter, manner and circumftances, would in all probability have been fully fet down: and have been declared whether it were a miracle wrought by God, a delufive apparition of Satan, the Soul of *Samuel*, or the Impofture of the Woman, the certainty of which had been mainly profitable and expedient for the people of God and his Church to have known. And if the Penman had it from the relation of *Saul* or ei-ther or both of his Servants, then it muft needs have been accord-ing to their deluded imaginations and their deceived apprehenfi-ons, as is moft rational to believe that it was; or if he had it from the Woman, or thofe of her family, (which is not rationally pro-bable) then it is fure to have been reprefented for the moft ad-vantage, and credit of the Womans skill and cunning. But the moft learned perfons do judge it to be related, meerly according to the deceived opinion and apprehenfion of *Saul*.

5. But to come more near the ftrefs of the bufinefs, though Mr. *Glanvil* confidently fay, that Mr. *Scots* Tenent, that the Wo-man was in one room and *Saul* in another, when the feat was acted, is but a pretty knack and contrivance, and but an invention with-out ground, and not as much as intimated in the Hiftory: Yet we muft foberly averr, that nothing is more plain in the Text, than ei-ther that they were in diverfe rooms, or that *Saul* faw nothing at all, but what he had from her relation, or the acting of a confe-derate, and this we fhall prove by thefe undeniable reafons. 1. Af-ter *Saul* had pacified the pretended fears of the Woman, who falfly counterfeited that fhe knew not *Saul*, *who was taller by the head aud fhoulders than any man in Ifrael*, the next thing we hear of in the Text is, *and when the Woman faw Samuel*: Now if they were both in the fame room, and *Samuel* a vifible object, how comes it to pafs that *Saul* faw him not? for if they were both in one room, and *Samuel* vifible, how is it that he did not or could not fee him? were his corporal eyes as blind, as the eyes of his underftanding? furely not. What fiction or invention muft falve this? furely Mr. *Glan-vil* muft pump to find it out. 2. The next thing is, that when the Woman faw (for blind *Saul* faw nothing) *Samuel*, *fhe cried with a loud voice, magnà voce*, or (as the Hebrew hath it) *in magnâ voce*. And (I pray you) if they had been both in one room, or near together, what need fhe to have cried with a great voice, might not an ordinary tone have made him to have heard her? What was he deaf as well as blind? Or it might be it was the more to a-mufe and amaze the wretched and deluded King, or to fhew the wonderfulnefs of the apparition fhe feigned that aftonifhment, the more to magnifie her skill and cunning. Well, admit thefe were fo, yet however it is manifeft, notwithstanding her great voice, that

Confid. about Witchcraft, p. 86.

Z.

as yet *Saul* saw nothing, but stood waiting like a drown'd Puppet to hear what would be the issue, for all he understood was from her cunning and lying relation. And so either thus far it is manifest that they were in distinct rooms, or there was nothing that he could see. 3. The next thing is, he saith, *be not afraid, what sawest thou?* that is, though I be *Saul*, yet be not afraid, I have sworn, and thou shalt receive no harm, but *what sawest thou?* As who should say, I see nothing as yet at all, but I suppose thou hast seen something; for otherwise his question doth not agree with the words the Woman spake before. But however it is manifest that as yet he saw nothing, and therefore rationally it must be supposed that they were in distinct rooms, or that there was nothing visible, that he could see. Further, his question is not in the present tense but of the time past, *what sawest thou?* or what hast thou seen? which could not be congruously spoken, if they had been both in one room, but however do undeniably conclude that as yet he saw nothing at all. 4. The next is the Womans lying and forged answer, thereby to magnifie her own craft, and the more to amuse and astonish poor deluded *Saul*, saying; *Behold I saw gods ascending out of the earth*. Well, it is still apparent that as *Saul* could not before see *Samuel*, now he neither seeth these Gods she telleth him of, nor any such thing: So that all that he apprehended was from her forged Stories, for he saw nothing as yet, either because he was not in the same room with her, or that there was no visible apparition. 5. Then he maketh another absurd question, like a distracted Man in the house of *Bethlem*, saying, *what form is he of?* when his question should have been, what forms are they of? for she spoke of Gods which are plural, and more than one, but he asketh in the singular, *what form is he of.* By all which it is manifest, that he yet saw nothing at all. For when we plainly see a thing, we do not usually ask others what form it is of, because our eyes can inform us of that. So that he saw nothing, either because he was not in the same room, or that there appeared nothing that was visible. 6. Now after all these ambiguous lies, and delatory cheats, the crafty quean doth begin to come more near, to give satisfaction to the blinded expectation of *Saul*, who all this while stood gaping to see the appearance of *Samuel*, and so she tells him (who was fit to believe any thing, though never so absurd, or impossible) *behold an old man comes up, and he is covered with a mantle*. In the beginning of the action, the Text saith, *and when the woman saw Samuel, she cried out*, then she said, *she saw gods ascending out of the earth*, and now after all this discourse and expence of time *Samuel* is but coming up, all was lies and delayes the more to blind and delude the poor credulous King. But yet thus far it is plain that *Saul* saw nothing at all, and so must needs all this while, either be in another room, or else for certain there was no apparition visible, and all the satisfaction that he had, was from the lying stories the Wo-

man

man told him. Now let Mr. *Glanvil* confider and anfwer, whether
it be not only intimated, but clearly holden forth in the Text that
either they were in two diftinct rooms, or that nothing vifible did
appear before *Saul*. 7. Now after all this the Text faith, *and
Saul perceived that it was Samuel*, the Hebrew word doth fignifie
to know or to perceive, and relates to the underftanding: but how
did he know, or perceive that it was *Samuel*? not by the fight of
his eyes, for we have made it plain that he was either in another
room, or that no vifible apparition prefented it felf before his eyes,
but he only perceived it by the defcription of the crafty Woman,
who knew well enough what habit or garments *Samuel* wore in
his life time, as one that was the moft publickly known Man in
Ifrael: and therefore the fubtil and crafty quean, knowing that
Saul only required *Samuel* to be brought up and no other, doth
at the laft frame her tale agreeable to *Sauls* defire, and fo defcribes
him an old Man, covered with a mantle, and fuch an one as *Saul* had
known him to be, while he was living. But if *Saul* had feen any
fuch thing as the fhape or form of *Samuel*, then the Hebrew Verb
thrice ufed in that action, that properly fignifieth to fee with the
eyes, would have been ufed in this place (as well as when it relateth what fhe faw) and not the verb for knowing or perceiving, that
relateth to the mind, and *Samuel* he faw not, but only believed the
lies fhe told him. For otherwife it would have been, And *Saul*
faw *Samuel*, and not, *Saul* perceived that it was *Samuel*, which he
could not do but only by her relation, and forged tales. 8. The
laft thing in this action, is, that *Saul ftooped with his face to the
ground, and bowed himfelf:* now to what did he ftoop and bow,
feeing he had feen nothing with his own eyes, neither knew any
thing that appeared, but as the Woman told him? Could it be to
any thing but to an imaginary *Samuel* and fuch an one as fhe had
defcribed, whom he conceited in his Phantafie to be *Samuel* himfelf? Surely in rational confequence it could be nothing elfe. For
all that fhe had done and faid before, being undeniably lies and
cheats, this alfo in juft and right reafon, muft be judged to be fo
alfo. So that it was either the Woman, that being in another room,
did change and alter her voice, and fo plaid the part of *Samuel*,
or elfe that fhe had a confederate knave, whom fhe turned out to
act the part of dead *Samuel*.

6. The laft thing that we fhall handle concerning this controverted fubject, is the examination of the grounds and reafons of thofe
that are of a different judgment, which may be comprifed in thefe
three feveral heads. 1. Some do conceive that it was the Body of
Samuel that was raifed up, and acted by his foul or by Satan. 2. Some
hold that it was *Samuels* Soul that appeared in the fhape and habit,
that he had living. 3. Others do pofitively affirm that it was the
Devil that affumed the fhape of *Samuel*, and fo acted the whole
bufinefs, by a compact betwixt him and the Woman. Thefe we
fhall confute in order.

1. That

1. That it was not the Body of *Samuel* that was raised up, nor the Soul joyned with it, that acted *Samuels* part, is manifest from these reasons. 1. Because *Samuels* Body had lain too long in the grave, for some account it near two years, and therefore must needs in a great part be corrupted, wasted and disfigured, that none could have certainly known that it was *Samuel*. 2. It must have been so putrified and stinking, that none could have endured near it, for the noisome and horrible smell. 3. Who should have covered it with the mantle, which had it been buried with him, must in so long a time, have been rotten and consumed? Surely there were no Taylors in the Grave, to make him a new one, but (in reason and likelihood) if it had been his Body, it should have appeared in Linnen, or a winding-sheet, if that had not been rotten likewise. 4. To raise a Body, so long dead, must needs have required an om-

Philipp. 3. 21. nipotent power, for it is the Almighty power of Christ alone, that raiseth up the vile Bodies of his Saints, and maketh them like his glorious Body. And therefore neither the woman with all her Divinations, nor all the Devils in Hell, nor any created power, but the Lord Almighty, could have wrought this miracle, who would never have done it, to gratifie the humour, or to magnifie the cheating craft of an idolatrous, wicked and couzening Witch.

Matth. 27. 52, And if the Devil or any created power could raise up the Body of
53. a departed Saint, then the rising out of the Graves of many Bodies of Saints, that had slept, and their coming into the holy City, and appearing unto many, after Christ was risen from the dead, had been no certain, or convincing argument, of the undoubted truth of the Divinity and Resurrection of our most Blessed Saviour. But they were most infallible evidences of them both, as saith the Father

Caten. Aur. S. *Hierome* in these words, *sic multa corpora sanctorum resurrexerunt,*
Tho. Aquin. in *ut dominum ostenderent resurgentem, & tamen cum monumenta*
Matth. 27. *aperta sunt, non ante resurrexerunt quàm resurgeret dominus, ut esset* *primogenitus resurrectionis à mortuis.* 5. That it was not *Samuels* Soul joyned with the Body, that acted this, we thus argue: That Tenent that is flatly contrary to the plain Doctrine of the Scripture, must needs be false. But this tenent of *Samuels* Soul acting in the Body after death, is flatly contrary to the plain Doctrine of the Scripture, *ergo* it is false. The major (we suppose) no Oxthodox Christian can justly deny; and the minor is proved thus. The Scrip-

Revel. 14. 13. ture doth assure us, that *those that die in the Lord* (as without all doubt *Samuel* did) *are blessed, and rest from their labours.* Therefore must this Tenent be abominably false: for if the Soul of *Samuel*, after his death had been brought again to act in the Body, then he had not rested from his labours, but had been disquieted, and brought to new trouble, to have been vexed to have seen *Saul* committing more wickedness than before, in taking counsel from a cursed Idolatrous Woman, such as the Lord had commanded to be destroyed. And there is no one point in all this transaction of *Saul* with the Witch, that speaketh her Imposture more apparently than

where

where this counterfeit *Samuel* faith, *Why haft thou difquieted me?*
As though the Saints of God after death could be difquieted by a
Devil, or a Witch, who (according to Gods infallible truth) are
bleffed, and reft from their labours, and are in the hands of the
Lord, where no Torments can touch them. And therefore none
would have fpoken thofe lying words, but a devilifh cheating queau,
or a damnable fuborned confederate.

6. If *Samuels* Soul was again joined to his body fo long after fe-
paration, and fo performed vital actions, who was the author of
this conjunction or union? could the Witch or the Devil or any
created power effect that union? Surely not, none but the almighty
power of Jehovah, who breathed into *Adam* the breath of life. And
therefore we are bold to affert (with all the company of learned
Chriftians) that this opinion is erroneous, impious and blafphemous.

2. The fecond opinion, that it was *Samuels* Soul that appeared
in his wonted fhape and habit, that he wore while he lived, hath
been ftrenuoufly maintained by the Popifh party, and as ftrongly
confuted by the reformed Divines. But we fhall not trouble our
felves and our readers with them all, but only urge two or three
that are moft cogent, thereby to anfwer Mr. *Glanvils* fopperies, and
they are thefe. 1. If it were *Samuels* Soul that appeared, it cannot be fuppofed to come contrary, or whether God would or not,
for hardly any rational Man (we believe) will affirm that, becaufe
God doth whatfoever he will, both in Heaven and Earth, and who
hath refifted his will? 2. And it cannot be rationally thought that
Samuel, who whilft he lived, was fo punctually careful to do nothing (efpecially in his prophetick office) but what he was commanded of God, would after his death run an errand without his
confent or licence. 3. And that his Soul did not come by the command of God is moft certain: Though Mr. *Glanvil* ask the queftion, who faith that happy departed Souls were never imployed
in any minifteries here below? To which (though we have anfwered it before) we now again reply, that all learned Divines of the
reformed Churches have faid, and maintained it, and fo do we
both fay and affirm, that they never were nor are imployed in minifteries here below, becaufe never created, nor ordained of God,
for any fuch end or purpofe, but there are legions of Angels, that
are ordained to be miniftring Spirits, and not the Souls of the Saints
departed this life. But Mr. *Glanvil* goeth further, and faith, that
Samuel was not raifed by the power of the Witches inchantments,
but came on that occafion on a Divine errand. And though we
have before unanfwerably proved in the general, that no Souls of
thofe that are dead do after death appear, or wander here below,
nor come fuch flevelefs errands, as he fuppofeth: yet we fhall add
one or two here in particular, to prove that *Samuels* Soul came not on
a Divine errand as fent by God, without which miffion it could not
have come at all. 4. For fourthly, if Mr. *Glanvil* had proved by
any argument, or colour of reafon, that his Soul had come upon fuch a
Divine

Divine errand it had been something, but he hath only laid down an affirmation, without either proof, reason or authority, and we may with as good reason deny it, as he affirm it, for bare affirmations prove nothing at all.   5. It is manifest that God in all his ordinances of providence, especially in the order of his miracles, doth work chiefly to confirm and witness truth, for that (as the worthy and learned *Stillingfleet* hath observed) is the most proper *criterium* of a miracle; and to send a Soul from the dead must needs be miraculous.   Now if the chief end in Gods working of miracles (for none else but he can work them) be to establish truth, and settle his own Divine and pure worship, then it cannot be to uphold lies and Idolatrous courses.   But if God should have sent *Samuels* Soul on a Divine errand, when the Witch was practising her Diabolical Divinations and cheating tricks, it had been to have countenanced and confirmed both *Saul*, and the Witch, in their wicked wayes, and to have contradicted his own law and command, which did positively order, that all that used Divinations should be put to death, and all those that sought for counsel from them to be severely punished. Now let Mr. *Glanvil*, or any other prove, that God orders that to be done by the dead, which he forbad to be done by the living.   6. If it had been the true *Samuel* that appeared, it is not rational, nor credible to imagine, that he would neither rebuke *Saul* for consulting with a Woman that practised those things, that were forbidden by the law upon pain of death; nor that he would either reprove, or punish so wicked a Woman, finding her in the very act.   We say it is not credible, unless we suppose *Samuel* less zealous for the law and commands of God, being dead, than he was for them being living.   Surely he

1 Sam. 15.33. that living *hewed Agag in pieces*, only because God had commanded he should be slain, would (if it had been the true *Samuel*, which without all question it was not) have done as much or worse, to the cursed and Idolatrous cheating Witch, though after his death, if he had come upon a Divine errand.   7. God should have shewed himself very mutable, if he had answered *Saul* in a miraculous way by a dead Prophet, that had refused to answer him by one living. And *Samuel* while living knew certainly that the Lord had rejected *Saul* from being King over *Israel*, and had testified unto him, that

Verse 29. the *strength of Israel would not lie, and that he was not like a man that he should repent*. But if it had been the true *Samuel* that had been sent to speak to *Saul*, he knowing both by his own knowledge and relation of *Saul* himself, that God had refused to answer him by Prophets, must in that conference both have made God a liar, and mutable, and also himself, who living had testified the contrary, and therefore it could not be either the true *Samuel* nor his Soul.   8. It is manifest that the Lord had before withdrawn his good Spirit from *Saul*, and an evil one from the Lord was come upon him; and therefore it was no way probable, that the Lord would in a miraculous manner answer such a wicked person, whom

he

he had utterly rejected as a reprobate. Neither is it like that God would shew him an extraordinary favour by a dead Prophet, that would not vouchsafe him his Spirit in an ordinary way. And *Samuel* that came not at him for a long time (though but a little distance asunder) while he lived, was not like to make so long a journey in a Divine errand to visit him after his death. 9. And if *Abraham* at the request of the rich Man *would not send Lazarus to warn his brethren, left they should come into that place of torment*, which bore with it a fair shew both of Charity and Piety; much less would God give way (or *Samuel* be desirous to come) to send a blessed Soul from its rest for such a frivolous matter, and in no wise to connive at the wickedness of both *Saul* and the Witch, and never move either of them to the amendment of their lives. 10. Where doth Mr. *Glanvil* find it mentioned in any part of Scripture? or where is it recorded in the writings of any reformed or Orthodoxal Divines? or where in any of their works is it declared, that ever any blessed Soul after death, was either sent, or did come upon a Divine errand to any here below? Is it not monstrous confidence (not to say impudence) to utter such groundless assertions, without any proof, reason, or authority at all? Let all learned and judicious persons consider and judge.

3. That the Devil assumed the shape of *Samuel*, and acted the whole business, is the opinion of all, or the most of the learned Divines of the reformed Churches, of whom we shall crave pardon, if we dissent from them, it being no fundamental of Religion, nor any Article of the Faith. And this we profess is not done out of the spirit of contradiction, nor for singularity, but only because (as we conceive) the Tenent hath no sufficient grounds neither from Scripture nor sound reason, to support it, and therefore we shall labour its confutation, by these ensuing arguments.

1. Because this opinion, that the Devil should perform this apparition, doth beg two suppositions, never yet sufficiently proved, and that have in them no certain truth. For first they take for an Hypothesis, that Devils are meerly and simply incorporeal Spirits, which we shall prove hereafter to be false. Secondly they take for another Hypothesis, that Spirits and Devils can assume what bodies they please, and appear in any figure or shape, which is a meer figment invented by the doating Schoolmen, as we shall sufficiently make good hereafter.

2. We are not of their opinion, that think, that the Devils do move, and rove up and down in this elementary world at their pleasure, to act what they list, and appear when, how and in what shapes they please, for then the World would be full of nothing almost but apparitions, and every corner replenished with their ludicrous tricks, as formerly in the times of blind Popery and ignorance, there was no discourse almost, but of Fairies, Hobgoblins, apparitions, Spirits, Devils and Souls, ranting in every house, and playing feats in every Town and Village, when it was nothing but the

superstitious

superstitious credulity, and ignorant fancies of the people, joined with the Impostures of the Priests and Monks. And if this were true, then how should Men know a true natural substance or body, from these fictitious apparitions? Nay how could a Man have known his Father or Mother, his Brethren or Sisters, his Kinsmen or Neighbours? might they not as well have believed them to be Phantasms, and assumed bodies, as real and true creatures?

3. But though faln Angels in respect of their malice, wicked wills, and envious desires whereby they seek (as much as in them lies) the ruine of all mankind both in Soul and Body, may in that particular end and regard, be said to be like roaring Lions going about and seeking whom they may devour, and compassing the earth and walking to and fro in it: yet we must affirm that in respect of executing their wicked, envious and malicious wills and desires, they are restrained, nay kept in the chains of everlasting darkness, from which fetters and chains they go not out, but when and so far as they are sent, ordered, licensed (or as some would have it worded) permitted, by the purpose and decree of the Divine and Almighties providence. So that it is most certain, that the faln Spirits cannot go forth of their chains, when they list, to act what mischief they would, contrary to the will of the Almighty, who hath fettered, and still keeps them in those chains: but when they are at any time let loose, it is only by the will, decree, licence and order of Jehovah, who sends them forth to accomplish his will, either for punishment to the wicked to inflict upon them his just judgments, for which they are the appointed ministers and executioners, and in the performance of these offices of his wrath, they are limited and bounded how far they shall proceed, and no further; or else they are sent forth to tempt, or afflict the godly for the trial of their faith, and herein they are so restrained and bounded by the power of the Almighty as they cannot act one jot beyond the limit of his commands or Commissions, as is manifest in the case of *David*, who was tempted by Satan to number the people, and in the affliction of *Job*, wherein he was bounded how far he should act, and no further. And when the evil Angels are thus sent forth, and limited by God, what, and how far they shall act, it is always for just and righteous ends, as in the case of *Ahab*, when a lying Spirit was sent by God into the mouths of his Prophets, that he might be perswaded to go up to *Ramath* *Gilead* that he might be slain there, or as it was for a judgment and destruction upon *Sennacheribs* Army, that *Jerusalem* might be saved and freed, and he sent back with shame and confusion into his own countrey, or it is to manifest his glory, goodness and mercy to his Saints, so *David* was moved to number the people, that falling under that temptation, and he and the people therefore plagued, might be brought to a greater degree of repentance, and to know that their defence stood not in the multitude of men, but in the benignity of Jehovah, who was their strength and their defender, and

1 Kings 22.

Isa. 37.

. and so *Job* was so sore afflicted, that his Faith and Patience might be made manifest, and remain for an example to all succeeding posterities. But it is utterly irrational and incredible that God would send the Devil (without whose mission he could not have done it) to appear in the shape of *Samuel*, either to magnifie the skil, or practice of a lewd, wicked, and Idolatrous Woman, which thing he had forbidden by his plain and open law, nor to gratifie the curiosity of a wretched Reprobate, such as was *Saul*, whom he had denied to answer by living Prophets, and therefore would not answer him by the apparition of a Devil, to have committed a counterfeit Imposture, in the shape of holy *Samuel*. And therefore we conclude, that it was no apparition of the Devil, but meerly the Imposture of the Woman, either alone, or with a Confederate.

There is also a fourth opinion concerning the transaction of this Woman of *Endor*, that holds, that it was neither the Body, or Soul of *Samuel* that was raised up, neither the Devil that appeared in his shape, nor that it was the Imposture of the Witch alone, or with a Confederate, but that it was the Sydereal, or Astral Spirit (as they are pleased to term it) of *Samuel* that was made to appear, and speak by the art and skill of the Woman. But because this Tenent is not of much Antiquity, nor hath many assertors of it, as also because it taketh that for an Hypothesis, to wit, that there are three parts in Man, the Body, Soul, and Spirit ; and that the Soul goeth immediately after death either to Heaven or Hell, the Body to the grave, and that the Spirit doth for a certain time after death wander in the air, and may be (by a certain kind of art) brought to appear visibly, and to give answers of all things that it knew living, which as yet hath never been sufficiently proved, therefore we shall pass it over here, having (perhaps) occasion to speak of it more largely hereafter.

We shall now come to mention some places in the New Testament that are produced by some, thereby to prove the great power of Devils and Witches in transferring and carrying bodies in the air, as is that of our Saviours temptation, where it is said that the Devil took him into an exceeding high Mountain, and that he set him upon the pinnacle of the Temple in *Jerusalem*, from whence they thus argue : That if the Devil had power to carry our most blessed Saviour in the air into an high mountain, and to set him upon the pinnacle of the Temple, that much more hath he power to carry the bodies of Witches who are his sworn vassals in the air, whither he pleaseth, or they desire. To annul the force of which objection we give these reasons.

1. If it were granted that the Devil did transport our Saviour *Reas.* 1. in the air, yet it will not follow that he can at any time when he pleaseth carry the Bodies of Men or Women so likewise, for no particular proposition will, according to the rules of art, infer a general or universal conclusion, nor one example or instance inductively prove a general practice ; one Swallow doth not make a

A a   Summer.

Summer. For though once when our bleſſed Saviour was baptized,
the Holy Ghoſt did deſcend like a Dove, and light upon him, it
will not follow, that in all other of his actions of preaching, or

Matth. 3. 16.
Luke 3. 22.
Judg. 15. 15.

working of miracles, the holy Spirit ſhould appear alſo in the form
of a Dove, nor when other Saints are Baptized will it follow that
it doth, or ſhould alwaies appear in the ſame form. And though
Samſon did once ſlay a thouſand of the *Philiſtines* with the jaw-
bone of an Aſs, it doth not follow, that either he did ſo in like
manner in every battel, or that every Man may do the like.

Reaſ. 2.
2. If it were granted that the Devil did carry Chriſts Body in the
air, it will not follow that he can do ſo at any other times, when he
pleaſeth, becauſe in the temptation of Chriſt there was an extraordinary diſpenſation of God for the ſame, which cannot be preſup-
poſed in the ordinary tranſportation of Witches, and therefore
the argument falls quite to the ground.

Reaſ. 3.
3. In the actions of Satan (eſpecially in elementary things, for
we ſpeak not of the acts of his will) the will, order and licence of
God is chiefly to be conſidered, becauſe his power (in reſpect
of execution) is under the power of the Almighty, ſo that he
can do nothing in this reſpect but what he is ordered and commanded to do. And therefore the end of the action is principally to
be regarded ; for if God ſhould have given way that . Chriſt ſhould
be carried by Satan in the air, it was for a glorious and good end,
that the obedience of his will to the Father might be ſhown, and
that his victory over the Devil might be made manifeſt : but in carrying the Bodies of Witches in the air, there can be no good, juſt or
pious end wherefore the Devil ſhould be licenſed, or permitted to
carry them in the air, except it were to promote filthineſs and a-
bominable wickedneſs, which were abſurd and blaſphemous to imagine. And therefore we may rationally and plainly conclude, that
the carrying of the Bodies of Witches in the air, by the power of
the Devil, is a falſe, wicked and impious opinion.

Reaſ. 4.
4. Some are of opinion that this whole tranſaction was viſible,
ſenſible and corporeal, as *Theophylact*, and many others. Some are
of opinion that it was wholly in a Viſion. And ſome take a middle way that it was partly ſenſible and viſible, and partly mental,
and by way of viſion. Of which opinion the great *Cameron* ſeems

Ezek. 8. 3.

to be, who compares it with that of *Ezekiel* who ſaith: *And the*
ſpirit lifted me up between the earth and the heaven, and brought me
in the viſions of God to Jeruſalem : And ſheweth that the word
Ἀνέλαβεν doth agree with the Hebrew word נשא, which is as appli-
cable to lifting up or carrying in a viſion, as to bodily tranſportation. And that it was either altogether, or partly in a viſion, the

Eſai: cap:
4. 5.

learned *Beza* gives us this note : *Hoc videtur ſatis oſtendere hæc om-*
nia per viſionem quandam, non corporali tranſvectione & oſtenſione
eſſe geſta, quomodo nempe humanitus videre potuiſſet omnia regna
orbis, & gloriam eorum in momento ? But though it be the more
ſound and rational opinion that the whole tranſaction was mental,

and

and in a vision, yet we shall not altogether stand upon that, but if it be granted that it was corporeal and visible, yet it doth not appear that our Saviour was in his Body carried by the power of the Devil in the air, either to the top of an high mountain, nor set upon the pinnacle of the Temple in *Jerusalem*, and that for these reasons. 1. Our Saviour did not go to undertake this combat with Satan unwillingly, that he need be constrained, or carried to try the utmost power and malice of the Devil, but readily and willingly by the conduct and leading of the holy Spirit, for the Text saith in *Matthew*; *Then was Jesus led up of the spirit into the wildernesß, to be tempted of the Devil:* And S. *Mark* saith; *And immediately the spirit driveth him into the wildernesß.* And S. *Luke* saith: *He was led by the spirit into the wildernesß.* *Beza* saith, *subductus fuit in desertum,* and *Tremellius* saith, *ductus fuit,* upon the place in S. *Matthews* Gospel. And in S. *Luke Tremellius* saith; *Et duxit eum spiritus in desertum,* and *Beza, actus est ab eodem spiritu in desertum.* And in S. *Mark Tremellius* saith, *deduxit eum spiritus in desertum,* and *Beza* rendreth it, *expellit eum spiritus in desertum.* And because of the Greek word which is there εκβάλλη, he addeth this note, *Non significatur expulsio violenta, sed vis divina, quæ Christum, (qui ad illud usq; tempus ut privatus vixerat) nova persona induit, ac luctæ proximæ & ministerio præparatur.* Therefore saith *Origen: Sequebatur plane quasi athleta ad tentationem sponte proficiscens, & quodammodo loquebatur: Duc quo vis, & invenies me in omnibus fortiorem.* So that it is most plain that he was no otherwise led or carried by Satan, but as he was led by the Holy Ghost, so that he went whithersoever Satan would desire him of his own mind and accord, and needed not to be carried by the Devil, for S. *Luke* useth the same Greek word both for the Holy Spirit leading of him, and Satans leading of him, so that Satan did not carry his body in the air, as Men vainly conceive. 2. Though S. *Matthew* use the word παραλαμβάνει, which may signifie *assumpsit*, he took him, and set him upon a pinnacle of the Temple, and took him into an high mountain; yet it cannot be understood thereby that he took him, and carried his Body, but that he went before, and led Christ to those places, that he thought most fit for him to prevail in his temptations, to which places Christ went not by an unwilling constraint or hurried and carried in the air, but by a ready willingness, as one that certainly knew, and was assured, that he should win the Victory where ever, or how great soever the combat and temptations were. And therefore S. *Luke* useth the same word from ἄγω, *duco*, both for the Spirits, and Satans leading, as signifying no more, but to go before, and lead the way, or to draw one to such or such a place by persuasion and desire, and not to be carried in the air, which appeareth to be a vain and forged interpretation, and not the true meaning of the places.

Concerning *Simon Magus* we have before in this Treatise sufficiently proved that he was only a deceiver and Impostor, and what

Matth. 4. 1.

Mark 1. 12.

Luke 4. 1.

Caten. Aur.
Tho. Aquin. in
Luke 4.

strange feats he had done to aftonifh, and ftupifie the *Samaritanes*, were only jugling knacks, or deceits by confederacy, and no fuper-natural things, fo that here we will fay no more, but only add: That though our Englifh tranflation fay that he bewitched the people of *Samaria* with forceries, and that he himfelf, when he beheld the miracles and figns that were done, wondered; yet the word that they tranflate in the one place bewitching, and in the other wondered, are both from one *Thema* which is 'εξίςημι, *de ftatu mentis dejicio, facio ut aliquis mente non conftet, perterrefacio, obftupefacio*. And therefore either it ought to be that the *Samaritanes* were aftonifht at the feats that *Simon* wrought, and that he himfelf was aftonifht at the miracles of *Philip*, or that they were both bewitched, for they were both under the fame amazement, and there is no reafon at all to give it one fenfe in one place, and a different one in the other.

Acts 3. 9.

We need not here fay any thing of *Elymas* who is ftiled a Magician, becaufe it is manifeft that he was a falfe Prophet, full of all fubtilty, and all mifchief, a Child of the Devil, and an enemy of all righteoufnefs: which character truly given to him by the un-erring fentence of S. *Paul*, may be really afcribed to the whole tribe and profeffion of fuch kind of feducers and deceivers. Like unto whom were thofe *feven Sons of Sceva a Jew*, who are called *exorcifts, that took upon them to call over them that had evil fpirits, the name of the Lord Jefus, faying, We adjure you by Jefus, whom Paul preacheth*, but were foundly beaten for their pains, a fit reward for fuch vagabonds; And if all that profefs or practife fuch wicked, vain and lying things were duely punifhed, the poor ignorant people would not be fo much abufed as they are.

Acts 13. 10.

Acts 19. 13, 16.

The other places in the New Teftament we have handled, and anfwered, and alfo have touched upon that Text in the *Galathians* where we fpoke of Fafcination, but left it be not fufficient, we fhall handle it fully here. The words are, *O foolifh Galathians, who hath bewitched you, that you fhould not obey the truth?* From whence they ufe thus to argue: If Witchcraft in the Apoftles time had not been known, and practifed, he would not have made ufe of that Phrafe then; concerning which we return thefe refponfions.

1. If we confider natural Fafcination was by the Philofophers and Poets only taken to be contagious fteams flowing from the eyes, or breaths of malevolent and envious perfons, that had fome infectious difeafes, as we fee in the Plague, Small-pox, *Lues Venerea*, forenefs of Eyes, *Tinea*'s, and the like, which are contagious to others that lie with them, or converfe near them, the infected atomes or fteams iffuing in a certain Sphear of activity, are received by the pores, or mouths of the found perfons, by which they come to be infected alfo. And this the Poet witneffed: *Nefcio quis teneros oculus mihi fafcinat agnos*. Now this being the common opinion, the Apoftle taketh the metaphor from thence, as who fhould fay, who with their virulent and poyfonous opinions have infected

you,

you, that you should not obey the truth. And this is the genuine meaning of that metaphorical phrase, and no other sense can rationally and congruously be put upon the place, and this conduceth nothing to that opinion of Witchcraft that we oppose. For *Philosophica seu Physica fascinatio non nisi impropriè dici potest fascinatio, propriè verò est contagio, seu infectio.* And therefore did the learned *Vallesius* to the same purpose speak this. *Sed neq; si quis pestilenti affectus febri, aut etiam sine febre deferens secum seminaria pestis alium intuens intuentem inficiat, dicetur fascinasse, sed peste affecisse.* *Delrio. l. 3. q. 4. sect. 1. Concl. 2.*

2. Some of the fathers (which may be offered for an objection) do seem to hold that S. *Paul* here meant of diabolical fascination, and so *Tertullian* in English thus: For there is also something amongst the Gentiles to be feared, which they call fascination, being a more unfortunate event of praise, and great glory: this we sometimes interpret of the Devil. And S. *Hierome* saith upon this place: Fascination is when some things by Magical illusions are shewed to the eyes of Men, otherwise than they are. Also Fascination is vulgarly called that, which doth hurt Children, for the eyes of certain persons are said to burn with looking, and this act of theirs is called Fascination, and it may be that the Devils are subservient to this Sin. And *Thomas Aquinas* saith: And this also may be done by Devils, who have power of moving false imaginations, and bringing them to the principles of the Senses, by changing the Senses themselves. From whence we may note these things. 1. That *Tertullian* saith that they sometimes interpret this of the Devil, but how truly or upon what grounds he sheweth not, and it seemeth that sometimes they did interpret it of something else, for so his words must needs imply. 2. Secondly, S. *Hierome* sometime calleth fascination Magical illusions, and sometime that which doth hurt Children, by the burning of some eyes ; and then comes in with a may be that the Devils are subservient to this sin. So that he is not certain in his opinion, nor truly knows what fascination is, but according to vulgar opinion, or blind conjectures. 3. And all that the Angelical Doctor saith, doth but amount to the delusion of the Senses, by false imaginations, so that here is no proof either of the Devil, or his instruments, to cause any real fascination. *Vid. Jo. Lazar. Guttier. de fascino.*

3. Those that hold that *Paul* did allude unto natural, or diabolick fascination, do but mean magical illusions, whereby the senses are abused and deceived, to take things to be that which really they are not, and so are but cheating Incantations and delusory Juglings, for as *Galen* (if that piece be truly his) saith: *Incantationes verba sunt decipientia rationales animas secundum spci inceptionem, aut secundum timoris incisionem.* So that though S. *Paul* had taken the metaphor from that which was commonly accounted fascination, there is no necessity, that therefore the metaphor must in all points be true: it is sufficient that the common opinion was so, from whose usage of such terms the Apostle useth the word, *Vid. Guttier. passim.* *Galen. de Incantat.*

to

to fascinate, or inchant. And of this opinion was S. *Hierome* him-self who saith thus much : *Dignè Paulum, qui etsi imperitus est sermone non tamen & scientia, debemus exponere non quod scierit esse fascinum, qui vulgò putatur nocere, sed usus sermone sit trivii, & ut in cætero, ita & in hoc quoq; loco verbum quotidianæ sermocinationis assumpserit.* So that from hence it is most evident, that the using of the word fascination by the Apostle, doth not inferr the being of the thing, but only the opinion of the vulgar, that believed things that were not. And of the same judgment is *Thomas Aquinas* in these words : *Propriè dicit Apostolus, quis vos fascinavit ? quasi dicat, vos estis sicut homo ludisicatus qui res manifestas aliter accipit quàm sint in rei veritate.* Therefore we shall conclude this point with the sentiment of S. *Hierome : Nunc illud in causa est, quod ex opinione vulgi sumptum putamus exemplum, ut quomodo tenera ætas noceri dicitur fascino, sic etiam Galatæ in Christi fide nuper nati, & nutriti lacte, & solido cibo velut quodam fascinante sunt nociti.*

4. But howsoever fascination might be understood, yet it is plain, that except the *Effluvia* or steams of Bodies that had contagious diseases, entring into other sound Bodies, and thereby infecting them with their noysome vapours, or Atomes, there is nothing, but what was vain belief and credulous superstition, as the learned *Vallesius* tells us in these words, thus rendered in English:

Vid. Valles. de sacr. Philosoph.

"But if this be the way or reason of fascination, any one may easily "understand, that fascination is a certain superstitious fear, arising "from foolish credulity, of which sort are many other things in the "life of Man, as for argument, that this opinion is more approved "of by Women than by Men, and far more of the unlearned than of "the learned. Although (he saith) I also see that there are those "amongst the learned that are rather lovers of subtilty than verity, "who take care to defend those things that the vulgar do admire. By "which they would be accounted judicious magical Juglers, and "Men skilful of secrets. And therefore he thus concludeth : There-"fore the name of fascination is ancient, and according to the an-"cient signification, it doth not signifie any natural disease, but a "vain superstition, arising from vulgar opinion, and therefore nei-"ther *Hippocrates*, nor *Galen*, nor any of the ancient Physicians, "that I know of do mention fascination, neither amongst the dif-"ferences nor causes of Diseases. From whence again is taken "no small argument of its vanity. Therefore we shall conclude this "point with that remarkable saying of *Galen. Falsæ etenim opiniones animas hominum præoccupantes, non solum surdos, sed & cæcos faciunt, ita ut videre nequeant, quæ aliis conspicua apparent.*

Galen l. 8. de compos. medic.

5. The Angelical Doctor with the consent of the most part of all the learned do affirm that the Devil by his own power cannot change corporeal matter, unless he apply proportionate actives to fit passives, to produce those effects he intendeth; As for instance, he can cause burning, because there is a combustive agent in nature; but

but if that were awanting, or if there were no combuſtible matter, how ſhould he cauſe any ignition? But if he be ſuppoſed to work diabolical faſcination, for which there is no agent in nature, it being but an imaginary thing in the heads of the deluded vulgar; then it will neceſſarily follow, that he can work no faſcination at all, and ſo the whole opinion of the Witchmongers falls to the ground. For it is manifeſt that there is contagion, by the infected *Effluvia* or ſteams iſſuing from a diſeaſed Body to another by which it may be contaminated, but otherwiſe there is no natural faſcination, nor any agent in nature to produce that effect, and therefore there can be no Diabolical faſcination at all.

CHAP. IX.

Of Divine permiſſion, providence and preſcience.

THere is no one thing that hath more promoted this falſe and wicked Tenent of a kind of omnipotency in Devils, and the exorbitant power aſcribed to Witches, than the miſunderſtanding of the true and right Doctrine of Divine Providence, and the admitting of a bare permiſſion in God as different and diſtinct from his providence. From whence it cometh to paſs that not only the vulgar, but ſuch as tread in the ſteps of *Arminius*, do hold a meer bare permiſſion, and that God ſits as a quiet beholder by his Preſcience from the event of things to ſee what will be effected by Devils and wicked Men, who in the mean time run and rove about, acting what, when and how they pleaſe, and that God hath neither hook in their noſtrils, nor bridle in their mouths, neither keeps them in any reſtraint, order or government, and ſo we muſt needs have a mad rule in this World, during this permiſſion and naked inſpection.

But that we may proceed in ſuch order, as may be clear and intelligible to the Readers, we ſhall here propoſe the ſtate of the matter that we undertake to confute, which is this: That there is not in God a nude, paſſive permiſſion, ſeparate from the poſitive and active decree, order and will of his Divine Providence and Government, but that he doth rule all things according to the power and determination of his own poſitive and actual will. And this we ſhall proſecute in this following order and particulars.

Thoſe that deny that there is in God a paſſive permiſſion ſeparate from his decretive and actual will in his providence are accuſed by others, thereby to infer the abſurdity, that God is the author or efficient cauſe of ſin; which pretended abſurdity, in truth and reaſon cannot be any, becauſe it is a ſimple and abſolute impoſſibility, that

God

God should be the author of sin as these arguments do sufficiently testifie.

Argum. 1.   1. That of necessity must be false, which the Scriptures do declare to be so, in open and plain terms.   But that God should be the author of sin or evil, the Scriptures do deny in open and plain

James 1. 13.   terms, as where the Text saith: *God cannot be tempted with evil*: where both the act, and the possibility of it is absolutely denied.

Psal. 5. 4.   Again: *For thou art not a God that hast pleasure in wickedness, nei-*

Deut. 32. 3.   *ther shall evil dwell with thee.*   Therefore it is false that God is, or can be the author of sin; and so by consequence the supposed absurdity is a meer impossibility; and an absurdity urged that is impossible, is most of all absurd.

Argum. 2.   2. He is *ens summè perfectum. & quicquid est in Deo, est Deus*; but sin howsoever understood, or accepted, is an imperfection, defect and an aberration from a just and perfect rule, and therefore it is simply impossible that God can be the cause of any thing that is imperfect, sinful or evil, if sin be considered as *malum culpæ.*

Argum. 3.   3. God is not under any binding law given to him by some other, for then he should cease to be supream, independent and omnipotent : Now to whom there is no law given to observe, there can be no

Rom. 4. 15.   transgression, for the Apostle saith, *where there is no law, there is no transgression*; and therefore it is simply impossible that God should be the author, or causer of sin, or evil, because there is no law that he can transgress against.

Argum. 4.   4. God prohibiteth and hateth sin, as the Scriptures do every where testifie, but God is the cause of nothing but that which he loveth, and therefore cannot be the cause of the evil of sin.   And to speak properly sin hath no efficient cause, but a deficient, such as is the will of faln Angels, and wicked Men, whose irregularity of will, from the command of God, is all the cause that sin and evil hath or can have.   An efficient cause is only of those things that are good, because every efficient cause doth by working put something in being : But privations (of which sort are sins) do put nothing in being, but do truly note the absence of beings.   Therefore did

De Civitat.   S. *Augustine* say well: *Mali causa efficiens nulla est, sed tantùm de-*

Dei, l. 2. c. 7.   *ficiens.*

Argum. 5.   5. That which properly hath an efficient cause, hath also an end properly so called : But sin hath not an end properly so called, because the end is being, and therefore good, and the perfection of

Gen. 1. 3.   the thing.   But the Scripture doth declare that *all things that God created were exceeding good* ; and that the cause of sin was Man, and

John 8. 44.   the Devil; for the text saith, that *the Devil was a murderer from*

1 John 3. 8.   *the beginning, and abode not in the truth*: And again, *He that committeth sin, is of the Devil, for the Devil sinneth from the beginning.* Therefore from hence it is clear, that God neither is nor can be the author or causer of sin.

Argum. 4.   6. That which God is the author of, doth not make Man worse, but

but sin doth make Man worse, therefore God is not the author of it. And all sin is perpetrated, because thereby it receeded from the order that respecteth God, as the ultimate end of all things; but God doth incline all things unto himself, as to the ultimate end, neither doth he turn them from himself, because he is *summum bonum.*   And further as *Fulgentius* saith : *Deus non est ejus rei autor, cujus est ultor. At Deus est peccati ultor, ergo non autor.* And therefore we conclude, that this is a vain pretence of an absurdity, because it is impossible that God should be the author or causer of sin.

Vid. Schar. de miser. hom. stat. sub peccato, c. 3.

Fulgent. lib. i. ad Monim.

This plausible pretence to seem to be zealous, not to make God the author of sin, we commend as allowable ; but it is but like the zeal of the Scribes and Pharisees, which was without knowledge, because they pretend that for an absurdity, that is a simple impossibility.   And they ought to remember the argument of *Job*, which is this : *will ye speak wickedly for God ? and talk deceitfully for him ?* For as we ought not to suppose, or imply him to be the author of sin ; so we ought not to rob him of his Glory, by detracting from his power and providence, nor in ascribing that unto Creatures, that is only due unto the Creator ; as those do that hold a nude passive permission in him separate from his will and decree in his providence. Neither doth the denying of this any way imply that he is the author of sin, for a providential permission we allow as the act of his will and decree, as we shall shew hereafter.

Job 13. 7.

Now concerning permission in God, being a suspension of his efficiency in regard of some acts permitted to the creatures, and that for just and good ends, the definition of it and its affections or properties are so darkly handled even by those that make most ado about it, that it would serve rather to divert Men from the right way than to guide them in it, or unto it. Therefore here we shall only note these three things, and pursue it more fully hereafter. 1. There must be the person or power permitting that hath ability, right and authority so to do.   2. There must be the person or power permitted that hath ability to perform the thing permitted, otherwise it would be in vain, and to no purpose.   3. There must be the thing or action that is permitted to be done, or brought to pass, by the person permitted to act, and that must not be impossible.

1. Before the Creation it is meerly improper to attribute permission unto God, because there was no person, nor power besides himself that could act any thing, and therefore could not be permitted, and so the correlative being awanting, both the relative and the relation betwixt them must necessarily fall to the ground, as having no existence ; and so it is impossible that permission should be in God when there was no Creature to be permitted, and so could not be attributed unto him before the Creation.

2. It is as improper to attribute permission unto God in respect of the Physical agency of second causes, because he not only worketh all in all, and by his Divine concourse and conservative power

B b   sustaineth

Heb. 1. 3.
Job 34. 14,15. *sustaineth all things by the word of his power,* and *Job* tells us: *If he gather unto himself his spirit and breath, all flesh shall perish toge-ther, and man shall turn again into dust.* Upon which place of the Hebrews S. *Chrysostome* saith thus: *Feratq; inquit omnia, hoc est,* Vid. Chrysost. in Loc. *gubernet omnia. Siquidem cadentia, & ad nihilum tendentia con-tinet. Non enim minus est continere mundum quàm fecisse: Sed si oportet aliquid quod admireris dicere, adhuc amplius est. Nam in faciendo quidem, ex nullis extantibus rerum essentiæ productæ sunt: in continendo verò, ea quæ facta sunt, ne ad nihilum redeant con-tinentur. Hæc ergo dum reguntur, & ad invicem sibi repugnantia coaptantur, magnum & valdè mirabile, plurimæq; virtutis judicium declaratur:* But also because he hath set all natural things their bounds, and ordered, decreed and determined their ends in acting. Now what he hath appointed, ordered and decreed to be the agen-cy of every creature, and determinated its end in acting, cannot properly be called permission, but his will, ordination and provi-dence. As if one should say he suffereth and permitteth the Sun and Moon to run their course, it is an improper expression and in-jurious to his wisdom and power in his providential government of the creatures, seeing that it is a certain truth, *Deus operatur in omni operante:* And *he hath appointed the Moon for seasons, and the* Psal. 104. 19. *Sun knoweth his going down.* And it is absurd to say he suffereth the Sea to Ebb and Flow, when he hath *set it a bound that it cannot pass over. For he commandeth, and raiseth the stormy wind,* Verse 9.
Psal. 107. 25.
Job 38. 11.
Jerem. 5. 22. *which lifteth up the waves thereof. And said, hitherto shalt thou come and no further: And here shall thy proud waves be staid.* And again, *Will ye not tremble at my presence saith the Lord, which have placed the sand for the bound of the sea, by a perpetual decree that it cannot pass it, and though the waves thereof toss themselves, yet can they not prevail; though they roar, yet can they not pass over it.* And therefore we may conclude that the whole Creation in respect of Physical agency is ruled according to those orders, and not by a fortuitous chance, or a bare passive permission. 1. For first all creatures have their Physical agency, and the affections and pro-perties thereof ordained by God in the Creation, and according to this they constantly act, except they be turned, altered, or suspend-ed by the Creator himself, and he doth immediately act in them all, and they cannot properly be said to be permitted. 2. They are upholden, sustained and conserved in their several conditions, by the word of his mighty power, his continual concourse and di-vine emanation, which if it should but cease one minute, the whole Creation would fall into that nothing, from whence his Eternal and Omnipotent *Fiat* did raise and call them forth, so that we dare affirm with profound *Bradwardine, Quod necesse est Deum servare quamlibet* De Causs. Dei,
l. 1. c. 2. p. 165. *Creaturam immediatiùs quacunq; causa creata.* 3. When he pleaseth he doth suspend the effects and agency of natural causes, as in making the Sun stand still in the victory of *Joshua,* and of the three Children in the fiery Furnace. Sometimes he causeth them to act contrary to

their

their innate powers and qualities, as in *making the shaddow go ten* Isai. 38. 8.
degrees back in Ahaz sun-dial: and in causing *the waters of the red*
sea, contrary to their natures, which are to tend downwards, *to* Exod. 14. 21,
be divided, and to go backward, and to be as a wall on the right '22, 23.
hand, and on the left, until Moses, and the children of Israel were
passed through. And by many other wayes and means doth he al- Id. v. 17.
ter and change the course of natural agents, to serve his will and
good pleasure in his mercy, or in his justice, and yet here is no bare
or passive permission. 4. Besides these he ordereth all the particular acts of natural agents, to be subservient unto his will: So when
Jonah fled to *Tarshish, the Lord sent forth a great wind into the sea,* Jonah 1. 4.
and raised a mighty tempest to overtake Jonah ; and when he was
cast into the Sea, *the Lord prepared a great fish to swallow him up,* Id. 2. 10.
and also the Lord spake unto the fish, and it vomited up Jonah up-
on the dry land. Now the wind was not carried nor the storm
raised, by a permissive power, but by the will and order of the
Lord Jehovah, who sent them, and directed them either by his immediate power, or by the ministry of his Angels; and though they
wrought according to their natural agency, yet the special ordering
as to the particular act was not by permission, but by the will and
appointment of his providence. Neither did the great fish come by
chance or permission, but God in his merciful providence had pre- Psal. 129. 91.
pared him for the preservation of *Jonah*, and caused him to be vomited on the dry land ; so that all creatures do not only continue
according to his ordinances, but also all elementary, and irrational creatures do praise the Lord by fulfilling his word, will and
providence. And lest we be either censured to wrest the Scriptures,
or to be single in this opinion, take the judgment of some few o-
thers. S. *Gregory* (as he is quoted by learned *Bradwardine*) tells Greg. 16. mor.
us thus much: *Quis de Deo ista vel desipiens suspicetur, qui nimi-* 4.
rùm dum sit semper omnipotens, sic intendit omnibus, ut assit sin-
gulis ; sic adest singulis, ut simul omnibus nunquam desit ; sic itaq;
exteriora circundat, ut interiora impleat; sic interiora implet, ut
exteriora circundet ; sic summa regit, ut ima non deserat ; sic imis
præsens est, ut à superioribus non recedat. And *Thomas Aquinas*
their great Schoolman (as the same author cites him) saith: *Quòd* Thom. de Christ.
Deus immediatè ordinat omnes effectus per seipsum, licet per causas Religion. 133.
medias exequatur, sed in ipsâ executione quodammodò immediatè
se habet ad omnes effectus, in quantum omnes causæ mediæ agunt in
virtute causæ primæ, ut quodammodo ipse in omnibus agere videatur,
& omnia opera secundarum causarum ei possunt attribui, sicut arti-
fici attribuitur opus instrumenti. Therefore we will conclude this
with that of S. *Augustine: Proculdubio nullus est locus ab ejus præ-*
sentia absens ; super omnem creaturam quippe præsidet regendo, sub-
tus est omnia sustinendo, non pondere laboris, sed infatigabili vir-
tute, quoniam nulla creatura ab eo condita per se subsistere valet, nisi
ab illo sustentetur, qui eam creavit. Extra omnia est, sed non exclu-
sus, intra omnia, sed non conclusus. And these places need no

fiction

fiction of an Hebraism to expound them, nor no device of a verb of an active termination, and a permissive signification to evade the pressure of this truth.   And therefore in respect of Physical agency

De Causf. Dei,
p. 171.

we are bold with *Bradwardine* to assert these three Corollaries.

   1. *Quod nulla res potest aliquid facere, sine Deo.*

   2. *Quod nulla res potest aliquid facere, nisi Deus per se & im-mediate facit illud idem.*

   3. *Quod nulla res potest facere aliquid, nisi Deus faciat illud idem immediatiùs quolibet alio faciente.*

   4. So that however permission may be understood, it must properly relate to intellectual and rational creatures, and that only and especially in respect of those actions which we call moral, that is, in regard of sin, evil or *malum culpæ*; for whatsoever is *malum pœnæ*, God is the author, causer and inflicter of, according to the Text:

Amos 3. 6.

Shall there be evil in a City, and the Lord hath not done it? To understand aright the nature of permission, we are to consider the affections, properties and adjuncts of it, both in regard of the person permitting, the creature permitted to act, and the thing permitted to be done, with all the circumstances about them, and these we shall take from their Ring-leader and great Champion *Arminius* himself in these points.

   5. And first in respect of the person permitting (he saith) it is necessary that he know, what, to whom, and the ability of performance, that is to be granted, or used, by the person permitted, and that the person permitting have power to permit and to impede, and also that he have the right and authority of permitting.   2. In the person permitted, it is necessarily requisite, that he have suf-ficient power to effect and perform the thing permitted, if not hin-dered; for otherwise it would be nonsense to say, that a person is

Vid. Twisse
Vindic. grat.
de permiss.
p. 341.

permitted to do an act that he hath no power to perform.   3. If the person permitted have sufficiency of power to perform the act per-mitted, yet there is also required a propension and disposition in the person permitted, to perform the thing permitted, otherwise the permission as to that act would be without a certain end, and so would be *in vagum*, inconstant and not to be performed, and therefore he concludeth thus : *Imò nec rectè dici potest quod alicui actus permittatur, qui actus illos præstandi affectu nullo tene-tur.*

   6. We shall omit the exceptions that the learned and subtile Dr. *Twisse* hath made against diverse particulars in these passages, and shall only fix upon one that is manifestly false (if he mean of permission in general which he confesseth.) For in the Angels and *Adam* before their falling and committing of sin, there was not any propension or disposition to sin, and therefore to this we shall give the most acute answer of Dr. *Twisse* in these words: *Nam licèt in-*

De permiss.
p. 342.

sit homini propensio ad peccandum (scilicet post lapsum) per modum dispositionis, quæ præcedanea sit permissioni actus peccaminosi; At in Adamo (ante lapsum) nulla inerat hujusmodi dispositio, aut ad
                           peccandum

peccandum propensio, ante peccatum ejus primum. Sed neq; in An-gelis, qui à statu suo ceciderunt. Secundo, ut ut dispositio, sive ha-bitus insit qui inclinet ad agendum, non est ex natura dispositionis sive habitus cujuscunq; ut faciat hominem propendere ad actum ali-quem particularem, cujus vel solius ratione dicitur permissio. And though it be granted that God did create the Angels, and *Adam in statu labili,* wherein they had a sufficiency of power or grace not to have sinned, or faln, and though that power or grace was not withdrawn from them, and that there was no coaction upon their wills to inforce them to sin; for if it had been so, their falls would have been no sin: so neither did God supply them with more assist-ing grace to have upholden them, for then their estate had not been labile, nor they in a possibility to sin. But it is manifest that they in their Creation were set in *æquilibrio,* and had equal power of freedom of will either to sin or not to sin, and so had no propensi-on or disposition at all to commit that sin, to which they were left by a free permission: and so propension and disposition to the act permitted (if permission be understood generally) had no place in the Angels nor *Adam* before their first sinning, according to the Text, *God made man upright,* that is like a straight or right line that fall-ing perpendicularly upon another right line, doth incline to nei-ther end of the line upon which it falls, so *Adam* was made up-right without any propension or inclination to sin at all. And if this propension and disposition be understood, and applied to Angels in their condition after their fall, then it is true they have not on-ly an inclination but a most strong will and desire to commit more evil and mischief than God in his goodness permits them to per-form, for *the Devil goeth about like a roaring Lion seeking whom he may devour,* and it was Satan that not only had a disposition, but *desired to sift* Peter *as wheat.* And it is manifest that wicked Men have a strong will and desire to commit mischief; but that God hath an hook in their Nostrils, and a Bridle in their Jawes wherewith he curbs and restrains them, that they cannot act out all the mischief that they intend, as is manifest in the example of *Sennacherib* and many others.

Eccles. 7. 29.

7. Permission must be referred and reduced to the will of God, for nolition is an act of his will as well as volition: and to speak properly and truly, permission is but an act of the Divine Will not to impede such or such particular actions of the creatures; and there-fore the same things will follow from his volition or his will *non impediendi,* as from his volition to the acts of a free agent, seeing neither do put coaction upon the will of the Creature that is to act. And that permission is an act of the Divine will, and to be reduced unto it *Arminius* confesseth in these words: *Permissionem ad genus actionis pertinere ex ipsa vocis flexione est notum, sive per se sive re-ductive, ut in Scholis loquuntur. Cessatio enim ab actu, ad actum quoq; est reducenda: causam autem proximam & immediatam habet voluntatem, non scientiam, non potentiam, non potestatem, licet*

Twisse de Per-miss. ut supra.

& ista in permittente requirantur. And when he defineth permission, he saith: *Permissio Dei, est actus voluntatis Divinæ*; than which nothing can be more clear. And not much different from this is the

definition of permission, that is given by learned *Junius* thus: *Est autem permissio actus voluntatis, quo is penes quem est alienas actiones inhibere, eas non inhibet, sed agentis voluntati permittit earum modum.* And again he saith: *Apud Deum verò Opt. Max. nulla est omnino permissio, nisi voluntaria: quandoquidem omnis divina permissio à principio interno est, id est, à voluntate ipsius, & movetur ad finem quem voluntas præfinivit ejus.* But we will con-

clude this with that of S. *Augustin* thus Englished: Not any thing
"cometh to pass, unless the Omnipotent will have it to be done, ei-
"ther that it may be done by his suffering, or by his Volition. Nei-
"ther is it to be doubted that God doth well, even by suffering
"those things to be done, that are done evilly; For he doth not
"permit but by a just judgment, and verily every thing is good
"that is just. Although therefore those things that are evil, in as
"much as they are evil, they are not good; notwithstanding, as
"they are not only good, but also as they are evil, it is good. For
"unless this were good that there should be evils, they would by
"no means be permitted of the omnipotent good, to whom with-
"out all doubt it is always as easy to do that which he would, as
"it is easy not to suffer that which he would not have to be. By
all which it is plain that his permission is the act of his Divine Will,
and if he would not have it done he would not permit it, and so
the same consequences will follow from Nolition, that follow from
Volition, in respect as they are both acts of the Divine Will.

8. It is a certain truth that all moral actions are performed by a
physical power in respect of the sustentation of the will in its natural being while it acteth, and that the creature is conserved even
in the act as it is natural, though there be obliquity in the will of
the creature acting in reference to the law given, or made known

unto it. And this *Arminius* acknowledgeth in these words: *Necesse itaq; est, ut cum Deus potentiæ creaturæ actum aliquem permittit, creatura illa conservetur, ut sit, & vivat, potentia ejusdem
permaneat, idonea ad actum producendum, nulla major vel æqualis
potentia opponatur, objectum deniq; offeratur, & potentia permittatur.* From whence therefore to instance in the first sin of the Angels and *Adam*, besides the equal power and liberty of will that
they had to sin or not to sin, it is manifest that God willed and determined not to withdraw his conservative power from them, but
that they might be and live in the very act of their sinning. Neither
did he withdraw that power they had, nor opposed a greater, or
equal power to impede them, much less did he create or infuse a-
ny evil into their natures, nor put upon them any coaction of will,
to inforce them to sin, but solely left them to the power and liberty of their own free wills. And though by his prescience he certainly
knew that they would sin and fall, yet he determined in his purpose not to hinder them, but by his providential decree did set

down

down how to guide and order that fall and defection the most advantagiously for his glory both in his Mercy and Justice. So that even in this there was no bare paſſive permiſſion, ſeparate and diſtinct from his will and decree in his providence, but only permiſſion to the moral act of their wills, which by his wiſdom, decree, and providence, he ordered for his own glory, according to the Text : *The Lord hath made* (or wrought) *all things for himſelf,* Prov. 16. 4. *yea, even the wicked for the day of evil.* The Hebrew word *hath wrought,* doth properly ſignifie, to work by poliſhing, trimming, or framing and fitting, ſo that the wicked (who have made themſelves ſo by the acts of their own wills) God by his decree and providence doth poliſh, fit and order for the ſetting forth of his own glory in framing the wicked for the day of evil, the evil of puniſhment and judgment.

9. Further it is neceſſary that the creature acting a moral act (eſpecially in this caſe of the Angels and *Adam* before their fall) have the liberty and freedom of will, and that the will at the inſtant of the act, be not reſtrained nor under a coactive power, for otherwiſe *malum culpæ* or ſin would ceaſe to be evil, and ſo there could be no ſin at all. And thus far, and in this peculiar reſpect only, the Angels and *Adam* before their acting of ſin, and in the very inſtant of the act it ſelf, were permitted, that is, God willed and determined not to impede them, but for the ordering of that ſin and fall, the permiſſion was conjoined with his will and providence, and not ſeparate from it, or a nude permiſſion.

10. That *malum culpæ,* or ſin doth ariſe by the occaſion of a law; for where no law is, there can be no ſin, and therefore the Apoſtle ſaith : *But ſin taking occaſion by the Commandment, wrought in* Rom. 7. 8. 11. *me all manner of concupiſcence.* So that ſin conſidered as it is ſin, is an Aberration or Deviation of the Will of the creature from the revealed law of the Creator, and hath ſimply and abſolutely no other cauſality, but only the deficiency and *αταξία* of the Creature to produce it, eſpecially in theſe caſes of the Angels and *Adam* in their firſt acts of ſin.

11. Now we will come to the application of this unto wicked Men as they are under original and actual ſins, and that in theſe few examples. 1. It is not by a bare permiſſive power, but by his will and order in his providence, for he *ſetteth up the wicked in ſlippery* Pſal. 73. 18. *places,* and *yet a little while and the wicked ſhall not be : yea, thou* Pſal 37. 10. *ſhalt diligently conſider his place, and it ſhall not be.* So *Cain* was ſuffered to ſlay his Brother *Abel,* but by and by he was ſent from the preſence of the Lord into the land of *Nod :* So he ſet up *Saul* to be *King* over *Iſrael,* and ſoon after rejected him, and alſo deſtroyed him : theſe were by providence, not only bare permiſſion. 2. For Pſal 75. 6, 7. *promotion cometh neither from the Eaſt nor the Weſt, nor from the South : But God is the judge, he pulleth down one, and ſetteth up another.* So wicked *Haman* was ſet up to be the higheſt in the Kingdom next *Ahaſuerus,* and got a decree to have all the Jewes put

to

to death, and had set up a pair of Gallows to hang *Mordecai* upon, and yet see the providence of God, who quickly brought him to be hanged upon them himself: and this will be further made out where we speak of providence.

12. Though those that ascribe so large a power unto Devils and Witches, do take it for granted that they are only under a bare passive permission, and that the faln Angels do act, what, when, where and how they lift, yet is it a meer falsity, for they are under the rule of Gods Divine Will, decree and providence, and do act nothing, but as and so far as they are licensed, ordered and limited by his will and providence, and are under a punctual restraint, nay kept in the chains of everlasting darkness unto the judgment of the great day, as we shall prove at full in that Chapter where we handle the knowledge and power of faln Angels. And therefore here we shall only say this, that if Devils could do as much mischief as they would, and were under no restraint or chains, then none of the godly would be left alive. But it is manifest that Devils do act nothing (excepting the obliquity and evil of their own wills) but meerly as instruments of the Divine Will and Providence, for as the Christian Philosopher saith : *Illa est impietas ; nimirum ea falso attribuere creaturis, quæ radicaliter Deo soli sunt propria, & inter cætera, actum aliquem peculiarem in diabolo esse existimare, qui non est originaliter à Deo, & consequenter immediaté, cum essentialis Dei actus sit per se sine divisione in omni re.*

Risp. Fludan. ad Lanov. p.18.

Greg. in Dialog. Concerning Divine prescience, which is as S. *Gregory* saith, *Præscientia est unamquamq; rem antequam veniat, videre, & id quod futurum est priusquam præsens sit prævidere,* we may only note his, That it is certain and infallible, as saith the Lord by the Prophet: *Isal. 42. 9.* Behold the former things are come to pass, and new things do I declare, before they spring forth I tell you of them : Also, *known unto God are all his works from the foundation of the World.* So *Augus. de Trinit. l. 15. c. 7.* "that his prescience is that infallible vision, by which he comprehendeth all what he knows by one eternal, immutable and ineffable "vision. But this prescience in God doth nor flow from the things that are to come to pass, but from his decree, by which all future *Ephes. 1. 11.* things are determined, who doth *all things according to the counsel Psal. 115. 3. of his own will,* for *God is in heaven, he hath done whatsoever he pleased.* But this prescience is not to be considered only by it self, as a bare vision, or inspection, but as it is coupled and joined with *Psal. 33. 13, 14, 15.* his providence, *For the Lord looketh from heaven, he beholdeth all the sons of men. From the place of his habitation he looketh upon all the inhabitants of the earth. Forming* (or framing) likewise *their hearts, and considering all their works.* And this prescience considered solely by it self, is not the cause of the things that come to *Vid. Rivet. de Provid. Dispus. I.* pass, for as the Father saith well: *Sicut tu memoria tuâ non cogis facta esse quæ præterierunt, sic Deus præscientia suâ non cogit facienda quæ sunt futura.* So that we conclude that God by a naked prescience *August. de lib. arbitr. l. 3.* doth not only behold infallibly the things that are to come, and so

io

is only a spectator of what Devils and wicked Men will do, but also that he doth order, rule and predesign all their works and actions.

1. As touching Gods Government and Administration of the World by his Divine providence, we shall in the first place lay down some of the definitions of it from the most sound and learned Divines of the Reformed Churches, and that in English, after this order. The acute and learned *Rivet* describes it thus: " Providence *Andr. Rivet. disputat. Thes. 1. p. 4.*
" is an ineffable force and virtue of the Divine Sapience and Po-
" tency, by which God doth conserve and govern to his own Glo-
" ry all his Works according to his eternal, most wise, and most
" free decree, and directing every thing in time unto its end. *Jo-*
hannes de Spina defines it thus : " Providence is the prescience and *De provid. Trac. p. 9.*
" counsel of God eternal, most free, immutable, most just, most
" wise, most good, whereby God worketh and determineth all good
" things in all, but doth only permit evil things, and doth dispose
" and direct all things to his own Glory and the Salvation of his elect.
And much to the same purpose doth *Lambertus Danæus* speak in
these words: " Providence is a most free and most powerful action *Isagog. Christ. c. 32. p. 52.*
" of God, by which he not only stirreth up and governeth univer-
" sals, but also singulars, in every one of their single actions. And
" (he saith) it is called a most free and most powerful act, because
" it can neither be hindered nor overcome by any law. And to
these for substance do agree *Calvin*, *Musculus*, *Beza*, *Zanchius*, and
the rest of all Orthodox Divines.

2. But we shall chiefly insist on that definition that is given by
learned *Piscator* in these words: " The providence of God is his
" eternal, most wise, most just and immutable counsel or decree,
" whereby he doth most freely govern all things by him created to
" the glory of himself, and the Salvation of his elect. To which he
giveth this explication: " That it doth consist of a Genus and *Exeget. Loc. 6. p. 143, 144. &c.*
" three differences. The Genus is the word *Decretum* which is
" illustrated by four adjuncts; Eternity, Sapience, Justice and Im-
" mutability. The first difference is taken from the objects; which
" are all created things. The second from the ends, which are two,
" the Glory of God, and the Salvation of the elect. The third from
" the effect, which is the government of things created, which Gu-
" bernation is illustrated by the adjunct which is liberty.

3. The parts of this definition are thus proved. 1. That the
providence of God is his counsel and decree, appeareth most plainly
from these Scriptures: *Peter* in his Sermon to the Jews upon the day
of Pentecost saith: *Him (that was Jesus) being delivered by the* *Acts 2. 23.*
determinate counsel and foreknowledge of God (τῇ ὡρισμένῃ βουλῇ ἢ προ-
γνώσει Θεῦ) ye have taken, and by wicked hand have crucified and
slain. And again the Church at *Jerusalem* in their prayers say thus:
Of a truth against thy holy Child Jesus whom thou hast anointed, both *Acts 4. 27, 28.*
Herod, and Pontius Pilate, with the Gentiles, and people of Israel
were gathered together, For to do whatsoever thy hand and thy coun-
C c   *sel*

sel determined (ἡ χεὶς σε ϰ᾿ ἡ βυλὴ σε περώεισι ϰοίας) *before to be done.*
2. That all things created (nay alfo thofe things which do feem to
happen fortuitoufly, or to be by permiffion, as finful actions) are governed and ordered by the providence of God, as thefe Scriptures

Heb. 1. 3.
will fufficiently demonftrate. *Chrift Jefus the fon of God, doth uphold* (or fuftain) *all things by the word of his power.* And doth not

Matth. 10. 29, our Saviour tell us : *Are not two sparrows fold for a farthing, and*
30, 31,
*one of them fhall not fall on the ground without your father ? But the
very hairs of your heads are all numbred. Fear ye not therefore, ye
are of more value than many sparrows.* That place concerning the
Cities of refuge, and the fleeing of the ignorant man-flayer thither

Deut. 19. 4, 5. is moft remarkable, and is this. *And this is the cafe of the flayer,
which fhall flee thither, that he may live: whofo killeth his neighbour ignorantly, whom he hated not in times paft, as when a man
goeth into the wood with his neighbour to hew wood, and his hand
fetcheth a ftroak with the ax to cut down the tree, and the head flip-
eth from the helve, and lighteth upon his neighbour that he die, he
fhall flee unto one of thofe Cities, and live.* And was not the action
of *Jofephs* brethren, fin and finful in felling of him to the Ifmaelites,

Gen. 45. 5.
and yet he acknowledgeth, *that God fent him before them to preferve life.* So that God brought good forth of evil, and doth order even the fins of the wicked to juft and good ends by his Di-

Prov. 16. 33. vine Providence. Again: *The lot is caft into the lap, but the whole
difpofing thereof is of the Lord.* So when the Men in the Ship with
Jonah did caft lots, by the Lords difpofing *the lot fell upon Jonah*
who was juftly guilty, and fo by providence pointed out. 3. That
God doth govern all things to his own glory is manifeft by thefe

Prov. 16. 4.
Texts: *The Lord hath made all things for himfelf: yea even the*
Rom. 9. 22, 23. *wicked for the day of evil.* And, *what if God, willing to fhew his
wrath, and to make his power known, endured with much long fuf-
fering the veffels of wrath fitted to deftruction: And that he might
make known the riches of his glory on the veffels of mercy, which
he had afore prepared unto glory?* And that he governeth all things

Rom. 8. 28, for the Salvation of his elect, is plain: *And we know that all things
30.
work together for good, to them that love God, to them who are the
called according to his purpofe.* So that if God be for the Elect,
who can be againft them? 4. That God doth govern all things
moft freely is clear, becaufe he is omnipotent and fupream, and
there is no power that can either impede, or conftrain him. *For he*

Pfal. 115. 3.
hath done whatfoever he would, both in Heaven and Earth. And

Rom. 9. 15, the Apoftle faith; *I will have mercy upon whom I will have mercy.*
18.
Therefore hath he mercy on whom he will have mercy, and whom

Job 34. 13.
he will he hardeneth. For *who hath given him a charge over the
earth? or who hath difpofed the whole world?*

4. The feveral ways that God ufeth in governing the creatures
in the world whether good or bad, may be comprifed in thefe four
ways. 1. He ruleth and ordereth them, by bending, inclining and
turning of their wills and intentions, to ferve and fullfil his decree

and

and pleasure.   So when the Brethren of *Joseph* were fully resolved
to murther him, God by the means of *Reuben* and *Judah*, so wrought ^{Gen. 37. 18,}
upon their minds and wills, that they were contented to sell him ^{19, 20, 26, 27,}
to the Ismaelites, that so the determinate counsel of God might be ^{50. 20.}
fulfilled; for though they intended it for evil, that he might never
return to his Father, nor to have his dream fulfilled that they might
bow down before him, yet God intended it for good, and so
brought it to pass.   And this he did not by changing or taking a-
way their natures, nor by putting a coactive power upon their
wills; but by inclining and bending them to his own purpose, so
that the act was the act of their own wills, but the moving of their
wills to spare his life was from the Lord : for as he that made the
eye must needs see, so he that made the will must needs have a power to move, incline and turn it.   And therefore the Father said
well, *Certum est, nos velle cum velimus, sed Deus facit, ut velimus
bonum.*   And it is apparent that the hearts of all men are in the hands
of the Lord, and he turneth and inclineth them according to his
will and purpose, as saith *Solomon*, *The Kings heart is in the hand* ^{Prov. 21. 1.}
*of the Lord, as the rivers of water : he turneth it whithersoever he
will.*   Upon which the note of *Tremellius* and *Junius* is this : *Est
quidem animus omnium hominum gubernaculum, quo velut naves in
mediis aquis reguntur corpora & actiones nostræ : tamen ne ipsorum
quidem regum animus ex seipso permovetur, impellitur, inhibeturque,
sed Deus in singulorum animis, veluti clavum tenet.*   And concern-
ing the wicked God saith : *I will harden the heart of Pharaoh, and* ^{Exod. 7. 3.}
multiply my signes and wonders in the land of Ægypt.   And again :
And *indeed for this cause, have I raised (made thee stand, feci ut ex-* ^{Id. 9. 16, 17.}
isteres, as Beza notes) thee up, for to shew in thee my power, and ^{Rom. 9. 17.}
*that my name may be declared throughout all the earth.   And as yet
exaltest thou thy self against my people, that thou wilt not let them
go ?*   And further the Text saith : *He turned their hearts, to hate his* ^{Psal. 105. 25.}
people, to deal subtilly with his servants.   2. God also ruleth and
ordereth his creatures by leading, drawing, inciting and moving
their wills to his own ends and purposes, as sometimes to good,
as in his own people : *For as many as are led by the spirit of God,* ^{Rom. 8. 14.}
they are the sons of God.   And so was our Saviour *led,* or driven
(ἐκβάλλει, ἤγετο, ἀνήχθη) *into the wilderness, to be tempted of the devil.* ^{Matth. 4. 1.}
To this agreeth the blessing and prophecie of *Noah: God shall per-* ^{Mark 1. 12.}
swade, or allure *Japhet, to dwell in the tents of Shem.*   Sometimes ^{Luke 4. 1.}
God inciteth the creatures to evil by the ministery of Satan, as is ^{Gen. 9. 27.}
manifest in these examples.   For the Text saith, *And again the an-* ^{2 Sam. 24. 1.}
*ger of the Lord was kindled against Israel, and he moved David a-
gainst them, to say, Go number Israel and Judah.*   And another place
saith : *And Satan stood up against Israel, and provoked David to num-* ^{1 Chron. 21. 1.}
ber the people.   Whereby it is plain that Satan was the instrument,
as sent and ordered of God to move *David* to number the people,
that thereby the King and people might be punished, and the King
thereby brought to a deeper sight of his sins, repentance, and a closer

C c 2   trusting

trusting and adhering to his God. So when the Lord intended to have *Ahab* to go up to *Ramoth Gilead* that he might be slain, he sent forth an evil Angel, to be a lying spirit in all *Ahabs* Prophets, 1 Kings 22.22. and said unto him, *Thou shalt perswade him, and prevail also : Go forth and do so.* So that what God orders, Satan doth but execute. So when God intended to punish and destroy *Abimelech,* and the Men of *Shechem,* he sent an evil spirit between them to divide them, and so accomplisht his will upon both parties, as saith the Text: Judges 9. 23, 56, 57. *Thus God rendred the wickedness of Abimelech which he did unto his father, in slaying his seventy brethren. And all the evil of the men of Shechem, did God render upon their heads: and upon them came the curse of Jotham the son of Jerubbaal.* 3. God ruleth his creatures by permission, or his will of not impeding them to act according to their wills and power, as in these cases. For God Psal. 81.11,12. speaking of his people of *Israel* saith : *But my people would not hearken unto my voice; and Israel would none of me. So I gave them up unto their own hearts lusts, and they walked in their own counsels.* Acts 14. 16. Agreeable to which is that in the *Acts : Who in times past suffered all nations to walk in their own ways :* which is as *Beza* notes: *Ex arbitrio suo vivere, nulla ipsis præscripta ratione religionis.* And Rom. 1. 24. in this sense, and to this purpose it is that *God gave (παρέδωκε) them up to uncleanness, through the lusts of their own hearts;* because of that horrible Idolatry that formerly they were guilty of. 4. God ruleth his creatures by his providence, sometimes by repressing, prohibiting and impeding the execution of their wicked wills, as is clear in the case of *Abimelech* King of *Gerar,* who took *Sarah Abrahams* Wife intending to have had carnal knowledge of her, Gen. 20. 6. but God plagued him and his Family, and said; *For I also withheld thee from sinning against me; therefore I suffered thee not to touch her.*

Now we shall come to consider how the faln Angels are under the rule and restraint of this Divine and all-governing providence, wherein we shall make it appear, that they act nothing in this elementary and sublunary World, after any corporeal manner, but as they are ordered, licensed and limited by the will and decree of the Almighty, and so do not wander and rove at their own pleasures to act in corporeal things, what, when and how they list, as the Witchmongers vainly suppose, and this we shall clear in these particulars.

1. It cannot rationally be supposed that God is less wise, in ruling and ordering the Prince of darkness, the Prince of Devils, and the head of all Rebellion and Rebels, than he is in ruling his Subjects and Servants, which are all wicked men ; but all these he ruleth with a rod of Iron, and breaketh them in sunder like a Potters vessel: And therefore much more hath he a restraint upon, and a rule over the faln Angels who kept not their first estates, and therefore are reserved in chains in darkness until the judgment of the great day.

2. As

2. As he is the Prince and Ring-leader of all Sin and Rebellion against God, though he yet have not his final punishment; unto which he is reserved for the judgment of the great day, and though he be not yet thrust into the abysse or great depth, nor into that everlasting fire that is prepared for him and his Angels; yet is he kept in chains and darknes, and can act nothing but as he is licensed, ordered and limited by the Almighty. Matth. 25. 41. Luke 2. 31.

3. And though he compass the earth to and fro, and walk about *like a roaring lion seeking whom he may devour*, yet is that but according to the malice and purpose of his wicked will, for in punishing or afflicting of the godly he must have licence from God first, or else he can do nothing in this Elementary World, as is most manifest in the affliction of *Job*, neither could he enter into the herd of Swine, but by Christs leave and order, nor deceive *Ahabs* Prophets but by order from the Lord.   And therefore an ancient Father said well : *Quod si super porcos potestatem non habent, multò magis nullam habent Dæmones contra homines factos ad imaginem Dei ; oportet ergo Deum solum timere, contemnere autem illos.* Thom. Aquin. Caten. aur. in Luc. 8. p. 200.

Therefore we shall conclude this briefly here, having occasion to handle it more fully hereafter, to wit, that the Witchmongers can have no shelter for their opinion from the Doctrine of Gods permission (if rightly understood) because God doth neither order, nor permit faln Angels to act any thing (especially in corporeal things) but what is for just, good, and wise ends, which cannot be shewed in these actions attributed to Witches.

CHAP. X.

Whether faln Angels be Corporeal or simply Incorporeal, and the absurdity of the assuming of Bodies, and the like consequents.

I Am not insensible what great censure I may incurr for entring upon such a ticklish and nice point as the corporeity or incorporeity of Angels, seeing it hath exercised and crucified the wits of the most learned in all ages, especially being but an obscure person, and not heightned with those lofty titles that usually elevate Mens fames, more by those attributes than by the weight and strength of their arguments.   Yet it being no necessary Article of the Christian Faith, but that a Man may lawfully defend either, it cannot rationally be judged by understanding Readers either to be pride or just offence for me to handle this subject.   For seeing that most of the Christian and Learned Fathers for the space of four hundred years after Christ, were of the opinion that they were corporeal,

real, it can be no novelty in me to revive or affert that opinion, and therefore I fhall labour to make it manifeft in this enfuing order.

1. There is a late way of arguing taken up by Dr. *Moore* and others, that they will undertake to prove a thing to be fo or fo, or elfe to make Man to deny his own faculties. And fo the faid Doctor *The immort. of the Soul, p. 7, 8.* doth undertake to prove the exiftence of immateral and incorporeal beings, or elfe he thinketh he bringeth Men to deny their own faculties : And thefe faculties he maketh to be, common notions, external fenfe, and evident and undeniable deductions of reafon. And concludeth that, what is not confonant to all or fome of thefe is meer fancy, and is of no moment for the evincing of truth or falfhood, by either its vigour or perplexivenefs. But this will not accomplifh the bufinefs he intends, for thefe reafons. 1. Becaufe there is not the common notion of a fpiritual and immaterial being in all or any Man, neither is it (to ufe his own words) true at firft fight to all men in their wits upon a clear perception of the terms, without any further difcourfe or reafoning, but is only a bare fuppofition without any proof or evidence at all. 2. The being of an immaterial and fpiritual fubftance can no way incurr into the fenfes nor affect them, becaufe it is manifeft (as *Des Cartes* hath fufficiently proved) that all fenfation is procured by corporeal contact, and not otherwife. And though we deny not that there have been, are and may be apparitions, that cannot be rationally fuppofed to be the ordinary *Phænomena* of corporeal matter, yet affecting the fenfes, there muft be fomething in them that performeth that effect, that is corporeal, or elfe the fenfes could not be wrought upon, for *immateriale non agit in materiale, nifi eminenter ut Deus.* 3. No right deductions can poffibly be drawn from the higheft power of ratiocination, where the underftanding hath no cognofcibility of the things that reafon would draw its conclufions from, for as the fame Doctor frameth his Axiome which is this : Whatfoever things are in themfelves, they are nothing to us, but fo far forth as they become known to our faculties or cognitive powers. But we affert (which we fhall make good anon) that our faculties or cognitive powers (how far foever fome would vainly magnifie and extol them) have not the power of underftanding beings that are fimply and abfolutely immaterial and incorporeal. 4. There is nothing that is more undoubtedly true than what the *Nov. Organ. lib. 1. p. 49.* Lord *Verulam* hath told us in thefe words : *Caufa vero & radix ferè omnium malorum in fcientiis ea una eft : quod dum mentis humanæ vires falfo miramur & extollimus, vera ejus auxilia non quæramus.* And again : *Subtilitas naturæ fubtilitatem fenfus & intellectûs multis partibus fuperat,* the which may be proved from many undeniable inftances, which need not here be mentioned, only we fhall add what the aforefaid learned Lord fpeaks to the fame purpofe *Ibid. p. 21.* which is this : "The fault of fenfe is twofold: For it either for-"faketh or deceiveth us. For firft there are many things that efcape "the fenfe, though rightly difpofed, and no way impeded either "by the fubtilty of the whole body or by the minutenefs of the
"parts

" parts, or by the diſtance of place, or tardity and velocity of motion,
" or by the familiarity of the object, or by reaſon of other cauſes.
" Neither again, where the ſenſe doth apprehend the thing, are
" thoſe apprehenſions ſufficiently firm. For the teſtimony and infor-
" mation of ſenſe is always from the Analogie of Man, not from the
" Analogie of the Univerſe. And it is altogether aſſerted with great
error, that ſenſe is the meaſure of things. Neither can theſe notions
the Doctor would make ſo clear, be had or gathered, without ſome
intimation from ſome of the ſenſes.

2. Further the Doctor tells us that the Idea of a Spirit is as eaſie
a notion, as of any other ſubſtance whatſoever. And he alſo ſaith : *An Antidot.*
" Neverthelesſ I ſhall not at all ſtick to affirm, that his Idea or notion &*c. p.* 12.
" (ſpeaking of God) is as eaſy as any notion elſe whatſoever, and *Immortal. p.* 21.
" that we may know as much of him as of any thing elſe in the
" World. This later he ſpeaketh concerning God. But that theſe
aſſertions are unſound, theſe following reaſons will ſufficiently e-
vince.

1. He doth define a Spirit thus : A Spirit is a ſubſtance penetrable *Reaſ.* 1.
and indiſcerpible. Now if it be true that he affirms before, that, " the
" ſubject, or naked eſſence, or ſubſtance of a thing is utterly uncon-
" ceiveable to any of our faculties, and that if we take away apti-
" tudes, operations, properties and modifications from a ſubject,
" that then the conception vaniſheth into nothing, but into the Idea
" of a meer undiverſificated ſubſtance, ſo that one ſubſtance is not
" then diſtinguiſhable from another, but only from accidents or
" modes, to which properly belongs no ſubſiſtence. So then if
we take away penetrability and indiſcerpibility, which are but the
modes and properties of a Spirit, whoſe genus he maketh ſubſtance
to be, then it vaniſheth into an indiſtinguiſhable notion, and ſo his
definition comes to nothing.

2. For if ſubſtances be known by their properties and modifica- *Reaſ.* 2.
tions, as we grant they are, the modifications and properties muſt
of neceſſity be ſome ways known unto us : but there are no ways
either by common notions, evidence of the ſenſes, or ſound deductions of reaſon that can certainly inform us of theſe properties or
modifications of penetrability and indiſcerpibility, and the Doctor
yet never proved either, but is only a bare ſuppoſition, and a melancholy figment.

3. He tells us that all ſubſtance has dimenſions, that is, length, *Reaſ.* 3.
breadth and depth, but all has not impenetrability, and boldly The Immort.
ſaith : It is not the Characteriſtical of a body to have dimenſions, *p.* 68.
but to be impenetrable ; to which we anſwer. It is ſtrongly aſſerted
by learned *Helmont,* that by the ultimate ſtrength of nature, bodies do ſometimes penetrate themſelves and one another, and to that
purpoſe he giveth convincing examples, and concludeth thus from
them. *Invenio equidem, naturæ contiguam dimenſionum penetra- De Injeſt.*
tionem, licet non ordinariam. And after ſaith thus : *Quibus conſtat p.* 598.
corpora ſolida, ſatis magna, penetraſſe ſtomachům, inteſtina, ute-
rům,

rum, *omentum, abdomen, pleuram. veficam, membranas inquam, tanti vulneris impatientes. Id eft, abfq; vulnere cultros per iftas membranas transmiffos. Quod æquivalet penetrationi dimenfionum, factæ in natura, absq; ope Diaboli.* And to the fame purpofe that moft acute perfon, Dr. *Gliffon*, handling this very point faith : *Verùm enimverò, fi fola quantitas actualis fit caufa impenetrabilitatis corporum (ut ex fupra dictis liquet.) eaq; fit naturaliter mutabilis; quid impedit ne fubftantia materialis aliam fubftantiam, mutatâ quantitate, novâq; fimul affumptâ utrifq; communi, penetret?* And therefore we may as confidently deny his affumption, that Impenetrability is the Characteriftical of body, as he affirm it without proof, and muft with all the whole company of the learned, affign Extenfion to be the true and Genuine Character of Body. And further he granting that fubftance hath length, breadth, and depth, we muft of neceffity conclude, that whatfoever hath thofe properties muft needs be material and corporeal, and fo that which he would make to be Spirit is meerly Body.

Dt Natur.Subft. Energ. p. 406.

Reaf. 4.

4. Whereas he faith that the notion of Spirit is as eafy a notion, as any other whatfoever, it is granted, but is not at all to the purpofe : for our inquiry need not be of the facility of a notion, but of the verity of it, that is, of the congruity and adequation of the notion and the thing from whence it is taken; otherwife though the notion be eafy, yet without an adequate congruity to the thing it is meerly falfe. As for inftance, when a melancholy perfon doth verily imagine himfelf to be changed into a Wolf or Dog, it is not only an eafy notion, but alfo it is truly a notion, and yet a falfe notion, becaufe there is no true congruity betwixt it and the thing from whence it is taken, the Body of the perfon fo conceiving, being not at all changed into Wolf or Dog, but ftill retaining its humane fhape and figure. And therefore the Lord *Verulam* doth to this point fpeak truly and clearly in thefe words: *Itaq; fi notiones ipfæ mentis (quæ verborum quafi anima funt, & totius hujufmodi ftructuræ ac fabricæ bafis) malè ac temere à rebus abftractæ, & vagæ, nec fatis definitæ & circumfcriptæ, deniq; multis modis vitiofæ fuerint, omnia ruunt.* And therefore the Doctor might very well have confidered, whether thefe his new notions had been fitly and rightly drawn from the things, to which he doth fo confidently affix them, before he had fo boldly afferted them, which though they be truly his notions, that is, that he did think, conceive, and frame them, yet they are not truly abftracted from the things: And fo he may be rather judged to be led by fpeculative and Philofophick Euthufiafm, than by the clear light of a found underftanding.

Nov. organ. p. 18.

Reaf. 5.

5. And concerning his Tenent that the Idea or Notion of God is as eafy as the notion of any thing elfe whatfoever, that the notion may be eafy we grant; but whether it be true and adequate, there lies the queftion. For thofe old Hereticks that held that God had Eyes, Ears, Head, Hands and Feet and the like, had an eafie notion of

of it, conceiving him to have humane members, but I hope the Doctor will not say that this notion of theirs was a notion truly drawn from the nature and being of God, becaufe there is no corporeity in him at all. And it is and hath been the Tenent of all Orthodox Divines, Ancient, Middle and Modern, that God in his own nature and being is infinite and incomprehenfible, and therefore there can no true and adequate notion of him, as being fo, be duly and rightly gathered in the underftanding of creatures; and fo the Doctors pofition or notion muft needs be Phantaftry and imaginary Enthu-fiafm. For as there are many things in nature that in themfelves are finite and comprehenfible, that as he grants of naked effence or fubftance are utterly unconceivable to any of our faculties; much more muft the being of God that is infinite and incomprehenfible, which are attributes that are incommunicable, be utterly unconceivable to any of our faculties. And it is but the vain pride of Mans Head and Heart, thereby to magnifie his own abilities, whereas the Text doth pronounce this of him, *For vain man would be wife; though he be born like a wild afs colt*; that lifts him up to Job 11. 12. conceit that he can fathom and comprehend the Infinite and Almighty, whom the Heaven of Heavens cannot contain, and therefore cannot frame a true notion of him, whom perfectly he doth not 1 Kings 8. 27. underftand nor comprehend, and the attributes of God are matters of Faith and not the weak deductions of humane reafon.

3. Thofe that feem to idolize humane abilities and carnal reafon, have not only applied thofe fo much magnified Engines to the difcovery of created things, wherein they have effected fo little, that fufficiently proclaims the invalidity of the inftruments or the inaufpicious application of them, or both, all the feveral forts of Natural Philofophy hitherto found out, or ufed, being examined, coming far fhort of folving the *Phænomena* of nature, when even the leaft animal or vegetable affords matter enough to puzle and *nonplus* the greateft Philofopher, fo that we may juftly complain with *Seneca*, that the greateft part of thofe things we know are the leaft part of thofe things we know not; Thefe engines (I fay) though proving ineffectual to find out the true notions and knowledge of natural things, have alfo (like the fiction of the Gyants) notwithftanding invaded Heaven, and taken upon them to difcover and determine of Celeftials, wherein it is in a manner totally blind, or fees but with an Owl-like vifion. For indeed the deciding of this point muft be taken from the Divine authority of the Scriptures, and the clear deductions that may be drawn from thence; for this is that clear light, that we ought to follow, and not the Dark-lanthorn of Mans blind, frail and weak reafon, for it is *a fure word of Prophecie whereunto* it is good *to take heed*, and not to *vain Philofophy, old Wives Fables*, or *oppofition of Sciences falfly fo called*. And therefore we fhall conclude this point here concerning the corporeity or incorporeity of Angels with that Chriftian and learned pofition of Dr. *Stillingfleet* in thefe words: "But although

D. d   "Chri-

" Chriſtianity be a Religion which comes in the higheſt way of cre-
" dibility to the minds of Men, although we are not bound to be-
" lieve any thing but what we have ſufficient reaſon to make it ap-
" pear that it is revealed by God, yet that any thing ſhould be
" queſtioned whether it be of Divine revelation, meerly becauſe
" our reaſon is to ſeek, as to the full and adequate conception of it,
" is a moſt abſurd and unreaſonable pretence.

    4. In handling this point of the corporeity or incorporeity of
Angels, we do here once for all exclude and except forth of our
diſcourſe and arguments the humane and rational Soul as not at all
to be compriſed in theſe limits, and that eſpecially for theſe reaſons. 1. Becauſe the humane Soul had a peculiar kind of Creation
differing from the Creation of other things, as appeareth in the
words of the Text. *And the Lord God formed man of the duſt of*
the ground, and breathed into his noſtrils the breath of life; and man
became a living ſoul. Upon which the note of *Tremellius* and *Ju-*
nius is, *anima verò hominis ſpiritale quiddam eſt, & divinum.* 2. Becauſe I find *Solomon* the wiſeſt of Men making this queſtion: *who*
knoweth the ſpirit of man, that goeth upward: and the ſpirit of the
beaſt, that goeth downward to the earth? 3. Becauſe it is ſafer to
believe the nature of the Soul to be according to the Analogy of
Faith, and the concurrent opinion of the learned, than to ſift ſuch
a deep queſtion by our weak underſtanding and reaſon. So having
premiſed theſe things, and left this as a general exception and caution, we ſhall proceed to the matter intended in this order.

    1. We lay it down for a moſt certain and granted truth, that
God ſimply and abſolutely is only a moſt ſimple ſpirit, in whom
there is no corporeity or compoſition at all, and what other things
ſoever that are called or accounted ſpirits are but ſo in a relative
and reſpective conſideration, and not in a ſimple and abſolute acceptation. And this is the unanimous Tenent of the Fathers,
Schoolmen and all other Orthodox Divines, agreeing with the
plain and clear words of the Scripture, as, *God is a ſpirit, and they*
that worſhip him, muſt worſhip him in ſpirit and in truth. And a-
gain: *Now the Lord is that ſpirit, and where the ſpirit of the Lord*
is there is liberty. Therefore we ſhall lay down this following propoſition.

    2. That Angels being created ſubſtances, are not ſimply and ab-
ſolutely incorporeal, but if they be by any called or accounted ſpirits, it can but be in a relative and reſpective ſenſe, but that really
and truly they are corporeal. And this we ſhall labour to make good
not only by ſhewing the abſurdities of that opinion of their being
ſimply ſpiritual, but in laying open the unintelligibility of that opinion, and by anſwering the moſt material objections.

    1. And firſt to begin at the loweſt ſtep, Body is a thing that af-
fecteth the ſenſes moſt plainly and feelingly; for though many bodies
are ſo pure, as the air, æther, ſteams of the Load-ſtone, and many
other ſteams of bodies, that they eſcape the ſight of our eyes, yet
    are

are they either manifest to our feeling, or otherwise made manifest by some sensible effect, operation, or the like; yet for all this, the intrinsick nature of body as such is utterly unknown unto us, for when we speak of the extension of body, as its Characteristical property, we do but conceive of its superficial dimensions, its internal nature *quatenus Corpus*, being utterly unknown unto us; it being a certain truth, that *Quidditates rerum, non sunt cognoscibiles;* and as D*r Moore* granteth, the naked essence or substance of a thing is utterly unconceiveable to any of our faculties. From whence we argue, *à minori ad majus,* that if the substance of a body, whose affections and modifications do fully incur into, and work upon our senses, be utterly unconceiveable to any of our senses, much more of necessity must the substance of a Created spirit, conceived as immaterial and incorporeal, be utterly unconceiveable to any of our faculties, because it hath no effects, operations, or modifications that can or do operate upon our senses.

2. And as we know not the intrinsick nature of body, so also *Argum.* 2. we are ignorant of the highest degree of the purity and spiritualness of bodies, nor do we know where they end, and therefore cannot tell where to fix the beginning of a meer spiritual and immaterial being. For there are of Created bodies in the Universe, so great a diversity, and of so many sorts and degrees of purity and fineness, one exceeding another, that we cannot assign which of them cometh nearest to incorporeity, or the nature of spirit. And many of these being compared with other more gross and palpable bodies, may be and are called and accounted spirits, though notwithstanding they be all Corporeal, and but under a gradual difference. So the vital part in the bodies of men are by Physicians called Spirits in relation to the bones, ligaments, musculous flesh and the like; nay even in respect of the blood, lymphatick humor, lacteal juyce, or the *succus nutritius nervosus,* and yet still are contained within the limits of body, and are as really Corporeal as any of the rest, and so are the air and æther. And those visible species of other bodies that are carried in the air and represented unto our Eyes, by which we distinguish the shape, colour, site and similitude of one body from another, though by the Schools passed over with that sleight title of qualities, as though they were either simply nothing, or incorporeal things, are notwithstanding really Corporeal, else they could not incur into, nor affect the visive sensories: And these do in the air intersect and pass through one another (as may be optically demonstrated) without Confusion, Commixion, or discerption, and may comparatively be accounted spirital and incorporeal, though really they be not so. But what shall we say to that wonderful body, Image or *Idolum* of our selves, and other things that we behold in a mirrour or looking-glass? must this be a meer nothing, or an absolute incorporeal thing? surely not. For it is as really a body as any in the Universe, though of the greatest purity and fineness of any that we know; and how near it

approaches to the nature of spirit, is very difficult (if not impossible) to determine; for if it did exist when the body or subject from whence it floweth were removed, it might rationally be taken for a Spirit, and with far more probable ground than many things else that have been vainly supposed to be Spirits. And that these visible shapes of things, and this Image in the glass, are not meerly imaginary nothings, but Corporeal Figures and steams, is most manifest, because they vanish when the body or subject is removed, because that *nullius entis nulla est operatio, & Incorporeum non incurrit in sensus,* and because they would pass through the glass, but only for the foil or *Bractea* laid on the otherside, by which the Image is reflected. So that if we have bodies of so great purity, and near approach unto the nature of spirit, we cannot tell where spirit must begin, because we know not where the purest bodies end.

Argum. 3.   3. D*r Moore* maketh substance to be the genus, and spirit and body to be the two species, so that body and spirit are of one generical Identity, and so there must of necessity some certain specific difference betwixt them be assigned and proved, or else the division is vitious, and the property of spirit not proved, and so their opinion of spirit falls totally to the ground. For we affirm (and shall prove) that though a difference be imagined and supposed, yet it was never yet sufficiently proved, for *omnia supposita, non sunt vera,* otherwise all the impossible figments and vain *Chimæra's* of melancholy and doting persons might pass for true Oracles : but it is one thing truly to understand, and another thing to imagine and fancy what indeed is not, nor ever was. And though the supposition seem never so probable and like, yet it will but at the best infer the possibility of such an imagined difference, but not prove it really to be so, and therefore here we shall retort the Doctors Axiom against him, which is this : "Whatsoever is unknown to us, or is "known but as meerly possible, is not to move us or determine us "any way, or make us undetermined; but we are to rest in the pre-"sent light and plain determination of our own faculties. Now that a spirit is penetrable and indiscerpible, may be imagined as possible to the fancies of some, but cannot be clearly intelligible to any sober mind; for to imagine, and to understand, are faculties that are very different, and however if such a difference be conceived as possible (which cannot enter the narrow gate of my Intellect) yet the difference of being penetrable and indiscerpible, is not to move us to determine that a spirit hath those distinct properties from bodies, because they are but known to us as meerly possible. And therefore that these two differences of penetrability and indiscerpibility assigned by D*r Moore,* are not sufficiently proved to be so, we shall give these reasons. 1. If bodies in the ultimate act of nature can penetrate themselves and one another, as *Helmont* and D*r Glisson* do strongly labour to prove, then penetrability is not the proper difference of spirit from body, because then common

The Immortal.
of the Soul.
Axiom. 2. *p.* 6.

                                                                    to

to them both.   2. But if it be taken for a truth (and the one of
neceſſity muſt be true) that bodies do not, or can poſſibly penetrate themſelves or one another, as the common tenent holdeth, and
ſeemeth moſt agreeable to verity, for it is ſimply unintelligible and
impoſſible to conceive, that two Cubes (ſuppoſe of Marble or
Metal) ſhould penetrate one another, and yet but to have the dimenſions of one, and to poſſeſs no greater ſpace than the one did
formerly fill: And if this be impoſſible and unintelligible in reſpect
of bodies, whoſe properties, aptitudes, affections and modifications are apparent to our ſenſes, then muſt it be more impoſſible and
unintelligible in ſubſtances ſuppoſed to be meerly incorporeal, becauſe they muſt needs be more pure and perfect, and therefore leſs
ſubject to ſuch unconceiveable affections; and however, it can be
no wayes known to our faculties or cognitive powers, that they
have any ſuch ſpecifical property or affection.   3. As it is not any
way manifeſt to any of our ſenſes, nor can be proved by any ſound
deductions of reaſon, ſo it cannot be manifeſted to be any innate notion ſhining from the Intellect it ſelf, and we ought not to take adventitious ones inſtead of thoſe that are innate, nor fictitious ones
for either, but to make a due diſtinction of each of them one from
another.   4. Neither is indiſcerpibility a proper difference of a
ſpiritual ſubſtance from a corporeal one, becauſe the viſible ſpecies
of things do in the air interſect one another, and ſuffer not diſcer-
pibility: and that theſe are bodies is manifeſt, becauſe they affect
the ſenſes; and therefore that which is a property of ſome bodies
cannot be the proper difference to diſtinguiſh a ſpirit from a body.
5. This is only an arbitrary and feigned ſuppoſition, and cannot be
proved either by the teſtimony of any of the ſenſes, by ſound reaſon, or innate notions; and what is or cannot be proved by ſome of
theſe (according to his own poſition) ought to be rejected.   And
therefore as indiſcerpibility is no proper difference of a ſpirit from
a body, no more is penetrability, which can no more be in a ſpiritual ſubſtance, than either in diſcreet quantity one can be two, or
two one, or in continuate quantity one inch can be two, or two can
become one.   Dr *Gliſſon* from his much admired *Suarius* the great
Weaver of fruitleſs Cobwebs, hath deviſed another difference of
ſpirit from body which he thus layeth down, as we give it in this
Engliſh.   " I aſſign (he ſaith) a twofold difference betwixt the ſub- *De natura ſub-*
" ſtance of matter and that of ſpirits.   The firſt is taken from the *ſtant. Enrrgetici*
" ſubſtantial (*à ſubſtantiali materiæ mole*) heap or weight of the *c. 27. p. 379.*
" matter.   For I (he ſaith) beſides the actual and accidental ex-
" tenſion, do attribute to the matter this ſubſtantial heap or weight
" which is denied to ſpirits.   But the ſign of this heap or weight is,
" that if the matter in the ſame ſpace be duplicated, triplicated, or
" centuplicated, that it will be made more denſe twofold, threefold,
" or an hundred fold.   And concludeth thus: I anſwer (he ſaith)
" that matter and ſpirit in this do agree betwixt themſelves, that
" they both are finite, and from thence that they have this com-
" mon

" mon,that neither of them can reduce themselves into a littleneſs that
" is infinite, or into an infinite magnitude. Therefore the difference
" betwixt them doth not conſiſt in this ; but in this, that a ſpirit whe-
" ther it be contracted or dilated, is not made more denſe or rare ; but
" on the contrary, matter, whether it be contracted or expanded, is
" made more denſe, or more rare. To which we return this reſponſion.
1. It is uſual with men, when by their wills and fancies they would
maintain an opinion that is weak and groundleſs, finding they cannot
clearly perform it, to bring in ſome ſtrange, obſcure or equivocal
word, thereby to make a flouriſh, though they prove nothing : So here
this learned perſon to make a ſhew to prove the difference of ſpirit
doth aſſign *moles ſubſtantialis* as peculiar to body, but not to ſpirit ;
but what is to be underſtood by *moles*, he might know his own
meaning, but I am ſure there are few others that do or can underſtand
it, and therefore is but a deviſed ſubterfuge to ſtumble and blind mens
intellects, and not to prove the thing intended. 2. If by the word
moles he intend weight or gravity (and what elſe it can ſignifie is not
intelligible) then it will not be a difference betwixt body and ſpirit,
becauſe gravity and levity are differences of bodies in reſpect of one
another, and therefore can be none as he aſſignes it. 3. To aſſert that
a ſpirit when contracted or dilated is not made more denſe or more
rare, but that matter whether it be contracted or expanded, is
made more denſe or more rare, is eaſily ſpoken, but not ſo eaſily
proved : and rude aſſertions without ſound proof, are of no validity,
and may with as good reaſon be denied and rejected, as affirmed or
received. 4. We have no denſity in bodies but in reſpect of the paucity and parvity of the pores, ſo that leſs of another body is contained
in them, and that is accounted rare that hath many or greater, and
ſo containeth more of another body in them, and are qualities or
modifications that only belong unto bodies, and not at all unto ſpirits, and is but precariouſly taken up by the Doctor without any
proof or demonſtration at all. 5. If ſpirits cannot expand themſelves into an infinite ſpace, nor contract themſelves into an infinite
littleneſs, then where are bounds and limits of this contraction and
expanſion, or how is it proved that they can do either? ſeeing they
are properties and affections of bodies and matter, and never were
proved to be peculiar to ſpirits.

Argum. 4. 4. Thoſe that are much affected to and zealous for experimental
Philoſophie, do often run into that extream, as utterly to condemn
and throw away all the ancient Scholaſtick Learning, as though
there were nothing in it of verity or worth : But this is too ſevere
and diſſonant from truth, as might be made manifeſt in many of
their Maximes; but we ſhall only inſtance in one as pertinent to our
preſent purpoſe, which is this : *Imaginatio non tranſcendit Conti-
nuum.* And this if we perpend it ſeriouſly, is a moſt certain and
tranſcendant truth; for when we come to cogitate and conceive of
a thing, we cannot apprehend it otherwiſe than as continuate
and corporeal ; for what other notions ſoever we make of things,
they

they are but adventitious, arbitrary, and fictitious, for even *non entia ad modum entium concipiuntur.*   And therefore thofe that pretend that Angels are meerly incorporeal, muft needs err, and put force upon their own faculties, which cannot conceive a thing that is not continuate and corporeal: But if they will truft their own Cogitations and faculties rightly difpofed, and not vitiated, then they muft believe that Angels are Corporeal, and not meerly and fimply fpirits, for abfolutely nothing is fo but God only.

5. If the Angelical nature were fimply and abfolutely fpiritual *Argum. 5.* and incorporeal, then they would be of the fame effential Identity with God, which is fimply impoffible. For the Angels were not Created forth of any part of Gods Effence, for then he fhould be divifible, which he is not, nor can be, his Effence being fimplicity, unity, and Identity it felf, and therefore the Angels muft of neceffity be of an effence of Alterity, and different from the effence of God. Now God being a fimple, pure, and abfolute fpirit in the Identity of his effence, if the Angels were fimply and abfolutely fpiritual and incorporeal, then they muft be of the fame effence with him, which is abfurd and impoffible; and therefore they have Alterity in them, and fo of neceffity muft be Corporeal, and not fimply and meerly fpiritual.   And that as much as, we contend for here is granted by Dr *Moore* in thefe words: " For (he faith) I look upon An-" gels to be as truly a compound Being confifting of foul and body, " as that of men and brutes. Whereby he plainly afferteth their Compofition, and fo their Alterity, and therefore that they muft needs have an *Internum* and *externum*, as the learned and Chriftian Philofopher Dr *Fludd* doth affirm in thefe words: *Certum eft igitur in-* *Vid. Rob. Fludd.* *effe ipfis (fcilicet Angelis) aliud, quod agit, aliud autem, quod* *utri. Cofm. Hift.* *patitur; nec verò illud fecundùm quod agunt, aliud quam actus* *Tract. 1. l. 4.* *effe poterit, qui forma dicitur; neq; etiam illud fecundum quod pa-* *c. 2. p. 110.* *tiuntur, eft quicquam præter potentiam, hæc autem materia appellatur.*

6. Therefore to conclude, thefe arguments do fufficiently and *Argum. 6.* evidently prove that Angels are either Corporeal, or have bodies united unto them, which is all one to our purpofe whether way foever it be taken. To which only we fhall add thefe authorities; and firft S. *Bernard* tells us thus much rendered into Englifh. " There- *Serm. 6. fup.* " fore (he faith) as we render unto God alone true immortality, *Cantic. p. 505.* " fo alfo incorporeity, becaufe he alone doth fo far tranfcend the " univerfal Corporeal nature of fpirits, that he doth not ftand need " of any body whatfoever, in any operation whatfoever, being " content with only a fpiritual nodd (or motion) when he will, to " perform whatfoever he pleafeth.   Therefore only that majefty of " his, is that, which neither for himfelf, nor for another, hath need " of the help of a Corporeal inftrument, by which omnipotent " will he is immediately prefent at every work.   And that of *Da-* *Lib. 5.* *mafcen* is full to the purpofe, which is this: " That Angels *quan-* " *tum ad nos*, are faid to be incorporeal and immaterial : but " compared

" compared to God, are found to be Corporeal and material. And of this opinion befides were *Tertullian*, S. *Auguftin*, *Nazianzen*, *Beda*, and many others, as may be feen in the learned Writings of *Zanchy* upon this fubject: with whofe words we fhall fhut up this particular: *Certum enim eft, ex iis quæ fcripturæ tradunt de Ange-lis, probabiliorem effe Patrum fententiam, quàm Scholafticorum: utram tamen fequaris, non multum peccaveris, nec propterea inter Hæreticos haberi poteris.*

And on the otherfide, if they be holden to be fimply and abfo-lutely incorporeal, then thefe abfurdities muft of neceffity fol-low.

1. If Angels be fimply incorporeal, then they can caufe no Phy-fical or local motion at all, becaufe nothing can be moved but by contact, and that muft either be by immediate or virtual contact, for the Maxime is certain, *Quicquid agit, agit vel mediatione fup-pofiti*, as when ones hand doth immediately touch a thing and fo move it; *vel mediatione virtutis*, as when a man with a rod or a line, doth draw a thing forth of the water, both of thefe do require a Corporeal contact, that is, that the fuperficies of the body move-ing or drawing, muft either mediately or immediately touch the fu-perficies of the body to be moved or drawn. But that which is abfolutely incorporeal hath no fuperficies at all, and therefore can make no contact either mediate or immediate; and therefore An-gels if fimply incorporeal, can caufe no Phyfical or local motion at all.

2. If Angels be abfolutely incorporeal, then they cannot be con-tained or circumfcribed in place, and confequently can perform no operation in Phyfical things. To which if they anfwer with *Thomas Aquinas: Quod circumfcribi terminis localibus eft proprium Cor-porum, fed circumfcribi terminis effentialibus, eft commune cuili-bet Creaturæ, tam corporali, quam fpirituali*; This aiery diftinction might have taken place, if *Aquinas* had fhewed us what effential terms and limitations are, but of this we have no proof at all, and what was never proved may juftly be denied. For what a definitive place is, was never yet defined, neither can we poffibly conceive an Idea or notion of any fuch thing, but only as we may make a *Chimæra* or figment of that which never was nor is. For though we may apprehend that they are not circumfcribed in place, as grofs bodies are, yet it is not to be doubted, but that they move from place to place, and do fo confift in fome place, that they occupy a certain fpace of place, and this is moft certain, if we believe (as we ought) thofe things which the Scriptures do declare concerning the miffion and motion of Angels. And therefore notwithftanding this frivolous and feigned diftinction, we may conclude with *Theo-doret, Angelorum naturam effe finitam, & circumfcriptam, eôq; opus habere loco.* Neither doth that avail to folve the bufinefs, and make this a good diftinction, which is brought by Dr *Moore*, to wit, that there are two acceptions of place, the one being imaginary fpace,

the

the other that place is the concave superficies of one body immediately environing another body, and that therefore there being these
two acceptions of place (he concludeth) that the distinction of
being there *Circumscriptivè & definitivè*, is an allowable distinction. But by the Doctors leave we must affirm, that what he saith is
not allowable, and that for these reasons.   1. Because imaginary
space hath no existence in nature, but only in the fancy of the Imaginant, *& entia rationalia, non sunt entia naturalia ex parte rerum existentia*.   2. Because it is a certain truth which *Des Cartes*
hath taught us, to wit :   That the names of place or space, do not
signifie any thing different from a body that is said to be in a place,
but only do design the magnitude, figure and site of it amongst
other bodies. And that this site may be determined, we ought to
have respect unto some other bodies, which we may consider as immoveable. And as we respect divers bodies, we may say that the
same thing at the same time doth change place and not change
place. As when a Ship is carried in the Sea, he who sitteth in the
Ship doth always remain in one place, if respect be had to the parts
of the Ship, betwixt which parts he keepeth the same site : And
the same person doth continually change place, if respect be had to
the shores, because he continually receedeth from some shores, and
cometh more near unto other.   3. Neither is this distinction good,
because as the same Author tells us : *Non etiam in re differunt spa-
tium, sive locus internus, & substantia corporea in eo contenta, sed
tantùm in modo, quo à nobis concipi soleat.* 4. Dr *Moore* granteth that spirits are substances and have extension, and we affirm
that nothing can be so but what is Corporeal, and consequently
must be in place circumscriptively, and therefore the fancy of a definitive place, is meerly a fictitious foppery, without ground or
reason.

And now let us examine the objections that are usually brought
against this opinion, the strongest of which is to this purpose; that
if Angels be Corporeal, then of necessity they must be mortal, alterable and destructible; to which I answer. 1. Because no Creaturely nature is or can be immortal, *per se & ab intrinsecâ & propriâ naturâ*, for God only is so as saith the Text, ὁ μόνος ἔχων ἀθα-
ναςίαν, *Who only hath immortality* ; Therefore the Angels whether
corporeal or incorporeal, are not immortal, neither by themselves
or their intrinsick nature, either (as the Schools speak) *à parte
ante, vel à parte post*, because God only is so, exclusively considered
in regard of any Creature, and so the objection is of no force. 2. The
Corporeity of Angels doth not at all hinder their immortality *à parte
post*, for as God is only immortal in respect of Essence, Eternity,
Infinity and Independency, so Angels nor any Creatures, are immortal in that point or respect, but only in regard of their dependency upon God, who by his conservative power doth keep them
by Christ, that for the time or duration to come, they shall not die,
perish, or be annihilated ; and this he can and doth as well perform

if

if they be corporeal as spiritual, even as he doth preserve and conserve the bodies of the Saints in their Graves until the general Resurrection, and in the World to come doth keep them in immortality; though they be changed and made spiritual bodies, yet they remain bodies still. For it is he *that sustaineth all things by the power of his word*; And it is he *that doth vivifie or quicken all things: and if he gather unto himself his spirit and his breath, all flesh shall perish together, and man shall turn again unto dust.* So that the objection is of no validity, because no Creature is kept in perpetual duration, *à parte post, ab intrinsecâ naturâ, sed ex causis conservantibus,* which is the good will, benignity, and blessed influence of *Jehovah*, and not from any internal creaturely power. 3. Every spiritual and incorporeal substance that is created, is as annihilable by the prime power that created it, as is a Corporeal created substance. And on the contrary, a Corporeal or material substance is no more capable of annihilation by any power or efficiency of second Causes, than an incorporeal and spiritual substance is; and therefore whether Angels be simply incorporeal, or that they be Corporeal, it neither maketh for nor against their immortality, which consists only in the benign emanation of the Divine conservative power of the Almighty: And therefore doth profound *Bradwardine* draw that invincible, and undeniable Corollary of verity, *Quod necesse est Deum servare quamlibet Creaturam immediatiùs quacunq; causa creata.* 4. Though the most of the bodies that are known unto us be divisible, alterable and discerpible, or dissipable in respect of our conceptions of them, yet actually we may find many bodies in nature that are not, nor ever were dissipated or dissevered *secundum totum*, though there may be alteration in their superficial parts, as the Earth, the Sun, Moon, the rest of the Planets, and those great and glorious bodies that we call Stars; so that for the duration of bodies *à parte post* we can conclude little of certainty. And as there are bodies that *secundum suum totum,* are not severed or dissipated, so there are some bodies that though they may suffer division and dissipation into smaller parts, yet do those parts though most minute, suffer no real transmutation, but remain of the same Homogeneous nature they were before, as is most manifest in Silver dissolved in *Aqua fortis*, wherein though it be so severed and dispersed, that it appear not at all unto the eye, yet may it be from thence recovered and redintegrated into its own nature as it was before. And also the Masters of the more abstruse Philosophy affirm to us upon their own certain experience, that though metallick *Mercury* may be divided into insensible and invisible Atomes, yet still it retains the nature of metallic *Mercury*, and that thus *Helmont* tells us: *Si non vidissem argentum vivum eludere quamcunq; artificum operam, adeò, quod aut totum avolet adhuc integrum, aut totum in igne permaneat, atq; utrolibet modo, servet impermutabilem sui ac primitivam identitatem, identitatísq; homogeneitatem anaticam: dicerem artem non esse veram, quæ vera est,*

sine

Hebr. 1. 3.
1 *Tim.* 6. 13.
Job 34. 14, 15.

D. Litbiâs. l. c.
8. *J.* 70.

ſine mendacio, atq; longè veriſſima. So alſo there are bodies which although they ſuffer diviſion and ſeparation by ſome other bodies diſſevering of them, yet by motion of coition they ſoon cloſe and redintegrate themſelves, having thereby ſuffered no detriment at all, as is moſt apparent in the pure body of the Æther, the viſible ſpecies of things, the images in a Looking-glaſs and in ſhadows, which are all bodies. So that ſeeing bodies, no more than Spirits to be annihilable by ſecond cauſes, and that there are ſome bodies that are not diſſipated *ſecundum totum*, and that there are others that though they are ſeparable into more minute particles, yet do they remain in Analytical and Homogeneous Identity, and that there are others that though they be actually for a ſmall moment divided, yet they do inſtantaneouſly coaleſce, and by coition unite themſelves; yet we may therefore rationally conclude, that corporeity, *quatenus* ſuch, doth not at all take away immortality *à parte poſt*, becauſe bodies as well as ſpirits may be kept in immortality by the conſervative concourſe of Divine Power, and ſo the objection utterly falls to the ground.

2. There is only another argument that the perſons of the other opinion have urged, ſuch as *Aquinas*, and the reſt of the Scholaſtick rabble, to wit, the Text in the Pſalm, which is this: *Who maketh his Angels ſpirits: his miniſters a flaming fire.* From whence they would poſitively conclude that they are ſpirits, and abſolutely incorporeal; but fail of their purpoſe for theſe clear reaſons. 1. The Text there cannot be rationally underſtood of their creation, or of their creaturely nature, but of their offices and adminiſtrations, becauſe the word uſed there is not from בָּרָא to create, or form forth of nothing, but from עָשָׂה *fecit*, that is by ordering them in their offices and miniſtrations. And again the word רוּחַ doth not alwaies or of neceſſity ſignifie an incorporeal thing but that which is a body, as the winds, and ſo doth *Luther* and diverſe others render it, and it is commonly attributed to beaſts as well as Men, as in that of *Solomon, Who knoweth the ſpirit of man that goeth upward, and the ſpirit of the beaſt that goeth downward to the earth?* Where the word ſpirit, which is all one in the Hebrew, is attributed to beaſts as well as to men, but no man ('I ſuppoſe) will believe that the ſpirit of a beaſt is ſimply incorporeal, and therefore by the word ſpirit in the Pſalm cannot neceſſarily be underſtood a ſimple incorporeal ſubſtance, and therefore the conſequence is not neceſſary.

But the Author of the Epiſtle to the Hebrews muſt needs be taken for the beſt Expoſitor of theſe words of the Pſalmiſt, who doth quote them only for this purpoſe, to prove that Chriſt in dignity and office is far above the Angels who are all ordered to ſerve and obey him, and are by their offices all but miniſtring ſpirits, ſent forth to miniſter for them who ſhall be heirs of Salvation. By which it is manifeſt that this place is to be underſtood of their miniſtration and offices, and not of their nature or ſubſtances. 2. They can no more be meerly and literally ſaid to be ſpirits, underſtanding

Objeſt. 2.

Pſal. 104. 4.
Heb. 1. 7.

ſpirit

spirit to intend an abfolute incorporeal fubftance, than his minifters
can be literally underftood to be flaming-fire, they muft either be
both literally true, which is abfolutely abfurd, or elfe thofe words
muft have a metaphorical interpretation, as they may and muft
have, and there is no inconvenience in that expofition. For as the
winds, which is but a ftrong motion of the air, and the fhining or
flaming fire, are two of the moft quick, agile and operative agents
that are known unto us in nature, fo the Angels and Chrifts Minifters are ftrong, quick and moft nimble and powerful in performing their offices and adminiftrations. Therefore we fhall conclude
Metaphyf. l. 2. this as *Scheibler* doth from S. *Auguftine: Nihil enim invifibile &*
c. 4. p. 222. *incorporeum naturâ credendum eft, præter folum Deum, qui ex eo in-*
Vid. Auguft. *corporeus & invifibilis dicitur, quia infinitus, & incircumfcriptus*
Tom. 2. l. de *eft, & fimplex, & fibi omnibus modis fufficiens fe ipfo, & per feip-*
fpir. & an. c. 8. *fum : omnis verò rationalis creatura corporea eft, Angeli & omnes Vir-*
tutes corporeæ funt, licet non fubfiftunt in carne.
   Now though we have fufficiently proved that they are corporeal,
that is, that they have bodies naturally united unto them, and fo
have an *internum*, or moving power, and an *externum*, or a part
moved, that is, as Dr. *Moore* confeffeth, a fpiritual and incorporeal
part, and a corporeal part or vehicle, yet to affign what kind of
bodies they have, or what proper difference there is betwixt their
fubftance and other corporeal fubftances is no eafie matter to determine. Only we fhall give two differences whereby they are diftinguifhed from other fubftances that are corporeal, and that as the
Scripture holdeth them forth unto us. 1. The firft differential diftinction is, that their bodies do not fuffer, or are altered or diffipa-
ted, by the moft ftrong, and operative fublunary agent that is known
unto us: Amongft which we have none of greater force and activity than our culinary fire, yet it is manifeft that that Element did
not work upon nor burn the Angel that appeared to *Manoah* and
Judges 13 20. his Wife, *who afcended in the flame of the altar*, and was not touched, or altered at all, which plainly fheweth that his body was not
to be wrought upon by the fierce flame of fublunary fire, and he
is there called the Angel of *Jehovah*. This alfo is confirmed by
Dan. 3. 24,25. that which *Nebuchadnezzar* faw, and confeffed, that though *there*
were three men only caft into the fiery furnace, yet he faw a fourth
(which by all the learned is judged to be an Angel) *and they had*
no hurt upon them, that is, the fire did not work upon their bodies to burn, alter, or confume them. So that in this the bodies
of Angels differ from the moft of other bodies, becaufe they do not
fuffer by fublunary fire, the moft violent agent that we know. And
this muft needs rationally be taken to be proper unto Angels in regard of their created natures, and not as fuperadded by a Divine
and Almighty Power, as in fome other cafes it may be granted.
   2. A fecond difference is, that what bodies foever fpirits or Angels
Luke 24. 39. have, or appear in, they have not flefh and bones fuch as Chrift
had in his true and numerical body in which he did appear after his
                                                        refurrection,

resurrection, which was the same individual body which he had
before he was crucified.   But though they have bodies, yet to feeling and tangibility they have not flesh and bones as humane bodies
have, which have a renitency and resistibility to our touch, which
their bodies have not, being as it were ethereal, airy and shadowy;
and yielding and giving way to the touch, and though to be divided and separated, yet, may be, do as soon close by counition, and
so suffer nothing at all by that division.

Concerning the properties of their bodies it seems to have been
the opinion of *Tertullian* (as I find him quoted by Mr. *Baxter*)
that they had thin pure and aereal bodies which they could dilate
and expand, condense and contract at their pleasures, and so frame
them into diverse and sundry shapes; his words are these: *Dæmones
sua hæc corpora contrahunt, & dilatant, ut volunt: sicut etiam
lumbrici, & alia quædam insecta.*   So we see that some worms and
insects will extend themselves into a vast length and smallness, that
they can pass through a very small hole, or passage, and again contract themselves into a great bulk, drawing in the length, and in-
creasing the breadth and thickness, which though it still be the same
corporeal substance, and in general doth, in what figure soever it
be brought into, but retain the same dimensions in respect of place,
yet in regard of accidental shape or figure it may change the dimensions in respect of one another, as one while to be more in longitude, and less in breadth and depth, and sometimes more in breadth
and depth, and less in length.   So may the bodies of Angels by
contraction and dilatation, sundry wayes alter their dimensions,
and consequently their shapes and figures, and all this according to
the motion and act of their own wills, so that still there must be limits
to these acts of distention and contraction, that they can do neither
in an infinite degree as either to become an insensible and indivisi-
ble prick, nor to be infinitely expanded or dilated, and this opinion
hath sufficiency of rationality and intelligibility in it. Of this very
point S. *Bernard* speaketh thus modestly: *Videntur Patres de hujusmodi diversa sensisse, nec mihi perspicuum est unde alterutrum
doceam: & nescire me fateor.*   And though we cannot punctually
enumerate, nor assign the certain properties of their bodies, yet we
may rationally conclude thus much. 1. That they being creatures
ordained for high and noble ends must needs have their bodies and
organs fitted and suitably proportioned to fulfil and accomplish
those ends, as doth most manifestly appear by the bodies and organs of all other creatures, which are most wisely and fitly framed
by the Almighty, according to the several ends and uses they were
created and ordained for. 2. It is most probable that considering
there are creatures that as their wills are moved by their passions
and affections can alter the colours and figures of their own bodies,
as is manifest in worms, and in the colours of the Chameleon, as it
is asserted by the experience of the learned Physician *Dominicus
Panarolus*, so from the less to the more, that Angels have bodies of
far

Saints Ever-
last. rest, c. 7.
part 2. p. 255.

Sup. cantic.
p. 504.

far more excellency to perform their miniftrations in, than thofe grofs and terreftrial bodies have that are here below. And it is no fmall wonder to obferve our ordinary *Gallus Turcicus vel Gallopa-vus*, how quiet and demifly fometimes he goes, and then again up-on the fuddain by fome emotion of fpirit, how will his train be advanced and extended, his barbles fwelled and puffed up, and the appendicle that comes over the bill or *roftrum*, be ex-tended or contracted at the pleafure of the animal: And much more to confider the quick and fuddain change of the colours of both thofe parts, as fometimes to a whitifhnefs, or an afh-colour, fome-times purple, fometimes blewifh, and fometimes pure red, fo quick a motion that creature can give to the fpirits and blood, that they can fo quickly alter and change, not only the colours, but alfo the magnitude. And much more may we rationally believe that Angels can alter and change the figure and colour of their bodies according to the miniftrations they are imployed about.

Mark 12. 25.   3. The Scripture informeth us that in or at *the refurrection, the bodies of men fhall be as the Angels that are in heaven, ficut Angeli:* Now this Analogy, comparifon, or affimilation, would be altoge-ther falfe if Angels had no bodies at all, but were meerly incor-poreal; then it would follow, that the bodies after the refurrection were made meer Spirits, and fo ceafed to be bodies, which is falfe according to the doctrine of S. *Paul,* who fheweth us plainly that after the refurrection they are changed in qualities into σώματα
1 Cor. 15. 44. πνευματικὰ *fpiritual bodies, for there is a natural* Soul or Animal *body,* and fo likewife, *there is a fpiritual body.* From whence we neceffarily conclude that Angels have Bodies, and that they are pure fpiritual ones.

Now we fhall come to the other point intended in this Chapter, that is to fhew that the opinion of Angels affuming bodies of the Elements here below, is a meer figment, as muft of neceffity follow if this be a truth that we have proved, to wit, that they have bo-dies; for then affuming of other bodies muft needs be in vain and to no purpofe: but we fhall alfo fhew the weaknefs and folly of that Tenent by thefe pofitive reafons following.

1. Thofe that maintain the affumption of bodies dare not affirm that they are fo invefted with thofe bodies, as are humane fouls with their bodies: for then there muft be vital union, which can-not be but by Divine Ordination: But it doth not any where ei-ther by Scripture, or found rational confequence, appear that ei-ther God appointed, or gave power to Angels to affume to them-felves bodies of what fhape they pleafed, or that he ordained a vi-tal union, betwixt the Angels and thofe bodies they are fuppofed to affume either by Creation, or Generation, and therefore if they did affume any fuch bodies it muft but be as we put on and off our Garments, or as Players put on and off their Perukes, Vizards and Garments according to the feveral things or perfons they intend to reprefent ad perfonate.

2. But

2. But the great question will be, who are the Taylors that shape and frame them these vestments? what! must it be themselves that shape and figurate these bodies, as snails are supposed to frame and make their shells and houses? Surely not, because if they be simply incorporeal, then they can make no contact with corporeal matter, and without a corporeal contact there can be no alteration nor organization of matter, and consequently they cannot frame or shape themselves such vestments; neither can any other actor or agent be assigned that can frame them, and therefore the Tenent is a most ridiculous figment. And again if they should have such solid bodies framed of the inferior Elements, as the body of a Serpent, as the Witchmongers do suppose the Devil assumed when he deceived *Evah,* and such bodies as Demons are vainly supposed to assume to carry the heavy bodies of Men and Women in the air, then those bodies must needs be of that solidity and compactness that they cannot suddainly be wasted and dissipated, and then doubtlessly we should find them sometimes, as we do the sloughs, *Exuvias,* or skins of Snakes, for they could not be consumed in a moment. And it were horrid to suppose that God should instantaneously create them, and as suddainly dissipate and waste them. So that in verity there is nothing of certitude, but it may be looked at as a Chimera and a Poetical Fable.

3. And if the Angels had not such bodily organs wherein they could move, walk, speak, and perform other such actions withal, before they assumed or crept into such vestments, their being inclosed and invested with them and in them would no more fit and inable them to walk or speak in them, than would an hollow Image inable a lame Man to walk, or a dumb Man to speak that were inclosed in them. Therefore (suppose) as the Witchmongers hold, that the Devil should appear to a Witch in the assumed shape of a Cat, Dog, Foal or such like, and walk and talk with him or her, if before that assumption of such a shape, the Devil could not walk and speak, the having crept into such a vestment would no more inable him to speak, than a dead Cat in an empty hogshead, or wind pent in an empty bladder.

CHAP. XI.

Of the Knowledge, and Power of faln Angels.

THese evil Angels of which we treat, did doubtless, before they left their habitation and did not keep their first estate, participate of the same knowledge and power, that those Angels still retain that did not fall into that defection and rebellion; so that our disquisition must be, what knowledge and power they
have

have loſt, and what they ſtill do retain, and this we may conſider in theſe particulars. 1. That there are many things of which they are totally ignorant and neſcient. 2. The knowledge that they have is dark and confuſed.

1. Concerning the firſt, this muſt of neceſſity be a certain rule that what the holy and elect Angels do not know, the evil and faln Angels muſt much more ignore, except the knowledge of evil and guilt, from which the good Angels are free; and theſe may be reduced to theſe few points. 1. We here may conſider that the knowledge of Angels, is to be reſtrained into theſe three ranks; firſt either their innate and congenerate knowledge, or ſecondly their infuſed or revealed knowledge by God in his Son Jeſus Chriſt, or thirdly their experimental knowledge that they gain by obſervation and experience, and it is of the firſt only that we ſpeak in this Paragraph, and the reſt we ſhall handle anon. 2. That our cogitations, deſires and affections are not known to the Angels, unleſs they manifeſt themſelves either by external ſigns, or effects, or be revealed from God; And theſe ways they may be known, but not otherwiſe; for it is manifeſt that Satan had darted it, or put it into the mind of *Judas* to betray Chriſt, yet had he ſo cunningly carried himſelf, that neither by any effect nor ſign did the Diſciples know it until our Saviour did reveal it unto them. So that the Scriptures do plainly inform us of the truth in this particular, as, *For what man knoweth the things of a man, ſave the ſpirit of man which is in him?* For this is only proper to God to ſearch the heart, and to underſtand the cogitations, as ſaith the Text : *For thou only knoweſt the hearts of the children of men*, he only knoweth them, and neither Angels nor men: and though the heart be deceitful and deſperately wicked, yet *God doth ſearch the heart, and try the reins.* So that if the good Angels do not know the cogitations, deſires and affections of Mens hearts, except God either reveal them unto them, or they be made manifeſt by ſigns and effects, much leſs muſt the bad Angels know or underſtand them. 3. Thoſe things that are meerly contingent, and thoſe which depend upon free will, cannot be known of the Angels, unleſs they be revealed by God, as is manifeſt by the Text. *Produce your cauſe, ſaith the Lord, bring forth your ſtrong Idols, or Diviners, ſaith the King of Jacob. Let them bring them forth, and ſhew us what ſhall happen : let them ſhew the former things what they be, that we may conſider them, and know the later end of them, or declare us things for to come. Shew the things that are to come hereafter, that we may know that ye are Gods : yea, do good, or evil, that we may be diſmayed, and behold it together.* And as the good Angels know not contingent things, or thoſe that depend upon free will, much leſs do the faln Angels underſtand them, as is manifeſt in theſe examples. The Angel that was ſent of God to warn *Joſeph to take the child Jeſus, and fly into Ægypt*, did not of his own innate knowledge, either in it ſelf, or in its cauſe (as the Schoolmen ſpeak) know that *Herod* would ſeek

the

1 Cor. 2. 11.

2 Chron. 6. 30.

Jer. 17. 9, 10.

Iſai. 41. 21, 22, 23.

Matth. 2. 13.

the child to deſtroy him, becauſe it was truly a contingent thing, and did only depend upon the free act of *Herods* will, and therefore by Divine Goodneſs and Providence it was, revealed to the Angel, thereby to preſerve the life of the child , and to fulfil the Scriptures.   Neither do the faln Angels know future events that are contingent, or depend upon the free will of men, as is manifeſt in Satans tempting and afflicting of *Job*, which he intended to have been his deſtruction, and therefore did falſly divine and foretel that *Job would curſe God to his face*, but the event was not according to his lying conjecture, but to the manifeſtation of *Jobs* Faith and Patience, and produced his glorious reſtoration.   So the lying ſpirit in the mouth of *Ahabs* Prophets, did not know that *Ahab* would go up to *Ramoth Gilead*, or that he ſhould be ſlain there, but that God did reveal it unto him, and ſent him forth with a powerful commiſſion to prevail.   So that all the predictions and Divinations of the Devil or his Angels are nothing but lying gueſſes and uncertain conjectures; for what can be expected from him *who was a liar from the beginning, and the father of lies?* Neither were his Idol-prieſts, Wizzards, Diviners or Prophets any better but meer conjecturers and lyars, as was moſt manifeſt in all thoſe Oracles that were amongſt the Grecians, which uttered nothing but cheats, lies, equivocations and ambiguous reſponſions.   And thoſe amongſt the Jews were no better, who took upon them to foretel and divine for others, but could not or did not foreſee their own deſtruction, as is manifeſt in *Ahabs* Prophets ſlain by *Elijah*, and the Prieſts of *Baal* ſlain by *Jehu*, and therefore muſt all thoſe needs be deceived that run to Divining Witches and Wizzards, of which ſort of couzeners we have too many.

And if againſt this it be objected that the Devils, did know and confeſs that Jeſus was the Son of God, and therefore if they could tell this that was ſo great a myſtery, much more eaſily may they know other inferior things, and ſo may foretel future contingencies, to which we give this reſponſion.   *Object.*

1. We only affirm that Devils did not know Chriſt by their innate or inbred knowledge, but they might know him by the revelation of the Father, and by the things that were written of him by the Prophets, and by the obſervation of thoſe things that were manifeſted at his birth, and ſhewed and done in his life time.

2. And it is manifeſt that God did not altogether intend to have him hidden from the knowledge of Devils, becauſe he ordered that *the ſpirit ſhould lead him into the wilderneſs, that he might be tempted*, that his power and victory might be ſhown over the Prince of darkneſs.   And the end that the wiſdom of God had in this, was that the Devils to their greater terror and horror might know their Conquerour, and by whoſe power they ſhould be tormented and thrown into the Abyſs or bottomleſs pit, and this made them cry out ſaying, *Art thou come to torment us before the time*, and alſo *force us not into the Abyſs or deep*.   Matth. 8. 29.

Luke 8. 31.

F f   3. The

3. The Devils might know this becaufe the Angels had proclaim-
ed his birth to the Shepherds, and told them, that *unto them was*
born that day, in the City of David, a Saviour which was Chrift
the Lord : And they might know it from the appearing of the Holy
Ghoft in the form of a Dove, and refting upon him, and by the
voice which faid from Heaven, *this is my beloved fon, in whom I*
am well pleafed. And they might know it by the conqueft that
Chrift had over the Devil, and by *their daily being caft out by the*
power of his word, and command, as by the finger of God.

4. The myfteries of Salvation cannot be known unto the good
Angels, but by Divine Revelation, much lefs unto the bad ones,
as witneffeth the Text : *For what man knoweth the things of a man,*
fave the fpirit of man which is in him ? even fo the things of God
knoweth no man, but the fpirit of God. The myfteries therefore
of Salvation, as they have been decreed by himfelf in his eternal
counfel, are not known unto the Angels, but by the revelation of
the fpirit of God and the complement and fulfilling of his promifes.
So concerning the reftauration or precife day and hour of the coming
of Chrift, do not the Angels in Heaven know, though their
knowledge be vaft and great, and therefore much lefs thofe faln
and rebellious Angels that are *chained in everlafting darknefs, un-*
till the judgment of the great day.

5. And as that which is not underftood of the bleffed and elect
Angels muft needs be unknown unto the faln Angels, fo likewife
there are many things known to the good Angels, that are hidden
or but conjectured at by the bad ones, as may be manifeft in thefe
inftances. 1. The bleffed Angels know and fee the face of the Father in beatifical vifion, as faith the Text : *Take heed that ye offend*
not one of thefe little ones; for I fay unto you, that in heaven their
Angels do always behold the face of my father, which is in heaven.
Upon which *Beza* hath this note: *Loquitur more feculi hujus, ubi*
confiftere in confpectu regis faciemq; ejus perpetuò videre poffe, fignum
eft domefticæ intimæq; familiaritatis. But the faln Angels are totally deprived of this bleffed Vifion, being caft forth of Heaven,
as faith the Text. *And the great Dragon was caft out, that old Ser-*
pent, called the Devil and Satan, which deceiveth the world: he
was caft out into the earth, and his Angels were caft ont with him.
And S. *Peter* tells us, *that God fpared not the Angels that finned, but*
caft them down to hell, and delivered them into chains of dark-
nefs. 2. And as they have loft the vifion and fruition of the mer-
cies of God, fo they have utterly loft the knowledge of his will,
concerning his Covenant of Grace and mercy to the elect, for they
are only miniftring fpirits fent forth to tempt to fin, to afflict and
punifh, and have ftill enough for the advancing of the Kingdom of
darknefs, but have no knowledge of faving grace nor the myfteries
of the Gofpel, but are all enemies and adverfaries to God and the
Kingdom of Chrift, and *goeth about feeking* continually *whom he*
may devour. But it is the bleffed elect Angels that are *miniftring*
fpirits

Luk. 2. 11.
Math. 3. 17.
1 Cor. 2. 11.
Math. 18. 10.
Revel. 12. 9.
2 Pet. 2. 4.

spirits, sent forth for to minister to them, who shall be heirs of Sal- Heb. 1. 14.
vation. 3. The good Angels have the blessed messages revealed
unto them for the assisting and delivering of the godly. So an Angel did comfort *Joshua,* and another warned *Joseph* to take the child Josh. 5. 13.
Jesus, and to fly into *Ægypt,* thereby to preserve the childs life ;
and an Angel delivered the Apostles forth of prison, and many such Acts 12. 7.
happy errands are made manifest unto them, and they imployed a-
bout them, of all which the faln Angels are utterly ignorant, and
they are concealed from them.

6. There are some things that the evil Angels know of, which the
blessed ones have no sensibility of, that is the knowledge of their
own guilt, and the experimental sense of the loss of Gods Favour,
Love, Grace and Mercy.

2. The second thing that we proposed to handle, is, that the
knowledge that the faln Angels have is dark and confused, which
is plain because *they are reserved in chains under darkness, unto the* Jude 6.
judgment of the great day. Now those that are kept or reserved in
darkness, must of necessity have their knowledge dark, and consequently confused ; and he also that is the Prince of darkness, and
the Father and Author of the works of darkness, must needs like
his children have his understanding darkned also. And therefore
we will conclude this point with the opinion of S. *Augustine* who
speaking both of the Angels that stood, and those that fell, saith
thus : *Ante peccatum autem tam isti quam illi perfectè omnia intel-* De Civitat.
ligebant. Accessit igitur istis propter peccatum aliquid tenebrarum. Dei, l. 9.
Proindè etiam tenebræ appellantur, & in tenebris esse dicuntur, cœ-
lesti illa luce destituti, & in locum caliginosum præcipitati. Vt in-
dè intelligamus nonnihil tenebrarum naturali etiam illorum menti
accessisse, in pœnam admissi peccati in Deum, Deiq; filium. But we
shall only here speak of their knowledge in reference to things acted
in this elementary and sublunary world, and that in these particulars.

1. Though they retain the same faculty of understanding that they
had before their fall, of the generation, motion and mutation of natural things here below, yet is it much darkned, and far inferior to the
knowledge of the good Angels in natural things , the one sort
living and abiding in light, and the other being shut up in darkness.

2. What knowledge soever they have by their natural faculties,
or that they may be supposed to gain by acquisition, is by them
gotten or learned for no other end, but for the hurt and destruction of mankind, and not as the good Angels who make use
of theirs for the benefit of those that shall be heirs of Salvation.
For as a good Physician labours and studies to know the nature and
virtues of Animals, Vegetables and Minerals, and their parts and
products, for the good and benefit of mankind, but a Witch or
poysoner laboureth to know their virtues thereby to destroy and
kill ; even so do the evil Angels, and not otherwise.

3. The knowledge of Devils whether natural or acquisitive is
spurious, erroneous, fallacious, deceitful and delusive; both in

F f 2   respect

reſpect of themſelves and others, for as ſaith the Scripture: *He was a murderer from the beginning, and abode not in the truth, becauſe there is no truth in him. When he ſpeaketh a lie, he ſpeaketh of his own: for he is a liar, and the father of it.* Therefore ſaith learned *Rollock* upon this very place: *Hoc eſt loqui ex ingenio ſuo, quod naturale eſt ſibi facere; ſuum enim & quod ex ſeſe depromptſit, non autem quod aliundè accepit, profert.* For as all the endeavours of the faln Angels tend to the ſeduction and deluſion of others, ſo are they, and were they the deceivers and deluders of themſelves: For it is moſt manifeſt that their minds are ſo obcæcated and covered over with darkneſs, that although they be not altogether in gene-ral deſtitute of the knowledge of that which is juſt and unjuſt, good and evil, pious and impious, yet they do not acknowledge their own ſin, as they ought, for they are ſo pertinacious in their ſin and wickedneſs, that they do not attentively perpend and con-ſider their own evil, and therefore are not truely ſenſible, or do underſtand that it is evil, and therefore are by the juſt judgment of God ſo abſolutely obcæcated that they cannot acknowledge their own evil and ſin. And as that knowledge they have is ſo darkned that they have deluded and deceived themſelves, ſo all their know-ledge in reſpect of others is erroneous, fallacious and lying, as the

Text witneſſeth of Antichriſt: *Even he whoſe coming is after the working of Satan, with all power and ſigns, and lying wonders: And with all deceiveableneſs of unrighteouſneſs, in them that periſh. And for this cauſe God ſhall ſend them ſtrong deluſions, that they ſhould believe a lie.*

4. In regard of the words, intentions and actions of wicked Men they both know and may foretel much, becauſe they are the Au-thors and deviſers of thoſe evils and wicked thoughts; as it was the Devil that puſhed on the Scribes and Phariſees to accuſe and put Chriſt to death, for it was *their hour and the power of dark-neſs,* and it was Satan that had darted it into the mind of *Judas Iſcariot* to betray his Maſter: And therefore the Devils might pro-bably (if not certainly) know that his death would be brought to paſs; ſo that they may eaſily foretel what themſelves have pro-jected and prepared inſtruments to accompliſh.

5. The acquired knowledge of the faln Angels muſt needs be great in regard of their vaſt multitudes and their being diſperſed in this caliginous air or Atmoſphere, for the Devil is called the Prince of the air (if that be literally to be underſtood) and he compaſſeth the earth and walketh to and fro in it, and *goeth about ſeeking whom he may devour,* and therefore by their agility of body and celerity of motion may eaſily know what is done and ſpoken, and may ſo very quickly convey it one to another, and ſo may moſt readily communicate things that are acted or ſpoken at an incredi-ble diſtance one from another; but yet all this no further than Di-vine Providence will permit and allow of.

6. The Witchmongers and others do attribute a kind of omnic ſcien

ſciency to Devils in reſpect of their acquired knowledge, which we
by no means can allow them, and that for theſe reaſons. 1. Though
it be granted that they do grow and increaſe in the knowlege of
ſin, evil, and wickedneſs, therewith to hurt, devour and deſtroy,
or gain more skill and craft to lie, cheat, delude and deceive; yet
that they either gain or gather any knowlege that is good, or for
any good end, is abſolutely falſe, for *they abode not in the truth,*
neither are they lovers of truth, but are utter Enemies to all good
knowledge and verity.   2. That they may be Maſters of all the arts
or wayes of deceit, lying, cheating and deluſion, is no way to be
denied; but that they ſhould (as many ſuppoſe) by reaſon of their
longevity and duration, learn and be perfect in any or all of the good
Arts or Sciences, is to me utterly incredible, becauſe they are the
Corruptors of all, but the perfectors of none, elſe ſhould they be
the greateſt Philoſophers in the World, which is falſe.   And therefore moſt Chriſtian and pious was that Sentence of that unjuſtly
cenſured Perſon *Paracelſus* in theſe words: *Et licèt Diabolus qui-* Dæmo. inſt.
dèm plurima machinetur : hoc tamen cum omnibus ſuis legionibus ver. l. p. 225.
præſtare minimè poteſt, ut vel abjectam ollam frangat, nedum ean-
dem faciat : multò is minùs quenquam occidere, aut jugulare poteſt,
niſt id mandato, permiſſu juſſuq; ac vi divina faciat.

The other main point that we undertake to handle in this Chapter, is, touching the power of the faln Angels, and that is to be conſidered in theſe three particulars : 1. In general in reſpect of their
power, either in ſpiritual and moral things, or in things natural.
2. Or in reſpect of ſpiritual and moral things in particular.   3. Or
in reſpect of Phyſical and ſublunary things.

1. And for the firſt it muſt of neceſſity be granted, that their
power ſince their fall is much diminiſhed, or at leaſt reſtrained and
chained and fettered up.   For they becoming Rebels againſt the Almighty, and not keeping their firſt Eſtate, but having left their own
habitation, it was moſt agreeable to the wiſdom and juſtice of God
to take away from them the greateſt part of that power and authority that he formerly had given them, and ſo to impriſon and chain
them up, that they might never be able to attempt or perform the
like Rebellion again; otherwiſe the Almighty ſhould not have
uſed that wiſdom that is ordinary with earthly Princes, who have-
ing overcome thoſe that rebelled againſt them, do not only diſ-
arm them, but alſo confine or impriſon them.   And to this very
thing do the Scriptures allude, when they ſay, that *they are deli-*
vered into chains of darkneſs, and that *they are reſerved in ever-*
laſting chains under darkneſs unto the judgment of the great day.
So that though the Devils ſtill retain their cruel, wicked and devouring will and mind; yet they are but like the Lyon within the
Bars of Iron, or *Bajazet* in the Cage of Iron led about by *Tamberlan,* and
ſo though they be never ſo cruelly bent to do miſchief, yet they are
under the Chains and cooped up in the Grates of Darkneſs, and kept
in Everlaſting Chains that they are never able to break or unlooſe.
                                                              And

And though he be called the God of this World and the Prince of it, yet that is not to be understood, that he is the Prince and Ruler of the Creatures of the World, or that he giveth riches, health, honour or the like, for those are the gift of God only and not of the Devil; but he is the God and Prince of the evil and wickednes that is in the World, for in that, and by that, he reigneth and ruleth; and to this purpose saith *Rollock* : *Damnatio est Satanæ, qui peccati author est. Nam vita hujus mundi est secundum principem cui potestas est acris, &c. Dicitur autem Princeps hujus mundi, quia per peccatum, & mortem regnat in mundo: ut enim teste Paulo, Regnum Dei positum est in justitiâ, & pace, & gaudio per spiritum sanctum, sic regnum Satanæ positum est in injustitia, & morte. Unde ipse propter peccatum per quod regnat, dicitur rector tenebrarum. Propter mortem per quam regnat, dicitur imperium mortis habere.* And upon this place St. *Augustin* saith thus : *Nunc Princeps hujus mundi ejicietur foras, absit ut Diabolum principem mundi ita dictum existimemus, ut eum Cæli & terræ dominari posse credamus: sed mundus appellatur in malis hominibus, qui toto orbe terrarum diffusi sunt. Sic ergò dictum est: Princeps hujus mundi, id est princeps malorum hominum qui habitant in mundo. Appellatur etiam mundus in bonis, qui similiter per totum orbem terrarum diffusi sunt: Ideò dicit Apostolus, Deus erat in Christo mundum reconcilians sibi: Hi sunt ex quorum cordibus principes mundi ejicientur foras.* And whereas also Satan is called *the Prince of the power of the air, that worketh in the Children of disobedience*, it is not literally so to be understood, as though he had the natural power of ruling the air, and causing of winds, hail, snow, frost, rain, thunder and lightning, for these are all ordered according to the will of divine providence and the causes that he hath established in the Elements: So *David* speaking of the Heavens, the Earth, and the Elements, doth conclude thus; *They continue this day according to thine ordinances, for all thy servants*: And it is he that ordereth all these, as saith the Text: *Who covereth the Heavens with Clouds, who prepareth rain for the earth, who maketh grass to grow upon the mountains. He giveth snow like wool, he scattereth the hoary frost like ashes. He casteth forth his ice like morsels: Who can stand before his Cold? He sendeth forth his word, and melteth them: he causeth his wind to blow, and the waters flow.* And all these fulfil the will and command of God, and not the will of the faln Angels; for the Text saith: *Fire and hail, snow and vapour, stormy wind fulfilling his word* ; so that if they have any thing to do in the sublunary changes or motions of Meteors, it is but only as instrumental and organical Causes, working meerly as they are ordered and acted by the first cause that worketh all in all, as the Christian Philosopher Doctor *Fludd* hath most learnedly proved in his Treatise of Cosmical Meteors, which I seriously commend to those that desire full satisfaction in this particular. But the Devil is chiefly called *the Prince of the power of the air*, because he is the proud, high, airy and

spiritual

Marginal notes: John 12. 31. — Ephes. 2. 2. — Rom. 14. 17. — Ephes. 6. 12. Heb. 2. 14. — Vid. Caten. Aur. Tho. Aquin. — Psal. 119 89. — Psal. 147. 8. 16, 17, 18. — Psal. 148. 8.

ſpiritual Prince and Ruler of wickedneſs in high or ſuper-cœleſtial
places, by which proud, airy, and ſpiritual wickedneſs, *he worketh* Epheſ. 6. 12.
*in the Children of diſobedience. For we wreſtle not againſt fleſh and
blood, but againſt principalities, againſt powers, againſt the rulers of
the darkneſs of this world, againſt ſpiritual wickedneſs in high places,* ἐν τοῖς ἐπουρανίοις. Upon which learned *Beza* ſaith thus : *Homines quorum fragilis & caduca eſt natura, cui opponuntur verſutiæ
ſpirituales, infinitis partibus potentiores.* And again, *Iſta nomina
tribuit Angelis malis, propter effectus, non quod eos ſuâ vi poſſint
præſtare, ſed quia illis Deus laxat habenas.* And therefore S. *Chry-* Homil. 22. ſ.
ſoſtom upon this place ſaith thus: *Mundi verò dominos eos vocat,* 257.
non quod mundum gubernent, ſed ſolet ſcriptura malos actus hunc Jo. 8.
*mundum vocare, ut quando Chriſtus dicit, vos non eſtis ex hoc mun-
do quemadmodum ego non ſum ex mundo.*

2. To conſider their power in ſpiritual and moral things particularly, we ſhall find they have no power in ſome things, but by
their fall have utterly loſt it, as is apparent in theſe few points:
1. They have loſt that freedom of will that they had by Creation,
and were partakers of before they fell, and agreeable to this is the
Theſis of learned *Zanchj,* which is this : "That all Devils have ſo Dt operib. Dei
"far their wills made obſtinate in ſins, the hatred of God, Chriſt, l. 4. c.6. p.175.
"and of Mankind, that from this evil they cannot will to repent,
"and thereby be ſaved; and this he thus proveth. 1. Becauſe in the
Scriptures they are called, πονηρὸς κατ' ἐξοχὴν, for they are now become ſuch, that they cannot be changed from their malice and
wickedneſs; becauſe it is become natural unto them. 2. From
whence it is manifeſt, that the whole time ſince their fall, never
yet any of them hath given any ſign of reſipiſcence. 3. If they
could repent and believe in Chriſt, then for them and their ſins
Chriſt alſo ſhould have died; for he ſaith, *that he prayed for thoſe* Jo. 17.
that were to believe in him; but they neither believe in him, neither did he die for them. 4. But the chief cauſe of their impeni-
tency is the juſt judgment of God, that hath given them up to
hardneſs of heart, becauſe they ſinned knowingly and wilfully
againſt the truth. And this point is ſufficiently proved by *Thomas
Aquinas,* the reſt of the Schoolmen and many others. 2. So that
as they have loſt freedom of will, ſo they cannot at all will or act
to be ſaved, or to repent. 3. And as they cannot will or act to repent or be ſaved, ſo the whole acts of their wills are evil, malicious
and wicked, *being liars and murtherers from the beginning.*

3. The third is to conſider their power in ſublunary and elementary things which is the moſt pertinent to our preſent purpoſe, it
being the thing that ſome have magnified even to a kind of omnipotency, and therefore we muſt the more narrowly ventilate and examine it, which we ſhall do in this order.

1. How great ſoever the power of the faln Angels may be ſuppoſed to be, yet neither in knowledge can they be deemed to be om-
niſcient, or in power to be omnipotent, becauſe they are created
Beings;

Beings, circumscribed, limited and finite, and consequently can perform no act that necessarily must require an omnipotent power, and so can neither create things *de novo*, annihilate or transubstantiate any Creature or substance, or pervert or put forth of order, the things that God by Creation, Decree and Providence hath set into their certain orders of Generation, alteration and corruption.

Ut supra.

2. How great soever their power may be supposed to be, yet rationally it must be taken for a truth, that they have not the same power that they had before their fall. For as *Zanchy* saith : *Certum est enim in universum, & in genere, hac etiam in parte illos punitos fuisse, ut non possint quicquid poterant, cum boni essent, nec etiam quicquid nunc velint.* Because the Holy Ghost beareth witness, *that they are bound in Chains*, and that Satan begged leave of God to invade *Job*, that they fought with the good Angels, but were overcome, and that they may be so resisted of believing men that they may be overthrown. *Ac væ nobis, nisi potentia Dæmonum infirmata esset, & à Domino comprimeretur, & compesceretur.*

*Zanch. de op.
Dei ut supra.*

3. And what power soever be granted to the faln Angels, yet it is by the opinion of all the learned, restrained only to these sublunary and inferior bodies, and that they have neither power by Creation or Ordination, to work upon, move, or alter things that are Angelical, Celestial, Ethereal and Superior, but only are chained in this Caliginous Atmosphere, and impure air. For it is manifest, that superior bodies work upon those that are inferior, but not on the contrary, neither have we any examples that can prove that they do operate upon Celestial bodies, and so their power (how great soever some may suppose it to be) is only restrained to these inferior sublunary things.

4. The operations and actions performed by the faln Angels, may be considered, either in the simple respect of their natural and created power, and this how great soever it was before their fall, is not only lessened, but that which remains, is limited and restrained with the Adamantine Chains of the decree of divine providence: or in respect of what power they may have superadded by God, when they are Commissionated and sent by God to effect some particular actions, as for example, *Moses* and *Aaron* had but the ordinary strength and power that was common to other men, before they were sent upon the message to *Pharaoh*, and made Instruments to deliver the Israelites, for then were they armed and indowed with the power of working great and stupendious Miracles. So it cannot rationally be imagined that the two Angels that were sent as Instruments to destroy *Sodom* and *Gomorrha*, did or could of their own proper, individual and created power, bring down Fire and Brimstone from Heaven to burn those two Cities, but that it was brought to pass by the Power of the Almighty, as granted and given to them for that judgment only, and not by that ordinary power that they could always exercise, for the Text saith:

Then

Then the Lord rained upon Sodom, and upon Gomorrha brimstone Gen. 19. 24.
and fire from the Lord forth of heaven. Neither can it rationally be
suppofed that one Angel hath by his created power, that ability,
that *he can flay in one night an hundred fourfcore, and five thou-* Ifai. 37. 36.
fand, as it is written *the Angel did in the camp of the Affyrians,* but
that it was brought to pafs by the power of Jehovah fuperadded
unto him, to work the great deliverance of *Hezekiah* and his people. Upon which place the learned Expofitor *John Calvin* faith
thus: *Solus quidem dominus fatis per fe poteft, ac certè folus nos
fervat: Angeli enim, manus quodammodo funt ipfius: Unde etiam
Virtutes & Poteftates vocantur. Interim hæc vis foli Deo tribuenda,
cujus organa tantummodò funt Angeli, ne in fuperftitionem incida-
mus.* From whence we may note thefe two things. 1. That even
Devils are but the organs and inftruments by which God accom-
plifheth his will, and executeth his wrath and juftice, and fo are
but as tormenters and executioners to act no more than what they
are appointed and commanded to do. 2. We may obferve that in
times paft they had large Commiffions given and great power fuperadded to perform great wonders for the deftruction of the wicked, which was done for great and extraordinary ends, fuch as in
thefe days the Lord doth feldom or never ufe, and therefore there
can be no reafon now fhewed why Devils fhould have any extraordinary power added unto them in working ftrange feats for
Witches and Sorcerers.

5. It will much conduce to the clearing of this point of the power
of Devils to examine into what place they are faln, or fince their rebellion into what Prifon they are fhut, and this we fhall give in the Thefis De op. Dei l. 4.
of learned *Zanchy* who faith thus: "All the evil Angels were c. 4. p. 174.
"thruft down from Heaven, into places that are below the Celefti-
"al Orbs, to wit into this air, and below, as it were into a cali-
"ginous Prifon, where they are referved unto the Univerfal Judg-
"ment as bound with chains. And this is plain from the words of
S. *Peter*, who faith: *For if God fpared not the Angels that finned, but* 2 Pet. 2. 4.
*caft them down to hell, and delivered them into chains of darknefs
to be referved unto judgment.* To which accordeth that of *Jude*:
And the Angels that kept not their firft eftate, but left their own ha- Jude 6.
*bitation, he hath referved in everlafting chains under darknefs, un-
to the judgment of the great day.* For as learned *Mufculus* tells us: *De-* Loc. Com. p. 12.
*cet Chriftianum hominem ea modeftia, & cautio, ut nihil affirmet, nec
fi quis alius affirmaverit, inconfideratè recipiat, quod non certo veritatis teftimonio è facris literis defumpto, confirmari queat.* To this we
fhall only add what the acute and learned Theologue *Amefius* notes
upon this place of *Peter*, which in Englifh is this: "In general (he
"faith) we are taught, that they did not keep their firft eftate, that
"is, they did forfake righteoufnefs and that ftation in which they
"were placed of God, and afterwards they have exercifed from the
"beginning, envy, lies and murther againft Men. Alfo (he faith) we
"are taught, that they were a great number that were partakers of

G g   "this

"this defection, and therefore the Apostle speaketh in the plural
"number. 1. They are said to be thrust down *in Tartarum* into
"Hell by reason of the commutation of estate and condition, because
"that from a most high condition, which they received by creation,
"they were cast down to an estate most low. 2. By reason of com-
"mutation of place, because they were thrust down from a place
"of beatitude, where they were conversant about the Throne of God
"with the rest of the Angels, into an inferiour place subject to sin
"and misery. But that this place is in the lowest parts of the earth,
"as the Papists do hold, cannot be made forth from the Scriptures,
"but rather the contrary, for they are said to be conversant, and
"to rule in the air, and to walk to and fro in the earth seeking the
"subversion of Men. This at the least is manifest from the Scri-
"ptures, and ought to satisfie those that are not too curious.
"1. That they suffer a great change of estate and condition. 2. That
"they are excluded and shut out from their first habitation.
"3. That they are in such a place where they suffer both the pain
"of loss and of sense. They are said to be delivered over to dark-
"ness, partly in respect of sin, and partly in respect of misery; for
"darkness in Scripture doth denote both: and they are said to be
"delivered in chains, by a metaphor taken from facinorous per-
"sons, that are condemned and kept bound in prison with chains,
"and the chains are these. 1. Obfirmation or obduration in sins.
"2. An utter despair of any freedom or deliverance. 3. A terrible
"expectation of extream misery, and an horrid fear of being cast
"into the abysse or deep. 4. The Providence of God which con-
"tinually watches over their custody, imprisonment, and punish-
"ment. They are said to be reserved to damnation, because they
"are so bound up in these evils and miseries, that they never can
"escape; and yet these are but the beginnings only of their miseries,
"for they are hereafter *to go into that everlasting fire, that is prepa-*
"*red for the Devil, and his Angels.*

Matth. 25. 41.

6. Though the Devils be said to be reserved in everlasting chains
of darkness, yet are they said sometimes to be loosed, and *to go to*
and fro in the earth, and to walk up and down in it, and *that Satan*
doth like a roaring lion walk about seeking whom he may devour.
Which must be understood (as we have shewed before) that in respect of his evil will, malice and envy, he seeketh and desireth the
overthrow of all mankind, but yet is so restrained that he doth but
act, what, where, when and so far only as God doth limit and order him. For though it be usually said that God doth permit him,
yet it cannot be understood as a bare and nude permission, as though
God should suffer him to go so loose and at liberty, that he may
exert and exercise his power to the uttermost, for then all the godly should be destroyed both in Souls and Bodies, and God should
only sit by as a bare spectator, not as an Orderer, Ruler and Governour, even as though an hungry fierce Lion that had been chained up in a grate, should be let loose to rage and run where he would,
and

Job 1. 7.

1 Pet. 5. 8.

and to kill and devour what he could, and thus the Witchmongers do fuppofe of him, which is falfe and contrary to the teftimony of Gods word. But when the Almighty maketh ufe of Satan or his Angels, they are only fo let loofe that he hath a hook in their Noftrils, and their Necks in a chain, that they can act no more nor no further than he ordereth, and gives them leave to accomplifh, and thus are they limited not only by his irrefiftible will and decree, but they are alfo watched over and ruled by the good Angels that are as it were their keepers and overfeers. So when the Devil is ufed as an inftrument to afflict Holy *Job,* he is firft let loofe to afflict him in his Children and Goods, but not to touch his Body; and the fecond time he hath leave and power given him to lay his hand upon *Jobs* Body, but not to take away his life: which do plainly fhew, that he is not only and barely fuffered to do what he will, but hath his limits fet how far he fhall act, and no farther. And when God maketh ufe of him for the punifhment of the wicked, he giveth him power, and ordereth him how far to act or prevail. As in the cafe of the lying fpirit in the mouth of *Ahabs* Prophets, the evil fpirit is fent forth with this commiffion, *And God faid thou fhalt perfwade him and prevail alfo: go forth and do fo.* By which it is manifeft that he prevaileth more by the virtue of Gods command and commiffion, than by his own proper created power. 1 Kings 22. 22;

7. It is manifeft that as the good Angels are the Minifters of God for the Salvation of mankind, fo the evil Angels are miniftring fpirits only feeking the deftruction and damnation of Men; and though God doth ufe the Miniftry of thefe that are evil and have an evil will, yet he ufeth them well, and to good ends, that is, as the executioners of his juftice to chaften the godly, and to reftrain, or deftroy the wicked. Therefore God and the Devil do not afflict, tempt or do any other thing for the fame ends; for God acteth to prove, preferve, and ftir up to goodnefs, but the Devil acteth to bring into fin and evil, to deftroy and to bring to defpair, as is manifeft in the Hiftory of *Job.* And therefore here we may confider the feveral ways wherein God ufeth the evil Angels as his inftruments, and that is in thefe particulars. 1. God ufeth him generally for temptation both of the good and the bad; fo he tempted *David,* Chrift and the Difciples, for Satan had *defired to fift them as wheat,* and therefore he is called ὁ πειράζων, the tempter: and thefe temptations are internal and fpiritual, for *we fight not againft flefh and blood, but againft fpiritual wickednefs in high places.* And in thefe as far as concerneth the faithful, he acteth but only as God permitteth or ordereth him, as is plain in the cafe of *David,* where one Text faith, *Jehovah moved David to number the people,* and in another place, *and Satan flood up, and moved David to number the people:* where it is to be noted that God did it as the director and orderer, and Satan performed it as his inftrument and fervant. And the Apoftle telleth us; *that God is faithful, and would not fuffer the believing Corinthians to be tempted above what they were* 1 Cor. 10. 13.

Vid. Lambert. Dan. Ifagog. c. 24. p. 68.

able,

able, but would with the temptation also make a way to escape, that they might be able to bear it. 2. God maketh use of him for the chastisement and affliction of the godly, as is most manifest in that of *Job*; but this only so far as he is limited, ordered and commanded from God and no further. 3. When Satan as a tormenting or punishing instrument is used of God, he hath his commission given him how far only he shall act and proceed, beyond which he cannot go one hairs breadth, as is manifest in the case of *Ahab* and the *Gadarens* Swine, so that we may conclude this with the learned Aphorism of *Piscator* in these words: *Etsi autem Satan seu Diabolus cum suis Angelis Deo & filiis Dei adversatur quantum in ipso est, nimirùm voluntate & conatu: non tamen effectu; ita nimirum ut vel fidelibus perniciem afferre, vel quicquam efficere possit quod Deus nolit. Deus enim illum potentiæ suæ fræno vinctum constrictumq; tenet: ut ea modò exequatur quæ ei divinitùs mandata, aut concessa fuerint.*

8. Lastly, we shall now examine the particulars wherein learned *Zanchy* doth acknowledge the faln Angels to have power over our and other sublunary bodies, and they are principally these.

1. Upon the supposition granted that the faln Angels have permission, he holdeth that by their own proper created natural power, they can as they please move in place: as to lift a Body up from the earth on high, and then to let it fall or throw it down to the earth; that they can transfer or carry a body from one City to another in a very short space of time: Lastly, that they can move and agitate bodies with every kind of local motion that none can resist them. And that therefore all those strange transportations of Witches in the air into forraign and far distant places (he holdeth) need not be thought strange or impossible, and that they may be done with great celerity, and in a short time. And this he thinketh he proveth by the example of *Philip, who when he had instructed the Eunuch in the faith and baptized him, was caught away by the spirit of the Lord, that the Eunuch saw him no more, and that he was found at Azotus.* Upon which we must make these animadversions. 1. That upon the supposition or ground that faln Angels are simply and meerly incorporeal, this must be false, for then they cannot move in place, nor agitate any bodies, as we have sufficiently proved before. 2. And though upon the supposition that they are corporeal, they may move in place, and may move and agitate other bodies, yet that must be understood in a proportionable measure, according to their power and strength, and not in an infinite, or indefinite respect; for though one Devil may be supposed to move or lift up that which would load an Horse, yet it will not follow that he can move or lift up as much as would load a Ship of a thousand Tun; and though one Devil might remove a Millstone by his own created power, yet it will not follow that he can remove the greatest mountain that is to be found. 3. And whatsoever motion Devils may have here in the air, or power to remove

and

Exagis. Aphor. 14. p. 133.

De oper. Dii. l. 4. c. 10. p. 186.

Acts 8. 39, 40.

and agitate bodies, yet the leaft of thefe cannot be performed but by licence and permiffion from God, which licence and permiffion is always for ends agreeable to his Wifdom and Juftice; but for God to licenfe or permit Devils to appear to Witches in the fhape of Cats, Dogs, Squirrels or the like, to the end to fuck upon their bodies or to have carnal copulation with them, or to tranfport them in the air to places far diftant, to dance, revel, feaft and to do homage to the Devil (as the Witchmongers alledge) is for fo impure, filthy, horrid and abominable ends, as can no way agree with the Wifdom or Juftice of the Almighty, and therefore muft needs be falfe and frivolous. 4. And that which the faln Angels are in the Scriptures recorded to have performed, may be confidered, whether they accomplifhed thofe things by their own created power, or by the power of God granted to them when they are fent forth to perform fuch or fuch an act: For as it may not be rationally granted that the two Angels that were inftruments for the deftroying of *Sodom* and *Gomorrha* did bring down fire and brimftone from Heaven by their own created power, nor that the deftroying Angel in *Egypt* did in one night kill all the firft-born by his own power, but by the power of the Almighty granted unto him in that miffion; fo it is not rational to fuppofe, that although Satan might by internal motions and fpiritual temptations prevail with the *Sabæans* and *Chaldæans* who were his Vaffals, wherein he could work what he would, to take away the Oxen, Affes and Camels of *Job*, and to flay his Servants: though (I fay) he might do this by his created power; yet that he fhould bring fire from Heaven to deftroy the fheep, or that he by his created power could raife fuch a wind, as could blow down the houfe in which the Sons and Daughters of *Job* were, and flay them, is not probable, but that it was performed by that affifting power that was granted him of God, to effect that affliction upon *Job*, that God had determined for the trial and manifeftation of his Faith and Patience, which cannot in any reafon be faid to be done by Devils in their tranfactions with Witches, and therefore muft needs be Fables and Chimeras. 5. And whereas he addeth that the Devils can perform all kind of motions with natural bodies, and that none can refift them, it is too large by far; for by that rule they might fhake and remove the earth, which they cannot do, for it abideth firm according to Gods appointment in the creation: And it is abfurd to think that the fuperior and good Angels cannot refift them, who have far greater force and might than the faln Angels have. 6. And whereas he would prove the power of Devils by that of the fpirit of the Lord conveying of *Philip* from the Ethiopian Eunuch, which fuppofing it to be a good Angel, it muft likewife be granted to be furnifhed from God to have that power to carry him away, and doth not neceffarily conclude that the Angel did it by its proper created power: neither is the confequence good, to argue that what a good Angel may do, that therefore a bad one may do the

fame

fame or the like, for their powers and ftrength are not equal, the one retaining what he had by creation, the other lofing much by reafon of his rebellion and fall ; as an outlawed perfon hath not in a civil refpect the fame power that another perfon hath that is under a legal capacity, and as a prifoner that is loaden with chains, gives and fetters, can neither walk, leap, or run fo faft, as he that hath none, no more can the fettered Devils move with that agility and celerity that the good Angels can do that have no fetters nor chains at all.

2. A fecond kind of actions that he affigneth unto Devils is, that they cannot only move bodies locally, but alfo can alter them diverfe and fundry ways, as to make hot things of cold, and fo on the contrary, white things of black, and black of white, and can make of fair things deformed ones, and fo on the contrary, and can make found bodies fick, and fick bodies found, affecting them with various qualities. But thefe particulars he leaves altogether without proof, except one Text in thefe words : *And he cried with a loud voice unto the four Angels to whom it was given to hurt the earth and the feas.* From whence we fhall obferve thefe things. 1. It is granted that God doth make ufe of evil Angels to punifh the wicked, and to chaftife and afflict the godly, and in the effecting of thefe things that they have a power given them to hurt the earth and the Sea and things therein, as to bring tempefts, thunder, lightning, plague, dearth, drought and the like ; but that in the effecting thefe things, they have a dative power above what they had in Creation, and that they are commiffioned and fent by God upon purpofe to fulfil and effect thefe things, and fo are as the organs and inftruments to perform the will of God in his juftice, and are always for fuch ends as tend to the Glory of the Creator : But for Devils to be fent to play fuch ludicrous, filthy and wicked tricks with Witches, as is commonly affirmed, fuits not at all with the Wifdom and Juftice or Glory of God, neither have we any fuch examples in holy Writ, no further, but that Devils only are Gods Executioners or Hangmen. 2. It doth no where appear that the Devils can alter, or change the fhape or qualities of things at his own will and pleafure, but the contrary is manifeft in the Priefts of *Baal* in the time of *Elijah* upon the Mount *Carmel*, where their Idols or Gods were to fhew their power by firing the Sacrifice, a thing which if Satan could have done for them with all his power, it had been moft advantagious for his Kingdom ; but it is evident that he neither did nor could procure as much fire as would burn the Sacrifice, though earneftly called upon by his beft Servants the Idolatrous Priefts. But thou wilt fay, his power was then reftrained and withholden at that time from effecting any fuch thing. Well, grant it were fo, what was the end that God ufed that reftriction upon him at that time for ? was it not becaufe God would not contribute to magnifie the Devils Kingdom ? nor to fuffer him any longer to deceive his people ? But to difcover the weak-

Apoc. 7. 2.

nefs

ness of his power, who is not able of his own created power, to bring forth fire where there is none, not able to break a paper window, unless he have leave and power given him from God. And therefore much less can, for the magnifying of his own power, and to dishonour the Creator, appear as a Cat, Dog, Squirrel or the like to Witches, suck upon their bodies, have carnal copulation with them, or transport them in the air, for this were to advance his credit too much, and utterly derogatory to the Glory of God. 3. Concerning Satans being an instrument and means to bring and cause diseases, it may be considered these two ways. 1. In an ordinary way he seduceth and draweth men to gluttony and drunkenness, by which way of ingurgitation and excess they draw and contract to themselves diverse Diseases, as Coughs, Catarrhs, Dropsies, Scorbutick Distempers and the like. Others he draweth to insatiable lust and concupiscence, that thereby they fall into the *Lues Venerea*, and the whole troop of those dire and horrid Symptomes that accompany it, whereby Men and Women undergo great misery, pains, sickness, and sometimes death. Sometimes he pusheth Men on so far in malice, wrath, choler and passion, and many other such like ways, that they wound, lame and sometimes kill one another; and in this sense he may be said to cause diseases diverse ways. 2. But there is another way more extraordinary wherein as an instrument he may be said to cause diseases and sometimes death, as in that case of *Davids* numbring of the people, where there died of the Pestilence seventy thousand, and though this Pestilence was sent by Jehovah, yet was a destroying Angel the instrument and minister in the execution of it, for the Text saith: *And when the Angel of the Lord stretched forth his hand upon Jerusalem to destroy it, the Lord repented him of the evil, and said to the Angel that destroyed the people, It is enough: now stay thy hand.* And *Herod* for assuming to himself that honour that was only proper to God, *was immediately smitten by the Angel of the Lord, and was eaten up of worms, and gave up the Ghost.* And the Psalmist saith: *He cast upon them the fierceness of his anger, wrath, indignation and trouble by sending evil Angels among them,* the Hebrew giveth it, the emission or sending out of evil Angels. From whence it is manifest that evil Angels are the organs and instruments of Gods wrath, and as Ministers cause Plague, Pestilence and other diseases. 3. Thirdly, there is another great question whether or not the Devil by his vassals, to wit, Sorcerers and Witches doth not cause diseases and death, as is believed by those vomiting up of strange things exceeding the bigness of the Gullet to get either up or down, of which we shall speak largely where we handle the opinion of *Van Helmont* concerning the actions of Witches: Here only we shall say thus much, that the Devil is author and causer of that hatred, malice, revenge and envy, that is often abounding in those that are accounted Witches, which desire of revenge doth stimulate them to seek for all means by which they may accomplish their intended
wickedness,

2 Sam. 24. 16.

Acts 12. 23.

wickednefs, and fo they learn all the wicked and fecret wayes of hurting, poyfoning & killing, but yet we affirm, that what evil foever they perform, it is by caufes and means that work naturally, and fo the evil is only in the ufe and application, and not in the efficients or means.

And whereas he holdeth that Devils as they can caufe Difeafes, fo they can cure them and take them away, we muft crave to be excufed if we cannot fubfcribe to his opinion, and that for thefe reafons.   1. Becaufe of their caufing of Difeafes we have fufficient evidence in the Scriptures, but of their curing of any, we have not any mention at all; and though fome will think this but weak becaufe it is negative, yet it is not probable, but as it expreffeth the one fully, fo it would have given fome hint of the other, if there had been any fuch matter.   2. But the Scriptures do inform us, that the gift of healing or curing Difeafes, is not in the power of Devils by their Creation, much lefs fince as a gift beftowed upon them, but floweth folely from God by the Miniftry of good Angels, of whom *Raphael* (that is, the Medicine or health of God) is the chief.   And that it is reckoned amongft the gifts of the Holy Ghoft is moft plain: *For to one is given by the fpirit the word of* 1 Cor. 12. 8,9. *wifdom, to another the word of knowledge by the fame fpirit. To another faith by the fame fpirit : to another the gifts of healing by the fame fpirit ;* but thefe gifts of healing are not given to Devils, but to the chofen ones of God. And the Pfalmift where he is fpeaking how God afflicted and brought low the people of *Ifrael* by reafon of their fins, Pfal. 107. 18, faith: *Their foul abhorred all manner of meat, and they drew near* 20. *unto the gates of death, but he fent his word and healed them.* And God declareth, that if his people *Ifrael* would keep his Statutes, he would bring none of thofe Difeafes upon them that he had threatned, for (he faith) *I am the Lord that healeth thee,* and this he doth by the miniftry of good *Angels,* or by natural means, and not by Devils.   3. That Devils are no caufers or inftruments in curing Difeafes is manifeft, becaufe that were to make him act contrary to his original deftination after his fall, wherein in his own propriety, *he is a murderer from the beginning,* and that both of fouls and bodies, and never did, nor doth any good to mankind, either fpiritual or natural, either real or apparent ; for that were to act contrary to his will, nature and difpofition, and contrary to the Ordinance and appointment of God who hath Created the deftroyer to deftroy.   Therefore Satan after his fall was not ordained of God to be an healer, preferver, or fanator of difeafes, but to Ifai. 54. 16. be a deftroyer, a wounder and murderer ; for his nature is become fo wicked and malignant, that his whole endeavour is the deftruction of mankind, both in fouls and bodies, and fo no healer, no not of the leaft infirmity.   4. But he is that grand Impoftor, that by lying, cheating and delufion, laboureth to make his Vaffals and others believe that he can cure and heal Difeafes, when he can do no fuch thing, and therefore hath and ftill doth amongft the Pagans, by the wicked Priefts his Slaves, make the people believe,

lieve, that if the ſick perſons be brought before their Idols, and there worſhip and pray, that they ſhall be Cured, when there is not any jot performed in the way of ſanation, but what is by natural means, fancy, and imagination, or what is pretended to be done ſo, by cheating, counterfeiting and impoſture. And the very ſame thing is practiſed by the Papiſts unto this day, in the pretence of their falſe and lying Miracles, fathered upon their Saints and Images, which are nothing elſe but lying cheats and Impoſtures, as we ſhall fully make manifeſt hereafter.   5. The Devil internally deludeth the minds of men, in making them believe, that Pictures, Charms, Amulets, and ſuch other inefficacious and ridiculous means, have power to Cure theſe and theſe Diſeaſes, when indeed they are meerly inoperative, and effect nothing at all; but yet the Witch-mongers will needs have them to be *media operativa*, when they are utterly inefficacious, and are only means of ſeduction and deluſion, to alter, change, or fortifie the imagination, by which alone the Cures (if any ſuch be effected) are brought to paſs, and not by any power of the Devil at all; and he operateth nothing at all in them, except a mental and internal deluſion, in making the Witch-mongers and others believe, that thoſe things are wrought by a Diabolical Power, which are only performed by the force of imagination, and a natural agency and virtue.   6. Again, where there are many occult and wonderful effects wrought by natural cauſes and agents, as by appenſions of vegetables, animals, or their parts, and minerals, by maguetiſm, as the Hoplochriſm, Sympathetic Powder, by Tranſplantation and many other very abſtruſe and ſecret wayes and means, the Devil laboureth to take away the glory of theſe ſanative effects, both from God and his Inſtrument which is Nature, and to have it aſcribed unto himſelf; and in this the Witchmongers do him no ſmall ſervice, in giving that power and honour unto the moſt wicked and wretched of all Gods Creatures, that is only due to the Creator, and to his inſtrument Nature. And to conclude this, I cannot but repeat that excellent and Chriſtian Sentence of *Helmont : Pigritiæ ſaltem enim immenſæ inventum fuit, omnia in Diabolum retuliſſe quæ non capimus.*   *De inject. mattrial. p. 598.*

3. A third kind of power that he aſcribeth unto Devils, is their changing and tranſmuting of bodies, which is either in regard of ſubſtantial transformations, or of thoſe that are but in the external figure or ſhape, or in the qualities, accidents and adjuncts only. Of real tranſubſtantiations, after a long diſpute, he granteth, that they cannot be brought to paſs but by a Divine and Omnipotent Power, which we have ſufficiently proved before, and therefore ſhall forbear to ſay any further of it here. And for what other portents, prodigies, or lying wonders he can perform, we ſhall here examine and diſcuſs them to the full in this order.

1. We ſhall paſs by what may be thought of the ſtrange feats the Magicians of *Pharaoh*, or *Simon Magus* did perform, as fully examined and concluded before, and ſhall give thoſe Texts of Scripture

that

that mention the figns and wonders that Antichrift and falfe Prophets, that are Satans Inftruments, can or do work, and they are

Deut. 13. 1, 2, 3, 5. thefe. *If there arife among you a Prophet, or a dreamer of dreams, and giveth thee a fign, or a wonder: And the fign or the wonder come to pafs, whereof he fpake unto thee, faying, Let us go after other gods (which thou haft not known) and let us ferve them: Thou fhalt not hearken unto the words of that Prophet, or that dreamer of dreams: for the Lord your God proveth you, to know whether you love the Lord your God with all your heart, and with all your foul. And that Prophet, or dreamer of dreams, fhall be put to death, becaufe he hath fpoken to turn you away from the Lord your God.* —

Deut. 18. 20, 21, 22. Another place is this: *But the Prophet which fhall prefume to fpeak a word in my name, which I have not commanded him to fpeak, or that fhall fpeak in the name of other gods, even that Prophet fhall die. And if thou fay in thine heart, How fhall we know the word which the Lord hath not fpoken? When a Prophet fpeaketh in the name of the Lord, if the thing follow not, nor come to pafs, that is the thing which the Lord hath not fpoken, but the Prophet hath fpoken it prefumptuoufly: thou fhalt not be afraid of him.* From whence we may take thefe Obfervations.

Obferv. 1. 1. That we may know he is a falfe Prophet, that fpeaketh a thing in the name of the Lord, if the thing do not come to pafs: But yet this muft be underftood with limitation, where God fendeth a Meffage by a true Prophet, where the thing is fpoken pofitively, but the condition is concealed, and not expreffed, as in the

Jonah 3. 4. Meffage of *Jonah* to *Nineveh: yet forty days, and Nineveh fhall be overthrown:* which was intended if they repented not, but implicitely was underftood (as the event fhewed) if they did repent, the

Orig. Sacr. l. 2. c. 6. p. 193. Lord would fpare them: of which Learned Dr *Stillingfleet* hath this Propofition: "Comminations of judgments to come do not in "themfelves fpeak the abfolute futurity of the event, but do only "declare what the perfons to whom they are made are to expect, "and what fhall certainly come to pafs, unlefs God by his mercy in- "terpofe between the threatning and the event. So that Commi- "nations do fpeak only the *debitum pœnæ*, and the neceffary obli- "gation to punifhment; but therein God doth not bind up himfelf "as he doth in abfolute promifes; the reafon is, becaufe Commina- "tions confer no right to any, which abfolute promifes do, and "therefore God is not bound to neceffary performance of what he "threatens.

Obferv. 2. 2. That there are thofe that do foretel, or fhew figns and wonders, that do come to pafs, and yet thofe that foretel them are falfe Prophets, becaufe fometimes God fendeth falfe Prophets with power to work figns and wonders, thereby to try his people, whether or no they will cleave unto him with all their hearts and fouls, or turn to other ftrange gods, or Idols; and this is ordered by the Providence of God for the trial of the faithful, as was in the Cafe of *Job*. But though thefe may be great figns and wonders to amaze and

and amuse men, and likewise come to pass, yet are they no true miracles, but are distinguished in this, that true miracles are alwayes for the establishing and confirmation of the true Doctrine and Worship of Christ, but the other are lying wonders, wrought only to try the godly, or for the deluding and punishing of those that received not the knowledge of the truth. And though there are, and may be signs and wonders that are wrought by Antichrist and false Prophets, by and in the power of Satan, yet these are all ordered by the Wisdom and Providence of the Almighty, and Satan is no more but an organ and instrument in the performance of them.

There are two other remarkable places of Scripture concerning the Devils power in working signs and wonders, the first of which is this : *For there shall arise false Christs and false Prophets, and* Matth. 24. 24: *shall shew great signs and wonders, insomuch that (if it were possible) they shall deceive the very elect.* The other is this : *Even him* 2 Thess. 2. 9; *whose coming is after the working of Satan, with all power, and* 10, 11, 12. *signs, and lying wonders : And with all deceiveableness of unrighteousness, in them that perish; because they received not the love of the truth, that they might be saved. And for this cause God shall send them strong delusion, that they should believe a lie. That they all might be damned, who believed not the truth, but had pleasure in unrighteousness.* From whence we may take these remarkable observations.

1. Though there arise false Christs, and false Prophets, and e- *Observ.* 1: ven the Antichrist himself, working after the power of Satan, with signs and lying wonders ; yet though Satan be the organ and instrument in performing these lying wonders, God is the Author and efficient cause that doth inflict them, because they are *mala pœnæ,* and come not by a bare permissive power, but are inflicted by him as punishments upon the wicked, even those that received not the love of the truth, and therefore these lying wonders cannot possibly deceive the elect, but prove all deceiveableness of unrighteousness in them that perish; and the reason why they are thus punished with the deceits and delusions of Satan, is because they received not the love of the truth, and therefore God doth send such strong delusion, that they might believe a lie, and this he doth rightly and justly, that as *Beza* notes, *Ita tamen ut soli increduli sint illius fraude perituri.* Upon which place learned *Rollock* tells us this : "We are (he saith) to observe "that Antichrist is nothing else, but Gods Executioner by whom "he punisheth those, by his just judgment, who have not received "the love of the truth, but have contemned the Gospel : which is "so far forth true, that if there had not been, and now were a con- "tempt of the truth, then altogether Antichrist had not been, that is, "the Executioner had not been, whom God sendeth to execute "his just judgment upon those that despise the truth of his Gospel. "So that it is manifest that God doth make a just, and good use of "the very malice, and lying nature of Devils, in punishing those

"that

"that did not receive the love of the truth, but deceiving them by "ſtrong deluſions that they might believe a lie; and this he doth "as ſent and commanded of God, and ſo cannot go one jot further "than his Commiſſion, or as far as he is limited by God.

Obſerv. 2.   2. We may obſerve that how great ſoever theſe ſigns and wonders be, yet they are but lying ones, both in regard of the end for which they are done, and in reſpect of their ſubſtance. And therefore how great ſoever the ſigns and wonders be that evil Angels do perform, yet they are totally different from true miracles, thoſe being alwayes wrought for the confirming of the true Doctrine and Worſhip of God, but theſe have their end only to eſtabliſh falſe doctrine, lies and erroneous opinions, or Idolatrous Worſhips. So they differ in their ſubſtance, for thoſe miracles that God ſheweth for the confirmation of his truth, are alwayes true and real, being againſt and above the whole power and courſe of nature, but thoſe wonders wrought by Satan are but deluſions, cheats, juglings and impoſtures, which though they may ſeem ſtrange to thoſe that are ignorant of their cauſes, yet do but all ariſe from natural cauſes, or from artificial cunning, confederacy and the like. And therefore we may conclude that what miracles ſoever are wrought by a Divine Power, tend to the overthrow of Satans power in the world, but all falſe miracles are wrought to uphold the power of Satans Kingdom in the world, and following deluſions, lies and falſe doctrines.

Obſerv. 3.
Stilling. Sacr.
p. 252.   3. Therefore what ſigns and wonders ſoever Satan doth work, they are no real and true miracles, for as Dr. *Stillingfleet* ſaith: "God alone can really alter the courſe of nature. I ſpeak not (he "ſaith) of ſuch things which are apt to raiſe admiration in us, be "cauſe of our unacquaintedneſs with the cauſes of them, or man "ner of their production, which are thence called Wonders; much "leſs of meer juggles and impoſtures, whereby the eyes of Men are "deceived; but I ſpeak of ſuch things as are in themſelves either "contrary to, or above the courſe of nature, *i. e.* that order which "is eſtabliſhed in the univerſe. And this cannot be altered by any diabolical power, but only by that which is Divine and Omnipotent, which never doth it but for conſiderable ends and important cauſes, as may be manifeſt from theſe unſhaken grounds. 1. That Devils can work no true miracles is manifeſt from the definition of a miracle which is this: *Verum miraculum eſt opus, quod fit præter, & contra naturam & ſecundas cauſas, cujus nulla Phyſica ratio poteſt reddi.* But Satan cannot alter or change the order and courſe of nature. Therefore Satan cannot work or effect a true miracle. The propoſition may be illuſtrated by an induction made of many great miracles, of which there is mention made in the Old and New Teſtament, all which are of that ſort, that are repugnant to the order and courſe of nature, and of which no natural or phyſical reaſon can be rendered and given. Such were the taking of *Enoch* and *Elias* into Heaven, the conſerving of *Noah* and his Family

mily in the Ark, the confusion of tongues at the building of *Babel*, the fecundity of *Sarah* being old and barren, the paſſage of the children of *Iſrael* over the red Sea and over *Jordan*, the ſtanding ſtill of the Sun in the battel of *Joſhuah*, its going back in the dial of *Ahaz*, its eclipſe at our Saviours ſuffering, the preſervation of *Daniel* in the Den of the Lions, and of the three companions of *Daniel* in the fiery furnace, the preſerving *Jonas* in the belly of the Whale, the raiſing up of the dead, and the curing of the Man born blind, and all the reſt of thoſe moſt true and wonderful miracles wrought by our bleſſed Saviour and his Apoſtles. 2. The aſſumption of the Syllogiſm is thus proved. It is the part of the ſame power to change the order of nature, and to create things that were not exiſtent, and ſo the mutation of the order of nature is a certain kind of new creation. But Satan hath not power, by which he can create things that as yet had no exiſtence, as all perſons of reaſon muſt needs confeſs. From whence it muſt follow that Satan hath not power to change the order of nature, and conſequently that he cannot work true and real miracles. 3. The working of true miracles is only a proper attribute of God, and incommunicable to any creaturely power, for the Text ſaith: *Bleſſed be the Lord God, the God of Iſrael, who only doth wondrous things.* And again, *thou art the God that doſt wonders.* And theſe two things the changing of the order of nature, and creation S. *Paul* attributeth to God as only proper to him: *God who quickeneth the dead, and calleth thoſe things that be not, as though they were.* Upon which *Beza* gives this note. *Eo qui vitæ reſtituit. Apud quem jam ſint, quæ alioqui reipſa non ſunt, ut qui vel uno verbo quidvis poſſit ex nihilo efficere.* Pſal. 72. 18. *Id.* 77. 14. Rom. 4. 17.

But if it be objected that though Satan and his Angels of themſelves, and by their own proper power, do not work true miracles, yet may not God work real miracles by them, as he did by the Prophets, Apoſtles and his Miniſters? It is anſwered: That the wonders which are wrought by Satan, do tend to that end, that they might confirm lies againſt God and his glory. But God doth not accommodate his power, to confirm lies, contrary to his glory, and againſt himſelf. Therefore Satan by the power of God, as his Miniſter, doth not work true miracles, for God doth uſe the ſain Angels as executioners of his wrath and judgments, for the afflicting and puniſhing of men, but when God worketh any thing for the good of mankind, either in Soul or Body, he doth not uſe Devils as his Miniſters, but the good and bleſſed Angels, who are miniſtring ſpirits ſent forth for the good of thoſe that ſhall be heirs of Salvation. *Vid. Rollot. in Theſſ.* 2.

And if it be queried, what things and of what ſort and kind, are thoſe wonders that are wrought by Satan and Antichriſt? I anſwer, that either they are indeed nothing but preſtigious juglings and illuſions: or if they be any thing, they are not brought to paſs contrary to the order of nature and ſecond cauſes, although they may

ſeem

seem so to us, who do not know the causes that are in nature, so well
as that old serpent : neither do we apprehend the manner by which
he worketh and acteth his tricks. From which ignorance it proceedeth, that those wonders, that in themselves are no true miracles,
nor done contrary to the order of nature, are by us taken to be true
miracles.

But we will draw towards a conclusion of this point, with that
definition and corollaries that learned *Zanchy* gives us in these particulars. *Miraculum (ait) igitur est externum & visibile, verum &*
simpliciter mirabile factum, ad optimos fines atq; imprimis ad salu-
tem hominum, & ad Dei gloriam promovendam editum. From whence
these points are to be observed.

Di Oper. Dei,
l. 4. c. 12.
p. 191.

1. That a Miracle is external and made visible. For so (he
saith) are all those things that we read of in Scripture that are taken to be true miracles : And therefore that the pretended invisible miracle of Transubstantiation (as they call it) in the ordinance
of the Lords Supper, is a meer figment, because no such thing was
ever made visible, or truely witnessed. But let us press this his argument a little further. If it be (as indeed it must be) a certain
property of a true miracle that it be external and visible, that there
may be witnesses of it, otherwise that which none ever saw or
knew may be the property of a miracle : Then those great wonders
that Witchmongers do affirm that the Devil worketh with and for
Witches, as having carnal copulation with them, sucking upon their
bodies, making a corporeal and oral league with them, carrying them
in the air, changing them into Cats or Dogs, must of necessity be a
meer figment and an impossibility : Because never yet seen, witnessed, or proved by any that were of sound judgment, right understanding or of clear reason, but are meerly the works of darkness,
having existence no where, but in the minds and brains of the Witchmongers, who are ruled by the Prince of darkness.

2. A miracle ought to be really and truly done, that is, that indeed it be such a thing as it appeareth, as the water that Christ
changed into Wine, was really such, that is, it was truely Wine to
the sight and taste of all those that drank of it. Therefore those
things that are brought to pass by the prestigious juglings of Devils and Magicians, are indeed no true miracles. And to apply
this to our present purpose, it is manifest that those things that
Witchmongers do believe that the Witches do or suffer, as to fly
in the air, to be present at dancings and banqueting, and yet to remain empty and hungry, and the like, are but meer delusory dreams
and cheating fancies in their brains, and if any thing be done *ad*
extra, it is but meerly as Juglers do by drawing the eyes from observing the manner of their conveyances, by substituting one thing
in the stead of another, and the like. So that at the best Satan in
respect of what he performeth in these aforesaid actions, is but as
a chief *Hocus Pocus* fellow, or Jugler, and one that acteth
to a worse end, than our common Juglers do, who act but to move
sport

sport and delight, and thereby to get something to be a livelihood, but Satan works his tricks to blind and delude the Soul, and to lead it to error and destruction.

3. A true miracle ought to be simply miraculous and wonderful, that is with and unto all. And such are those miracles, whose causes are hid from all, and therefore are those things that are done contrary to the order of nature, by the only virtue and power of the Almighty God. Therefore those things that are done by natural causes, though occult to many, as are oftentimes done by Devils, are no true miracles. From whence therefore we may conclude, that whatsoever is performed in Physical actions, by natural causes, (and it is the general Tenent of all, that Devils in these cases can work nothing but by natural causes,) are no miracles, and that as they are agents, are not evil, but only become so in the use and application.

4. Every true miracle is wrought above all for most good ends, and especially for the Salvation of Men, and the true Glory of God. By this particular therefore all those signs and wonders that are wrought by Devils, are excluded from the name of true miracles, because they are all wrought for evil ends, and contrary to the Glory of God, and for the deceiving and perdition of Men. And therefore all prodigies wrought by Devils, are called lies.

4. The fourth and last particular that he setteth down, that the Devils have power in, and operate here below, is, that they can insinuate themselves into and penetrate our bodies, and so move Men diverse ways, driving them into the solitary places and Monuments, and by throwing them into the fire or water, by strange tearing and tormenting of them, and by many other ways, of which we shall only note these few things.

1. It is manifest that in the times of our Saviours being here upon earth, and his Disciples, that there were many Demoniacks or Men possessed with Devils, or Men that were devillished, or over whom the Devil exercised an effective and ruling power, and the reason was plain and manifest, for our blessed Saviour being to establish the Doctrine of the Gospel, by great and true miracles, it was necessary that there might be fitting subjects for the effecting of such stupendious miracles in and by, and therefore the Father in his providence had prepared and provided Lunaticks, Demoniacks, those that were born blind, and other strange Diseases that the power of Christ and his Apostles might be manifest in their miraculous cures. But whether or no that Devils have at all times the same power over mens bodies is much to be doubted, there being not the same causes or ends for permitting the same now that was at that season, as we perhaps shall shew hereafter.

2. The manner of the Devils possessing of the minds and bodies of Men, he laboureth to prove, to be essential and personal, and not virtual and effective, which he thinketh he sufficiently proveth by the words *to enter*, and *to dwell*, of which we shall only say this.   1. That

1. That upon the ſuppoſition that Devils are corporeal and have thin, pure and etherial bodies, it may be granted that they may really and ſubſtantially enter into bodies, for he ſaith: *Dæmones autem habent corpora aerea, & aere etiam ſubtiliora & tenuiora. Deindè, ut* Tertullianus *ait, Dæmones ſua hæc corpora contrahunt, & dilatant, ut volunt, ſicut etiam lumbrici, & alia quædam inſecta. Ita difficile illis non eſt penetrare in noſtra corpora.*

*Vid. Dialog.
diſc. of Spir.
and Devils,
Dialog. 2.
p. 34. &c.*

2. But ſecondly, there is none of thoſe places that he citeth, nor any other that ſignifieth a local, or perſonal poſſeſſion, or any ſuch local inherency in the bodies of Men, but only a ſpiritual rule, he (that is Satan) *worketh in the children of diſobedience,* or an effective dominion over them, by which he doth actually afflict, vex and torment Men ſundry and diverſe ways. Neither is the word *Dæmonizomenos* tranſlated or underſtood by learned Men of an eſſential, or perſonal poſſeſſion of Devils to be inherently in men, but only of an effective dominion in afflicting and tormenting of them.

3. And this is moſt manifeſt, that as the Text ſaith, *that Chriſt* Epheſ. 3. 17. *may dwell in your hearts by Faith,* where it were abſurd to underſtand by Chriſts dwelling in the hearts of the faithful, a perſonal, eſſential or ſubſtantial dwelling, but only an effective one, becauſe he worketh effectually in them by his ſpirit: Even ſo were it abſurd to take the other places of entring into, and dwelling there, in ſo groſs, and literal a ſenſe, as perſonally to inhabite, but only effective by his power and dominion. For though the Text John 13. 2. 27. ſaith; that *after the ſop, Satan entred into Judas,* yet in the ſame Chapter the Evangeliſt expoundeth what manner of entrance it was; not a perſonal one, but an effective one by putting, or darting it, βιβλικότος, into *Judas* heart to betray his Maſter. And whereas it is ſaid that Satan had filled the heart of *Ananias* to lie to the Acts 5. 3. Holy Ghoſt, no man can rationally underſtand it of a perſonal and eſſential repletion, but only of an effective one, having by his power ſeduced the heart of *Ananias,* and filled it with deceit by his effectual operation, and not otherwiſe. And whereas it is ſaid Luke 8. 33.
Mark 5. 13.
Matth. 8. 32. by S. *Luke* and S. *Mark,* of the legion of Devils that our Saviour did caſt out, that they entred into the ſwine, ειςῆλθεν εἰς τοὺς χοίρους· S. *Matthew* makes it clear, ſaying, *they went into the herd of ſwine,* εἰς τὴν ἀγέλην τῶν χοίρων, *in gregem,* or as *Tremellius* renders it *ad gregem porcorum,* by which it is manifeſt that they did go amongſt, or into the herd of Swine, and put them into ſuch a fright or fury, by an effective power working upon them, that they ran down a ſteep place into the Sea, and periſhed in the waters; but not that they did perſonally and eſſentially enter into the bodies of the Swine, for that were abſurd and needleſs, for the Swineherd can with his Horn and Whip drive them without creeping into their bellies, and much more might the Devils drive them into the Sea (according to the Proverb, They muſt needs run whom the Devil drives) without a perſonal and local being in their bellies

as though a Piper cannot effectively play feveral tunes upon his Pipes, except he creep into them.

CHAP. XII.

If the Devil, or Witches have power to perform ftrange things, whether they do not bring them to pafs by meer natural means, or otherwife. And of Helmonts *opinion concerning the effects caufed by Devils or Witches.*

HAving handled the knowledge and power of the faln Angels as far forth as there is any thing manifefted in the Scriptures, or that may be deducted from thence by found reafon, and finding their knowledge and power to be much lefs in thefe inferior bodies and elements than is commonly fuppofed ; we are now to proceed to examine what they do fimply of their own power, and what they perform by natural means.   And firft it cannot be denyed but that they can of themfelves dart in evil thoughts, fuggeftions and temptations into the minds of Men immediately of their own power, as alfo to allure Men to fin by the irritation of external objects prefented to the fenfes, as alfo by means of the phantafie, and efpecially by the melancholy humour which is *Balneum Diaboli.* But fecondly the great queftion is, what they work in elemental and corporeal things, and whether it be not only by natural means, as the applying of fit actives to agreeable paffives, whereby the acts afcribed unto them are performed, or not?   Which we affirm from thefe grounds.

1. Becaufe it is the common and unanimous opinion of Philofophers, Theologues and Phyficians, that what the Devils operate *Vid. Gutter. de* in fublunary bodies , or in caufing difeafes in humane bodies, *Fafcino dub. 5.* is by the applying fit actives to convenient paffives , by which *p. 125.* the effects are brought to pafs.   And this is an argument fufficiently preffive, and convincing, if there be any force in arguments brought from humane authority, efpecially confidering that no other caufes befides what are natural, could ever yet be affigned, much lefs proved.

2. And this is more plain if we confider what the Author quoted laft in the Margent faith to the fame purpofe, *Dæmon propria virtute nequit tranfmutare materiam corpoream, nifi adhibeat illi activa proportionata effectibus quos intendit.* As for example, the Devil may caufe burning, by reafon that there is a combuftible fubject, as alfo a fiery and burning agent in nature, and this agent being fire, being applyed to combuftible matter would produce that effect which we call cremation, or burning: But if there were

no

no combuſtible matter in nature, or that there were no igneous a-
gent, then it is plain, the Devils could produce no burning at all;
and ſo where there is no agent and patient in nature, to produce
the effect intended, (as in pretended faſcination there is neither)
there ſuch an effect could not poſſibly be produced: ſo that from
hence it muſt neceſſarily follow, that Devils can operate nothing in
corporeal matter, but by applying fit agents to convenient patients, and therefore *Helmont* ſaid well: *Quaſi Satanas ſupra naturam
eſſet, operareturq; naturæ impoſſibilia. Dono quidem, modum ope-
rando exoticum: at ſane ad intra naturam coerceri oportet.*

3. And that many ſtrange things that are vomited up by ſuch as
are ſuppoſed to be bewitched do proceed from natural cauſes, and
that the Devil worketh no more in them but by inſtigation, to
move wicked perſons (ſuch as are commonly thoſe that are accounted Witches) to give and adminiſter ſtrange things, Philters, or
ſecret poiſons, to ſuch as they would kill, torment, make mad, or
draw to unlawful love, or rather luſt, as may be made manifeſt
from the teſtimonies of perſons of unqueſtionable veracity and
judgment, ſome few of which we ſhall here relate. *Philip Salmuth*
chief Phyſician to the Prince of *Anhalt* recordeth this which we
ſhall give in Engliſh: "The Daughter of a certain Inkeeper was
"deſperately in love with a principal Nobleman. To whom go-
"ing away ſhe offers a moſt beautiful apple. This he ſuſpecteth
"and throweth into a Basket. After three days he remembers it,
"and looks at it; and then it altogether appeared blackned. He
"expecteth for the ſpace of other three days, and then findeth abund-
"ance of little Frogs there. Therefore he returneth into that Inn,
"where the Maid lived, and doth counterfeit ſickneſs and huge tor-
"ments. The Maid willeth him to uſe warm milk. That he pour-
"eth upon the Frogs, who take it greedily, and by little and lit-
"tle do increaſe. But he every day feigneth greater pains, where-
"upon the Maid pitying him doth will him to take the urine of
"a Mare newly made and warm. This he alſo poureth upon the
"Frogs, whereupon they die. After ſome time the ſervant of ano-
"ther Nobleman is afflicted with miſerable torments, and there
"is ſuſpicion of a Philter given by a perſon of quality. They exhi-
"bite Mares urine, and ſhe vomiteth up two Lizards, and two
"Frogs. By which it is manifeſt that ſuch ſtrange vomitings up of
Frogs, Lizards, Askers and the like, though attributed to Witchcraft, and the operation of Satan, do but proceed from natural
cauſes. And doubtleſs the ſperme, or *ova ranarum*, were but conveyed into the Apple, that ſo by the heat of the Stomach, and
the Chylus, (that is like warm milk) they might grow and increaſe.
And this kind of witching, or ſecret poyſoning, we grant to be too
frequent and common, becauſe thoſe perſons commonly accounted
Witches are extreamly malicious and envious, and do ſecretly and
by tradition learn ſtrange poyſons, philters and receipts whereby they do much hurt and miſchief. Which moſt ſtrange wayes of
poyſoning

*Dr injecl. ma-
terial. p. 597.*

*Obſ. Medic.
Cent. 1. c. 70.
p. 45.
Hiſt.* I.

poyſoning, tormenting, and breeding of unwonted things in the
ſtomach and bellies of people, have not been unknown unto many
learned men and Philoſophers, but they reſpecting the good of
mankind, and the multitude of evil minded perſons, have altogether forborn openly to mention ſuch dangerous receipts in their
writings, or at the beſt ſo to publiſh them, that not one of a thouſand could underſtand what they intended, and ſo theſe ſecrets of
miſchief are for the moſt part kept in obſcurity, amongſt old women, ſuperſtitious, ignorant, and melancholy perſons, and by them
delivered over from hand to hand, and commonly one learns it of
another according to the Proverb, Popery and Witchcraft go by
Tradition. And to this very purpoſe I cannot but inſert that re-
markable paſſage of *Paracelſus* in theſe words. *Poſſem equidem (ait)* *De Peſtil. Tract.*
2. p. 388.
peculiarem de ipſis tractatum edere, ut artes ac machinæ illarum
manifeſtarentur. Sed propter malitioſos iſta talia pennâ ſeu calamo
minimè evulganda ſunt, multa enim flagitioſa ſimul induci poſſent :
quæ ſatius eſt reticeri. And that ſtrange productions may be brought
to paſs, and ſtupendious effects brought into action, from ſecret and
hidden natural cauſes, that are better known to thoſe malicious
perſons that are accounted Witches, than others, may be made ma-
nifeſt by another obſervation ſet down by the forementioned *Sal-* *Obſerv. Medici*
83. p. 99.
Hiſtor. 1.
muth, and is this : " *Galen* and others have recorded, that the ſa-
" liva, or ſpittle of a mad dog, if it touch an human body, and be
" not forthwith waſhed off, may cauſe madneſs. But in the *Hydro-*
" *phobia*, there is ſo great force of the poyſon, that the perſons that
" are bitten do alſo piſs or void by urine, little whelps, or pieces
" of fleſh like them, as *Avicenna lib. 3. Fen. 6. tr. 4. c. 7.* hath de-
" livered, though doubted of by others. But (he ſaith) I cer-
" tainly know notwithſtanding that of ſuch *ſaliva* or ſpittle only
" left in the Garment, after biting, have Worms been breed, plainly
" reſembling little Whelps with their heads. For a mad Dog did
" meet a Servant Maid of an honeſt Matrons going to the Market,
" and flies furiouſly and violently at her feet. She that ſhe might
" avoid the danger, inclineth her ſelf, and a little bendeth her knees,
" whereupon the Dog doth with his teeth catch hold of her Gar-
" ment, and eſpecially the ſeam or low ſelvidge, and did bark a lit-
" tle while, and forthwith ran away. Which being done the Maid
" remained terrified, and at the firſt doubted whether the Dog was
" mad or not, but having recollected her ſelf, ſhe ſuſpecteth his ra-
" biouſneſs, becauſe he had been very familiar, even almoſt dome-
" ſtick with her. Therefore ſhe returneth home, and hangeth the
" torn Garment upon a piece of wood in the Houſe. But afterwards
" upon the fourth day ſhe goeth to it, with an intent to mend it.
" But oh a wonderful thing, ſhe findeth Worms altogether like lit-
" tle Whelps in the head, to be bred in thoſe places of the hem
" in which the Dog had faſtned his teeth, and thoſe as a new Mira-
" cle (as they did call it) were ſhewed unto certain of the Neigh-
" bours being called together.

4. Ano-

4. Another instance to prove the strange effects that may be produced by natural Causes, and yet are so occult, stupendious, and unusual, that they are commonly fathered upon Devils, when they have no more at all to do in or about them, but only the mental perswading of the persons to use them to wicked and destructive ends, as those wonderful compositions that produce the Plague and such like grievous Diseases and Symptoms; For this kind of *veneficium* (call it Witchcraft if you please) is and hath been often practised by most horrible, malevolent, and wicked persons, who by an art more than Diabolical (especially in respect of the end and use) have so framed, and prepared, and commixed things naturally, that in the form of unguents have produced the Plague and divers other most pernicious and venefical Diseases, which may be confirmed by undeniable examples, of which we shall give some

Quercet. Rediv. Tom. 3. p. 38. Histor. 1.

few. *Josephus Quercetanus*, that famous Chymist and Physician to *Henry* the Fourth of *France*, tells us thus much : "The Contagion "of the Plague is not only contracted by the mediation of the air "and water, things in a manner universal, or from other things more "particular, as vestments, linnen, and other moveable things in-"quinated by the attraction of pestiferous Atomes : But also by "the detestable Crafts, and Diabolical Arts of certain most wicked "persons, which we call poysoners, or witches, by means of which "they contemperate and mix certain poysons into the form of an "unguent, and use to rub some of it upon the handle of doors, so "that those that do but lightly touch them, are forthwith infected "with the Plague, this subtile poison forthwith creeping by the "pores of the skin into the extremities of the veins, is quickly com-"municated to the heart, to which human industry can hardly ad-"minister any remedy. Unto which the Lord *Verulam* gives this cau-

Syl. Syl. Cent. 10. 564.

tious attestation : *Pestem quoq; excitavit Januarum, rimarum, alio-rumq; inunctio, non tam ex contactu, quam quod homini in more po-situm, si quid humidi adhærescat digitis, naso illud admovere. Mo-neri se patientur, apud quos ea inolevit consuetudo, ut præcaveant.*

De Præstig. Dæm. lib. 3. c. 36. p. 265. Histor. 2.

Johannes Wierus a learned Physician, and a person of credit and veracity, reciteth this History from *Antonius Sabellicus, Ennead. 4. lib. 4.* This strange venefice or witchcraft, was practis'd at *Casal* in the City of *Salassia*, a Region of *Italy*, in the year of our Lord God 1536. "About forty persons men and women, amongst whom "there was one Hangman, had combined and sworn together, That "seeing the Plague had ceased that before did rage, they would "compound an unguent, with which the handles of the doors being "besmeared, they should be infected that touched those handles. "They did also prepare a Powder which being secretly sprinkled in "the Garments, should produce the Plague. The Villany lay hid "for some certain time, and many were taken away of such as were "joined in blood or affinity: Also money was given (as was said) "to the Poysoners, instead of inheritance. But when they had mur-"thered the Brother and only Son of one *Necus*, and that scarcely "others

" others than the Mafters of Families themfelves, or their Sons, did
" perifh: And that alfo they had marked, that into what Houfes
" thofe Confpirators had infinuated themfelves, that thofe for the
" moft part did perifh into whofe Houfes they entred : but the Con-
" fpiracy being found out, they were all put to death with moft ex-
" quifite torments. They alfo confeffed, that they had determined
" to kill all the Citizens upon a Feftival day, by anointing the Seats,
" and to that purpofe they had prepared twenty Pots full of that
" pernicious and hellifh Ointment. And *Paracelfus* tells us, that at *De Peftil. lib.*
" St. *Vitum* and *Villacum* , certain of the Poyfon-makers in the *Tract.2. p. 388.*
" time of a Plague, did take the Earth and Duft from the Graves *Hiftor. 3.*
" of thofe that had been buried, and did fo prepare it with their
" Magical Art, that they raifed up a moft cruel and raging Plague,
" whereby many thoufands of men were infected and flain. But that
the manner of that preparation is by no means to be revealed. Thofe
that defire more fatisfaction in this particular may have recourfe to
that learned Treatife, *de Pefte,* written by the learned and induftrious *Matthias Untzerus.*

5. But there is no where a more ftrange accident written, than *Stow. Annal:*
what is recorded in our own Annals in the year 1579. the nineteenth *p. 681.*
year of the Reign of Queen *Elizabeth*, in thefe words :   " The *Hiftor. 4.*
" 4, 5, and 6. days of *July*, were the Affifes holden at *Oxford*,
" where was arraigned and condemned one *Rouland Jenkes* for his
" Seditious Tongue, at which time there arofe fuch a damp, that
" almoft all were fmothered, very few efcaped that were not taken
" at that inftant: The Jurors died prefently : Shortly after died
" Sir *Robert Bell*, Lord Chief Baron, Sir *Robert de Olie*, Sir *William*
" *Babington*, Mr *Weneman*, M^r *De Olie*, High Sheriff, Mr *Davers*,
" Mr *Farcurt*, Mr *Kirle*, Mr *Pheteplace*, Mr *Greenwood*, Mr *Fofter*,
" Serjeant *Baram*, Mr *Stevens*, &c. There died in *Oxford* 300. per-
" fons, and fickned there but died in other places 200. and odd,
" from the fixth of *July* to the twelfth of *Auguft*, after which day
" died not one of that ficknefs, for one of them infected not ano-
" ther, nor any one Woman or Child died thereof. This is the punctual relation according to our Englifh Annals, which relate nothing
of what fhould be the caufe of the arifing of fuch a damp, juft at
the Conjuncture of time when *Jenkes* was Condemned, there being
none before , and fo it could not be a Prifon Infection, for that
would have manifefted it felf by fmell or by operating fooner. But
to take away all fcruple, and to affign the true Caufe, it was thus :
It fortuned that a Manufcript fell into my hands, collected by an
antient Gentleman of *York*, who was a great obferver and gatherer
of ftrange things and facts, who lived about the time of this accident happening at *Oxford*, wherein it is related thus : " That
" *Rouland Jenkes* being imprifoned for treafonable words fpoken
" againft the Queen, and being a Popifh Recufant, had notwith-
" ftanding during the time of his reftraint, liberty fometimes to walk
" abroad with a Keeper; and that one day he came to an Apothecary,
                                                           " and

"and shewed him a receipt which he desired him to make up; but
"the Apothecary upon the view of it told him, that it was a strong
"and dangerous receipt, and required some time to prepare it, but
"also asked him to what use he would apply it? he answered to kill
"the Rats that since his Imprisonment spoiled his Books; so being
"satisfied he promised to make it ready.   After a certain time he
"cometh to know if it were ready, but the Apothecary said the
"ingredients were so hard to procure that he had not done it, and
"so gave him the receipt again, of which he had taken a Copy,
"which mine Author had there precisely written down, but did
"seem so horribly poysonous, that I cut it forth lest it might fall
"into the hands of wicked persons.   But after it seems he had got
"it prepared, and against the day of his tryal had made a week or
"wick of it (for so is the word, that is, so fitted, that like a Can-
"dle it might be fired) which as soon as ever he was Condemned
"he lighted, having provided himself a Tinder-box and Steel to
"strike fire. And whosoever should know the ingredients of that
"Wick or Candle, and the manner of the Composition, will easily
"be perswaded of the virulency and venenous effects of it, and this
"in him in regard of the use and end was meerly Diabolical, though
"the agency and effects were meer natural.

    6. It is very strange to consider what learned and grave Authors
have left recorded of the Ligation or binding of Husbands that they
might not be viripotent, or be able to have to do with their Wives
for a longer or a shorter time; nay some even have proceded so far as
to write it, and seem also to believe it; that by venifice or Witchcraft, the virile members may be quite taken away; as is related by

De morb. venefic. *Codronchius,* of a certain young man that had his members quite
l. 3. c. 5. taken away by a Woman Witch, which notwithstanding she restored
Histor. 5. again, by beating and putting her in the fear of death. And of this
incredible story, *Sennertus* a professed maintainer of the impossible

De fascino lib. power of Witches, doth notwithstanding give this censure. " The
6. Part 9. c. 5. " Devil doth often delude men by prestigious and jugling deceits,
p. 680. "and perswadeth them that he hath brought such Diseases as indeed
"are none at all, as this taking away the virile member, related by
"*Baptista Codronchius.* For although some be of that opinion, that
"the genital members may really be taken away and restored by the
"Devil: notwithstanding (he saith) I had rather hold with those
"that believe such things are meer juglings and delusions; seeing
"it is not in the power of the Devil to restore unto man a member

Syl. Syl. Cent. 9. "lost or taken away.   The most learned Lord *Bacon* doth affirm,
Exper. 888. "that this kind of Ligation or binding, to make men impotent for
Ibid. Cent. 10. "Coition, is frequent in *Santonne* and *Gascoigne*, and is used to be
959. "done upon the Marriage day, and that it is often performed by
"the Mothers to prevent that incantation by others, and that they
"may loose it when they please.   And doth think it no light mat-
"ter because punishable by their laws. And saith after, If it exceed
"not nature it hath its force from the Imagination of the binder of

"the

" the virile member, and adds : *Putem ego illud ab incantatione*
alienum esse, quia non à certis personis tantum (quales incantatores)
sed à quolibet fieri potest. But that which puts it forth of all doubt
that it is nothing but melancholy, and the abuse of the fancy, is manifest from the observation of perspicacious *Salmuth*, which is this:
"I have known two (he saith) who did imagine themselves impo- *Obs. Medic. Cent.*
"tent to the act of Venery, and thought themselves maleficiated *2. p. 96.*
" or bewitched, when as before they had afforded themselves suf- *Hist. 6.*
" ficiently strenuous in that warfar also with their Wives. But
" both being (he saith) handled and cured by me, as persons me-
" lancholick and Hypochondriacal , have afterwards sufficiently
" laughed at themselves. But I did conjecture them to be melan-
" cholick by this, because they did complain, that about that act
" they were overwhelmed with an heap of Cogitations. From
" whence it is manifest from what cause that effect did proceed.
" And therefore it is deservedly doubted of *Wierus*, whether or no
" there be any true impotency at all , but what is from natural
" Causes.

7. That the most of those vomitings of strange things is only
caused from natural Causes, as poysonous Potions, Philters and
the like, is manifest by another example given us by that famous
Chymist and learned Physician of *Frisuiga* in *Bavaria*, *Martinus*
Rulandus, which is this: " *David Held* Student in the Arts about *Curat. Emp.*
" the twentieth year of his Age did receive from a wicked Wo- *Cent. 91. p. 222.*
" man Cakes, which he did eat, and departing from her forthwith *Hist. 7.*
" in the way he began to doat, and being brought home he began
" to rage more, and fell into madness. And to help this madness
" the Students came unto me and declare the insanity, the Philter
" that he had taken, and his being infected or brought into that
" madness by it, and desire some help against it. To oppose which
" (he saith) I gave six Ounces of my *Aqua Benedicta*, which I
" commanded straightway to be given him in the name of *Jesus*.
" And this being taken soon after by vomiting he cast up the Philter,
" or invenomed Cakes that he had swallowed, which being cast
" upon the Earth, they did with the admiration of the by-standers
" begin to wax hot and to boil, as meat with the fire doth grow
" hot and boil. So that this poison being cast up as a thing unhoped
" for, soon after the insanity is driven away, and within two days
" his understanding was perfectly restored, and by the power of the
" Almighty did totally recover. So that it is manifest that these
kind of people that are commonly called Witches, are indeed (as
both the Greek and Latin names do signifie) Poysoners, and in respect of their Hellish intentions are Diabolical, but the effects they
procure flow from natural Causes. If any require more ample
satisfaction in this point, they may find divers Histories recorded
in *Schenkins* his Observations, *lib. 7. de venenis*, to verifie this particular.

8. There is no one Argument that doth more confirm, that what
effects

effects foever Devils, or thofe called Witches do bring to pafs in humane bodies, are wrought by natural means, and proceed from natural caufes: Becaufe what difeafes foever are cured by natural caufes and agents, muft of neceffity be brought into humane bodies by natural means. But many difeafes attributed to the Devil, or Witches as inftruments, have been cured by natural means and applications, as we fhall prove both by authorities and matters of fact. And therefore thofe difeafes muft of neceffity grow and arife from natural caufes. And for authority we find *Helmont* affirming thus much: "And alfo partly the curing of thefe difeafes is to be "had by certain Simples, to which the omnipotent goodnefs hath "given a gift from the beginning of the Creation, of refifting, "preventing and correcting of *Veneficia*, Witchcrafts, or poyfon-"ings, and of bringing forth things injected. For (he faith) cer-"tain Simples do drive away evil fpirits (a miferable company of "Men, who give worfhip to Gods, that are not able to refift the "natural efficacy of Simples) and reckons fome that take away "the penetration of the formal light tied to the excrements. Some "do hinder the touch, entrance or application. And that there "are many fuch like, that do correct the poyfons, and kill them. "And chiefly he commendeth the *Electrum minerale immaturum* of " *Paracelfus*, the *Phu* of *Diofcorides*, being a kind of Valerian with "purple flowers, and likewife there commemorateth diverfe o-"thers.

To confirm this affertion of *Helmonts*, we fhall tranfcribe what the Honourable perfon Mr. *Boyle* hath fet down to this purpofe. "Since the beginning of this Effay (he faith) I faw a lufty, and ve-"ry fprightful Boy, child to a famous Chymical Writer, (I judge "it to be *Joachimus Poleman*) who as his Father affured me and "others, being by fome enemies of this Phyficians, when he was yet "an infant, fo bewitcht that he conftantly lay in miferable torment, "and ftill refufing the breaft, was reduced by pain and want of "food, to a defperate condition, the experienced relator of the "ftory remembring that *Helmont* attributes to the *Electrum mine-"rale immaturum Paracelfi*, the virtue of relieving thofe, whofe "diftemperscome from Witchcraft, did according to *Helmonts* pre-"fcription hang a piece of this noble mineral about the infants "neck, fo that it might touch the pit of the Stomach; whereup-"on prefently the child, that could not reft in I know not how "many dayes and nights before, fell for a while afleep, and wa-"king well cried for the Teat, which he greedily fuckt, from " thenceforth haftily recovering, to the great wonder both of the "Parents, and feveral others that were aftonifht at fo great and "quick a change. And though I am not forward (he faith) to "impute all thofe difeafes to Witchcraft, which even learned Men "father upon it; yet it's confiderable in our prefent cafe, that what-"foever were the caufe of the difeafe, the diftemper was very great, "and almoft hopelefs, and the cure fuddenly performed by an out-
"ward

Inj:calat. mod. intvand. p.603, 604.

Ufeful. of Exper. Philof. p. 214. *Hift.* 8.

"ward application, and that of a Mineral, in which compacted fort
"of bodies the finer parts are thought to be lockt up. Another
example he giveth us in these words: " The same *Henricus ab*   Ut supra p.217.
" *Heer* among his freshly commended observations, hath another   Hist. 9.
" of a little Lady, whom he concludes to have been cast into the
" strange and terrible distemper, which he there particularly re-
"cords, by Witchcraft. Upon so severe an examination of the
"Symptomes made by himself in his own house, that if, notwith-
"standing his solemn professions of veracity, he mis-relate them not,
"I cannot wonder he should confidently impute so prodigious a
"disease to some supernatural cause. But though the observation,
"with its various circumstances, be very well worth your perusing;
"yet that, for which I here take notice of it is, what he adds about
"the end of it, concerning his having cured her, after he had in
"despair of her recovery sent her back to her Parents, by an out-
"ward medicine, namely, an Oyntment which he found extolled
"against pains produced by Witchcraft, in a Dutch book of *Ca-*
"*richter*'s (where also I remember I met with it set down a little dif-
"ferently from what he delivers.)

But to conclude this tedious particular, I shall only add one ob-   *Observ. Medic.*
servation more from learned *Salmuth*, which is this: "The ser-   34. p. 127.
"vant Maid (he saith) of *Cæsars à Breitenbach* was taken with a   Hist. 10.
"most intense pain of her left arm, which when it did not at all
"remit or abate, but that the dolour was augmented more and
"more, and that no tumour, nor any other preternatural thing did
"outwardly appear, the beholders did fear some sort of venefice or
"Witchcraft. Therefore they apply a well tryed medicine, which
"in such a case is said to be much approved, to wit red Corals well
"beaten with the leaves of Oak, and with Rose-water brought
"into the form of a Cataplasm, and leave it on for the space of 24
"hours. In which space of time the place is brought to suppura-
"tion, and within as many more hours, the same remedy being apply-
"ed again, the abscess is broken, and in it needles, hairs and burnt
"coals are found. All these together with the Amulet they put
"into an hole made with an Augur or Gimlet in the root of an
"Oak, towards the East, in the morning before the Sun rise, and
"they stopped up the same hole with a wedge or pin, made of the
"wood of the same Tree. The pain thereupon plainly ceaseth,
"and the place is with other medicaments brought to Cicatriza-
"tion. But some deriding such things, and thinking them to be
"prestigious delusions, do pull them forth of the hole again. Here-
"upon forthwith that miserable servant was again afflicted with
"cruel pains, more raging than the former. Therefore they repeat
"the former medicaments, and more copious matter doth issue
"forth, which being taken together with the Amulet, and put in
"the former place in the Oak, all the pains did forthwith vanish,
"and she afterwards lived altogether sound. And so I conceive
that by these reasons, authorities and instances of matters of fact,

K k   it

it is sufficiently proved, that what Devils or Witches work in humane bodies or in corporeal matter, is by applying fit actives to suitable passives, and so the effects are only produced by natural causes and means, which was the thing I undertook to make good.

The next thing that in this Chapter we have to consider and examine is the opinion of *Johannes Baptista van Helmont*, that great Physician, Philosopher and Chymist, which we shall open in these particulars.

1. He reciteth a large Catalogue of things, that are in a most strange manner brought or injected into the bodies of Men and Women, as darts, thorn-pricks, or pins, chaff, hairs, dust of wood that hath been sawed, little stones, egg-shels and pieces of pots, hulls and husks or swads, insects, things of linen, needles and the instruments of artificers, which have been injected insensibly, and entred altogether in an invisible manner, but were detained and ejected with direful pains and tortures. And that sometimes they are greater than the holes or passages by which they are intromitted.

2. And to confirm this assertion he bringeth instances of matters of fact, as these following. " For (he faith) of late there was a part

Hist. 1.   " of an Oxe-hide injected by the pores of the skin, it being in-
" tire, which the Chirurgeon did draw forth with a pair of For-
" ceps, it being of the magnitude of the ball of a Mans hand, the
" Apostume first being ripened. And a Witch burned at *Bru-*
" *ges*, did confess, that she had injected that hide into the good
" man. So (he faith) we have in times past seen at *Lira* the chil-
" dren of *Orphans* to have cast up by vomit an artificial Horse and

Hist. 2.   " Cart, drawn forth by the hands of the by-standers; to wit a
" foor footed board accompanied with its ropes, and wheel. And
" what way soever it were placed, it was easily greater than the
" double throat. Further he faith, I have seen at *Antwerp* in the year
" 1622. a young Maid, who had vomited, perhaps two thousand
" pins conglomerated together, and with them hairs and filth. Ano-
" ther Maid (he faith) at *Mechlin* in the year 1631, who we being
" present, did vomit up shavings of wood or chips, cut off in
" plaining with the Hatchet, with much slimy stuff, to the magni-
" tude of two fists. It is (he faith) a frequent thing every where
" admitted by learned Men. Upon which we will only give these
Animadversions.

Anim. 1.   1. That things as strange as these, that *Helmont* seems to avouch of his own sight and knowledge, are also attested by other persons of great learning and credit, as, besides what we have immediately before shewed from *Salmuth*, of the needles, hairs and burnt coals that came forth of the Maids arm, these examples may ratifie. We will pass by *Sprenger, Bodin, Remigius* and *Del Rio* as Pontificial Authors, and therefore partial and interested, only in the first place

Pract. l.7.c.25.   we shall give this from *Alexander Benedictus*, who telleth this:
Hist. 3.   " That he saw two Women his neighbours upon one day, being in-
" fected

"fected by potions of evil medicaments, who afterwards were
"wonderfully tormented with strange vomitings: That the one
"cast up with great strainings an head bodkin very great bended
"like an hook, with a great lump of Womens hair, wrapped with
"the pairing of nails, who died the day following. The other vo-
"mited up a Womans Quoif, pieces of glaſs, with three dried
"pieces of a Dogs tail that was hairy, ſo that ſhe had voided
"by vomiting as much, (if ſet together,) as would have equa-
"lized the quantity of the whole tail. But the moſt strange story
"that poſſibly can be read is recorded by *Thomas Bartholinus* who
"was Phyſician to *Frederick* the third King of *Denmark*, of *Anna*
"*Erici*, who vomited up at ſeveral times a piece of ſharp wood, *Hiſt. Rar. Anat:*
"great ſtore of black blood, an hem or fring of ſilk or linen cloath *Cen. 1.Hiſt. 52:*
"of a blew colour, ſowed with a green thred, in which were hid *p. 73.*
"three pieces of lead, two pieces of glaſs, three Almonds, three *Hiſt. 4.*
"pieces of a Tobacco-pipe, and white ſtones or flints : And after-
"wards many other horrid, ſtrange and incredible things that may
"be read in the place quoted in the Margent.

2. It would ſeem a point of ſtrange Scepticiſm or infidelity to *Anim.* 2.
diſtruſt and reject theſe relations as lies and fictions, ſeeing the
Authors that recite them do for the moſt part atteſt them upon their
own view or knowledge, or at leaſt from unqueſtionable eye-witneſſes, and that they were Men of great Reputation and Credit,
that lived in ſeveral Countrys, and in different times, and therefore
could not conſpire in a lie.

3. But notwithſtanding all this, we find perſons of great learning *Anim.* 3.
and ſober judgments, to uſe much heſitation about theſe things, and
either to ſuſpend their belief of them, as having never ſeen any
ſuch things themſelves, and therefore may well conclude as many
Wiſe Men do, that he that hath ſeen a thing may better believe
it than he that hath not ſeen it, or elſe are utterly diffident and believe no ſuch matters of fact at all. And indeed there is no greater
folly than to be very inquiſitive and laborious to find out the cauſes
of ſuch a Phenomenon, as never had any exiſtence, and therefore
Men ought to be cautious and be fully aſſured of the truth of the
effect, before they adventure to explicate the cauſe. And I find
both my Lord *Bacon*, and that honourable and learned perſon
Mr. *Boyle*, when they have occaſion to mention theſe things, do it
with extream caution, and always with an If or ſome other note
of ſignal dubitation, and alſo the Lord *Mountaigne* in his Eſſays,
and our Countreyman Mr. *Osburne* (no contemptible perſons) in
his writings ſeem utterly diffident of any ſuch matter.

4. Again if we conſider how eaſy a thing it is, for the moſt vi- *Anim.* 4.
gilant, attentive and wiſeſt perſon either to impoſe upon himſelf,
being drawn by thoſe overruling notions that he ſuckt in from his
childhood, whereby the will and affections being never ſo little
byaſſed the judgment will be preſently ſwayed that way: or how
ſubject the moſt wary and perſpicacious perſon is to be impoſed

upon by the cunning craftiness or confederacy of others, or drawn to believe a meer impossibility, by the perseverant asseverations of what others have seen and known, may certainly induce us, though not utterly to reject all relations of this nature, yet to stand like *Janus* in this field of doubtful perplexity.

Anim. 5.   5. If to this we add the consideration, how rare and seldome these things happen, and how long (though it argue but negatively) many Physicians have practised, and yet have never met with any such strange accidents : and withal that many of these vomitings of strange stuff, and the like have been meer counterfeit juglings and Impostures, as was manifest in the Boy of *Bilson Sommers* of *Nottingham* and diverse others: besides, I that have practised Physick above forty years could never find any such thing in truth and reality, but have known many that have counterfeited these strange vomitings, and the like, which we and others have plainly laid open and detected. So that though we shall not simply deny the verity of these relations, so we cannot but believe, that some of them have been cheats and delusions, and others meer mistakes of ignorance and vain credulity, and in the belief of any of them, that we ought to proceed with much cautiousness and careful foresight.

3. The next thing that *Helmont* lies down (after he thinketh that he hath proved the matters of fact sufficiently) is the assigning of the true cause (as he thinketh) of the bringing to pass these wondrous effects ; And these he maketh twofold, first the Devil, by reason of the league with the Witch, doth bring and convey the things to be injected to the place, or near the object, and makes them invisible by his spiritual power : Secondly that the Witch by the strength of her imagination and the motion of her free will, (which he holds to be the only peculiar prerogative of mankind, and to remain both with Men and Women after the fall, namely a power by their free wills and force of imagination, to create or frame seminal and efficacious Ideas to work as it were *ad nutum*) doth convey or inject these strange things into the bodies of those they would hurt or torment, and that in this case as the ultimate attempt of nature, there is and may be a penetration of dimensions, and these things he attempteth to prove after this manner, which we shall first amply lay down and relate, and afterwards we shall give some notes and observations upon them, as things of great weight and consideration.

Reas. 1.   " 1. He granteth that the evil spirit hath a power motive, yet " therewith cannot hurt the innocent as he pleaseth. And further " he tells us that these injected things do enter invisibly. And that " this one thing is meerly Diabolical. For the most miserable scof-" fer (he saith) seeing he hath nothing that is real left to his liberty, " yet he hath vain appearances : Because he is the Father of lies, he " feigneth those things and maketh them to appear falsly, or other-" wise than they are, from the beginning of the World. And in
                                                              " these

"these juglings the Man that is the Devils bondſlave worketh no-
"thing at all. But by what manner the Devil maketh things viſi-
"ble in themſelves to be inviſible, or how he involves them in his
"inviſible ſpirit, he confeſſeth that he is not a ſedulous ſearcher
"of the works of Satan, that belong unto him in propriety. And
"therefore that the Devil doth transfer the things to be injected,
"being made inviſible, unto the object, the Idea of humane de-
"ſire directing. And becauſe it is not permitted to the Devil, to
"enter into Man, much leſs that he may hurt him, and leaſt of all
"with an inviſible burden; therefore he uſeth the free motive
"power of the Man bound unto him. The Man doth therefore
"impreſs his free motive Blas into the body made inviſible, but
"the Devil doth carry it unto the Man, into whom it is to be in-
"jected. And as a knife by the deſire and conſent of the perſon
"wounding is fixed into the fleſh of him that is wounded: So this
"body made inviſible by the Devil, is injected into the body of
"the perſon to be inchanted, by the Idea of the motive power of
"the Witch: Satan conſpiring to this becauſe of the purpoſed di-
"rection of hurting the perſon.

"2. Truly I believe (he ſaith) that it doth fight with Piety, if a
"power exceeding nature be attributed to the Devil. As though
"Satan ſhould be above nature, and ſhould operate things impoſ-
"ſible to nature. I grant that the manner is exotick and ſtrange,
"but yet notwithſtanding it ought to be contained within the li-
"mits of nature. And if it be ſaid: the manner is unknown by
"which nature ſhould do it. The manner is alſo equally unknown
"by what means Satan ſhould do it. Therefore they gain nothing
"who refer the work of nature unto the Devil. But whether they
"offend or not, let others look to it. For at leaſt it is an inventi-
"on of immenſe ſloathfulneſs, to refer all things to the Devil that
"we do not underſtand. Neither would I (ſaith he) have the De-
"vil called upon to ſatisfie our queſtions by a temerarious attributi-
"on of power. *Reaſ. 2.*

"3. Therefore (he ſaith) I will ſhew, that the aid of Satan is
"not at all needful, that ſome ſolid body may be drawn without
"the comminution of it ſelf, by a paſſage far leſs than it ſelf. For
"the evil ſpirit, though he have a motive Blas; yet notwithſtand-
"ing it is againſt piety, that he can hurt the innocent at his plea-
"ſure. Which certainly ſhould come to paſs, if every where he
"could inject theſe things, according to his nefarious will, for (he
"ſaith) I have ſeen theſe things happen to innocent children, to
"Virgins that were pious and devoted to God after a ſingular man-
"ner. And to prove this point he giveth theſe inſtances. *Corne-*
"*lius Gemma de Coſmocriticis* doth recite that he had ſeen a piece
"of three pounds or 48. ounces weight, of a braſs Cannon, which
"a Maid the Daughter of a Cooper had voided by ſtool, with its
"characters or letters, together with an Eele wrapt in its ſecun-
"dines. But it is impoſſible to nature to melt powdered metal in *Reaſ. 3.*

Hiſt. 1.

us,

" us, and to be detained so many months in its pristine figure in the
" Intestines, or that the Eele should so often be made into small pow-
" der and to arise again from death. And that pieces of wood and
" leather should so often be turned into small powder, and again

Hist. 2.   " restored into their former condition. For (he saith) I have seen
" at *Bruxells* in the year 1599. that an Oxe having taken three
" Herbs did vomit a Dragon with a tail like an Eele, a body as of
" leather, a Serpentine Head, and not less than a Partridge. There
" is (he saith) an History of a Polonish Countryman, seen lately

Hist. 3.   " of the Son of the Lord *Ericius Puteanus*. A certain rustick did
" attempt himself to cut the Squinsie that he had in his throat with
" a short Knife, which at unawares he swallowed, and that at the
" length he did void the same at the right side of the *Abdomen*, or
" lower belly, with much rotten matter after great tortures, and
" survived in health. Also at *Vilvordia* in the year 1636. a Coun-
" tryman known unto me (he saith) intending to feed a Cow, did
" daily give her a bowl, in which he had boiled Pot-Herbs with
" bran. At last she waxeth leaner more and more every day, and be-
" gun to halt upon the right thigh: The Cow being killed, the short
" Knife of his Wives bended back into the haft of Box, is found
" hid betwixt the ribs and the shoulder blade :   For the Country
" Woman in cutting the rape root, had left her Knife amongst the

Hist. 4.   " Pot-Herbs, and the Cow by drinking had swallowed it. Also (he
" saith) *Ambrosius Paræus* relateth a story of a certain man whom
" Thieves had compelled to swallow a Knife, which he afterwards
" being found did void by an Apostume of the side. *Alexander Be-*
" *nedictus* (he saith) doth mention another, to whom an Arrow
" had penetrated into his back, the hook of which of the breadth
" of three fingers he did void by stool without hurt.   The same
" Author relateth of a certain Girl of *Venice* who had swallowed
" a Needle, and that after two years she voided it by urine, crusted

Hist. 5.   " over with a stony substance. Also (he saith) *Antonius Beneve-*
" *nius* doth relate, that an Hetruscan Woman had swallowed a Cop-
" per Needle or Pin, which three years after she voided at the Na-
" vil, and was found. *Valesius de Taranta* (he saith) mentioneth

Hist. 6.   " a Girl of *Venice* (perhaps the same) who voided by urine a Pin
" of three fingers long. A certain Capucine at *Eburum* called *Bullo-*
" *nius*, by Sirname *Hamptean*, did with much aversion of mind
" drink up an huge living Spider, which he had seen fall into the
" Chalice in the time of the Sacrifice of the Mass.   Within a few
" days he had a Phlegmon or bile that did arise in his right thigh,
" and with much rotten matter from thence he voided the whole

Hist. 7.   " Spider, but being dead. A young Merchant of *Antwerp* being
" playing at *Venice* in his mouth with an unripe Ear of Barley, did
" swallow the same with an huge fear of suffocation: From thence
" after three Weeks in the left side above the Girdle, an Apostume
" appeared, and at the length with the rotten matter the same Ear
" of a yellow colour is extracted whole.   And he escaped sound.
                                                                   " With

" With *Fernelius* a Student is related to be cured by him who had
" voided an Ear of Corn by the ribs. Alfo Writers do commemo-
" rate, that the young one fometimes dead and wafted in the Womb,
" hath voided the bones through the Womb, the belly, by the na-
" vil, and fometimes by the fundament. More things of this nature
" do every where occur amongft Authors worthy of credit.

4. From which matters of fact he thus concludeth : " By which *Reaf.* 4.
" (he faith) it is manifeft, that folid bodies fufficiently great, have
" penetrated the Stomach, the Bowels, the Womb, the Caul, the
" lower Belly, the skin upon the infide of the Ribs, the Bladder,
" Membranes (he faith) impatient of fo great a wound. That is
" to fay, that Knives have been tranfmitted through thefe Mem-
" branes without wound, which is equivalent to the penetration
" of dimenfions made in nature without the help of the Devil. And
" that an human body may be drawn through a fmall hole, through
" which a Cat might only pafs, but not through a Wall. Verily
" that the Devil cannot break a paper Window without the confent
" of his Mafter, is (he faith) manifeft by the procefs and arreft of
" *Ludovicus Godfredus* the Witch, pronounced at *Aix* in *Narbona*,
" the laft of *April* 1611. I pray you where have the three pounds
" of brafs, of the Cannon of War, marked with its letters, laid hid?
" how for fo many months hath the drofs fhined, in what part was
" the piece of brafs greater than the inteftine contained? While I
" was (he faith) fhewing a neceffary vacuity in the air, I promifed
" that I would declare, that although the penetration of bodies by
" the primary law of nature, and by the common way of Artificers
" be forbidden : notwithftanding that while a body doth totally
" pafs over into the dominion of the fpirit, and is carried over, and
" is by that as it were weakened ; then bodies do naturally and mu-
" tually penetrate one another, at leaft in that part that is porous :
" Becaufe that the fpirit then doth inclofe the body under it felf,
" and therefore as it were taketh away the dimenfions.

5. And to confirm and open this point more fully, he faith: *Reaf.* 5.
" I will premife fome things. The defire of eating Mufcles did in-
" vade a Woman with Child. And fhe eateth fome of them fo very *Hift.* 1.
" haftily, that fhe did devour the raw fhells, twice or thrice broken
" with her teeth. Thereupon by and by within an hour, fhe bring-
" eth forth a found and adult Child, with the fame half-chewed fhells,
" and wounded in the belly. Therefore the fhells without the aper-
" ture of the membranes, had forthwith penetrated the Stomach,
" Womb and Secundines : or elfe there were new fhells generated
" upon the young Child. Neither could this later be true. For they
" were the true fragments of the Mufcles, and not figuratively fra-
" med to the imitation of them. Furthermore, the appetite is not
" carried to a thing unknown : Therefore the appetite of eating
" the Mufcles was not of the Child, but of the Woman. Therefore
" it was not neceffary that new Mufcles fhould be generated about
" the Child ; for they were defired by the Mother that they might
                                                          " become

"become nutriment to her, not the Child. Otherwise by the same
"argument of Identity, what things foever fhould by the appetite
"be defired, fhould be generated about the young Child ; of whom
"when they could not be digefted, they fhould be always either
"left remaining about the Child, or fhould there putrefie. Which
"is falfe both ways: for if it fhould putrefie, that which is defired
"would caufe abortion; or if it were conferved there, it would be
"found regularly. For the Child is only nourifhed by the Navil:
"Therefore thofe external Mufcles could neither be wifhed by the
"Child, nor could be profitable unto it , and by confequence,
"were neither for an end made anew, but fent to the young one by
"reafon that it was an uterine appetite. The appetite is always di-
"rected from the end; but the Woman with Child defired the
"Mufcles not the fhells, neither that the Mufcle being a living ani-
"mal might remain in its former ftate, in which it was unprofitable
"to the Mother, nor could fatisfie her appetite ; and therefore much
"lefs hath had occafion of generating new and unprofitable fhells
"about the young one. But however it be taken, the appetite was
"not to the fhells twice or thrice broken. For if the Fifhes had been
"taken forth of the fhells, fhe had eaten the fifh the fhells being left.
"Therefore the concomitance and concifion of the fhells were acci-
"dental to the appetite. I fuppofe truly (he faith) that as the de-
"fire, terrour, &c. do generate feminal Idea's, which the hand of
"the Woman with Child doth fend down to the young one, and
"doth depinge or figurate it in a fet time : So the joy of finding
"that which the appetite did defire, doth bring that very thing to
"the Child. So verily the heavinefs of heart of him that fwallowed
"the Knife, the horror of having drunk the Spider, and of the Ear
"of Barley devoured, did repel or drive back thofe things beyond
"the membranes not able to fuffer a wound without death. And
"thefe things (he faith) of things injected, entring by the ordi-
"nary power of nature, without the fufpicion of Diabolical co-
"operation.

Reaf. 6.   6. Now he proceedeth to prove penetration of dimenfions by
natural power in another way. "Something like to thefe (he faith)
"appeareth in things that from within are to without taken away,
Hift. 1.   "which I will difpatch (he faith) in one or two examples. The
"Wife of a Taylor of *Mechlinia*, feeth a Souldier before the doors
"to lofe his hand in a conflict : Forthwith being ftricken with
"horror, fhe brought forth a Daughter with one hand, the other
"awanting, with the ftump all bloody, which hand of hers could
Hift. 2.   "not be found, and the flux of blood killed the Child. The Wife
"of *Marke de Vogeler*, a Merchant of *Antwerpe* in the year 1602.
"feeing a Souldier begging whofe right Arm an Iron Bullet in the
"Siege of *Oftend* had taken away, and which he carried about as
"yet bloody ; by and by after that fhe brought forth a Daughter
"wanting an Arm, and that the right one too, the fhoulder of whom
"being yet bloody the Chirurgion ought to confolidate. She hath
"Married

" Married to a Merchant of *Amſterdam*, by name *Hoochcamer*, and
" is yet living this year 1638. But the right Arm was no where to
" be found, neither the bones or any corruption did appear, into
" which the Arm might be waſted in a little hour. But the Souldier
" not being ſeen, the Child had two Arms, neither could the Arm
" that was torn off be annihilated. Therefore the Womb being ſhut
" the Arm was taken away. But who tore it away naturally, and
" whither was it taken ? certainly trivial reaſons do not ſquare or
" agree in ſo great a portent or Paradox. I am not he that will ſay
" theſe things. I will ſay this at the leaſt : That the Arm was not
" taken away or torn off by Satan. Furthermore it was of leſs weight
" to carry away elſewhere the Arm torn off, than to have torn
" the Arm from the whole body without death. The Wife of a Mer- *Hiſt.* 3.
" chant (he ſaith) known unto us, as ſoon as ſhe heard that thir-
" teen were to be beheaded (it happened at *Antwerpe* in the time of
" the Duke of *Alva*) and Women with Child are led with inordi-
" nate appetites, ſhe determined to ſee the decollations. Thereupon
" ſhe aſcends the Chamber of a Widdow that was a familiar friend
" to her that lived in the Market-place. And the ſpectacle being
" ſeen, forthwith the pain of Child-birth took her, and ſhe brought
" forth a full grown infant with a bloody neck, whoſe head did no
" where appear.

7. From theſe moſt ſtupendious and almoſt incredible ſtories, he *Reaſ.* 7.
draweth theſe concluſions. "I do not find (he ſaith) that human
" nature doth abominate the penetration of dimenſions, ſeeing it is
" moſt frequent to the ſeeds of things. For in the ſeeds of things,
" that primevous Energie of penetrating bodies, doth yet conſiſt, but
" not ſubject to force, art or human arbitrement. For there are ma-
" ny bodies many times more ponderous than the matter of which
" they are framed. It is neceſſary (he ſaith) that more than fifteen
" parts of water do fall in together into one, that one part of gold
" may from thence be made. For weight is not made of nothing :
" but argueth the ponderating matter in the ballance. Therefore
" water doth naturally penetrate its body ſo often as the gold doth
" overweigh the water. Therefore the domeſtick and daily progreſs
" of ſeeds in Generations, doth require that the body doth penetrate
" it ſelf by condenſation, which is altogether impoſſible to an Ar-
" tificer. We grant (he ſaith) that there are pores in the water,
" theſe notwithſtanding cannot contain ſo much as fourteen times
" the quantity of its whole. Therefore it is ordinary, that ſome
" parts of the water do penetrate themſelves into one place.

8. And to illuſtrate this going before he ſaith : "By an example, *Reaſ.* 8.
" *Aqua fortis* doth by its ſpirit make Braſs, Iron or Silver remain-
" ing opacous in their natures ſo tranſparent that they cannot be
" ſeen, and doth paſs the metal thorough filtring paper, which
" otherwiſe will not tranſmit, no not the moſt ſmall powder, which
" metal doth eſſentially remain ſtill a metal *in ſpecie* or kind. But
" not that the ſimilitude of penetration of dimenſions doth uniformly

L l   " ſquare

" fquare with the propounded example of the metal. Becaufe rea-
" fons do not agree to fo great a Paradox, wherein (he faith) I
" willingly acknowledge the manner to be indemonftrable *à priori.*
Even as no man can know by what means the Idea impreffed in the
feeds doth figurate, direct, and difpofe the things that it hath
framed. And therefore we are forced to hunt forth the fame *à
pofteriori.*

Reaf. 9.   9. From all which he draweth this Conclufion. " There is there-
" fore another far different power of incantation, befides the Devils.
" And therefore natural and free. He hath no Dominion over the
" juft. But if the power of inchanting were free to the Devil, alfo
" it would be equally free to him to kill by a Knife or a Maul. And
" fo none fhould be free. Therefore the Witch (he faith) doth,
" *per ens naturale*, form imaginatively a free Idea, which is natural
" and noxious. Which Idea Satan cannot form. Becaufe that the
" formation of Idea's do require the Image of God and a free power :
" And therefore the Witches do operate by a natural force, no lefs
" againft the juft and innocent, than againft wicked men. Seeing
" that inchantments do more eafily infect Children than thofe of ripe
" age, fooner Women than ftout Men : A certain natural power is
" fignified to be limited to the inchantment, to which it is eafily
" refifted by a ftout and couragious mind. The Devil therefore
" offereth filth and poyfons to his Clients, that he may knit fermen-
" tally Idea's formed in the Imagination of the Witches unto them.
" And he preferveth that Ideal poyfon, that it may not be blown
" away with the wind, or being covered in the earth, it be not de-
" ftroyed by putrefaction. But he carrieth that poifon locally near
" to the object, to be inchanted : But to apply it, or carry it in-
" to the man, he by no means is able. And therefore the Witch
" doth alfo fend forth another *executive medium*, or mean emana-
" tive and commanding, which mean is the Idea of a ftrong defire.
" For it is infeparable to the defire to be carried about things wifh-
" ed for. To all which the Devil as a Spectator doth affift in the
" conduction.

Reaf. 10.   10. " For (he faith) in truth, I have demonftrated already, that
" operative means are folely in the power of man. For only God is
" the moft chiefly glorious Creator, to be infinitely praifed, who
" hath Created the Univerfe forth of nothing. But man as far forth as
" he is the Image of God doth forth of nothing create certain *Entia*
" *rationis*, or *non*-Entities in their beginning, and that in the pro-
" per gift of the Phantaftical virtue. Which are notwithftanding
" fomething more than meerly a privative or negative being. For
" firft of all while thefe conceived *Idea*'s do at length cloath them-
" felves in the fpecies or fhape fabricated by the Imagination, they
" become Entities now fubfifting in the middeft of that Veftment,
" to which by the whole they are equally in them. And thus far
" they are made feminal and operative Entities : of which, to wit
" their affumed fubjects are forthwith totally directed. But this
                                                       " power

"power is given to man alone. Otherwiſe a ſeminal power to pro-
"pagate, is given to the Earth, to Bruits, Plants, &c. Alſo the Dog
"by his madneſs can transfer or change his ſpittle or *ſaliva* into
"poyſon, becauſe it is peculiar to his kind or ſpecies. Which alſo
"is obvious in divers poyſons of animals. But to form Idea's ab-
"ſtracted from their ſpecies and adjacent proprieties, that is given
"to none but man.

Having thus far at large traced his footſteps in theſe abſtruſe and
myſterious matters, we ſhall come now to examine them and make
ſome obſervations upon them. And although we may be ſharply
cenſured for taking upon us to queſtion the things that he hath
aſſerted, having been *ſuo gradu* an Adeptiſt, a perſon of profound
judgment, great experience, general learning, high reputation, and
now generally followed as the Chief Standard-bearer for Philoſophy, Phyſick and Chymiſtry, that many eſteem it no ſmall glory
to be called and accounted an Helmontian. Yet notwithſtanding
this we ſhall note ſome obſervations in this order.

1. He holdeth that the Devil doth only make the things inviſi- *Obſerv. 1.*
ble, or hides them by his ſpirit, and brings them near to the object
into which they are to be injected, and that the Witch by the ſeminal Idea of her imagination, and the ſtrength of her deſire as
the agent, or efficient cauſe, doth inject or thruſt them into the
body of the perſon, intended to be hurt or tormented; whereby he
neceſſarily ſuppoſes a league or contract betwixt the Devil and the
Witch, and therefore he calls them the Devils clients and thoſe
that are bound unto him. But what kind of contract this ſhould
be, explicite or implicite, internal and mental, or corporeal and
viſible, he tells us not; the latter of which we utterly deny, that it
is in the power of the Devil to practiſe when he pleaſeth, as we
have before with ſufficient arguments demonſtrated at large. And
for an implicite or mental league, we grant that all thieves, murderers, theſe kind of malicious and poyſoning Witches and all o-
ther wicked perſons are bound in a ſpiritual contract unto him: For
he is the ſpirit that *worketh in the children of diſobedience.*
And what wickedneſs ſoever he hath tempted and drawn them unto, to be willing to commit, he prompteth and puſheth them on
with all his skill and power to perpetrate and execute the ſame.
But ſtill this is to be underſtood only of his ſpiritual and inviſible
aſſiſtance, and not of any viſible or corporeal aid, for elſe (as this
Author confeſſeth) he might as well kill with a knife or a maul.
And therefore we cannot here paſs by the bold and groundleſs (if
not impious) aſſertion of *Sennertus*, who though a very learned *De Incant.*
perſon in diverſe parts of humane literature, yet drawn with *p. 677.*
the ſway of popular opinion, did moſt miſerably lapſe in affirming that
although Witches do purpoſe to hurt men, yet "that they neither
"do nor can effect thoſe things, but that the Witches being caſt in-
"to a profound ſleep, the Devil in the mean time acteth thoſe things
"by himſelf; and thinks he proves this ſufficiently by a fabulous
"and

"and lying ſtory feigned to be told of a Witch, that being in a "deep ſleep, when ſhe waked, told that ſhe had been transformed "into a Wolf, and had torn in pieces a Cow and a Sheep, which were found to be ſo, and therefore the Devil muſt needs have done it. But in this he neither nameth the place, time, nor Author to avouch it, and therefore all reaſonable Men may judge how palpable a falſity it is, for then if true it would follow that none could be ſafe, and that the Devil might kill immediately with ſwords or knives, which he cannot do.

Obſerv. 2.   2. Whereas he holdeth that the Devil doth bring or convey the things to be injected near unto the place, and that he offereth filth and poyſons to his clients, that thereby he may fermentally conjoin the Ideas of theſe formed in the imaginative faculty with theſe. If the Devil be taken to be meerly and ſimply incorporeal, then he cannot remove matter (as we have before proved) and ſo cannot convey the things near to the object ; and if he be taken to be corporeal (as we have aſſerted) his help is needleſs, becauſe the Witches may do it themſelves, as we find ſufficient ſtories of their hide-
De Lithiaſ. ing of ſtrange and poyſonous things under the threſholds of houſes
c. 8. p. 75. and Churches ; and to this purpoſe this ſame Author telleth us this
Hiſt. ſtory : "A certain perſon (he ſaith) did by cuſtome uſe to make "water in a corner of the Court, whereupon he was afflicted with "a bloody and cruel Strangury. And all the remedy of the Phy-"ſicians proved in vain, except that as often as he did drink of Birch-"Ale he did find a ſignal eaſe : But as oft as he roſe and walked, "and made water in the ſame place, ſo often his pains did return. "At the laſt a pin of old black Oak-wood is eſpied to be fixed in "the place where he uſed to make water. Which being pulled "forth and burned he remained free from the bloody Strangury, by "drinking Ale of Birchen-twiggs. Alſo (he ſaith) that he re-"membred, that *Karichterus* had written that he had looſed ſuch "kind of inchantments by only piſſing through Beeſomes of Birch. Now from hence it is plain that this making water conſtantly up-on this pin of old black Oak-wood did cauſe his bloody Stran-gury, and that the pulling of it up and burning of it, was with the help of the Birchen Ale the cure ; but it can no wayes be judged neceſſary that the Devil ſhould fix the Oak pin there , but that the Witch might do it himſelf. Neither can it be thought to be any power given by the Devil to the Oaken pin, that it had not by nature, for in probability it will conſtantly by a natural power produce the ſame effect ; only thus far the Devil had a hand in the action, to draw ſome wicked perſon to fix the pin there where the Man was accuſtomed to make water, thereby to hurt and torture him, and ſo was only evil in reſpect of the end.

Obſerv. 3.   3. We obſerve and affirm that whatſoever effects are brought to paſs by that which is commonly called and accounted Witch-craft, if they be not brought to paſs by jugling, confederacy, de-luſion and impoſture (as the moſt of them are, if not all) then
they

they are performed either by meer natural causes, or the strength of the Witches fancy, and most vehement desire of doing of mischief to those she hateth, or by both joined together, and that Satan is no further an author or actor, but as he leadeth and draweth the minds of the Witches to do such mischievous actions, and pusheth on to seek about to learn of others such secret poysons, charms, images and other hidden things, that being used so or so, may produce such destructive ends as their wicked and diabolical purposes are led to, and in this sense they are his clients, and bounden vassals, and not otherwise.

4. The stories that he relateth are either all to be taken to be *Observ. 4.* true, or none of them; and if they be all alike equally to be credited, then it will undeniably follow, that they were all alike produced by natural causes, and so no need at all of the Devils assistance in performing of them, no more than by working upon the minds of such as used those natural means to a wicked and mischievous end. For first he giveth these instances of things that were very strange that were voided either by vomit or stool, by the ordinary power of nature, without suspicion of diabolical cooperation, as the voiding of the piece of the brass Cannon with its letters, with the Eele wrapped in its secundines: The Dragon that the Oxe voided by taking three herbs, with a tail like an Eele, a body like or of leather, with a Serpentine head, and not less than a Partridge: The knife that the Thieves forced a man to swallow, which he voided by an Apostume in the side, and was after found: also the arrow head of three fingers broad strucken into the back, and after voided by stool, with diverse such which we recited before. And that these being solid bodies should have penetrated and passed through parts that are impatient of wounds, and in which a wound is mortal, must of necessity be very wonderful, and might as soon and upon as rational grounds be taken to be diabolical, as those that he enumerateth to be so: For from these it is manifest that either nature put to her last pinch doth make penetration of dimensions, or else so inlarge the pores, that those solid bodies may pass without wound, which (if seriously considered) is a stupendious operation and effect. And as there needeth no cooperation of a diabolical power, for the performing of these, no more needeth there any concurrence of Devils to the others, that to that purpose he relateth. Only here is all the difference: these are wrought by the ultimate endeavour of the *Archæus* to save life, without the concurrence of external causes; the others (that are therefore called diabolical) are commonly wrought for a bad end; namely to hurt or to take away life, and have an external cause, to wit, the force of the Witches imagination and strong desire of doing of mischief, which is stirred up to that end by Satan, and therefore in regard of the end are devilish, though they be both wrought by the agency of nature, the one in the body of the imaginant, the other in the body that the Witch intendeth to hurt by the force of her
imagina-

imagination and vehement defire, whereby a feminal Idea is created or formed, which is fufficiently operative to accomplifh the end intended.

Obferv. 5.   5. The arguments that he bringeth to prove penetration of dimenfions to be in nature, or fomething equivalent thereunto, feem to be ftrong and convincing. For in the generation of things, whofoever fhall ferioufly and ftrictly mark, fhall find (as he alledgeth) that the fpirit of the Archeus (though not altogether incorporeal) doth in the feeds of things penetrate it felf, and their parts one another, which he further maketh good by the inftance of Gold generated of water; for it muft of neceffity be, that more than fifteen parts of water muft fall in or penetrate one another, that from thence one part of Gold may be made, for weight is not of nothing, but argueth the matter ponderous in the Ballance. Therefore naturally the water muft fo oft penetrate its body as the Gold doth preponderate the water. And though it be granted that the water hath pores, yet notwithftanding it cannot contain fo much as fourteen times, it whole. And therefore he irrefragably concludeth : *Eft ergo ordinarium in natura, quod aliquæ partes aquæ fe penetrent in unicum locum.* And this he backs with an unanfwerable ftory of a Woman that longing for Mufcles, did in greedinefs eat fome of them with the fhells twice or thrice broken with her teeth, and that fhe brought forth a child with the fame half eaten fhells, and a wound in the belly ; therefore thofe fhells had penetrated the ftomach, womb and fecundines, or otherwife the force of the Archeus had opened the pores and letten them pafs in an unconceiveable manner. So that if thefe things be granted to be true (and we confefs we know not how they can be anfwered) then there need no diabolical power be brought to folve the injecting of ftrange things into mens bodies, feeing nature is fufficient of it felf, and therefore we can allow no power at all unto Devils in effecting thefe things (if they be truly done, and be not delufions) but only in drawing the minds of the Witches to thefe wicked and mifchievous courfes; and therefore the Lord *Bacon* faid profoundly

Syl. Syl. Cent.
10. p. 556.
and wifely thefe words: *Ut in operationibus illis earumq; caufis error cavendus eft, ita quoq; danda vel imprimis opera eft, ne effecta nobis imponant, temere judicantibus talia effe, quæ eoufq; nondum procefferunt. Sic prudentes judices, præfcripta velut norma, fidem haberi temere nolunt confeffionibus fagarum, nec etiam factorum contra illas probationi. Sagas enim turbat imaginationis vertigo, ut putent fe illud facere, quod non faciunt, populumq; hîc ludit credulitas, ut naturæ opera imputent fafcino.*

Obferv. 6.   6. And to confirm this point he addeth far more ftupendious matters of fact than the former, of things that were within, being taken to without or invifibly conveyed away, as the woman at *Mechlin* that faw the Souldier in a conflict lofe his hand, and forthwith brought forth a Daughter wanting an hand, which was never found, and the wench died of the Hæmorrhage. Another

at

at *Antwerpe* seeing a Souldier begging with his right arm shot off and bloody, forthwith brought forth a Daughter wanting the right arm whose bloody shoulder the Chirurgeon cured, and she was married after; and that the arm was never found, neither did there appear any bones or putrefied matter into which the arm might waste. Also another Woman going to see the Decollation of thirteen men, did soon after bring forth a mature Child with a bloody neck, the head no where appearing.   I confess it would rack the judgment even of the most credulous to the highest pitch to believe these unparallel'd Stories; but the Author relating them as of his own knowledge, and being a person of unquestionable veracity, I cannot conceive how they can rationally be denied, especially finding Mr *Boyle* to affirm, that in those experiments (much more relations of matters of fact) that *Helmont* avouched upon his own knowledge, he durst be his Compurgator. Who would not believe but that these things could never have been done, but by a supernatural and Diabolical power, but that this Author (to which all judicious persons in reason may adhere) doth utterly deny; that the arm was either pull'd away or conveyed none can tell whither, by Satan, and therefore that in such a strange Paradox, trivial reasons are not to be allowed; and it were too much sloathfulness to ascribe all effects unto Satan, of which we are ignorant. And therefore if an hand, an arm, nay an whole head, could be separated from the rest of the body, and conveyed forth of the Womb by the *Archeus* or natural spirit, thereunto excited by the impression of horror and terror in the Women: In like manner by the same power of the natural spirit of man or woman, excited by a vehement and fierce imagination to revenge and to do mischief; may strange things be injected (if there can be any sound proof of such a matter of fact) into the bodies of such men or women as the Witches intend to do hurt unto, and yet Satan hath no more hand in it, but only as a spiritual agent to move the wills of those wicked and malicious people to do mischief unto those that they hate, though without cause. And the great secret of that which may be called Witching, is the learning of others, who likewise have had it by tradition, the great force of imagination, and the natural spirit with the ways and means how to excite it and exalt it; herein stands the mystery of all Magick, and it becomes only evil in the use and application, and they are to be condemned that use it to such devillish ends; even as those that use those good Creatures that nature doth produce to poysonous, wicked, and destructive purposes. And lastly, here we may note, that if things or bodies that are without may be injected into the bodies of others, by the force of exalted imagination and a vehement desire, then the same power that doth inject them through skin, flesh and bones, must also be able to bring them near to the place, and need not at all the assistance of Satan, because it is far easier to carry them near the place, than to thrust them into the body; and so this Author hath here introduced the

Devils

Devils aid to bring them to the place to no purpose, and never
yet proved either by reason or matter of fact, that ever Satan did
any such thing, and so is a meer supposition without proof.

Observ. 7.   7. The other matters of fact that he relateth are prodigious,
and are brought to prove that Satan is an actor to convey these
strange things into the bodies of men, and are these. A piece of
an Oxe Hide taken forth of a mans Arm, so also that *Equuleum*, a
Wood-Horse, or a four-footed board with a wheel and ropes twice
as broad as the gullet. Another that vomited up perhaps two thousand pins conglomerated together, with filth and hairs; another that
vomited up, he being present, wooden Chips that had been cut off
with the Hatchet in smoothing of wood, with much slime to the
bignefs of two fifts, of which we shall note these Conclusions. 1. It
doth no way appear (if these things be granted to be true, both
for matter and manner) neither doth he offer to prove it, that
these are any more than the former Diabolical, but only in the
end, because they are for the hurt and destruction of mankind
and not otherwise; and there being no proof of the Devils Cooperation any further but in working upon the minds of those
that are agents and inftruments to bring these things to pass, we
may very well reject those things that are suppofed, but not proved. 2. The ejecting or voiding of such ftrange things as here
he hath related, doth not necessarily suppose their injection
or thrufting in, because they may be bred there by natural Caufes,
so Worms of many forts and strange Figures, alfo Frogs, *Dracuncu-
los* and Askers have been voided; and doubtlefly bred there by
natural causes, and were not injected or thruft in, and for proof of
this I refer the Reader to the relations of learned *Schenchius lib.*
3. *p.* 363. of those ftrange forts of Worms and other Creatures that
he from divers Authors fheweth have been vomited up, which without all fcruple, were not injected, but bred there. To confirm this
and to prove what strange things are sometimes bred in Apoftumes
and Tumors, we shall tranflate a paffage or two, and firft take this
from *Levinus Lemnius* that learned and famous Phyfician of *Zeland*,
who writeth thus : " Alfo forth of fordid Ulcers and Impoftures

De occult. nat.
mirac. l. 2. c.
40. p. 325.
"(he faith) we have known that the fragments of nails, hairs,
"fhells, little bones and ftones have been taken forth; which were
"concreted and grown together forth of putrid humours: As alfo
"little creatures, worms with tails, and little beafts of an unaccu-
"ftomed form, caft up by vomiting, efpecially in thofe who were
" oppreffed with contagious difeafes, in whofe urines I have often
" difcerned to fwim little Animalcles like to Pifmires, or to thofe
" creatures we obferve in the eftival months to move in the celefti-
" al dew here in *England* we call it Woodfoar, or Cuckow-fpit-
tle. Take another from that learned and expert Chirurgeon

De Tumor. l. 6.
c. 19. p. 158.
Ambrofius Paræus where he is fpeaking of ftrange tumors, in thefe
words : " Alfo in thefe tumors being opened thou maift fee bodies
" of all kinds, and far differing from the common matter of Tumors,

"as

" as ftones, chalk, fand, coals, cockles, ears of corn, hay,
" horn, hairs, flefh as well hard as fpongious, grifles, bones and
" whole Animalcles, as well living as dead. The generation of
" which things (by the corruption and alteration of the humors)
" will not much aftonifh us, if we confider, that even as nature hath
" framed Man as a Microcofm forth of all the feeds and elements
" of the whole great world, that he might be as it were the lively
" image of that great world : So in that Microcofm, nature
" hath willed, that all the fpecies of all motions and actions
" might be manifeft, nature being never idle in us, as long as matter
" is not a wanting to work upon. So that it is moft plain that
thefe ftrange things may be bred within, and fo the opinion of injecting them, is but a meer figment. 3. Neither can the vomiting up
of fuch ftrange things as he relateth, conclude neceffarily that they
were injected either by the power of Satan or the Witch, becaufe
they may be performed by jugling, fleight of hand, confederacy
and the like, as was manifeft in the Boy of *Bilfon*, and diverfe
that we have known, that had made fome numbers of others to
believe that they had voided ftrange things, as pins, needles,
crooked-knitting-pricks, mofs, nails, and the like; but upon a ftrickt
fearch, have but proved delufions and fleight, fuch as our common
Hocus Pocus Men ufe, when they make the people believe they
fwallow a long pudding of white tinn, and again pull it forth of their
mouths, or in pulling ribbins, or laces of diverfe colours forth of
their throats. 4. And again the moft of thefe relations are but
commonly taken upon truft from the affirmations of the by-ftanders
who might be confederate parties, or ignorant perfons, and fo
eafily deceived; and it appeareth not that *Helmont* was by at the
very inftant when the children vomited up the wooden horfe, or
fourfooted board, but that it was the by-ftanders that drew it
forth, who might be parties to the cheat, or be themfelves deluded,
and fo aver it pertinaciously to others. For I have in my practice
known a young Wench about 9 or 10 years old, who that fhe *Hift.*
might be pittied and have an idle life, had made her Father and
Mother believe that quick worms came forth at her ear, and alfo I
taking her into mine own houfe fhe had perfwaded all the family
that it was true, and did often open her head-cloaths, and holding
down her ear a quick worm would drop forth of the hair, who
notwithftanding by diligent watching, was found out to get them
privately from under ftones or wood, and fo did cunningly
convey them into her hair, but being difcovered, was by due correction reclaimed, and fo the wonder ceafed. And it is as common
to miftake things, either by abfolute judging them to be fuch a
thing indeed, when it hath but fome flender refemblance of it, or
by judging a thing to be really fo, becaufe of fuch a name but metaphorically given unto it; fo it is ufual to call a *Carcinoma* in the
higheft degree *Lupus* or a Wolf, becaufe as a Wolf is a moft voracious creature, fo this ulcer is the moft devouring of all others; and

therefore

therefore have we known after that such have been by incision eradicated by our selves and others, and exposed to the view of the vulgar people, they would presently most earnestly affirm to others that they had seen it, and that it was a living creature, and had mouth, eyes and ears; so far will ignorant mistake induce credulity.

Observ. 8.   8. That the force of imagination accompanied with the passions of horror, fear, envy, malice, earnest desire of revenge, and the like, is great upon the body imaginant, as also upon the *fœtus* in the womb, is acknowledged by all. But that it can at distance work upon another body, though denied by *Fienus* and the whole rabble of the Schoolmen, yet is strongly proved by this learned Author, and allowed of by all others that truly understood the operations of nature, which we also take to be a certain truth, and do assert that if those people that are esteemed Witches, do really and truly (of which we utterly doubt) inject any of these strange things into the bodies of men, that they are brought to pass meerly by the imagination of the Witch; and the Devil acteth nothing in it at all, but the setting of his will upon that mischief. As for the handling the dispute concerning the manner of the injecting of these strange things, so strongly pursued by this Author, *Sennertus* and others, we shall totally supersede and suspend our judgment, until the *ὅτι* be sufficiently proved (which yet lies under water, and unseen) and then it will be time enough to dispute the manner, when the matter is certainly made evident. Therefore we will shut up this with that modest and grave advice of the Lord *Syl. Syl. Cent.* Bacon in these words: *Ideo cogemur in hac inquisitione ad nova* *10. p. 583.* *experimenta confugere; ubi directiones tantùm eorum præscribi possunt, non ulla positiva in medium adferri. Si quis putet subsistendum nobis fuisse, donec tentamentis res penitus innotuisset, (ut fecisse nos ubiq; probant alii tituli) sciat dubia nos fide amplecti quæcunq; imaginationis effecta circumferuntur, animum tamen esse illa per otium exigere ad Lydium veritatis lapidem, id est, experimentorum lucem.*

CHAP.

CHAP. XIII.

That the ignorance of the power of Art and Nature and such like things, hath much advanced these foolish and impious opinions.

THE opinions that we reject as foolish and impious are those we have often named before, to wit, that those that are vulgarly accounted Witches, make a visible and corporeal contract with the Devil, that he sucks upon their bodies, that he hath carnal copulation with them, that they are transubstantiated into Cats, Dogs, Squirrels, and the like, or that they raise tempests, and fly in the air. Other powers we grant unto them, to operate and effect whatsoever the force of natural imagination joyned with envy, malice and vehement desire of revenge, can perform or perpetrate, or whatsoever hurt may be done by secret poysons and such like wayes that work by meer natural means.

And here we are to shew the chief causes that do and have advanced these opinions, and this principally we ascribe to mens ignorance of the power of Nature and Art, as we shall manifest in these following particulars.

1. There is nothing more certain than, that how great soever the knowledge of Men be taken to be, yet the ultimate Sphere of natures activity or ability is not perfectly known, which is made most manifest in this, that every day there are made new discoveries of her secrets, which prove plainly that her store is not yet totally exhausted, nor her utmost efficiency known. And therefore those Men must needs be precipicious, and build upon a sandy foundation, that will ascribe corporeal effects unto Devils, and yet know not the extent of nature, for no Man can rationally assign a beginning for supernatural agents and actions, that does not certainly know where the power and operation of nature ends.

2. And as it is thus in general, so in many particulars, as especially in being ignorant of many natural agents that do work at a great distance, and very occultly, both to help, and to hurt, as in the weapon salve, the Sympathetick powder, the curing of diseases by mumial applications, by Amulets, Appensions and Transplantions, which all have been, and commonly are ascribed unto Satan, when they are truly wrought by natural operations. And so (as we have sufficiently manifested before) by many strange, and secret poysons both natural and artificial, that have no bewitching power in them at all, but work naturally, and only may be hurtful in their use through the devilishness of some persons that use them to diverse evil ends.

3. There is nothing that doth more clearly manifest our scanted

M m 2   knowledge

knowledge in the secret operations of nature, and the effects that she produceth, than the late discoveries of the workings of nature, both in the vegetable, animal and mineral Kingdoms, brought dayly to light by the pains and labours of industrious persons: As is most evident in those many elucubrations, and continued discoveries of those learned and indefatigable persons that are of the Royal Society, which do plainly evince that hitherto we have been ignorant of almost all the true causes of things, and therefore through blindness have usually attributed those things to the operation of Cacodemons that were truely wrought by nature, and thereby not smally augmented and advanced this gross and absurd opinion of the power of Witches.

4. Another great means in advancing these Tenents hath been Mens supine negligence in not searching into and experimenting the power of natural agents, but resting satisfied in the sleepy notions of general rules, and speculative Philosophy. By which means a prejudice hath been raised against the most occult operations of nature, and natural magick (which is(as *Agrippa* truly said) " The comprizer of great power, full of most high mysteries, and "containeth the most profound contemplation, nature, power, "quality, substance and virtue of most secret things, and the know- "ledge of all nature) to be condemned, as the work of the Devil "and hellish fiends, which is the handmaid and instrument of the Almighty. And from this diabolical pit of the ignorance of the power of nature (especially when assisted by art) have sprung up those black and horrid lies in the mouths of *Erastus*, *Conringius* and above all of *Kircherus*, denying the possibility of the transmutation of metals, by the power of Art and Nature, and ascribing the performance thereof by *Paracelsus*, *Lullius*, *Sendinogius* and others to the Devil; so malevolent do men grow when they are led by nescience and ignorance.

De occult. Phi-
los. l. 1. c. 2.

5. The ignorance of the strange and wonderful things that Art can bring to pass hath been no less a cause, why the most admirable things that Art bringeth to pass by it are through blind ignorance ascribed unto Devils, for so have many brave learned Artists, and Mechanicians been accused for Conjurers, as happened to *Roger Bacon*, Dr. *Dee*, *Trithemius*, *Cornelius Agrippa*, and many others, when what they performed was by lawful and laudable art. The strange things that the Mathematicks and Mechanicks can perform are hardly to be enumerated, of which were those most wonderful catoptrical glasses mentioned by *Nicero*, *Aquilonius*, *Baptista Porta* and many others, those wonderful engines in the shape of Birds, Men, Beasts, and Fishes that do move, sing, hiss and many such like things mentioned by *Heron* of *Alexandria*, and our Countryman Dr. *Fludd*; and those that would have more ample satisfaction concerning the stupendious things that are produced by art, may receive most large satisfaction in reading that most learned and elaborate Epistle written as a preface before the Book of
Johannes

Johannes Erneftus Burgravius called *Biolychnium vel de lampade* *Vid. Th. iir.*
vitæ & mortis, by *Marcellus Vranckheim* Doctor of both laws, as *Chym. Vol. c.*
alfo in reading that profound and myfterious piece written by *Ro-* *p. 943.*
ger Bacon, de admirabili poteftate artis & naturæ, & de nullitate
magiæ, with the learned notes of Dr. *Dee* upon it, of which he
faith this : *Vt videatur quod omnis poteftas magica fit inferior his*
operibus & indigna. And therefore there can be nothing more
unworthy, than for any man, that pretendeth to any portion of
reafon, fo far to dote, or fuffer himfelf to be led with ignorance
and rafhnefs, as to afcribe thofe ftrange things that Nature and Art,
or both joined together do produce, unto Devils : And yet there
is nothing that is more common not only by the blind vulgar,
but even by thofe that otherwife would be accounted learned, and
wife enough ; pride and folly attendeth the moft of the Sons of
Men.

6. Another grofs miftake there is, in fuppofing thofe ftrange
things that are performed by vaulters, tumblers, dancers upon
ropes, and fuch like, not poffible to be done but by the affiftance
of the Devil, when they are altogether brought to pafs and effected by ufe, cuftome, exercife, nimblenefs and agility of body. And
yet we have known fome not only of the popular rank, but many
that thought themfelves both wife, learned and religious that
have been fo blind as to father thefe things upon Devils and feri- *Hift,*
oufly to feem to believe, that the actors of thefe things had made
a league and compact with the Devil, by whofe help they performed them. And I do remember that a pretty active young man,
within thefe few years went about in this North Countrey with a
neat Bay Mare for money to fhew tricks, which were very odd
and ftrange, for if fhe had been blindfolded, and feveral pieces of
money taken from feveral perfons, and wrapped in a cloath, the
Mare would have given every one their own piece of money ; and
this and many other feats fhe plaid, were not only by the common
people, but by others that fhould have been more wife, judged to
be performed by no other means but by the Devil, and fome were
fo ftark mad as to believe and affirm that the Mare was not a natural one, but that it was the Devil that plaid thofe ftrange tricks
in the fhape of a Mare : when more fober judgments knew that they
were performed by the mafters eye, and rod directing the Mare.
Error & credulitas multum in hominibus poffunt.

7. In like manner are often both thofe that are learned, as well
as the vulgar moft wofully impofed upon by the odd and ftrange
feats performed by Legierdemain, fleight of hand, and by wonderful things brought to pafs by fubtile and cunning Impoftors that
act by confederacy, and the like, of which we have given fome
inftances before in this treatife. And it was no evil piece of fervice,
that Mafter *Scot* did in his book of the difcovery of Witchcraft,
when he laid open all the feveral tricks of Legierdemain and fleight
of hand, thereby to undeceive the ignorant multitude ; and that
is

is no lefs praife-worthy that is performed by the Author of that little treatife called *Hocus Pocus junior*, where all the feats are fet forth in their proper colours, fo that the moft ignorant may fee how they are done, and that they are miracles unknown, and but bables being difcovered, which treatife I could commend to be read of all Witchmongers and vain credulous perfons, that thereby their ignorance may be laid open, and they convinced of their errors.

8. The ignorance or miftaking of thefe things, joyned with the notions Men have imbibed from their infancy, together with irreligious education, are the true and proper caufes, that make fo many afcribe that power to Devils and Witches, that they neither have, or ever had, or can ever bring into act. And therefore it behoveth all that would judge aright of thefe abftrufe matters, to labour to underftand the fecret operations of nature, and the ftrange works of art, to diveft themfelves of their falfe imbibed notions, and truely and rightly to underftand the Articles of the Chriftian Faith, to be daily converfant in reading the Scriptures, they will then be more fit to judge of thefe things, and not to call light darknefs, nor darknefs light.

CHAP. XIV.

Of diverfe Impoftures framed and invented to prove falfe and lying miracles by, and to accufe perfons of Witchcraft, from late and undeniable authorities.

IN the treatife preceeding we have often made mention of delufions and Impoftures, which we fhall largely handle in this place: and though Mr. *Glanvil*, and others do object, that though many pretended poffeffions or Witchcrafts have been proved to be meer couzenings and impoftures, yet therefore it will not follow that all are fo. To which we fhall render thefe anfwers.

1. If it do not neceffarily conclude, that they are all impoftures, yet it gives a moft fhrewd caufe of dubitation that they may be fo. And the objection depends not upon a neceffary connexion betwixt the fubject and predicate, for fome being direct and palpable Impoftures, it is not of neceffity, but by contingency or accident that the others are not fo, and ought firft to have been proved, which never yet was performed.

2. But we affirm that a general conclufion drawn from an inductive argument is good and found, where no inftance can be clearly made out to the contrary. But as yet no true inftance, really and faithfully attefted, hath ever been brought to prove that any

of

of thefe things that we deny, were ever effected by diabolical power. For who were ever by and prefent, that were perfons of fincerity and found judgment, that could truly teftifie and averr that
the Devil in a vifible and corporeal fhape made a contract with
the Witch, or that he fuckt upon his, or her body, or that he had
carnal copulation with them, or that faw when the Witch was really changed into a Dog or a Cat, or that they flew or were carried in
the air ? Seeing no inftance can be given to prove any of thefe to be
undoubted truths, it muft needs follow that they are meer figments, or at the beft all but abfolute Impoftures. And again it is but
precarious, and *petitio principii*, to imagine that any perfons have
vomited up or voided ftrange things that faw or knew that they
were injected by Devils, for they were either naturally bred there,
or elfe were meer Impoftures and delufive Juglings.

And therefore we fhall propofe fome Hiftories of ftrange and
prodigious cheats and Impoftures from late and unqueftionable authorities, whereby all the reft may be judged and difcerned; of which
take this for one.

" 1. *Elizabeth Barton* of *Kent* (by thofe that laboured to cry   *Hift.* 1.
" up her horrible cheats for miracles, otherwife called the holy
" Maid of *Kent*) and others were in the twenty fifth year of King
" *Henry* the Eighth attainted of High Treafon, for that under co-
" lour of hypocrifie, Revelations and falfe Miracles practifed by *Vid. Stat. Pul-*
" the faid *Elizabeth*, they confpired to impugne and flander the *ton,* 25. *year Hin.* 8. *c.* 12.
" divorce between the King and Queen *Katherine* his firft Wife,
" and the laft Marriage between him and Queen *Anne* his fecond
" Wife, to deftroy the King, and to deprive him of his Crown.
Her falfe and feigned miracles, and the fubtile and cunning con-
trivances that were brought to pafs by the help of her confederate accomplices, and her and the others open confeffion of them
may be found at large in *Hollingfhead, Stow,* and the writings of *Vid Chron.*
Mr. *Lambert,* whither for brevities fake I remit my reader, and *Hollingfhead. Stow An. Hen.*
fhall only give it here in the words of *Speed,* which are thefe: 8. 25. *p.* 1013.
" The Romanifts (he faith) much fearing that *Babel* would down,
" if Queen *Anne* might be heard againft wicked *Haman,* fought to The Pope.
" underprop the foundations thereof with certain devices of their
" own : and that the fame might pafs without note of fufpicion,
" they laid their forgery even upon Heaven it felf; whofe pre-
" tended oracle *Elizabeth Barton* (commonly called the holy Maid
" of *Kent*) was made to be; and the pillars of this godlefs Fabrick
" were *Edward Bocking* a Monk by profeffion, and Doctor of Di-
" vinity, *Richard Mafters* Parfon of *Aldington,* the Town where-
" in fhe dwelt; *Richard Deering* a Monk, *Hugh Rich* a Friar, *John*
" *Adeftone* and *Thomas Abell* Priefts, put to their helping hands;
" and *Henry Gould* Batchelor of Divinity, with *John Fifher* the re-
" verend Father of *Rochefter* imployed their pains to dawb thefe
" downfalling walls with their untempered morter. The Scribes
" that fet their pens for her miracles, were *Edward Thwaites* Gen-
                                                    " tleman,

"tleman, and *Thomas Lawrence* Register, besides *Haukherst* a Monk,
" who writ a letter that was forged to be sent her from Heaven;
" And *Richard Risby* and *Thomas Gould* were the men that disper-
"sed her miracles abroad to the world. This holy Maid *Eliza-*
"*beth* made a Votaress in *Canterbury*, was taught by *Bocking* her
" Ghostly Father, and suspected Paramour, to counterfeit many
" feigned trances, and in the same to utter many virtuous words
"for the rebuke of sin, under which more freely she was heard a-
"gainst *Luthers* doctrine, and the Scriptures translation, then de-
"sired of many: neither so only, but that she gave forth from
" God and his Saints by sundry suggestive Revelations, that if the
" King proceeded in his Divorce, and second Marriage, he should
" not raign in his Realm one month after, nor rest in Gods favour
" the space of an hour. But the truth discovered by Gods true
" Ministers, this oracle gave place as all other such did, when Christ
" by his death stopped their lying mouths: For her self and seven
" of her disciples were executed for Treason at *Tiburn*, and the o-
" ther six put to their fines and imprisonment. To which he sub-
joineth this story of the like nature. "With the like counterfeit
" Revelations and feigned predictions this generation of hypocrites
" had brought *Edward* Lord *Stafford* Duke of *Buckingham*, un-
" to his unhappy end, by the working of *John de la Court*
" his own Confessor, together with *Nicholas Hopkins* a Monk of
" the Carthusian Order in the Priory of *Henton* in *Somersetshire*,
" who by his visions from Heaven forsooth, heartned him for the
" Crown; But before his own Coronet could aspire to that top,
" he worthily lost both head and all upon *Tower-hill* for his Trea-
"son, *Anno Domini* 1521. Unto such sins the world was then
" subject, and into such conceits their reputed holiness had brought
"them, not only among the simple and unlettered, but even with
"them that seemed to be learned indeed: For by certain predi-
" ctions foreshewing a great deluge, Prior *Bolton* of S. *Bartholo-*
"*mews* in *London*, was so fearful that he built himself a house up-
" on the height of *Harrowhill*, storing it with provisions necessary
" to keep himself from drowning in *Anno Dom.* 1524.

Hist. 2.　　2. And that we may be certified how frequent and common these
counterfeited Impostures have been, and yet are practised, take
this other from undoubted authority. The 15 of *August* being
Stow's Chron. "Sunday in the 16 of the raign of Queen *Elizabeth*, *Agnes Bridges*
p. 678. "a Maid about the age of 20 years, and *Rachel Pinder* a Wench a-
"bout the age of 11 or 12 years, who both of them had counter-
" feited to be possessed by the Devil (whereby they had not only
" marvellously deluded many people both Men and Women, but al-
"so diverse such persons, as otherwise seemed of good wit and
" understanding) stood before the Preacher at *Pauls-cross*; where
" they acknowledged their hypocritical counterfeiting with peni-
" tent behaviours, requiring forgiveness of God and the world, and
" the people to pray for them. Also their several examinations
"and

" and Confeſſions were there openly read by the Preacher, and after-
" wards publiſhed in print , for poſterity hereafter to beware of
" the like deceivers. From whence we may take theſe two Obſervations.

1. We may from hence note, how ſubject the nature of man is *Obſerv.* 1.
both to deceive and to be deceived, and that not only the common
people, but alſo the wiſer and more learned heads may moſt eaſily
be impoſed upon. And, that therefore in things of this nature and
the like, we cannot uſe too much circumſpection, nor uſe too much
diligence to diſcover them.

2. We may note, that when ſuch ſtrange Impoſtures or falſe Mira- *Obſerv.* 2.
cles are pretended, there is commonly ſome ſiniſter and corrupt end
aimed at, under the colour of Religion, and that thoſe that are
moſt ready to publiſh ſuch things as true Miracles and Divine Revelations, are generally thoſe that did complot and deviſe them. And
therefore the greater number they be that cry them up, and the more
eſteem the perſons are of that blow abroad ſuch things, the greater
ſuſpicion we ought to have of the falſity and forgery of them. Always
remembring that the greater the fame and number of the perſons
are that conſpire and confederate together, the greater things they
may bring to paſs, and be more able to deceive, as was manifeſt by the
Prieſts attending the Oracles ; who, though they laboured to father
their predictions upon ſome Deity, yet it was manifeſt that it was nothing elſe, but their own Confederacy, Impoſtures and Juglings.

3. But theſe Diabolical Counterfeitings of poſſeſſions, and the *Hiſt.* 3.
maintaining of the power of diſpoſſeſſion and caſting forth of Devils, was not only upheld and maintained by the Papiſts to advance their ſuperſtitious courſes ; but alſo in the ſaid time of Queen
Elizabeth, there were divers Non-Conformiſts, to gain credit and
repute to their way, that did by publick writing labour to prove
the continuation of real poſſeſſions by Devils, and that they had
power by faſting and Prayer to caſt them out. Of which number
were one Mr *Darrell* and his Accomplices, who not only writ divers Pamphlets in the poſitive defence of that opinion, but alſo
publiſhed certain Narrations of ſeveral perſons, that they pretended
were really poſſeſſed with Devils, which were caſt forth by their
means in uſing Faſting and Prayer. Which writings were anſwered   *Vid.* A Book
by Mr *Harſnet* and others, and their Theory not only overthrown,   called , *A diſ-*
but their practice diſcovered to be counterfeiting and Impoſture.   *covery of frau-*
Whereupon there were divers perſons ſuborned to feign and counter-   *dulent practiſes*
feit poſſeſſions, as *William's Sommers* of *Nottingham*, who by the Exor-   *concerning pre-*
ciſts was reported to have ſtrange fits, paſſions and actions ; which   *tended poſſeſſi-*
are at large deſcribed and ſet forth in that learned Treatiſe, *Dialo-*   *ons.*
gical Diſcourſes of Spirits and Devils, written about the ſame time
by *John Deacon* and *John Waller*, Miniſters , and of divers other
perſons who likewiſe pretended the ſame counterfeit poſſeſſions.
And though the ſaid forged and feigned poſſeſſions were ſtrongly
maintained by their Abettors, and the matters of fact audaciouſly
aſſerted

Vid. ibid. Dia-log. II. p. 352. afferted to be true; yet after the faid *Darrell* and his Accomplices were examined by the Queens Commiflioners, all was made apparent to be notorious counterfeiting, cheating and impofture, both by the confeffion of *Sommers* himfelf, and by the Oaths of feveral Deponents. Neither was that difcourfe containing the certain poffeffion of feven perfons in one Family in *Lancafhire*, at *Cheworth* in the Parifh of *Leigh*, in the Year 1594. (though believed by many for a truth, becaufe of the ftreight tale told by the faid *Darrell* in that Narrative) of any better grain, but full of untruths, impoffibilities, abfurdities and contradictions.

Hiſt. 4.

Vid. The cunning of the Boy of *Bilſon, p. 55.*   4. Our next inftance fhall be a moft ftrange Impofture acted in the time of King *James*, and in a manner known unto the whole Nation; that is of the Boy of *Bilſon* in *Staffordſhire*, in the year 1620. by name *William Perry*, whofe condition as he had been taught, and fo left by the Popifh Priefts, take as followeth. " This "Boy being about thirteen years old (but for wit and fubtilty far "exceeding his age) was thought by divers to be poffeffed of the "Devil, and bewitched, by reafon of many ftrange fits and much "diftemper, wherewith he feemed to have been extreamly affected. "In thofe fits he appeared both deaf and blind, writhing his mouth "afide, continually groaning and panting, and (although often "pinched with mens fingers, pricked with Needles, tickled on his "fides, and once whipped with a Rod, befides other the like ex-"tremities) yet could he not be difcerned by either fhrieking or "fhrinking to bewray the leaft paffion or feeling. Out of his fits "he took (as might be thought) no fuftenance which he could di-"geft, but together with it, did void and caft out of his mouth, "rags, thred, ftraw, crooked pins, &c. Both in and out of his fits "his belly (by wilful and continual abftinence defrauding his own "Guts) was almoft as flat as his back, befides, his throat was fwoln "and hard, his tongue ftiff and rolled up towards the roof of his "mouth, infomuch that he feemed always dumb, fave that he would "fpeak once in a Fortnight or three Weeks, and that but in very few "words.

    "Two things there were which gave moft juft caufe of prefump-"tion that he was poffeffed and bewitched; one was that he could "ftill difcern when that Woman (which was fuppofed to have be-"witched him) to wit *Jone Cocke* was brought in to any room "where he was, although fhe were fecretly conveyed thither, as "was one time tryed before the Grand Jury at *Stafford*: The fe-"cond, that though he would abide other paffages of Scripture, "yet he could not indure the repeating of that Text, *viz. In the* "*beginning was the word, &c.* *Jo.* I. *ver.* I. but inftantly rolling "his eyes and fhaking his head, as one diftracted, he would fall "into his ufual fits of groaning, panting, diftraction, &c. In which "plight he continued many months, to the great wonder and afto-"nifhment of thoufands, who from divers parts came to fee him. Thus much of his cunning.

Yet

Yet notwithstanding, this most devillish and cunningly contrived counterfeiting and dissimulation was discovered and fully detected by the sagacity of that pious and learned person, Dr *Thomas Morton* then Bishop of *Coventry* and *Lichfield :* To whose memory I cannot but owe and make manifest all due respect, because he was well known unto me, and by the imposition of whose hands I was ordained Presbyter when he was Bishop of *Durham*, and also knew his then Secretary, Mr *Richard Baddeley*, who was the Notary, and writ the examination of this crafty Boy. The manner how such a doubtful and intricate piece of Imposture was found out and discovered, you may read at large in the Treatise called *a Discourse concerning Popish Exorcising*. And his publick Confession we shall give in the Authors own words: "He was finally brought again "to the Summer Assizes held at *Stafford*, the 26. of *July*, *Anno* "1621. where before Sir *Peter Warburton* and Sir *Humfrey Winch* "Knights, his Majesties Justices of Assize, and the face of the Coun- "ty and Country there assembled, the Boy craved pardon first of "Almighty God, then desired the Woman there also present to for- "give him ; and lastly, requested the whole Country whom he had "so notoriously and wickedly scandalized, to admit of that his so "hearty Confession for their satisfaction.

"And thus it pleased God (he saith) to open the eyes of this "Boy (that I may so say) *luto* with the Clay of the Romish Priests "lewd Impostures, and *sputo* with the spittle of his own infamy, to "see his errors and to glorifie the God of truth. And though many such Impostures as this have in several ages been hudled up in darknes and recorded for true stories, by those that were Partizans to them and Confederates with them, yet doubtless were but of the same stamp with this, and might all as well have been discovered, if the like care, skill and industry had been used.

5. No less villanous, bloody and Diabolical, was the design of *Thompson alias Southworth*, Priest or Jesuit, against *Jennet Bierley*, *Jane Southworth*, and *Ellen Bierly* of *Samesbury* in the County of *Lancaster*, in the year 1612. the sum of which is this. "The said "*Jennet Bierley*, *Ellen Bierley*, and *Jane Southworth*, were Indicted "at the Assizes holden at *Lancaster* upon *Wednesday* the nineteenth "of *August*, in the year abovesaid, for that they and every of them "had practised, exercised, and used divers devillish and wicked "Arts, called Witchcrafts, Inchantments, Charms and Sorceries, in "and upon one *Grace Sowerbutts*. And the chief witnes to prove "this was *Grace Sowerbutts* her self, who said that they did draw "her by the hair of the head, and take her sense and memory from "her, did throw her upon the Hen-roost and Hay-mow ; did appear "to her sometimes in their own likenes, sometimes like a black "Dog with two feet, that they carried her where they met black "things like men that danced with them, and did abuse their bodies ; "and that they brought her to one *Thomas Walsham's* House in the "night, and there they killed his Child by putting a nail into the

Hist. 5.

Vid. The arraignment and tryal of Witches at Lancaster, 1612.

N n 2   "Navil;

"Navil, and after took it forth of the Grave, and did boil it, and
"eat fome of it, and made Oyl of the bones, and fuch like horrid
"lies. But there appearing fufficient grounds of fufpicion that it
was practifed knavery, the faid *Grace Sowerbutts* was by the wifdom, and care of Sir *Edward Bromley* Knight, one of his Majefties
Juftices of Affize at *Lancafter*, appointed to be examined by *William Leigh* and *Edward Chifnal* Efquires, two of his Majefties Juftices of peace in the fame County, and fo thereupon made this free
confeffion. Being demanded "whether the accufation fhe laid upon
"her Grandmother, *Jennet Bierley*, *Ellen Bierley* and *Jane South-
"worth*, of Witchcraft, *viz.* of the killing of the child of *Thomas
"Walfhman*, with a nail in the Navil, the boyling, eating and oyl-
"ing, thereby to transform themfelves into divers fhapes, was true ?
"fhe doth utterly deny the fame, or that ever fhe faw any fuch
"practifes done by them. She further faith, that one Mr. *Thomp-
"fon*, which fhe taketh to be Mr. *Chriftopher Southworth*, to whom
' fhe was fent to fay her prayers, did perfwade, counfel and ad-
"vife her, to deal as formerly hath been faid againft her faid Grand-
"mother, Aunt and *Southworths* Wife.

"And further fhe confeffeth, and faith, that fhe never did know,
"or faw any Devils, nor any other vifions, as formerly hath been
"alledged and informed.

"Alfo fhe confeffeth, and faith, that fhe was not thrown, or
"caft upon the Hen-rouft, and Hay-mow in the Barn, but that fhe
"went up upon the Mow by the wall fide. Being further demand-
"ed whether fhe ever was at the Church, fhe faith, fhe was not, but
"promifed hereafter to go to Church, and that very willingly ; of
"which the author of the relation gives this judgment.

"How well (he faith) this project, to take away the lives of
"three innocent poor creatures by practice and villany, to induce
"a young Scholar to commit perjury, to accufe her own Grand-
"mother, Aunt, *&c.* agrees either with the title of a Jefuit, or
"the duty of a religious Prieft who fhould rather profefs fincerity
"and innocency, than practife treachery! But this was lawful, for
"they are Hereticks accurfed, to leave the company of Priefts, to
"frequent Churches, hear the word of God preached, and profefs
"religion fincerely.

Hift. 6.   6. But we fhall fhut up the relating of thefe prodigious and
hellifh ftories, of thefe kind of couzening and cheating delufions
and impoftures, with one inftance more that is no lefs notorious
than thefe that we have rehearfed. About the year 1634 (for
having loft our notes of the fame, we cannot be fo exact as we
fhould) there was a great pretended meeting of many fuppofed
Witches at a new houfe or barn, in *Pendle* Foreft in *Lancafhire*,
then not inhabited, where (as the accufation pretended) fome of
them by pulling by a rope of Straw or Hay, did bring Milk, Butter, Cheefe, and the like, and were carried away upon Dogs,
Cats or Squirrels. The informer was one *Edmund Robinfon* (yet
living

living at the writing hereof, and commonly known by the name
of *Ned* of *Roughs*) whose Father was by trade a Waller, and but
a poor Man, and they finding that they were believed and had incouragement by the adjoyning Magistrates, and the persons being
committed to prison or bound over to the next Assizes, the boy,
his Father and some others besides did make a practice to go from
Church to Church that the Boy might reveal and discover Witches, pretending that there was a great number at the pretended
meeting. whose faces he could know; and by that means they got
a good living, that in a short space the Father bought a Cow or
two, when he had none before. And it came to pass that this said
Boy was brought into the Church of *Kildwick* a large parish Church,
where I (being then Curate there) was preaching in the afternoon,
and was set upon a stall (he being but about ten or eleven years
old) to look about him, which moved some little disturbance in
the Congregation for a while. And after prayers I inquiring what
the matter was, the people told me that it was the Boy that discovered Witches, upon which I went to the house where he was to
stay all night, where I found him, and two very unlikely persons
that did conduct him, and manage the business; I desired to have
some discourse with the Boy in private, but that they utterly refused; then in the presence of a great many people, I took the Boy
near me, and said: Good Boy tell me truly, and in earnest, did
thou see and hear such strange things of the meeting of Witches,
as is reported by many that thou dost relate, or did not some person teach thee to say such things of thy self? But the two men not
giving the Boy leave to answer, did pluck him from me, and said
he had been examined by two able Justices of the Peace, and they
did never ask him such a question, to whom I replied, the persons
accused had therefore the more wrong. But the Assizes following
at *Lancaster* there were seventeen found guilty by the Jury, yet
by the prudent discretion of the Judge, who was not satisfied with
the evidence, they were reprieved, and his Majesty and his
Council being informed by the Judge of the matter, the Bishop of
Chester was appointed to examine them, and to certifie what he
thought of them, which he did; and thereupon four of them, to
wit, *Margaret Johnson, Francis Dicconson, Mary Spenser,* and *Har-
grives* Wife, were sent for up to *London,* and were viewed and examined by his Majesties Physicians and Chirurgeons, and after by
his Majesty and the Council, and no cause of guilt appearing but
great presumptions of the boys being suborned to accuse them
falsely. Therefore it was resolved to separate the Boy from his Father, they having both followed the women up to *London,* they
were both taken and put into several prisons asunder. Whereupon
shortly after the Boy confessed that he was taught and suborned to
devise, and feign those things against them, and had persevered in that
wickedness by the counsel of his Father, and some others, whom
envy, revenge and hope of gain had prompted on to that devillish
design

deſign and villany ; and he alſo confeſſed, that upon that day when he ſaid that they met at the aforeſaid houſe or barn , he was that very day a mile off, getting Plums in his Neighbours Orchard. And that this is a moſt certain truth, there are many perſons yet living, of ſufficient reputation and integrity, that can avouch and teſtiſie the ſame; and beſides, what I write is the moſt of it true, upon my own knowledge, and the whole I have had from his own mouth more than once.

Thus having brought theſe unqueſtionable Hiſtories to manifeſt the horrid cheats and impoſtures that are practiſed for baſe, wicked and devilliſh ends, we muſt conclude in oppoſing that objection propoſed in the beginning of this Chapter, which is this : That though ſome be diſcovered to be counterfeitings and impoſtures, yet all are not ſo, to which we further anſwer.

Reaſ. 1.   1. That all thoſe things that are now adayes ſuppoſed to be done by Demoniacks or thoſe that pretend poſſeſſions, as alſo all thoſe ſtrange feats pretended to be brought to paſs by Witches or Witchcraft, are all either performed by meer natural cauſes (for it is granted upon all ſides that Devils in corporeal matter can perform nothing but by applying fit actives to agreeable paſſives.) And miracles being long ſince ceaſed, it muſt needs follow, that Devils do nothing but only draw the minds of Men and Women unto ſin and wickedneſs, and thereby they become deceivers, cheats and notorious impoſtours: ſo that we may rationally conclude that all other ſtrange feats and deluſions, muſt of neceſſity be no better, or of any other kind, than theſe we have recited, except they can ſhew that they are brought to paſs by natural means. Muſt not all perſons that are of ſound underſtanding judge and believe that all thoſe ſtrange tricks related by Mr. *Glanvil* of his Drummer at Mr. *Mompeſſons* houſe, whom he calls the Demon of *Tedworth*, were abominable cheats and impoſtures (as I am informed from perſons of good quality they were diſcovered to be) for I am ſure Mr. *Glanvil* can ſhew no agents in nature, that the Demon applying them to fit patients, could produce any ſuch effects by, and therefore we muſt conclude all ſuch to be impoſtures.

Reaſ. 2.   2. It is no ſound way of reaſoning, from the principle of knowing, either thereby to prove the exiſtence of things, or the modes of ſuch exiſtence, becauſe the principle of being is the cauſe of the principle of knowing, and not on the contrary, and therefore our not diſcovering of all Impoſtures that are or have been acted, doth not at all conclude the reſt that paſs undiſcovered, are diabolical or wrought by a ſupernatural power; for it ought firſt to be demonſtrated that there are now in theſe days ſome things wrought by the power of Devils, that are ſupernatural, in elementary and corporeal matter, which never was nor can be, as from the teſtimonies of all the learned we have ſhewed before. And therefore a man might as well argue that there are no more thieves in a Nation, but thoſe that are known, and brought to con-

dign

digu punishment, when there may be, and doubtless are many more; so likewise there are many hundreds of Impostures, that pass and are never discovered, but that will not at all rationally conclude that those must be diabolical that are not made known.

CHAP. XV.

Of divers Creatures that have a real existence in Nature, and yet by reason of their wonderous properties, or seldom being seen, have been taken for Spirits, and Devils.

BEfore we come to speak of Apparitions in general, we shall premise some few things by way of caution, because there is not one subject (that we know of) in the World that is liable to so many mistakes, by reason of the prepossessed fancies of men, in adhering to those fictions of Spirits, Fairies, Hobgoblins, and many such like, which are continually heightned by ignorant education, and vain melancholy fears. We shall not mention those many apparitions that are frequently practised by forgery and confederacy, for base ends and interests, as have been commonly used in the time of Popery, and attempted in our dayes, though with little success. As also by other persons for base lucre or worse intents, of which we have known some notorious ones that have been discovered. Neither shall we speak of those feigned ones that have been practised to hide thievery and roguery, as we once knew that certain persons who stole mens sheep in the night, did carry them a- *Hist. 1.* way upon a thing made like a Bier covered with a white sheet, by which means those that saw them took it to be an apparition, and so durst not come near them, and so the most part of the people of 3 or 4 Villages were terrified, and the report was far spred that it was a walking spirit, and yet at last discovered to be a cunning piece of knavery to hide their theft withal. Neither shall we say any thing of those ludicrous apparitions that are often practised to terrifie, abuse, and affright others. But we shall here give the relation of some strange creatures, that seldom being seen or found, have induced more ignorant persons to take them for Demons, and these we shall enumerate in this order.

1. It hath been, and still is a strong opinion amongst the vul- *Hist. 2.* gars and Witchmongers also, that Witches transforming themselves into diverse shapes, did in the night time enter into peoples houses, and then and there suck the breasts or navils of infants in their Beds or Cradles, that thereby they were weakned or confumed away; which inveterate opinion was the more firmly believed, because children that at night were very well, in the morning were

Centur. 1. Hist. 9. p. 18.

were found to be very ill, and to have been sucked in the places aforesaid. To clear which point take thisObservation from the learned pen of *Thomas Bartholinus* that was Physician to *Frederick* King of *Denmark*, in English thus. "Three infants (he saith) of the "*Pastor Fionens* at *Lyckisholm*, which is a noble Mannor belonging "to the very illustrious Lord *Christian Thomæus Sehsted*, the Kings "Chancellor, *Eques Auratus*, and a most renowned Senator of "*Denmark*, my *Mecænas*, that were sleeping in their accustomed "Chamber, were not long after troubled with an unwonted be- "wailing and inquietude, that they felt themselves to be sucked or "milked of something. The nipples of their breasts being diligent- "ly handled by the Parents did confirm the Childrens suspicion, be- "cause they did hang out like a Womans that did give suck. And "to prevent this fascination, the nipples of the breasts were anoin- "ted with preservatives against poyson and other bitter things. Here- "upon their Navils were so worn with vehement suction, that not "only they were prominent or did hang out, but also did as it were "shew the greatness of the mouth that had sucked by the impression "remaining. But the Infants being carried forth of the Chamber, "did from thenceforth rest free from any suction, especially being "carried in peoples arms. And this *Caprimulgus* or Goat-milker, is "by *Bellonius* said to be in *Crete* of the bigness of a Cuckow, being "very hurtful to the Goats, insomuch that it sucketh milk from "their dugs on the nights. By which we may plainly understand, how Creatures that are but seldom seen, or whose properties are unknown, may easily effect those things that ignorant heads may impute unto Witchcraft.

De quadr. l. 1. p. 862.

2. It is no less believed by many, that those kind of Creatures which are called Satyres are but a kind of Demons; for learned *Gesner* reckoning them to be a kind of Apes, doth tell us this: "Even as (he saith) the Apes *Cynocephali*, or with Dogs-heads, "have given the occasion of the Fable, that some have thought such "to be men: So Satyrs being also a rare kind of Apes, and of "greater admiration, some have believed them to be Devils: also "of some men deluded by the Poets and Painters, as also Statua- "ries, who have feigned that they had Goats feet and horns, the "more to augment the admiration and superstition, they have been "thought Devils: when in Ape-Satyres there is no such thing to be "seen. And this opinion hath been the more strengthened because the most of the Translators have in the Old Testament rendered the word שעיר (which properly signifieth an happy man or beast) a Goat, a Satyre, (as *Gen.*27. *ver.* 11. *Esau my Brother is a hairy man*; where the very same word is used) Demon, or Devil. But it is plain that it did and doth signifie no more but only Satyrs, as will appear by these reasons. 1. First, as our English Translators have truly ren-

Isai. 34. 14.

dred it in that of *Isaiah*, *And the Satyre shall cry unto his fellow*: for it is certainly related, both by ancient and modern Navigators, that in those desolate Islands where there are store of them, they

will

will upon the nights make great fhouting and crying, and calling one unto another. And in another place of the fame Prophet it is faid by the fame Tranflators, *and Satyres fhall dance there*; dancing Ifai. 13. 21. being one of the properties of that hairy Creature, as a thing it is much delighted with, and fo are but Satyres that are natural Creatures and not Devils. 2. And though the fame Tranflators have rendred the plural of the fame word, by the name Devils, yet it there Levit. 17. 7. properly fignifieth alfo Satyres; for though in another place it be faid; *they facrificed to devils, not to God*, and fo again by the Deut. 32. 17. Pfalmift, for *they facrificed their fons and daughters unto devils*; Pfal. 106. 37. where in both places the word is שׁעִירים *vaftatoribus*, to the deftroyers or to Devils; becaufe in thofe Idols the Devils were worfhipped, and thereby deftroyed the fouls of men : 3. Yet it is manifeft that their Idols were formed in the fhape of Satyres, in a moft terrible manner; for the late and moft credible travellers that have been in thofe parts of *Afia*, where thofe Idolatries are ftill upholden, do unanimoufly relate that they make their Images or Idols that they worfhip, as terrible and frightful as they can devife, as may be feen in the relations of the Travels of *Vincent le Blanc, Mandelflo*, and *Ferdinand Mendez Pinto*, and Mr *Herbert* our Countryman gives us the Idol of the Bannyans in the ugly fhape of a monftrous Satyre. 4. So that though this worfhipping and facrificing, in refpect of its abominablenefs, filthinefs and Idolatroufnefs, was yielded to Devils, which fpiritually and invifibly ruled in thefe Children of difobedience, and was the Author of all thofe delufions and impoftures; yet it doth no where appear, that it was Demons in the corporeal fhape of Satyres (as many have erroneoufly fuppofed) no more than the golden Calves that *Jeroboam* made, were real Devils : but thefe Idols were made in the figure or fhape of Satyrs or hairy Creatures, as faith the Text: *And he ordained him Priefts for the* 2Chron. 11.15. *high places*, and for the hairy Idols or Satyres, *and for the Calves that he had made*. It is the fame Hebrew word here that our Englifh Tranflators render Devils, that in the two former places of *Ifaiah* they tranflate Satyres; and as the Calves are not rendred Devils, why fhould the Images that were like Satyres be tranflated fo? Surely the Devil was as much in the Calves, and as much worfhipped in thofe dumb Idols as he was in the dumb and dead Idols or Images of the Satyres, and fo no more reafon to call the one Devils than the other. But that which totally overthrows the conceit that they fhould be real Devils in corporeal fhapes and figures, is this, that both the Calves and the Images of thefe Satyres were made by *Jeroboam* : now it is manifeft that he could not make a real Devil, but only Images of Calves and Satyres, wherein and whereby the Devils might be worfhipped in thofe Idolatrous ways.

So that it is moft apparent, that thefe Satyres being feldom feen and of ftrange qualities, have made many to believe that they were Demons; nay it feems their Images and Pictures have been taken for Devils, and yet are but meer natural Creatures, and by learned men

accounted

accounted a kind of Apes, which we shall now prove by an undeniable instance or two ; and first this from the pen of that learned
Hist. 3.
Observ. Medic.
lib. 3. *c.* 56. *p.*
283.
Physician *Nicholaus Tulpius,* who saith thus : " In our remembrance
" (he saith) there was an Indian Satyre brought from *Angola* ; and
" presented as a gift to *Frederick Henry* Prince of *Aurange.* This
" Satyre was four-footed and from the humane shape which it seems
" to bear, it is called of the Indians *Orang antang, homo silvestris,*
" a wild man, and of the Africans *Quoias morron,* expressing in lon-
" gitude a Child of three years old, and in crassitude, one of six
" years. It was of body neither fat nor lean, but square, most able
" and very swift. And of its joints so firm, and the Muscles so large,
" that it durst undertake and could do any thing ; on the foreparts
" altogether smooth, and rough behind, and covered with black
" hairs. Its face did resemble a man, but the nose broad and crook-
" ed downwards, rugged and a toothless female. But the ears were
" not different from humane shape. As neither the breast, adorned
" on both sides with a swelling dug (for it was of the feminine Sex)
" the belly had a very deep navil ; and the joints, both those above
" and those below, had such an exact similitude with man, that one
" egg doth not seem more like another. Neither was there a-want-
" ing a requisite commissure to the arm, nor the order of fingers to
" the hands, nor an humane shape to the thumb, or a prop of the
" legs to the thighs, or of the heel to the foot. Which fit and decent
" form of the members, was the cause that for most part it did go
" upright : neither did it lift up any kind of weight less heavily than
" remove it easily.

" When it was about to drink it would hold the handle of the
" Kan with the one hand, and put the other under the bottom of the
" Cup, then would it wipe off the moysture left upon its lips, not
" less neatly than thou shouldest see the most delicate Courtier.
" Which same dexterity it did observe when it went to bed. For
" lying her head upon the Pillow, and fitly covering her body with
" the Cloaths, it did hide it self no otherwise, than if the most de-
" licate person had laid there.

Hist. 4.
" Moreover the King of *Samback* (he saith) did one time tell
" our Kinsman *Samuel Blomart,* that these kind of Satyres, especi-
" ally the Males in the Iland of *Borneo,* have so great boldness of
" mind and such a strong compaction of Muscles, that they have often
" forceably set upon armed men ; and not only upon the weak sex of
" Women and Girls ; with the flagrant desire of which they are so
" inflamed, that catching them often they abuse them. For they are
" highly prone to lust (which is common to these, with the lustful
" Satyres of the ancients) yea sometimes so keen and salacious, that
" therefore the Indian Women do eschew the Woods and Groves as
" worse than a Dog or a Snake ; in which these impudent animals
" do lie hid. And that this lascivious animal is found in the Eastern
" Mountains of *India* ; as also in *Africa,* between *Sierra, Liona,*
" and the Promontory of the Mountain, where (perhaps) were
　　　　　　　　　　　　　　　　　　　　　　　　　　　" those

"those places where *Plinius lib.* 5. *cap.* 5. affirmeth that upon the
"nights there was seen to shine frequent Fires of the Ægipanes, and
"to abound with the lasciviousness of the Satyres, who do love
"craggy Dens and Caves, and shun the society of mankind, being
"a salacious, hairy, four-footed Creature, with human shape and a
"crooked nose. But that the foot of this Creature neither hath hoofs
"nor the body every where hairs, but only the head, shoulders and
"back. The rest of the parts are smooth, and the Ears are not
"sharp.

So that from hence it is undeniably true, that there are such
Creatures existent in nature, and have been either taken for Devils
or the Apparitions of Demons in this shape of Satyres, as Doctor
Brown hath well observed in these words : " A conceit there is (he
"saith) that the Devil commonly appeareth with a cloven foot or
"hoof, wherein although it seem excessively ridiculous, there may
"be somewhat of truth; and the ground thereof at first might be
" his frequent appearing in the shape of a Goat, which answers
"that description. This was the opinion of ancient Christians con-
"cerning the Apparitions of *Pans, Fauns* and *Satyres,* and in this
"form we read of one that appeared unto *Antony* in the Wilder-
"ness. The same is also confirmed from expositions of holy Scrip-
"ture ; for whereas it is said ; Thou shalt not offer unto Devils, the
"original word is *Sehhirim,* that is rough and hairy Goats, because
" in that shape the Devil most often appeared, as is expounded by
"the Rabbins, as *Tremellius* hath also explained.

Enq. into vulg.
err. l. 5. p. 271.

But saving the reputation of learned Saint *Hierome* and Dr *Brown,*
it is but a supposition unproved that ever the Devil appeared in the
shape of a Goat, the rise of the opinion was only because the Devil was worshipped in an Idol made in the shape of a Goat.

3. In a few ages past when Popish ignorance did abound, there
was no discourse more common (which yet is continued amongst
the vulgar people) than of the apparition of certain Creatures
which they called Fayries, that were of very little stature, and being
seen would soon vanish and disappear. And these were generally
believed to be some kind of Spirits or Demons, and *Paracelsus* held
them to be a kind of middle Creatures, and called them *non-Ada-
micks,* as not being of the race of *Adam* ; but there are Authors
of great credit and veracity, that affirm, there have been Nations
of such people called Pygmies. And though Doctor *Brown* hath
learnedly and elegantly handled the question, "Whether there have
"been or are any such dwarfish race of mankind, as but of three
"spans, not considering them singly but nationally, or not, and
"hath brought the most probable arguments that well can be, to
"prove that there are not nor have been any such race of people
"called Pygmies, yet doth he moderately conclude in these words.
"There being thus (he saith) no sufficient confirmation of their
"verity, some doubt may arise concerning their possibility; where-
"in, since it is not defined in what dimensions the soul may exercise

Enquir. into
vulg. errors.
l. 4. c. 11.
p. 207.

"her

Mund. Subter.
l. 8. Sect. 4.
c. 4. p. 101.

Idea Idear. ope-
ratr. c. 6.

Hist. 5.

Demonstr. Thes.
p. 679.

"her faculties, we shall not conclude impossibility, or that there
"might not be a race of Pygmies, as there is sometimes of Giants,
"and so may take in the opinion of *Austine*, and his Commentator
"*Ludovicus Vives*. And though *Kircherus* with his wonted impu-
"dence do conclude in these words : *Fabulosa itaq; sunt omnia,
qua de hujusmodi Pygmais veteres Geographi à simplici populo sola
relatione descripta tradiderunt* : Yet (I say) notwithstanding these
negative arguments, I give the relation of others (that are of as
great or greater credit) in the affirmative. And thus much is affirmed by that most sagacious and learned person *Marcus Marci*, a late
Physician of no mean judgment, who saith thus: *Quicquid tamen
sit de his, Pygmaos & olim fuisse, & nunc esse affirmamus*. And besides the testimony of *Aristotle, Solinus, Pomponius Mela*, and *Ælian*,
he relateth these. "But those (he saith) that have in our age viewed
"the World, the same do testifie also, that there are yet Pygmies in
"the Island of *Aruchet*, one of the *Moluccas*, and in the Isle *Cophi*,
"and such *Pigasetta* affirmeth that he saw. And though Doctor
Brown seem to sleight it, yet (according to the Proverb) *one eye-
witness is more to be credited than ten that have it but by the ear*.
Odericus in his History of *India* doth report also, "that there are
"such people of about three spans high, which also is confirmed
by the later *Odericus*. And to these affirmative proofs we shall
add that of the learned Philosopher and Physician *Baptista Van
Helmont*, in English thus. "A Wine Merchant (he saith) of our
"Country, a very honest man, sailing sometimes to the *Canaries*
"or Fortunate Islands, being asked of me his serious opinion and
"judgment upon certain Creatures, which there the Children as
"oft as they would did bring home, and did name them *Tudesquil-
"los*, or *Germanulos*, that is little men; (the Germans call them
"*Eard-Manlins*) for they were dead Carkases dried almost three
"foot long, which any one of the Boys did easily carry in one
"hand, and were of an human shape : But the whole dead Carkase
"was transparent like Parchment, and the bones were flexible as
"grisles. Also the bowels and intestines were to be seen, holden
"against the sun, which, when after I knew to be a certain truth,
"from the Spaniards born there, I considered, that in these days the
"off-spring of the Pygmies were there destroyed.

From whence all understanding and unpartial judgments may
clearly perceive, that these kind of Creatures have been really existent in the World and are and may be so still in Islands and Mountains that are uninhabited. and that they are no real Demons, or
non-Adamick Creatures, that can appear and become invisible when
they please, as *Paracelsus* thinketh. But that either they were truly
of human race endowed with the use of reason and speech (which
is most probable) or at least that they were some little kind of
Apes or Satyres, that having their secret recesses and holes in the
Mountains, could by their agility and nimbleness soon be in or out
like Conies, Weazels, Squirrels, and the like.

4. It

4. It hath been no lefs a miftake about thofe Fifhes that are called *Tritones, Syrenes,* Meir-maids, or Marine, and Sea-Men, and Women, which have been by many fuppofed and taken to be Spirits, or Demons, and commonly Nymphs, when indeed and truth they are reall creatures, as thefe examples do make manifeft.   The firft of which we fhall recite from the faithful pen of that learned Anatonift *Thomas Bartholinus,* who was Phyfician to *Frederick* the third King of *Denmark,* in thefe Englifhed words: "Various things "(he faith) of Meir-maids are extant delivered in the monuments "of the Ancients, that are partly falfe, partly true.   It is not far "from a Fable that they held, that they did imitate the voices "of Men and Women.   But that there are beafts found in the Sea, "with humane faces (he faith) I fhall not deny.   But I will not (he "faith) fum up the accounts of the ancients.   For they are full of "the ftories of Meir-maids.   Amongft the later Authors, thefe have "here and there handled this argument, *Scaliger (in lib.* 2. *Hiftor.* "*Anim. t.* 108.) *Rondoletius, Licetus (de Spont. vin. ort.) Mar-*"*cus Marci (de Ideis) P. Boiftuan (Hiftor. Gall. prod. T.* 1. *c.* 18.) "At *Enchuyfen* in *Holland* (he faith) the fhape of a certain Meir-"maid is to be feen painted, that formerly had been caft upon the "fhore, by the force of the waters.   It is (he faith) in the mouth "of our common people, that a Meir-maid was taken in *Denmark,* "that did fpeak, foretel things to come, and fpin.   A Father of "the Society of *Jefus* returning forth of *India* to *Rome,* had feen "a Sea-Man there adorned with an Epifcopal Mitre, who did feem "to have in the next corner, hardly born his captivity; but being "let loofe, and turned into the Sea, did feem to render thanks for "his liberty, by bowing of his body before he went under water, "which (he faith) the Jefuit was wont to tell to *Corvinus* the el-"der, as his Son (he faith) told me at *Rome.*   But this being but a ftory told to *Bartholinus* at the fecond hand, and but primarily from the mouth of a Jefuit (who doubtlefs had fome defign in it) I leave it to the judgment of the Wife and Prudent.   But he proceeds thus.   "It is (he faith) moft certain that fifhes are to be "found in the Ocean, that reprefent Terreftrial Animals in fhape: "As the Sea-Fox, the Wolf, the Sea-Calf, the Dog, the Horfe, *&c.* "Therefore why fhould we deny humane fhape to Sea-mon-"fters?   Certainly alfo in the earth there are Apes, which want-"ing reafon, do exprefs the external fhape and geftures of Man. "All Sea-monfters of this fort we referr (he faith) to the kind of "*Phoce* or Sea-Calves.   There was (he faith) in the age we live "in a Sea-Man taken by the Merchants of the *Weft-India* Compa-"ny, and diffected at *Leiden* by *Peter Pavius, John de Laet* being "prefent my friend (he faith) and while he lived, a great and moft "knowing perfon of the things of *America* and of Nature.   The "head and the breaft even as far as the navil was of an humane "fhape, but from the navil even unto the extremities, it was de-"formed flefh, without the fign of a tail.   But that I may not (he
                                                                "faith)

Centur. 2.
Hiftor. 11.169.

Hift. 6.

" faith) feem to impofe upon the Reader, the hands and ribs are to
" be found in my Study or Clofet, which I owe to the kindnefs of
" the praifed *Latius*. We have (he faith) annexed the Picture of
" both, as well of the Meirmaid erect, as of the image of it fwimming,
" that we might fatisfie the dubitation of all men. The hand doth
" confift of five fingers, as ours do, with as many articulations as
" ours, but that only is fingular, that all the bones of the fingers
" are broader and compreffed, and a membrane doth joyn them
" together in courfe, as in volatiles, as Geefe, Ducks, &c. which do
" help to ftretch forth the foot in the water. The extremity of
" the two middle fingers are broader, the extremities of the other
" two fharp. The *radius* and cubit are very fhort, for the con-
" modioufnefs of fwimming, fcarce the length of four fingers breadth.
" Neither is the draught of the fhoulder more ample. The ribs
" are long and thick, almoft exceeding common humane ribs a third
" part.

" Of the ribs (he faith) are beads turned or thrown, a prefent
" remedy for the pain of the Hemorrhoides, which the praifed *Latius*
" hath obferved by experience. Alfo (he faith) that Bracelets being
" made of the bones of this kind of *Phocas* carried to *Rome*, applied
" to the wrift do appeafe the Hemicrany, and fwimming of the head,
" which comes again, if they be laid away, as (he faith) the moft
" illuftrious Nobleman *Caffianus à Puteo*, (moft worthy of Roman
" Purple) hath told me. The fame Noble *Puteus* (he faith) hath
" fhewed me the picture of a Meirmaid in his Clofet, which not
" many years before, was driven to the fhore of *Malta*. A certain
" Spaniard (he faith) told me, that Meirmaids were feen in *India*
" having the Genital members of Women, like thofe of humane
" kind, fo that the Fifhers do bind themfelves with an Oath to the
" Magiftrate, that they have no copulation with them. *Bernardi-*
" *nus Ginnarus (lib. 1. c. 9. de Indico itinere, edit. Neap. 1641.)*
" doth relate that Meirmaids are feen, in the vaft River *Cuama*,
" near the head of *Good-hope*, which in the middle fuperior part are
" like to the form of men, that is, with round head, but immediately
" joyned to the breaft, without a neck, with ears altogether like
" ours, and fo their eyes, lips and teeth. And that their dugs be-
" ing preffed do fend forth moft white milk.

Therefore he concludeth: "There is (he faith) fo great diffe-
" rence of the form of Meirmaids, with the Ancients and Moderns,
" that it is no wonder, that fome do account them figments. We
" have (he faith) the hands to be feen with eyes, and we fhew the
" Meirmaids to be fuch, as in truth they are feen to be. Neither do
" the hands and ribs deceive, whofe Pictures we have given framed
" according to the truth of nature.

Hift. 7.   5. But befides thefe there are other Fifhes or Sea-monfters, that
Genial. dier. in all parts refembled Men and Women, as thefe examples make
l. 3. c. 8. p. 134. manifeft. *Alexander ab Alexandro*, a perfon of great learning
and experience, relateth: "That in *Epirus* a *Triton* or Sea-Man was
                                                              "found,

" found, who forth of the Sea did ravish Women being alone upon
" the shore : But being taken by cunning, he did resemble a Man
" with all his members, but did refuse meat being offered, so that
" he died with hunger and wasting, as being in a strange element.

6. Also *Ludovicus Vives* doth tell us this story : "In our age (he *Hist.* 8.
" saith) with the *Hollanders*, a Sea-Man was seen of many, who al- *Lib. de verit.*
" so was kept there above two years, he was mute, and then be- *fid. Christ. l. 2.*
" gun to speak : But being twice smitten with the Plague, he is let
" loose to the Sea rejoicing and leaping.

7. In the year of our Lord 1403. there was taken a Sea-woman *Hist.* 9.
" in a lake of *Holland*, thrown thither forth of the Sea, and was car- *Vid. Idem*
" ried into the City of *Haerlem*; she suffered her self to have garments *Idear. operat.*
" put upon her, and admitted the use of bread, milk and such like *c. 6.*
" things : Also she learned to spin, and to do many other things af-
" ter the manner of Women, also she did devourly bend her knees
" to the image of Christ crucified, being docible to all things, which
" she was commanded by her Master, but living there many years,
" she always remained mute.

8. To these we shall conclusively add one story of sufficient cre- *Hist.* 10.
dit from our own English Annals, which is this : "In the year *Stows Annal.*
" 1187. being the 33th year of the Reign of *Henry* the second, *p. 157.*
" near unto *Oreford* in *Suffolk*, certain Fishers of the Sea took in
" their nets a fish having the shape of a man in all points, which fish
" was kept by *Bartholomew de Glanvile*, Custos of the Castle of
" *Oreford*, in the same Castle, by the space of six months and more
" for a wonder; he spake not a word. All manner of meats he did
" gladly eat, but most greedily raw fish after he had crushed out
" all the moisture. Oftentimes he was brought to the Church
" where he shewed no tokens of adoration. At length when he
" was not well looked to, he stole away to the Sea, and never after
" appeared. The learned Antiquary Mr. *Camden* tells this same *Britan. p. 412.*
story from *Radulphus Coggeshall*, an ancient writer, and that "*Ca-*
" *pillos habebat, barbam prolixam & pineatam, circa pectus nimium*
" *pilosus erat, & hispidus :* and concludeth : *Quicquid nascatur*
" *in parte naturæ ulla, & in mari esse, & non omnino commentitium*
" *est.*

By all which examples we may be rationally satisfied, that though
these creatures have a real existence in nature, yet because of their
strange natures, shapes and properties, or by reason of their being
rarely seen, they have been and often are not only by the common people but even by the learned taken to be Devils, Spirits or the effects of Inchantment and Witchcraft. And therefore
men that would judge aright must take heed that they be not deceived and imposed upon by relations of this nature, and also of
all such things as may be acted by Imposture and confederacy, and
those other Physical things that are brought to pass by natural *Lib. de Spectr.*
causes, divers sorts of which are recited by *Ludovicus Lavaterus* very *prim. part.*
largely, to which I recommend those that desire further satisfaction *c. 11. p. 61.*
in those particulars. CHAP.

CHAP. XVI.

Of Apparitions in general, and of some unquestionable stories that seem to prove some such things. Of those apparitions pretended to be made in Beryls and Crystals, and of the Astral or Sydereal Spirit.

IN this Treatise we have before sufficiently proved that the denying of the existence of such a Witch as doth make a visible contract with the Devil, or upon whose body he sucketh, or that hath carnal copulation with a Demon, and that is transubstantiated into a Cat or a Dog. or that flyeth in the air; doth not inferr the denial of Spirits ei-her good or bad, nor utterly overthrow the truth of apparitions, or of such things as seem to manifest some supernatural operations. And therefore here we shall fully handle the question of Apparitions, and things that seem to be of that nature, and that in this order.

1. We shall not meddle with Apparitions in the large extent of the word, for so it may comprehend the appearing of new Stars, Comets, Meteors and other Portents, and Prodigies, which (though unusual and wonderous) have yet their production from natural causes. But only here we shall treat of such apparitions as are taken to be performed by supernatural creatures, or in such a way and by such creatures as we commonly account to be different from (if not above) the power of ordinary and visible nature, as of Angels good or bad, the Souls of men departed, or their Astral Spirits, or of some other creatures that are, or may be of a middle nature.

2. As for the apparitions of good Angels sent by God in times past, both in sleep and otherwise, the Scriptures do give us most full and ample assurance, as these few instances may undeniably demonstrate. 1. That *an Angel of the Lord* (that is a good Angel) *did appear* visibly *unto Manoah and his wife*, and did vocally and audibly talk and discourse with them both, and did after in both their sights openly and visibly *ascend in the flame that did arise from the altar*. Now a more plain and indubitable apparition visibly seen and audibly heard than this cannot be found nor read of, having the unquestionable authority of sacred writ to avouch it. 2. Another parallel unto it, and of equal authority, verity and perspicuity, is the sending of the Angel *Gabriel* unto the Virgin *Mary*, her seeing of him, hearing of his salutation, having discourse with him, and seeing his departure, both which are undoubted testimonies of the true, and real appearance of good Angels even to sight and hearing. 3. That sometimes the good Angels have been sent to the servants of God, and have appeared and spoken unto them in dreams; as that *the Angel of the Lord appeared unto Joseph*

in

Judg. 13.

Luke 2. 26. to 39.

in a dream, and bade him to take unto him Mary his wife, which ^{Math. 1. 20.} wasa bleffed, and clear apparition, though in a dream in his fleep. And likewife by the appearing of an Angel unto him in a dream, *he was warned to take the child, and his mother, and to flee into* ^{Math. 2. 13,} *Ægypt,* and alfo again *was commanded by an Angel, after the death* ^{13, 19.} *of Herod, that appeared in a dream, and bade him to take the young child and his mother, and to go into the land of Ifrael.*

3. Of the vifible apparition of evil Angels we fcarce have any evidence at all in the Scriptures, except we fhould take fuppofals for proofs, or difputable places to be certain demonftrations, or wreft and hale the word of God to make it ferve our preconceived opinions. For I do not find any one place in all the Scriptures, where plainly and pofitively any apparition of evil fpirits is recorded, or that by any rational and neceffary confequence fuch a vifible appearance can be deduced or proved : For we have clearly proved that the tempting of *Evah* by the Serpent doth not neceffarily inferr, that it was by a vifible apparition, but by a mental delufion; and that that of *Saul* and the Woman of *Endor,* or the Miftrifs of the bottle, was neither *Samuel* in Soul and Body, nor his Soul alone, neither the Devil in his fhape we fuppofe we have evinced paft anfwer; and that the tempting of our bleffed Saviour by Satan was internal or at leaft the greateft part of it; fo that there doth remain but little of certain proof of the apparition of Devils in that grofs manner, and fo common and frequent as many do too peremptorily affirm: yet for all this we think it rational to grant, that as God hath in times paft often fent meffages by good Angels, for the teaching, counfelling and comforting of his fervants, both audibly and vifibly to be perceived; fo alfo that fometimes God might not only fend evil Spirits internally and mentally to deceive and feduce the wicked, as in the cafe of the lying fpirit in the mouth of *Ahabs* Prophets, but alfo vifibly to appear to terrifie, punifh and deftroy the wicked, or to make way for the manifeftation of his glory. And the Scriptures that mention Demoniacks, and fuch as are commonly faid to be poffeffed, (though that were not by an effential inhefion, but by an effective operation both upon the Souls and Bodies of the perfons that were fo affected and afflicted) do plainly fhew that the operative effects of the Devils power was both heard and feen by their words and actions. So the Devils ufing the organs of the man in whom was the legion of them, *they* ^{Luk. 8. 26. to} *befought Chrift not to command them to go out into the deep, but* ^{37.} *befought him to fuffer them to go into the herd of fwine:* Which " plainly fheweth that their words were audible, and were heard " of the multitude that were by, and the acts that they performed " were vifible enough, for by the power of the Devil *he brake the* " *chains* and fetters, wherewithal he was bound, *and was driven* " *of the Devil into the wildernefs,* and that thefe Devils went forth " of the man, *and entered in amongft the herd of fwine,* by whofe ef-" fective power *the fwine ran violently down a fteep rock into the*

" fed,

" *sea, and were drowned.* And this doth plainly manifest the present operation of the Devils, that was apparent both by the words and actions, that were both to be seen and heard ; so that this in that large sense, that it is usually taken in, was a real apparition of Devils, or at least equivalent thereunto.   For we do but here inquire after such appearances of Devils, that do necessarily infer their presence in operating so in and upon creatures or corporeal matter, that by sight, hearing, or other of the senses, it may certainly be manifest to work above the ordinary power of nature, and may induce us rationally by the testimony of our senses, to believe that those things are brought to pass by those creatures that we call Demons, as many of these persons, who were said to have been or to be afflicted with Devils, were in the days of our blessed Saviours remaining in the flesh.

4. But though it be never so freely and fully granted, that in the ages and times mentioned in the Old and New Testament (nay it may be for a century or more after) there were persons that were possessed and afflicted with Devils, and also that for that time there were many miracles wrought : Yet now it will be said that miracles are totally ceased as not being any way necessary to confirm the Gospel, which is now established and setled.   This we confess is so strongly and convincingly proved by the Divines of the reformed Churches, that we account him wilfully blind that will oppose it.   Yet notwithstanding all this that miracles are totally ceased, I grant that there are some strange things that have happened in late ages, and some in our own time, that cannot be any way solved by meer ordinary natural causes, and apparitions made by some kind of creatures that must be derived from some such causes as those of good or bad Spirits, or from creatures of the like nature.   And that though miracles be ceased, it will not therefore follow that every thing that hath a cause above or differing from the usual and ordinary course of nature, must be also ceased, for *quanquam nunc non sint miracula, possint tamen esse miranda* : and though that miracles be ceased, yet it will not follow that apparitions are so also, because apparitions are not miracles ; for a good Angel to be sent and to appear, cannot be said to be a miracle, because it is the end for which he was created, they (that is the Angels) *are all ministring spirits sent forth for the good of those that shall be heirs of Salvation.*   And it cannot be said otherwise of evil Angels or of any other creatures that may make these apparitions, for as they are and must be creatures, so there is and must be some certain ends, for which they were created and are imployed unto.

5. But to prove the truth of apparitions, or other strange Phenomena's equivalent unto them, as to have been truly performed as matters of fact is extream difficult and almost impossible, because the Histories and relations of things of this nature are most strangely fabulous, and therefore are by no means to be relied upon, as will most
manifestly

manifeftly appear by undeniable reafons, if we examine them in divided members in this order.

1. The Hiftories and relations that are given either by the Poets, or moft of the ancient Philofophers, of thefe things, are fo feemingly impoffible, and fo extreamly fictitious, as he muft of neceffity have in a manner totally forfaken his own reafon, that can give any credit at all unto them. And efpecially they are fo fraught with the horrible fables of the numeroufnefs of their feigned gods, demigods, fpirits, hobgoblins, *Lares, Lemures,* Mens fhadows and the like, that they would make a man believe that the world was full of nothing elfe, and this was chiefly done to uphold their Idolatrous and fuperftitious Religion. And all thefe kind of authors that have written from the time of *Homer* until the end of the ages in which the two *Plinies* and *Plutarch* lived, have but run the fame courfe, all their relations tafting of the leaven of impoffibilities, fuperftition and fabuloufnefs.

2. And if we look into the Pontificial Writers, efpecially thofe that have recorded ftories of this nature fince the fixth century, we fhall find fuch a Rhapfodie, and heap of Bombaft lies and invented fables both of apparitions and Witches, that no rational man can well give affent to one of a thoufand of them, they feem fo incredible, that they would rather make a wife man diffident of all fuch matters of fact, than to yield credit to any. And a man might as reafonably believe the forged and lying miracles of *Mahomet,* as thofe monkifh fables. For the extream defire that thofe Authors had to advance their falfe and feigned Doctrine of Purgatory, and thereby to uphold the gain and benefit that was gotten by injoining fuch and fuch penances and eleemofynary deeds to redeem Souls from thence, did drive them on to invent thoufands of falfe ftories of the apparitions of Souls after death, which had not one jot of truth in them at all.

3. Thofe that are called the Reformed Divines (becaufe they returned to that pure and true Doctrine and Worfhip, that had been fettled and practifed in thofe foregoing ages that were truly Catholick and Apoftolick) being altogether intent about the main and principal points of the Faith, and thofe that concerned the true worfhip of God, did take little heed to the matters of this nature, as being more circumftantial, and therefore not by them accounted fo effential and neceffary. From whence it came to pafs that *Lambertus Danæus, Hemmingius, Eraftus* and others, did without due examination and circumfpection receive the opinions and ftories of the Papifts hand over head. From whence (I conceive) it came to pafs that *Ludovicus Lavaterus* a learned Divine of the reformed Religion at *Zurich* did write a book of apparitions and fuch matters, but brought no other proofs of the truth of thefe things *de facto,* but the often repeated ftories of Heathenifh Authors, and fome few from Ecclefiaftick Authors, that are of dubious credit, but not any one of his own knowledge.

6. But

6. But if we come to consider the Histories of late that are reported of apparitions, and such like things that must of necessity have something in them, that resembles a supernatural cause, we may in part receive more ample satisfaction, which will be manifest in these few following particulars.

1. *Meric Casaubon* Doctor of Divinity, in his treatise of Credulity and Incredulity (sometimes by us quoted before) hath strongly indeavoured to make good all those impossible and absurd things that are ascribed unto Witches : which though he hath pitifully failed to perform, yet hath he said enough that may serve to prove that there are many strange things that seem to prove the being of Demons or Spirits, though he have not brought any one story of his own knowledge or that was done in his time.   And we have shewed before that apparitions are no certain ground for Christians to believe the existence of Demons by, but the word of God.   But in his Preface to that piece of the relation concerning Dr. *Dee*, he relateth two stories told by that venerable and learned Prelate Bishop *Andrews* to his Father *Isaac Casaubon*. " The one (he saith) " concerning a noted or at least by many suspected Witch or Sor- " ceress, which the Devil in a strange shape did wait upon (or for " rather) at her death.   The other concerning a Man, who after " his death was restored to life to make confession of a horrible " murther committed upon his own Wife, for which he had never " been suspected.   And both these (he saith) that learned Bishop " did believe to be true, but for one of them it seems, he did un- " dertake upon his own knowledge, to wit that of the apparition, " and the other he had from an eye-witness.   And considering the condition of Bishop *Andrews* both for learning and piety, the relations are of much weight, and they may be seen at large in the fore-cited Preface.

2. I cannot but much wonder that Dr. *Henry Moore*, a grave person, and one that for many years hath resided in a most learned and flourishing Academy, whose name is much taken notice of both at home and abroad, having published so many books, should make such bad choice of the Authors from whom he takes his stories, or that he should pitch upon those that seem so fabulous, impossible and incredible.   And that I may not seem to tax him without cause, I desire the Reader to peruse his two relations, the one of the Shoomaker of *Breslaw* in *Silesia*, Anno 1591. the other of *Johannes Cuntius* a Citizen of *Pentsh* in *Silesia*, and to tell whether he can rationally believe those things either to have been true or possible.   And as for the Author *Martinus Weinrichius* a Silesian Physician, I cannot find any thing either of his fame or writings, and it is most strange that he should be omitted by that diligent and unpartial Author *Melchior Adams*; And there had been far better Authors and of more credit to have pitcht upon for such like stories, than either *Bodinus* or *Remigius*; neither can there be much credit given to any of the stories that he relates, except it be that

of

of the Pied-Piper, which some do interpret far otherwife.

3. " There was a Treatife called, the Devil of *Mafcon*, or a true
" relation of the chief things which an unclean fpirit did and faid at
" *Mafcon* in *Burgundy*, in the Houfe of M[r] *Francis Perreaud* Mini-
" fter of the reformed Church in the fame Town, written by the
" faid *Perreaud* foon after the Apparition which was in the year
" 1612. but was not publifhed until the year 1653. which was 41.
" years after the thing was faid to be acted. It feems it was tran-
" flated by D[r] *Peter Du Moulin*, the Son of the learned and reve-
" rend *Peter Du Moulin*, at the requeft of the honourable and learn-
" ed perfon M[r] *Boyle*. The moft of the things had been known unto
" M[r] *Du Moulin* the Father, when he was Prefident of a National
" Synod in thofe parts, to whom alfo the faid *Perreaud* was well
" known, who was a religious, well poifed, venerable Divine. And
" M[r] *Boyle* faith, that he had had converfe with this pious Author
" at *Geneva*, and had inquired after the Writer, and fome paffages
" of the Book, which overcame all his fetled indifpofednefs to be-
" lieve ftrange things. The Character given of this Author, and
" the affent of fuch learned perfons to the things related, have gain-
" ed an ample fuffrage to give credit to them alfo. But notwithftand-
" ing all this, there are many paffages in the relation that a quick-
" fighted Critick would find to be either contradictory or incon-
" fiftent, and it cannot rationally be thought that he was a Caco-
" demon, his actions were fo harmlefs, civil, and ludicrous; and if
" he were to be believed (and in fome things he did fpeak truth,
" and the Minifter himfelf M[r] *Perreaud* did in fome things give cre-
" dit to him) he was no Devil, but hoped to be faved by Jefus
" Chrift. But whether a Devil or not, yet the ftory for fubftance
" doth fufficiently prove the exiftence of fuch kind of Demons,
" that can work ftrange and odd feats.

4. M[r] *Baxter* a perfon of great learning and piety, whofe judgment bears great fway with me, fpeaking of Apparitions faith thus:
" I know many are very incredulous herein, and will hardly be-
" lieve that there have been fuch Apparitions. For my own
" part (he faith) though I am as fufpicious as moft in fuch reports,
" and do believe that moft of them are conceits or delufions, yet
" having been very diligently inquifitive in fuch Cafes, I have re-
" ceived undoubted teftimony of the truth of fuch Apparitions,
" fome from the mouths of men of undoubted honefty and godli-
" nefs, and fome from the report of multitudes of perfons, who
" heard or faw. Were it fit here to name the perfons, I could fend
" you to them yet living, by whom you would be as fully fatisfied
" as I: Houfes that have been fo frequently haunted with fuch
" terrors, that the inhabitants fucceffively have been witneffes
" of it.

7. Though fome of thefe laft recited teftimonies might fufficiently
convince the moft obftinate and incredulous, that there are Apparitions and fome other fuch ftrange accidents that cannot be folved

The Saints Ever-lafting reft. c. 7. p. 255.

by

by the fuppofed principles of matter and motion, but that do neceffarily require fome other caufes, that are above or different from
the vifible and ordinary courfe of nature ; yet becaufe it is a point
dark and myftical, and of great concern and weight, we fhall add
fome unqueftionable teftimonies, either from our own Annals, or
matters of fact that we know to be true of our own certain knowledge, that thereby it may undoubtedly appear, that there are effects that exceed the ordinary power of natural caufes, and may for
ever convince all Atheiftical minds, of which in this order.

Stow. p. 605.
Hift. 1.
1. "In the firft year of *Edward* the Sixth, *Anno Domini* 1551.
" on St. *Valentines* day, at *Feverfham* in *Kent*, one *Arden* a Gentle-
"man was murthered by procurement of his own Wife ; for the
" which fact fhe was the fourteenth of *March* burnt at *Canterbury :*
" *Michael* Mr *Arden's* Man was hang'd in Chains at *Feverfham*, and
"a Maiden burnt: *Mosbie* and his Sifter were hanged in *Smithfield*
" at *London :* *Greene* which had fled, came again certain years after,
" and was hanged in Chains in the High-way againft *Feverfham*, and
"black *Will* the Ruffian , that was hired to do that act, after his
"firft efcape was apprehended, and burnt on a Scaffold at *Flufhing*
"in *Zealand.*

P. 1708.
The fame horrid murther is more at large related by *Hollingfhead*,
who lived at that time, and had information of all the particulars,
who faith thus much more. " This one thing (he faith) feemeth very
"ftrange and notable touching Mr *Arden*, that in the place he was
"laid, being dead, all the proportion of his body might be feen two
"years after and more, fo plain as could be, for the grafs did not
"grow where his body had touched, but between his legs, between
"his arms and about the hollownefs of his neck, and round about
"his body : And where his legs, arms, head, or any part of his bo-
"dy had touched, no grafs growed at all of all that time. So that
"many ftrangers came in that mean time, befide the Townfmen, to
"fee the print of his body there on the ground in that Field, which
"Field he had (as fome have reported) cruelly taken from a Wo-
" man, that had been a Widdow to one *Cooke*, and after Married to
" one *Richard Read* a Marriner, to the great hinderance of her and
"her Husband the faid *Read*, for they had long enjoyed it by a
"Leafe which they had of it for many years not then expired. Ne-
"verthelefs he got it from them, for the which, the faid *Reads*
" Wife not only exclaimed againft him in fhedding many a falt tear,
" but alfo curfed him moft bitterly even to his face, wifhing ma-
"ny a vengeance to light upon him, and that all the World might
"wonder on him, which was thought then to come to pafs, when
" he was thus murthered and lay in that Field, from midnight till
" the morning, and fo all that day, being the Fair-day, till night, all
"the which day there were many hundreds of people came won-
"dring about him. From whence we may take this Obfervation.

Obferv.
As it is moft certain that this is a true and punctual relation given
us by *Hollingfhead*, as being a publick thing done in the face of a

Nation, the print of his body remaining so long after, and viewed and wondered at by so many; so that it hath not left the least starting hole for the most incredulous Atheist to get out at. So likewise it may dare the most deep-sighted Naturalist, or unbelieving Atheist; that would exalt and so far deifie Nature, as to deny and take away the existence of the God of Nature, to shew a reason of the long remaining of the print of his body, or the not growing of the grass in those places where his body had touched for two years and more after? Could it be the steams or Atoms that flowed from his body? then are why not such prints left by other murthered bodies? which we are sure by sight and experience not to be so. And therefore we can attribute it justly to no other cause but only to the power of God and divine vengeance, who is a righter of the oppressed, fatherless and Widdows, and hears their cries and regardeth their tears.

2. "In the second year of the Reign of King *James* of famous *Hist. à.* "memory, a strange accident happened, to the terror of all bloody "murtherers, which was this; One *Anne Waters* enticed by a lover *Sir Rich. Ba-* "of hers, consented to have her Husband strangled, and then buri- *kers Chron.* "ed him secretly under the Dunghil in a Cow-house. Whereupon *fol. 448.* "the man being missing by his Neighbours, and the Wife making "shew of a wondering what was become of him, it pleased God "that one of the inhabitants of the Town dreamed one night that "his Neighbour *Waters* was strangled, and buried under the Dung-"hill in a Cow-house, and upon declaring his dream, search being "made by the Constable, the dead body was found as he had dream-"ed, and thereupon the Wife was apprehended, and upon exami-"nation confessing the fact was burned. But we shall give it more at large as it was taken from the mouths of *Thomas Haworths* Wife, her Husband being the dreamer and discoverer, and from his Son, who together with many more, who both remember and can affirm every particular thereof, the Narrative was taken *April* the 17*th* 1663. and is this.

"In the year abovesaid, *John Waters* of *Lower Darwen* in the "County of *Lancaster* Gardiner, by reason of his calling was much "absent from his Family: In which his absence, his Wife (not with-"out cause) was suspected of incontinency with one *Gyles Haworth* "of the same Town; this *Gyles Haworth* and *Waters* Wife conspired "and contrived the death of *Waters* in this manner. They con-"tracted with one *Ribchester* a poor man to kill this *Waters*. As soon "as *Waters* came home and went to bed, *Gyles Haworth* and *Waters* "Wife conducted the hired Executioner to the said *Waters*. Who "seeing him so innocently laid betwixt his two small Children in "Bed, repented of his enterprize, and totally refused to kill him. "*Gyles Haworth* displeased with the faint-heartedness of *Ribchester*, "takes the Axe into his own hand, and dashed out his brains: The "Murderers buried him in a Cow house, *Waters* being long missing "the Neighbourhood asked his Wife for him; she denied that she

"knew

"knew where he was. Thereupon publick search was made for him
"in all pits round about, lest he should have casually fallen into any
"of them. One *Thomas Haworth* of the said Town Yeoman, was
"for many nights together, much troubled with broken sleeps and
"dreams of the murder ; he revealed his dreams to his Wife, but she
"laboured the concealment of them a long time :   This *Thomas*
"*Haworth* had occasion to pass by the House every day where the
"murder was done, and did call and inquire for *Waters*, as often
"as he went near the House.   One day he went into the House to
"ask for him, and there was a Neighbour who said to *Thomas Ha-*
"*worth*, It's said that *Waters* lies under this stone, (pointing to the
"Hearth-stone) to which *Thomas Haworth* replied, And I have
"dreamed that he is under a stone not far distant.   The Constable
"of the said Town being accidentally in the said House (his name
"*Myles Aspinall*) urged *Thomas Haworth* to make known more at
"large what he had dreamed, which he relateth thus. I have (quoth
"he) many a time within this eight weeks (for so long it was since
"the murder) dreamed very restlesly, that *Waters* was murdered
"and buried under a broad stone in the Cow-house; I have told my
"troubled dreams to my Wife alone, but she refuses to let me make
"it known: But I am not able to conceal my dreams any longer, my
"sleep departs from me, I am pressed and troubled with fearful
"dreams which I cannot bear any longer, and they increase upon
"me. The Constable hearing this made search immediately upon it,
"and found as he had dreamed the murdered body eight weeks bu-
"ried under a flat stone in the Cow-house; *Ribchester* and *Gyles Ha-*
"*worth* fled and never came again. *Anne Waters* (for so was *Waters*
"Wifes name) being apprehended, confessed the murder, and was
"burned. From whence we may observe this.

Observ.   1. That this is the full and punctual relation of this bloody and
execrable murder from *Haworths* Wife (who then was a very old
Woman) and the Son, and differs not a jot from what Sir *Richard*
Baker writes, but only they say his brains were dashed out with an
Axe, and he saith he was strangled, which is only a circumstance of
the manner, but in the matter they both agree, that it was a certain
truth that *Waters* was murdered, and Sir *Richard Bakers* information might fail in that particular of the manner of it. And if it be
thought strange that the two little Children did know nothing of
it, it is certain that they were much too young, and said that they
were twins, not above half a year old.   But the only matter that
we have brought it for, is the extraordinary way of its discovery
by *Thomas Haworths* dreaming, in which point both the relations
closely agree, and was the chief and only reason why Sir *Richard*
Baker put it in his Chronicle. And the same also more at large *Stow*
hath recorded in his Chronicle.   Now what should the cause be
that *Thomas Haworth* should be hindred of his sleep, and have rest-
less dreams, and that his dream should hit so punctually of the place
where he was buried, more than any other person in the same Town ?
                                                                                Certainly

certainly it cannot be referred to fortune and chance, for they have no caufality at all, and are but only names that we impofe upon certain effects and accidents: *Te facimus fortuna Deum, cæloq; locamus,* as faid the Poet. Neither can it rationally be thought to be melancholy, becaufe that though it be a fubtil humour, and render thofe that are affected therewith very imaginative and thoughtful, yet fuppofing *Thomas Haworth* to be of that temperament and difpofition, it might make him more deeply to think and meditate upon the rumour of *Waters* being awanting or upon fufpicion of his murder, but could not in dreams inform him to know precifely the place where he was buried. And if fome fhould imagine it to be the Soul of the murthered perfon *Waters,* as doubtlefs a Papift would be ready to affirm, yet is that opinion directly contrary to the Scriptures, and fufficiently confuted by the reformed Divines. And if it fhould be referred to the operation of the Aftral or Sydereal fpirit, that is an opinion but imbraced by few, and is hard to prove to be a certain verity, of which we fhall fpeak largely anon. Neither can it by any found reafon be thought to be the Devil, becaufe it is manifeft that God doth not ufe the miniftry of evil Angels for any good end, as for the difcovery of murther, and the bringing of the guilty perfons to condign punifhment; but on the contrary he ufeth their fervice for to tempt, feduce, deceive, punifh and torment. Therefore we conceive that it was brought to pafs by the finger of God, who either immediately by himfelf, or by the miniftry of a good Angel, did reprefent thofe dreams to *Thomas Haworth,* and revealed the precife place of *Waters* burial.

3. "About the year of our Lord 1623 or 24 one *Fletcher* of *Hiſt.* 3. "*Rafcal,* a Town in the North Riding of *Yorkſhire* near unto the "Foreft of *Gantreſs,* a Yeoman of good Eftate, did marry a young "lufty Woman from *Thornton Brigs,* who had been formerly kind "with one *Ralph Raynard,* who kept an Inn within half a mile from "*Rafcall* in the high road way betwixt *York* and *Thuske,* his Sifter "living with him. This *Raynard* continued in unlawful luft with "the faid *Fletchers* Wife, who not content therewith confpired the "death of *Fletcher,* one *Mark Dunn* being made privy and hired "to affift in the murther. Which *Raynard* and *Dunn* accomplifh- "ed upon the *May-day* by drowning *Fletcher,* as they came all "three together from a Town called *Huby,* and acquainting the "wife with the deed fhe gave them a Sack therein to convey his "body, which they did and buried it in *Raynards* backfide or Croft "where an old Oak-root had been ftubbed up, and fowed Muftard- "feed upon the place thereby to hide it. So they continued their "wicked courfe of luft and drunkennefs, and the neighbours did much "wonder at *Fletchers* abfence, but his wife did excufe it, and faid "that he was but gone afide for fear of fome Writs being ferved "upon him. And fo it continued until about the feventh day of "*July,* when *Raynard* going to *Topcliffe* Fair, and fetting up his "Horfe in the Stable, the fpirit of *Fletcher* in his ufual fhape and

"habit

"habit did appear unto him, and faid, Oh *Ruph*, repent, repent,
"for my revenge is at hand ; and ever after until he was put in the
"Goal, it feemed to ftand before him, whereby he became fad and
"reftlefs : And his own Sifter over-hearing his confeffion and relati-
"on of it to another perfon, did through fear of lofing her own
"life, immediately reveal it to Sir *William Sheffield*, who lived in
"*Rafcall*, and was a Juftice of Peace. Whereupon they were all
"three apprehended and fent to the Gaol at *York*, where they
"were all three condemned, and fo executed accordingly near to
"the place where *Raynard* lived, and where *Fletcher* was buried,
"the two men being hung up in irons, and the woman buried un-
"der the Gallows. I have recited this ftory punctually as a thing
that hath been very much fixed in my memory, being then but
young, and as a certain truth, I being (with many more) an ear-
witnefs of their confeffions and an eye-witnefs of their Executions,
and likewife faw *Fletcher* when he was taken up, where they had
buried him in his cloaths, which were a green fuftian doublet pinkt
upon white, gray breeches, and his walking boots and brafs fpurrs
without rowels.

Obferv.   Some will fay there was no extrinfick apparition to *Raynard* at
all, but that all this did only arife from the guilt of his own confcience, which reprefented the fhape of *Fletcher* in his fancy. But
then why was it precifely done at that time, and not at any others?
it being far from the place of the murder, or the place where they
had buried *Fletcher*, and nothing there that might bring it to his
remembrance more than at another time, and if it had only arifen
from within, and appeared fo in his fancy, it had been more likely to
have been moved, when he was in, or near his backfide where the
murthered body of *Fletcher* lay. But certain it is that he affirmed
that it was the fhape and voice of *Fletcher*, as affuredly to his eyes
and ears, as ever he had feen or heard him in his life. And if it
were granted that it was only intrinfick, yet that will not exclude
the Divine Power, which doubtlefs at that time did labour
to make him fenfible of the cruel murther, and to mind him of the revenge approaching. And it could not be brought to pafs either by
the Devil, or *Fletchers* Soul, as we have proved before ; and therefore in reafon we conclude that either it was wrought by the Divine
Power, to fhew his deteftation of murther, or that it was the Aftral
or Sydereal Spirit of *Fletcher*, feeking revenge for the murther, of
which more anon.

Hift. 4.   4. About the year of our Lord 1632. (as near as I can remember having loft my notes, and the copy of the Letter to Serjeant
Hutton, but am fure that I do moft perfectly remember the fubftance of the ftory) near unto *Chefter* in the ftreet, there lived
"one *Walker* a Yeoman-man of good Eftate, and a Widower, who
"had a young Woman to his Kinfwoman that kept his Houfe, who
"was by the Neighbours fufpected to be with child, and was to-
"wards the dark of the evening one night fent away with one
                                                        " *Mark*

" *Mark Sharp* who was a Collier, or one that digged coals under
" ground, and one that had been born in *Blakeburn* Hundred in
" *Lancaſhire*, and ſo ſhe was not heard of a long time, and no noiſe,
" or little was made about it. In the winter time after one *James*
" *Graham* or *Grime* (for ſo in that Country they call them) being
" a Miller, and living about two miles from the place where *Walker*
" lived, was one night alone very late in the Mill grinding Corn,
" and as about twelve or one a clock at night he came down the
" ſtairs from having been putting Corn in the Hopper, the Mill
" doors being ſhut, there ſtood a Woman upon the midſt of the
" floor with her hair about her head, hanging down, and all bloody;
" with five large wounds in her head : He being much affrighted
" and amazed, begun to bleſs him, and at laſt asked her who ſhe
" was, and what ſhe wanted ; to which ſhe ſaid, I am the Spirit of
" ſuch a Woman, who lived with *Walker*, and being got with
" child by him, he promiſed me to ſend me to a private place, where
" I ſhould be well lookt to until I was brought in bed, and well
" again, and then I ſhould come again, and keep his houſe. And
" accordingly (ſaid the apparition) I was one night late ſent away
" with one *Mark Sharp*, who upon a Moor (naming a place that
" the Miller knew) ſlew me with a pick (ſuch as men dig coals
" withal) and gave me theſe five wounds, and after threw my bo-
" dy into a coal-pit hard by, and hid the pick under a bank; and his
" ſhoos and ſtockings being bloody he endeavoured to waſh, but
" ſeeing the blood would not waſh forth he hid them there. And
" the apparition further told the Miller that he muſt be the Man to
" reveal it, or elſe that ſhe muſt ſtill appear, and haunt him. The
" Miller returned home very ſad and heavy, but ſpoke not one
" word of what he had ſeen, but eſchewed as much as he could to
" ſtay in the Mill within night without company, thinking there-
" by to eſcape the ſeeing again of that frightful apparition. But
" notwithſtanding one night when it begun to be dark, the appa-
" rition met him again, and ſeemed very fierce and cruel, and threat-
" ned him that if he did not reveal the murder ſhe would continu-
" ally purſue and haunt him. Yet for all this he ſtill concealed it,
" until S. *Thomas* Eve before *Chriſtmas*, when being ſoon after Sun-
" ſet walking in his Garden ſhe appeared again, and then ſo threat-
" ned and affrighted him that he faithfully promiſed to reveal it
" next morning. In the morning he went to a Magiſtrate and made
" the whole matter known with all the circumſtances, and diligent
" ſearch being made, the body was found in a coal-pit, with five
" wounds in the head, and the pick and ſhooes and ſtockings yet
" bloody, in every circumſtance as the apparition had related un-
" to the Miller. Whereupon *Walker* and *Mark Sharp* were both
" apprehended, but would confeſs nothing. At the Aſſizes follow-
" ing (I think it was at *Durham*) they were arraigned, found guil-
" ty, condemned and executed, but I could never hear that they
" confeſſed the fact. There were ſome that reported that the ap-

"parition did appear to the Judge or the Foreman of the Jury,
"(who was alive in *Chester* in the ftreet about ten years a-go, as I
"have been credibly informed) but of that I know no certainty.
There are many perfons yet alive that can remember this ftrange
murder, and the difcovery of it, for it was, and fometimes yet is
as much difcourfed of in the North Countrey as any thing that almoft hath ever been heard of, and the relation printed, though now
not to be gotten. I relate this with the greater confidence (though
I may fail in fome of the circumftances) becaufe I faw and read
the Letter that was fent to Serjeant *Hutton*, who then lived at
Goldsbrugh in *Yorkshire*, from the Judge before whom *Walker* and
Mark Sharp were tried, and by whom they were condemned, and
had a Copy of it until about the year 1658. when *I* had it and many other books and papers taken from me.

Obferv.   And this I confefs to be one of the moft convincing ftories (being of undoubted verity) that ever I read, heard or knew of, and
carrieth with it the moft evident force to make the moft incredulous fpirit, to be fatisfied that there are really fometimes fuch things
as apparitions. And though it be not eafy to affign the true and
proper caufe of fuch a ftrange effect, yet muft we not meafure all
things to be, or not to be, to be true or falfe, according to the extent of our underftandings, for if there be many of the *magnalia
naturæ* that yet lie hidden from the wifeft of men, then much more
Rom. 11. 33. may the *magnalia Dei* be unknown unto us, *whofe judgments are
unfearchable, and his wayes paft finding out.* And as in the reft we
cannot afcribe this ftrange apparition, to any diabolical operation,
nor to the Soul of the Woman murthered, fo we muft conclude
that either it was meerly wrought by the Divine Power, or by the
Aftral fpirit of the murthered Woman, which laft doth feem moft
rational, as we fhall fhew hereafter.

Hift. 5.   5. To thefe (though it be not altogether of the fame nature)
we fhall add one both for the oddnefs and ftrangenefs of it, as alfo
becaufe it happened in my time, and I was both an eye and ear-
witnefs of the trial of the perfon accufed. And firft take a hint of it
from the pen of *Durant Hotham*, in his learned Epiftle to the *My-
fterium magnum* of *Jacob Behemen* upon *Genefis* in thefe words:
"There was (he faith) as I have heard the ftory credibly reported
"in this Country a Man apprehended for fufpicion of Witchcraft,
"he was of that fort we call white Witches, which are fuch as do
"cures beyond the ordinary reafons and deductions of our ufual
"practitioners, and are fuppofed (and moft part of them truly)
"to do the fame by the miniftration of fpirits (from whence under
"their noble favours, moft Sciences at firft grew) and therefore
"are by good reafon provided againft by our Civil Laws, as being
"ways full of danger and deceit, and fcarce ever otherwife ob-
"tained than by a devillifh compact of the exchange of ones Soul
"to that affiftant fpirit, for the honour of its Mountebankery.
"What this man did was with a white powder which, he faid, he
                                    "received

"received from the Fairies, and that going to a Hill he knocked
"three times, and the Hill opened, and he had access to, and con-
"verse with a visible people; and offered, that if any Gentleman
"present would either go himself in person, or send his servant, he
"would conduct them thither, and shew them the place and persons
"from whom he had his skill.

To this I shall only add thus much, that the man was accused for *Vid. i Jacob.* invoking and calling upon evil spirits, and was a very simple and *c. 12.* illiterate person to any mans judgment, and had been formerly very poor, but had gotten some pretty little meanes to maintain
himself, his Wife and diverse small children, by his cures done
with this white powder, of which there were sufficient proofs,
and the Judge asking him how he came by the powder, he told a
story to this effect. "That one night before day was gone, as he
"was going home from his labour, being very sad and full of hea-
"vy thoughts, not knowing how to get meat and drink for his
"Wife and Children, he met a fair Woman in fine cloaths, who
"asked him why he was so sad, and he told her that it was by rea-
"son of his poverty, to which she said, that if he would follow
"her counsel she would help him to that which would serve to
"get him a good living; to which he said he would consent with
"all his heart, so it were not by unlawful ways: she told him that
' it should not be by any such ways, but by doing of good and cu-
"ring of sick people; and so warning him strictly to meet her there
"the next night at the same time, she departed from him, and he
"went home. And the next night at the time appointed he duly
"waited, and she (according to promise) came and told him that
"it was well that he came so duly, otherwise he had missed of that
"benefit, that she intended to do unto him, and so bade him fol-
"low her and not be afraid. Thereupon she led him to a little Hill
"and she knocked three times, and the Hill opened, and they went
"in, and came to a fair hall, wherein was a Queen sitting in great
"state, and many people about her, and the Gentlewoman that
"brought him, presented him to the Queen, and she said he was
"welcom, and bid the Gentlewoman give him some of the white
"powder, and teach him how to use it; which she did, and gave
"him a little wood box full of the white powder, and bad him
"give 2 or 3 grains of it to any that were sick, and it would heal
"them, and so she brought him forth of the Hill, and so they parted.
"And being asked by the Judge whether the place within the Hill,
"which he called a Hall, were light or dark, he said indiffe-
"rent, as it is with us in the twilight; and being asked how he got
"more powder, he said when he wanted he went to that Hill, and
"knocked three times, and said every time I am coming, I am
"coming, whereupon it opened, and he going in was conducted
"by the aforesaid Woman to the Queen, and so had more powder
"given him. This was the plain and simple story (however it may
"be judged of) that he told before the Judge, the whole Court,
"and

"and the Jury, and there being no proof, but what cures he had
"done to very many, the Jury did acquit him: and I remember the
"Judge said, when all the evidence was heard, that if he were to
"assign his punishment, he should be whipped from thence to Fairy-
"hall, and did seem to judge it to be a delusion or an Imposture.
From whence we may take these observations.

Observ. 1.   1. Though Mr. *Hotham* seem to judge that this person accused
had the white powder from some Spirit, and that one also of the
evil sort, and upon a contract, by the ingaging of his Soul, we
have before sufficiently proved the nullity of a visible and corporeal
contract with the Devil; neither was it yet ever proved that the Devil did any good either real or apparent, but is the sworn enemy
of all mankind, both in their Souls and in their Bodies, but this
powder wrought that which was really good, namely the curing
of diseases, and therefore rationally cannot be thought to be given
from an evil spirit.

Observ. 2.   2. Some there were that thought that the simple man told a plain
and true story, and that he had the powder from those people we
call Fairies, and there are many that do believe and affirm that there
are such people, of whom *Paracelsus* hath a Treatise of purpose,
holding that they are not of the seed of *Adam*, and therefore he
calls them *non*-Adamicks, and that they have flesh and bones, and
so differ from spirits, and yet that they can glide through walls and
rocks (which he calleth their Chaos) as easily as we through the
air, and that they get children, and are mortal like those that
Hieronymus Cardanus relateth that appeared to his Father *Facius
Cardanus*, and these he calleth *Pygmæi, Silvestres, Gnomi* and *Um-
bratiles*; but his proof of their existence to me doth not seem satisfactory, what others may think of it I leave to their demonstrations,
if they have any.

Observ. 3.   3. Some there were (and those not of the meer ignorant sort)
that did judge, that though the Man was simple, yet that the story
that he told was but framed and taught him, the better to conceal
the person from whom he received the white powder. For they
thought that some notable Chymist, or rather an Adeptist, had
in charity bestowed that powder upon him, for the relief of himself
and family, as we know it hath often happened to other persons, at
other times and places. And this last opinion seems most consonant to reason, and I the rather believe it because not many years
after, it was certainly known, that there was an Adeptist in that
Countrey, and we ought not to fetch in supernatural causes to solve
effects, when natural causes may serve the turn.

    6. The last thing of this strange nature, that we shall instance in,
is concerning the bleeding or cruentation of the bodies of those
that have been murthered, I mean of such as have been murthered
by prepense malice, and upon premeditated purpose; for the bodies of others that are killed by chance-medley, and by man-slaughter, we do not read nor find any examples, that ever their bodies
did

did bleed. And though we have not been ocular witness of any such bleeding yet are there records of such accidents given us by many learned and credible authors that a man might almost be accounted an Infidel not to give credit to them, and that both of those that have bled when the murtherer hath not been present, and also of those that have bled the murtherer being present. And first of those bodies that have issued blood, when the murtherer was not by.

Gregorius Horstius a Physician of great experience and learning, and of no less integrity, recordeth this story, thus Englished. " In " the year of our Lord 1604. the twenty sixth day of *December* a " young Nobleman of twenty five years old, was shot at with a ' Gun in the night time about nine a clock from an high window "of an house, in the Town of *Blindmarck* in lower *Austria*, and the " bullet entring his left breast went forth at his right side and so " forthwith died in the place. The dead body being viewed again, ' and the wound confidered, the same quantity or bigness both of ' the entrance and out-going are found with great plenty of blood " issuing. The following day being the twenty seventh of *Decem-* "*ber* in the morning, the body of the murthered young man hath ' other cloaths put upon it and so is kept quiet for the space of " two days. Furthermore upon the thirtieth of *December* he is laid "upon the Bier, and kept in the Church. and that without any "further motion, where nevertheless from the upper wound the ' fresh blood did daily flow, until the eighth of *January* 1605. from "which time the Hemorrhage ceased. But again the thirteenth of "*February*, about noon, the flux of blood by the lower wound for " an hour or two was observed to issue, as though the slaughter had " been newly done. In the mean time the habit of the whole body " was such, as did most easily agree to what it was living, the co- "lour of his face remained even unto his burial ruddy and florid, "the vein appearing in his forehead filled with good blood: no "sign of an incipient putrefaction appearing for so many weeks, no " stink, or ungrateful odour, which otherwise doth accompany "dead bodies within a few days, was here found at all: The fin- "gers of the hands remained soft, moveable, or flexible, without "any wast, the natural colour being not very much changed, ex- "cept that in process of time, about the last week before burial, " they begun in a certain manner to wax livid in the extremities.

7. This following he giveth to prove, that as cold constringeth and shuteth up the veins, so heat doth open them, and cause the blood to flow, and faith: " This is proved a few years since by ex- "perience in an infant slain by a most wicked Mother forthwith af- "ter it was born, and thrown from the Tower of a Noble Baron of "upper *Austria* into a ditch that was full with water ; which after "five weeks by good fortune was found and taken out. And forth- "with (he faith) the Mother not present, it being then not known "who was the Mother, when it felt the force of the external air, it be-
"gun

Hist. 6.

Append. de Cruent. Cad 3-ver. p. 143.

Hist. 7.

Ibid. p. 154.

"gun to diftil forth very fresh blood, becaufe the pores, which by rea-
"fon of the cold, were fhut that the blood could not flow, were then
"unlockt and opened by the heat of the ambient air. And thus
much of thofe that havè bled, the murtherers not being prefent.

Hift. 8.

8. Next we fhall give fome examples of thofe that have bled
when the murtherers have been brought into the prefence of the body
Obferv. l. 2. murthered or caufed to touch it, and this *Francifcus Valeriola* doth
fol. 202. atteft with an ample faith that he himfelf faw: "When (he faith)
"*James* of *Aqueria,* a Senator of *Arles,* was found dead of a wound,
"& that he that gave that wound was apprehended by the Magiftrate,
"and brought into the view of the dead body, that he might acknow-
"ledge the perfon murthered and confefs the fact, by and by the bub-
"ling blood, all the by-ftanders looking on, begun to come forth,
"with much fervour and bubbles, from the wound and the noftrils.

Hift. 9.

9. Take this other as it is cited by *Gothofredus Voigtius,* in this
Delic. Phyf. manner: "In the year 1607 the 25 of *April* a certain Shepherd in
Sect. I. Artic. I. "*Spain* being feeding his flock was flain by two Noblemen, and his
p. 5. "body thrown into a company of bufhes. The Judges of the fame
"place, having much and daily fought the Shepherd, after four
"days at length find his body in the bufhes. But becaufe that mur-
"der was committed, no witnefles being by, the fufpicion fell upon
"the two Noblemen, inhabiting in the neareft place, who being ta-
"ken were haled to the body of the perfon murthered. But what
"comes to pafs? The firft fcarce with his eyes had lookcd upon the
"dead body, but behold, the blood in plenty begun to flow from
"thence. But the other coming near, the very right hand of the
"perfon murthered did firft of all fhew to thofe that were by the
"wound, and afterward the murderer himfelf. Which being done,
"forthwith the two Gentlemen (or Nobles) did of their own accord
"confefs that they were the Authors of the murther, and did re-
"ceive the punifhment that was worthy of their deeds.

Hift. 10.

10. Another very remarkable one we have from the fame Author
Ut fupra p. 9. cited from *Cantipratanus lib. 2. mirac. c. 29.* in this manner. "It
"happened (the Author faith) in the year of Chrift 1271. in the
"Town Pfortzheim, that a certain moft wicked old Woman fa-
"miliar with the Jews, did fell them a girl of feven years old, and
"without parents, to be flain. Her therefore in fecret her mouth
"being ftopt, fetting her upon linnen cloaths, they wound almoft
"in all the junctures of the members with incifions, and with great
"endeavour prefs forth the blood, and receive it moft diligently in
"the linnen cloaths. But fhe being dead after great pains, the
"Jews throw her body into a running water near the Town, and
"laid an heap of Stones upon it. But after the third or fourth day
"her body is found by Fifhers, by means of her hand ftretched forth
"towards Heaven, and carried into the Town, the people with a-
"bomination crying forth that fo great a wickednefs was perpetra-
"ted by the Jews. And the Marquifs of *Baden* being near, went
"unto the Corps, and ftraightway the body ftanding upright did
                                                      "ftretch

" ftretch forth its hands unto the Prince, as though it would im-
" plore the revengment of blood, or perhaps mercy. But after half
" an hour it difpofed it felfupon its back, after the manner of thofe
" that are dead.   Therefore the wicked Jews being brought to the
" fpectacle, forthwith all the wounds of the body burft forth,
" and in teftimony of the horrid murder , poured forth great plen-
" ty of blood, whereupon the Jews were put to death.

   11. Another the fame Author relateth from *Jacobus Martinius* Hift. 11.
in Difp. de Cognitione fui, propl. 8. who faith : " In the year of *Ut fupra p. 54.*
" our Saviour 1503. a certain Inn-keeper, by name *Buggerlinus,* with
" whom a certain poor Merchant or Pedlar had laid up his money or
" ftock, occafion being taken by the Inn-keeper he kills him in a
" Wood, and buries him privately ; but afterwards when he was
" found, the fufpicion of the murther fell upon the Inn-keeper. For
" that Pedlar had a bended knife or dagger at his girdle, which
" they took, and fhewed to the Inn-keeper, asking him, if he knew
" it? But behold affoon as he took it in his hand it fweat drops of
" blood, whereby the murtherer being affrighted, confeffed the
" murther, and fo was Executed.

   12. We have alfo a punctual Hiftory to this purpofe, related by Hift. 12.
Hollingfhead, Stow, and Sir *Richard Baker,* from *Roger* of *Winchefter,* Vid. Hiftor.
of King *Henry* the fecond, which is this : " This King, when he Thuan. l. 32.
" was carried forth to be buried was firft apparelled in his Prince-
" ly Robes, having his Crown on his Head, Gloves on his Hands,
" and Shoes on his Feet wrought with Gold, Spurs on his Heels,
" a Ring of Gold on his Finger, a Scepter in his Hand, a Sword by
" his Side, and fo was laid uncovered having a pleafant counte-
" nance : which when it was told to his Son *Richard,* he came with
" all fpeed to fee him, and as foon as he came near him, the blood
" gufhed out of the nofe of the dead Corps in great plenty, even as
" if the fpirit of the dead King had difdained and abhorred the
" prefence of him, who was thought to be the chief caufe of his
" death.   Which thing caufed the faid *Richard* to weep bitterly,
" and he caufed his Fathers body to be honourably buried at *Fon-*
" teverard.

   14. The laft ftory that we fhall relate of this nature, is from a Hift. 13.
Minifter that is learned, fincere and of great veracity, who had it from
thofe that were eye-witneffes, and is this : " In the year of our
" Lord God, 1661. *January* 30th on *Saturday* at night about nine of
" the Clock, did *John How* of *Bruzlington-Bank,* at the foot of
" an Hill (which is about two miles diftant from *Bifhop-Awkland*) mur-
" ther *Ralph Gawkley,* who was a Glover in *Bifhop-Awkland* : This
" *How* was the next day apprehended and brought to touch *Gawk-*
" leys Corps, the lips and noftrils of the dead body wrought and
" opened as he touched (which made him afraid to touch the fe-
" cond time) then prefently the Corps bled abundantly at the no-
" ftrils in the fight of Mr. *Robert Harrifon* the Coroner (now Te-
" nant at *Bifhop-Awkland* to Mr. *Franckland,* from whom I had the

                                        " relati-

"relation) of *Anthony Cummin* and his Brother, *&c.* of the Jury,
"and of a great many towns people, who were then prefent. So
'·*How* was Executed the next Affizes after at *Durham:* Wit-
"neffes againft him were *Anne Wall*, whom he alfo wounded, yet
"fhe efcaped with her life, and *How*'s own Wife, at the motion
"of her own Father (a very honeft Man) who bid her tell the truth,
"and fhe fhould never want help.

Some may think that I have been too large and tedious in heap-
ing fo many ftories concerning the bleeding of the bodies of thofe
that have been murthered; but I did it for this reafon, becaufe there
are many that think it but to be a Fable of the credulous vulgar,
and others think that it is but an ordinary matter that happens to
any bodies that are dead, and no extraordinary or fupernatural thing
in it at all. But whofoever fhall but ufe fo much patience, as ferioufly to read and confider thefe felect Hiftories that we have recited,
may eafily be fatisfied, both that fuch bleeding is abfolutely true *de
facto*, and alfo that there is fomething more than ordinary in it, and
therefore we fhall inlarge in thefe obfervations.

Obferv. 1.   1. It will not be found to hold touch upon diligent obfervation
and ftrict inquiry, that all dead bodies do bleed frefh and rofie
blood, efpecially after the third or fourth day, or after fome weeks,
as divers of the inftances above given do manifeftly prove; and
therefore is an accident incident to fome dead bodies and not to all.
And it will as far fail, that wounded bodies, that have been flain in the
wars, after the natural heat be gone, will upon motion bleed any
frefh or crimfon blood at all; for we our felves in the late times of
Rebellion have feen fome thoufands of dead bodies, that have had
divers wounds, and lying naked and being turned over and over, and
by ten or twelve thrown into one pit, and yet not one of them have
iffued any frefh and pure blood: Only from fome of their wounds,
fome fanious matter would have flowed, putrefaction beginning by
reafon of the moifture and acidity in the air, but no pure blood,
and therefore is not a common accident to all humane bodies that
die naturally or violently, but only is peculiar to fome, and efpecially to thofe that are murthered by prepenfed malice, as appeareth in the Hiftories recited above.

Obferv. 2.   2. We fhall acknowledge with *Gregorius Horftius*, *Sperlingius*
and *Gothofredus Voigtius*, that fometimes the bodies of thofe that
have been murthered do bleed, when the murtherer is not prefent, as
is manifeft from the fixth Hiftory recited from *Horftius* of the young
Man of twenty five years old, that bled fo long and fo often,
though the murtherer was not prefent; from whence they conclude
that the prefence of the murtherer, is not a neceffary caufe of the
bleeding of the murthered body; and therefore that the bleeding
of the body is not always a certain and infallible fign of difcover-
ing the murtherer? To which we reply, that the iffuing of frefh
and crimfon blood from the wound or the noftrils of the perfons
body that hath been murthered, is always a certain fign that the

Corps

Corps that doth so bleed was murthered, because those that die naturally or violently by chance, man-slaughter or in the war, do not bleed, as hath been proved before. Again, if the murtherer be certainly known, or have confessed the crime, in regard of the final cause which is discovery, there is no reason why the Corps should bleed: And though the presence of the murtherer may not be the efficient cause why the Corps doth bleed, yet is it the occasional, as is manifest undeniably by sundry of the Histories that we have related, where the murtherers had not been certainly known but by the bleeding of the body murthered.

3. Whereas the three Authors above named, thinking they have *Observ. 3.* sufficiently confuted those that ascribed this effect of the bleeding of the dead body to Sympathy or Antipathy, or to the moving of the bodies, or heat in the air; have assigned the cause to be the beginning of putrefaction in the bodies murthered, by which a new motion is caused in the humors, and so in the blood, by which means it floweth afresh: against this these two reasons oppose themselves. 1. Must putrefaction needs begin at that very moment, when the murtherer toucheth the body? For in divers of them there was no bleeding until the murtherers were present or did touch the bodies, and their touching could not cause the beginning of putrefaction, and soon after their removing the bleeding hath ceased, so that putrescence *in fieri* cannot be the cause of the fresh bleeding. 2. Putrefaction beginning could not be the cause why the murthered Shepherds body in the ninth History should with its hands point to the wound, and to the murtherers, nor that the hands of the Wench murthered by the Jews, in the tenth History, should be stretched forth to the Prince of *Baden*, or that the Lips and Nostrils of the Body of *Gawkley* should work and open at the touch of the murtherer *How*; this must of necessity proceed from some higher cause than putrefaction, or any other they have laid down.

4. But though it should be acknowledged, that in some of these *Observ. 4.* bleedings there were something that were extraordinary or super- natural, yet as learned *Horstius* tells us: "It is (he saith) an incon- *Append. de cru.* "venient Tenent of those that hold, that the Souls of those that *Cadav. p. 154.* "are murthered, wandering about the Bodies, by reason of the ha- "tred they bear towards those that were their murtherers, do cause "these bleedings: but this in Philosophy cannot stand, because "the separate form can by no means operate upon the subject any "longer. And (he saith) the same thing in Theologie seems to be "very impious; because the Souls of the dead are without mun- "dane conversation, as is sufficiently manifest from the History of "the Rich Man and *Lazarus, Luke* 16.

"5. And if some should refer these effects immediately unto God. *Observ. 5.* "as many learned Authors have done; as though God by this "means would sometimes make known those that are guilty: or to "refer this unto the Devil, as though he would sometimes elude

R r 2 "the

"the Judges, and to do this that so the innocent might be punish-
"ed with the wicked ; We answer (he saith) to this briefly,by add-
"ing this only, that a supernatural cause is not rashly to be feigned
"where a natural one is ready at hand.   And if there be such ex-
"amples, which cannot be reduced to these aforesaid natural cau-
"ses, of which sort many are related by *Libanius part* 2. *fol.* 172.
"then we can by no reason be repugnant, but that they are preter-
"naturally brought to pass. And of this opinion are most of the Pontificial Writers, that thereby they might the better maintain their
Tenent, that miracles are not ceased ; though we do not understand
that if we should grant, that in these things there should be some
concurrence of Divine Power more than ordinary, that therefore it
must be a miracle, for it is yet not infallibly concluded what a miracle is, and every wonderful thing is not therefore concluded to
be a miracle, and a miracle being not absolutely defined, what is not
one cannot be certainly resolved.

Observ. 6.   6. Some there are that ascribe these strange bleedings of murthered bodies, and of their strange motions, with the sweating of blood,
as upon the Pedlars bended dagger or knife, mentioned in the ele-
venth History, unto the Astral or Sydereal spirit (and that not im-
probably ;) that being a middle substance, betwixt the Soul and the
Body doth, when separated from the Body, wander or hover near
about it, bearing with it the irascible and concupiscible faculties,
wherewith being stirred up to hatred and revenge, it causeth that
ebullition and motion in the blood, that exudation of blood upon
the weapon, and those other wonderful motions of the Body, Hands,
Nostrils and Lips, thereby to discover the murtherer, and bring
him to condign punishment.   Neither is any Tenent yet brought by
any, that is more rationally probable to solve these and many other
wonderful Phenomena's than this of the Astral Spirit, if it can be
but fully proved that there is such a part of Man that doth separately exist, which we shall endeavour to prove ere we end this
Chapter.

Observ. 7.   7. But it is granted upon all sides, that if the murtherer be brought
to the presence, or touch of the person murthered, and not quite
dead, that then the wounds though closed and staid from bleeding,
or the nostrils, will freshly break forth and bleed plentifully.   The
reason is obvious, because the Soul being yet in the Body, retaining its power of sensation, fancy and understanding, will easily
have a presension of the murderer, and then no marvail that through
the vehement desire of revenge, the irascible and concupiscible faculties do strongly move the blood, that before was beginning to
be stagnant, to motion and ebullition, and may exert so much force
upon the organs as for some small time to move the whole body,
the hands, or the lips and nostrils.   So that all that is to be done,
is but to prove, that the person murthered is not absolutely dead,
and that the Soul is not totally separated or departed forth of the
Body, and this we shall do by undeniable proofs, as are these that follow in this order.   1. Though

1. Though we generally take death to be a perfect separation of the Soul from the Body, which is most certainly a great truth, yet when this is certainly brought to pass, is a most difficult point to ascertain, because that when the Soul ceases to operate in the Body so as to be perceived by our Senses, it will not follow; that therefore the Soul is absolutely departed and separated.

2. It is manifest that many persons through this mistake have in the times of the Plague been buried quick, and so have some Women been dealt withal that lay but in fits of the suffocation of the Womb, and yet were taken to be dead. So that from the judgment of our Senses, no certain conclusion can be made that the Soul is totally departed, because it goeth away invisibly; for many that not only to the judgment of the vulgar, but even in the opinion of learned Physicians, have been accounted dead, yet have revived, *Observ. Medic. p. 617, 618.* as learned *Schenckius* hath furnished us with this story from *Georgius Pictorius*, "that a certain Woman lay in a fit of the Strangula-"tion of the Womb, for six continual days without sense or moti-"on, the arteries being grown hard, ready to be buried, and yet "revived again, and from *Paræus* of some that have lain three days "in Hysterical suffocations, and yet have recovered, and of divers "others that may be seen in the place quoted in the Margent.

3. So that though the organs of the Body may by divers means, either natural or violent, be rendered so unfit, that the Soul cannot perform its accustomed functions in them, or by them; so as they may be perceptible to our senses, or judgments; yet will not that at all conclude, that the Soul is separated, and departed quite from the Body, much less can we be able to define or set down the precise time of the Souls abode in the Body, nor the ultimate period when it must depart, for the union may be (and doubtless is) more strong in some than in others, and the Lamp of life far sooner and more easily to be quenched in some than in others. And the Soul may have a far greater amorosity to stay in some Body that is lively, sweet, and young, than in others that are already decaying and beginning to putrifie, and it may in all probability both have power and desire to stay longer in that lovesome habitation, from whence it is driven away by force, especially that it may satisfie it self in discovering of the murderer, the most cruel and inhumane disjoyner of that loving pair that God had divinely coupled together, and to see it self, before its final departure, in a hopeful way to be revenged.

4. If we physically consider the union of the Soul with the Body by the mediation of the Spirit, then we cannot rationally conceive that the Soul doth utterly forsake that union, untill by putrefaction, tending to an absolute mutation, it be forced to bid farewel to its beloved Tabernacle; for its not operating *ad extra* to our senses, doth not necessarily inferr its total absence. And it may be that there is more in that of *Abels blood crying unto the Lord from the ground*, in a Physical sense, than is commonly conceived, and

and God may in his juft judgment fuffer the Soul to ftay longer in the murthered Body, that the cry of blood may make known the murtherer, or may not fo foon, for the fame reafon, call it totally away.

There is another kind of fuppofed Apparitions, that are believed to be done in Beryls, and clear Cryftals, and therefore called by *Paracelfus Ars Berylliftica*, and which he alfo calls Nigromancy, becaufe it is practifed in the dark by the infpection of a Boy or a Maid that are Virgins, and this he ftrongly affirmeth to be natural and lawful, and only brought to pafs by the Sydereal influence, and not at all Diabolical, nor ftands in need of any Conjuration, Invocations or Ceremonies, but is performed by a ftrong faith or imagination. And of this he faith thus : *Sed ante omnia (ait) notate* *Explic. Aftro. p. 654.* *proprietatem Beryllorum. Hi funt, in quibus fpectantur præterita, præfentia, & futura. Quod nemini admirationi effe debet, ideò, quia fydus influentiæ imaginem, & fimilitudinem in Cryftallum imprimit, fimilem ei, de quo quæritur.* And a little after he faith : *Præterea fyderibus nota funt omnia, quæ in natura exiftunt. Cumq; Aftra homini fubjecta fint : poteft is utiq; illa in fubjectum ita cogere, ut voluntati ejus ipfa obfecundent.* What truth there may be in this his affertion, I have yet met with no reafons or experiments that can give me fatisfaction, and therefore I leave it to every Man to cenfure as he pleafeth.

Hift.

The only ftory that feems to carry any credit with it, touching the truth of Apparitions in Cryftals, is that which is related of that great and learned Phyfician *Joachimus Camerarius* in his Preface before *Plutarchs* Book *De Defectu Oraculorum*, from the mouth of *Laffarus Spenglerus*, a perfon excellent both for Piety and Prudence, and is in effect this : " *Spengler* faid, that there was one " perfon of a chief family in *Norimberge*, an honeft and grave Man, " whom he thought not fit to name. That one time he came unto " him, and brought, wrapt in a piece of Silk, a Cryftalline Gemm " of a round figure, and faid that it was given unto him of a cer- " tain ftranger, whom many years before, having defired of him en- "tertainment, meeting him in the Market, he took home, and "kept him three days with him. And that this gift when he de- "parted, was left him as a fign of a grateful mind, having taught " fuch an ufe of the Cryftal as this. If he defired to be made more " certain of any thing, that he fhould draw forth the glafs, and will " a male chaft Boy to look in it, and fhould afk of him what he "did fee? For it fhould come to pafs, that all things that he requi- "red, fhould be fhewed to the Boy, and feen in the Apparition. "And this Man did affirm, that he was never deceived in any one "thing, and that he had underftood wonderful things by the boys " indication, when none of all the reft did by looking into it, fee " it to be any thing elfe but a neat and pure Gemm. He tells a great " deal more of it, and that doubtful queftions being afked, an an- "fwer would appear to be read in the Cryftal: but the Man being
                                                              "weary

" weary of the ufe of it, did give it to *Spengler,* who being a great
" hater of fuperftition, did caufe it to be broken into fmall pieces,
" and fo with the Silk in which it was wrapped, threw it into the
" fink of the Houfe.

I confefs I have heard ftrange ftories of things that have been revealed by thefe fuppofed apparitions, from perfons both of great
worth and learning; but feeking more narrowly into the matter I
found them all to be fuperftitious delufions, fancies, miftakes, cheats
and impoftures. For the moft part the child tells any thing that
comes into his fancy, or doth frame and invent things upon purpofe,
that he never feeth at all, and the inquirers do prefently affimilate
them to their own thoughts and fufpicions. Some that pretended
to fhew and foretel ftrange things thereby to get money, have been
difcovered to have had confederates, that conveied away mens goods
into fecret places, and gave the cunning Man notice where they
were hid, and then was the child taught a ftraight framed tale, to
defcribe what a like Man took them away, and where they were,
which being found brought credit enough to the couzeners, and
this I knew was practifed by one *Brooke* and *Bolton.* Some have had
artificial glaffes, whereinto they would convey little pictures, as
Dr. *Lambe* had.

It being manifeft by what we have laid down that there are apparitions and fome fuch other ftrange effects, whereby murthers are
often made known and difcovered, and alfo having mentioned that it
may be moft rationally probable that they are caufed by the Aftral
or Sydereal Spirit, it will be neceffary to open and explain that
point, and to fhew what grounds it hath, upon which it may be
fettled, which we fhall do in this order.

1. There are many (efpecially Popifh Authors thereby to uphold their Doctrine of Purgatory) that maintain that they are the
Souls of the perfons murthered and deceafed, and this opinion,
though unanfwerably confuted by the whole company of reformed Divines, is notwithftanding revived by Dr. *Henry Moore,* but
by no arguments either brought from Scripture, or grounded upon any folid reafons, but only fome weak conjectures, feeming abfurdities, and Platonick whimfies, which (indeed) merit no refponfion. And we have by pofitive and unwrefted Scriptures, in
this Treatife afore proved, that the Souls of the righteous are in
Abrahams bofom with Chrift at peace and reft, and that the Souls
of the wicked are in Hell in torments, fo that neither of them do
wander here, or make any apparitions; for as S. *Auguftine* taught
us: *Duo funt habitacula, unum in igne æterno, alterum in regno
æterno.* And in another place: *Nec eft ulli ullus medius locus, ut
poffit effe nifi cum Diabolo, qui non eft cum Chrifto.* And *Tertullian* and *Juftin Martyr,* two moft ancient writers do tell us: "That
" Souls being feparated from their Bodies, do not ftay or linger up-
" on the earth: And after they be defcended into the infernal pit,
" they do neither wander here upon their own accord, nor by the

*Immort. of the
Soul. c. 16.
fect. 8. p. 296.*

*De Verb. Apoft.
lib. Serm. 18.
Idem contr. Pe-
lag. c. 28. Tom. 7.*

" power

"power and command of others; But that wicked spirits may coun-
"terfeit by craft that they are the Souls of the dead, *Vid. Lavate-*
"*rum de Spectris secunda parte c. 5.*

2. We have also shewed that these apparitions that discover
murther and murtherers and brings them to condign punishment,
cannot be the evil Angels, because they are only Ministers of torture, sin, horror and punishment, but are not Authors of any good
either Corporeal or Spiritual, apparent or real. So that it must of
necessity be left either to be acted by a Divine Power, and that either by the immediate power of the Almighty, for which we have
no proof, but only may acknowledge the possibility of it ; or mediate by the ministery of good Angels, which is hard to prove,
there being no one instance, or the least intimation of any such matter in all the Scriptures, and therefore in most rational probability,
either relations of matters of fact of this nature are utterly false, or
they are effected by the Astral spirit.

3. Concerning the description of this Astral Spirit or Sydereal
Body, (for though it be as a spirit, or the image in the looking-glass,
yet it is truly corporeal) we shall give the sum of it, as *Paracelsus*
in his magisterial way, without proof doth lay down. "He posi-
"tively holdeth that there are three essential parts in Man, which
"he calleth the three great substances, and that at death every one
"of these being separated, doth return into, or unto the Womb
"from whence it came ; as The Soul that was breathed in by God,
"doth at death return unto God that gave it : And that the Body,
"that is to say, that gross part that seems to be composed of the two
"inferior Elements of Earth and Water, doth return unto the Earth,
"and there in time consume away, some bodies in a longer time,
"some in a shorter : But the third part which he calleth the Astral
"Spirit, or Sydereal Body, as being firmamental, and consisting of
"the two superior Elements of Air and Fire, it (he saith) returneth
"into its Sepulcher of the Air, where in time it is also consumed,
"but requireth a longer time than the body, in regard it consisteth
"of more pure Elements than the other, and that one of these A-
"stral Spirits or Bodies doth consume sooner than another, as they
"are more impure, or pure. And that it is this spirit that carrieth a-
"long with it the thoughts, cogitations, desires and imaginations
"that were impressed upon the mind at the time of death, with the
"sensitive faculties of concupiscibility and irascibility. And that
"it is this spirit or body (and not the Soul that resteth in the hands of
"the Lord) that appeareth, and is most usually conversant in those
"places, and those negotiations that the mind of the person living
"(whose spirit it was) did most earnestly follow, and especially
"those things that at the very point of death, were most strongly
"impressed upon this spirit, as in the case of the person murthered,
"whose mind in the very minute of the murther, receiveth a most
"deep impression of detestation and revenge against the murtherer,
"which this spirit bearing with it, doth by all means possible seek
"the

Vid. lib. Sagac.
Philos. passim.

"the accomplishment of that revenge, and therefore doth cause
"dreams of discovery, bleedings and strange motions of the body
"murthered, and sometimes plain apparitions of the persons mur-
"thered, in their usual shape and habit, and doth vocally and au-
"dibly reveal the murther with all the circumstances, as is apparent
in the two forementioned Histories of the apparition of *Fletcher*
to *Raynard*, and of the Woman murthered by *Mark Sharp*, to the
Miller *Grimes*.

4. And this Astral Spirit is no more than that part in Man that is commonly called the sensitive Soul, and by the Schools is commonly defined thus: *Anima sentiens est vis, quæ apprehendit & percipit ea quæ ex-
"tra ipsam sunt.* And this is corporeal, and (as Dr. *Willis* holdeth) *De Anim. Brut.*
"mortal and coextended with the Body, and that it hath the power *c. 1, 2.*
"of imagination, appetite, desire, and aversion and the like, and in a
"manner, a sensitive way of ratiocination, and yet is distinct from the
"rational Soul or *Mens* that is incorporeal, immortal, and far more ex-
"cellent. And perspicacious *Helmont* holding this sensitive Soul to
be distinct from the *mens* or immortal and rational Soul, saith thus:
*Est ergo anima sensitiva, caduca, mortalis, mera lux vitalis data à
patre luminum, nec alio modo verboq; explicabilis.* But of the rational Soul he saith: *Ipsa autem mens immortalis, est substantia lu-
cida, incorporea, immediate Dei sui imaginem referens, quia eandem in creando, sive in ipso Empsychosis instanti, sibi insculptam sus-
cepit.* So that both these late and learned Authors hold, that in
every Man there are two distinct Souls, the sensitive that is mortal,
corporeal, and coextended with the Body, and the rational, that
is immortal and absolutely incorporeal: so that though in words
and terms they seem to differ, yet in substance they agree. For
the Hermetick School, the Platonists, *Paracelsus, Jacob Behemen,*
and others do hold three parts in Man which they call, Soul, Spirit and Body, and these two last Authors do hold the body to be
one part in Man, and two Souls besides, the sensitive and rational
that are two distinct parts, the one corporeal and mortal, and the
other incorporeal and immortal, and so they do but nominally
differ. And now our task must be to prove, that first there are
such three parts in Man, and that after death they do separately exist, which we shall attempt in this order.

1. Though arguments taken *à notatione nominis*, do not necessarily prove, yet they illustrate, and render the case plain and intelligible; and we shall find that the *Hebrews* have three distinct appellations for these three parts. As for the Soul, either rational or
sensitive, or vital spirit, they use *Nephesh* which is common to brutes
and reptiles as well as to Man, as saith the Text: *And to every beast Gen. 1. 30.
of the earth, and to every fowl of the air, and to every thing that
creepeth upon the earth in which there is a living soul, Nephesh Haiah.*
And therefore to distinguish the rational and immortal Soul, from
this which is sensitive, mortal and common with brutes, the Text
saith: *And the Lord God formed man of the dust of the earth, and*
S s   'breathed

breathed into his nostrils the breath of life, and man became a living soul. Upon which *Tremellius* gives us this note: *Vt clarius appareret discrimen quod est inter animam hominis, & reliquorum animantium : Horum enim animæ ex eadem materia provenerunt, unde corpora habebant, illius verò anima spiritale quiddam est & Divinum.* And upon the words; *Sic fuit homo. Id est (ait) hac ratione factum est, ut terrea illa statua animata viveret.* Another word they use, which is *Ruah,* and this is also generally attributed

Eccles. 3. 21.

to Men and Beasts, as the words of *Solomon* do witness. *Who knoweth the spirit of man that goeth upwards, and the spirit of the beast that goeth downward to the earth?* And in both these, touching both Man and Beast, the word *Ruah* is used as common to them both; and sometimes it is taken specially for the rational immor-

Ibid. 12. 7.

tal Soul, as, *And the spirit shall return unto God who gave it.* Also they have the word *Niblah,* and *Basar,* that is, *corpus, caro,* or *cadaver,* and by these three they set forth, or distinguish these three parts. And the Grecians have likewise their three several names for these parts, as ψυχὴ, *anima, vita,* which is taken promiscuously sometimes for the rational and immortal Soul, as in this

Matth. 10. 28.

place; *And fear not them which kill the body, but are not able to kill the soul: but rather fear him which is able to destroy both soul and body in hell.* And it is taken for the life in that of the *Acts:*

Acts 20. 10.

And Paul said, Trouble not your selves, his life is in him. Also they have the word Πνεῦμα, *Spiritus, ventus, spiritus vitæ,* being variously taken, yet sometimes for the rational and immortal Soul,

Luke 23. 46.

as *Father into thy hands I commend my spirit.* So they have the word Σῶμα, *Corpus,* the body or gross and fleshly part. And to these accord the three Latine terms for these three distinct parts; *Anima, Spiritus* and *Corpus.*

2. This opinion of these three parts in Man, to wit Body, Soul and Spirit, is neither new, nor wants Authors of sufficient credit and learning to be its Patrons. For *Hermes Trismegistus* an Author

Mens ad Herm. p. 21.

almost of the greatest Antiquity saith thus: καὶ ὁ μὲν Θεὸς ἐν τῷ νῷ, ὁ δὲ νοῦς ἐν τῇ ψυχῇ, ἡ δὲ ψυχὴ ἐν τῇ ὕλη. That is, *God is in the mind, the mind in the soul, and the soul in matter.* But *Marsilius Ficinus* gives it

Pimand. c. 12. p. mihi 451.

thus: *Beatus Deus, Dæmon bonus, animam esse in corpore, mentem in anima, in mente verbum pronunciavit.* And further addeth: *Deus verò circa omnia, simul atq; per omnia, mens circa animam, anima circa aërem, aër circa materiam.* And some give it more fully thus. *God is in the mind, the mind in the Soul, the Soul in the Spirit, the Spirit in the blood, and the blood in the Body.* But besides this ancient testimony, it is apparent that the whole School of the Platonists, both the elder and later were of this opinion, and also the most of the Cabalists: For *Ficinus* from the Doctrine of of *Plato* tells us this: *Humanæ cogitationis domicilium anima ip-*

Comment. in Conviv. Platon. p. 400.

sa est. Animæ domicilium spiritus. Domicilium spiritus hujus est corpus. But omitting multitudes of others that are strong Champions for this Tenent, we think for authorities to acquiesce in that

of

of our moſt learned Phyſician and Anatomiſt Dr. *Willis*, and in thoſe that he hath quoted, which we ſhall give in the Engliſh: Firſt he ſaith : "Leſt I be tedious in rehearſing many, it pleaſeth "me here only to cite two Authors (but either of which is a Troop) "for the confutation of the contrary opinion. The one (he ſaith) "is the moſt famous Philoſopher *Petrus Gaſſendus*, who *Phyſic. ſect.* "3. *lib. 9. c.* 11. doth divide, *toto Cælo*, (as is ſaid) the mind of "man, from the other ſenſitive power, as much as is poſſible to be "done, by many and moſt ſignal notes of diſcrimination, yea diſ-"joining of them (as it is ſaid in the Schools) by ſpecific differen-"ces : Becauſe when he had ſhewed this to be corporeal, extended, "naſcible and corruptible, he ſaith the other is an incorporeal ſub-"ſtance, and therefore immortal, which is immediately created, "and infuſed into the body by God ; to which opinion he ſheweth "*Pythagoras, Plato, Ariſtotle*, and for the moſt part all the ancient "Philoſophers, except *Epicurus*, did much agree; excepting not-"withſtanding that they did hold, as not knowing the origin of "the Soul, which they judged to be immortal, that it being cropt "off from the ſoul of the world, did ſlide into the body, and that it "was poured again into the Soul of the world either immediately, or "at the laſt mediately, after its tranſmigration into other bodies.

The other ſuffrage (he ſaith) upon this matter, is of the moſt learned Divine Dr. *Hamond*, our Countryman, who opening the Text *Epiſt. Theſſalo.* 1. *c.* 5. *v.* 23. to wit, *your whole ſpirit and ſoul and body &c.* "He ſaith that Man is divided into three parts. "1. To wit, into the body, by which is denoted the fleſh and the "members. 2. Into the vital ſoul, which in like manner being ani-"mal and ſenſitive is common to man with the bruits. 3. Into the "ſpirit, by which the rational ſoul, that was firſt created of God, "is ſignified, which alſo being immortal doth return unto God. "*Annot. in Nov. Teſtam. lib. p.*711. This his expoſition he con-firmeth by Teſtimonies brought from Ethnick Authors, and alſo from the ancient Fathers. From all which the learned Dr. doth make this concluſion: "And from the things above (he ſaith) it is "moſt evidently manifeſt, that man being as it were an Amphibious "animal, or of a middle nature and order betwixt the Angels and "bruits, with theſe he doth communicate by a corporeal ſoul, fra-"med of the vital blood and the ſtock of animal ſpirit, joyned "likewiſe in one ; and with the other he communicates by an in-"telligent ſoul immaterial and immortal. And thus much for ar-guments brought from humane authority, which are prevalent, if they be brought affirmatively (as theſe are) from learned men or Artificers, and ſo we ſhall proceed to further kind of proofs.

Ibid. p. 74.

3. But an argument ariſing from Divine Authority is of the moſt force of all, and therefore let us a little ſurvey the Text it ſelf, which in our Engliſh Tranſlation is thus: *And the very God of peace ſanctifie you wholly : And I pray God your whole Spirit, and Soul, and Body be preſerved blameleſs, unto the coming of our Lord*

1 Theſ. 5. 23.

Lord Jesus Christ. The Apostle having given the believing *Thessalonians* all the spiritual counsel that could be necessary, to bring them to the perfection of sanctification, doth pray for them, that the God of peace would sanctifie them wholly, or as the word ὁλοτελεῖς signifieth (as *Arias Montanus* hath rendered it) *omninò perfectos,* altogether perfect; And that the whole, ἐλόκληρον, that is the whole part, portion or lot (for so the word properly signifieth) which he nameth by *Spirit, Soul and Body, to be preserved blameless, unto the coming of our Lord Jesus Christ.* And therefore to this doth learned *Beza* add this note: "*Tum demùm igitur (ait)* "*homo integer sanctificatus fuerit, quum nihil cogitabit spiritus,* "*nihil appetet anima, nihil exequetur corpus, quod cum Dei volun-* '*tate non consentiat.* And before he had said: Therefore *Paul* by "the appellation of spirit doth signifie the mind, in which the "principal stain lieth: and by the Soul the rest of the inferior fa- "culties, and by the body the domicile of the Soul. And in ano-
Ephes. 4. 17. "ther place he saith: The mind is become vain, the cogitation ob- "scured, the appetite hardened. And to the same purpose doth learned *Rollock* upon the place say thus much: "Sanctification, or "transformation is not of any one part, but of all the parts, and of "the whole man. For there is no part or particle in man, which "was not deformed in that first fall, and made as it were monstrous. "Therefore μεταμόρφωσις, or transformation ought to be of the whole "man and of every singular part of him. And further he saith: For "the whole man the Apostle hath here the enumeration of his prin- "cipal parts. And they are three in number, Spirit, Soul and Body. "By the spirit (he saith) I understand the mind, which the Apostle "*Eph.* 4. 24. calleth *the spirit of the mind,* and this is no other "thing than the faculty of the rational mind, which is discerned "in invention, and in judging of things found out. By the name "of soul (he saith) I understand all those inferior faculties of the "mind, as are the animal which are also called natural. The body "doth follow these parts, to wit that gross part which is the in- "strument by which the spirit and soul do exert their functions and "operations. By all which it is most clear, that though they call them faculties, yet they are distinct essential parts of the whole man, which is most manifest, in that the body, though one of these three, cannot be a faculty, but a meer instrument, and yet is one of the essential parts, that doth integrate the whole man. But whosoever shall seriously consider, how little satisfaction the defi- nition of a faculty given by either Philosophers or Physicians, will bring to a clear understanding, may easily perceive, that distinct parts are commonly taken to be faculties.

4. The first argument that this learned Physician urgeth, to prove that there are two Souls in man, the one sensitive and corporeal, the other rational, immortal and incorporeal, is in this order. "But
Ut supra c. 7. *p. 74.* "(he saith) whereas it is said that the rational soul doth by it self "exercise every of the animal faculties, it is most of all improbable, "because

'becaufe the actions and paffions of all the animal fenfes and moti-
"ons are corporeal, divided and extended to various parts, to per-
" form which immediately the incorporeal and indivifible foul (if
" fo be it be finite) feemeth unfit or unable. Further (he faith)
" what belongeth unto that vulgar opinion, that the fenfitive foul
" is fubordinate to the rational, and as it were fwallowed up of it,
" that that which is the foul in brutes, in man becomes a meer pow-
" er; thefe are the trifles of the Schools. For how fhould the fen-
" fitive foul of man, which before hath been in act a fubfiftent, ma-
" terial and extended fubftance, lofing its effence, at the advent of
" the rational foul, degenerate into a meer qualitie? But if it be
" afferted that the rational foul, by its advent alfo doth introduce
" life and fenfation, then man doth not generate an animated man,
" but only a formlefs body, or a rude heap of flefh.

 5. Another argument he ufeth to prove thefe two fouls in man
is this: "Therefore (he faith) it being fuppofed that the rational
" foul doth come to the body before animated of the other corpo-
" real foul, we may inquire, by what band or tye, feeing it is a pure
" fpirit, can it be united to this, feeing it hath not parts, by which
" it might be tied, or adhere to the whole or any of the parts? And
" therefore he thinketh that concerning this point it is to be faid
" with moft learned *Gaffendus*: That the corporeal foul is the im-
" mediate fubject of the rational foul, of which feeing it is the act,
" perfection, complement and form, alfo by it the rational foul is
" made or becometh the form and act of the humane body. But
" feeing that it doth fcarce feem like or neceffary, that the whole
" corporeal foul fhould be poffeffed of the whole rational foul;
" Therefore it is lawful to determine that this rational foul, being
" purely fpiritual, fhould refide as in its Throne, in the principal
" part or faculty of it, to wit in the imagination, framed of a fmall
" portion of the animal fpirits, being moft fubtile, and feated in the
" very middle or center of the brain.

 6. Another chief argument that he ufeth to prove thefe two
fouls in man, is the ftrife and difagreements that are within man:
"Becaufe (he faith) the intellect and imagination are not wont to
" agree in fo many things, but that alfo the fenfitive appetite doth
" diffent in more things: From whofe litigations moreover it fhall
" be lawful to argue, that the moodes of the aforefaid fouls, both
" in refpect of fubfifting and operating, are diftinct. For as there is
" in man a double cognitive power, to wit the intellect and ima-
" gination, fo there is a double appetite, the Will proceeding from
" the Intellect, which is the Page or fervant of the rational foul,
" and the fenfitive Appetite, which cohering to the imagination,
" is faid to be the hands, or procuratrix of the corporeal foul.

 7. To thefe we fhall add, that when the underftanding is truly
enlightened with the fpirit of God, and led by the true light of the
Gofpel, in the ways of Chrift, then is man faid to be fpiritual, becaufe the carnal mind and the fenfitive appetite are fubdued and
brought

brought under to the obedience of Chriſt by his grace. So alſo when
Epheſ. 4. 18. the underſtanding is darkned, as ſaith the Apoſtle; *Having the un-*
derſtanding darkened, being alienated from the life of God thorow
the ignorance that is in them, becauſe of the blindneſs of their hearts.
Then man becomes wholly led with the carnal and ſenſual appetite, and is therefore called ψυχικὸς ἄνθρωπος, the natural, animal or
ſoully man: And in both theſe conditions the organical body is
led and acted according to the ruling power, either of the Spirit
of God, and ſo it is yielded up a living ſacrifice to God; or of the
ſpirit of darkneſs, corruption, and the ſenſitive appetite, and ſo is an
inſtrument of all unrighteouſneſs. By all which it is moſt manifeſt
that there are in man theſe three parts, of Body, Soul, and Spirit,
which was the thing undertaken to be proved.

    8. Laſtly as to this point, it is a certain truth that two extreams
cannot be joined or coupled together, but by ſome middle thing
that participateth or cometh near to the nature of both. So the
Soul which (by the unanimous conſent of all men) is a ſpiritual
and pure, immaterial and incorporeal ſubſtance cannot be united to
the body, which is a moſt groſs, thick and corporeal ſubſtance,
without the intervention of ſome middle nature, fit to conjoin and
unite thoſe extreams together, which is this ſenſitive and corporeal
Soul or Aſtral Spirit, which in reſpect of the one extream incorporeal, yet of the moſt pure ſort of bodies that are in nature, and
that which approacheth moſt near to a ſpiritual and immaterial
ſubſtance, and therefore moſt fit to be the immediate receptacle of
the incorporeal Soul: And alſo it being truly body doth eaſily
join with the groſs body, as indeed being congenerate with it, and
ſo becomes *vinculum & nexus* of the immaterial Soul and the more
groſs body, that without it could not be united.

    Now having (as we conceive) ſufficiently proved that there are
in man theſe three diſtinct parts of Body, Soul, and Spirit, in the next
place we are to ſhew that theſe three may, and do ſeparately exiſt,
and that we ſhall endeavour by theſe reaſons.

Reaſ. 1.
Eccl. 12. 7.

2 Cor. 5. 1.
    1. It is manifeſt by Divine Authority that *the ſpirit*, that is the
rational, immortal and incorporeal *ſoul, doth return to God that*
gave it. That is not to be annihilated or to vaniſh into nothing,
but to abide and remain for ever or eviternally. For the Apoſtle
ſaith: *For we know, that if our earthly tabernacle or houſe were*
diſſolved, we have a building of God, an houſe not made with hands,
eternal in the heavens. By which it is manifeſt that the immaterial
Soul doth exiſt eternally *ex parte poſt*, as the Schools ſay, and alſo
the groſs body being ſeparated from the immortal Soul, doth by
it ſelf exiſt until it be conſumed in the grave, or by corruption be
changed into earth, or ſome other things, or that the Atomes be
diſperſed, and joined unto, or figurated into ſome other bodies.
So it is moſt highly rational that this ſenſitive Soul, or Aſtral Spirit, which is corporeal, ſhould alſo exiſt by it ſelf for ſome time,
until it be diſſipated and waſted, in which time it may (and doubtleſly

leſly doth) make theſe apparitions, motions and bleedings of the murthered bodies.

2. Upon the ſuppoſition that the rational Soul be not *ex traduce,* *Reaſ.* 2. but be infuſed after the bodily organs be fitted and prepared, which is the firm Tenent of all Divines Ancient, middle and Modern, and muſt upon the granting of it to be ſimply, and abſolutely immaterial and incorporeal (which is indiſputable) of neceſſity be infuſed, becauſe no immaterial ſubſtance can be produced or generated by the motion of any agent, that is meerly material, or forth of any material ſubſtance whatſoever. And therefore I ſay that the Soul being infuſed, it muſt of neceſſity follow the organized body, that could not exiſt (except as a lump of fleſh) without the corporeal ſenſitive ſoul; which muſt of neceſſity demonſtrate, that as they did ſeparately exiſt before the union of the Soul and Body, ſo they alſo do exiſt diſtinctly after their ſeparation by death; and ſo the Aſtral Spirit may effect the things we have aſſerted.

3. And if the experiment be certainly true that is averred by *Bo-* *Reaſ.* 3. *rellus, Kircher, Gaffarel,* and others (who might be aſhamed to affirm it as their own trial, or as ocular witneſſes, if not true) that the figures and colours of a plant may be perfectly repreſented, and ſeen in glaſſes, being by a little heat raiſed forth of the aſhes. Then (if this be true) it is not only poſſible, but rational, that animals as well as plants, have their Ideas or Figures exiſting after the groſs body or parts be deſtroyed, and ſo theſe apparitions are but only thoſe Aſtral ſhapes and figures. But alſo there are ſhapes and apparitions of Men, that muſt of neceſſity prove that theſe corpo- *Hiſtor. rarior.* real Souls or Aſtral Spirits do exiſt apart, and attend upon or are *Obſ. 62. p. 325,* near the blood, or bodies; of which *Borellus* Phyſician to the King *326.* of *France,* gives us theſe two relations.

1. *N. de Richier* a Soap-maker (he ſaith) and *Bernardus Ger- Hiſt.* 1. *manus* from the relation of the Lord of *Gerzan,* and others, diſtilling mans blood at *Paris,* which they thought to be the true matter of the Philoſophers-ſtone; they ſaw in the cucurbit or glaſs body, the Phantaſm, or ſhape of a Man, from whom bloody rayes did ſeem to proceed, and the glaſs being broken they found the figure as though of a ſkull, in the remaining fæces.

2. There were three curious perſons alſo at *Paris,* that taking *Hiſt.* 2. the Church earth-mould from S. *Innocents* Church, ſuppoſing it to be the matter of the ſtone, did diſtill it and work upon it, and in the glaſſes they did perceive certain Phantaſms or Shapes of Men, of which they were no little afraid.

3. Our Countryman Dr. *Flud* a perſon of much learning and *Hiſt.* 3. great ſincerity, doth tell us this well atteſted ſtory: " That a cer- *De Myſt. Sang.* " tain Chymical Operator, by name *La Pierre,* near that place in *Pa- Anatom. c. 6.* " *ris* called *Le Temple,* received blood from the hands of a certain *p. 233.* " Biſhop to operate upon. Which he ſetting to work upon the *Sa-* " *turday,* did continue it for a week with divers degrees of fire, " and that about midnight the *Friday* following, this Artificer ly-

"ing

" ing in a Chamber next to his Laboratory, betwixt sleeping and
" waking, heard an horrible noise, like unto the lowing of Kine,
" or the roaring of a Lion; and continuing quiet, after the ceasing
" of the sound in the Laboratory, the Moon being at the full by
" shining enlightening the Chamber, suddenly betwixt himself and
" the Window he saw a thick little cloud, condensed into an oval
" form, which after by little and little did seem compleatly to put
" on the shape of a Man, and making another and a sharp clamour,
" did suddenly vanish.   And that not only some Noble Persons in
" the next Chambers, but also the Host with his Wife, lying in a
" lower room of the house, and also the neighbors dwelling in the
" opposite side of the street, did distinctly hear as well the bellow-
" ing as the voice, and some of them were awaked with the vehe-
" mency thereof.   But the Artificer said that in this he found so-
" lace, because the Bishop of whom he had it, did admonish him,
" that if any of them from whom the blood was extracted, should
" die in the time of its putrefaction, his Spirit was wont often to ap-
" pear to the sight of the Artificer, with perturbation.   Also forth-
" with upon *Saturday* following he took the retort from the Fur-
" nace and broke it with the light stroak of a little key, and there
" in the remaining blood found the perfect representation of an hu-
" mane head, agreeable in face, eyes, nostrils, mouth and hairs,
" that were somewhat thin and of a golden colour.   And of this last
" there were many ocular witnesses, as the Noble Person Lord of
" *Bourdalone*, the Chief Secretary to the Duke of *Guise*, and that
" he had this relation from the Lord of *Menanton* living in that house
" at the same time, from a certain Doctor of Physick, from the owner
" of the house, and many others.

So that it is most evident that there are not only three essential,
and distinct parts in Man, as the gross body, consisting of Earth and
Water, which at death returns to the earth again, the sensitive and corporeal Soul, or Astral Spirit, consisting of Fire and Air, that at
death wandereth in the air, or near the body, and the immortal and incorporeal Soul that immediately returns to God that gave
it: But also that after death they all three exist separately; the Soul
in immortality, and the body in the earth, though soon consuming;
and the Astral spirit that wanders in the air, and without doubt
doth make these strange apparitions, motions, and bleedings; and so
we conclude this tedious discourse with the Chapter.

CHAP.

CHAP. XVII.

Of the force and efficacy of Words or Charms, whether they effect any thing at all or not, and if they do, whether it be by Natural or Diabolical virtue and force.

THere is nothing almost so common not only in the Poets (who have been the chief disseminators of many such things) but in most of other Authors, as the mention of the force of Charms and Incantations: And yet if we narrowly search into the bottom of the matter, there is nothing more difficult than to find out any truth of the effects of them, in matters of fact; and therefore that we may more clearly manifest what we have proposed in this Chapter, we shall first premise these few things.

1. Those that take the effects of them to be great. as many Divines, Philosophers, and Physicians do, suppose no efficacy in them solely, holding that *quantitates rerum nullius sunt efficaciæ,* but that they are only signs from the Devil to delude the minds of those that use them, and in the mean time that the Devil doth produce the effects. But it had been well, if those that are of this opinion, had shewed us the ways and means how the Devil doth operate such things, seeing he can do nothing in corporeal matter but by natural means : So that either we must confess that there is no force at all in Charms, or that the effects produced are by natural means.

2. Neither can we assent fully to those that hold, that the force of imagination can work strange things upon other bodies, distinct and separate from the body imaginant, upon which it is not denied to have power to operate very wonderful things; and that for the reason given by the most learned Lord *Verulam,* which is this: *Experimenta quæ vim imaginationis in corpora aliena-solidè probent, pauca aut nulla prorsus sunt; cum fascini exempla huc non faciant, quod Dæmonum interventu fortasse non careant.* [*Syl.Syl.Cent.10. p. 583.*]

3. I said *not assent fully,* because there are some reasons that incline me to believe the possibility of it, though there be hardly found any experiments that solidly prove it. For as the said Lord *Verulam* saith again : *Movendi sunt homines, ne fidem detrahant operationibus ex transmissione spirituum, & vi imaginationis, quia eventus quandoq; fallit.* [*Ibid. p. 554.*] And there are so many learned Authors (though Dr. *Casaubon* according to his scurrilous manner stiles them Enthusiastical *Arabs*) of all sorts, that do stifly maintain the power of the imagination upon extraneous bodies, with such strength of argument, that I much stagger concerning the point, and therefore dare not say my assent is fully to either. For learned Dr. *Willis* having (as we conceive) unanswerably proved that there

T t   is is a twofold Soul in Man, and that the one which is the fenfitive, is corporeal, though much approaching to the nature of fpirit, how far the force of imagination, which is its inftrument, may reach, or what it may work at diftance, is not eafy to determine. And if the Soul, as *Helmont* laboureth to prove, by the Prerogative of its creation can when fufcitated by ftrong defire and exalted phantafie operate *per nutum*, then it muft needs follow, that it may work upon other bodies than its own, and fo ufing Words, Charms, Characters and Images may bring to pafs ftrange things. But if thefe three conclufions be certain and true, written by the pen of a moft *Medicina Mag-* learned, though lefs vulgarly known Author, to wit : " 1. The *nitica p. 14,* " Soul is not only in its proper vifible body, but alfo without it ; *17, 19.* "neither is it circumfcribed in an organical body. 2. The Soul "worketh without, or beyond its proper body commonly fo cal-"led. 3. From every body flow corporeal beams, by which the " Soul worketh by its prefence, and giveth them energie and pow-"er of working : And thefe beams are not only corporeal, but of "divers parts alfo: If thefe (I fay) be certain, then doth the imagi-nation work at diftance by means of thofe beams, and confequent-ly Words and Charms, and fuch like may be the means and inftru-ments, by which the imagination (being the principal power of the fenfitive Soul) may operate ftrange things at diftance, and fo that not be vain which learned *Agrippa* tells us.

> *Nos habitat, non Tartara, fed nec fydera Cœli :*
> *Spiritus in nobis qui viget, illa facit.*

And we have before fufficiently proved, that the fpecies of bodies are corporeal, and it is plain, that thefe operate upon our eyes at a vaft diftance, and do interfect one another in the air without con-fufion. And we muft in all reafon acknowledge that the fenfitive Soul, muft needs be of as much purity, and energie as thofe that we call the fenfible, or vifible fpecies of things, and then it muft neceffarily follow, that it by the means of the imagination may o-perate at a great diftance, and fo words and charms may from thence have power and operation. For learned *Agrippa* that great Philofo-pher, and mafter of lawful and natural Magick and not of that which is accounted diabolical (as the wretched pen of *Paulus Jovius* hath painted him) holds this : *Quod unicuiq; homini impreffus eft Character Divinus, cujus vigore poteft pertingere ad operandum mirabilia.* Which if fo, then many words, charms and the like, have a natural efficacy to work wonderful things, and that at a great di-ftance alfo.

4. I cannot likewife but take notice of another caution, very pertinent to our prefent purpofe, given us alfo by the faid Lord *Ve-* *Vt fupra p.555,* *rulam,* and in Englifh is this : "Again men are to be holden back *556.* "from the peril of credulity, left here they too much rafhly incline "with an eafy faith, becaufe they often fee the event to anfwer to "the operations. For the caufe of the fuccefs is to be referred of-"ten to the forces of the affections and imaginations in the body
"that

"that is the agent, which by a certain fecondary reafon may act in a
"diverfe body. As for example: If any one carry about the figure
"of a Planet or a Ring or a part of fome beaft, being certainly per-
"fwaded, that it will prove helpful unto him in promoting his love,
"or that he may be preferved from danger or wound in battel, or
"in ftrife that he may overcome &c. it may render his wit more
"ftirring, or may add fpurs to his induftry, or may cherifh confi-
"dence and hold up conftancie, from which perchancie he might
"have flided. Now who is ignorant what induftry and a mind te-
"nacious of its purpofe, may defign and bring to pafs in civil af-
"fairs? Therefore (he concludeth) he fhould err and deceive and
"be deceived, who fhould afcribe thefe things to the force of ima-
"gination upon the body of another, which his own imaginati-
"on worketh in his own body. And therefore this may caution all
that would judge aright of the force and effects of words and
charms that they may perhaps neither flow from the nature or efficacy of the words, nor from the force of the imagination of him
or her that pronounceth, writeth, giveth or applieth the charm,
but from the imagination and belief of the perfon to whom they
are applied, and for whom they are intended. For it is manifeft
by common experience (and we our felves have known it to be
certain) that thefe charms either pronounced, or written and hung
about the patients neck, have produced the greateft effects, upon
fuch as are of the weakeft judgment and reafon, as Women, Children, and ignorant and fuperftitious perfons, who have great confidence in fuch vain and inefficacious trifles; and that they feldom
or never produce any effects at all, upon fuch as are obftinate Infidels in the belief of their operations, and I fear we fhall not (or
very hardly) find any inftance to make this good, that they effectively work upon fuch as are utterly diffident of their force or
power.

5. It hath fometimes been a queftion, Whether a rational Phy- Cent. Problem.
Dcad. 2. p. 38.
fician in the curing of melancholy perfons, or others in fome odd
difeafes, ought to grant the ufe of Characters or Charms, and fuch
ridiculous adminiftrations? Which is decided in the affirmative,
that it is lawful and neceffary to ufe them, by that able and learned Phyfician *Gregorius Horftins*, by eight ftrong and convincing
arguments. And we our felves having practifed the art of medicine
in all its parts in the North of *England*, where Ignorance, Popery,
and fuperftition doth much abound, and where for the moft part
the common people, if they chance to have any fort of the Epilepfie, Palfie, Convulfions or the like, do prefently perfwade themfelves that they are bewitched, fore-fpoken, blafted, fairy-taken,
or haunted with fome evil fpirit, and the like; and if you fhould
by plain reafons fhew them, that they are deceived, and that there
is no fuch matter, but that it is a natural difeafe, fay what you can
they fhall not believe you, but account you a Phyfician of fmall or
no value, and whatfoever you do to them, it fhall hardly do them

any

any good at all, because of the fixedness of their depraved and pre-possessed imagination. But if you indulge their fancy, and seem to concur in opinion with them, and hang any insignificant thing about their necks, assuring them that it is a most efficacious and powerful charm, you may then easily settle their imaginations, and then give them that which is proper to eradicate the cause of their disease, and so you may cure them, as we have done great numbers. Here it is most manifest that the charm or appension hath no efficacy at all, and yet accidentally, it conduces to settle their fancies and confidences, which conduceth much to their cures. And from hence it comes to pass that by reason of the fixed belief of the party to whom the charm is applied, there are many helped, when the causality and efficiency is solely in the person imaginant and confident of receiving help by the means of the charm, and no efficacy at all in the charm it self, nor no diabolical concurrence, besides what obliquity may be in the minds of the actors, nor no agency in the imagination of the charmer, to produce the effect: yet because often people are cured thereby, the common people (and sometimes the learned also) do attribute the whole effect unto the charm, when indeed it effecteth nothing at all. And to this pur-

De Fascino lib. 1. c. 5. p. 22. pose *Varius* doth quote a passage from *Galen*, which is this: *Sunt quidam natura læti, qui quando ægrotant, si eos sanos futuros medicus confirmet, convalescunt; quorum spes sanitatis est causa: & medicus si animi desiderium incantatione, aut alicujus rei ad collum appensione adjuverit, citius ad valetudinem perducet.*

But we now come to examine if we can find any convincing examples, from Authors of credit, that in words, characters and charms there is any force or efficacy; and this we shall endeavour from the best and most punctual Authors, that have come within the compass of our knowledge, or reading, and that in this order, to which we shall add some observations.

1. I think there are few that have been, or are Students or Practitioners in the Art of Medicine, that have not either heard, or read the writing of that most able and learned person *Johannes* *De abdit. rer. caus. l. 1. c. 11. p. 65.* *Fernelius* who was Physician to the most Christian King of *France* *Henry* the second, who in that most profound piece that he writ, *De abditis rerum causis*, gives us as an ocular witness this relation.

Hist. 1. "I have (he saith) seen a certain Man, who by the virtue or force "of words did brings various Specters, or Apparitions into a look-"ing-glass, which did there so clearly express forthwith either in "writing or in true images, whatsoever he commanded, that all "things were readily and easily known to those that were by.

Observ. 1. 1. From hence we may observe, that *Fernelius* seeing this (as he saith) with his eyes, cannot (being so great a Scholar, and a circumspect person) be imagined to have been deceived, or imposed upon; though as much as he relates might have been brought to pass by the artificial placing of the glass, and having several images and things written moved by a confederate placed in some secret corner,

corner, where the images might fitly be reflected from the glafs to the fight of the by-ftanders, or by fome other means performed by the optical fcience and confederacy. And it is no fure ground to introduce a Demon, to act the bufinefs, when artificial means may rationally folve the matter, neither was it impoffible but he might miftake in the conjecture of the caufe of thofe Phenomena.

2. And though he feems by his preceeding difcourfe, to believe it to have been caufed but by a league and compact betwixt the perfon that fhewed it, and fome Cacodæmon: yet he bringeth no better proof for it, than the rotten authority of *Porphyrius* and *Proclus*, and no convincing argument that Demons can perform any fuch ftrange matters. And however if they were the meer apparitions of evil fpirits, it is much to be wondered that *Fernelius* would be prefent at any fuch finful and dangerous fights, or have fuch familiar converfation with any of that damned crew, feeing he there faith: *Quæ omnes prorfus vanæ & captiofæ funt artes.* *Obferv. 2.*

3. If thefe Apparitions were caufed by Cacodæmons, then there was no efficacy in the words at all, they were nothing but the fign of the league betwixt the evil fpirit, and the perfon that reprefented them; and then he need not have faid, that they were derived into the glafs *vi verborum*, and fo this will not prove that it was effected by force of the words. But if all this that he relates, did proceed but from lawful and natural caufes, as *Paracelfus* ftrongly holds (the glafs being but made as that which he faw in *Spain*, of the *Electrum* that he mentions) then the words might be efficacious, and fo it is a punctual inftance to prove that words are operative, which is the thing *de facto*, that we here feek after. *Obferv. 3.*

2. The next Hiftory to this purpofe we fhall take from *Antonius Benevenius*, as we find him quoted by that learned perfon *Marcellus Donatus*, and likewife Dr. *Cafaubon* (for I have not the book by me) who renders it thus. "A Souldier had an arrow fhot "through the left part of his breaft, fo that the iron of it ftuck to "the very bone of the right fhoulder. Great endeavours were u- "fed to get it out, but to no purpofe. *Benevenius* doth fhew, that "it was not feafible without prefent death. The Man feeing him- "felf forfaken by Phyficians and Chirurgeons, fends for a noted "*Ariolus* or Conjurer: who fetting his two fingers upon the wound, "with fome Charms he ufed, commanded the iron to come out, "which prefently without any pain of the patient, came forth, and "the Man was prefently healed: And this the Doctor, who I pre- "fume had the book, faith, that *Benevenius* faith *vidimus* we have "feen it, which *Marcellus Donatus* faith, the Author afcri- "bed to the virtue of the words, and others to the force of imagi- "nation. *Hift. 2.* *De Medic. Hiftor. mirab. lib. 2. c.1.p.26. Of Credul. and Incred. p. 85.*

1. Here we may obferve, that this may either be brought to pafs by the efficacy of the words or charms that he muttered, and then we muft needs confefs that charms are of great and ftupendious force: or that it might be effected by the imagination of the Charmer, *Obferv. 1.*

and

and then we muſt ſuppoſe (which the moſt do deny) that the imagination of the perſon imaginant, hath power to operate upon extraneous bodies, if it had power to cauſe the iron to come without
harm forth of the wounded Souldiers body, or it may be cauſed
(and that in moſt probability) by the imagination of the party
wounded being excited and rouſed up by the uttering of the charm,
in which the patient (in all likelihood) had no ſmall confidence.
And ſo however the charm was an accidental cauſe, or (as they uſe
to ſay) *cauſa ſine qua non*, of the bringing forth of the iron.

Hiſt. 3.
Lection. in
Fen. 2. *Avicen.*

3. Another Hiſtory we muſt borrow from the aforeſaid two Authors *Donatus* and Dr. *Caſaubon*, which they have tranſcribed forth
of *Johannes Baptiſta Montanus*, becauſe I have not the Author by
me, and is this : "My ſelf with mine eyes, you may (he ſaith) be-
' lieve me, have ſeen it : A certain man who when he had made a
" circle and drawn ſome characters about it, and uttered ſome words,
" he did call together above a hundred Serpents. And further ſaith,
" that though he did murmur certain words, yet he holdeth, that
" the bringing of the Serpents together was not performed by the
" force of the words, but by the power of a ſtrong imagination,
" and that ſome by the ſtrength of imagination, not of words, are
" ſaid to draw forth darts, and to cure wounds.

Obſerv I.

1. And here we may take notice that this is a punctual and poſitive Hiſtory, plainly declaring the matter of fact, in calling together above an hundred Serpents, and this muſt be done either
by the force of the words, or by the ſtrength of the perſons imagination, or both, unleſs we muſt admit the Devil to perform it,
which may vainly be ſuppoſed, but cannot be proved, by what natural means he ſhould bring it to paſs. But however the relation
is very credible, *Montanus* being a famous Phyſician and Profeſſor
at *Padua*, and affirms it as ſeen with his own eyes.

Hiſt. 4.
Inſtit. de mag.
Infam. p. 92.

4. To theſe we may add one of ſufficient credit from the learned
Maſius, as it is cited by *Wierus*, and Dr. *Caſaubon* (which may be
we have related before, but not to this purpoſe) and is this : "I al-
" ſo (he ſaith) have ſeen them who with words (or charms) could
" ſtop wild beaſts, and force them to await the ſtroak of the dart :
" who alſo could force that Domeſtick beaſtly creature, which we
" call a Rat, as ſoon as ſeen, amazed and aſtoniſhed to ſtand ſtill, as
" it were immoveable, until not by any deceit or ambuſhes, but
" only ſtretching their hands, they had taken them and ſtrangled
" them. This is from his own ſight, and he a Man of undoubted
veracity.

Hiſt. 5.

5. Another take from the credit of Dr. *Caſaubon* who fathers it
upon *Remigius*, but confeſſeth that at the time of his writing the ſtory he could not find it in *Remigius* his Book, and is this. "I have ſeen
" a Man (ſaith he) who from all the neighbourhood (or confines)
" would draw Serpents into the fire, which was incloſed within a
" magical circle ; and when one of them, bigger than the reſt,
" would not be brought in, upon repetition of the charms before
                                                    " uſed,

"used, he was forced, and so into the fire he did yield himself with
"the rest, and with it was compassed.

6. To these we shall adjoin another story written from *Wierus* by *Hist.* 6.
Dr. *Moore* thus: "And (he saith) *Wierus* tells us this story of a Antidot. a-
"Charmer at *Saltzburg*, that when in the sight of the people he gainst Atheism
"had charmed all the. Serpents into a ditch and killed them, at *c. 2. p. 165.*
" last there came one huge one far bigger than the rest, that leapt
"upon him and winded about his waste like a girdle, and pulled
"him into the ditch, and so killed the Charmer himself in the con-
"clusion. And this great Serpent the Doctor taketh (in his Ap-
pendix) to be a Devil, or a Serpent actuated and guided by him,
but upon what grounds of reason I can no way understand.

These are the most material passages that in our reading we
can find in credible and learned Authors, to prove thereby the effects of charms *de facto*, and we confess they are all short, and not
sufficiently evidential, as such a case may justly require ; and therefore we shall here add some testimonies of good Authors that do
strongly affirm and aver the same. As not to stand upon the authorities of the Cabalists, Platonists or Arabians, we find the truth
of the charming of Serpents avouched by *Paracelsus* (whose credit in this point, may be equivalent to any others) who saith thus :
"But (he saith) answer me from whence is this, that a Serpent in *Archidox.*
" *Helvetia*, *Algovia*, or *Suevia*, doth understand the *Greek Idiom*, *Magic. l. i.*
" *Osy, Osya, Osy, &c.* When notwithstanding the Greek tongue is *p. 695.*
"not so common in this age, with the Helvetians, Algovians, or
"Suevians, that the venenous worms should be able to learn it ? Tell
"me (he saith) how, where and from what causes, Serpents do un-
"derstand these words, or in what Academies have they learned
"them, that they should forthwith at the first hearing of those
"words, stop their ears, with their tail turned back, lest
"they should be compelled to hear the words again reiterated ?
"For assoon as they hear them, they contrary to their nature and
"cunning do forthwith lie immoveable, and do pursue or hurt no
"man with their venemous biting, when notwithstanding other-
"wise they on the sudden fly from the noise of a mans going as soon
" as they hear it, and turn into their holes. From whence it is manifest that *Paracelsus* knew of his own experience that the charm
(which it seems he knew) would make Serpents lie immoveable,
and so that there was power and efficacy in words naturally without superstition to work and operate.

Also the learned person *Tobias Tandlerus* Doctor of Physick and
publick Professor at *Witteberge*, in his smart and pithy Oration *de* *p. 88.*
fascino & incantatione, tells us this : " That *Tuccia* a Woman be-
"longing to the Temple of *Vesta* being accused of Incest, did by
"the help of prayer carry water in a sieve, as *Pliny* witnesseth :
" *lib. 28. c. 2. natur. Histor.* Who there with many examples, doth
"extol the efficacy of words. And further sa th: They are found
"that stay wild beasts with words, that they escape not the throw-
"ing

"ing of the dart. And those that render Rats being seen in any
"place, stupid with secret murmuring, that they may be taken with
"the hand and strangled.

Pro. 2. *c.* 11.
p. 220, 241.

Augerius Ferrerius, whom *Thuanus* calls *Medicus Doctissimus*, in
his treating of Homerical medication, after he hath quoted *Galen's*
recantation from *Trallianus*, and divers arguments and examples
to prove the efficacy of words, charms and characters from him,
from *Aetius* and others, he concludeth thus: *Quorum experientiam
cum ob oculos positam, & tot illustrium virorum authoritate confir-
mata videris, quid facies? Nam iis quæ sensibus exposita sunt con-
travenire, sani hominis non est: Doctorum vero experimenta infir-
mare, temerarium.*

Lastly, for authorities sake we shall add the opinion of sagacious
Helmont, who writ a Book by him styled, *In verbis, herbis, & la-
pidibus est magna virtus*; and of the efficacy of words saith only
thus much: *De magna virtute verborum quædam ingenuè dixi, quæ
magis admiror quam applico.* By which it is manifest that though
Helmont did not make use of words or charms, yet knowing the efficacy of them he could not but admire them.

These authorities joyned with the examples may suffice to convince any rational man that at some times and places, and by some
persons, the using of charms have produced strange effects: and
therefore taking the matter of fact to be a truth, we should come
to examine the cause of these effects; but first it will be necessary to
premise some cautions and necessary considerations, which we shall
pursue in this order.

*Histor. Natur.
lib.* 28 *c.* 2.
p. 397.

Consid 1. 1. We are to consider the intricacy and difficulty of this point,
which hath exercised the wits of the learned in all ages, and forced
Pliny to say: *Maximæ quæstionis, & semper incertæ est, valeantne
aliquid verba & incantamenta carminum.* And again more particularly: *Varia circa hæc opinio, ex ingenio cujusq; vel casu, mulce-
ri alloquio foras: quippe ubi etiam Serpentes extrahi cantu cogiq;
in pœnas, verum falsumne sit, vita non decreverit.* It seems by *Pliny*
that learned men of old have been very much divided in their opinions about this matter, insomuch that he dares not take upon
him to decide it, but leaves it free to every man to believe as they
shall see cause. And therefore we ought not to be condemned, if
we do not absolutely decide it neither, it is enough if we bring so
much light to the matter that it may be better understood, though
not absolutely determined, *In magnis voluisse sat est.*

Consid. 2. 2. Again we are to note that some Authors of great credit and
learning do hold these things to be but meer *Aniles fabulæ*, of which
opinion (it seems) *Aristotle*, and *Galen* were, though *Trallianus*
doth affirm (though some say falsly) that he made a retractation of
that opinion, and this was the judgment of the learned Spaniard
Valesius, who in his book, *De sacra Philosophia*, hath taken great
pains to perswade men, though he deny not supernatural operations
by Devils and Spirits, that inchanting by magical words are impossible

poſſible, and whatſoever is alledged by any ancient or late writer to that purpoſe, he doth reject as meerly fabulous. But upon as good grounds may any one reject this his ſingle opinion as fabulous, becauſe there are a whole cloud of witneſſes againſt him, of as great credit and authority as himſelf, and experience every day will make it manifeſt, that great effects do follow from the appenſion of charms and characters, not determining here whether they cauſe thoſe effects cauſally as efficients, or but meerly accidentally and occaſionally, and therefore in this point Dr. *Caſaubon* ſaith well: "As for *Valeſi-* "*us* opinion (he ſaith) though a learned Man, and for ought I know "Pious and Wiſe; yet it is no wonder to me, that any one man, "though pious and learned, ſhould fall into an opinion very Para- "doxical and contrary to moſt other mens belief, eſpecially in a thing "of this nature, which moſt depends of experience.

Vid. Credul. and Incredul. p. 101.

3. Notwithſtanding all this, for the moſt part all charms, ſpells and characters are inefficacious, fallacious, ſuperſtitious and groundleſs, and hardly fit for an honeſt and wiſe man to uſe, except only to ſettle the imaginations of patients, that they may more readily and hopefully take thoſe things that may effectually cure them. I ſay for the moſt part, not alwayes, becauſe I grant that they do ſometimes either efficiently or accidentally produce real effects. But that they are ſometimes fallacious is manifeſt in the Charmer of *Saltzburg*, who though with his charms he could prevail againſt the little ſerpents, yet that one that came prevailed againſt him, and threw him into the ditch and killed him. And how vain it is to put any confidence in theſe idle trifles, and how fallacious and ineffectual and deſtructive they are, may appear by two deplorable examples. *Amatus Luſitanus* a learned and experienced Phyſician, and a man of great repute and veracity doth relate this: "That in "the end of the Spring, the Summer coming on, two young men "did go from *Ancona* to the City *Auximum*, and by the way, the "one of them turning aſide to make water, found a Viper in an hole "at the bottom of a Tree, with a great deal of rejoicing, but with "an unhappy ſucceſs. He did contend with his companion, that "he could take the Viper with his hand, without any hurt, and "did brag that with the murmuring of certain words, he could "make all Serpents obey him, lying ſtill as ſtupid. The other did "laugh him to ſcorn. At laſt they come to a wager. But the Viper "more audacious than was right, remained always truculent and "unaltered. At laſt when he ſtretched forth his hand to take her, "it being ſtirred up with a mad and venemous fury, lifting up the "neck did bite him in the finger, which beginning to pain him, "he quickly put his finger to his mouth perhaps to ſuck forth the "blood, but within a ſmall while the unhappy young-man died by "his own fault, neither did medical helps yield him any ſuccour, "but he might have eſcaped, if he had not put the poyſon of the "Serpent to his mouth. And this wofull example may be a ſuffici- ent warning to all that they be not too haſty to put confidence in

Conſid. 3.

Centur. 3. Cu- rat. 14. Hiſt. 1.

theſe

Hift. 2.   thefe fallacious trifles.   Another ftory we fhall give of our own knowledge, and is this. " I had difmembred a pretty Young-mans " leg by reafon of a Gangrene, his name *Robert Taylor*, a good Scho-" lar, and had been a Clerk to a Juftice of Peace, and about three " weeks after when the ftump was near healed, I being gone from " home, his Mother lying in the fame room with him, but having " gotten too much drink, he calling upon her to help him to the " Clofe-ftool, but fhe not hearing, he fcrambled up himfelf as well " as he could, but hit the end of the ftump that was not quite clo-" fed, whereby the arteries were opened, and a great Hemorrhage " followed.   And there being an honeft fimple man that owed the " houfe where he lay, having a vain confidence that with a charm " he faid he had , he could undoubtedly ftay the bleeding, and " therefore would not fuffer them to call up my man to ftay the Flux " until day; which continuing fo long, the vain and fruitlefs charm " prevailing nothing, though my man when he came did ftop it, " yet had he loft fo much blood that he died the next day; and this may ferve for a fufficient caution againft vain confidence in charms.

Confid. 4.   4. Further we are to confider, that there are many notorious impoftures, frauds and cheats committed upon the poor ignorant, credulous and filly common people, while fome make the people believe that their difeafes are inflicted by fuch and fuch Saints, and therefore they muft ufe fuch and fuch ftrange luftrations, fuffumigations and other vain fuperftitious Rites and Ceremonies.   Others pretend to drive away evil Spirits by exorcifms and conjurations, and others to cure all difeafes (in a manner) with words, charms, characters, amulets, and the like, when the moft of thefe pretenders are meer ignorant Knaves and Impoftors, that do nothing but cheat the too credulous people of their money, and defame and difhonour the moft noble Art of Medicine, of which we have known divers forts, fome of which we have mentioned before in this Treatife.

De Morbo Sacro lib. Sect. 3. f. 301.   To fuch as thefe that ancient Author (fuppofed by fome to be *Hippocrates*) *De morbo facro*, doth give fufficient reproof, and of whom he faith thus: *Ac mihi certè qui primi hunc morbum ad Deos retulerunt. tales effe videntur, quales funt magi, expiatores, circulatores, ac arrogantes oftentatores, qui fe valde pios effe plurimumq; fcire fimulant.*   A moft large Catalogue of thefe kind of peftiferous impoftors, and many others, you have at full and to the life painted forth by *Paracelfus* in his Preface to his lefs Chirurgery, where he hath fufficiently ftigmatized them with all thofe wicked marks and brands that juftly belong unto them.   The fame alfo is fully performed by learned *Langius* in his Epiftles, to whom I referr the readers.

Confid. 5.   5. We are to confider that though we fhould grant that words or charms had in them no energie, nor efficiency at all, by any natural power, and that the Devils power doth not concur to make them operative; yet (as we have partly fhewed before) they are of
fingular

singular use and benefit to a learned Physician, whereby he may settle the fancies of his patients, to cause them more chearfully and confidently to commit them to his hands, and to take what he shall order and prescribe them, and this manner of their use is no way to be dispraised or condemned, and we leave it as excepted forth of the dispute we have in hand.

There are chiefly three opinions, amongst those that grant the truth of the matter of fact concerning the proper cause of these effects produced by words. 1. Of which the first sort are those that hold there is no efficiency at all in the words themselves, which are nothing but the sign of the league and compact betwixt the Charmer and the Devil, and that whatsoever is brought to pass is only effected by the Devils power, and of this opinion are the greatest part of the learned. 2. Are those that hold that the words or charms are but means to heighten the imagination, and that it is the strength of the exalted imagination only that produceth those things that seem to be effected by those words or charms, and of this opinion was *Avicen* and many of the Arabians, *Ferrerius, Montanus* and many others. 3. There are those that hold that there is a natural efficiency in words and characters rightly fitted and conjoined together in proper and agreeable constellations, and of this opinion were *Johannes Ludovicus de la Cerda, Johannes Brarus Camisius Lusitanus, Paracelsus, Galeottus Martius, Henricus Cornelius Agrippa*, and many others; and of these we shall speak in order.

1. The first opinion doth take up a false supposition for its ground, to wit that the Devil doth make a visible and corporeal league with the Charmer, by virtue of which compact the effects are produced; and if this compact be not explicite, yet it may be implicite, and so the Devil operateth the effects, thereby to draw the Charmer into his league and service. But we have before sufficiently proved the nullity of any such Covenant, and shewed plainly that it is a false, impious and diabolical Tenent, and that there is not, nor can be any other league betwixt the Devil and wicked men, but what it spiritual, internal and mental, and therefore that the Devil doth not bring those effects to pass, by pretence of a league, that hath no being or existence. *Reason 1. against this opinion.*

2. We have proved by the unanimous consent of all the whole army of the learned, that the Devil can work no alteration or change in natural bodies, but by the applying of fit agents to agreeable patients; but what agent could the Devil have applied to make the iron that stuck in the Souldiers shoulder-bone related by *Benevenius*, to come forth without pain? surely none at all. For where an agent in nature is awanting to produce an effect, there the Devil must needs also be lame, and can effect nothing; and if either the words had a sufficient natural power to cause the iron to come forth, or the Souldiers imagination exalted by confidence in the Charm and Charmer, then the Devils help is in vain implored, *Reason 2. against this opinion.*

implored,

implored, or he brought into be an actor of that he hath no power at all to perform, and there was no other natural agent applied, and therefore it must of necessity be one of the two that produced the effect, and not a Demon.

Reason 3. against this opinion.
Vid. Spong.
Fosteriana expressio. c. 2. p. 7, &c.

3. It cannot in any reason be imagined that the Devil, that for the space of above five thousand years hath been the bitter and inveterate enemy to the health of Man both in Soul and Body, should now be become a Physician & an healer. We read that God sent forth evil Angels amongst the people, but he sent forth his word and they were healed. But it is manifest that the evil Angels since their fall, are ordained of God to be the instruments and organs for the executing of his wrath, and the good Angels are his ministring Spirits for the good of his people both in Souls and Bodies: and therefore that the Devil should be the author, or instrument of curing any disease at all, were to make him to act contrary to that end for which God hath ordained him, for he is the destroyer, that is ordained to destroy, but not to heal.

Reason 4. against this opinion.
Vid. Miscell.
Medic. Sutt.
lib. 6. Epist. 17.
p. 284.

4. But we shall take another argument or two from the learned pen of *Henricus Brucæus* in his Epistle to *Thomas Erastus*, where about this point he saith this: "What is that (he saith) that the "most of the Grecian Physicians were ignorant of Demons; or that "it should be agreeable to truth, that they have not judged that "Demons had any power either in inflicting or taking away any dis-"eases? For that sentence of *Hippocrates*, that there is somewhat "that is divine in diseases. *Galen* doth shew in his Comment how it "is to be understood, and *Hippocrates* himself in that Treatise of the "Falling-sickness doth sufficiently open it. Notwithstanding these "chief men being Physicians and Philosophers, by whom the power "of natural things and words was principally looked into; they "were more willing to assent to things that were evidently apparent, "than take away the force of incantation by it self. By it self (he "saith) Because they have had no remembrance of Demons, from "whom the causes of such effects, which follow incantations, do seem "only they can possibly be derived.

Reason 5. against this opinion.

5. Before he argueth thus: "But the curation of diseases, which "are performed by conjurations and imprecations, he ascribeth "unto the Devil. Notwithstanding (he saith) some things do move "a scruple to me, because that some things of them do seem to be "of that kind, which cannot at all be referred to Demons, in "which no league or compact doth seem to interceed. For leagues "or compacts seem to be contracted, for that also those things com-"prehended are to be performed to those that Covenant, that by "that means those that Covenant with him, may be withdrawn "from the worship of the true God, or that some may be confirmed "in their impiety. Which causes in Men to whom the true God is "utterly unknown, have no place; for neither are they to be with-"drawn from the true God, whom they altogether ignore, or to be "confirmed in impiety, when they have been brought up in the "worship

" worſhip of Idols from their tender years. For (he ſaith) *Aloiſius*
" *Cádamuſtus* in the 18 Chap. of the Indian Navigations relateth, that
" Serpents ſeeking to deſtroy Sheep in the Kingdom of *Senega,*
" which is given to Idolatrous Worſhip, they will on the night aim
" by heaps at the Sheep-folds, from whence they are driven away
" with certain conceived words, and this reaſon is not unknown to
" many others.   And that *Trallianus* where he treateth of the ſtone,
" acknowledgeth the force of incantations in healing of diſeaſes,
" and he witneſſeth that *Galen* himſelf, taught by experience, did
" come over to this opinion.   For though *Galen* before (as we have
ſhewed) did account charms but as *Aniles fabulæ*, yet this Author *Trallianus* doth quote a piece of *Galens*, wherein he maketh a
retra&ation of that opinion, and it ſtandeth with good reaſon that
it might be ſo, *Trallianus* living near his time, and ſo might (notwithſtanding what *Guitterrius* bawleth to the contrary) have that
part of his writing that ſince might be loſt; for I remember *Paracelſus* ſomewhere ſaith that in his travels he found the works of
Galen, far more genuine and incorrupt than thoſe that were publiſhed and extant.

6. A further reaſon this Author gives us thus: " Furthermore Reaſon 6. a-
gainſt this opi-
nion.
" (he ſaith) that it is not impious to frame to cure a diſeaſe with
" conceived words, and cannot be perſwaded to believe it, eſpe-
" cially ſeeing that thoſe diſeaſes that are cauſed by Magick, are *Ut ſuprá.*
" only to be cured by Magick.   But (he ſaith) I confeſs that com-
" pacts with Demons are not to be entred into, but that compacts
" being entred into with others, ſhould paſs to another, and ſhould
" bind with the ſame impiety, that is not agreeable to truth, ſeeing
" that the conſent of thoſe that make the league, doth effect and
" confirm the compacts.   Which if it be (he ſaith) far abſent from
" us (that is a compact) and in the uſe of conceived words, by
" which the malady is taken away, there be contained nothing that
" is impious, and that we implore the divine aſſiſtance; I do not
" ſee (he ſaith) any thing hurtful to Religion, nor unbeſeeming
" a good and Pious Man.   For as if things that are ſalutiferous to
" mankind, ſhould come from Men that were Atheiſts, we ſhould
" imbrace them, not reſpecting the Authors: So if (he ſaith) things
" that are profitable ſhould be ſhewed of a Demon, I ſhould not think
" they were to be rejected.

7. Laſtly he ſaith: ' Why may we not alſo refer effects in the Reaſon 7. a-
gainſt this opi-
nion.
" ſanation of diſeaſes, which do accompany the enunciation or de-
" ſcription of conceived words, to thoſe we call good or guardian
" Angels? Why ſhould we not judge that theſe would be as ready
" to eaſe and help, as others to hurt, eſpecially in diſeaſes, where
" we are deſtitute of natural helps?   And this opinion (he ſaith)
" *Conſtantinus magnus* did approve, *Codicis lib. 9. tit. 10. leg. 4.*
" The Science of them (he ſaith) is to be puniſhed, who being skill-
" ed in Magical Arts are diſcovered either to endeavour the im-
" pairing the health of men, or the drawing of chaſt minds to luſt.
                                                              " But

Hist.

"But for seeking remedies to humane bodies, they ought not to be
"punished. But perhaps thou wilt say, that words are in vain mut-
"tered forth, unless a compact do interceed. But that which hap-
"pened (he saith) at *Lipsick* some twelve or fifteen years since, doth
"refell this opinion, where a little Wench, that by reason of her
"age did not know what she did, while she imitated the whole a-
"ction of her nurse, which she had often seen her use, and there-
"with stirred up tempests; herewith the little Wench raised up
"such Thunders and Lightenings, by which a Village, not far
"from the City was burned: As (he saith) D. *Nenius* told him,
"and was a thing known to innumerable Citizens. For the Wench
"being brought to the Court, it was debated whether by law she
"could be punished, but it was decided by the opinions of the
"Lawyers, that she could not be punished, seeing that by reason of
"her young age, she was altogether ignorant of what she did.

8. We cannot also but remember here some notable passages of
Paracelsus where he is speaking of the power of faith and strong
confidence, meerly considered as a nude and natural power: And
affirming its great force and operation to effect strange things, he

De superst. &
Ceremon. l.
p. 451.

saith: "But truly we cannot deny, but that spirits do commix them-
"selves with such a faith, in celebrated feasts, and the like, as
"though they had performed those things. But not at all they,
"but faith only doth these things: As if a Man had honey, and did
"not know from whence it came, nor what kind of creature did
"make it, and the Beetle should brag that she had made it. So
the Devils though they perform nothing at all, but the effects are
meerly produced by the power of a natural or miraculous faith,
yet they glory as though they had done them (in all things being liars and deceivers) and therefore do they what they can to
confirm and raise up ceremonies and superstitions; From which
commotions faith is brought forth, and faith worketh those strange
effects, and therefore by reason of the superstition used, the Devils
would make men believe that they are authors of those strange
effects, which are onely wrought by the Power of an humane
Faith, that they might rob God of his Glory and have it ascribed
unto themselves. And therefore no persons do the Devils more
service than those that ascribe those works unto them that are
wrought by natural power and the strength of humane faith. From
whence he concludeth thus: *Eodem modo fides est in homine, ut
laqueus quo strangulatur fur, ad multa utilis sit. Ea fides facit, ut
fiat. Si fides etiam in filum lineum est, similiter fit. Interim tamen hoc nec Diabolus facit, nec fur, nec laqueus, nec carnifex: sed
adulterina tua fides, quam non impendis ut debebas.*

Having sufficiently (we suppose) proved that in the producing
the effects by words or charms, the Devil doth operate nothing
at all in them, but only as a lying deceiver and Impostor, laboureth to have the honour of those effects ascribed unto him; we shall
now come to the second, and that is those that hold that the effects

are

are folely produced by the force of the imagination and faith of the Charmer, and fo that imagination doth work further than the proper body of the imaginant, upon other extraneous bodies, and that the words or characters avail nothing, but the fortifying and exalting of the faith of the Operator, to prove which are brought thefe arguments.

1. When the Difciples asked our Saviour, Why they could not *Argum. 1.* caft forth the Devil out of the child that was lunatick, and fore vexed, and oft fell into the fire, and into the water, he told them; *Becaufe of their unbelief,* and faid : *For verily I fay unto you, if ye* Matth. 17. 20. *have faith as a grain of muftard feed, ye fhall fay unto this mountain; remove hence to yonder place, and it fhall remove, and nothing fhall be impoffible unto you.* Upon which place learned *Beza* gives us this note : *Non fidem illam generalem & hiftoricam intelligit : Nec etiam fidem juftificantem. Sed illam demum fpecialem, & quibufdam Chriftianis particularem, quâ animus quodam fpiritûs fancti impulfu ad res mirandas perficiendas impellitûr, & iftâ vocatûr fides miraculorum.* And againft diffidence our Saviour orders the Matth. 10. 1. remedy of fafting and prayer. But this was a power given by Chrift unto them, which they (it feems) had loft, and are here taught to refufcitate it by prayer and fafting. Others take it to be a natural power of faith or ftrength of imagination in all men, which they may ftir up by fafting and prayer, therewith to operate that which is good, but being fufcitated by the means of images, pictures, fuperftitious ceremonies, and the like, and fo may effect either good or bad; but this later opinion we reject as unfound, and contrary to the Scriptures; and fo the argument doth prove very little.

2. *Helmont* holdeth, "that every man, in refpect that they have *Argum. 2.* "been partakers of the image of God, hath power to create cer- *Vid. de injecl.* "tain entities, by the power of imagination, and that thefe con- *mater. 661,* "ceived Ideas do cloath themfelves with a body in the fhape of the 602. "image fabricated in the imagination, and it is by thefe that thofe "ftrange things are effected, that are falfly attributed to Demons. And that man folely hath this power. Which (if his argument be well grounded) doth prove plainly, that thefe ftrange effects are brought to pafs by the fole power of the phantafie of the perfon imaginant, or ufing the charms, and neither by the power of the Devil nor of the charms.

3. The argument to prove thefe things by, that they are brought *Argum. 3.* to pafs by the ftrength of imagination, ufed by *Cornelius Agrippa,* is this : *Non mediocri experientiâ (ait) comprobatum eft, inftant à De occulta Phi*natura homini, quandam dominandi, & ligandi vim: And that *lof. lib. 3. c. 40.* there is an active terror in man, (if it be rightly refufcitated in him, *p. 137.* and that he know how to direct and make ufe of it) impreffed in him by the Creator, which is as it were a terrifical character and fignacle of God inftamped upon man, by which all creatures do fear, and reverence man, as the image of his Creator, and as by the law of creation, to be Lord, and to bear rule over them all. And hefe

here I cannot but mention that lepid(though tedious & ludicrous)tale

Of Credul. and Incredul. *p.* 110.

that Dr. *Caſaubon* gives us of an horſe-rider called *John Young*, "that "could tame the moſt fierce Bulls and unruly Horſes, as alſo by pipe-"ing to make the moſt couragious and fierce Maſtiff to lie cloſe "down and to be quiet, by the force of his imagination and charms. "And this *John Youngs* Philoſophy was agreeable to this of *Agrippa's*, "to wit, That all creatures were made by God, for the uſe of Man "and to be ſubject unto him, and that if men did uſe their power "rightly, any man might do what he did. *Fides ſit apud autho-rem.*

Argum. 4.

4. *Avicenna, Algazel, Alkindus, Marſilius Ficinus, Jacobus de Forlnio, Pomponatius Paracelſus* and others, do ſometimes hold "that the Soul (the ſenſitive and corporeal it muſt be underſtood) "not by a nude apprehenſion, or meer impery, but by the emiſſion "of ſpirits (or corporeal beams, as we have ſhewed before) do "work upon external bodies, and ſo move and alter them. Some-"times they hold, that the whole Soul (ſenſitive muſt be meant) "doth go quite forth of the Body, and wander into far diſtant pla-"ces, and there not only ſee what things are done, but alſo to act "ſomething it ſelf. And to this opinion (only meaning of the im-mortal, and immaterial Soul) Dr. *Moore* and Mr. *Glanvil* do ſeem to agree, namely that the Soul may for a time depart forth of its Bo-dy, and return again. And to prove this the argument of *Avicen* is this: Superior things (he ſaith) have dominion over the inferior,

Vid. Thom. Fien. de virib. imagin. Quæſt. 12. *p.* 202. *&c.*

and the Intelligences do rule and change corporeal things. And that the Soul is a ſpiritual and ſeparable ſubſtance. And therefore after the ſame manner, may act in corporeal things, and change them as may be ſeen at large, with reſponſions in the book of *Fienus*.

Now we come to the third and laſt opinion of thoſe that poſi-tively hold, that there is a force in words and characters (if right-ly framed) to effect ſtrange things withal, and this is as ſtrongly denied by many. Therefore we ſhall only offer the moſt convin-cing arguments, that we meet withal, and leave it to the cenſure of others, and that in this order.

But before we enter upon the poſitive arguments, we think it fit, leſt we be miſtaken (though in part we may have touched ſome of them before) to lay down ſome few cautions and conſidera-tions, which we ſhall do in this manner.

Conſid. I.

1. It is to be taken for a certain truth, that the greateſt part of thoſe pretended charms and characters that are in this our age uſed by ignorant, ſuperſtitious, and cheating impoſtors; are utterly falſe, and of no power or efficacy at all. And this was underſtood

*De mirab. pot. Art.& Nat.c.*2.

by our learned Countreyman *Roger Bacon*, who tells us thus much. "For without all doubt (he ſaith) all of this ſort now a days are "falſe, or doubtful or irrational, and therefore not at all to be

De Occult. Philoſ. p. 484.

"truſted unto. And to this doth *Paracelſus* fully agree, ſaying: "All characters are not to be truſted to, or any confidence to be "placed in them, nor in like manner in words. For the Nigro-"mancers

" mancers and Poets, being very laboriously imployed about them,
" have filled all Books with comments proceeding forth of their
" brains, wanting all truth and foundation, of which some thousands
" are not worth one deaf nut.

2. Yet for all this we are to consider, that all of them are, not _Consid._ 2.
totally to be rejected, for _Bacon_ tells us : " That there are certain de-
" precations of ancient times instituted of men, or rather ordained _Vid. ut supra._
" of God and good Angels, that are both true and efficacious; and
" such like as these may retain their first virtue. As in some Coun-
" treys (he saith) yet some certain prayers are made upon red hot
" iron, and upon the water of the flood, and likewise upon other
" things by which the innocent are tried, and the guilty condemn-
" ed. And this was the trial that by the Saxons (when used in _Eng-
land_) was called Ordeall. Therefore _Paracelsus_ saith thus : _Re-
peto ergo, characteribus & verbis non omnibus fidendum esse, sed
eligenda & retinenda, quæ recta, genuina, ex fundamento veritatis
deprompta, ac multoties probata sint_, which is counsel good, sound
and profitable. And somewhere he tells us that even those true and
genuine characters and Gamahuis that were rightly fabricated under due constellations, and were in old time efficacious, may have
now lost their virtue because the configurations of the Heavens are
altered.

3. Many of these strange characters or words were not by wise _Consid._ 3.
men inserted into their works, that thereby any strange things might
be wrought by them, but were invented to conceal those grand
secrets that they would not have to be made known unto the unworthy. And therefore _Bacon_ gives us this profound and honest _Ubi supra._
counsel : " So therefore (he saith) there are very many things con-
" cealed in the books of the Philosophers, by sundry ways : In
" which a Wise Man ought to have this prudence, that he pass by
" the charms and characters, and make trial of the work of nature
" and art : And so he shall see, as well animate things, as inanimate,
" to concur together, by reason of the conformity of nature, not
" because of the virtue of the charm or character. And so many
" secrets both of Nature and Art are of the unlearned, esteemed to be
" magical. And Magicians do foolishly confide in charms and cha-
" racters, judging virtue to be in them, and because of their vain
" confidence in them, they forsake the work of Nature and Art, by
" reason of the error of charms and characters. And so both these
sort of Men are deprived of the benefit of wisdom, their own fool-
ishness so compelling them.

3. The same most learned Countryman of ours _Roger Bacon_, _Consid._ 4.
doth further give us this advice saying : " But those things that are _Ut supra 1. 2._
" contained in the books of Magicians ought by right to be ba-
" nished, although they have in them something of truth : Because
" they are mixed with falsities, that it cannot be discerned betwixt
" that which is true, and that which is false. And also Impostors and
" ignorant persons have feigned and forged divers writings under

X x

" the

"the names of ancient wise men, thereby to allure the curious, and
" to deceive the unwary, which with great care and consideration
" we ought to eschew. To the same purpose *Paracelsus* doth cau-
"tion us in this point. *Cuilibet ergo promptum sit, characteres &*
" *verba quævis discernere posse.*

Consid 4. 4. But for all this (as we have often intimated before) charms
and characters though in themselves of none effect, may conduce
to heighten the fancy and confidence of a Patient, and render him
more willing to take those things that may cure. And to this purpose, the forementioned Author *Roger Bacon*, from *Constantine*
the Physician tells us thus much : " But it is to be considered, that
"a skilful Physician, or any other, that would excite and stir
"up the mind, may profitably make use of charms and characters
"though feigned, not because the characters or charms themselves
" do operate any thing, but that the medicine may be received
" with more desire and devotion, and that the mind of the Patient
"may be stirred up, and may confide more freely, and may hope
" and rejoice; Because the Soul being excitated, can renew many
" things in its proper body, so that from infirmity it may be re-
" stored to health by joy and confidence. If therefore (he saith)
" a Physician to magnifie his work, that the Patient may be raised
" up to hope and confidence, shall do any thing of this nature, not
" for fraud, but because of this, that he may confide, that he may
" be healed, it is not to be condemned. We brought this authority
to confirm what we had asserted before; and that these things are
wonderfully prevalent, we have before shewed examples.

Argum. I. 1. There are some, that to prove that words and characters have
a natural efficacy do alledge some passages of Scripture, which we
shall propose as very probable, but not as necessarily convincing,
Numb. 6. 27. and the first is this: *And they shall put my name upon the children
of Israel, and I will bless them.* Which some understand that the
name *Jehovah* which they call *Tetragrammaton*, was worn upon
them, and that thereby they were blessed, and from thence they
suppose that Hebrew names, especially that, are very efficacious and
Ezek. 9. 4, 6. powerful. Another is : *The man cloathed in linnen, that had the
Ink-horn by his side,* is commanded to set a mark, or (as some read
it) a *Tau upon those that mourned.* This is the name of a letter the
" last in the Alphabet, and hath in the old books of the Hebrews (as
" *Schindlerus* tells us) the figure of a cross, and such like the *Sa-*
" *maritans* use to this day. From whence by *Tau*, some in *Eze-*
" *kiel* do understand the figure of the Cross of Christ.

Explic. 2. 2. But to explicate what is meant by charms and characters, we
are to note that it is not to be understood of those words that are
by humane institution significant according to the imposition of
men, nor of any sort of charms or characters, but of such, as by
wise men are duly fitted and joined together, in and under a right
and favourable constellation, for it is from the Influence of the Stars
(as we have proved before) that words, charms, images and characters

racters do receive their energie and virtue. And to this purpose is the true rendition of the words in the Psalm. *Which hearkeneth* [Psal. 58.] *not to the voice of those that mutter, the conjunction of the learned joyner.* That is, that the Serpent doth not hearken unto, or obey the charms that are framed or joined together by the learned joiner or framer of charms. So that there is a great learning required to frame and compose charms rightly that they may be efficacious. For *Paracelsus* witnesseth that Serpents once hearing an efficacious charm do forthwith stop their ears, lest they should hear the words repeated again. Of both these sorts the learned *Roger Bacon* doth [Ut sup.] tell us this: "Of characters therefore according to the first man-
' ner, it is so to be judged as we have shewed in common speech:
" But of sigills and characters of the second manner, unless they be
" made in elected seasons, they are known to have no efficacy at all.
" And therefore he that doth practise them, as they are described in
" books, not respecting but only the figure that the exemplar doth
" represent, is judged of every wise man to do nothing. But those
" which know to perform their work in fit constellations according
" to the face of the Heavens; those may not only dispose characters
" but all their works, both of Art and Nature, according to the
" virtue of the Stars. But because it is a difficult thing to under-
" stand the certainty of Celestials in these things, therefore in these
" things there is much error with many, and there are few that un-
" derstand to order any thing profitably and truly. And to this
purpose *Paracelsus* tells us: "Certain Chirurgical Arts in- [Chirurg. major. c. 8. p. 22.]
" vented of the first improvers of Astronomy, by which admirable
" things were (by an Ethereal virtue) performed. But these after
" the decease of the ancient Magicians, were so lost, were as scarce
" any footsteps do now remain. But it was the Art of Celestial im-
" pressions, that they might draw down, the influent action, into
" some corporeal substance. The thing is plain by example. The
" seed of a Rose doth obtain the virtue and nature of a Rose, yet
" for all that it is not a Rose, but when being put into the earth,
" it doth sprout, then at the last it produceth a Rose. By the same
" reason, there are certain celestial virtues and actions in being,
" which being sown into Gemms, which were called of the ancient
" Magicians, *Pcantides* and *Gamahii* (otherwise *gemmæ hujæ*) from
" whence they have afterwards sprung up, no otherwise than seed,
" which doth fall from the Tree, and doth regerminate. This was
" that Astronomie of the ancient *Ægyptians* and *Persians*, by which
" they did adorn Gemms with celestial virtues. Neither are these
" things forthwith to be reputed impossible: For if we believe, that
" the Heaven doth send the Plague and other diseases upon us, why
" may we not hope, that the benignity of its virtues may be com-
" municated to us also? In like manner if the Heaven doth act upon
" the bodies of men, why may we not think that they may wrest their
" darts into stones? Many are touched with such like celestial darts
" which a Magician who hath skill of the Firmament, may easily (if

"they

"they be noxious) shun: or if they be benign shall, by putting
"some body, communicate it to that body, that now that body may
"fully obtain into it self the virtue of that dart or influence. From
"whence stones are found amongst the *Ægyptians*, which being born
"do cause diseases: But again there are others, that do throughly
"make found those diseases. So (he faith) we have seen *Gemmas*
"*Huyas*, that is *Peantides*, wherein the sign of the *Sagittary* was
"insculped against weapons, which were prevalent against wounds
"made with Swords. Also we have known (he faith) that Magi-
"cians have rendered stones efficacious to cure Feavers: nor only
"to have made them strong to cure diseases, but also wounds,
"and their symptoms, to wit, the Hæmorrhage, the Sinonia (or
"finew-water) Convulsions, and the Epilepfie. But as in that age
"the use of these was frequent, and the authority great; so by lit-
"tle and little the fophistications of false Philofophers being in-
"creafed, they have come into defuetude and contempt, and o-
"ther childifh things have been fubftituted in their places. But
"thefe Stones (becaufe now the fite and influx of the Heavens are
"plainly otherwife than they were in times paft) are no more fo effi-
"cacious as they were then, therefore it is convenient that they be
"prepared anew.

"The Art Magick, becaufe it was more fecret, nor known to
"vulgar Philofophers, both becaufe it did ingenerate wonderful
"virtues, not only to Stones, but alfo to fuch like words, begun
"to be called the preftigious Art by an odious term. For men be-
"ing unskilful of thefe things, who notwithftanding did ufurp the
"title of the Art unto themfelves, addicted themfelves unto artifi-
"cious operations, croffes and exorcifms: From thence the vul-
"gar, being unskilful of the Magical Art, have begun to attribute
"this virtue to exorcifms, characters, fhort prayers, fignacles,
"croffes, and to other frivolous things. But the matter (he faith)
"is quite otherwife: for the conftellation under which the ftones and
"words are prepared, doth induce the virtues, not exorcifms.

And being entred upon this particular, we shall add fome things
to this more fully, as firft this from the great *Georgius Phædro*, who
faith, after he had fhewed the great virtue of fome Roots and Herbs
in curing wounds and ulcers: "But a Characteriftical cure is that,
"which exercifeth its natural power by words pronounced, written
"or ingraven, by the qualities celeftial and various influences of
"the Stars, being friendly to our bodies. And to this doth fully
"agree, what is written by *Trallianus* at large and *Angerius Fer-*
"*rerius* in his Chapter *de Homerica medicatione*, whither I referr
"the Reader, and conclude this explication with that fentence of
"*Paracelfus: Præterea fyderibus nota funt omnia, quæ in natura*
"*exiftunt. Unde (inquit) fapiens dominabitur aftris, is fapiens,*
"*qui virtutes illas ad fui obedientiam cogere poteft.*

Chirur. Minor. p. 78.

Explic. Aftro-nom. p. 654.

Argum. 3.   3. What is here fully explicated as alfo what we have formerly in
this Treatife proved both by reafons, authorities and examples doth

fufficiently

sufficiently manifest the great power of Celestial Bodies upon inferior matter, and that according to the aptitude and agreeableness of the matter prepared, and the configuration of the Heavens at the time elected, the powerful influence of the Stars and Planets is received into the subject, according to the purpose it was intended for. So that from hence it will clearly follow, that if fit and agreeable words or characters be framed and joined together, when the Heavens are in a convenient site and configuration for the purpose intended, those words and characters will receive a most powerful virtue, for the purpose intended, and will effectually operate to those ends by a just, lawful and natural agency, without any concurrence of Diabolical power, superstition or ceremonies, and this is that which was laboured to be proved.

4. *Thomas Bartholinus* that most learned Physician, and experienced Anatomist (though his credit be laboured to be eclipsed by Dr. *Casaubon*, who is always more ready to ascribe power unto Devils, the worst of Gods creatures, than either to God or Nature) doth (touching this point) asserts this: "Notwithstanding (he " saith) that words framed or shut up in a certain Rhythme, may " without any superstition work some such like thing as the curing " of the Epilepsie. For first, the air is altered by the various prola- " tion of words, as well that air, which doth enter into the lit- " tle pores of the vessels ending in the skin by transpiration, as that " which is carried into the Ears, Nostrils, and Lungs. 2. The " state being different of the words uttered, doth impress a diffe- " rent force, which the unlike constitution of the rough Artery, and " of the rest of the instruments of speech, whether that state be hot " or cold, it impresseth a virtue, which doth either acuate or make " grave. 3. The breath is heated by the various prolation of words, " which either alone, or bound up in the Rhythme doth califie cold " things, and discusseth flatulencies. And these may have a great diversity in operation, according as the air and breath, and the several kinds of Atomes in them, may be ordered in their site, motion, and contexture, so that thereby the various effects may be produced, without Cacodemons, or vain superstition.

Argum. 4:
Histor. cent 2.
Histor. 78.
p. 280.

5. And if we consider it seriously there is something more than ordinary in this place of Scripture. *And it came to pass, that when the evil spirit from God was upon Saul, that David took an harp, and played with his hand: so Saul was refreshed, and was well, and the evil spirit departed from him.* Upon which learned *Tremellius* gives us this note: " That evil spirit, that is, those phan- " tastical pangs, or that furious rage, which did proceed from that " evil spirit, did cease. So that it is manifest that it was the natural efficacy of the melodious sound made by *Davids* playing upon the Harp, whereby the Atomes of the air were put into such a motion, site and contexture that thereby they became repugnant and antipathetical to those contrary Atomes, that were by the means of the evil spirit stirred up in the sensitive Soul of *Saul,* by which

Argum. 5:
1 Sam. 16. 14,
23.

he

he was terrified or tormented, and by overcoming them. and diffi-
pating of them, he came to be refreshed, and for a time those effects
wrought by that evil spirit ceased.   So that the argument lies plain
thus : If the melody of tunes or sounds modulated upon an Harp,
have power to refresh the mind, and to cause the rage of an evil
spirit to cease; then may words rightly framed in agreeable
Rhythmes, which are but modulated tunes or sounds, ease sick persons, and remove diseases: But the former is true by the testimony
of this Scripture, and so also is the later.   Neither is the objection
of *Hieronymus Jordanus* against this of any force at all, where he
saith that the reason of sweet Harmony, and magical words, are
very far different.   But it had been suitable for him to have shewed us, wherein that difference doth lye, and not to have put it off
with such a pittiful shuffle, as that it is obvious to Tyronists. This
is (indeed) a shift used by many, that when they are not able to solve
the argument, they put it off with some impertinent diversion, or
passe by it with some ironical Sarcasm.   But I must tell him that
tunes and sounds, that are framed by art in the best ways that can
be devised, thereby by modulating of the air, to cause it to have
several effects upon the auditory organs, differ not at all from
right framed charms and characters, that by disposing the atomes
of the air several ways, do produce various effects ; I say there is
no difference, except that constellated words may be more efficacious than Musick, because they are by a most curious and secret art,
not only composed and joined together, but also are prepared at
such chosen and fit times, that the Heavens may more powerfully infuse their virtues and influences into them, which is not observed in
the composition of tunes.

De eo quod Di-
vin. est in mor-
bis. c. 52.
p. 183.

Argum. 6.
Vid. Athan.
Kercher. l. mag-
net. muf. p.761.
&c.
Et Monfelt. in-
fect. Theatr.
p. 220.

6. There is no one thing (if true, and that *Kercherus* and others
have not told us abominable lies) that hath more induced me to believe that there is some natural virtue in words and charms composed
in a right way or Rhythme, than because those that are stung, or
bitten with the *Tarantula* or *Phalangium*, are cured with Musick,
and that not with any sort of Musick, but with certain proper and
peculiar tunes, which are diversified according to the colour of the
Tarantula that gave the venemous prick or bite, and so by dancing
they sweat forth the poison. And *Kercherus* further tells us not only
that those that are stung with the *Tarantula* are cured with Musick,
but that the *Tarantula*'s themselves with dance, when those tunes
are modulated   that are proportionable and agreeable to their humors.   Now if tunes modulated in proportionable and sympathi-
zing ways agreeable to the humours, do cure those that are stung,
then much more may words and charms rightly composed and joined together, and that in a due selected time under a powerful constellation, produce such effects as to cure diseases, and move animals to divers and various motions ; for betwixt the prolation of
words putting the Atomes of the air into a fit motion, site, figure,
and contexture suitable to perform the end intended, and the vi-
                                                                    brating

brating and various figuring the air in its motion by mufical tunes, there is no difference at all in refpect of the material or efficient caufe, and fo either of them may produce like effects.

7. There is alfo an experiment that hath been fufficiently tryed *Argum.* 7. and attefted, which doth much induce me to believe that there is efficacy in words and charms above their fignificancy by impofition and inftitution, and that is this. They take two Lutes rightly ftringed and laid upon a long table, and then they lay a light ftraw, chaff, or feather upon the Unifon ftring of the one, and then they ftrike, or move the Unifon ftring of the other Lute, that lieth at the other end of the Table, by which motion of the Unifon-ftring at the one end of the Table, the ftraw, chaff or feather upon the Unifon-ftring of the Lute at the other end of the Table (though it be of the longeft fort) will by the vibration of the air be moved, or ftruck off, and yet it will not do it, if the ftraw be laid upon any other ftring, and then the Unifon of the other Lute moved: By which it is manifeft that the ftriking or moving the Unifon-ftring of the one Lute doth fo figurate and difpofe the Atomes of the Air, that they are fit and apt to move the Unifon-ftring of the other Lute, and fo to make the ftraw fall off, as being of an agreeable mood and temper for the fufception of the motion, which the reft of the other ftrings (being of different degrees and nature) are not: for the maxime is true, *Quicquid recipitur, recipitur ad modum recipientis.* And this being fo, it muft needs be alfo granted that words and rhythms fitly joined and compofed, being pronounced do put the atomes of the air into fuch a fite, motion, figure, and contexture, that may at a diftance operate upon the fubject for which they are fo fitted and produce fuch effects, as they were compofed and intended for: efpecially being framed under powerful and fuitable conftellations, from whence they receive their greateft force.

8. The chiefeft objection that is ufually brought againft the na- *Argum.* 8. tural agency of fitly compofed words or rhythms is a maxim of the Schools, ill underftood and worfe applied, which is this: *Quantitates rerum, nullius funt efficacia:* unto which we fhall render thefe refponfions.

1. If quantity be taken mathematically, and abftractly, then it is true, that it is of no efficacy or operation, becaufe it is then only *ens rationis,* and doth only exift in the intellect, and fo can operate nothing *ad extra.* But if it be taken concretely, phyfically, and as materiate, than it is of force, and very operative, as two pound quantity of lead will weigh down one pound of the fame lead, and two ounces quantity of the fame Gunpowder, will carry a bullet of the fame quantity further, and more forceably, than one ounce of the fame will do: And one fcruple of white *Hellebor* may be taken, when a Drachm will kill, and a fire of a yard Diameter will warm a man at a greater diftance than a fire but of one foot diameter.

2. Figures, characters, words or fpeech are (indeed) properly

Vid. Syſtem.
Harm. Log-Hin.
Alſtedii. p.251.

no quantities: For figures and characters are only delineations and circumſcriptions of ſome kind of matter, and are all, whether natural or artificial, properly contained under quality, and denoting what figure or Form the thing is of. Figure therefore properly is attributed to artificial things, as to a circle, a ſquare, a triangle, and the like; and form to animate things, as to a Man, an Horſe, an Oxe, and the like: And ſo characters whether ingraven in metals, gemms, ſtones, clay, plaiſter or wood, or written upon parchment, paper, or the like, of what figure or form ſoever they be, are but qualities, and do qualifie the matter according to the form and figure impreſſed in the ſubject matter, which being artificially done, the matter is the patient, the figure or character is the exemplar cauſe, and the force that maketh the impreſſion is the efficient cauſe, and that theſe as qualities have ſome efficacy, no rational man can deny.

3. But to make it more clearly manifeſt, let us ſuppoſe three various figures that are Iſoperimetral, as a circle, a plain ſquare, and an equilateral triangle: Though they be all of equal circumference, yet ſhall the circle contain more than either the ſquare, or the triangle; and therefore learned *Ramus* doth lay down this rule.

Geom. l. 19.
p. 144.

Circulus è planis Iſoperimetris inæqualibus eſt maximus. But when the queſtion is asked, what is the cauſe, why a circle of figures of equal circumference, contains the moſt? The anſwer is commonly made, *Quia omnium figurarum perfectiſſimus, & capaciſſimus eſt circulus*; but if it be again urged, what is the cauſe, that a circle of an equal circumference to a plain ſquare, ſhould be more capacious than the ſquare? Here (the thing being found true by ocular experience) the capaciouſneſs of the circle, more than the ſquare (they being both of equal circumference) can be aſcribed to nothing elſe at all, but only to the figure, and therefore of neceſſity, figures have in them ſome efficiency.

4. That which we call ſpeech, or oration, is conſidered three ways. 1. That which is mental and only conceived in the mind, and not expreſſed. 2. That which is expreſſed or uttered by the vocal organs. 3. And that which is written. And theſe are called mental, vocal and written. The two, that is, mental, and that which is written, are referred to the predicament of quality. And whereas oration vocal is by ſome referred to the predicament of quanti-

Vid. Logic.
Syſtem. Harmon.
Alſtedii. p.249.

ty, as it is the meaſure of ſounds and ſyllables, as it is pronounced, whereof ſome are made long, and ſome ſhort; and ſo while diſtinct ſounds and ſyllables are uttered in a certain mood, they are ſaid to be meaſured, and to belong to quantity: But if we will underſtand aright, one thing in different reſpects may belong both to the predicament of quantity and quality. So the prolation of ſounds or ſyllables in reſpect of their modification, and comparing one to another, ſome may be long, and ſome may be ſhort, and have a different part of time in their pronunciation, and ſo may Analogically, and by way of ſimilitude, be ſaid to be meaſured, and conſequently referred to the predicament of quantity. Yet if we conſider

sider speech or oration, which consists of sounds and syllables, in relation to the efficient cause, the material and instrumental, which is the breath of Man by his several organs, moving, modulating and figuring the air (which is the subject matter) into diversity of sites, motions, contextures and moods, then we must conclude that words, charms or rhythms, having efficient, material and instrumental causes, do belong to the predicament of Quality, and are of great force and virtue naturally, notwithstanding all that is or can be objected to the contrary.

5. Lastly, we are to consider that the breath of Man being variously modulated by its passage from the lungs, by the throat, palate, tongue, and other vocal organs, doth make such several impressions and configurations of the moved atomes in the air, that thereby so great a diversity of impulses or sounds are made upon the drum of the ear, that thereby naturally we are able to distinguish one from another. Now humane institution found forth the ways of making these several sounds, or tones, to be appropriated to such and such things, or to signifie the diversity of creatures and things, according to the several compacts and agreements of Men amongst themselves, so that what one sound doth signifie in one language, may signifie another thing in another. So that not considering the institution or invention of this or that significancy of several sounds in several languages, every sound, or articulate prolation, doth naturally make a distinct and several impulse upon the ear, and thereby the senses, and consequently the mind are variously affected by them. And therefore the younger *Helmont* doth give us an apposite passage, or two to this purpose, Englished thus: "For as in those of ripe years, certain musical mo-*Alphabet. Na-* " dulations being heard, do often so efficaciously imprint in the *tur. p. 20.* " mind the Idea of the voice and tones, that diverse do sensibly feel " them for so long a time in themselves, as it were yet sounding, " that they cannot, when they would, be freed from them: From " whence also (he saith) the word *inchanting* seemeth with the La- " tines and Gauls to have drawn its original. So the Idea of our " Mothers tongue impressed in infants, doth so long adhere there, " that to them about to speak afterwards, it doth as it were place, " and order the tongue, and so is the only one mistress of their speech. And again he saith: "If in times past there were found those, who *Ibid. p. 52.* " by the benefit of musical instruments could move and mollifie the " mind of Man various ways: How much more humane voice, if " it being moderated by prudence, do break forth from a living spi- " rit, shall not only have power to effect those things, but also those " that are far greater?

Having thus far largely handled this point, we shall only recapitulate a few things, and so conclude this Treatise.

1. It being granted, that great effects have been produced by words, charms, rhythmes, and tunes, we have removed all diabolical concurrence to those effects, except what may be mental and internal,

ternal, as in all wicked persons, when they use natural means to a wicked and evil end, and that (as we conceive) by sufficient and convincing arguments: And especially because, where there is no natural agent, there the Devil can operate nothing at all, and if there be a natural agent, his concurrence is not necessary.

2. As for the force of imagination upon extraneous bodies, we cannot in reason affirm it to be none at all, neither dare, or will we assert that its power (in that respect) is so vastly great, as many do pretend.

3. And for what strange effects soever, that are true and real, that do follow upon the use of words, charms, characters, rhythms, and the like, we do confidently affirm, that they are effected by lawful and natural means, but withal that of this sort in this age, few or none are found out that are efficacious. But that error, credulity, ignorance and superstition do put great force, and stress upon these things, when really they produce no effects at all,

---

The *Alarm* that the Pendle-forest *Witches gave to all this Kingdom, that they were sent for to* London, *great sums gotten at the* Fleet *to shew them, and publick Plays acted thereupon ; and the Original Examination coming lately to the Authors hand, it is desired the Reader will after these words Page* 277. *line* 4. [and had incouragement by the adjoining Magistrates] *peruse these following Depositions,* viz.

The

The Examination of Edmund Robinson *Son of* Edmund Robinson *of* Pendle-Foreſt *eleven years of age, taken at* Padham *before* Richard Shutleworth *and* John Starkey *Eſquires, two of his Majeſties Juſtices of the Peace within the County of* Lancaſter, *the* 10th *day of* February, 1633.

"WHO upon Oath informeth, being examined concerning
"the great meeting of the Witches of *Pendle*, ſaith that
"upon *All-Saints-day* laſt paſt, he this Informer being
"with one *Henry Parker* a near door-neighbour to him in *Wheatley-*
"*lane*, deſired the ſaid *Parker* to give him leave to gather ſome
"Bulloes which he did ; In gathering whereof he ſaw two Gray-
"hounds, *viz.* a black and a brown ; one came running over the
"next field towards him, he verily thinking the one of them to be
"Mr. *Nutters*, and the other to be Mr. *Robinſons*, the ſaid Gen-
"tlemen then having ſuch like. And ſaith, the ſaid Grayhounds
"came to him, and fawned on him, they having about their necks
"either of them a Collar, unto each of which was tied a ſtring : which
"Collars (as this Informer affirmeth) did ſhine like Gold. And he
"thinking that ſome either of Mr. *Nutters* or Mr. *Robinſons* Fa-
"mily ſhould have followed them ; yet ſeeing no body to follow
"them, he took the ſame Gray-hounds thinking to courſe with
"them. And preſently a Hare did riſe very near before him. At
"the ſight whereof he cried, Loo, Loo, Loo: but the Doggs
"would not run. Whereupon he being very angry took them,
"and with the ſtrings that were about their Collars, tied them to
"a little buſh at the next hedge, and with a ſwitch that he had in
"his hand he beat them. And in ſtead of the black Grayhound
"one *Dickenſons* Wife ſtood up, a Neighbour whom this Informer
"knoweth. And inſtead of the brown one a little Boy, whom this
"Informer knoweth not. At which ſight this Informer being a-
"fraid, endeavoured to run away : but being ſtayed by the Wo-
"man (*viz.*) by *Dickenſons* Wife, ſhe put her hand into her pocket,
"and pulled forth a piece of Silver much like to a fair ſhilling, and
"offered to give him it to hold his tongue and not to tell: which
"he refuſed, ſaying, Nay thou art a Witch. Whereupon ſhe put
"her hand into her pocket again, and pulled out a thing like un-
"to a Bridle that gingled, which ſhe put on the little Boyes head :
"which ſaid Boy ſtood up in the likeneſs of a white Horſe, and in
"the brown Grayhounds ſtead. Then immediately *Dickenſons*
"Wife

"Wife took this Informer before her upon the said Horse and car-
"ried him to a new house called *Hoarstones* being about a quarter
"of a mile off. Whither when they were come, there were divers
"persons about the door, and he saw divers others riding on
"Horses of several colours towards the said House, who tied their
"Horses to a hedge near to the said House. Which persons went
"into the said House, to the number of threescore or thereabouts,
"as this Informer thinketh, where they had a fire, and meat roast-
"ing in the said House, whereof a young Woman (whom this In-
"former knoweth not) gave him Flesh and Bread upon a Trencher
"and Drink in a Glass, which after the first tast he refused and
"would have no more, but said, it was naught.

"And presently after, seeing divers of the said company going
"into a Barn near adjoining, he followed after them, and there he
"saw six of them kneeling, and pulling all six of them six several ropes,
"which were fastened or tied to the top of the Barn. Presently
"after which pulling, there came into this Informers sight flesh
"smoaking, butter in lumps, and milk as it were flying from the
"said ropes. All which fell into basons which were placed under
"the said ropes. And after that these six had done, there came o-
"ther six which did so likewise. And during all the time of their
"several pulling they made such ugly faces as scared this Informer;
"so that he was glad to run out and steal homewards: who imme-
"diately finding they wanted one that was in their company, some
"of them ran after him near to a place in a High-way called *Bog-
"gard-hole*, where he this Informer met two Horsemen. At the
"sight whereof the said persons left following of him. But the
"foremost of those persons that followed him, he knew to be one
"*Loind's* Wife: which said Wife together with one *Dickensons*
"Wife, and one *Jennet Davies* he hath seen since at several times
"in a Croft or Close adjoining to his Fathers house, which put
"him in great fear. And further this Informer saith, upon *Thurs-
"day* after *Newyears-day* last past, he saw the said *Loind's* Wife
"sitting upon a cross piece of wood being within the Chimney of
"his Fathers dwelling house: and he calling to her, said Come
"down thou *Loynd's* Wife. And immediately the said *Loynd's*
"Wife went up out of his sight. And further this Informer saith,
"that after he was come from the company aforesaid to his Fathers
"house, being towards evening, his Father bad him go and fetch
"home two Kine to seal. And in the way in a field called the *El-
"lers*, he chanced to hap upon a Boy, who began to quarrel with
"him, and they fought together, till the Informer had his ears and
"face made up very bloody by fighting, and looking down he saw
"the Boy had a cloven foot. At which sight he being greatly af-
"frighted, came away from him to seek the Kine. And in the way
"he saw a light like to a Lanthorn towards which he made haste, sup-
"posing it to be carried by some of Mr. *Robinsons* people; but
"when he came to the place, he only found a Woman standing
"on

"on a Bridge, whom when he faw he knew her to be *Loind's*
"Wife, and knowing her he turned back again: and immediate-
"ly he met with the aforefaid Boy, from whom he offered to run,
"which Boy gave him a blow on the back that made him to cry.
"And further this Informer faith, that when he was in the Barn,
"he faw three Women take fix Pictures from off the beam, in
"which Pictures were many Thorns or fuch like things fticked in
"them, and that *Loynd's* Wife took one of the Pictures down,
"but the other two Women that took down the reft he knoweth
"not.   And being further asked what perfons were at the afore-
"faid meeting, he nominated thefe perfons following, *viz. Dick-*
"*enfons* Wife, *Henry Priestleys* Wife, and his Lad, *Alice Hargreene*
"Widow, *Jane Davies, William Davies,* and the Wife of *Henry*
"*Fackes,* and her Sons *John* and *Miles,* the Wife of   *Den-*
"*neries, James Hargreene of Marfdead, Loynd's* Wife, one *James*
"his Wife, *Saunders* his Wife, and *Saunders* himfelf *ficut credit,*
"one *Laurence* his Wife, one *Saunder Pyn's* Wife of *Barraford,*
"one *Holgate* and his Wife of *Leonards* of the Weft clofe.

Edmund Robinfon *of* Pendle *Father of the aforefaid* Edmund Robinfon *Mafon informeth,*

"THAT upon *All Saints day* laft he fent his Son the aforefaid
"Informer to fetch home two Kine to feal, and faith that his
"Son ftaying longer than he thought he fhould have done, he went
"to feek him, and in feeking of him heard him cry pitifully, and
"found him fo affrighted and diftracted, that he neither knew his
"Father, nor did know where he was, and fo continued very near
"a quarter of an hour before he came to himfelf.   And he told this
"Informer his Father all the particular paffages that are before de-
"clared in the faid *Robinfon* his Sons information.

Richard Shutleworth.

John Starkey.

FINIS.

The Printer defires the Reader to excufe
fome literal faults, as *Nandeus* for *Naudeus*, *Libanius* for *Libavius*, and the like, the Author
writing a very fmall hand, and living at great diftance that his perufal could not be gotten.

www.ingramcontent.com/pod-product-compliance
Lightning Source LLC
Chambersburg PA
CBHW051114120726
47905CB00005B/1278